Murder

Books 7 to 9

Murder in Room 346

Murder of a Silent Man

Murder has no Guilt

Phillip Strang

BOOKS BY PHILLIP STRANG

DCI Isaac Cook Series
MURDER IS A TRICKY BUSINESS
MURDER HOUSE
MURDER IS ONLY A NUMBER
MURDER IN LITTLE VENICE
MURDER IS THE ONLY OPTION
MURDER IN NOTTING HILL
MURDER WITHOUT REASON

DI Keith Tremayne Series
DEATH UNHOLY
DEATH AND THE ASSASSIN'S BLADE
DEATH AND THE LUCKY MAN
DEATH AT COOMBE FARM

Steve Case Series
HOSTAGE OF ISLAM
THE HABERMAN VIRUS
PRELUDE TO WAR

Standalone Books
MALIKA'S REVENGE

Copyright Page

Dedication

For Elli and Tais who both had the perseverance to make me sit down and write.

Murder in Room 346

Phillip Strang

Chapter 1

'Coitus interruptus, that's what it is,' Detective Chief Inspector Isaac Cook said. It was to be the only attempt at humour that day, and even then, it was in bad taste. On the bed, in a downmarket hotel in Bayswater, lay the naked bodies of a man and a woman.

'Bullet in the head's not the way to go,' Larry Hill, Isaac Cook's detective inspector, said. He had not expected such a

1

flippant comment from his senior, not when they were standing near to two people who had, apparently in the final throes of passion, succumbed to what appeared to be a professional assassination.

'Do you recognise him?'

'James Holden, from what I can see.'

'And the woman?'

'According to the driving licence in her purse, her name was Helen Langdon. There's an address in Kensington, good street.'

'Judging by her clothes, she had plenty of money.'

'An attractive woman, or at least, she was.'

Isaac Cook could understand what his DI meant. The woman was not so attractive sprawled across the bed, the blood congealing on her and the sheets.

'No idea what she saw in him,' Larry said.

'Rent by the hour?'

'Not according to her handbag. There's a business card. She worked for the man.'

Gordon Windsor, the crime scene examiner, came over. 'Apart from you two talking while I'm trying to focus, I'll give you what I've found so far.'

'You know this will be all over the media within the hour,' Isaac said.

'James Holden, moral crusader, a proponent of the sanctity of the marital bed, man and wife. It's bound to be.'

'The man preaches one thing, practises another.'

'They've all got hidden secrets. Anyway, this is what we have,' Windsor said. 'Helen Langdon, age thirty-two, James Holden, age seventy-two. Both have been shot in the head.'

'Whoever did this knew what they were doing,' Larry said. 'Somehow the person managed to get into the room unseen, and then get close enough to the pair to hold the gun to each of their heads.'

'They were occupied, maybe they didn't look,' Isaac said.

'We'll check, but it's clear that they were indulging in sexual intercourse.'

'The man was seventy-two,' Isaac said.

'It's alright for you young studs,' Windsor said, 'but let me tell you, life is not over at fifty.'

'But James Holden was not fit, and he was always preaching against this sort of thing,' Larry said.

'I can only give you the facts,' Windsor said. 'Why the man was here with a young woman is for you to find out. And why he was killed, that's up to you. Their bodies will be with Pathology later today. I suggest you ask there in a day or so for any more information, but they'll only confirm what I've just said.'

Isaac knew that Windsor was correct in his evaluation. They had known each other for many years, he, the first-generation English-born son of Jamaican parents, and Gordon Windsor, the smallish, rotund man in his late fifties.

Back in the office at Challis Street Police Station, Sergeant Wendy Gladstone, the best person if you needed to find someone, and Bridget Halloran, who ran the office, would already be preparing the case for the prosecution.

Wendy and Bridget were firm friends, sharing a house since Wendy's husband had died and Bridget had kicked out her layabout live-in lover.

DI Larry Hill maintained an uneasy truce with his wife and her faddish diets, but he was looking a lot better since she and his DCI had ganged up on him to moderate his food intake and the pints of beer.

The only thorn in the side of the Homicide department was Seth Caddick, a man who had once temporarily occupied Isaac's seat as the senior investigating officer in Homicide, only to be unceremoniously eased out after Isaac had solved the case, but now he was back, and this time as his senior. The sycophantic, and to Isaac incompetent, Caddick had somehow managed to attain the rank of Detective Superintendent, and he was in Detective Chief Superintendent Richard Goddard's office, and he was in charge.

Isaac Cook had respected Goddard, a man who had got on the wrong side of the London Metropolitan Police commissioner, Alwyn Davies. Caddick, a man who for some reason always came up smelling of roses, had been quick to claim it was his leadership that ensured the enviable success rate of the Homicide department, when it was clearly Isaac and his team.

Not that it concerned Isaac unduly, as Goddard had explained that Caddick's tenure was to be short-lived, but it was already five months, and the man continued to irritate and interfere.

***

Back in the office at Challis Street, Isaac gathered the team. He had phoned Caddick out of courtesy, knowing the man's reaction if he was ignored. Isaac had come close to insubordination on a couple of occasions, and Goddard, his former senior, had told him to play the game and not to rile the man.

Isaac wasn't sure how much longer he could put up with Caddick. The man continued to be a mediocre performer, and morale was down, with a few people transferring out of Challis Street, some others just resigning. So far, none of Isaac's core team had left, and he was hopeful he could keep it that way.

'Bridget, what do we have?' Isaac asked. The woman was computer-savvy, and she could find out things about a person that no one else could.

'James Aloysius Holden, age seventy-two, married to Violet Holden, two children. John, age thirty-seven, a lawyer. His sister, Linda, age thirty-three, a social worker.'

'Helen Langdon was younger than his daughter,' Larry said.

'It sounds indecent to me,' Wendy said.

'Bridget, carry on. We can discuss the age difference afterwards.'

'James Holden, Member of Parliament, self-professed moral crusader, a staunch advocate for prison reform and controls on the internet. And also, a believer in one man, one woman, and total fidelity.'

'Not practising what he preaches,' Larry said.

'They're all the same,' Wendy said. She was in her fifties, troubled with arthritis, and putting on weight after giving up a lifetime habit of smoking. She was not an admirer of those born with a silver spoon in their mouth, or the hypocrites in society who preach one thing, do another.

'Not all,' Isaac said, 'but in this case, there's some explaining to do. What do we know about his wife?'

'She's been notified,' Bridget said.

'Wendy, it may be best if you come with me. Do we have her address?' Isaac said.

'Ebury Street, Belgravia. We can be there in twenty-five minutes.'

As Isaac and Wendy were preparing to leave, in walked their superintendent, Seth Caddick. 'Where are you off to?' he said.

'We're going to interview the dead man's wife,' Isaac replied.

'Very well. Keep me updated, and make sure your report is in on time.'

Caddick walked out of the office. Larry turned to Isaac. 'How can you put up with him, guv?' he said.

'Play the game, play the game,' Isaac said. 'The man's only keeping the seat warm.'

'For you?'

'That's the word,' Isaac replied with a wry smile.

'And who'll run Homicide?'

'Are you up to it?'

'I reckon so. I just need to pass one more exam, and then I'll be looking for a promotion.'

'As long as you stay with Homicide.'

'My wife's not so keen, not after the time I ended up in the hospital courtesy of a local gang.'

'That can happen walking down the street,' Isaac said, realising that it wasn't entirely accurate. The only reason Larry had not died was due to the ineptitude of his assailants. He had been interviewing a homeless man who had witnessed a murder. His attackers had subsequently dealt with the witness with a knife in the heart.

After the short discussion with Larry, Isaac and Wendy drove out to Ebury Street. 'Nice houses,' Isaac said.

'Out of my budget,' Wendy replied. She feigned disinterest, although Isaac knew she appreciated the beauty of the buildings.

Outside the Holden home, an elegant three-storey, late Georgian, white-painted house, a uniform stood. 'The media has been around. I'm here to deter anyone knocking on the door,' he said. Wendy could tell that he would have preferred to have been anywhere else than at the door of a moral crusader's home, as it was cold and raining, not an unusual occurrence for the time of year.

From inside the house, the door was opened by a man in his thirties. 'My mother is resting,' he said.

Ushered into a room on the left of the hallway, the two police officers waited. A woman entered and placed a tray on the table in front of where they sat. 'Madam will be here soon. The tea's freshly brewed,' she said before leaving.

Violet Holden entered the room. She was helped by John Holden, her son. 'It's come as a great shock to my mother, to all of us,' he said. He was a man of about medium height, his hair cut short, his fingernails manicured, his suit of the best quality.

'Thank you for coming,' Violet Holden said.

'I'm sorry that it's under such circumstances.'

'Is it true what they're reporting?' the woman asked. 'We'd been married for over forty years. I thought I knew the man, and this has come as a shock.'

'His death?'

'I assumed he'd die in the Houses of Parliament, or in some committee or other, even in one of those prisons he frequented, but they're reporting that he was found in bed with another woman. Was it Helen?'

'Helen Langdon. Yes, it was. What can you tell me about her, about your husband?'

'My husband was a saint. It must have been her.'

'Can we come back to your husband,' Isaac said. Holden's wife was taking it badly, but he wasn't sure if it was because of her husband's murder or his adultery.

'What do you want me to tell you? He can't have been with that woman willingly.'

'Unfortunately, there's no question that he was.'

'Is this necessary? My mother is under a great deal of strain,' John Holden said.

'If Mrs Holden is up to it, we should continue,' Isaac said.

Violet Holden patted her son on the arm. 'I'll be fine,' she said.

'Your husband was at a hotel in Bayswater. Do you know of any reason why he would choose there?'

'To be with Helen?'

'Yes.'

'We had advised our father about employing her, but he wouldn't listen,' John Holden said.

'Why?'

'Our father was a great believer in the rehabilitation of criminals after they had served their sentences. Helen had spent time in prison.'

Isaac turned to Wendy. 'Bridget missed that,' he said quietly, ensuring that no one else heard.

'Her name in prison was Helen Mackay.'

'*The* Helen Mackay!'

'She changed her name on leaving prison at my father's suggestion.'

'And your father was part of the rehabilitation process?'

'She was released due to him.'

'Have you met her?' Wendy asked.

'On several occasions. She was pleasant and respectful, devoted to James,' Violet said. 'And now my husband's association with her has got him killed.'

'Until you mentioned her name, we had assumed the reason for their deaths was your husband,' Isaac said.

'Who would have wanted to kill my husband?'

'He must have made powerful enemies. His attempts at censorship must have raised the hackles of a few.'

'My husband wasn't an idealistic bigot. He was a man who had a strong conviction of what was right and wrong.'

'And he's strayed,' Isaac said.

'My husband was a complex man. There were times when his moral crusade became too much for him. Times when he needed to let off steam.'

'This is not the first time?'

'It's the first time with a woman. Sometimes he wanted to come home, put his feet up, have a drink of something strong.'

'Mother, I don't think you should be saying this,' her son said.

'Why not? They're police officers, and they need to know certain facts. And what does it matter? Your father, my husband, has been caught in bed with another woman, and not only that, with Helen Mackay. How do you think your father's legacy is going to stand up when it's revealed that he's been caught in flagrante delicto with a woman who bashed her elderly husband to death with a hammer?'

'Her defence argued it was self-defence, mitigating circumstances,' Isaac said.

'Did anyone believe her when she said she had married for love?' Violet Holden said.

'Did you?' Isaac said.

'Nobody did. Her husband was wealthy, old, and likely to die at any time, and there in the court was a woman in her twenties with a dubious past. The popular press had condemned her the moment she entered the court.'

'The judge believed her. That's why she only received seven years.'

'Out in four. My husband believed in her as well, and then she slept with him, destroying his reputation.'

'Mrs Holden, you don't believe that your husband was coerced, do you?'

'My husband was the same as any other man. Underneath that exterior there was a man of flesh and blood. A man who liked the occasional drink, the occasional woman, the occasional sin.'

'Was this the first time?'

'With Helen, yes.'

'With others?'

'I never knew, although I suspected he did from time to time.'

'Mother, you're maligning my father.'

'Don't pretend, John. You knew what he was like, the same as you.'

Chapter 2

'Moral crusader, serial philanderer, is that what we've got here?' Larry Hill said. The team were back in Homicide at Challis Street Police Station. Thankfully, Detective Superintendent Seth Caddick was not in the building; he was at his favourite place, Scotland Yard, pressing the flesh of whoever he could find, especially Commissioner Alwyn Davies.

Isaac Cook, once seen as an example of the modern police force, knew his star was not shining brightly with the commissioner. When it had been Commissioner Shaw in charge of the London Metropolitan Police, and Richard Goddard his chief superintendent, Isaac's moves on the promotion ladder seemed fine, but he and Goddard had languished under Davies, and Isaac was still a DCI and Goddard had been sidelined into Public Relations.

The problem with Alwyn Davies, according to Isaac and Goddard, was that the man was an incompetent who surrounded himself with other incompetents. There were others, Detective Superintendent Seth Caddick included, who believed that Davies was a man who recognised true ability. It was an impossible situation, Isaac knew, and he had put up with Caddick for almost half a year, and he intended to see the demise of the man's career. The only problem was that as the Homicide team succeeded, so did Caddick, and the man was not slow in pointing it out.

The one skill that Caddick had, apart from irritating Isaac, was that he was an accomplished public speaker. At the wrap-up press conference after someone had been charged with murder, Caddick was able to give the impression that he had single-handedly solved the crime, with Isaac and his team mere functionaries following instructions.

Richard Goddard had been willing to acknowledge his team's contribution, but in front of a microphone and a camera the man was a wet blanket. It had been Isaac who had saved him on several occasions from the ignominy of saying something silly and fluffing his speech. Caddick didn't need any such help, although the interviewers invariably wanted to hear from the tall, good-looking and very dark DCI, not from a dishevelled-looking man with a Welsh accent.

'What do we have on James Holden?' Isaac asked his team. The initial research from Bridget Halloran in the office had been precise, but nothing of a surprise, as the man was well known to the general public.

'Apart from the fact that he was seventy-two with a wife and two children?' Bridget said.

'We need something more than that.'

'James Holden was elected to parliament thirty-three years ago. He held the post of Minister of Health in a previous government, but currently is in opposition.'

'Not much chance of their being returned to power anytime soon,' Wendy Gladstone said.

'Regardless of his party's electoral prospects,' Isaac said.

'James Holden took up the cause of declining moral standards eight years ago,' Bridget continued. 'He's stated on many occasions, passionately in the Houses of Parliament, that more should be done to encourage the institution of marriage, and that graphic violence and sex on the internet and the television are detrimental to society. In the last few years, he's taken on prison reform. According to him, prison is there for rehabilitation, not just for punishment. Holden has made an effort to take recently released prisoners who showed remorse for their crimes and to find them suitable employment, not a dead-end job paying the minimum wage.'

'Helen Langdon, is she one of these prisoners?' Isaac asked.

'Helen Langdon, previously known as Helen Mackay, had served four years of a seven-year sentence for the second-degree murder of Gerald Adamant, a man who had inherited a fortune from his father at the age of fifty. At the time of his marriage to Helen Mackay, he was sixty-eight, she was twenty-four. The media soon dug up dirt on Helen, not that there was much. She had briefly appeared onstage at a risqué club, but apart from that, she's clean. Her family were found to be decent people with a daughter who, through no fault of her own, men lusted after. According to

Helen, it was love for Adamant, the only person who had seen her inner self, and Adamant, if you remember, wasn't a bad-looking man. He certainly looked younger than his age, and she definitely looked older. The marriage cost plenty, the honeymoon even more, and for a few years, no more was heard of them, apart from Adamant's philanthropic work, his wife at his side.'

'And then?' Isaac said.

'Adamant is dead, Helen is charged with murder. According to her, the marriage was fine. He treated her well, she loved him. And then, one day, he snaps, accuses her of sleeping with other men, never loving him.'

'Any truth in his accusations?'

'No proof was ever found. The evidence at the trial showed that Gerald Adamant and his wife did have a good marriage, and there was no indiscretion by either person.'

'But she killed him.'

'The two of them are in the kitchen of their house. Renovations are going on, he's got his hands around her throat. She grabs hold of a hammer lying to one side and strikes him on the head to make him back off. Adamant died later that day. The rest you know.'

'Let us give the woman the benefit of the doubt,' Isaac said. 'Is there any information as to how she came to be working for Holden?'

'Holden was known for his frequent visits to the prisons throughout the country. On one of these prison visits, he befriends Helen Mackay – she's reverted to her maiden name – and subsequently makes an impassioned plea for her release, due to disputed evidence at her original trial.'

'Since her release, she's been vindicated of the crime,' Larry said.

'Carry on, Bridget.'

'Helen Mackay changed her name on her release. She had a degree in accountancy; his organisation needed an accountant. After a couple of years, Helen Langdon, as she is now known, was largely forgotten.'

'She was living well in Kensington,' Wendy said.

'Adamant's family, supporters of hers during the original trial, bequeathed her the apartment and sufficient money to live.'

'She wasn't entitled to more?'

'A pre-nuptial had been signed. Technically, she was entitled to nothing, but Adamant was a good man, so was his family, and Helen had made the man happy, even if she ultimately killed him.'

'It's one hell of a story,' Larry said.

'Life is often stranger than fiction,' Isaac said.

***

Violet Holden, as distraught as she was, realised the situation was delicate. Her husband, believed by the man in the street to be a moral man, had a dark side. Not that she had been under any illusion for many years, not since the first time he had erred. Back then, their son was up and walking, no more than one year old, and in walked the father, a look of guilt on his face.

That time he had confessed, as he would every time afterwards. That was why she had been able to tell the police in all honesty that her husband had only been with Helen the one time. If he had lived, he would have come back to the family home and confessed, and each time there'd be the pledge that he would never do it again. Violet knew full well that he would; not often, but often enough.

'Why was he with her?' Linda Holden, the younger child of James and Violet, said. Her mother knew that Linda was an unattractive woman of thirty-three, having inherited her father's bulbous nose and his blotchy skin, and her mother's slender frame. The mother consoled herself with the knowledge that her daughter had a kind heart, like her father.

'It's not the first time,' her mother replied.

'But Helen, why her?'

Violet, an attractive woman, a beauty in her youth, knew why, even if the daughter did not. Helen Langdon, regardless of her history, was a beautiful woman, the sort of woman that her husband liked.

Violet remembered when they had met, she and James. He had not been a handsome man, but he had an inner strength, an inherent sense of decency. He was also the most intelligent man she had ever met, able to converse about any subject that interested her. They had become a couple, and they married within six months; he, a virgin, she, not so chaste.

They had been happy years before their son had come along, time enough for James to be elected to parliament. Even then he had been an ardent moralist, a clear and concise debater, a man going places, and in politics that meant the prime ministership. But then, another general election and James Holden was in opposition, a repeating event in the intervening years until his death. It was that first time he realised he had joined the wrong party, but there was no changing. He was not like Winston Churchill who had managed to move across the political divide; he was James Holden, a loyal party member, an ardent believer in doing the right thing, regardless of personal cost.

'She was devoted to your father, you knew that,' Violet Holden said.

'But why the two of them in bed?'

'There was empathy between the two of them, almost a melding of the minds. It's as if they were father and daughter.'

'How could he? It's almost obscene.'

'It was inevitable. Your father, like all great men, needed to rebel occasionally.'

'Are you saying that Helen offered herself as the object of his rebellion?'

'Helen would have done anything for him.'

'Aren't you upset, Mother?'

'Your father's legacy must be preserved; his good work must continue. Linda, you must be the one.'

'But I don't have my father's skills.'

'Yes, you do. It is for all of us to be willing to portray my husband, your father, as the man he was, a man who was flawed. His indiscretion with Helen must be used to portray him as a sinner who repents, a man who would admit all to his family.'

'And Helen?'

'She was a good person, regardless of her past and what has occurred. We will not conduct vendettas against anyone. We, the Holdens, will be the face of equanimity, of kindness, of charity to all.'

'It'll be hard for John,' Linda said.

'Then we must work hard to bring him around. He has a mean streak, and he will want to portray Helen as a wicked woman.'

'Not as someone he loved, but who ultimately rejected him for his father.'

'Precisely, and John doesn't have your and your father's kind nature,' Violet said.

Chapter 3

Isaac recognised trouble, not with a capital T, but with a capital C: Caddick. The man was sitting in Isaac's office; he appeared to be friendly, which meant only one thing, he was going to be difficult.

'Now, look here, Cook, I want this case run by the book. Commissioner Davies is taking a keen interest in this police station, especially this department, and James Holden was well respected. There's bound to be a lot of focus on us to provide results.'

'On me,' Isaac corrected the man.

'You think you're so smart, don't you? Well, let me tell you, I'm the superintendent, you're not, and unless your attitudes changes, I'll have you out of here in a flash.'

So much for the friendly, Isaac thought. He could see the hand of the commissioner in Caddick; he was not going to rise to the bait.

'We've just taken on the case. You're not expecting us to solve it that quickly, are you?' Isaac replied.

'I am. The demands on my budget are too much as it is. I'll not be paying for you and your mollycoddling of your people. And if your sergeant is too old, replace her. I can find you someone else, younger, keener, more willing to get out there and mix it on the street.'

'Sergeant Gladstone pulls her weight. She'll not let this department down.'

'On your head. I'm just giving you fair warning.'

Straight out of the Alwyn Davies book of policing, Isaac thought but decided to say no more. His superintendent had irritated him, not for the first time either. Isaac had wanted to tell the man that he was a snivelling little weasel, not even competent to shine the boots of his predecessor, Detective Chief Superintendent Goddard. Goddard had confided to Isaac that the forces were continuing to rally, and ongoing discussions were being conducted to allow Commissioner Davies to resign with grace, which would probably amount to a hefty payout, and possibly a knighthood.

Isaac had baulked at the mention of the knighthood. 'I thought they were awarded after you had done something, not destroyed it.'

'That's not how the real world works, and you know it,' Goddard had replied.

There was plenty to do, but Caddick's visit had left Isaac devoid of enthusiasm. He got up from his desk and walked out of his office.

Isaac sat down next to Wendy Gladstone. He could see she was struggling, and Caddick was right in that her performance was down from a year previously. He also knew that he would protect her at all costs. The times when she was needed out on the street, she had never let him down, and she was totally loyal to him, as were the others in the office. Isaac knew that Caddick's approach did not work. People under pressure perform as long as that pressure is reasoned and progressive, not by threatening their jobs.

'We need to find out why they were shot,' Isaac said. 'What do we know about Helen Langdon?'

'I can check out where she worked, talk to her colleagues. They're bound to be in shock after the executive director and the financial controller are both killed.'

'And in the same bed. Let's go, I'll come with you,' Isaac said. 'After five minutes with our senior, I need to be out of here.'

'Begging your pardon, sir, but Superintendent Caddick is a pain in the rear end,' Wendy said.

'Don't even think it, don't ever say it. You know how we're meant to act with the man.'

'It's hard. Sometimes I feel that I could tell him what I think of him.'

'I know what you mean,' Isaac said. 'Where's Larry?'

'He's back out at the crime scene. The CSIs are wrapping up. He wants to see what he can find out.'

'If it's a professional slaying, then probably not much.'

'There are still cameras in the street. Bridget can look through them once we have some idea of the murderer. She's collating what she can find on Holden and Langdon. It's a sorry mess, that's what it is.'

'A mess. I'm not so sure about the sorry. James Holden can only blame himself.'

'What did you make of Holden's wife?' Wendy asked.

'There's not much to say. She looked upset.'

'She was, but she wasn't surprised her husband had been in another woman's bed.'

'How can you know?'

'I observed her reactions when she spoke. She wasn't happy about the situation, although she was shocked it was Helen Langdon.'

***

The offices of James Holden's organisation were located in Paddington, no more than a six-minute drive from Challis Street. Isaac parked the car in a bay reserved for the executive director. 'He'll not need it today,' he said.

Inside the office, freshly painted judging by the smell, a middle-aged woman sat behind reception. 'Can I help you?' she said.

'Detective Chief Inspector Cook, Sergeant Gladstone,' Isaac said.

'You're here about James?'

'That's correct.' Isaac took note of the fact the woman did not mention Helen.

'It's a sad day. Everyone's a bit lost. His daughter's here if it's any help.'

'It will be.'

Isaac and Wendy took a seat. Isaac flicked through some brochures on the table in the reception area; Wendy checked the news on her phone. After a few minutes, Linda Holden appeared. 'We've been discussing what to do. We need to make a press statement.'

'I'll be asked to give a press conference at some stage,' Isaac said.

The three walked through the offices to the rear of reception. It was a better office than Homicide, Wendy had to admit.

'What can I do for you?' Holden's daughter said. 'As you can understand, I'm not really in the mood to answer too many questions. I should be with my mother.'

'That's understood. In fact, we're surprised to see you here.'

'I wouldn't be, but my father's work is important. It can't be allowed to fail.'

'Tell us, how do you plan to handle your father's death? How will you word your press statement?' Wendy said.

'How can we be accurate and ignore the fact he was murdered?'

'You can't,' Isaac said, 'but you're the second person in this office who has purposely not mentioned Helen Langdon.'

'We decided the best way to deal with the media would be for us not to mention Helen.'

'She worked here?' Isaac said.'

Yes, and very efficiently.'

'Then some advice. Don't ignore her, and don't try to hide the fact she was in bed with your father.'

'We thought it would be best.'

'Maybe you did, and if you were dealing with friends and relatives, then fine, but you're not. You're dealing with the British press, and they'll smell a rat if you try to hide the truth.'

'Then what do we say?'

'Words to the effect that tragically James Holden and Helen Langdon were killed in Bayswater today. The full details of how they died and what the motive was behind the slayings are still unclear. The police are conducting an investigation, and it would be inappropriate to comment further until more information is available. In the meantime, the good work of Mr Holden and his team of loyal supporters will continue.'

'You said everything without saying it,' Linda Holden said.

'You've not lied. You've acknowledged that Helen was killed, yet you've given no details.'

'And later on, when the press continues to pry?'

'The matter is with the police. It would be inappropriate to comment or speculate.'

'But everyone will know the truth.'

'It'll be headline news tomorrow, but you've not fuelled the fire.'

'Thank you. We'll follow your advice. I've made a note of what you just said.'

'Now, coming back to our investigation. What is your position in the organisation?'

'I was here in an advisory capacity, but now I'll be taking my father's position.'

'Are you qualified?' Wendy asked.

'I hope so. My father schooled me well in his beliefs. Beliefs I share as well.'

'Your father has died, upsetting in itself, no doubt. What we need to know is why?'

'My father did not make enemies intentionally, and he was not a firebrand. He was pragmatic, fully cognisant that in all of us is the need to rebel, to be bemused by the frailties of the human condition. He only wanted to control the descent into barbarism, not to curtail it totally.'

'Barbarism?'

'My father believed society was descending into a moral abyss as a result of modern technology. His opponents portrayed him as puritanical, against anything and everything. He was not that, but he held views, dated in modern society, which he put forward. He was vigorously opposed to the gratuitous sex and violence that pervade our lives.'

'There are people making fortunes out of those. They would be powerful enemies.'

'Potentially, but my father had little impact. However, I will continue the fight on his behalf and in his memory.'

'Helen Langdon?'

'My father had in the last few years become passionate in his desire to modernise the penal system in this country, more in line with the Scandinavian countries, where a prisoner is treated with respect, where conjugal visits are allowed, and for the more trusted, weekend leave. He saw the current system in England as regressive, whereby the felon is punished, not redeemed.'

'Helen Langdon?'

'She is not the only one that my father helped. He met her three years ago in prison. He spent time with her, as he did with the other prisoners, but her case seemed unique. The press had lambasted her when she married Gerald Adamant, criticised her when she gave the impression of loving her husband when she had given them no cause to doubt her sincerity.'

'Did you like Helen?' Wendy asked.

'Yes, I did, so did everyone in this office. Not forsaking her beauty, and the fact that most men swooned in her presence, she was a capable and devoted member of the team.'

'Is that for us, or is that a genuine answer?'

'It's genuine. Even the Adamant family spoke for her at her retrial. It's unlikely they would have done so if they had any doubts.'

'At the first trial?' Isaac asked

'They still spoke on her behalf, but the public interest was too intense. An acquittal then would have received too much negative comment. Helen served her time and then came here.'

'Her relationship with your father?'

'She was devoted to him.'

'Intimate?'

'Not that any of us knew. Their relationship seemed to transcend the physical. What they have done has shocked us all.'

'Was your mother shocked?'

'Inspector Cook, my father was not a saint, nor was he a martyr. He was a man, the same as you. No doubt he had the same desires and lusts that we all do, yet he kept them in check most of the time.'

'It was not the first indiscretion?'

'It was to me, although my mother may say otherwise. Whatever the outcome of his and Helen's murders, I will hold my father in the highest esteem.'

'And Helen?'

'If she had erred, the same as my father, then we will forgive her.'

***

Larry questioned the concierge at the hotel in Bayswater, although the title of concierge pinned to the lapel of the man's collar seemed inappropriate. A third-rate hotel in Bayswater was not the Savoy, and the so-called deluxe suite where the two bodies had been discovered was neither luxurious nor well-maintained.

'I found them there, lying on the bed,' the concierge said. 'I saw them come in. I thought she was on the game, and he was one of her marks. How was I to know it was high and mighty James Holden.'

'You've heard of the man?'

'Who hasn't, always preaching to the converted. For me, I do what I want, when I want, and watch what I want. It's alright for him, rich and powerful. If he wants a woman, he can get one anytime.'

'And the woman he was with?'

'She oozed a good time. No doubt that's what he got until someone put a bullet through his head. Shame about her, though.'

'Why?'

'Good looker. Would have fancied her myself. Mind you, if she were selling herself, it would have taken more than a week's salary for a night with her.'

'She wasn't selling herself. She was a colleague.'

'He may have been an old fool, but I'll give him his due, he knew how to pick his colleagues. In this hotel, there are only the cleaners, the day manager, and a lady who does the accounts. I wouldn't give any of them one, but Holden's woman, anytime.'

Larry studied the man: overweight, the top button of his shirt undone. His hair was long and greased back. Altogether, a poor specimen of a hotel employee, and someone who wouldn't be averse to looking through a crack in a door to watch the action.

'Who did they sign in as?'

'Mr and Mrs Smith, what else?'

'Do they still do that? Larry asked.

'Of course not. Bob Cleveland and Mary Gold.'

'This is a murder, not the time for you to make cheap attempts at humour.'

'It's not the first body in this hotel. The occasional guest dies here; first murder, though. Will it be on the news tonight?'

'It probably will. If you're interviewed for the television, I should remind you that we'll be watching. If you attempt to gain financially or if you're withholding vital information, then you will be charged with perverting the course of justice, do you understand?'

'I understand, I've been through the rigmarole before.'

'You've been in prison?'

'Two years for stealing. This hotel is the only place that would give me a job.'

'If you want to keep it, what's the truth?'

'Okay, he's been here before.'

'With the woman?'

'No, another one.'

'Her name?'

'She's a regular around here. No one signed in. He just paid his money, the same as he always does, and I gave him the key. It's not recorded in the books.'

'Which means you've made yourself some money on the side.'

'A few of the local women use this place. It's not much, but it's discreet. No wonder Holden brought the classy woman here. Mind you, she looked better than this place. Who was she, by the way?'

'You'll find out soon enough. In the meantime, I need a statement and a proof of address from you. Any peepholes in the doors or the walls upstairs?'

'I'm not into that. I've done my time, been punished. That's the problem with all of you. Once a criminal, always a criminal.'

'They're both dead, upstairs in your hotel. Where were you? What did you hear?'

'Nothing. They were up on the third floor, and this is an old building, not like the type they build these days.'

'Are there any cameras in here?'

'Only in reception.'

'We'll need the video.'

'It hasn't worked for six months, and it's not me, it's the management. They don't want to waste the money.'

'Someone came into this hotel and killed two people. Did you see anyone suspicious?'

'There's always one or two that look suspicious, but they come in with a local whore.'

'These local women, where do they live, who are they? We'll need to interview them, as well as the men they were with.'

'Not much chance there, and they don't sign in, just slip me the money.'

'Your job after this becomes known?'

'Non-existent. Yet again, a man trying to reform is forced back into crime by those upholding it.'

'Work with me, and I'll make sure you keep your job. How do I contact your management?'

'To report me?'

'No. To let them know that I'll be giving you an assistant for a few nights and that you, as the concierge, have been more than helpful.'

Chapter 4

John Holden attempted to be busy, but he could not focus. Not only was there the distraction of his dead father, but there was also the increasing media interest in how he died, and how the man had been in bed with a woman younger than his daughter, a woman that the man's son had come to love.

Not that there had ever been any physical contact with Helen. As she had freely admitted when John had pledged his desire to be with her, it was the father she loved, not the son.

There was a client Holden needed to deal with, a man who would require all of John Holden's legal skills, yet he could not give the man what he wanted. He knew he should be upset over his father's death, but he could only feel sadness for Helen, as well as the hurt he had felt when she had been found in bed with his father. James Holden, he knew, was a fraud. He had seduced his son's one true love, even though John had confessed this love to him on more than one occasion.

Helen's reply to John had always been the same: 'My need of men has passed. They have only caused me problems.' John knew it was only the talk of someone who had spent four years in jail. Helen Langdon was a woman who needed a man, a woman who needed him, but she had rejected him, discarded him as if he was an old sock.

John Holden was angry, and his anger could not be abated. He wanted to sit down and cry, he wanted to lash out, he wanted someone to pay, but the person responsible was dead. He had never been fooled by his father, an eccentric who went around preaching goodness and love and family values, yet couldn't keep his trousers on if there was an attractive woman nearby. And it wasn't as if the man was handsome, not like the son. Holden got up from where he was sitting and stood in front of a mirror in his office in Mayfair. He studied his features. 'Perfection,' he said out loud. So loud that his personal assistant in the other room knocked on his door. 'Are you alright, Mr Holden?'

'Fine, thank you,' he replied. He straightened his tie, dabbed at the moistness around his eyes, and opened the door to the other room. 'I'll see my next client now,' he said.

***

Seth Caddick did not like DCI Isaac Cook, the senior investigating officer in Homicide at Challis Street. He needed to remove him from his position and to bring in his man, someone who would respect him, the same way he respected Commissioner Davies.

Caddick, a realist, knew that Isaac was competent, but he was not his police officer, he was the former superintendent's, the high and mighty Richard Goddard, a man who could play the political game as well as he could. A man who had succeeded because he had been friendly with the previous commissioner, Lord Shaw, and now Cook, Goddard, and Shaw were plotting to bring down Alwyn Davies. Caddick knew he had to do his part; he had to get rid of Cook.

'Watch out for Cook, the man's no fool,' Alwyn Davies had said in his office at Scotland Yard the previous day. 'Caddick, you're my man, and I'll protect you, but you're not up to the standard required for a superintendent.'

'I thought I was doing a good job,' Caddick had protested.

'You're not listening. You've succeeded well enough by claiming credit for others' work. No problem in itself, it happens all the time. Politicians claim they fixed the economy when the previous government had put in place the plans for recovery. I've claimed credit for the previous commissioner's efforts, and you've claimed credit from Goddard and Cook.'

'What are you saying?'

'The honeymoon period's over. It's up to you to prove yourself. It's for you to make your mark.'

'And how am I meant to do that?'

'You need Cook out and our man in. Cook's good on his feet, and with an audience that's listening, he's believable. You're good as well, but you don't look as impressive as Cook. People instinctively are drawn to him.'

'Is that an insult, sir?' Caddick asked. He was not used to criticism, especially from Davies.

'It's a fact, and you've got to do something about it.'

'I'm doing the best I can. We're bringing in the results.'

'You're not, Cook is. Is our man ready to take over from Cook?'

'He's available.'

'Then you need him, and soon. Goddard's in the background, stirring the pot.'

'Can't you transfer him out?'

'Goddard's got powerful friends. Men who are looking for the opportunity to pounce and evict me from this office. I've no intention of giving them the satisfaction, and you're not helping.'

'If you can't get rid of Goddard, then how can I get rid of Cook?'

'You've got to ride the man, you've got to prove he's not doing his job. His team, what about them?'

'They're loyal to him. I tried to get rid of Sergeant Gladstone. She's getting close to retirement, and she's not in the best of health.'

'And?'

'Cook said she was fine.'

'Is she?'

'She's Cook's person.'

'What have you done about it?'

'Nothing more at present.'

'Then do something. Get her checked out, make sure her health is up to scratch. What about her policing skills, reporting?'

'She's not computer literate.'

'Then subject her to the full treatment. Make sure she's on the list for early retirement, but whatever you do, you've got to undermine Cook, get him out. His replacement is a good man. He can do Cook's job, you can't.'

'But...'

'Don't but me, Seth. I'm under pressure, and if I go, you'll not be far behind. I put you in Goddard's position to support me, and so far, you've been a liability. At some stage, when they're ratcheting up the pressure on me, they'll be looking at my appointees and those I've sidelined, and you'll be subjected to a full audit of your policing skills, your ability to perform as a superintendent. And you know what they'll find?'

'No, sir.'

'They'll find someone who has been promoted without the necessary checks, and it'll reflect on me. I'm giving you two months with this, and then…'

'Goddard?'

'If it gives me a few months, I'll put him back at Challis Street.'

'But they'll see it as a weakness on your part.'

'What do I care, as long as I'm still in a job.'

'And me?' Caddick asked.

'Don't worry, I'll find you somewhere else.'

***

With Larry following up on the other woman who had been at the hotel in Bayswater with James Holden, Isaac and Wendy took the opportunity to make contact with the Adamant family.

Gerald Adamant, the dead patriarch, had inherited a mansion and its expansive grounds from his father on his death. His father had made a fortune in business; his son, Gerald, had every intention of enjoying the wealth.

He had been in his late twenties when he had married his first wife, the daughter of an investment adviser. Soon, in rapid succession, two children, Archie then Abigail.

'We're here because of the death of Helen, your father's third wife,' Isaac said. A maid brought in tea for those in the visitor's room of the Adamants' Victorian mansion. Also present were Archie, Abigail, now forty-one, and Howard, the son of Adamant's second wife. He was twenty-nine, and as Isaac had observed, not as impressive a figure as his step-siblings.

Archie was forty-three. He was erect, well-spoken. His sister, Abigail, was attractive. Not as beautiful on the eye as Helen Langdon had been, but still agreeable. Wendy thought she looked like someone who was into horses. The youngest, Howard, sat casually on a sofa. He was wearing a tee-shirt and jeans. Wendy's summation was that he spent the father's money, did little to earn any for himself.

'We had great respect and love for Helen,' Archie said. 'Her death has come as a shock to us.'

'She killed your father. How could you feel anything but loathing for the woman?'

'She made him happy.'

'And you loved your father that much, you agreed to him marrying a woman younger than any of you?'

'Not at first. We were suspicious of her motives, and her first impression in this house was not favourable. She was all over our father, and exceedingly pleasant to us.'

'Sickening,' Abigail said.

'And what about you, Howard?' Wendy asked.

'I didn't like it, especially when she tried to mother me.'

'Let me explain on behalf of Howard,' Archie said. 'Howard had found Helen on the internet. He's good with technology, that's why he makes more money than either my sister or myself.'

Wendy realised she had judged the cover, not the book, in the case of Howard Adamant.

'I write programs for computers. People buy them, I make a bundle,' Howard said, slightly more interested than before.

'She was more Howard's age,' Archie said. 'He didn't like it because he fancied her.'

'And what's wrong with that. She was a good-looking woman,' Howard said. 'You couldn't keep your eyes off her.'

'I'm not saying I could.'

'We are aware of Helen's attributes. We've been told about her by the Holden family.'

'How are they taking it?'

'Stoically. How about you three?'

'In time, Helen proved to us that she cared for our father,' Abigail said. 'To him, she was his wife, to us, she was a sister. We all grew very fond of her. Our mother, Archie's and mine, had died young, and then Howard's mother passed away a few years ago. Both wives had loved him, as he had them.'

'Is there any more that we should know about your mothers?' Isaac asked.

'Howard's mother was a few years younger than our father. Our mother was the same age as him,' Abigail said. 'Our father was a well-respected member of society, who we thought at first had gone slightly mad when he arrived at the house with Helen.'

'Trying to regain lost youth with a younger woman,' Archie said.

'Much younger,' Howard said, 'and yes, I did fancy Helen. I wanted her, even made a pass at her, but she wasn't like that. She looked it, but she was a decent person.'

'Your relationship with her, eventually?'

'I still fancied her, and she knew it. It became a joke between us, nothing more. I'll not say a bad word about her.'

'Yet the woman killed your father?' Isaac said.

'Helen had seen a change in his behaviour for a few months. She had confided in us, asked our advice,' Abigail said.

'And what did you say?'

'We pleaded with our father to see a specialist, but he wouldn't hear of it. Our father was conscious of his own mortality, and he wasn't willing to admit he was getting old.'

'The young wife?'

'At first, but he loved Helen as much as she loved him.'

'And your reaction when your father died?' Wendy asked.

'We were shocked and upset. We blamed Helen, called her some wicked things, but then came the autopsy, and the pathologist stating our father had a brain tumour and it could have been responsible for his aggression. They did find bruising around Helen's neck.'

'Did you speak to Helen before her trial?'

'I did,' Abigail said. 'She was contrite, emotional, and sorry for what she had done.'

'Did you believe her?'

'I wasn't sure what to believe. She had killed our father, the result of a violent confrontation. At the trial, the first trial, the experts for the defence and the prosecution were arguing as to whether a brain tumour could have been responsible for our father's aggression.'

'And what did you believe?'

'We all wanted to believe that Helen was innocent. She was family, she was important to us.'

'At the first trial, you, Archie, made a plea on behalf of the family.'

'It was obvious Helen was going to prison, but the experts were in conflict. We just wanted it to be known we did not hold any blame against her.'

'It's an unusual reaction,' Isaac said. 'Normally, the family of the deceased are vehement in their condemnation. Why are you so different?'

'Because we knew our father, we knew Helen. If it had been us, we would have acted in the same way.'

'Had it happened before?'

'Once or twice. He hit me once for no reason,' Abigail said.

'And when was this?'

'When I broached the idea of him visiting a specialist.'

'Was anyone else present?'

'It was only me.'

'Had Helen raised the subject with him?'

'On one occasion. He didn't like it, but he didn't hit her. She was afraid to talk to him again, that's why I tried.'

'Your stepmother was in jail. What did you do?'

'Archie's a lawyer. He put together a team to examine the evidence. That's when we came across James Holden.'

'You knew the man?'

'We all did. He visited Helen in jail. I went with him the first time,' Abigail said.

'After that?'

'He'd go on his own, once or twice a month. We could see whenever we visited her that she was becoming enamoured of Holden, not that we discouraged it.'

'It was Holden who managed to get her out of prison,' Isaac said.

'He approached us, asked us to write a letter stating our non-objection, and in time she was released. Six months after her release, new evidence from another expert showed that more research had been done in America on the effect of a brain tumour pressing on certain parts of the brain. It was accepted, and the conviction against Helen was quashed.'

'Did you keep in contact after her release?'

'We did, not often though. Helen seemed to want the past behind her, and we understood. She was always welcome here though, and she'd phone occasionally. I doubt if we saw her more than three or four times since her release.'

'And now, to find out that she has been in bed with Holden?' Isaac said.

'We knew of her affection for the man, but he was married,' Abigail said. 'We reserve our judgement on Helen, but we'll never waiver in our support for her. She was an important part of our father's life.'

Outside the mansion, as Isaac and Wendy were preparing to leave, he asked 'What did you make of what they said?'

'Helen Langdon is either due for sainthood, or we've been fed nonsense.'

'They did support her at the trials. For Helen's benefit, or was there an ulterior motive?'

'You don't buy their holier than thou attitude?' Wendy said.

'Too good to be true,' Isaac said. 'Get Bridget to dig in the dirt, find out what she can about the Adamants.'

Chapter 5

With Helen Langdon, née Mackay, identified as the woman who had been killed with James Holden, as well as the woman who had killed Gerald Adamant, public sentiment towards her vacillated. Some saw her as the callous murderer of an old husband; others, as the falsely maligned and loyal wife of a man who had gone mad. Her parents' home was surrounded by the press and gawping onlookers when Isaac and Wendy arrived. Barricades had been erected in the street, a uniform stationed at the front door.

'It's been madness,' the uniform said. 'The poor parents inside are doing their best to cope, and the mongrels outside are making it into a party. We even had an ice-cream van parked on the other side of the road. It was doing sterling business until we moved it on.'

Isaac had seen it too many times. A murder, someone's misfortune, and the bizarre, the plain nosey, were incapable of showing any compassion for those trying to deal with the emotions and the raw nerves. Mr and Mrs Mackay seemed to be two such people.

'Helen, she was a good daughter,' her father said.

'I'm sorry,' Isaac said, 'but I must ask you certain questions.'

'We understand,' her softly spoken mother said. 'We've not slept since it happened, not certain if we will ever again.'

Wendy could see the emotions on their faces. She felt as if she should go over and put her arm around the mother but decided not to. It was a formal interview, and the parents may have some information that would not be revealed if there was overfamiliarity.

'When did you last see your daughter?' Isaac asked.

'The day she died. She popped in for a cup of tea, unannounced.'

'Her mood?'

'She was cheerful, enjoying being unknown.'

'She would be known around here?' Wendy said.

'Not here. We moved from our previous house. The notoriety was too much, the parents of a murderer, not that we ever believed it.'

'Why? Your daughter married an older man. If I'm not mistaken, Gerald Adamant was older than you, Mr Mackay.'

'He was. He wanted to call me Dad. I wasn't having any of it. It was always Gerald and Frank whenever we met.'

'Was that often?'

'Not often. Helen, she was busy with Gerald's philanthropic pursuits, but she phoned every week. Once we had got over the initial shock of the age difference, we accepted them as a married couple.'

'Did Helen have a penchant for older men?'

'Do you mean, was she wiggling her arse to seduce them? Is that what you're saying?'

'Frank, she's our daughter. You can't say that about her,' Betty, Helen's mother, said.

'It's what they said in the newspapers. It's what the two police officers here want to ask, but they'll be polite. Am I correct, Inspector Cook?'

'I would have used different wording, but yes.'

'You know of Helen's history. It was the same when she was young. Fourteen and then she starts filling out. The local youths can't handle it, but Helen's not like that. She was studious, always got good marks at school, and then she goes to university, a good degree, but what happens? The boss is after her, the men in the office fancy their chances, but all Helen wants is to do her job, meet a nice man, and settle down. She tried it once, lived with him for a few months, the date is set for the marriage, and then he takes off. After that, she's upset, so she appears onstage at a club.'

'We're aware of this?'

'Bare breasts, plenty of flesh. Not that Helen liked it, but she had become tired of using her brain, only for men to see below her neck. Anyway, after a year or so, Gerald walks into her life. We warned her about older men, but she said she was fine with him, and she was. At least, up until that fateful day when he tried to kill her, and she hit him with the hammer.'

Wendy could see the mother sobbing. She relented and went and put her arm around the distraught woman; Isaac understood why she did so. He had once had to tell the parents of a young man of seventeen that he had blown himself up and twenty others in a terrorist attack. The memory of the mother's reaction still haunted him, even after so many years.

'Your relationship with the Adamants?'

'The younger son could be surly, but he was decent enough, the same as his brother and sister.'

'Surly?'

'He fancied Helen, more her age than his father was, but she was committed to Gerald, and the younger son, a smart man by all accounts, wasn't her kind of man. She told us he reminded her of all the men she had met before. She offered them companionship and an intelligent woman. All they saw was a quick lay. Apologies for my speaking about my daughter like that, but with us, Helen was very open. It was the way we liked it with her. She wasn't only our daughter, she was also our friend.'

'The Adamants supported her at her trial.'

'They did, and very commendable of them, but with so much publicity, and Helen looking the way she did, the sentiment of the jury was against her. We used to visit her in prison at every opportunity, and then, there was James Holden.'

'Did you meet him?'

'On many occasions. Another decent man, the same as Gerald.'

'Older?'

'Helen had enjoyed being married to Gerald. He treated her well, never flaunted her, and he always included her in his conversations, entrusted her to help with his philanthropic work. She told us that James Holden was the same as Gerald and he was going to get her out of prison. We could see she was becoming close to the man, and even though he was married, and we warned her, the heart doesn't know such boundaries.'

'After her release?'

'She went to work for Holden, although the salary wasn't much. Not that Helen needed it. The Adamants ensured she had an apartment and some money.'

'I must ask this,' Isaac said. 'Helen, as you say, was a good person, so was Holden, yet they ended up in a hotel together.'

'We've tried to understand why,' Betty Mackay said, temporarily revived by Wendy's ministrations. 'As much as she may have loved James, he was still married. She would not have considered it for one moment, not our Helen.'

'But she did. The facts are clear, and we need to know why. Mr Mackay, do you have any thoughts?'

'No more than my wife. Helen would have only agreed if it was for James's well-being, but he was older than me. The passion doesn't run as strong, the need to rush off to a hotel for a little romance doesn't seem plausible. That's more the folly of teenagers in love, not an old man and one of his employees.'

'Regardless, it did happen,' Isaac said, 'and not only that, we know that James Holden had been there with another woman in the past.'

'Then we are lost as to why Helen was there with him unless it was important. Are you sure they were involved?'

'We're sure. There's proof.'

***

Two men waited in the reception of the hotel in Bayswater. Neither man was comfortable with the other: the concierge because his money-making venture, his time with one of the whores instead of payment, would be curtailed, and the other man, Police Constable Trevor Greenock, because he was fastidious about personal hygiene, and the concierge stank.

'What time does this woman come in?' Greenock asked.

'It depends. Some nights she doesn't come in at all.'

'Attractive?'

'I'd say so,' the concierge said, although not as attractive as the murdered woman had been, he knew that. He had seen them through the peephole, seen the old man's attempt at lovemaking, imagined it was him, young and virile, with her. If it had not been for the bell on reception, another whore bringing her mark in, he would have stayed watching Holden and the woman; he would have seen who shot them.

'It's not much of a hotel is it,' Greenock said. He was a tall man with black wavy hair. Two years with the police, and his first stakeout. He had changed his police uniform for an assistant manager's at the hotel. Tomorrow he'd have a talk to Homicide and see if he could move over on a more permanent basis.

'Some of the women who come in here aren't much either.'

'Then why was Holden here?'

'You'd better ask him.'

'He's dead, that's why I'm asking you,' Greenock said. He could sense the unpleasant man knew more than he was letting on.

'Sometimes men like a bit of the rough, a woman off the street. Men like Holden, I see them in here occasionally. They spend their lives being respectable, law-abiding citizens, when all they want to do is rebel, the same as all of us. But it's not possible, you know that, not in the long term anyway. They come down here. One was even a vicar, not that he realised that I knew.'

'How did you know?'

'My father, he was keen on the church. Every weekend we'd be there. Everyone gives away what and who they are by the way they walk, their mannerisms.'

'Regular Sherlock Holmes, aren't you?'

'Not me. I've read all his books, and he's right. You watch the next one that comes in.'

Soon after, a woman, dressed in a white blouse with a red skirt, walked in through the door. The man was dressed casually, an open-necked shirt, a pair of jeans.

'The usual, Joyce?' the concierge said.

'I'd say by the way he walked he was a police officer,' Greenock said.

'I'd have him down as an army officer. Why the police?'

'I've seen him around, not that I've ever spoken to him, and he didn't recognise me.'

'Any problem for him?'

'Not if he's off duty.'

A forty-five minute wait, another woman. 'It's her,' the concierge said.

'Excuse me. I'm Police Constable Greenock. I've a few questions if you don't mind.'

The man she had come in with attempted to rush out of the hotel. Greenock had pre-empted him by remotely locking the entrance door. 'You'll not get out of here. And besides, it's the lady that interests the police, not you.'

'I've not done anything,' the woman protested. 'I'm registered, legal, even pay my taxes.'

'I'm here about a man you brought in here in the past.'

'I'm like a priest. I don't tell on anyone. They pay their money, they have their fun, and that's it.'

'Your name, sir?' Greenock said, turning to the flustered man.

'It'll ruin me.'

'Were you here on the night of the murder?'

'I read about it, James Holden. This is my first time here.'

Greenock looked over at the concierge. He shook his head, indicating the man had lied.

'Okay, I'll tell you what we'll do. If you provide me with evidence as to who you are, you can leave now. I've got your photo, and I'll check your phone before you leave. I'll just take a few contacts off it, phone them up if we can't contact you, tell them that we're looking for a man who had been with a prostitute in Bayswater. I'm sure we'll find you soon enough.'

'Conrad Evans, I'm a builder in the city. I was on my way home. It's been a long day, and I see Daisy here, and she beckons me over. That's the truth, believe me.'

'I do. Your identification and your phone.'

Greenock picked up his phone while the man fumbled in his wallet. 'Send a car,' he said. 'You'll need to come to the station with me,' he said to the woman.

'What for? Business has been quiet. You'll have to feed me if you want to talk.'

'Pizza?'

'That'll do.'

Her client left, a police car arrived. 'I'll look past your taking backhanders from the whores this time,' Greenock said to the concierge.

'Don't worry. Your Inspector Hill fixed it with the management. I work with you; he'll protect me.'

'The long arm of the law protecting the villains. Whatever next?'

'It was the long arm of the law that put me inside in the first place.'

'You'll be here tomorrow?'

'I hope so. It's a lousy job, but it does have benefits.'

'Joyce?'

'You've got it.'

'You're a foul man,' Greenock said. 'Don't think tonight has been a pleasure for me.'

'I've got a thick skin. Nothing you say will affect me.'

'No doubt it won't. I hope you enjoy your time with Joyce.'

'More than you will with Daisy.'

Chapter 6

At Challis Street Police Station, the prostitute sat quietly in one corner, eating a pizza. 'Not much to look at,' Wendy said.

Isaac thought his sergeant was harsh in her criticism. He could see the woman had the look of the street and the needle marks on her arms were not the best, but considering the life the woman had led, she had fared better than most.

'What are you looking at?' the woman said, lifting her head away from the pizza.

'Nothing,' Isaac said. 'When you're ready.'

'Are you going to charge me?'

'There's no charge. We've just got a few questions.'

'Okay, let's get on with it. I've lost enough money tonight because of you.'

Inside the interview room, Daisy sat on one side, Isaac and Wendy on the other. 'Could we have your correct name, please?' Isaac said.

'Elizabeth Wetherington.'

'Miss Wetherington…'

'Call me Daisy, everyone else does.'

'Daisy, we are interested in a man you took to the hotel several times in the past.'

'How do you expect me to remember. I go there, they have what they want, and then they leave. I don't get to study them, not even talk to them most of the time.'

'According to the concierge, you took this man to the hotel two weeks ago on a Thursday. Can you remember back to that day?'

'My memory's not so good.'

'What does it need to help it?'

'Money would help.'

Wendy studied the woman: peroxide blonde, heavy on the make-up, bright-red lipstick, a drawn face.

'There's no money in here,' Isaac said. 'The best you could do is to give us your information and then you're out of here.'

'Okay, a Thursday two weeks ago. It was a busy night, made some good money.'

'And what's good money?' Wendy asked.

'Five hundred pounds at least.'

'And then you spent it shooting up.'

'Maybe I did, maybe I didn't.'

'I'll show you a photo,' Isaac said. 'If you recognise him, let me know.' Isaac pushed the photo of James Holden across the desk. Daisy picked it up and studied it for a few seconds.

'He always treated me well, paid more than the others.'

'Why did he pay more?'

'I don't know, guilt maybe. Some of them regret what they've done afterwards. Some of them are in tears because they've cheated on their wives.'

'Does that worry you?'

'The tears or the cheating?'

'The cheating.'

'Why? Should it? I'm not their social worker. I'm a working woman trying to survive. If they want me, they pay. If they don't, they can keep on walking by, but him, he doesn't. He phones me up, we meet outside the hotel, sometimes inside. We go up to the room, and that's it. Fifteen minutes later I'm back on the street looking for another man.'

'Not much of a life, is it?' Wendy said.

'I was married once. He used to beat me. Out on the street is better than that, and anyway, I'm used to it.'

'What can you tell us about the man in the picture?' Isaac said.

'He never gave me a name. He's polite, a little on the old side, but he manages.'

'With your help,' Wendy said.

'That's what he pays for. Once it's over, he gives me my money and leaves. He's not much into conversation. It's purely business. I've got the commodity, he's got the money.'

'Are there many like him?'

'Not many. Most of them are rough, drunk from a night out at the pub, some are violent.'

'Coming back to the man in question,' Isaac said. 'What else can you tell us about him.'

'Nothing really. As I said, he didn't talk much.'

'Why do you think he paid you for sex?'

'I've no idea. Most of them have an unhappy home life. Some want to tell me about it, but I'm not interested. But with him, nothing. I just assumed he wanted a bit of the rough.'

'And you're the rough?'

'You know what I mean. There's no baggage with me, no pretending it's love. It's into the room, strip down, a couple of minutes fumbling around, him on top of me, me on top of him, and that's it.'

'Clinical,' Wendy said.

'No doubt, but, as I said, I was married once. I don't want to pretend to be in love only to be thrown across the room on another night.'

'Do you watch the television, read the newspapers?' Isaac said.

'Not me. I've no time for television, and I'm not interested in the news.'

'The man we are questioning you about was murdered. Did you know that?'

'Not me.'

'He was murdered in the hotel where you met Constable Greenock. It was the room you normally use.'

'And you think I'm involved?'

'He was with another woman.'

'And I could have been murdered if I had been with him?'

'We don't think so. I suggest you read the newspaper in future. The man's name was James Holden. Have you heard of him?'

'Not me.'

'He's well known. A member of parliament, a moral campaigner.'

'And he was with me. If I'd known, I would have charged him double.'

'The woman's name was Helen Mackay. Have you heard of her?'

'Helen, sent to prison for murdering that old man?'

'Yes, that's her.'

'Before she latched on to him, we used to work together in Soho.'

'On the street?'

'Not Helen. She was down on her luck, the same as me, and we're in this club, strutting around with next to nothing on.'

'Was it a strip club?' Wendy asked.

'They called it a gentlemen's club, not that many of the customers were. All they wanted to do was to grab us, make us sit on their laps, and let them fondle our breasts.'

'And you let them?'

'Why not? They were generous with their tips.'

'And Helen, was she into this?'

'The men wanted her, more than me, more than any of the other girls.'

'You've not answered my question.'

'Helen kept her distance. She was a classy woman, and then, one day, she's gone. We were all envious of her, but she never fitted in.'

'Why's that?'

'As I said, she didn't belong. She was a beautiful woman, not like us.'

'You still look okay,' Wendy said.

'Sure, but Helen was in a league of her own. She could have made plenty of money, set herself up as a high-class escort. She always said she wanted to settle down, find a man who treated her well. She was intelligent, advising us on how to live our lives, where to invest our money.'

'Were you and the other women resentful?'

'Of Helen? No way. We all loved her.'

'When she killed her husband?'

'I wanted to be a character witness, but her lawyer wasn't too keen. Anyway, in the end, her dead husband's family said a few words for her.'

'Were you at the trial?'

'Every day. I couldn't help her, but she was my friend.'

'When she came out of prison, did you make contact with her?'

'I contacted her once, but she was distant. It was clear she wanted to put the past behind her, so I left her alone.'

'And she ended up with your man in your room at the hotel.'

'I don't get that,' Daisy said.

'Nor do we. You're free to go,' Isaac said.

'I hope you find who did it. Helen was my friend. I'll be sad tonight. I think I'll go home.'

'What did you reckon?' Wendy said after Daisy had left, a police car organised to drop her one street from the flat she shared with another working girl.

'Holden wanted Helen, fixated on her, and he couldn't have her, but he can have an old friend.'

'There's more than a few psychoses there.'

'How did Holden know that Daisy wouldn't be at the hotel on the night he went with Helen? Why that hotel?'

'As I said, the man had some issues.'

'You're right,' Isaac said. 'We need to find out what they were.'

***

Isaac met up with Richard Goddard, Homicide's former chief superintendent. Caddick would have regarded it as gross disloyalty; Isaac considered it necessary.

'How is it in Public Relations?' Isaac asked as the two men sat down for lunch at a pub on the other side of the River Thames.

'It's a hard battle convincing anyone the Met is on top of their game. Commissioner Davies is making a right hash of it, and now he's planning to bring in another lackey to lord it over us.'

'Can he?'

'They're trying to get him out, but it takes time, and in the interim, he'll do what he wants.'

'Can't they stop him? There are procedures in place to control who is hired, who is fired.'

'The man's fighting back, pushing the envelope. He'll claim discretionary powers, and what is anyone going to do? Subject him to a disciplinary hearing, invite the press in to watch? Our commissioner is a caged animal. He'll do whatever's necessary to survive.'

'If you were in his position?'

'Are you saying I'm as bad as him?'

'Not at all, sir, but you're a political animal. Can't you play the system? Take some shortcuts, put Davies under pressure?'

'From Public Relations? It's hardly likely, and besides, I'm a chief superintendent. There's more than a few ranks separating me from Davies.'

'Then bring them on board.'

'Some are on board, but no one's willing to show their hand just yet.'

'And in the meantime, the Met goes down the tube, us with it?'

'Regardless of Davies and Caddick, you've got a job to do. What's the situation with James Holden?'

'Any murmurings from where you are?'

'There's concern at Westminster. The man was a politician, and they're all watching.'

'There'd be a few skeletons down there.'

'I know of some,' Goddard said.

'If Holden is held up to ridicule, then eventually the press will start looking into the behaviour of others.'

'They're always trying, but so far they've not found anything.'

'Why's that?'

'The relationship between those in power and those in influence is still strong.'

'Influence? You mean those who control the television channels and the newspapers?'

'Yes. Mind you, social media is an issue. That can't be controlled.'

'Holden wanted it curtailed,' Isaac said.

'He wanted to control the sex and the violence, not the truth.'

'That's the problem. Once you start putting clamps in place, you escalate into other areas that should be sacrosanct.'

'Freedom of the press?'

'Exactly.'

'Do you think the media moguls would care if Facebook and Twitter were throttled?'

'No. Is that what Holden was doing?'

'Indirectly.'

The two men had been talking for over thirty minutes and had not ordered. Isaac called over the waiter. 'Two of your specials, a bottle of wine.'

'What's the occasion?' Goddard said.

'It's good to be here, sir.'

'Caddick, how's he performing?'

'He's learning. He's picked up the clichéd responses, found himself some sycophants, as well as a lady to deal with his paperwork. She's efficient and apparently loyal.'

'Talk to her, find out if she is.'

'Undermine him from within?'

'Don't try it. That'll get you suspended. Those who are pandering to him, important?'

'No. They're moderate performers, but they'll keep him informed.'

'Then do your job, solve the case,' Goddard said. 'What is it with Holden? How come he gets himself murdered with a woman who had spent time in prison?'

'She was declared innocent at a retrial.'

'Maybe she was, but mud sticks, and it's stuck to Holden's legacy, threatening to undo his good work.'

'Good work?'

'His work with the prison system, that's well-founded. It was a creaking institution, in need of a clean broom. If his party had been elected to power, he would have become the Secretary of State for Justice. No possibility his death is politically motivated?'

'None we can see at the present moment.'

'Caddick is aiming to bring his man in to take your place,' Goddard said.

'He tried it once before.'

'This time he might succeed. Don't give Caddick a chance to unseat you.'

'Can I stop him?'

'Only by good policing.'

Chapter 7

Linda Holden, the head of the organisation that her father had set up to combat declining moral standards, realised she had been given the poisoned chalice. With her father's death, and his subsequent exposure as a man who preached one thing, did another, his star had fallen.

Isaac and Larry knew when they visited James Holden's offices that the man once held in such high esteem had erred more than once. According to Daisy, the prostitute, she had been four times in that hotel with him: the same room, the same bed.

Holden taking Helen Langdon there too, and using the same bed, seemed unusual.

Bridget was delving into the man's childhood, attempting to understand what drove him and whether it was hereditary. John Holden, the son, it had been found, had a history of violence when he was younger, a need to cause trouble. Isaac saw him as a possible suspect, but he would have had to know of his father's peccadilloes, as well as where he went with Helen and when.

'It's not been easy,' Linda Holden said. Isaac and Larry were in her office. Another lady had brought them a coffee each from the machine in the office kitchen. To Isaac, it was not up to the standard of the coffee he usually purchased at a café near Challis Street. However, he thanked the lady for her kindness.

'What do you mean?' Isaac said, looking at Linda. He could see she was struggling to manage, her desk cluttered with papers.

'My father was regarded by some as a saviour. A man who stood up for the common man, the decent man, but now…'

'Social pariah?'

'No one's listening. That's the problem: put yourself on a pedestal, and you're soon knocked off.'

'It was your father's doing,' Isaac said.

'And Helen's. We trusted her, even welcomed her into our home, and then she goes and sleeps with our father. Do you know why?'

'What did you know of Helen's past life?'

'I read the transcript of her first trial.'

'Then you know about the club.'

'Our parents taught us not to be judgemental, to take people as you find them.'

'With Helen, was that possible?'

'Yes. My opinion of her has been shaken, but I still regard her as a friend.'

'Then you must have some ideas as to why she was in that hotel with your father.'

'Was it the first time?'

'In that hotel with Helen, but he had been there before.'

'Who with?'

'A woman who had known Helen before she went to prison; before she married Gerald Adamant.'

'After my father met Helen, he had her checked out. She was in prison for killing her husband. My father had to be sure she was worthy of his help.'

'And what did he find out?'

'The report's here. I read it two days ago for the first time.'

'Damning?'

'I've made you a copy.'

'We'll read it back at Challis Street. Tell us, what did you gain from the report?'

Linda Holden sat back, reflected on what to say. 'Everyone she came into contact with had only good things to say about her. She had been an accountant before, competent according to her boss.'

'She had trouble with him.'

'She had that effect on men, even my brother.'

'What about him?'

'He was in love with her, but she rejected him.'

'How did he take it?'

'Badly.'

'Your brother, he doesn't seem as agreeable as you.'

'John's got a temper, and he was upset over Helen. He blows hot and cold sometimes, but he was always polite with her, distant with my father.'

'No love lost?'

'My brother respected our father, although he didn't always follow his advice. There were a few instances when John was younger, drunkenness, occasionally sneaking a girl into his bedroom.'

'Normal for a young man,' Isaac said.

'Normal for me,' Larry said.

'My father wasn't upset over what he had done. My father was a pragmatist, but he had a reputation to uphold, a reputation that depended on his family, as well.'

'And a teen has hormones driving him in another direction.'

'Would your brother be capable of murder?' Isaac said.

'Not John. Don't think because I told you about him and my father that he'd be capable of that. He admired my father, loved Helen. He'd not do anything to either of them.'

'How about the people in this office? Some must have been suspicious of the special relationship between Helen and your father.'

'We all knew, even our mother, but we trusted Helen.'

Isaac was always suspicious when everyone told him that the person was a saint, would never harm a fly. Experience had taught him that everyone was flawed, even the righteous.

'What about you?' Isaac said. 'What's your secret?'

'What do you mean?'

'No one's perfect. Your father's been murdered. Nobody has the luxury of privacy. We'll dig deep if you don't tell us.'

'Apart from an inappropriate love affair in my twenties, there's nothing. I'm married now, have been for twelve years, two children.'

'Inappropriate?'

'He was married. It ended badly.'

'How?'

'His wife found out. There was a scene where she confronted us in the hotel room.'

'How did she find out?'

'I never knew. I was heartbroken, but time heals.'

'And the man?'

'He went back to her. I see them from time to time.'

'Socially?'

'Not socially, but we move in the same circles.'

'Anything said?'

'Nothing.'

'Does your husband know?'

'No.'

'Your father, your mother?'

'I can't be sure. And besides, it was a long time ago.'

***

James Holden's body was released from Pathology and handed over to the family. They had asked for respect and to be able to grieve in peace – it was not to happen.

At the church James and Violet Holden attended every Sunday, the vultures were waiting, cameras at the ready. Isaac had seen them on his arrival and had asked the uniforms to make sure they didn't get too close.

John and Violet Holden were the first to arrive. Soon after, Linda Holden, accompanied by her husband and two children. Isaac noticed a few politicians, everyone from James Holden's office.

'Not much of a showing,' Wendy said. She sat at the back of the church with Isaac. They hadn't been invited, but it was an excellent chance to watch the reactions of the people, to see if there were any unknown faces.

'Under the circumstances, it's the most that could be expected. The family's been ostracised since his murder. Why was he in that hotel?'

'With that woman.'

'It'll become clearer in time, but if Helen Langdon is so important, then why a flea-bitten hotel frequented by prostitutes?'

'You don't buy the idea that he may have had some sordid perversion, a need to demean Helen, to blame her for his weaknesses.'

'Not with her, I don't.'

'Then what?'

'I don't know. What do you reckon to the family?'

'His wife seems upset, so does his daughter. The son appears ambivalent.'

At the front of the church, the priest went through the funeral service, both John and Linda reading from the bible, Linda also delivering a eulogy, failing to mention the circumstances of her father's death.

At the end, the coffin was borne away on the shoulders of six men, one of them John Holden, another Linda's husband.

'What do we know about the husband?' Wendy said, as the coffin passed by.

'Married to Linda for twelve years, the CEO of a manufacturing company. Not much to tell about him.'

'Any reason to believe he might be involved?'

'You can check him out if you like, but I'm suspicious of John Holden. His alibi is weak for the night of the murder.'

'At home reading. A single man in his forties. It doesn't sound natural.'

'Gay?'

'He was keen on Helen.'

'Why Helen? He's not a bad-looking man. There must be plenty of opportunities for him.'

Outside the church, the cortege left, the hearse in front, two limousines carrying the Holden family following.

'Not much more to be gained here,' Wendy said.

'Caddick's trying to get me out. I've received some information.'

'What will you do?'

'Solve this case. He'll not act if I do, and he'll not act to remove me at this time.'

'He'll wait until the right time, take credit for your good work.'

'That's how it works,' Isaac said.

'Not in my book, it doesn't.'

'Your book's an old edition.'

'It's the edition I prefer.'

'This time, I intend to fight fire with fire.'

'You're going to take him on, get him out of Challis Street, bring back Chief Superintendent Goddard?'

'When the time's right.'

'That's not like you, guv.'

'These are unusual times. The old rules no longer apply.'

'Be careful. It could backfire.'

'That's why I'm forewarning you. I don't want anyone else involved.'

'We'll be right behind you, you know that.'

'I know, but I'll not be able to help you if I don't succeed.'

***

Back at Challis Street, Bridget Halloran was keen to bring the team together. 'I've been through the report that Linda Holden gave us,' she said.

The four were sitting in Isaac's office. 'What have you found?' Larry asked.

'I cross-referenced the club where Helen and Daisy had worked.'

'Anything interesting?'

'Ben Aberman, the owner of the club, disappeared while they were both working there.'

'Suspicious?'

'Not at the time. The man had incurred significant debt, and it was thought he had left the country. No one's ever reported him missing or attempted to find him.'

'Was the club a front for prostitution?' Wendy said.

'They all are,' Isaac said.

'According to what we know, Helen Langdon was not prostituting herself, although Daisy probably was.'

'Is there any more to Aberman disappearing?'

'The ownership of the club changed overnight.'

'And the debts?'

'They disappeared.'

'Are you suggesting Aberman was murdered?'

'It's a possibility. Also, his house has remained empty.'

'Men such as Aberman change their names all the time,' Larry said.

'That's why there's never been an investigation, and would the police be interested in the disappearance of a man such as Aberman?'

'Not unless there was a crime to answer for,' Isaac said.

'Is the club still operating?' Larry asked.

'I'll give you the address. Don't expect too much when you get there. It looks seedy.'

'We won't.'

'And don't touch the women,' Wendy said.

'Would we ever?' Larry replied.

***

Two funerals in as many days. The funeral of James Holden had been poorly attended; the funeral of Helen Langdon, née Mackay, not so. This time, the church was overflowing. In the front pew, Frank and Betty Mackay. Behind them Linda Holden and the three Adamants, Archie, Abigail, and Howard.

'We had to come,' Abigail Adamant said. 'A mark of respect for her.'

'The other people here?' Isaac said.

'They're supporters of what my father was trying to achieve, people that he's helped,' Linda Holden said, turning around from where she was sitting.

'They weren't present at your father's funeral.'

'Some were, but the others, they're fresh out of prison. They don't want publicity, and there were cameras at my father's.'

'There are cameras outside.'

'Most of them came in through a side entrance. I organised a bus for them, and besides, Helen was one of them.'

Abigail Adamant read from the bible, one of the women who had come on the bus gave a eulogy about what an inspiration Helen had been. Linda Holden also got up and made a speech on behalf of Helen, noting that she was an exceptional woman and their lives had been better for knowing her. No mention was made of James Holden.

At the end of the service, Helen's father, Archie and Howard Adamant, as well as three men from the bus, carried the coffin to the waiting hearse. Isaac gave Wendy his handkerchief as she was overcome with emotion. 'It's so sad,' she said.

'What was she, do we know?' Isaac said.

'Not really, although I feel sad for her parents.'

'We've got work to do. I need to go with Larry to this club.'

Chapter 8

The night of Helen Langdon's funeral, two men entered the Dixey Club in Bayswater. 'It's not much,' Larry said. Both men were dressed casually, no ties, no signs of being police officers.

'Do you want to be up at the front? It'll cost extra,' a burly, heavily tattooed man said.

'We're fine, wherever,' Isaac said.

'Suit yourself. Up front, the girls get friendly.'

'We should have accepted his offer,' Larry said. 'It seems obvious, our refusing. As if we disapprove.'

'I do.'

'That's not the point. We're here to check out the place, not offer a comment.'

Isaac looked for the man from before. 'Up front,' he said.

'That'll cost you.'

'Okay, put it on the card.'

Hastily moved to the front, the two men sat perilously close to where a woman rotated around a pole. 'It's a meat market,' Isaac said.

'It's where you're meant to be enjoying yourself. You'll have to stop scowling.'

'What if we're recognised?'

'How? I can barely see you in here. The women are well lit, though.'

'You're enjoying this, aren't you?'

'I'm enjoying seeing you squirm. She's not a bad looker, the one on the stage. How much do you reckon? A hundred?'

'Are they all available?'

'Most would be, but Daisy said that Helen wasn't.'

'How could she not be in here?'

'Helen was a rare beauty, everyone's told us that. She's the drawcard, the others are what's available. What did you reckon to Daisy?'

'She's had a tough life.'

'Helen would have if she had stayed here. But then, she was a smart woman. Even if men had not taken her seriously, seen her as a plaything, it's hard to understand what brought her to a place like this.'

The two men's conversation was disturbed by the female from the pole coming in their direction. Larry slipped a five-pound note into her bra; she went away looking for someone more generous. She found him and sat on his lap, continuing to gyrate. Larry watched the action; Isaac pretended not to.

'You don't like the women?' the man from before said.

'Yes, we do,' Isaac said.

'Then don't go skimping on the tips. She's worth more than a measly fiver.'

'It's a rough place,' Isaac said when the man had gone away. 'How can we claim this on expenses?'

'With Richard Goddard, it wouldn't have been a problem. Caddick may not be so easy.'

'It's still a legit expense.'

'Don't worry, he'll sign eventually. His sort of place, I would have thought,' Isaac said.

'What are you going to do about him?'

'We ride out the storm. The man won't last forever.'

'Hey, look at her. She's better than the other one,' Larry said as another female walked onto the stage. Around the two men, the other patrons were clapping.

'Some of them would be in here every night,' Isaac said.

'And around the back.'

'It's not licensed for prostitution.'

'What does it matter? It goes on. These women work on tips, and what they can make on the side. Even then, the management will take a percentage.'

'I still find it hard to believe Helen Langdon worked here.'

'You think there was another side to the woman before she gave up on being an accountant?' Larry said.

'It's possible.'

'We'll check it out.'

'This is not my kind of place,' Isaac said. 'Let's go.'

***

Isaac, not feeling pleased with himself for enjoying the cavorting females at the Dixey Club, although he'd not admit it to his DI, was in the office early the next day. He had dwelt on what they had seen at the club, reflected on the woman that Helen Langdon had been. Isaac was convinced she wasn't as chaste as she had been portrayed.

The team were in the office; Larry, not an early morning person, arrived last.

'We checked out the club last night,' Isaac said.

'Did you enjoy it?' Wendy asked.

'Not particularly,' Isaac said, not wanting to admit the truth. It was as if entry somehow detached the patron from the reality of the outside world. A place where the basest desires were permitted, even encouraged. The men in the audience, what little he had seen of them, had been nudging each other, pointing at the women, making suggestive gestures. The women looked annoyed, yet moved in their direction, allowing them to sample the goods, ensuring that the men stuffed random notes in their underwear.

'Are you going back?' Wendy asked.

'Ben Aberman, any more updates?' Isaac asked.

'I found records of Helen working there, Daisy as well,' Bridget said. 'The dates correlate with Aberman's disappearance, although Helen left two days after the man disappeared. Daisy stayed for another three months.'

'Any more about what Helen did there? From what we could see, all of the women were willing to let the men paw them.'

'Helen must have,' Wendy said.

'Daisy said she didn't and she wasn't into selling herself.'

'Aberman's disappearance and Helen leaving the club two days later is more than a coincidence. Daisy must know more than she told us.'

'We need to talk to her again. Would you like me to deal with it?' Wendy said.

'Take her for a meal. She looked as though she could do with one. Talk to her woman to woman,' Isaac said.

'I know what to do, guv.'

'Aberman's house, do you have an address, Bridget?'

'It's in the country. I'll give it to you.'

***

'What do you hope to gain from this?' Larry said as he and Isaac drove out to Aberman's house.

'Helen Langdon's story is a lie. As though she orchestrated this whole subterfuge.'

'But why?'

'I don't know, and that concerns me. If she could maintain a cover for so long, what else is she capable of?'

'Gerald Adamant?'

'What if she did kill him, and not in self-defence?' Isaac said.

'The woman admitted to killing him. She served time in prison.'

'She was even the one who phoned the police to give herself up, which tends to destroy my argument.'

'I can see what you're getting at,' Larry said. 'Ben Aberman.'

'What if she killed him? We don't know how and why, and maybe it's a red herring.'

'If she's working in the club, and the men are keeping their distance, and she's not selling herself, it can only mean one thing.'

'She was Aberman's woman.'

'Too many loose ends. She was an accountant, a reputable firm. No doubt she was annoyed with all the attention, the lewd comments, but she was a smart woman, and there are laws in this country. She could have done something about it, other than take off her business suit and gyrate around a pole, and what if some of her former clients or former work colleagues came in?'

Aberman's house, better than expected, sat on the edge of the village. Larry got out of the car and opened the gate for Isaac to drive in. An old lady appeared from one side of the house. 'What are you doing here? I'll call the police.'

'We are the police,' Larry said. 'We're following up on Mr Aberman's disappearance.'

'I'll need to see your identification.'

'No problems. And you are?'

'I live next door. I keep a watch on the house for Mr Aberman.'

'He's been missing for a long time.'

'A woman comes here sometimes. She gives me some money for my trouble.'

'How often?' Isaac said, having joined Larry and the old lady outside the front door of the house.

'Sometimes she phones, but every month some money, not that I need it.'

'When was the last time you saw Mr Aberman?'

'It's a few years. He's overseas.'

'What can you tell us about him?'

'He used to come here most weekends. He was always pleasant to me, always brought some flowers or chocolates. He worked in London.'

'Do you know what sort of business?'

'He said he was in the entertainment business. That explained some of the people I saw here.'

'What sort of people?'

'Show business types, expensive cars, fur coats, parties on the lawn at the back.'

'And then he left?'

'One day he's here, the next he's gone. I thought it strange at the time as he always came over to my house to say goodbye. He was a gentleman. And then a woman turns up, tells me he's travelling, and would I look after the house. Not that there's much to do. A man comes once a month to mow the lawn, and I dust inside the best I can, but that's about it.'

'Can you describe the woman?'

'Laura. An attractive woman, younger than him.'

'Was she here most weekends?'

'Not always, and then she disappeared for a few years, but the money still came through.'

Isaac looked at Larry, knew what he was thinking.

'It's important,' Isaac said. 'Can you describe this woman in detail?'

'She looked no older than my granddaughter, and she's not yet thirty. She spoke nicely, always very polite.'

'When was the last time you saw her?'

'Two weeks ago.'

'Her car?'

'She didn't drive. There's a railway station here, and it's not far to walk.'

'I've a photo. Can you tell me if it is her?' Isaac said as he handed the woman the picture.

The old woman took out her glasses from the pocket of the coat she was wearing, Isaac and Larry were champing at the bit, waiting for an answer. The woman took her time.

'Yes, that's her. That's Laura, such a nice person. Or I think it is. She dresses differently when she comes here, more sombre. She always has dark sunglasses on, never takes them off, not even when she comes in my house for a cup of tea. A lovely person, and so was Mr Aberman. I hope he'll be back soon.'

Chapter 9

Wendy arrived outside Daisy's flat at nine in the morning. If the woman had been working at night, she would be asleep, not that it would discourage Wendy from knocking. The flat, three floors up and with no lift, proved difficult for the police sergeant.

Where Daisy lived was not affluent, not for someone who could make five hundred pounds in one night, but then, Daisy, like a lot of the other women selling their wares on a street corner or in a club, had a problem. It had been clear when the woman was at

Challis Street Police Station that she was a drug addict, the worst kind.

Wendy knocked on the door, more firmly the second time. A woman poked her head out from a door opposite. 'There's a key under the mat,' she said. Wendy could see the block of flats catered to the ladies of the night.

'Thank you.' Wendy bent down, steadying herself on the wall in front of her. She picked up the key and inserted it into the lock. Inside the flat were signs of neglect: unwashed dishes, a cat that looked as if it was in need of a feed, a discarded syringe. Wendy moved through the flat, opening the first bedroom door. A woman, semi-comatose, briefly stirred. 'Close the door, I'm trying to sleep.'

'Sorry,' Wendy said. She moved on through the flat, stepping over a pile of discarded clothes. She opened one door to find out it was the bathroom, its condition the same as the rest of the flat. The third door, where she gently knocked before entering, was slightly ajar.

On the bed, Wendy could see the form of a woman under the blankets. 'Daisy, it's Sergeant Gladstone,' she said.

With no sign of movement, Wendy moved closer to the bed. She pulled back the blanket, then picked up her phone and dialled Isaac. 'There's another one,' she said.

'Daisy?'

'Not long by the looks of it.'

You know the procedure. We'll be there as soon as we can.'

Wendy phoned Gordon Windsor, the CSE. 'One hour, secure the location,' he said.

With the crime scene investigation team on their way, Wendy phoned for two uniforms to come to the flat and establish a crime scene. She then went into the other room where Daisy's flatmate was asleep and nudged her to wake up.

'Go away. Can't you see I'm asleep?'

'Sergeant Wendy Gladstone, Challis Street Police Station. Your sleep will need to wait.'

The woman stirred after Wendy had prodded her two more times, receiving a few expletives in return. Finally, she stood up, naked, and Wendy could see the woman was similar to Daisy: the gaunt frame, the result of drugs rather than food, the needle marks, the blotched body. Reaching for a top and a skirt, the woman turned to face Wendy. 'Did you get a good look?' she said.

'Nothing that interests me. Did you hear what I said before?'

'Something about the police.'

'That's correct. Sergeant Wendy Gladstone. I need you out of this flat.'

'What for? I've done nothing wrong.'

'Apart from selling yourself and jamming needles in your arm, you've probably not. Besides, I'm not here about you.'

'Then what do you want?'

'Your flatmate, Daisy. She's dead in the other room.'

'Oh.'

'Is that all you've got to say?'

'What do you want me to say? She was going to OD sometime. The same as me, I suppose.'

'She did not OD, she was murdered,' Wendy said.

'Who'd do that?'

Unable to do anything more with the woman, Wendy grabbed a coat from the back of the woman's door, took her by one arm, and moved her out of the flat, avoiding the traffic areas as much as possible. A uniform was coming up the stairs. 'I'll take it from here,' he said.

Downstairs, Wendy put the woman in her car and turned on the heater. 'Stay here, I'll be back.'

'Don't worry about me. I've still got some sleeping to do.'

Isaac and Larry had arrived. Wendy went over to where they were parked. 'Was she shot?' Isaac asked.

'Not this time. There's a cord around her neck.'

'The flatmate?'

'She's in my car. A herd of elephants could have gone through the flat. She wouldn't have heard anything.'

'We'll need to interview her.'

'Here or at Challis Street?'

'Challis Street. She can't go back into the flat, and there's nowhere else.'

'There's another woman in the flat opposite. We'll need to talk to her.'

'We'll deal with it,' Larry said. 'Find out what you can from the flatmate.'

Gordon Windsor arrived. 'Have you been in?' he said.

'Wendy found the body,' Isaac said.

'Have you touched anything?' Windsor said to Wendy.

'No more than was necessary. The flatmate's in my car.'

'I'll send someone to take her prints. We've got yours on file.'

'There's a woman in the flat opposite that we need to question,' Isaac said.

'Go ahead, but wear foot protectors, gloves outside of the woman's flat. There may be some evidence on the landing. Professional, was it?' Windsor said as he kitted up, preparing to enter the building.

'There's been no violence, no sign of the place being disrupted, although that's not so easy to tell.'

'The woman?'

'A prostitute. We interviewed her at Challis Street the other day.'

'Not another of your murder enquiries where the bodies keep piling up, is it? You may as well let me know so I can arrange extra personnel.'

'There'll be more,' Isaac said. 'Larry, kit up. We need to talk to the neighbour.'

Wendy left the men and walked back to her car. The flatmate was fast asleep in the back seat. Wendy opened the door, and the woman woke up with a start. 'This man needs to take your fingerprints. We need to eliminate you from the crime.'

'What crime?'

'Your flatmate, Daisy.'

'What about her?'

'She's dead. I told you before. Someone's killed her.'

'It wasn't me.'

'We know that, but the crime scene examiners need to eliminate your prints when they're checking the flat.'

'What about me?'

'We'll go to the police station. We'll have a chat, and then I'll see that you have accommodation. I'll also make sure you get some food.'

'It's not food I want.'

'That I can't supply. If it becomes an issue, we'll bring in a doctor.'

***

Isaac and Larry climbed the stairs to the neighbour's flat. Her door was open on their arrival, a police constable barring the woman from leaving. 'He won't let me out,' she said.

'A few questions and then we'll make sure you can leave.'

'I've got to work.'

'What do you do?'

'Not what they were up to. I've got a job. A place that makes meat pies.'

'Any good?' Larry said.

'I'll eat them, doubt if they'll serve them up in a fancy restaurant.'

'Can we come in?' Isaac said.

'What about my job?'

'Can you phone, tell them you'll be in late?'

'I've no credit on my phone, and the phone in here doesn't work.'

'You can use my phone,' Isaac said.

'Don't worry, it'll be fine. You better come in.'

The two men entered the flat. It was tidy, even if the paint was peeling, but there was a distinct smell of sewage emanating from the bathroom.

'I do my best,' the woman said, 'but the landlord, he doesn't care.'

'You've got a lease and a number for a plumber. Phone him up.'

'The landlord, he'll make an excuse, have me out of here in a minute.'

'Using a property without the owner's permission for the purpose of prostitution invalidates the lease. That's the reason you don't phone him up.'

'I don't like to advertise what I do. That's why I use the meat pie story.'

'Your name?' Isaac said.

'Hailey Ashmore.'

Isaac studied the woman. She certainly looked better than Daisy had that day in Challis Street, and there were no signs of drug use. Her manner, apart from at the door, was calm.

'Busy, are you?' Larry said.

'I do what's necessary. Life's not always fair.'

'We're here to investigate the death of Elizabeth Wetherington, also known as Daisy.'

'She was always going to come to a sticky end.'

'Why?'

'She's out at all hours, and then she has the occasional man over. I can hear them going at it from here.'

'No doubt they can hear you.'

'Not me. My clients, they're special.'

Isaac knew they were not. Special clients do not visit rundown flats that smell of sewage and cheap perfume.

'Did you see or hear anything last night?'

'Not me.'

'On your own?'

'Don't ask me his name.'

'Why?'

'I don't know it.'

'You're occupied for thirty minutes, and then he leaves.'

'I give my men a good time. It's more than a quick screw with me and out of the door. You're a good-looking man, I could give you a special rate.'

'We're here to discuss Daisy. How well did you know her?'

'Not that well. We'd talk outside on the landing, sometimes.'

'Her flatmate?'

'Gwendoline, she calls herself. You'd think she was a fairy with a name like that. A right tart.'

'Why do you call her a tart? You're here selling yourself.'

'Daisy was bad enough, but her flatmate is worse.'

'What do you mean?'

'I was coming back here one night with a gentleman friend, and there she was on the stairs, her skirt hitched up around her arse, a drunk going for dear life. My friend, he wanted to leave, but I made him come in, gave him a special treat.'

Isaac did not want to hear what the special treat was. 'Last night, when you weren't taking one of your gentlemen friends to paradise and back, did you hear anything unusual?'

'Not me. I've no idea what time the two of them came home, or who they were with. That's the honest truth.'

Both Isaac and Larry weren't convinced they had been told the full truth, but there was no more to be gained in the flat, and the smell was becoming nauseous. 'We'll take you out of here if you want,' Larry said.

'Don't bother. I've got someone coming over later.'

***

At the police station, Wendy sat with Gwendoline. A café across the road had sent over a full English breakfast, which the flatmate was devouring as if she hadn't eaten a decent meal for a long time.

'Gwendoline, what's your real name?' Wendy asked.

'Kate Bellamy.'

'Your age?'

'Is this necessary?'

'I'm afraid it is. You were in the flat when your flatmate was murdered.'

'I didn't kill her.'

'We've discounted you for the present. What can you tell us about last night?'

'Not a lot. It was a quiet night, just a couple of men.'

'Barely enough to pay the rent?'

'It'll be better tonight, but now I've got to find somewhere to live.'

'Do you have anywhere?'

'One of the other women on the street, she's looking for someone to share.'

'And the flat where you are now?'

'It was in Daisy's name. I just paid my share. The landlord's not going to have much success claiming the rent from her.'

'He may ask you to pay.'

'If he's a nuisance, I'll pay him off.'

'With money?'

'What do you think?'

Wendy had found in Daisy a vulnerable person destroyed by drugs. She wasn't so sure of Gwendoline. The woman was a drug addict, her arms testament to the fact, but with a full stomach, she was no longer showing the signs of severe addiction.

'Daisy was killed, which means someone must have entered your flat, walked along the hallway outside of your door, killed her, and then walked past your door again on the way out.'

'What do you want me to say?'

'I want you to tell me the truth. I want to know if you heard anything?'

'Sometimes Daisy has someone over. Sometimes I do. We mind each other's business. There was a noise, about two in the morning.'

'How do you know the time.'

'I'm giving you the facts I can remember. Whether they're accurate or not, I wouldn't know.'

'Why not?'

'Daisy and me, we're night owls. When it's dark, we go out to work. I had come home early for once, but I'm going nowhere, and besides, I'm not feeling so good.'

'Any reason?'

'I don't feel good a lot of times.'

'You've seen a doctor?'

'What for? He'll only tell me what to do.'

'And what's wrong with that?'

'I've got to earn a living. I don't have time for healthy food and exercise, and I'm not going to get off my back and find an honest job.'

'Is it better to have a sweaty man on top of you than a regular job?'

'The money's better.'

'The way you live doesn't show it.'

'Maybe it doesn't, but I've got a problem.'

'The same as Daisy, heroin.'

'She was crazy for it. I'm not so bad. If someone had snuck into her room last night, she wouldn't have known.'

'How would they have got into the flat?'

'How did you?'

'The key under the mat.'

'Sometimes we come home, can't remember where the key is, sometimes without a handbag.'

'Why?'

'Some of the men, they aren't so good. They don't want to pay, see us as tarts, and either they hit us, or they take our handbags, phones, as well.'

'Rough life?'

'You get used to it. What else do you want? I saw nothing, did nothing. Daisy's dead, she's not the first one that's died.'

'What do you mean?'

'Drugs. It'll kill me eventually.'

'I could get treatment for you.'

'Don't bother. I need to get into my room, get my clothes.'

'I'll take you back, and then take you where you want to go.'

'The police, they're not like you. Some of them move us on, some of them take liberties.'

'They'd be liable to internal discipline if they were discovered.'

'Don't worry. I'll not tell you who they are.'

Chapter 10

Seth Caddick sat in his office and looked out of the window. His conversation with Commissioner Davies had left him perplexed. He knew the man would not protect him, and it was up to him to secure his position. He enjoyed the rank of detective superintendent, and that everyone called him sir, except Isaac Cook, who was liable to forget.

'Chloe,' he called out through the open door. Caddick's secretary came in.

'You wanted me,' she said. Caddick had brought her in from his previous station. The opportunity to appoint someone local had been there, but who in the Met could be trusted. Chloe, he knew, was as loyal to him as she was to her job.

'Wendy Gladstone. We've got to remove Cook's support mechanism.'

'A medical?'

'When's it due?'

'Two months.'

'Bring it forward. Four weeks' time, and then I want her retired due to health reasons.'

'You'll need to give her notice of the medical.'

'Then do it today and make the appointment. I want a full check-up, no letting her pass because she's getting old. After that, we'll go for Larry Hill. He's not looking so good.'

'He looks fine to me,' Chloe said.

'He was badly beaten before. It must have had some effect.'

'Can't you just remove DCI Cook?'

'It's better to follow the procedure, and besides, I need him to wrap up the murder of James Holden.'

'And the women who've been killed.'

'Two whores. They don't matter.'

'Be careful. Helen Langdon was well connected.'

'How? She murdered Adamant, bedded Saint Holden, destroyed his reputation. There'll not be much interest in her.'

***

James Holden had been a complicated man. A man whose inner demons tormented him, the occasional urge to give in to temptation. Violet, his wife, had recognised it early in their marriage; she had decided not to allow it to destroy the love she had for the man, the inherent goodness in him.

After the first time, and each and every time after that, he had come to her and confessed. Not that she wanted to hear, but she knew that with honesty comes respect, even love. And now the facts were out. He had been with another woman, a now-dead prostitute by the name of Daisy, and there it was, emblazoned across the television. She had seen the black policeman, Isaac Cook, waylaid on his way out of the building where the woman had died. His inability to avoid making a statement, offering the usual platitudes: unable to make a comment at this stage, investigations are ongoing, charges will be laid soon.

Violet wondered who the charges would be laid against. Would it be her son? He had the anger, but why a prostitute of no importance? And there was Helen. She had a past history, and somehow it was tied to this other woman. It concerned Violet, having seen her son John's fits of violence as a child, the pulling off of a butterfly's wings, the senseless killing of a cat that had strayed into the garden, the embarrassment of explaining to the neighbours that she and James were not sure where they had gone wrong.

Violet remembered John's anger when Helen had rejected him. She realised the signs were there all along, the glances between James and Helen, brushing against each other in the office, the whispered conversations. She had wanted to confront her husband, but she had not. After all, hadn't he been honest in the past. And now, the man was dead, as was Helen. Was it the first time James had slept with Helen? Violet thought, and why had Helen not wanted her son? He was a man more her age, a man who would have given Helen children, yet the woman had wanted older men, men with one foot in the grave. Men who would die from a hammer blow to the head, and now from a bullet. If Helen had not died, Violet would have thought her responsible for James's demise. It could not be her, but it could be John. She hoped it was not.

***

'Aberman's next-door neighbour identified Helen Langdon,' Isaac said. It was 6 a.m. in the office, a good time for Isaac to lay out the plan for the day, not so good for the others.

'Inconclusive, guv. The neighbour is getting on a bit, and any woman covered up could have been mistaken for Helen Langdon,' Larry said.

'That's why we're not placing emphasis on it for the present moment, and where's the tie-in?'

'Wendy, apart from your medical, what have you got?'

'I can't pass it, and you know it.'

'You will. You're on an exercise routine. We'll get you fit. How's your blood pressure, lung capacity?'

'Fine. I had myself checked out a few months back, no serious damage. It's arthritis, that's what it is. I just can't move as fast as before.'

'Fast enough for this department.'

'It's our superintendent, isn't it?' Wendy said.

'He's weakening my base, going for the kill,' Isaac said.

'You don't intend to let him win, do you?'

'Not this time. We fight fire with fire. How's your health, Bridget?'

'Fine, but I'm not up for a medical.'

'Every morning, you've got to take a one-hour walk with Wendy, and easy on the food. No more hamburgers, greasy chips. From now on, it's salads and eating healthily, chicken if you're desperate.'

'Me, as well?'

'Bridget, you're to set Wendy an example.'

'Don't worry, Wendy. We'll get you through this,' Bridget said to her friend.

A period of magnanimity existed in the office, only to be disturbed by Caddick coming in the door. 'DCI, what's going on?'

'We'll talk later,' Isaac said to his team.

'One more murder. Is that right?' Caddick said as he sat down on a chair in Isaac's office.

'We know the woman had been an acquaintance of Helen Langdon.'

'Did she kill Langdon and Holden?'

'She's not involved.'

'Then why has she been killed?'

'It was in my report.'

'Too busy last night to read it. Give me the shortened version,' Caddick said.

That's what I gave you, you pompous fool, Isaac thought. Instead, he said, 'Before Helen Langdon married Gerald Adamant, she worked in a club.'

'What sort?'

'Gentlemen's.'

'Strip joint?'

'Yes.'

'Call it what it is. Don't go giving me the benefit of your fancy education. A spade is a spade, a place where the women prance around with nothing on is a strip joint. Do I make myself clear?'

'Yes, you do.'

'And it's sir to you. Your insubordination is wearing thin. I've put up with it till now on account of your past record. Dismal to me, but there are others who think you're special. And as for your staff…'

'Are you about to launch into a tirade about them?'

'A critical observation. They're a tired bunch of individuals, not worthy of feeding.'

'Sir, you, as a detective superintendent, must realise that derogatory remarks about personnel are an actionable offence. You could be reported for what you've just said.'

'Just you try it, Cook.'

'I intend to register a formal complaint against you in line with regulations.'

'I'll have you out of here in an instant.'

'Not while the complaint is ongoing, you won't. You'll have to give your reasons, and believe me, you'll not win.'

'Cook, it's you or me.'

'That's fine by me. Let's see how you get out of this one.'

'Do you want to make a comment here about me?' Caddick said.

'Not a chance. We'll wait until the hearing into my complaint comes up.'

'Is this how you spoke to Goddard?'

'Detective Chief Superintendent Goddard was a competent man. It wasn't necessary.'

'And I'm not?'

'I've nothing more to say. If you have no more to add to our conversation, I'll wish you goodbye. I've got three murders to solve.'

After Caddick had left, red in the face, Larry came into Isaac's office. 'You've made a cross for yourself to bear. Was it wise?'

'Probably not.'

***

The Dixey Club did not appreciate a visit from Homicide. It was still early in the evening, a few hours before the entertainment began. Isaac was pleased the lights were on. At the back door of the club, which opened onto an alley, two uniforms had been stationed in case someone wanted to slip out.

'You can't come in here,' the burly man from Isaac and Larry's previous visit said.

'DCI Cook. I've got a warrant.'

'We're clean, nothing to see here.'

'We've got a few questions. Is the manager here?'

'I'm the manager.'

'No, you're not. He's got an office out the back. We'll find him.'

Wendy walked through the place, saw the pole in the middle of the stage, walked through a door behind it, found some women in early for the night's entertainment. 'Sergeant Wendy Gladstone,' she said.

'We've done nothing wrong,' one of the women said. Wendy had seen the photos of the ladies on display outside: beautiful, fresh and young, and one of them of a more youthful Helen. Those preparing themselves were not. They didn't have much in the way of clothing, although one was dressed as a cowgirl, another as a nurse. The third, Wendy was not sure what she was meant to represent, but it looked weird to her.

'I'm not saying you have, but I've a few questions.'

Wendy could see the women were nervous.

'I'm not here for you three. If you've committed any crime, that's not my interest. There were a couple of women who worked here some years ago.'

'I've only been here two,' the youngest of the three said.

'Maybe you don't know. How about you?' Wendy said, looking at one of the girls, although she was well over thirty, probably closer to forty.

'I've been here a while. Who do you want to know about?'

'One was Daisy. The other one was named …'

'Helen, that's who you mean, isn't it?'

'Yes. What do you know about them?'

The woman dressed as a cowgirl, straightened herself on her chair. 'Daisy, she was game for anything.'

'Explain "game",' Wendy said.

'The men, they get carried away, wanting to do things they're not meant to.'

'Such as?'

'Exposing themselves, grabbing too much of us.'

'It's on display,' Wendy said.

'So's the meat at the butchers, but you don't go prodding it.'

'Do you object?'

'Not if they're paying and it remains light-hearted, but some of the men, well, you know?'

'I don't. I've not frequented these places.'

The youngest of the three spoke. Wendy realised she was dressed as an astronaut, although not from NASA. 'Some of them, they think because we strip on the stage, let them take a few liberties, that we're prostitutes, available to the highest tipper.'

'Aren't you?'

'Sometimes we'll negotiate a special deal, but we'll not do it on the stage or in the audience. We've some standards.'

'Daisy?'

'She was always available. She could have made herself plenty of money, apart from her addiction.'

'And you three?'

'I was into drugs a few years back,' the eldest said. The other two are clean.'

'So why be here?'

'Life's expensive, you know that,' the youngest said. 'I can make more here in two days than working all week in a regular job.'

'So how many days do you work here?'

'Four, and sometimes a Saturday.'

'Which means?'

'The rest of the week is free.'

'To do what?'

'There are one or two men.'

'Escort?'

'They pay plenty. I'm buying myself a flat, putting myself through university.'

'Are there beds out back?'

'Are you here to arrest us?'

'I'm with Homicide. We deal with murders, not who you screw on the premises.'

'Sometimes it happens,' the oldest of the three said.

'I'm not involved, I've got my men to consider. They don't want the goods damaged,' the youngest one said.

'Okay, enough about you three and this place, what about Daisy and Helen?'

'Daisy, she'd play the men, let them go further than they should. Sometimes, the management wanted her to go easy, but she was a drawcard, the same as Helen.'

'How?'

'Daisy, she's the rough, Helen, she's the pure. Helen, she'd get the men excited, playing to the crowd, teasing them, pulling back. Once they've lined up a likely mark, Daisy would come along, make sure the man or men were stuffing plenty of money into whatever she was wearing. Later Daisy would take them around the back and fleece some more money out of them.'

'Helen?'

'Never in this club. She played her part, that was all, and she was good.'

'Did you like her?'

'Everyone liked Helen, and now she's dead.'

'So is Daisy.'

'Daisy was always going to end up that way.'

'You knew about Helen marrying, and then killing her husband?'

'We knew.'

'What did you think?'

'She wasn't the sort of person to kill anyone.'

'But she could strut herself here, bait the men.'

'It doesn't make us all murderers, does it?'

'I'm trying to understand the woman.'

'Mind you, her becoming involved with Ben Aberman was not expected.'

'Why?'

'Aberman, he owned this place.'

'And he disappeared,' Wendy said. 'What's the full story?'

'Helen wanted more than this club. She told us she wanted to find a decent man to look after her.'

'A sugar daddy?'

'Not Helen. She was good at detaching herself. In here, she'd play the tart, outside she'd not want to associate with us.'

'What can you tell us about Ben Aberman?'

'He was a rogue, but he was a decent man, and he treated the girls with respect.'

'Were they living together?'

'We knew Helen would spend the night with him sometimes, and he was really keen on her.'

'And Helen?'

'She said she didn't love him, and it was just a business partnership.'

'What do you think she meant?'

'No idea really. She wasn't even escorting, and she could have made plenty of money. We never really understood why she was here.'

'Aberman disappeared,' Wendy said.

'We were told he went overseas.'

'And Helen's reaction?'

'She was ambivalent, told us not to worry, and that he would turn up in a few days.'

'And then Helen left.'

'Two days later, she's gone, never even said goodbye.'

'Did you look for her?'

'We did for a few days, but she'd left where she was living, never left a forwarding address. We assumed she was with Ben, but then, not long afterwards, she lands herself a rich man and marries him.'

'Did you ever speak to her again?'

'None of us did. She was the one that got away.'

Chapter 11

Out front in the club, the manager stood with Isaac and Larry. 'Ben Aberman, before my time,' he said. 'Sorry, can't help you.'

Isaac had met his type before: only interested in a profit, not caring how it was earned.'

'Your name?'

'Barry Knox.'

'You're soliciting on these premises. We know it, so do you. What do you want? This place to be closed down, or do you want to cooperate?'

'I'll need my lawyer here.'

'That's up to you, but you're opening up in sixty minutes. You'd better get him here fast.'

'You can't close me down.'

'You're up to your neck in crime. I was here the other night with DI Hill. We saw what was going on.'

'Harmless fun.'

'Are you dealing in drugs here?'

'We're clean. The place is legit, more than I can say for two undercover police officers casing the joint.'

'It's called policing. If you try it on us, I'll haul you down the police station and throw you in a cell for the night.'

'You can't talk to Mr Knox like that,' the tattooed man, who had been there on Isaac and Larry's first visit to the club, said.

'We can. And as for you, back off,' Isaac said. 'Do you have a record, been involved in any crime lately? And what do you know about this place, have you taken any liberties with the women?'

'You've no right.'

'I've every right. I need answers as to what happened to Ben Aberman, and what about Helen and Daisy, and don't make out you don't know who I'm referring to. Men like you don't move far. You would have been here then, so would your manager, or if he wasn't, he'd know people who were, people who know the true story.'

'Okay, you've made your point,' Knox said. 'It's best if you come into my office.'

The four men walked the short distance to the office. In the room, a monitor showed the stage, another showed the patrons, and another the room where the women gave the patrons individual attention.

'You've got a licence for that?' Isaac asked, pointing to the bed in the bare room.

'It's our first aid room,' Knox said.

'Knox, you'd better start talking.'

'Ben Aberman, I knew him, so did Gus. He wasn't pulling in the money, and his lenders were anxious. I came in to run the place and make it financially sound.'

'The lenders?'

'You don't go to the bank to open a strip club.'

'Loan sharks?'

'Businessmen. It's all legal. Aberman signed the documents, agreed to the terms and conditions.'

'Back then, you had Helen and Daisy, the double act. This place must have been making money.'

'Maybe it was, or maybe Aberman was creaming more off the top than he should have.'

'Which is it?'

'Aberman, he owned this place, but he wasn't honest with his financial backers, delaying the repayments.'

'Are you one of the backers?'

'Not me. I'm just the person sent in to make it pay.'

'Is it now?'

'We get by.'

'Which means it is, but you don't declare it.'

'Inspector Cook, we're a business. We make money, we spend money. How we structure our finances is not your concern. You're after Aberman, am I correct?'

'What about Gus here? What's he got to do with Aberman?'

'I did nothing with the man. He was my friend,' Gus said.

'Where's Aberman?' Isaac asked.

'I don't know, and that's the honest truth.'

'We know that Aberman does not own this club. Was the signing over of the business legal, or was his arm bent?'

'I wouldn't know. I'm just the humble manager,' Knox said.

'Did Gus force Aberman to sign the business over. What had Aberman been subjected to before he signed? What happened afterwards?'

'Aberman, he was reluctant, but they wanted to get their money. I'll swear on my mother's grave that nothing happened to him.'

'I pity your mother if she's dead. Aberman, he's forced to sign, and then he's dumped in a river somewhere, or taken out to sea. Did he cry when you threw him over the side?' Isaac said.

'You've got this all wrong. Aberman's out of the country.'

'Where?'

'He doesn't send me postcards. Helen, she knew.'

'She's dead, so is Daisy. Mr Knox, there are too many coincidences pointing back to this place and to you. And why did Helen leave the club two days after Aberman vanished, Daisy within three months?'

'She didn't want to work here without Aberman, and Daisy, we got rid of her in the end.'

'That's probably the first truthful answer you've given. Daisy was a hopeless drug addict, probably too much for even this club to handle. Helen, why two days? Did she know the story, did you pay her off?'

'I've told you the truth. What more do you want from me?'

'Was Helen involved with Aberman?'

'They were cosy.'

'Sleeping together?'

'Aberman was a snake.'

'So why was Helen with him?'

'I don't know. You could have asked her if she was alive.'

'Do you and your kind have any decency left in you? You killed Aberman, but you couldn't kill Helen. We know of her hold over men. Did she have it over you? Did she have it over Gus?'

'Helen was not as good as you make her out to be. Helen and Aberman made a good team, and then he's not around, and Helen's out of here in two days. We paid her up, it's in the books.'

'Aberman's house?'

'What about it?'

'If the man's got debts and the loan sharks...'

'They're businessmen, tough businessmen,' Knox corrected Isaac.

'Okay, have it your way,' Isaac said. 'These businessmen would not have allowed Aberman's house to remain in his name. They would have wanted it as security.'

'If they knew about it.'

'They did. The man had parties there. Parties attended by the cream, sour probably, of the criminal classes.'

'There was an agreement,' Knox said. 'If Aberman gave the clubs he owned over to them willingly, then the debt was absolved.'

'And where does Helen come into this?'

'Aberman made it clear she was to have the house if she wanted it.'

'But it's in Aberman's name.'

'Which proves he's still alive, paying the bills.'

'Why did he want to let Helen have the house?'

'Aberman was a sentimental fool. He'd fallen in love with the woman, the same as that old man she married, the same as that old fool she was shot with.'

'Was Helen capable of love?'

'I wouldn't know. She was a beautiful woman, but she never came near me.'

'Why?'

'Look at me. The manager of a strip joint.'

'So was Aberman.'

'Was he? The man had more than a few interests around here. He had plenty of money.'

'Then why not pay his debts?'

'He didn't get the money in the first place by giving it away.'

'Aberman's dead,' Isaac said. 'We'll find out what happened to him. In the interim, I'd suggest you tone down your activities here. Otherwise, there'll be another raid, and the police won't be walking out of here empty-handed.'

***

'Look at this,' Isaac said, pushing the opened letter across his desk to Larry. The two had just returned to Challis Street after visiting the Dixey Club.

'Are you surprised?'

'Not even a warning. I'm to present myself in two weeks for a disciplinary hearing.'

'DCS Goddard can't get you out of this.'

'I should have been more careful with Caddick, but the man's a bore. He doesn't know what he's talking about half the time, and the other half, he's sucking up to Davies.'

'What will you do?'

'I'll mount a vigorous defence.'

'It'll not work, and you know it. You told him what you thought of him, didn't you?'

'I did, and he's kept out of the way for a few days. No doubt working overtime on setting up my impending demise.'

'That serious?'

'They have the power to stand me down.'

'They could do that now.'

'Not Caddick. He wants these murders solved. That's why he's going for two weeks. He's hoping we'll be close by then, and he can step in and take the glory.'

'What about us?' Larry said.

'Solving these murders is always the best defence.'

'You were shot in the shoulder once before, got a medal,' Larry said.

'Are you suggesting I do that again?'

'Desperate times demand desperate measures.'

'Okay, Larry, enough of your jokes. What did we reckon of Barry Knox?'

'We should call in Bridget and Wendy.'

With the four in the office, Isaac took control. 'Bridget, what do we have on Barry Knox?'

'Minor hooligan. He's been arrested for pimping, spent six months in prison before getting out on a technicality.'

'Technicality?'

'The arresting officer had falsified some entries in his notes. Apart from that, Barry Knox is clean. He's managed a few clubs in the area, mostly seedy, and he's been at Dixey's since Aberman disappeared.'

'And the women at the club, Wendy?'

'One or two convictions against the oldest two for prostitution, nothing against the other woman.'

'Why's that?'

'A sign of the times. The young woman is studying for a degree and paying off a mortgage. She needs the money, and casual work in a shop or with a catering company doesn't pay the bills. She can get up on that stage, makes a few hundred for the night and survive.'

'Escorting?'

'Probably. They were honest about Helen and Daisy, gave some insights about Aberman.'

'Gus, the heavy?'

'According to the women, he's not too bright, but loyal, polite to the women, never takes advantage, although he's always peering into the changing room.'

'He'll see more on the stage, and Knox has a camera on the bed at the rear of the building. Which of your women were using it?'

'They weren't willing to admit it to me. The oldest one would be the most likely, but I've no proof.'

'Don't worry. We're after a murderer or murderers, not fallen women. Aberman, any luck finding him, Bridget? And if it was Helen, who was paying for the electricity, the rates, why was the house empty?'

'The rates are paid from an account in London,' Bridget said. 'There's a solicitor's firm that's taken responsibility.'

'The address?'

'It's in your inbox.'

'Larry, let's go,' Isaac said.

'Don't you want to stay and prepare your defence,' Larry said.

'Defence? Wendy said.

'I'm up before a disciplinary hearing,' Isaac said. 'Don't worry about it. You focus on passing your medical. I can deal with our superintendent. And get Gordon Windsor and his crime scene team primed to check out Aberman's house.'

'You don't think…?'

'I don't think anything at the present moment, but Helen Langdon's been murdered for a reason, as has James Holden. What if it's to do with Aberman's disappearance? Maybe Helen did love James Holden, told him her story. The man wasn't judgemental, no reason to be, but with Adamant, she was always careful.'

Chapter 12

'Can I help?' a polite young woman said from behind her desk. The firm of Slaters and Partners occupied two offices on the fourth floor of an office block in Mayfair.

'Detective Chief Inspector Cook, Detective Inspector Hill. We'd like to talk to one of the senior partners,' Isaac said.

'Mr Slater is in. I'll let him know you're here. You don't have an appointment, I suppose?'

'We're here on official business.'

'Please take a seat. I'm sure he won't be long.'

The two men settled on a leather sofa in the corner of the reception area. 'Attractive,' Larry said.

'I didn't notice.'

'Come off it. You're on your own again. It can't be much fun.'

'I've got you and Homicide,' Isaac said. 'What more could I want?'

'And Caddick for the argumentative mother-in-law.'

'My life is complete.' Isaac realised the relationship with his DI had become more cordial in recent months.

'Mr Slater will see you now,' the lady at reception said.

Isaac and Larry entered Slater's office. 'Always pleased to meet members of our fine police force. What I can do for you.'

'There's a property in the village of Bray. It's a two-storey, three- or four-bedroom house. It's been unoccupied for some years.

'Mr Aberman's house?'

'That's it.'

'What do you want to know?'

'We need to contact Mr Aberman.'

'I can't help you there.'

'You do pay the bills for the place?'

'That's correct. I have sufficient funds deposited in a trust account to cover the bills.'

'Did Mr Aberman set it up?'

'Yes, just before he went overseas.'

'Have you spoken to him since.'

'There's been no reason to. The instructions were clear. The house was to be maintained, the rates were to be paid, and a small account set up, with a debit card sent to a nominated address.'

'And you never queried this?'

'I've no reason to. London, especially the better areas, is awash with empty houses, absent landlords. My instructions were clear, and I've carried them out to the best of my ability.'

'You mentioned a debit card?'

'Yes. The balance of the account is kept at one thousand pounds.'

'Do you have an address for the card?'

'I've always sent it to a post office box.'

'Is that unusual?'

'A little strange, I'll grant you. Some people are reclusive, or they do not want their identities revealed. As long as I conduct my business according to the law, then I have no reason to concern myself.'

'You must be curious,' Larry said.

'Why? If Mr Aberman wants to act in a certain way, then I don't interfere.'

'Two people he knew have been murdered. We suspect Aberman has been as well. We need to prove our suspicion. Have you ever met a Helen Langdon or a Helen Mackay?'

'No.'

'You seem certain.'

'I watch the news. I'm aware that a Helen Langdon was found dead with James Holden. I take it that is the woman you're referring to.'

'It is.'

'Then I've not met her, not even spoken to her.'

***

It took a few days before all the paperwork was in place. The notification had been given to Slater, Aberman's solicitor, and Ben Aberman's next-door neighbour had been informed.

Four vehicles stood in the driveway of Aberman's house, with a uniform out on the street to deal with the onlookers. 'Just routine,' if anyone asked them.

Gordon Windsor walked around the house with Isaac, Slater having given them a key. 'It's musty in here,' Windsor said.

'What will you find in here?'

'No idea. The garden interests us more. We've got a couple of ground penetrating radars. They should pick anything up.'

'How long before you have an answer?'

'One, two days, to cover the grounds. And then we'll check the house. There's a cellar. It looks clean, but we don't know for certain until we check it. Are you sure Aberman's dead?'

'It's a strong possibility. If he is, and he's here, then Helen Langdon's not looking so good.'

Isaac walked out of the front door of the house and walked around to the next-door neighbour. 'Mrs Hawthorne, you've been informed?'

'Is Mr Aberman buried there?'

'We've not been able to find him. The woman who used to come here, we believe her name was Helen Langdon.'

'Is she dead?'

'If it's confirmed she was the woman you spoke to, then yes?'

'Such a lovely woman. She gave me a vase for my house once. She said it came from her house.'

'Do you still have it?'

'It was too nice to use. It's still in the paper she wrapped it in.'

'Can we check it?'

'If you like.'

Isaac made a phone call. Grant Meston, Windsor's deputy, came over.

'Mrs Hawthorne has a vase in her house. The lady who used to check on Aberman's house gave it to her. There may be fingerprints.'

'I'll check it out now. It shouldn't take long.'

Isaac left Meston with the old lady and returned to the back of Aberman's house. A grid pattern had been laid out in the garden, and the two machines were going up and down at a slow pace. 'We can't hurry this,' Windsor said. 'It's been a few years, the ground's bound to have compacted.'

'Are you certain with the machines?'

'If there's a body, we'll find it. Grant said you may have a lead next door.'

'Fingerprints on a vase. If they're Helen Langdon's, then it's a further tie-in to the Dixey Club and Barry Knox.'

'Nasty piece of work, is he?'

'He's not someone you'd want to invite around your house. Denied everything, of course.'

'Don't they always.'

'The man's gone from pimping to running a strip club, so he's suspect to start with, and his bodyguard, he's the violent type. The sort of person who could kill Aberman.'

From the far end of the garden, one of the CSIs raised his hand. 'Over here,' he shouted.

'A result?' Isaac said.

'Don't get too excited. It could be a cat or a dog buried there. Whatever it is, it'll take most of the day to confirm.'

Grant Meston reappeared. 'Perfect prints,' he said.

'Whose?'

'Helen Langdon.'

Isaac phoned Larry and Wendy. 'It's confirmed. Helen Langdon was the mysterious woman at Aberman's house.'

'What next?' Wendy asked.

'We'll meet later tonight. The CSIs have found something in the garden.'

'Aberman?'

'Unknown. They're erecting a crime scene tent. From here on in, it's down to being on the ground and slowly sifting through the soil.'

A voice came from another part of the garden. 'Over here.'

'It's going to be a busy day,' Windsor said.

'Okay, call me when you have something,' Isaac said.

***

Isaac could see no advantage in staying around Aberman's house, and with a disciplinary hearing pending, he had to prepare his defence. Helen Langdon seemed the reason for the double killing at the hotel in Bayswater, but the waters were becoming muddied. It was now known that she had been involved in a relationship with Ben Aberman, the previous owner of the Dixey Club.

Larry was checking on the Adamants, trying to understand why and how Helen had married the father, whether the man's death had been as a result of his madness or whether he had been murdered.

Larry found the youngest child, Howard, at his place of work, the family home. 'How much money can you make doing this?' Larry asked, as Adamant sat in front of his monitor.

'It depends. Some weeks, a few thousand, others as much as fifty or sixty.'

'Serious money.'

'Hard work, long hours.'

'That's what I've got,' Larry said.

The man opposite continued working, although he was communicative. 'I've got to finish this today,' he said. 'Have you found out who killed Helen?'

'Not yet. She seems to have led a varied life.'

'What do you mean?'

'Before she met your father, she was performing in a club.'

'We know that. Dixey's. It's a dive.'

'You've been there?'

'Once or twice with some friends.'

'When Helen was performing?'

'Not then. They still had her picture outside, although I can understand why.'

'Why's that?'

'You've been?'

'Twice.'

'They're not much, the ones up on that stage. Helen, she must have been the star performer.'

'She was.'

'I can't imagine her with the men, the same as the others.'

'She wasn't, although she played along.'

'How do you know?'

'Some of my friends, they'd seen her there, but I never did.'

'You fancied her?' Larry said.

'Who wouldn't? She was more my age than my father's, but he had the money.'

'Apparently, the money wasn't that important to her.'

'What do you reckon? You're the policeman.'

'Money's always important, so's love. Helen seemed to prefer older men, no doubt they treated her better.'

'More likely to forgive and forget, and she flattered their egos. I would have taken her in an instant, but she'd seen through me.'

'What do you mean?'

'I was in my early twenties. I was into anything in a skirt.'

'It wouldn't have been serious with you, just another woman.'

'Maybe, maybe not, but I wasn't into settling down. Helen, if she wanted security and a decent man, that wasn't me, not back then.'

'And now?'

'I've grown up, money in the bank. Sometimes the stress of my work gets to me, and the idea of hitting the clubs, chatting up a woman doesn't appeal anymore. It's a shame about Helen. If she was in that room with James Holden, there was a reason; maybe it was love, but whatever it was, she's blameless.'

'Why so much devotion to the woman from everyone we've met? And we've been to Dixey's, we've spoken to your family, to Holden's family. What is it?'

'I don't know. Are you suspicious?'

'Nobody's that good. Everyone's got something they'd rather hide, skeletons best left hidden.'

'But you know her skeletons. She performed in that club, danced naked, took money from depraved onlookers.'

'Depraved?'

'You've been. What do you think?'

'You're right, I suppose.'

'It's the permissive society. If you want some titillation, to get laid, you just need to go out of a Saturday night, any pub, and there are plenty of females waiting for a man.'

'Is that what you do?'

'I've one or two women I can phone up. I'm doing alright for myself,' Howard Adamant said.

Larry could only agree with the man as he left the house. Outside, a Porsche, and the chance of a few women at the weekend. He remembered back to when he had been Adamant's age, a lowly police constable, a fifteen-year-old car. His chances had not been so good, but he had managed. His wife had been a Saturday night pickup, and they were still together after many years.

He envied the young man his good fortune but did not want it for himself. If he could just make it to detective chief inspector, he'd be satisfied.

Chapter 13

'You'd better get back to Aberman's house,' Gordon Windsor said on the phone.

'What is it?' Isaac said.

'We've found human remains.'

'Aberman?'

'It needs Forensics and Pathology to confirm. I'd say it was male judging by the clothes, but apart from that, I'd only be guessing.'

'I'll take your guess.'

'It's been here for five to ten years, maybe longer. There's no chance of facial recognition. Does the man have a relative we can use for DNA?'

'We've not looked.'

Isaac ended the call and phoned Larry. 'I've got Bridget and Wendy in the office. I need you out at Aberman's as soon as possible. Wendy and I will meet you there.'

'What's up?'

'A body. We're assuming Aberman's. Bridget, check if Ben Aberman has a close relative. Also, dental records.'

Larry was at Aberman's house within forty minutes, Wendy and Isaac not far behind. In the driveway was the next-door neighbour. 'Is it Mr Aberman? she asked.

'We've no idea yet. We'll come and talk to you later.'

'Such a nice man. Whatever next?'

'You didn't know of the man's history?'

'I told you before. He was in the entertainment business. He used to have all these attractive people down for the weekend.'

Isaac didn't feel it necessary to tell the woman that the attractive people were probably criminals and ladies of the night.

The three police officers kitted themselves up in overalls, foot protectors, and gloves. They proceeded around to the back of the house. In the far corner of the garden were a crime scene tent and Gordon Windsor. 'There are another couple of places to check. We were lucky with this one.'

'Not so lucky for the man in the hole,' Wendy said.

'Any sign of how he died?' Isaac asked.

'Bullet in the head, the hole's clearly visible,' Windsor said.

'What was it wearing?'

'A shirt. A pair of trousers, no shoes. He's laid out straight.'

'Are you saying they gave him a proper burial.'

'No. Whoever put him in that hole wanted to make sure he'd not be discovered. It's a deep hole, at least four feet. Normally, someone would just scrape off the topsoil and bury him, but not with this one.'

'Eventually the body would have been discovered,' Larry said.

'Would it?' Windsor said. 'That's not an assumption I'd make. He's buried under a compost heap, next to a fast-growing bush, plenty of roots. In time the body would have decayed into the soil.'

'Why in this garden?' Isaac said. 'There must be better places to bury a body.'

'It depends where the man was murdered. We're going through the house now. Nothing yet, and after so many years, and especially if someone's attempted to clean up, we may not find much.'

'Check for Helen Langdon's prints in the house.'

'We know what we're doing.'

'It's not looking good for the woman,' Wendy said.

'We'll go and have a conversation with the lady next door,' Isaac said.

'It'll be best if I go alone. An old woman might feel intimidated by you two.'

'Very well, you deal with it. Larry and I, we'll stay here, see what else they discover.'

***

Wendy knew it was better for her to talk to the next-door neighbour, a softly spoken woman. In her house, not as grand as Aberman's but still impressive, Wendy took a seat in the kitchen. 'What can you tell me about Mr Aberman?'

'He was a good neighbour, although I only saw him on weekends. The woman who used to come here was always polite.'

'Are you shocked by what we've found in Mr Aberman's back garden?'

'I don't know what to think. I've lived here for a long time, and it's the first time anything like this has happened.'

'It takes time to digest. Mrs Hawthorne, Ben Aberman had a dubious background.'

'Not Mr Aberman?'

'Your Mr Aberman was involved with criminals. The woman who visited you, she used to perform in one of his clubs. She was Aberman's girlfriend.'

'I never saw her at any of the parties.'

'Tell me about these parties,' Wendy said.

'They were loud, and sometimes they went on late.'

'You didn't complain?'

'I liked them. Some of the others around here would phone the police, but I used to watch from an upstairs window.'

'Did Mr Aberman know?'

'I told him once. He thought it was hilarious, invited me over the next time they had one, but that never happened.'

'He disappeared?'

'I thought he'd gone overseas, and then his friend turns up and asks me to keep an eye on the place.'

'I need you to think back to the last time you saw Mr Aberman. Is that possible?'

'He arrived at the house with some other men. I waved to him, but he didn't see me.'

'Anything else? The car they arrived in, the other men?'

'The car, it was black. It looked expensive, but I don't know what it was. I remember it being there for a long time, overnight, but there was no noise.'

'Did anyone go out into the garden at the back? You've seen where the crime scene investigators are.'

'Two men were digging a hole. I thought it was strange, but then, I'd seen the parties.'

'These parties, risqué?'

'Oh, yes. I'm not a prude. Some of the others in the area are, but I wasn't worried if they ran around half-naked.'

'What were they doing?'

'I was young once. I could only envy them.'

'The sort of things you wouldn't want a child to see?'

'I'm the only one who can see over the fence. Mr Aberman had good privacy, but my room upstairs can see right over. Some of them at the party, well, later on, they're on the grass.'

'And?'

'You know.'

'Indulging in sexual intercourse?'

'We used to call it screwing, but I suppose you're the police. You have to use the official term, make it sound dirty.'

'We use your word, but I thought you'd be offended.'

'My husband and I, we were broadminded.'

Wendy looked at the old woman, a gentle and kind soul, who had her family photos lined up on a table in the sitting room, a woman who treasured her knick-knacks, a woman who was not offended by the behaviour next door.

'Tell me about the men digging?'

'There's not a lot I can tell you. It was dark, and I couldn't really see them.'

'Did they see you?'

'Not me. I was careful to stay hidden. I get up in that room, the lights off, and I peer through a gap in the curtains. The two men, one was taller than the other, they didn't say much, only stopped for a rest every fifteen minutes. I could see they both smoked.'

'After they finished digging the hole?'

'I fell asleep before then. It was boring.'

'Did you fall asleep when they had the parties.'

'Not then. I loved to watch.'

'Mrs Hawthorne, you're terrible. A woman your age,' Wendy said, although it was said with humour.

'The mind's willing, even if the body isn't.'

'You said the car left in the morning.'

'It wasn't there, but it could have left during the night.'

'Did you hear any noises, any names mentioned?'

'Nothing, and my hearing's fine.'

'No gunshot?'

'Nothing. Do you think the woman who came here knew there was a body in the garden?'

'We don't know.'

'You could ask her. She gave me a phone number.'

'She'll not answer,' Wendy said.

'Any reason why?'

'The woman you know has died. She's been murdered.'

'Such a nice person. What a shame.'

'A shame, as you say.'

***

With the recovered body from Aberman's back garden with Pathology, the Homicide team gathered at Challis Street. Isaac was about to go through what they had so far when his phone rang.

'Linda Holden. Can you come to my office?'

'Is it important?'

'Yes. I've found something,' the woman said as she ended the phone call.

'Larry, you better come with me,' Isaac said. 'Wendy, can you focus on finding any relatives of Ben Aberman. Bridget, whatever you can.'

'Aberman was divorced,' Bridget said. 'Wendy could try there first. I've got an address for the ex-wife, no idea what sort of reception she'll receive.'

'I can handle myself,' Wendy said.

'You know what we want. We'll go and see what Linda Holden has, and then we'll swing by the Dixey Club, see what Knox and Gus have to say for themselves.'

'You should take Aberman's neighbour. She'd love it,' Wendy said.

'More than me,' Isaac said.

The two police officers arrived at Linda Holden's office. The place was almost empty.

'We've had to let most of them go,' Linda said on their entering.

'Why's that?'

'We survive mainly on benefactors, some wealthy, some through donations on our website, but with all the negative publicity, we're not bringing in enough money. Another month and we'll close the door.'

'Your mother?' Larry asked.

'She's confused as to what's happened. The Daisy woman, what about her?'

'Your father met her on an occasional basis. Their relationship was purely commercial.'

'But not with Helen?'

'That's what we've always believed. Helen, whatever else she was, was not a common prostitute.'

'Our father was obsessed with her. He was even considering leaving our mother.'

'You have proof?'

'I found some letters from him to her. I don't know if he sent them, and if he did, then why are they in this office?'

'Why are you telling us?' Isaac said.

'I'm closing this place down. I don't want any loose ends.'

'I thought your father's work was important.'

'Have you turned on the television lately?'

'Your father's no longer seen as the beacon of morality.'

'That's why I'm showing you these letters. They may help to explain my father's behaviour, they may not.'

'Your brother?'

'He's still angry. Although I think he's over the worst of it. He had been in love with Helen.'

'He could have killed her and your father?'

'If my brother had seen these letters, he would have been angry enough to do something.'

The truth is always the best approach,' Isaac said.

Larry took one of the letters and glanced through it. 'Not unusual for a man as he's getting older, the need to relive his youth, but, as you say, it was more than love.'

'That's Helen, isn't it? She has this power over men.' Linda said.

'Have you ever heard of a Ben Aberman?' Isaac said.

'Should I?'

'It's before Helen's time in prison. The man goes back to when she was performing. He was the owner of the club.'

'What about him?'

'We found a body in the back garden of his house. It had a bullet wound in the head.'

'Do you suspect the same person killed my father and Helen?' Linda said.

'There's a few years between the deaths. Up until the last few weeks, Helen had been paying regular visits to the house,' Isaac said.

'Did anyone know Helen? Do you think she killed her husband?' Linda said.

'Our primary focus is her death, not who she may have killed. Adamant treated her well. Even his children and they were older than her, treated her with respect.'

'Then maybe my father had no chance.'

'Maybe,' Isaac said. John Holden concerned him, and his sister had been right. The letters which Isaac now had in his pocket could have tipped James Holden's son over the edge from insanely jealous to vengeful and violent.

Chapter 14

'Christine Aberman?' Wendy said at the door of a smart terrace house in Chelsea.

'If it's about Ben, it's been years since I've seen him.'

'Sergeant Wendy Gladstone, Challis Street Police Station. I've a few questions.'

'Come in. You'll have to mind the house, we've got the painters in.'

'We?' Wendy said.

'My husband and I.'

'You've remarried?'

'Two years ago. A good man, more than I can say of Ben. I've kept his surname, though.'

'What did you know about your husband's business?'

'He ran some clubs, downmarket, sleazy.'

'Did it concern you?'

'No, should it?'

'Have you been to the clubs?'

'Never. He wanted me to go, to see where he made his money, but watching vacuous women gyrating around on a stage does nothing for me.'

'When did you divorce your husband?'

'Ten, maybe eleven years. The marriage had slowly been going downhill, and then he was staying away of a night every week or so. I smelt a rat.'

'What did you do?'

'I confronted him. He admitted he'd been fooling around, and that was that: no drama, no hysterics, no accusing the other. We phoned up a solicitor friend of ours. He came over to the house, dealt with all the paperwork. This house was part of the settlement.'

'It's very nice.'

'I know it is, and now my new husband is here with me.'

'What does he do?'

'Bank manager. It's not very glamorous, and it doesn't pay much, but that's not the point, is it?'

'What do you mean?'

'He's reliable, he treats me well, and he doesn't cheat on me.'

'Did you ever meet a Helen or a Daisy?'

'I never met any of his women, and besides, what's this about?'

'Your husband's house in the country. We've found a body in the back garden.'

'And?'

'You don't seem concerned.'

'My husband mixed with some unsavoury characters. If there's a body at the house, I'd not be surprised. Is it Ben?'

'We'll need to conduct further tests.'

'What do you want from me?'

'Dental records, or somewhere we can obtain them. Also, DNA.'

'I can give you the name of a dentist he used to use.'

'A photo?'

'It's a few years old.'

***

The Dixey Club with the lights on and in the middle of the day was not the same as Isaac and Larry had seen it previously. It was still too early for the women to be on the premises, although the manager, Barry Knox, was, as was his heavy, Gus.

'What do you want?' Gus said.

'Knox here?' Isaac said.

'He's busy unless you've got a warrant.'

'I've got a police car outside. It wouldn't take much to get a few uniforms to haul you off to the police station, let you cool your heels for a few hours.'

'On what charge?'

'Letting minors in, selling drugs.'

'I've not done that.'

'If you haven't, then you're the only door manager in the area who hasn't. We could always give you a strip search, check out where you live.'

'Okay, you've made your point. I'll get Knox for you.'

'Bit tough there,' Larry said.

'We need to put the pressure on these two. Knox knows something, and Gus, he's the guy who does the dirty work.'

After a few minutes, long enough for Isaac and Larry to look around the place, Barry Knox emerged. 'I've got a busy workload. Is this important?'

'The parties at Aberman's, did you ever attend?'

'What did I tell you last time?'

'Last time, you were playing us for suckers. We can either talk here or down at Challis Street. Which do you prefer?'

'We've done nothing wrong. We have all the licences in place.'

'What about the bed at the back? Is it licensed? What do you do with the video of the men with your women on the bed? Share it amongst your friends, indulge in a little blackmail?'

'The camera is for security. The bed is for first aid. We've been through this before. If you're trying to wind me up, you're wasting your time.'

'I could have you for half a dozen violations. What I want to know is why you and Gus were in Aberman's garden digging a hole late at night.'

'Are you serious? I'd been to his parties a few times, but it wasn't for gardening.'

'Cocaine, women, alcohol?'

'Why not? Aberman may have had his faults, but the man knew how to live, and he used to get some classy women there.'

'And the women were available?'

'That's why they were there.'

'Our crime scene investigation team have found a body buried in Aberman's garden. We also know two men dug the grave. One was short, looked like a weasel. The other one was tall, heavily-built, similar to a wrestler. Sound familiar?'

'You can't go insulting me like that,' Knox said.

'I can and I will until you start talking. Helen, was she ever at one of those parties?'

'I saw her there once, but she didn't take part. I told you before, she was strictly in the club as eye candy. She'd get the money from the men, and then Daisy and the other women would go in for the kill. Helen, she was Aberman's woman, and if anyone touched her, he'd have Gus take him out the back door.'

'A severe beating?'

'They'd not come back here again,' Gus said.

'Let's come back to what we were talking about,' Larry said. 'Ben Aberman has these parties. They're wild, and there's plenty of wrongdoing, but we're not interested in any of that. We're interested in why a body is buried in his garden. Now, the question once again. Did you two bury the man?'

'It wasn't us.'

'But you know who it was.'

'Gus,' Knox looked over at the heavy, 'it's up to you. What do you reckon?'

'I'm not going to jail for something I didn't do.'

'Do you want to tell us down at Challis Street or are you going to give us a statement here?'

'Okay, Cook,' Knox said. 'Here's what we know. Ben Aberman, he's a good operator, making good money, but he flies close to the wind, takes a few chances. He's keen to open two more clubs, but he needs money, and you've seen his house. Not the sort of place that a few clubs such as Dixey's will get you. The man borrows to maintain his expansion plans, his lifestyle. His parties are notorious, and he foots the bill, and the whores don't come cheap. He's over-extended, the lenders are calling in the money. Aberman's panicking, borrowing here and there, wherever he can. Eventually, he runs out of time, and the lenders come in here and take him.'

'Gus?' Isaac said.

'I'm only the hired help. The people who came here scared me. They were really mean. I act tough, but I'm not about to kill anyone.'

'Carry on, Knox.'

'I'm brought in as the replacement manager of this club, plenty of money, some bonuses.'

'Bonuses?'

'One or other of the women.'

'Helen?'

'She was promised, but two days later, she's out of here. Daisy's left, the poor substitute.'

'After Aberman left, what happened?'

'Not a lot. I was told Aberman had signed over the clubs, but for some reason, the house stayed in his name. That's the honest truth. Whatever happened, we don't know.'

'But you heard rumours?'

'There's always rumours, but me and Gus, we didn't give much credence to them.'

'What were they?'

'Helen had negotiated on Aberman's behalf, and for whatever reason, they agreed to the deal. And then two days later, Helen left the club. The word is that he's gone overseas, but I can't buy that. For one thing, the man's got a house and a lifestyle. And where overseas? That would need money, and Aberman, even if he was nothing else, was an Englishman. He had no connections overseas we knew of.'

'Is this just you two, or are there others who doubt the story?'

'We live on the edge, you know that, DCI. People come, people go. We don't have the luxury of asking too many questions, otherwise…'

'You disappear.'

'Aberman's not around, the club's still open. That's all we know.'

'You weren't surprised about Aberman's garden.'

'One night, a couple of years back, one of the lender's heavies is in here. He's had a few to drink. We know we need to look after him, so we bring him into the office. He wants to drink. We join in. He starts drifting in and out of consciousness. He starts talking, tells us about Aberman.'

'What did he say?'

'We're just making conversation, not trying to pry.'

'And?'

'The heavy, he's an ugly man, goes by the name of Pete. He says Aberman's pushing up daisies.'

'He's dead.'

'That's what we thought he meant, and he said afterwards it wasn't daisies, it was a bush of some description. He didn't say what type, probably didn't know.'

'Did you think it was Aberman's garden?'

'Only when you mentioned the body. Anyway, the man fell asleep, and the next morning, when he woke up, he didn't remember the night before. What was on top of the body?'

'A bush,' Isaac said.

'We've been honest with you two,' Knox said. 'Now, give us a break and don't ask us to repeat what we've just told you in a court of law.'

***

Graham Picket, the pathologist, a taciturn man, never appreciated having Isaac in his office, and now he had the full ensemble: Isaac, Larry, Wendy, and Gordon Windsor.

'What is it with you, DCI?' Picket said. 'I have the body for two hours, and you're bashing my door down for an answer. Your sergeant has brought me the dental records of a Ben Aberman.'

'Confirmed?' Isaac asked.

'I'll need longer to conduct a full autopsy, but the body, what's left of it, and the dental records match. If you go away, then I'm willing to state that the body in my care is that of Ben Aberman.'

'Thank you. A full report as soon as possible,' Isaac said.

With the confirmation the team had expected, the investigation had taken a different direction. Initially, it had been about a man and a woman naked and dead in a hotel. Then there was a prostitute, a former friend of the dead woman, who had died, and now a club owner, which indicated that organised crime was involved.

'It's not over,' Isaac said. Back in the office at Challis Street, the team were focussing on the situation. They were all fired up, ready to discuss the case and to get back out on the road, when the booming voice of their superintendent interrupted them.

'They're piling up again, DCI,' Seth Caddick said.

'It's under control,' Isaac said.

'You must be joking. Maybe I should come down here and give you a hand.'

'If you do, sir, I'll register a complaint.'

'Suit yourself. Remember the disciplinary hearing's next week.'

'I've not forgotten,' Isaac said.

And with that, the obnoxious Caddick left.

'He's baiting you, sir,' Wendy said.

'And doing a good job,' Isaac replied. 'Ignore the man and ignore what could happen. We need to focus on what we have. Larry, an update from you.'

'So far, our focus has been on Helen Langdon, not James Holden.'

'Is there a point?'

'Purely conjecture. Helen Langdon, the sinner redeemed, is looking increasingly suspect. And why Daisy? The woman left the club a long time ago, and she was only murdered after Helen. And what is this control that Helen has over Aberman's murderer?'

'She must have known he was buried in the garden,' Wendy said.

'A logical deduction. And how does she pull this off, this subterfuge? She came from an average family, average education, and, apart from her looks, she seems to be able to control whoever.'

'Men with their tongues hanging out,' Bridget said.

'Not so flippant as it sounds,' Isaac said. 'She's able to control men by her sexuality, but she doesn't give in. Apart from Aberman, we've found no other behaviour unbecoming of the woman. Are we sure that Helen and Aberman were sleeping together?'

'That's what we've been told,' Wendy said.

'But no proof. We know she married Adamant, and that was consummated, and there's a clear indication she had had sex with Holden, but no proof with Aberman. And if the man's killed, did she know, did she agree? She has his house, it's empty, and she could have moved in, but she didn't. Why not? All the bills have been paid, and she even had a debit card for the incidentals.'

'What about the solicitor who was looking after it for Aberman? He must have some correspondence with whoever's paying the money. If it's not Aberman, then who and why?'

'We're ruffling the feathers of some serious criminal figures,' Larry said.

'How do we get to them?'

'Knox mentioned Ugly Pete.'

'How do we find him?'

'I'll use my contacts,' Larry said.

'Fine, you follow up on him. Wendy, see what you can find out about Aberman and Helen. See if anyone is certain of their relationship, or whether it's just smoke and mirrors, and if it is, why? Bridget, do some research into Aberman's solicitor.'

Chapter 15

Nicholas Slater, the senior partner at the legal firm that Aberman had used, was not in a good mood when Isaac and Wendy entered his premises. 'I'm severely embarrassed,' he said.

'Your client does not appear to be Ben Aberman, does it?'

'I have carried out my duties meticulously.'

'Let's go back to when you took over the responsibility for the Aberman house,' Isaac said.

'Mr Aberman has entrusted me with his legal work for many years.'

'You've met him?'

'A long time ago. I knew his wife as well. I only visited his clubs the one time when there was a dispute over an alcohol licence.'

'Mr Slater, there are serious concerns regarding your propriety. When you visited the club, was Helen Langdon on the stage?'

'Aberman introduced me to a woman once. It was probably her.'

'How can you be unsure? The woman's picture has been in the newspapers, on the television.'

'Okay, it was Helen.'

Slater phoned for his receptionist to bring in refreshments. After the tea had been delivered, Slater spoke. 'Ben Aberman was a friend. We had known each other for many years, and I dealt with all his legal work. In the last couple of years, before he disappeared, he had become more erratic.'

'Any reason why?'

'Aberman was interested in expanding. He had split from his wife, a calming influence, and he was enjoying the freedom.'

'The women in the club?' Wendy said.

'Yes. Before that, he had regarded the clubs as places to make money, but there he is, early fifties, recently separated, and in a harem.'

'Helen Langdon?'

'Ben, he wants to make his mark. He makes contact with some people who'll help him out. I advised him against it, but he wasn't listening.'

'Can you prove your objection?'

'It's on file. Ben agreed to take the money from these people. I wasn't involved.'

'Did you see the paperwork?'

'There wasn't any. He was dealing with gangsters. They lent the money, you paid them back with interest, or they'd come and take it with force.'

'Aberman's got the money. He's done his homework. Why then, does he get into financial trouble?'

'He had lined up the purchase of another club, paid money upfront, and then the deal collapsed. Ben was frantic. He's down fifty thousand pounds, the lenders are after him, and he can't pay.'

'How do you know this?'

'He asked me to get him out of trouble.'

'What did you do?'

'I advised bankruptcy as the final solution, or to just walk away from the clubs, but Ben, he wasn't listening.'

'Bankruptcy wouldn't have been an option. The people he was dealing with would have still wanted the money.'

'I've always suspected the premises Ben had been looking at belonged to those who had lent him the money. They forced him into trouble, knowing full well that Dixey and the other clubs were cash cows.'

'Cash cows?' Wendy said.

'It's a financial term,' Isaac said. 'The clubs have been set up, and they're making a profit. All the gangsters need to do is to maintain the business and cream off as much money as they can. Aberman did the hard work, they reap the rewards.'

'Ben, he was a fool,' Slater said. 'He decided to take them on.'

'You know a lot about this.'

'Ben's a friend. I advised him to prepare to leave the country. He was still not listening, but at least he was willing to consider my suggestion.'

'And when he disappeared?'

'I assumed he'd left the country. I already had access to one of his accounts. Out of friendship, I looked after the house for him.'

'That still doesn't explain Helen Langdon or the house being empty.'

'Helen, she's Ben's woman. Two weeks after my last contact with him, she entered this office. She was upset.'

'Why are you telling us this now?' Isaac asked.

'The situation is dangerous. Finding his body will only open old wounds. You're becoming involved in something dangerous. I hope you're prepared.'

'Are you?'

'I'm not sure I can be.'

'Continue,' Isaac said.

'The woman was not sure what to do. She told me this story about Ben, and how he'd got himself out of trouble by signing over the clubs, and she was going to look after the house for him."

'The money on her debit card?'

'That's covered. I asked her where Aberman is. She told me it would be best if I don't ask. Only that Ben's fine, and he'll be back one day.'

'Were you suspicious?'

'Ben always had a sense of the dramatic. After one year, more or less, the relationship with Helen is working fine. The house is empty, the woman is paying regular visits, and there's nothing more for me to do. I've other clients, and I gave little thought to Aberman.'

'Until?' Isaac said.

'Why do you say that?' Slater said.

'There's always an "until". You wouldn't be opening up to us unless there was a reason. You told us you didn't know Helen Langdon before, that you'd never met her.'

'Occasionally, Helen would phone me up.'

'Why?'

'She wanted to let me know that she was still around, and any attempt by me to enter the house would be met with retribution.'

'She knew what was in the house,' Wendy said.

'If she knew, then you did,' Isaac said to Slater.

'I did not. It was an unusual request, but I complied.'

'But the man was a friend who walked on the wild side. You must have been suspicious.'

'I was.'

'What did you do?'

'Several weeks ago, I was near to the house. I had a key in my pocket. It was an overcast day, and there was no one in the street. I took the opportunity to look around the house.'

'What did you find?'

'Nothing. It was not in good condition, and there was dust everywhere. I stayed about ten minutes and left.'

'No one saw you?'

'The old lady next door saw me leaving.'

'Did she talk to you?'

'No. I was too far away, but Mrs Hawthorne, she knew who I was. Before her husband died, I used to do some legal work for him.'

'Then what happened?'

'Nothing for a few days, and then Helen phoned me. She's angry, telling me I'd violated her trust, and our relationship would be severed forthwith.'

'What did you say?'

'Nothing. She hung up, and that was the last time I heard from her.'

'And when she ended up dead with James Holden?'

'I recognised her, knew her death was probably related to Ben Aberman. I was scared, not sure what to do.'

'Why was she killed?'

'She must have known that Ben Aberman was dead. But in all the years, she never dropped her guard.'

'What about the four years she was in jail?'

'I still received email correspondence.'

'Not from jail you wouldn't. Slater, you know more than you're telling us,' Isaac said. 'Unless you start giving us the truth, we'll be suspicious of you. You're too close to the action, maybe you killed Aberman. Maybe you're involved with these gangsters.'

'I'm innocent, believe me, but those that killed Aberman, they're dangerous. If they know I've been talking to…'

'They'll have you killed?'

'Yes. Even now, they're watching me.'

'Why would they be watching you? Apart from the one visit to the house, you've acted correctly.'

'I don't know why, and that's what frightens me. Helen, she could tough it out, but not me.'

'We've been told of a heavy who goes by the name of Pete. Any ideas?'

'I received a phone call,' Slater said.

'When?'

'Two days ago.'

'What did the person say?'

'I don't know who he was, only that he told me to be careful in what I said to you. I told him I knew nothing, but he didn't believe me.'

'Neither do we,' Larry said. 'You went into the house, you were curious, suspected something. I put it to you, Mr Slater, that you've always known Aberman to be dead and buried in that garden. Were you one of those at the house the night he died? Was it you who cleaned the house afterwards? And who was it who dug the hole in the garden? And who are the people who threatened the man and let Helen have the house, and why?'

'Helen, she was two-timing Aberman.'

'With who?'

There was a sound of shattering glass, a spray of blood, and Slater collapsed forward on his desk.

'He's been shot!' Isaac said. Both police officers moved from where they were and took shelter to one side of the window. Slater's receptionist opened the door on hearing the noise – another shot, and she collapsed to the ground.

Larry dropped to the floor and crawled over to where she was. He gently lifted her head. 'She's dead,' he said.

Isaac was on the phone, calling for backup. Wendy was on the way, as were Gordon Windsor and Caddick. The situation was dangerous. A quick glance by Isaac had shown a rooftop on the other side of the road. He couldn't see anyone there.

A phone call. Isaac answered. 'Specialist Firearms Command here. What's the situation?'

'Two dead. We'll try and move out of the line of sight.'

'Fifteen minutes, stay alive.'

'Slater knew the full story,' Larry said from his position on the ground next to the dead woman. 'She opened the door at the wrong time.'

Forty minutes later, the all-clear. 'No one up there,' the leader of the specialist firearms team said. 'A difficult shot, not sure I could have made it.'

Inside Slater's office were a team of medics, not that they could do much. Slater had been shot in the back of the head, his receptionist in the front.

'Nasty,' Caddick said as he entered the crime scene.

'Slater was about to tell us who had killed Aberman.'

'Out of here, everyone,' Gordon Windsor said. 'Isaac, you've got a right mess here. We'll need time on this one.'

Outside the building there was an ambulance; a medic checked out Isaac and Larry. Apart from shock and their clothes being covered in blood and shattered glass, they were declared fit.

'What's happened here?' Caddick asked.

'The man was covering for Aberman's murderers. He was about to give us a name.'

'The woman?'

'We think she was innocent. She's only worked for Slater for a few months.'

'Where to from here?'

'Apart from a shower and a change, we've another possibility.'

'Not for me to comment under the circumstances,' Caddick said, 'other than to say we're all pleased that you both are alive.'

'Thank you, sir,' Isaac said.

Caddick left, Wendy came over. 'We're dealing with dangerous people,' she said.

'Larry and I need two hours. We'll meet in the office, go over what we've got. Windsor can keep us updated, although we were there, we know what happened.'

'We need a name,' Larry said.

'Whoever they are, they're watching.'

'But why Aberman's garden? If they had killed him somewhere else, even thrown him overboard out at sea, we wouldn't be investigating his murder.'

'More questions,' Wendy said. 'I'll stay here for now, and we'll meet in two hours.'

Chapter 16

Larry's wife freaked out when he returned home. 'Not again. It's too dangerous,' she said. He tried to offer an explanation, but she wasn't listening. Isaac had no such person to complain. He was still on his own. The romance with the woman he had met in Brighton, a one-hour thirty minutes' drive to the south of London, had bloomed for a while, but then it had cooled down within a couple of months.

As he stood under the shower, lathering soap over and over again to remove the blood, the scent of death, he wondered if it was normal that the death of a solicitor and his young receptionist did not affect him.

He left the shower, dried himself, and put on a clean set of clothes. He put his old clothes in a large evidence bag, rather than dropping them off at the dry cleaner's. Caddick would have to sign expenses for their cost.

Two hours after leaving the solicitor's office, the team assembled at Challis Street. Bridget, as usual, was concerned and fussing. 'It must have been terrible,' she said.

'I could do with a pizza,' Isaac said.

'I'll order one,' Bridget said.

'Make that two.' Larry added his order.

'Three,' Wendy said.

Isaac could see Larry was suffering delayed shock. He made a phone call to the first aid officer in the building. She came down, gave Larry a tranquilliser and told him to take it easy, to go home and rest.

Larry thanked her, did not respond to her suggestion.

'You'd better not drive,' Isaac said.

Chief Superintendent Goddard phoned. 'I've requested a new date for your disciplinary hearing,' he said. 'With the recent developments, they've agreed. Also, Wendy Gladstone's medical, that's on hold.'

'Caddick?' Isaac said.

'Forget about him for now. You and Larry could have been shot. He'll keep out of your way for now, or if he's smart enough, he will.'

'Caddick and smart? Oxymoron, sir.'

'He's struggling to get his budget approved. Questions are being asked as to his effectiveness. There's an internal audit of all the senior officers. He's one of them.'

'Did Davies put that forward?'

'A government watchdog has made the recommendations. Davies will play it smart and put his full weight behind it.'

'Lord Shaw, DCS Goddard?'

'Don't go fishing, Isaac. Just be thankful that someone's still got the gumption to stand up and be counted.'

'How's Davies's position?'

'Don't expect him to depart soon. Worry about solving the current murders and try to make sure no one else dies.'

'We'll try our best, sir.'

Goddard ended the phone call. Isaac turned to the team. 'Wendy, your medical's been put on hold. Also, my disciplinary is off for now.'

'Caddick?' Larry said.

'He's got his own problems.'

'I'll go and see Mrs Hawthorne again,' Wendy said.

'Slater said he knew her, and she had seen him the day he visited Aberman's house. Mrs Hawthorne may well have enjoyed the spectacle of the parties, but she's nosey. Aberman was tortured, there must have been some noise.'

'I'll check out Slater's other clients,' Bridget said.

'Larry and I will revisit the Dixey Club,' Isaac said. 'Knox and Gus will be nervous now. If Slater can be killed, so can they, and they know who the villains are.'

***

Barry Knox was not pleased to see Isaac and Larry. It was late in the day when they arrived at the club. On the stage were two women, one upside down on the pole, the other teasing the patrons in the front row, tempting them to part with their money.

'You're here about Slater?' Knox said as Isaac and Larry entered his office. On the screens in one corner were the women out front, the audience, and the bed at the back of the establishment.

'Are you still looking at that bed?' Isaac said.

'First aid requires constant vigilance.'

'Did you know Slater?'

'He used to come along to Aberman's parties. Couldn't get enough of what was on offer.'

'What else can you tell us about him?'

'Not a lot. I never knew he was a solicitor until I saw a photo of him on the television.'

'We were there when he was shot,' Larry said.

'So much for the protection of the law,' Knox said. 'Don't bother offering me protection if I turn Queen's evidence.'

'Are you considering it?'

'I've nothing to tell you. I'm clean.'

'Twenty-four hours down at the police station may do you some good.'

'You can't hold me. I've done nothing wrong.'

'In this club? I'm sure if the vice squad come through here, they'll find something.'

'Okay, what do you want?'

'The truth.'

'Aberman, he was borrowing money.'

'We know this. And then he was in trouble.'

'That's it.'

'Who brought you in here to run this club?'

'The new owners.'

'Who are they?'

'I don't know.'

'What do you mean?'

'It's the honest truth. Apart from Ugly Pete, the heavy I told you about before, I've met no one. Our communication is by email and messaging.'

'An unusual relationship.'

'It suits me. I'm left to run the club, give them an agreed percentage of the takings, and I keep the rest after expenses.'

'Good money for you?'

'It's good. The women aren't complaining either. I expect the best, I pay the best.'

'They weren't bad-looking, the two out front,' Larry said.

'They're not. I've brought in some new women.'

'Slater was shot just as he was about to give us names,' Isaac said. 'Names you know. There's no window here, so nobody's going to take you out. It's either here or Challis Street.'

'These people don't mess around. If I tell you any more, I'm dead.'

'And if you don't, you're in jail.'

'Okay, Slater's death has got us all jumpy. Gus, he's taken off, trying to get some distance. I told him he's wasting his time, but then, he's not very bright.'

'What are you going to tell us?'

'Ugly Pete frequents a pub in Kensington, the Finborough Arms.'

'What does he look like?'

'I told you before. He's ugly, like a mongrel dog. And don't ask me any more. I still value my life, worthless as it may be to you.'

Chapter 17

Isaac realised that the murder enquiry had taken a turn for the worse. Before they had been looking for the murderer of two people in a hotel room, one a moral crusader, the other a former prisoner. Since then, a prostitute had been murdered, as well as a solicitor and his receptionist. And now there was the complication of the discovery of another body, Ben Aberman.

Isaac met his former senior not far from Scotland Yard.

'Public Relations isn't all it's cracked up to be,' Richard Goddard confessed.

'Davies didn't put you there to enjoy it,' Isaac said. 'He wanted you out of the way. It looks as though he's succeeded.'

'His time's coming, but that's not why we're meeting, is it?'

'I need to run the case past you.'

'Caddick?'

'The man's a fool. His advice is worthless.'

'What have you got?'

'Helen Langdon, four years in prison for killing her husband, subsequently acquitted. James Holden, moral crusader, member of parliament. The two of them are found naked in a hotel room, a bullet in the head each. Another prostitute, Daisy, a former work colleague of Helen's when they were both stripping, also murdered. Daisy was also meeting with Holden for the purpose of prostitution. We've assumed that Helen did not know about this.'

'That's three.'

'We discover the body of Ben Aberman, the owner of the club where the two women had worked. He was also Helen's lover during that period. Aberman's house has been empty for a long time. Helen had been looking after it, along with a solicitor who was paid by Aberman. We were with the solicitor when he was killed. His receptionist, young and new at the firm, walked in the door and was shot too.'

'What's the common thread?'

'Helen Langdon, but she's dead. We've been looking for a murderer amongst Helen's circle of acquaintances, but now we're dealing with organised crime.'

'Is there any possibility James Holden was the primary target, and the subsequent deaths have been an unfortunate consequence?' Goddard said.

'It was a consideration initially. Holden was critical of the amount of dubious material that could be downloaded from the internet. He was a vocal supporter of tightening censorship guidelines, applying restrictions.'

'Are you suggesting a rethink?'

'Not totally. The discovery of Aberman's body has brought in an added complication. The earlier murders were the work of an individual, the later murders, as well as Aberman's, have the hallmarks of a crime syndicate.'

'The crime syndicate is more immediate. They don't mess around, could even take you out if you get too close,' Goddard said.

'What can be done about Caddick? He's a liability to Homicide and the ongoing investigation.'

'Davies will play his hand at some stage. The man knows Caddick is not up to the task. His strategy now is to bring back those who are. He'll make the normal platitudes about staff rotation, multitasking, and so on, but we'll know what it is.'

'A stalling tactic?'

'Davies may outlast us all.'

'A dreadful thought,' Isaac said.

***

Nobody expected Gus, the Dixey Club's bouncer and doorman, to walk into Challis Street Police Station. It was nine in the evening, and the team in Homicide were wrapping up for the day.

For three days, Caddick had not been seen: a training course for senior police officers. Larry had offered a comment when he'd heard about Caddick and training. Isaac had told him to be careful what he said and to whom.

'I've come to give myself up,' Gus said as he sat in the interview room.

'Do you need legal representation?' Isaac asked.

'Not this time.'

'What are you confessing to?'

'I was there the night Aberman died.'

'We've no one who can identify you. Why are you here?'

'They killed Slater. They'll kill me.'

'Did you kill Aberman?'

'No.'

'Did you bury him?'

'Yes.'

'What crime did you commit?'

'I helped bury the body, didn't tell you the truth. I was at Ben Aberman's house that night. They were upstairs with

Aberman, working him over, trying to get him to sign over the clubs.'

'And you were downstairs watching the television.'

'Something like that.'

'Gus, you may fool others, but you don't fool us. Roughing a man up is one thing, shooting him in the head is another.'

'It was more than roughing him up.'

'The full story. We'll be recording this,' Isaac said.

'As long as you protect me.'

'Your full name?'

'Guthrie Boswell.'

Once Gus had been cautioned and advised of his rights, Isaac addressed him.

'In your own words.'

'Ben wasn't a bad man. He'd been running Dixey's for a few years. He treated the women well, especially Helen.'

'Were they lovers?'

'Yes. Ben was an ambitious man, wanted to do more. He borrowed money, gets into trouble.'

'How do you know this?'

'I was in the club. I'm the dumb muscle man, that's what everyone thinks, but I watch and listen.'

'And check out Aberman's office when he's not there.'

'Maybe there's some of that.'

'The night of Aberman's disappearance, what can you tell us?' Larry said.

'It's late, two in the morning. Ben in his office totalling up the money. I'm out front closing up.'

'Anyone else in the building?'

'The women have all left. Daisy's gone off with one of the customers. Helen went home on her own.'

'Aberman's home?'

'He had a flat not far from the club. She'd probably gone there, but I can't be certain. There's a knock on the door, I open it, and a gun is shoved in my face.'

'What did you do?'

'What anyone would do. I let the gun in.'

'How many men?'

'Three, and they're all armed. They demand to see Ben. I take them to his office. We've had problems with men demanding protection money before.'

'What has happened in the past?'

'Ben pays those who come in, and then afterwards, he finds out who they are. After that, they never return. The three guns, they're in Ben's office. One of the men is after the money owing. Ben, a stubborn man, is refusing. In the end, the men come out of the office with Ben held firmly between two of them. One of the men points a gun at me.'

'Did he speak?'

'He said either I'm with them, or I'm dead on the spot. Now, I'm not too smart to figure out what's going on most of the time, but this time, I know.'

'You went with them.'

'I figured Ben needed help, although I couldn't do anything in the club.'

'Ben was a friend?'

'He treated me well. I wasn't about to have my head blown off for him, but I owed him something.'

'Did you drive to Aberman's house in Bray?'

'That's it. Slater's already there. He's got some papers he wants Ben to sign.'

'And Ben refuses?'

'That's Ben.'

'Slater, what does he say?'

'I'm not that close, and they've handcuffed me. What I can make out is that Slater's trying to explain the situation.'

'Aberman's still not signing?'

'No. They take Ben into another room and start working on him. I can hear them from where I am, but I can't do anything.'

'No one in the area heard them?'

'These men, they're professionals. Ben had a gag so he couldn't scream, and the men, they're not talking, just hitting. They tell me he's going to sign or else they'll kill me first, then him. I'm panicking.'

'What did you do?'

'They gave me the option. Either I help them, or I'm dead.'

'You chose to help.'

'Whatever happened, I figured that Ben would still be alive, so would I, if I helped.'

'You trusted these men?'

'What option did I have? Ben looks at me, I say sorry, but he either signs or we're dead.'

'Then what?'

'They offered him the chance once again to sign, but he refused. They kept hitting him, and then one of them started on him with a lighted cigarette. Ben was in agony. I pleaded with him to sign, but he won't. In the end, they hooked him up to a handheld generator. He signed then.'

'Did they release him after he signed?'

'No. I go into the other room to figure out what to do next. I wanted Ben and me out of there, but the men with Slater, they don't look to be the forgiving kind. One of them came up to me.'

'What did he say?'

'He told me again, that I'm either with them or I'm not. I'm dragged into the other room, and there's Ben, his head covered in blood. The gun must have had a silencer as I never heard any sound.'

'You're freaking out, you're next. What do you do?'

'I've no option.'

'You were one of those who buried Ben in the back garden?'

'I helped to dig the grave.'

'And who was the other man?'

'Pete, that's all I know.'

'Ugly Pete?'

'Don't say that to his face. He's an angry man. He was the one who shot Ben.'

***

'You've charged the man with accessory to murder, is that it?' Superintendent Caddick said on his return from the course.

'It won't be long,' Isaac said. 'We've a lead on the murderer.'

'It's Holden that Commissioner Davies is interested in, not the owner of a strip club.'

'Murder's equal in the eyes of the law, the penalty is the same.'

'You've been meeting with Goddard from what I hear.'

'Is there a problem?'

'Suit yourself, but I'm in charge of this place, not him.'

'He's a personal friend,' Isaac said.

'Soon to be out on his ear.'

'Is he?'

'Goddard, he's playing politics. One wins, another loses.'

'Are you, Superintendent Caddick, intending to be one of the winners?'

'That I am.'

'For myself, I intend to succeed by good policing.'

'That's the problem, Cook. You're an idealist. The world is not what you believe. You've seen into the gutter on enough occasions. You know that people such as yourself are doomed to lose.'

'That's your view, not mine.'

'Very well. How long before you bring in Holden's killer?'

'Soon.'

'We'll see. You're off the disciplinary for now after the shooting in the solicitor's office. Made yourself some sort of hero, but how did they know you were there and what was being said?'

Several minutes after Caddick had left, Larry came into Isaac's office. 'He's right,' he said.

'Caddick, I don't think so.'

'I'm not saying he came up with an original thought, but how did they know what we were talking about, and why shoot Slater when we're in his office? They could have done that anytime.'

'Ugly Pete, any success?'

'I've got a lead on him and an address. I've got men keeping a watch on his house. The moment he's spotted, we're going in.'

'The pub?'

'He's keeping away from there. If he killed Aberman, and he knows that Gus is in custody, he would realise we're looking for him.'

'How did you get the address?'

'Ugly Pete's not a popular man. He's known for his rough tactics, and there are a few who wouldn't mind seeing him off the street for a while.'

'More than a while if he killed Aberman. Could he be the sniper at Slater's?'

'It's not likely. The man's not fit, moves slowly, and he's not known for using a gun. He's more into fists.'

'According to Gus, he killed Aberman.'

'Gus is scared of what could happen to him, or is he trying to shift the blame?'

'Either. We'll need Ugly Pete in here to know the truth. And Helen Langdon? She's the tie-in between Aberman and Holden. How could so many people be so wrong about her?'

'Focus on Ugly Pete. He'll help to fill in the blanks.'

Chapter 18

Wendy Gladstone maintained her visits out to Mrs Hawthorne, Aberman's neighbour. The woman was forgetful and glad of the company. After her third visit, Wendy could recite the Hawthorne family history, of how her husband had made his money in the city, how Mr Aberman had moved in several years after her husband had died, and how the man had helped her when she needed it.

'We've found one of the men who dug the hole in Mr Aberman's garden,' Wendy said.

'There were two.'

'We've got a description and a name for the other one. Mr Slater, the solicitor, do you remember him?'

'Yes. My husband used him occasionally.'

'He was at the house the night that Mr Aberman died.'

'He may have been. It was dark that night, and there were no lights in the driveway.'

'We've also been told that he would attend the parties.'

'I can't remember seeing him there, but that's not surprising.'

'Why?'

'I can't see very well, really. I could tell if it was a man or a woman, but apart from that, it wasn't so easy.'

'We have reason to believe Mr Slater was involved in Mr Aberman's death.'

'My husband didn't like the man, but he thought he was competent.'

'On the night Mr Aberman died, you said you didn't hear any noise.'

'There was some noise, but it wasn't a party. There were no women there.'

'What sort of noise?'

'Voices, that's all.'

'We know that Aberman was shot in the house. Are you saying you didn't hear the shot?'

'I went to sleep early. No party, no fun.'

Wendy realised the woman could offer little more. She left and walked around to Aberman's house. In the driveway, a car. 'Mrs Aberman, this is a crime scene,' she said.

'I just wanted to see the place.'

Wendy found the woman's presence disturbing. 'We need to talk,' Wendy said.

'If you want. Here?'

'Not here. I suggest we go and sit in my car.'

Seated in the car, Wendy turned to the woman. She could see that the ex-Mrs Aberman was not comfortable with the situation. 'You knew your former husband owned this place?'

'He bought it before we separated. When we divorced, I kept the house in London, he kept this one.'

'Which one do you prefer?'

'I always preferred this one, but Ben liked to have his parties.'

'And this house was better?'

'Yes.'

'You knew about the parties while you were married?'

'They were tamer when I lived with him, and Ben, he behaved himself. He changed with time, became more of a risk-taker, and some of the people he associated with, well, they were disturbing.'

'Explain.'

'More criminal. Some of them were charming, especially the more important ones, but they'd arrive with extra men, men who'd sit outside in the car or lean against it. I think some of them carried guns.'

'Tell me about the parties when you were here.'

'Ben liked to entertain. I would go on about the cost, but he said it was good for business. Not that I understood how, but the man was a good provider, so I left him to it.'

'Women?'

'There'd be women, and yes, couples were pairing off, but it was nothing serious. And Ben stayed with me. Sure, there was too much alcohol, and some of the guests were into cocaine. I would have preferred a quiet night at home with a bottle of wine, but that wasn't to be. It was the parties that drove us apart.'

'Helen?'

'I'd heard the rumours about her, but I ignored them. I married Ben when we were both young, and he was always faithful. I knew about the clubs, can't say I approved, but Ben liked to live on the edge, and in time I accepted his unusual way of making an income.'

'The man changed?'

'Not for a long time.'

'The suspicious signs?'

'Lipstick on the collar, not kissing me on coming home, straight in the shower. The signs were there, but for a long time I ignored them. I just didn't want to believe them.'

'What convinced you?'

'I paid someone to check out the club. A private investigator. He visited the club, found my husband in a compromising position with one of the women. I know people expect the owner of a strip club to be nefarious, but Ben wasn't like that. We were a conventional married couple at home, but in the club, he was the sleazy manager of a sleazy club. Almost like play acting.'

'What happened when you found out about the other woman?'

'I confronted him. He admitted to his guilt, and that was that.'

'You must have seen him from time to time.'

'I did for a few months, and then, after that, rarely.'

'Did you know Nicholas Slater?'

'We used the man for the purchase of the house in Bray. I didn't like him very much.'

'He was shot.'

'I know.'

'And yet you come to this house knowing full well that whoever shot him could be watching this house.'

'In the event of Ben's death, this house belongs to me. It was in the divorce settlement.'

'Your husband disappears for years, and you were never suspicious?'

'What could I do? And besides, I had no need of the house. I was, am, comfortable with what I've got, and I don't have the searing ambition that Ben had, but now the house is here, and I'd like it back.'

'He was killed in the house.'

'I know, and probably I'll sell it.'

'Can you prove the house is yours?'

'Yes, I can. Slater and my solicitor drew up the agreement. I have a document at home signed by both parties.'

***

On the fourth day of staking out Ugly Pete's house, he appeared. By that time the two teams that had been rotating to watch the house were bored, and if it had not been for one of the men looking over towards the house at the last minute of their shift, they would have missed him.

Ugly Pete's house, 34 Victoria Street, Croydon, was not everyone's idea of a desirable residence. It was on the rougher side of the area and getting rougher. On the footpath outside, a broken chair had been dumped for the council to pick up. Inside the front gate were an old bicycle, a discarded child's toy.

Isaac and Larry drove over to the man's house, even though it was one o'clock in the morning. At the back of the house, two uniforms waited. Out front, an armed response team. The man inside was known to be dangerous and probably armed.

Sergeant Gaffney of the Specialist Firearms Command knocked on the door – no response. He hit it harder the second time. A window opened upstairs. 'What do you want?' a gruff voice said.

The light of a street lamp shone in the man's face. 'I can see why they call him ugly,' Larry said.

'Police,' Gaffney said.

'Can't a man have a good night's sleep?'

'If you open this door, we can resolve this in a few minutes.'

The head at the upstairs window pulled back. 'He's getting ready to make a run for it,' Isaac said.

Gaffney gave the instruction. 'This man is regarded as extremely dangerous.' With that, another officer took hold of a battering ram and slammed it into the front door. It opened with no difficulty. A man was coming down the stairs in a hurry. 'Police,' one of the officers shouted. A short scuffle, an attempt to draw a weapon, and then Ugly Pete was handcuffed and in the back of a marked police car.

'Where to?' the driver of the car asked.

'Challis Street Police Station. Put him in one of the holding cells for now,' Isaac said.

He and Larry entered Ugly Pete's house and looked around, careful not to disturb anything. Downstairs was spartan and not clean. Upstairs, only one of the rooms had a bed. It was dirty; the sheets had not been changed for some time.

'We need a weapon,' Larry said. 'I'll stay and check the place.'

'Do we need the crime scene examiners here?' Isaac said.

'Not yet. There's been no crime here except against good taste.'

***

'I've done nothing wrong,' Ugly Pete said. He was in an interview room. He had accepted legal aid. Wendy had one conviction against him, his lack of hygiene; the man stank of body odour and stale beer.

'Your full name,' Isaac said.

'Peter Foster.' Isaac could tell the man had not shaved or showered for several days. His face was marked, the result of childhood acne, his nose twisted to one side. He was also short, matching the description that Gus and Mrs Hawthorne had given.

Isaac was sure that Ugly Pete was Ben Aberman's killer, but he didn't look to be the sort of person to admit to anything. The only witnesses on that night were the old lady next door – and it had been dark, and her eyesight would not have been that good – and Gus, the Dixey Club's doorman.

'Mr Foster, you are aware of the Dixey Club?'

'Not me.'

Isaac leant over to the man's solicitor. 'I suggest you advise your client to answer questions when given. We know that Mr Foster frequents the area near to the club. A denial does not assist his case.'

'What case is this?' Ugly Pete said.

'You've been informed. The murder of Ben Aberman.'

'Who?'

'Mr Foster, we can confirm that you were at a house in the village of Bray when Ben Aberman was killed. We have two witnesses who will confirm that.'

'Was I? That's news to me.'

'Ben Aberman, the owner of the Dixey Club, was beaten and tortured in that house. He was then shot, a bullet in the head.'

'What's that to do with me?'

'We have a witness who will testify that you shot the man, and then you buried him in the garden of the house.'

'Not me. I've killed no one.'

'Are you going to continue to deny your knowledge of this house?'

'I've never been there.'

'Stupidity is not a defence,' Wendy said.

'If you've no proof, then why is my client here?' the legal aid said.

'Ben Aberman had a woman. She called herself Helen.'

'I don't know her either,' Foster said.

'She was a dancer at the club. She was recently shot in a hotel in Bayswater, together with a man. Also, she had a friend, Daisy, who was murdered.'

'Are you trying to pin all of them on me?' Ugly Pete said.

'Not all. You did not kill the two in the hotel, nor Daisy. Those killings required a person of stealth. You're not stealthy, more brute muscle. Another two murders, Aberman's solicitor and his receptionist. Yet again, you could not have done it. It would have required an agile man to be on the roof opposite their office.'

'You've got nothing on me,' Foster said.

'You're a man with a record. How many times have you been charged with assault, how many convictions?'

'I'm a violent man, but it doesn't make me a killer.'

'Mr Foster, you know who the men are who gave Aberman the money, the men who wanted it back. Aberman, we know, was not a person to be intimidated. That's why you went to work on him in Bray, why you killed him, and why you and Gus, the doorman at the Dixey Club, buried Aberman in the garden. Gus is going down for enough years as it is. He'll identify you as the killer if it reduces his sentence. And what about your fingerprints at the house?'

'I wore…'

'Gloves, is that what you were about to say?'

'My client is not in a position to continue this interview. I am requesting that this interview is reconvened at a later time when Mr Foster has had a chance to change his clothes and to have a shower.'

'I don't think Ben Aberman had such courtesy when he was being beaten and tortured by Mr Foster,' Isaac said.

'My client vigorously denies his involvement.'

'Mr Foster, we will be charging you with the murder of Ben Aberman. The person who buried the body with you will testify it was you who was the murderer.'

'I'm innocent.'

'The only way you can hope for some leniency is if you tell us who were the other men at Dixey's the night you took Aberman. We know there were three. Who were the other two? And who or what is the organisation that Aberman signed the clubs over to? What is Helen Langdon's significance in this?'

'My client needs time to consider his position,' the legal aid said.

'Thirty minutes.' Isaac said.

Chapter 19

Isaac took the opportunity of a break in questioning Ugly Pete to phone Larry.

'I've found a weapon at Ugly Pete's house,' Larry said. 'It took me a while. I just followed the dust in the house, found a clean spot. It was there, under a floorboard.'

'Forensics, how long before they can give us a positive that it's the weapon that killed Ben Aberman?'

'It's fitted with a silencer. Not legal in the UK, but Ugly Pete wouldn't care. I'll take it to Forensics myself. We should have an answer today.'

'The man's playing tough. He doesn't want to admit to anything.'

'If he's convicted of Aberman's murder, he's not likely to see freedom for a long time.'

The interview reconvened. Isaac had more ammunition with which to get the reluctant man to talk.

'My client wishes to make a statement,' the legal aid said. Isaac thought he was too young to be a solicitor.

'When he's ready,' Isaac said.

'I, Peter Foster, did not kill Ben Aberman. I knew of the Dixey Club, having been there on a few occasions. At one time, I was hired to visit the club in the early hours of the morning with two others. I do not know their names. The purpose of the visit was to escort Mr Aberman to his house in Bray. There was a Mr Slater present. After we had delivered the man, I left.'

'Is that it?' Isaac said.

'That's all I've got to say,' Ugly Pete said.

'Your solicitor has not advised you well. Although in his defence he does not know of your history, nor of certain facts. Before we go any further, let me outline what we know,' Isaac said. 'We have found a weapon at your house. Hiding it under a floorboard was not enough to deter Detective Inspector Hill. It is fitted with a silencer and is almost certainly the weapon that killed Ben Aberman. We do have a bullet from where the murdered man was buried. Also, we have Guthrie Boswell's testimony that Mr Foster killed Aberman, and that he and Mr Foster buried the body in the garden.'

'I had to do it,' Foster said, leaping to his feet.

'Why?'

'If I hadn't shot him, they would have shot me.'

'That's not a defence,' Wendy said.

'I received this phone call. The man's insistent it's a pickup, a roughing up, make him sign a piece of paper. Nothing more, I swear it.'

'Your speciality?'

'That's what I do. Men such as Aberman get down in the dirt. They don't like it when they're called to account.'

'Why kill Aberman?'

'I don't know, but that's what I was told to do.'

'By who?'

'Slater.'

'And he's dead.'

'I only ever received text messages to be at a certain place at a certain time. The money's paid into my account.'

'You had the gun. You could have refused.'

'Not with the people Slater represented.'

'Which people?'

'People who stay hidden, people who would have me killed. That's the truth.'

'Who are they?'

'I don't know. You can keep me in here for as long as you like. I can't tell you any more.'

***

Linda Holden closed her father's morality campaign office the day after Ugly Pete was charged with the murder of Ben Aberman. One week later her brother, John, was dead.

'He'd been depressed for some time,' Linda said when Isaac met her at her family home.

'Your mother?'

'She's not been the same since our father died, almost reclusive.'

'Why was your brother depressed?'

'With John, you couldn't be sure. He'd attempted suicide before. This time he stepped in front of a train. He wanted to let us know that the guilt lies with us.'

'And does it?'

'My mother feels guilt, I don't. John was a weak person, always ready to blame his problems on others. Our father had no time for him.'

'Was it mutual?'

'They rarely spoke, and once Helen had made it clear she did not want his son, their relationship became worse.'

'I have to ask. Would John have been capable of murder?'

'He would have hated his father being in that room with Helen, but I still don't think he could have killed them.'

'Sisterly love protecting you from the truth?'

'It could be.'

'We have reason to believe that Helen Langdon was a fraud. The more we discover, the deeper we go, we find more negative aspects of the woman. In your time with her, did you ever sense anything unusual?'

'She was besotted by my father, that was clear, but if, as you say, she was a fraud, how much was genuine?'

'Why the hotel room?' Isaac said.

'Our father strayed occasionally, but why with Helen? And what about Gerald Adamant?'

'There's a new investigation into his death.'

'Is the verdict against Helen likely to be changed?'

'That's not our primary concern. We're focussed on who killed your father and Helen,' Isaac said. 'Regardless of what or who she may have been, the two were shot in that room. We've focussed on Helen because she has a past, but it's always possible that the murderer was targeting your father, and if he was, then why, and why in a hotel room? It would have been easier to kill him elsewhere.'

'Maybe Helen being with him was the reason. Maybe they wanted to destroy his reputation by exposing him as a debaucher, not a paragon of virtue.'

'Outside of that room, his murder would have strengthened his moral campaign, but in that room, regardless of his dying, he becomes painted as the sinner.'

'And with Helen Langdon, the wife of Gerald Adamant, the man she killed.'

'Whoever killed him knew what they were doing,' Isaac said.

***

Isaac's conversation with Linda Holden had offered him a fresh approach to the first murder investigation. He was in his office at Challis Street. The team were there.

'James Holden's son has committed suicide. His father's morality campaign office has closed.' Isaac said.

'It's not surprising after he's caught in a hotel with a former stripper,' Wendy said.

'That's the issue, isn't it? The man's reputation destroyed in an instant.'

'Did the killer get a tip-off, two birds with one stone?'

'Daisy knew them both. Maybe she recognised them going into the hotel, told someone. And whoever killed the two lovers killed her to tie up loose ends.'

'Was your concierge on duty the time they were killed?'

'Yes.'

'We need him in here now.'

Larry left Challis Street and drove the short distance to the hotel. Inside, at reception was another person. The hotel still had the look of neglect, and a woman could be seen sneaking in with her man for the hour. 'Is the other concierge here?'

'The hotel fired him,' the new concierge said. Larry looked at the man: Slavic, poor English, unpleasant look.

'Do you know where he is?'

'He found a job around the corner. And what's it to you?'

'Challis Street Police Station. Detective Inspector Larry Hill, or didn't you see my ID card when I showed it to you?'

'I saw it. Serge, he's a friend of mine, that's all.'

'Why was he fired?'

'He was letting people into the hotel without paying.'

'You're doing the same from what I can see.'

'Serge, he asks too many questions.'

'What sort of questions?'

'The sort I don't ask.'

'Are you going to continue talking nonsense, or am I going to haul you down the police station?'

'People come in here, people go out. They pay their money, sign in the book. Apart from that, I don't care what they do, with whom, and how. That way, I keep my job and make a little extra on the side. But my friend, he's inquisitive, wants to see what they're up to, who's with who. The management finds out that he's been spying on people. They're not happy, he's sacked.'

'Are you still letting the prostitutes in?'

'As long as they pay.'

'The management, they get a percentage of what you take?'

'That's the agreement.'

'Did you know Daisy?'

'She used to come in here occasionally.'

'She was killed because she knew the two in room 346.'

'I wasn't here that night.'

'What about the room?'

'It's still closed. It's being repainted.'

'Take me up there,' Larry said.

'I can't. I've got to man the desk. I can give you a key.'

Larry took the key and walked up the stairs to the third floor. Outside the murder room, he paused. Down the hallway, the sound of a woman with her customer: she making the mandatory noises; he attempting to pretend it was love. It was clear the man was drunk. Larry opened the door to the murder room. In the middle of the barren room was the bed where the two had been shot. A trauma scene clean-up team had been through the room. There was no sign of what had happened, only a faint whiff of cleaning fluids. The carpet that had been on the floor had been removed, as had the mattress and the sheets. In the wardrobe, there was nothing, not even a wire coat hanger. Larry looked in the bathroom, yet again spotlessly clean. He imagined there'd be couples in the future, lying on the bed, making love, not knowing that once two others had died violently on it. Larry closed the door on his way out.

Downstairs, he gave the key to the concierge and left. No words were exchanged. It was not far to walk to where Serge, the previous concierge, was.

'I can't tell you any more,' he said. Larry could see the hotel was better than the previous one, and Serge had cleaned himself up.

'No ladies of the night?' Larry said.

'They're strict here.'

'No more peeping, no more taking money to turn a blind eye.'

The concierge did not respond to the bait. 'I've told you all I know. The last time I pointed out someone to the police, she ended up dead.'

'What is it you've not been telling us?'

'What do you want me to tell you? The room was on the third floor, I'm on the ground floor. Two people come in, they pay for a room. She's attractive, he's older.'

'You didn't think it suspicious?'

'We're a hotel. If they pay their money, don't steal the contents from the minibar, what is there to be suspicious about?'

'You were watching couples in their rooms.'

'Who said I did?'

'Don't deny it.'

'Sometimes, when it's quiet, I like to look around.'

'Small hole in the wall?'

'Yes.'

'You couldn't resist Helen Langdon. The woman was beautiful, not like the women who normally came in, not like Daisy.'

'The hotel was quiet. I sneak away for a few minutes. I had the key to the next room. There's a small hole in the wall behind a picture.'

'What did you see?'

'The two of them in bed.'

'Sleeping?'

'Screwing.'

'You're excited, enjoying the spectacle. Then what happens.'

'The bell on reception goes. I've got a remote that beeps. I leave them to it.'

'How much longer before they're dead?'

'According to your people, fifteen minutes, maybe thirty.'

'At the reception, what do you find?'

'Another woman with her customer.'

You give them a key?'

'She's a regular. I know she'll fix up the money later, and besides, the man looks as if he's in need of her.'

'What do you mean?'

'He's pawing her, trying to kiss her.'

'Her reaction?'

'She's playing along. The man looks as if he's got money.'

'Who was the woman?'

'Daisy's flatmate.'

'Gwendoline?'

'That's her. She's been in the hotel more often than Daisy.'

'Why didn't you tell us this before?'

'Tell you what? You were looking for a man, not a prostitute.'

'And you didn't want us to find out about your snooping.'

'What are you going to do about it?'

'Nothing. We've got to find this woman. Does she stand on a street corner near here?'

'The same places as Daisy.'

Larry left the man and phoned Wendy. 'Meet me in Bayswater. We need to find Daisy's flatmate, Gwendoline. You know her better than me.'

***

Larry and Wendy drove around the area looking for the usual spots where the women congregated. Gwendoline was nowhere to be seen. Eventually, the two of them visited the brothels in the area. Around the back of Paddington Station, they found the prostitute. She was sitting on a leather sofa on the first floor of a brothel. On either side of her were two other women; one was South American, the other looked Asian.

'They're probably in this country illegally,' Wendy said.

'We're here for Gwendoline, not them.'

'What do you want?' Daisy's flatmate said.

'We've some questions for you.'

'I'm busy, come back later.'

'Later doesn't work for us,' Larry said. He could see the woman was agitated. She was wearing a dress so short that her underwear was visible. She was not wearing a bra.

'Five minutes, that's all I can give you.'

'We need you down at the police station. You can go like that or do you want to change?'

'I don't want any trouble in here,' the madam of the brothel said. Wendy saw a woman in her fifties, almost certainly an ex-prostitute. In the corner of her mouth a cigarette, its ash ready to fall on the floor.

'It's not as good as the hotel you used to use,' Wendy said to Gwendoline.

'It's safer here.'

'What do you mean?'

'Daisy, she was murdered, and then those two in that room at the hotel.'

'Did you use that room?'

'Sometimes.'

'Gwendoline, I don't want the police in here,' the madam said. 'Go with them, come back later.'

The prostitute picked up her coat and left with Larry and Wendy. She complained, although no one was listening. At Challis Street, she was placed in one of the interview rooms and given a cup of tea, as well as some biscuits. 'I'm hungry,' she said.

'Pizza?'

'Hawaiian.'

Twenty-five minutes later, with the woman fed, Larry and Wendy commenced the interview.

'You were in the hotel on the night of the murders in room 346.'

'A waste of time for me.'

'What do you mean?'

'I'm doing a favour for Daisy. She says the man pays well, and he'll see me right.'

'Why didn't she take him?'

'She wasn't feeling well, and the man phoned at the last minute.'

'You agreed?'

'Why not? I met him at the hotel, and we went up to the room.'

'Which room?'

'The one opposite the murders.'

'What happened?'

'He gave me a drink. I wake up three hours later.'

'Was the drink drugged?'

'I suppose so. Anyway, I've got a throbbing headache. I put on my clothes and leave the hotel, that bastard on the door wanting his money, as well.'

'Your customer, did he pay you?'

'No.'

'There's a murder in the room opposite. You're unconscious, the man you're with has disappeared. Doesn't that sound coincidental to you?'

'I don't get involved, the first rule for people like me. We don't ask for their life story, or whether life has treated them bad or good. We're not a confessional, either. It's sex and out of the door.'

'Did this man murder Helen Langdon and James Holden?' Larry asked.

'He could have killed me,' Gwendoline said.

'You were his way into the hotel. Did the concierge see you downstairs?'

'He did.'

'Describe this man?'

'What's to describe. I don't check them out, prefer to look away.'

'Regardless of whether you look or not, what can you tell us about him?'

'Average height, white. He spoke well.'

'Did he give a name?'

'Dennis, but that's probably not his name.'

'Why?'

'Most of them make up a fancy name. Somehow it helps them to deal with the guilt.'

'Is that why you're Gwendoline instead of Kate Bellamy?'

'The men want the strange names, I only want their money. There's no guilt from me. I'm a spaced-out junkie, nothing more, nothing less.'

'Let's come back to this man. Did you have sex with him?'

'No. He gave me the drink and then nothing.'

'Did you believe him to be the murderer?'

'I didn't think about it. He probably was, but I don't know. I was frightened.'

'Daisy, what did she say?'

'She said she was surprised. He had always been fine with her. A few days later, she's murdered in our flat.'

'It's probably the same man. Why did he leave you alone? You could identify him, the same as Daisy.'

'I couldn't. I told you, I don't study the men. With them, I'm an empty vessel. Mentally, I'm detached. If you ask me about the men from last night, I couldn't give you detailed descriptions.'

'Do you dislike your life?' Wendy asked.

'It's not my choice. I'm addicted, that's all. The men feed the habit, I forget.'

Chapter 20

Isaac sat with Violet Holden; she was subdued. Linda Holden sat close by.

'Mrs Holden, I'm sorry about your recent losses, but there are questions I must ask,' Isaac said.

'Please ask.'

'Mother's on sedatives,' Linda said.

'I'll take it easy. Please say if you have anything to add.'

'I will. The last few weeks have been difficult.'

'Mrs Holden, Linda, I want to update you on our enquiry. There are some concerns that you may be able to clarify.'

'We'll do what we can,' Linda said.

'We know of Helen's background, although it's still difficult to understand what was in her mind. All indications are that she and James Holden were killed because of her. She had probably known of the death of Ben Aberman, a former lover, and where he was buried. For whatever reason, she kept it secret. There's also her marriage to Gerald Adamant. Every person we've spoken to saw it as a love match.'

'You're not sure now,' Violet Holden said.

'It was everyone's faith in Helen that ultimately led to her reduced sentence after she killed Adamant with a hammer.'

'If people had not believed in her?'

'Without the character witnesses, she may have been found guilty of first-degree murder. That's conjecture on my part. Is it possible that Mr Holden was the intended target? He must have upset a few people over the years.'

'He was introducing a bill into parliament that would have given sweeping powers to block websites that showed dubious content.'

'Those safeguards are in place now,' Isaac said.

'They're subject to intervention, debate. He wanted to set up a team of people whose decisions would be final. They could switch off a site on picking up an offensive word, a suggestive image.'

'Can't they do that now?'

'They can, but the technology's improving. He knew he would have the civil libertarians against him, as well as those who uphold the freedom to see and do what we want.'

'Once you start, where do you end?'

'My father saw that throttling all of it was a better alternative than what we have now,' Linda said.

'Have there been any threats?'

'There are always threats, but my father ignored them.'

'If he had died as a martyr, then his reforms would have been implemented.'

'As a sinner, they will not.'

'Was Helen complicit?'

'How? She was killed in the bed next to my father.'

'Helen loved James,' Violet said.

'How do you know?' Isaac said.

'I was married to James for a long time. He was infatuated with her, no doubt thought it was love. With her, it was. Whatever she may have done or been, with James, she was honest.'

***

Barry Knox knew he was implicated, if not by actual deed, then by association. He had known of the death of Ben Aberman on the night he was led away by Ugly Pete and his associates, ultimately forcing Gus, his former doorman, to become an accessory to murder. Knox knew that Gus was not a murderer, never had been. He had been guilty of unjustifiable violence, but that was how the man operated. And strip clubs needed someone strong enough to deal with a group of men out on the town, determined to get drunk, and then believing that the girls on the stage were offering more than was available.

Knox knew the police were not fools, and, if it were not for the murders, the club's activities would be investigated further. Then they would find the videos of the customers with the girls, the profits from selling them on the internet, the fact that most of the girls were selling themselves, and he was their pimp. He made a phone call to someone who understood.

'I can't protect you for much longer,' Knox said. 'If Helen hadn't been killed, no one would have ever known about Aberman, and nobody would have visited this club.'

'Why are you calling me now? That was never agreed to.'

'Am I the only one living who knows the truth?'

'You'll not speak.'

'Why?'

'You only live as long as you are of use.'

'And what use am I?'

'I may have need of you in the future.'

'That was the last time, I told you that before.'

'If I go down, you go down, and I know of your history, what you are capable of. You were put in that club to ensure the truth was never revealed. You have served your purpose well, but you are not indispensable.'

'What about Gus? He did what was expected, but he's in jail.'

'He was never important. Knox, don't call me again. If I need you, you'll be contacted.'

Knox walked around the club, surveyed his domain. He had enjoyed it once, but now he despised it, and all on account of one man. He knew his life was forfeit if he stayed, but how could he leave? Wasn't that how they operated, those who had killed Aberman and the others? Hidden behind the scenes, nameless, while others did their dirty work, suffered for them. If he went to the police with what he knew, what could they do? They could not protect him, not totally, and there were crimes he was answerable for, crimes they would not turn a blind eye to. He walked backed to his office. The club was due to open in another hour, and his new doorman did not know the ropes yet. He needed training.

***

Wendy Gladstone had not been satisfied with Ben Aberman's widow's reason for being at the house in Bray. She decided to visit her at her home in Chelsea. She found the woman in a good mood.

'I've secured the house in Bray,' Christine Aberman said.

'It's a good job his body was found,' Wendy said. She had had a restless night with arthritis and was not in the mood for polite conversation.

'This house has been good to us, but my husband, he wants the quiet life, the same as I do, and with its sale, we'll be able to retire. I may even join in some of the village activities.'

'How long have you known that your husband was dead?'

'Ever since you found his body.'

'How long have you suspected?'

'For a few years. Our marriage ended, but it wasn't acrimonious. He used to keep in touch on an occasional basis, birthday card, that sort of thing, and then nothing.'

'You didn't approach the police with your concerns?'

'What did I have? The former owner of a strip joint has disappeared. What would you have done?'

'His disappearance would have been registered as a missing person.'

'Exactly, and then, even if the police were interested, there'd be the dumb questions. Why did a strip club owner disappear? What makes you think he's dead? Was he involved in drug dealing, prostitution, illegal sex-trafficking? My husband would not appreciate questions being asked about his wife's first husband.'

'You did nothing.'

'There was nothing I could do. I still regarded Ben as a friend, but he had become an absent friend. In time, I forgot about him and moved on with my life.'

'All the time knowing there was a house in Bray for you.'

'It wasn't that important. This house is paid off, we're not short of money, and what if I had tried to declare him dead?'

'The questions you were worried about,' Wendy said.

'If he hadn't been found, we would have stayed living here. It's a bit like winning the lottery. Before you win it, you survive. Afterwards, you wonder how you managed to live before.'

'Slater, what can you tell me about him?'

'We knew him, used him to purchase the house. Apart from that, not a lot. He'd sometimes come to the house in Bray, came to one or two of the parties, enjoyed himself.'

'Did Slater take advantage of the women?'

'He did.'

'And it didn't concern you?'

'I was younger then, less critical.'

'Was Daisy one of the women?'

'She was there a few times, never Helen, if that's what you're going to ask.'

'We know that Slater was present when your husband was murdered. Did you have any suspicions the man was crooked?'

'No.'

'You're a smart woman. You're at a party with drunken men, whores. You must have formed an opinion.'

'I knew the sort of men Ben associated with. He was not a dishonest man, but he was involved in a dishonourable profession. Slater, he was involved in shady deals, I know that.'

'How?'

'Ben told me.'

'Anything more?'

'No more than that. I didn't want the details.'

Wendy could see the woman was not comfortable with discussing her past life. If she had been an innocent bystander, then why be nervous? If she was involved, then why deny it? Associating with criminals, ensuring there were women available, may not have been everyone's idea of a party in the countryside, but it wasn't necessarily illegal.

'You're holding back,' Wendy said. 'You couldn't be married to a man for so many years and not be aware of what he was up to, who he was associating with.'

'I can't say any more.'

138

'Can't? Are you being threatened?'

'It's hard to explain.'

'I've got all day,' Wendy said.

'Ben was associating with the wrong kind of people, I could see that. At first, the men at the parties were the same as Ben. Purely interested in having a good time, running clubs. At the last party I attended, this was three years before he disappeared, there had been an argument between Ben and another man. He had turned up at the door, and he wasn't there for a good time.'

'Who do you think it was?'

'I had no idea at the time. He was well-dressed in a suit, in his late fifties. Apart from that, there's not a lot I can tell you. The two men went into another room, Slater joined them, not that he was happy as he had been occupied in another room with one of the women. Thirty minutes later, all three men emerged, and they're cheerful.'

'Then what?'

'Slater goes back to the woman, and the mysterious man leaves.'

'What did Ben say?'

'A minor dispute, that's all.'

'But you didn't believe him.'

'That's when I knew he was in too deep. That's when I decided not to attend any more parties.'

'Did you ever meet Helen?'

'Never. I knew he was playing the field, but I never knew who, and that's the truth.'

'This man you saw with your husband and Slater, does he frighten you?'

'I remember his eyes. They were cold. He was an attractive man, not like some of the others. He was a man used to people doing what he wanted. He could have killed Ben.'

'How do we find him?'

'He's dead.'

'How do you know this?'

'I know his name.'

'What was it?'

'Gerald Adamant.'

Chapter 21

The revelation of a tie-in between Helen Langdon's former husband and a former lover came as a surprise to the team in Homicide. On the one hand, was a man known for his philanthropy, on the other, a man who had criminal connections.

The team were in Isaac's office at Challis Street. 'Is she certain?' Isaac asked Wendy.

'She didn't make the connection at the time, knowing nothing about the man, other than what she had heard about him.'

'She kept this quiet from us.'

'She was the only one who saw him at the party, except for Aberman and Slater.'

'And they're both dead. She's worried she'll be next.'

'Is there another side to Gerald Adamant we don't know?' Larry said.

'The man's always come across as clean,' Isaac said. 'Bridget, what do you have?'

'Gerald Adamant, seventy-three when he died. The family money came through significant investments in Africa. It was his grandfather who made a fortune, his father who invested it wisely, and Gerald who devoted their wealth to worthy causes.'

'Has he worked? What's his education?'

'He went to Eton, then Oxford, majoring in Economics. After university, he worked as an investment analyst at the family firm, did well according to the reports. On the death of his father, he appointed someone to run the company. He was a clever man, and there are no black marks against him. He married in his thirties, Archie and Abigail the result of that union. His wife died of cancer, he married again, a woman who's twenty years younger than him. She had a child, Howard. The marriage broke down; they divorced. Howard stayed with the father; the mother took off overseas. After some years, Gerald Adamant married Helen Langdon. The rest you know.'

'We need to know what Adamant was doing with Aberman,' Larry said.

'But how? There's no one alive to tell us now,' Wendy said.

'There are Adamant's children,' Isaac said as he picked up his phone. 'Mr Adamant, we need to talk.'

'If it's important.'

'It is.'

'We can meet at the house, two hours.'

'Your sister and brother?'

'I can't answer for them. If you want them there, you can give them a call.'

'That'll not be necessary. We want to talk to each of you individually.'

Isaac and Larry arrived at the Adamants' house earlier than the two hours. Isaac parked the car on the gravel driveway and looked around him. He and Larry walked over to the expansive lawn in front of the house; a peacock strolled by.

'The upkeep must cost plenty,' Larry said.

'There's no shortage of money. I checked out the Adamants' investment company on the internet. They posted record profits at the end of the last financial year.'

'I hope this is important,' Archie Adamant said once the three of them were seated in the library.

'It is. Mr Adamant, did your father know Ben Aberman?'

'Not to my knowledge, but I wouldn't have known all his movements or all his acquaintances.

'You know who he is?'

'I was at Helen's trial, and Aberman's been on the television. I know he was Helen's lover before she met my father.'

'Apart from a shared history through Helen, we were unaware that the two men knew each other.'

'Did they?'

'We have a witness to them meeting the one time at Aberman's house in Bray.'

'Then I can't help you. Our father never mentioned it. Is it suspicious?'

'We're not sure. Two months after their acrimonious meeting, Aberman disappears, now known to have been murdered. And Nicholas Slater, Aberman's lawyer, who was also present at their meeting, was shot in the head as he was just about to tell us who is behind the group that took over Aberman's businesses.'

'Are you implying that my father was a criminal?'

'What do you reckon? Your father could have been involved in Aberman's death. He couldn't have been involved in Slater's.'

'Are you accusing me of Slater's murder?' Adamant said.

'We're police officers. We're putting forward scenarios, evaluating reactions, exploring the possibilities.'

'You'll get no reaction from me, other than disdain that you could consider my father was involved.'

'If your father was involved with Aberman's death, you could be involved with Slater's.'

'That's illogical and insulting.'

'Why? You've got money, a good life. Maybe it's a little boring, the same as it was for your father. He met Aberman, sensed an opportunity for adventure. He'd not be the first honest person to be seduced by the glamour of crime.'

'Are you suggesting that Helen passed herself on to our father after her lover was murdered?'

'I wasn't, but it's possible. What if Helen knew about your father? What if she saw her survival in aligning with him, playing the dutiful wife? The greatest confidence trick of all time, the charming older man, the devoted younger wife. How much did they manage to scam out of your father's rich friends?'

'You cannot continue to denigrate the memory of my father with such nonsense. He loved Helen, she loved him, and as for this criminal theory, that's all it is.'

'I hope you're right. But if it's proved right, she was more calculating than we had previously thought. If her lover is killed, and she knows she's about to die as well, she then inveigles her way into your father's affections. And when she is ready, she killed your father. Did you, Mr Adamant, love her too? Don't answer. I know what it is.'

'Everyone loved her, even Howard. That's how it was with the woman.'

'And once she's got you all where she wants you, she kills your father, calls for your sister.'

'But Helen went to prison.'

'She had weighed up the options. It was either a sentence for first-degree murder or, with mitigating circumstances, it's second-degree or manslaughter. She's prepared to do her time, but along comes James Holden. He falls for her, uses his influence, and she's out in four years.'

'What sort of woman could contemplate such a thing?'

'A woman who would have made plans. And once she was out of prison, you gave her a flat, money as well. Did she sleep with you by way of thanks?'

'No. She was too good a person for that.'

'Which means you loved her, saw yourself as not worthy. Is that why you killed her? Who was it who phoned you? Daisy? The concierge?'

'This is all wrong. I'm not guilty of what you have said. As to why our father was with Aberman and Slater, I don't know,' Archie Adamant said.

***

'It's a good theory,' Larry said as he and Isaac drove away from Adamant's house.

'Can you believe that Gerald Adamant is the Mr Big of the group that took over Aberman's business and then killed him?' Isaac said.

'It's not impossible. Could Helen maintain this hatred for so long, and then kill Adamant for no return?'

'Her parents may be able to shed some insight on the woman.'

'Then we'd better go and visit them,' Larry said.

'I'll go with Wendy. She can talk to the mother,' Isaac said.

Frank and Betty Mackay were pleased when Isaac and Wendy knocked on their door. 'We've not been far since it happened,' Frank said. 'We talk about her all the time. What she had done, where she had been. It's still hard sometimes, but we battle on.'

'A cup of tea, Mrs Mackay?' Wendy said.

'Please excuse my bad manners. I'll go and put the kettle on.'

'I'll give you a hand.'

In the kitchen of the small house, Wendy took the opportunity to speak to Helen's mother. 'Mrs Mackay, we're confused. We can't decide whether your daughter is the victim of an unforeseen chain of circumstances or whether she had been manipulating them.'

'She still died in that hotel room,' the mother replied. Wendy could see that she was still emotional.

'That doesn't make sense, I'll agree, but before that, even before she started working in the Dixey Club, what was she like?'

'She was a lovely child, always cared for us. Even then, she was the one the school friends gravitated to. I can't remember how many times she had them over here, always happy, playing the music too loud.'

It was clear to Wendy that Helen Langdon's mother wanted to remember the child, not the adult, not the victim of a murderer's bullet. 'After Helen left school, where did she go?' Wendy knew, but she wanted the woman to open up.

'University, and then to an accountant's firm in London. We thought she was going to be okay.'

'What do you mean?'

'Sometimes with Helen, we couldn't be sure what she was thinking. I'd ask, only to be told, "It's nothing, Mum, nothing to worry about".'

'But you did worry.'

'Maybe if I had seen it.'

'Seen what?'

'A coldness towards people. She would be friendly, loving with us, but she could be remote at times.'

'Intelligent?'

'Exceptional. It certainly didn't come from us. She rarely studied for an exam, just seemed to breeze through.'

'Photographic memory?'

'They said it was at the school.'

'Why did she leave the accountant's and go and work in Dixey's?'

'She never attached much importance to her looks.'

'She was beautiful,' Wendy said.

'It meant nothing to her. She knew she had this ability over people, and she knew how to manipulate them.'

144

'Did you have problems with young men when she was in her teens?'

'We knew she was sleeping with one or two of them. I questioned her once about it. She told me not to worry as she had no intention of falling pregnant or in love.'

'What did you and your husband do?'

'Apart from worry? There wasn't a lot we could do, and she never snuck a boy into the house. In fact, we never saw her with a steady boyfriend. Occasionally she'd meet one, do what she wanted, and come home.'

'No emotions from her, no sneaking in the door?'

'With Helen, she'd come in the door, tell us what she had just done, then sit down and watch the television with us. In time, we had to accept it, and she wasn't coming to any harm. She was the ideal child, never forgot our birthdays, occasionally bought me a box of chocolates.'

'After she left home?'

'She'd come home every weekend while she was at university, never brought a friend. And then she was working, doing well. After one year or thereabouts, she was on a stage.'

'How did you find out?'

'The usual. She came home, announced she was now a dancer.'

'Did she elaborate?'

'No. We were upset, but she said not to worry.'

'Did you know Ben Aberman?'

'We never met anyone, not then. We did meet Gerald Adamant and his family.'

'Did you approve?'

'Initially, no. The man was much older than Helen, but she was happy. In time, we came to accept it.'

'Your daughter was arrested for his murder. How did you and your husband react?'

'We're shocked. Helen's never shown any violence before. We drove up to where she was being held. Helen's in a cell. She said that Gerald went crazy and she had to stop him. Outside, Gerald's children. They're upset over their father's death, over Helen being charged. They can't believe she's guilty, neither can we.'

'Mrs Mackay, would you be surprised if I told you that Helen may have killed him not in self-defence but as a premeditated attack?'

'I'll never believe that of Helen.'

In the other room, Isaac spoke with Helen's father. 'Is it possible that Helen was not the innocent she portrayed herself to be?' Isaac said.

'She never portrayed herself as innocent, just a victim of circumstance.'

'What do you mean?'

'This hold she had over people.'

'Could you see through it?'

'When she was a child, I could.'

'Dixey's?'

'I went once, tried to plead with her to come home.'

'Did you see her on the stage?'

'No, I left before then. She said she was fine, life was good.'

'Did you believe her?'

'Helen had no issues with what she was doing.'

'Do you believe she was capable of love?'

'With her parents, yes. With the men, no.'

'Gerald Adamant?'

'We hoped she was, but we could never be certain.'

'We have serious doubts about their relationship, although we believe she was in love with James Holden.'

'The proof?'

'His wife said it was love. She had seen them together in Holden's office, at the Holden house.'

'Is that why they were in that room when they were shot?'

'We believe so.'

'I read about Aberman,' Helen's father said. He had initially cheered up on talking about his daughter, but now he was sad again.

'Did you meet him?'

'I met a man when I entered the club, a big man, gruff voice.'

'That's probably Gus, the doorman and bouncer. He's charged with being an accessory to Aberman's murder.'

'Is Helen involved? She always had an unusual outlook on life, a detachment. She had no concept of what was moral and what was not. She had her set of values, and that was that.'

'Did you talk to her about it?'

'When she was younger. Not that she ever caused any trouble, and her school marks were excellent. And then, there was the university and the accountant's, and then…'

'She was in a strip club,' Isaac said.

'She threw all that she had away for nothing. Did she kill Aberman?'

'Do you believe she could?'

'Helen was capable of anything, good or bad. To her, there was no difference.'

'It must be painful for you to be so honest.'

'The truth is best served by my openness. My wife will try to cover for her, but what good will it do? If Helen is guilty, it will come out eventually.'

'Helen did not kill Ben Aberman; however, Gerald Adamant's death is suspicious.'

'Whatever the truth, we'll have to deal with it,' Frank Mackay said.

Isaac could see a devastated man who had learnt to deal with the reality of his daughter. He had seen through her, but others continued to believe in her.

Chapter 22

Isaac and Wendy arrived back at Challis Street. As they entered the building, Superintendent Seth Caddick was waiting.

'It's a good job I caught you. In my office, five minutes,' Caddick said to Isaac.

'What now?' Isaac whispered to Wendy as the man walked away.

'He was smiling, it can only be good news,' Wendy said.'

'Good for who?'

Isaac walked up the stairs to the third floor, part of his keep fit regime to avoid taking the lift as much as possible.

'You've been questioning Archie Adamant, accusing him of being involved,' Caddick said as Isaac settled himself on the hard chair opposite the man's desk.

'We're reopening the case into his father's death. I was attempting to make him open up.'

'And did he?'

'Not really. There are hidden layers to this case, and Adamant knows some of them.'

'And you feel that upsetting Adamant is one way of achieving this?'

'I do. Adamant and anyone else who is not totally open.'

'He's made a complaint.'

'It's a murder enquiry. I'm not going easy on him just because his father was murdered.'

'I'm not expecting you to.'

'Then why am I here?'

'There's an audit of Homicide.'

Isaac knew it to be the expected audit of the superintendent, not the department.

'We're ready,' Isaac said.

'Not with all these murders unsolved.'

'The investigations are proceeding satisfactorily.'

'You've solved one murder. That leaves five. What about Gerald Adamant's death? Is it murder?'

'It's a theory at this time.'

Isaac sensed a change in his superintendent, a change he did not like. The man wanted a favour; he wasn't sure if he could give it, not sure how to avoid it.

'What do you need from me to solve Holden's murder?' Caddick said.

'No more than we have at present. Why are you asking?'

'Commissioner Davies has thrown me to the wolves. An unfavourable audit of Homicide will reflect badly on me.'

'It will reflect badly on us all, but where's the problem? Our record is sound, our reporting is up to date, and we, as a team, are conscious of budgetary constraints. What do you have to worry about?'

'Goddard was a good man, knew what he was doing,' Caddick said.

'That's not what you said before.'

'I understand your animosity. I'm an ambitious man, the same as you.'

'We have little in common,' Isaac said.

'If I receive a negative mark, it will reflect on you and your department.'

'You'll make sure it does.'

'Not me, not this time. I'm offering a truce, the chance to protect each other.'

'I will do my duty as a detective chief inspector. What more can I do?'

'Davies is attempting to consolidate Homicide departments, get rid of Challis Street.'

'The man never gives up.'

'He's a survivor, so am I, so is Goddard, and so are you. Any attempt to reduce staffing levels, the number of Homicide departments, will affect you as much as me.'

'Not Davies,' Isaac said.

'I know it,' Caddick replied. 'We need each other. Goddard's not coming back, so we'd better come to an arrangement. If I don't present us well enough to the auditors, it's my head and your department.'

***

Ben Aberman's former wife finally had possession of the house in Bray. Before she moved in, she had the place painted inside and out. Her husband was not so keen, as he had to commute the extra distance to London each day. 'I've longed for this day for so long,' she said as he attempted to carry her over the threshold, a mock attempt at pretending it was their first night together as man and wife.

The fact that he pulled a muscle in his lower back dampened the moment. Later that day, she walked around the garden, keeping her distance from where her dead husband had been found. 'We'll cover the area with concrete, put up a pergola,' she said.

Her husband, a calm and steadying influence, only nodded. Whatever she wanted, he knew she'd get. He had not wanted to enter the house as it reignited memories in his wife, memories she had kept repressed. He had looked upstairs and into the room where Aberman had been shot. It had been a bedroom, now it would be a study for him. A reminder that Ben Aberman was dead and he was not coming back, thankfully.

***

The reopening of the investigation into the death of Gerald Adamant had certain repercussions. The majority of those who had been close to the man and to Helen would have preferred it to be left alone. There was a cherished memory of the man, a fondness for the woman, and both were flawed. Helen's flaws were all the more apparent after her murder and more so after her past life had been exposed again. Not that it was a great secret before, as she had never attempted to conceal it totally, but now the gutter press was digging in the dirt, trying to find out the salacious, interviewing those who had known her. If they couldn't get what they wanted, they made it up.

As far as the media was concerned, Helen Langdon did not gyrate on that pole at Dixey's, she was taking the men into the back room. And as for Holden, she seduced him, dragged him into that hotel, and then a jealous ex-lover, probably a criminal, had come in and in a rage of jealousy shot Helen and Holden.

The truth, Isaac knew, was what people believed. No amount of explaining the facts at a press conference, or if he agreed to an interview, would change what people thought. James Holden, as a result, regained some respectability. Many in the community believed in what he had been trying to achieve, and some were willing to admit that he had erred, not because of his weaknesses, but because societal values and the openness of modern-day England had corrupted even him.

All that Isaac knew was that his department had reached a critical juncture in the investigation. The murders appeared to have ceased, everyone's dirty linen was out in the open.

Caddick was a nuisance, now looking to Isaac and his team to get him out of trouble, and even Isaac wasn't sure what to do. Other stations, other police officers, were concerned about the consolidation of various departments, the shutting down of some stations, even reducing police numbers out on the street. Isaac knew it was a retrograde step, and even Davies couldn't do anything about it, other than take advantage to strengthen his position, weaken others.

The first that Isaac heard by way of confirmation that Richard Goddard's star was again in the ascendancy was when Bridget came bursting into his office. 'DCS Goddard's coming back.' The second was when the man put his head around the door. 'Caddick's gone,' Goddard said. One-minute Caddick was on the phone, the next he was out of the front door.

Isaac rushed over to warmly shake Goddard's hand; the others in the office, likewise.

Goddard made an impromptu speech. 'Thanks for welcoming me back. Commissioner Davies has great faith in this department, a faith that you will show is fully justified.'

'Superintendent Caddick?' Wendy asked.

'He's been assigned a position in a regional station. He will retain the rank of superintendent.'

Inside Isaac's office with the door closed, Isaac asked his senior, 'What's the truth?'

'Davies is playing for time. If he puts me here, then he's shown that he has taken notice of the criticism levelled at Caddick. He'll take the flak for removing me and others and strengthen his position, turn it to his advantage.'

'Caddick?'

'Davies has protected him. A regional station, lower responsibilities, and not subjected to the same scrutiny as we are.'

'He left in a hurry, no coming in here to say goodbye.'

'The man was thankful to be out of here. He made no friends here.'

'We'll not miss him. We can rely on you to deal with the audit.'

'I will. However, James Holden?'

'It all points to Helen Langdon as the primary target, although there were others who bore a grudge against Holden. Since then, as you well know, there have been several other murders.'

'I've kept up to date with the case,' Goddard said.

'We believe the murderer entered the hotel with another prostitute. He drugged her – she woke up later – and then walked across the passageway, entered the room, and then shot the two of them in bed.'

'The other prostitute?'

'Gwendoline. She's still alive, although her previous flatmate, Daisy, is not.'

'And Adamant?'

'In light of what's happened, what we've found out, his death is suspicious,' Isaac said. 'And Slater's and his receptionist's deaths, they could be related to Aberman.'

'Wherever Helen Langdon moved, death seemed to follow,' Goddard said.

'They're all interconnected, and just focussing on who shot the first victim is going nowhere. The man with Gwendoline is not easy to trace.'

'Any clues?'

'Nothing significant from the prostitute. The normal – average height, average weight, hat pulled forward.'

'Did anyone else see him?'

'The concierge at the hotel, but he wasn't looking either. He keeps his eyes down, takes the money off the woman and hands her the key. He had a good little number there, but he couldn't stop peeping into the rooms.'

'No more from him?'

'Nothing.

'If Gwendoline remembered anything, she'd probably be dead now.'

'It's her only protection. The man killed two people in cold blood, and then another prostitute later; a third wouldn't concern him.'

'If he were paid for two, he'd not kill any more unless he was compromised,' Goddard said.

***

Wendy dropped in on Mrs Hawthorne, Aberman's next-door neighbour. It had become a weekly routine, and the woman always seemed to remember something on each occasion. She found her not to be her usual cheerful self.

'What's the problem?' Wendy asked as she sat down in the front room.

'It's her next door. She reckons I'm nosey, always looking over the fence. She used to be friendly in the past, but now, it's as if she's hiding something.'

Wendy thought the woman's observations were nothing more than feeling unneeded. In all the years since Aberman had disappeared, she had kept watch on his house, but now, her looking over the fence from behind a drawn curtain in an upstairs window was not wanted. Wendy left the house and walked next door.

At the front door was Ben Aberman's ex-wife. 'She's been accusing us in the neighbourhood of killing Ben,' she said. Wendy could see that the woman was agitated.

'Is that it?'

'Not totally. My husband, he's not so keen on the place. I thought it would be relaxing here, but he wants to go back to London.'

'And you?'

'I'm staying. Mrs Hawthorne, if she continues, will have a writ against her for slander. There are a few others around here who'll back me up.'

'You know some of the locals?'

'One or two. I lived here for a while, and they didn't like it when I left, and then Ben was flaunting the debauchery.'

'Debauchery?'

'You know what I'm referring to, the same as the nosey old woman next door does. This place was depraved, women everywhere, and not too fussy who was watching.'

'Ben?'

'I was told he behaved himself, not sure if that's true.'

'Who told you?'

'Some of those who attended.'

'Important people?'

'I never pried into who they were.'

'We were told Ben paid for everything.'

'He did.'

'But how? He couldn't have afforded the parties that often.'

'Every other week, regular as clockwork. Arrive at the house eight at night on Saturday, leave midday on Sunday.'

'But you attended the parties.'

'The earlier ones, but they were tame by comparison. It was only after we separated that they changed, Ben changed.'

'The people who attended?'

'I've told you all this before. Slater was there, so were some of the girls from the club. Not the one that was killed with James Holden. I told you I saw Gerald Adamant at the house once, angry as well, but that was a long time ago. Apart from that, no one I knew.'

'Your husband?'

'We met some time after. He never met Ben.'

Wendy wasn't sure where the conversation was heading. She'd been invited in, and she approved of the work that had been done in the house. It was freshly painted, and there was a pleasant feel to the house. It was hard to envisage it as a den of iniquity, but that was what it had been once.

'What about where they buried Ben?'

'We're putting a concrete slab over it.'

'No issues moving into the house, considering?'

'I'm not squeamish. My husband is.'

'I feel that you know more than you ever tell us,' Wendy said. 'You knew the people who came to the parties while you were here. Who were they?'

'Slater, my husband. The others I never knew. Barry Knox, he used to come here.'

'Gus, the doorman at Dixey's?'

'He was here, but I can't remember him taking an active part unless getting drunk qualifies.'

'Any dubious characters?'

'None that I remember.'

Wendy knew the woman was lying. She had played the game strategically. She was isolated from the parties, from the deaths, and now she was back at the house in Bray. Wendy was not sure of her innocence. She had divorced Ben Aberman several years before his death, and her life since then had been one of normality. With no more to be achieved, the police sergeant left the house and headed back to Challis Street and the police station.

Chapter 23

Barry Knox looked at the monitor in his office. He could see the club was filling up, and his decision to bring in fresh women was working. His new doorman, a tough, tattooed individual by the name of Doug, was not as good as Gus. He'd upset the women backstage on a couple of occasions by walking in and staring while they were preparing to go up on stage.

Knox had had to explain to Doug, a former bouncer at an illegal gambling club, that the women didn't mind being gawped at up on stage where they were being paid. However, backstage they hung on to their modesty for as long as they could. Knox did not elaborate that they found Doug repulsive. Gus, not the most attractive of men, had always been pleasant to the women, opening the door for them, helping them to carry their bags into the club. Doug was not.

The bed in the rear room was unused, the occasional favour from one of the women to Knox missing. A better class of women, a better return on the investment, but no more late-night romance.

Knox was pleased with the way the business was going; he was not pleased with the man sitting opposite.

'He said he knew you,' Doug said as he let the man into the office.

'Did you check him out?'

'He showed his ID.'

After Doug had left, Knox turned to Isaac. 'Are you here to ask questions? I've told you all I know.'

'Not all.'

'What do you mean?'

'Ben Aberman's ex-wife. What can you tell me about her?'

'She never came in here, and besides, when I took over, Aberman was with Helen.'

'You used to go to the parties out at Aberman's house before you took over here.'

'Sometimes. I was running another club. He invited me as a courtesy. I'd return the favour.'

'Did you have parties?'

'Not me. I didn't have that sort of money, but we swapped girls at the clubs. If one of them was off ill or absent or overdosed, we'd send one of ours over.'

'The parties at Aberman's house when his wife was there, what were they like?'

'The later parties were better.'

'Regardless, what were they like?'

'Plenty of alcohol, plenty of women.'

'Did his wife take part?'

'Not that I saw. Mind you, I was always busy.'

Yet again, Isaac realised that the ex-Mrs Aberman was somehow involved. She had always given the impression of non-involvement in her husband's business affairs, yet she attended the parties, even turned a blind eye to the shenanigans.

'Aberman used to throw a lot of money around. These parties couldn't have been cheap.'

'That was Aberman. He always liked to put on a show. I never understood how he did it, but I was glad of the invite.'

'You went to every one?'

'Not all of them. We weren't that friendly, it was just business.'

'Gerald Adamant, what can you tell me about him?'

'Not much, apart from him marrying Helen. After she left here, nobody heard from her for a few months, and then, all of a sudden, she's being squired around the town on Adamant's arm. The first time Daisy saw her picture in a newspaper, she was in here showing me.'

'Daisy, was she surprised?'

'Daisy and Helen, they'd been sort of friends in the club, although, with Helen, you never knew if she was a friend or whether it was something else.'

'What do you mean?'

'I'm not sure how to explain it. She came to the club, got up on the stage, and she was a great performer. She knew how to excite the men, and then she'd finish for the night, get dressed in regular clothes and walk out of the door.'

'What else?'

'Before she moved in with Aberman on a semi-permanent basis, no one knew where she went after she left the club.'

'You know a lot about this woman,' Isaac said.

'Not me, but there she is with Adamant, and then she marries the man. There was plenty of gossip about her. Most of the girls here on that pole, they're looking for the knight in shining armour, ready to take them away from all this and into a life of luxury, the loving husband, the house in the country. Normal childhood dreams, but with them, they carried on into adulthood. It's the life they lead, I suppose.'

'Do you want out?'

'A regular job, plenty of money? Of course I do. What do you think I'm doing here, living on the edge, wondering when the next gangster is coming to knock on the door, to tell me my number's up?'

'Is that likely?'

'Who knows. We're strictly legal here, but our protection comes at a cost.'

'Who owns this club? It's never been explained.'

'As I've told you before, a consortium of businessmen.'

'But you must have met them?'

'Not me. I've met the man who put me in this job, but apart from that, I haven't, and that's the truth.'

'I'm interested in Gerald Adamant. How did he come to know Helen?'

'I'm not sure. Some of the women said he used to come into the club.'

'Gus?'

'He said he did, but I wouldn't place too much credence on him.'

'Why?'

'Gus only sees the people of a night time when it's dark.'

'I need to meet this consortium,' Isaac said.

'They'll not talk to you, even if you can find them.'

'Why?'

'They're secretive.'

'Why are they secretive? You're legal.'

'Social stigma. Businessmen are after a good return on their money, and these clubs can be money in the bank, only it doesn't look good on their financial returns. It won't help their reputations, their being involved in strip clubs, prostitution, drug dealing.'

'You said there was no prostitution or drugs here.'

'There isn't, but people always associate these places with crime and sin.'

'How do you see it?'

'A night out with the boys, a chance to get drunk, to have a laugh and a look at the women. We're entertainment for the grown-ups.'

***

Back at Challis Street Police Station, Isaac called the team into his office. Chief Superintendent Goddard came as well, although he did not stay long. He gave the obligatory words of encouragement and left hurriedly, another meeting, another chance to press the flesh.

'Wendy, anything more?' Isaac said. He was sitting upright, his arms resting on his desk.

'I'm not sure I understand Ben Aberman's widow. Before, at her house in Chelsea, she was pleasant. Now, out at Bray, there's a hardness in her. She's fallen out with the next-door neighbour, accused her of prying.'

'Was she?'

'Probably.'

'You think the ex-Mrs Aberman is hiding something.'

'Yes, I do.'

'Bridget, what do we have on her?'

'Christine Aberman, married to Ben for fifteen years, no children. Originally trained as a nurse, although she's not worked for the last twenty years. She's from London, the same area as Aberman. She divorced Aberman, moved in with William Ecclestone, a bank manager, although she still uses Aberman as her surname. The house in Chelsea is beyond a bank manager's salary.'

'It was part of the divorce settlement, according to her,' Wendy said.

'It was. I have a copy of it, as well as the division of the assets,' Bridget said. 'There was no money owing on the house.'

'Could he have made this amount of money with Dixey's and two other clubs?' Larry said.

'His tax returns indicate he could not, although I assume there's a lot of black money.'

'Would he be subject to a tax audit?' Wendy said.

'Unlikely,' Isaac said. 'He'd use smart accountants to head them off, and his records would be meticulous.'

'They are,' Bridget said.

'And the house in Bray?'

'Yet again, paid off.'

'It's still suspicious,' Isaac said.

'He may have inherited money.'

'Would Aberman's ex-wife know?'

'Maybe. We could ask her.'

'Wendy, set it up. I'll go with you,' Isaac said. 'Before we wrap up, what about the consortium that took over Aberman's assets?'

'I can't make the connection to anyone. Slater was their mouthpiece.'

'He's dead, but the clubs are still running. Who are they reporting to?'

'Barry Knox would know,' Larry said.

'It's possible, but he's not talking, or he's scared.'

Chapter 24

Christine Aberman did not appreciate the visit by Isaac and his sergeant so soon after the previous visit. She was in the garden. As Wendy walked out to meet her, she glanced around at the house next door. She was sure the curtains had moved in the window that Mrs Hawthorne used for spying.

'You've ended up a very wealthy woman. Why have you kept both houses?' Wendy said.

'Good fortune, I suppose,' the woman said as she got up from her sitting position on the ground.

'It's more than that. The men who took your husband's clubs would not have hesitated to take this house. We've always assumed it was because Helen Langdon had some relationship with them, but it could be you.'

'I resent your aspersions. I was a loyal wife to Ben, even when he bought the first club. I didn't approve back then, I don't approve now. If this house and the one in Chelsea are the results of those places, then some good has come of them, but that's all.'

'Was Gerald Adamant at the parties more than the one time?'

'I told you I saw him here the one time.'

'Soon the pieces will fall into place. If we find out you're lying, it will reflect badly on you. I suggest you tell us what you know before it is too late.'

'Okay, Adamant sometimes came to the parties. I never saw him with any of the women.'

'But Adamant is known as a philanthropist,' Wendy said.

'He wasn't back then. Maybe he distanced himself afterwards, but he was up to no good when I met him.'

'Tell us about him.'

'He was a charming man, very polite. He'd come to the parties, not every time, and he and Ben would sit down and talk. Back then, they were friends, or they appeared to be.'

'What do you mean?'

'Adamant had my husband killed.'

'Are you certain?'

'It's the only explanation. I knew Ben had taken up with Helen and he was even considering marrying her.'

'How do you know this?'

'We were divorced, but we kept in contact. He phoned to tell me about Helen, told me she was a good woman.'

'Did he tell you about her working in the club?'

'He tried to explain that she was a free spirit.'

'Did you believe him?'

'I believed it was what he thought, but he was naïve. If she was wrapping herself around a pole with no clothes on, she was more than a free spirit.'

'What did you think she was?'

'I didn't think anything. Ben was keen on her, and there's no way I was going to dissuade him. Anyway, three weeks later, he's dead.'

'Do you believe that Gerald Adamant was involved with the group that took over Ben's clubs?'

'He was the group.'

'This house?'

'Slater phoned me, asked if I'd accept the house for not asking too many questions.'

'And you agreed?'

'Yes. I had committed no crime.'

'Did you believe Ben to be dead?'

'I was told he had gone overseas, and that he'd be back one day, but I didn't believe it. I didn't know he was buried in this garden.'

'Why didn't you move in?'

'That was the deal. Helen would look after the place for Aberman, maintain the pretence that he was coming back. If I had moved into the house, it would have been suspicious, and one thing Adamant did not want was anything obvious.'

'The philanthropy of the man?'

'Gerald Adamant used his charitable causes as the perfect cover. The man enjoyed living on the edge, being smarter than the next man. And then Helen kills him, claims it's self-defence, even got Adamant's children to act as character witnesses.'

'Who's running Adamant's criminal enterprises now?'

'Why are you asking me? Talk to Barry Knox, he'll know.'

***

The revelations of Christine Aberman had cleared the way forward for Homicide.

'Bridget, what do we have on Adamant's children that we didn't know before?' Isaac asked.

'Archie, the eldest. He's forty-three. Then there's Abigail, forty-one, and Howard, the younger son, the child of Gerald's second wife, he's twenty-nine.'

'Discount Howard,' Isaac said.

'Any reason?' Larry said.

'Too young.'

'But he's smart. The man can achieve plenty with a computer.'

'Okay. Leave him in for now. Let's focus on Archie.'

'Archie, short for Archibald, is a lawyer, practises in Paddington. He takes care of the family's business interests.'

'Any evidence that Archie could have taken over his father's criminal interests?'

'Is Christine Aberman's testimony enough to convince us that Gerald Adamant was behind the takeover of Aberman's clubs?' Larry said.

'It's the missing link that ties Aberman and Adamant, and Helen to Adamant. Helen knew that Adamant ordered Aberman's death. She knows where he is and she lays in a plan to snare the man.'

'But why wait so long before killing him?'

'Helen's smart. She knows that if she had killed him before they were married, then it's murder. If she married him, then killed him on their wedding night, then it's the same. But she waits, redeems herself in society.'

'It worked,' Wendy said.

'A remarkable woman,' Isaac said.

'Do you think so?' Bridget said.

'To achieve what she did, even if it was murder. She kept focussed all those years, never once letting her guard drop, and then she killed the man who had killed Aberman.'

'Do you think she loved him?' Wendy said.

'We'll never know.'

'We need to prove that Gerald Adamant was responsible for Aberman's death,' Isaac said. 'Larry, we'll go and visit his daughter. She may be the easiest to deal with.'

***

Abigail Adamant, a woman who did little other than spend the family money on frivolities, had not been easy to find. In the end, Bridget found her through accessing her Facebook account; she was at a restaurant in Chelsea.

'Miss Adamant, the death of your father's widow,' Isaac said once he and Larry had separated the woman from her friends.

'Call me Abigail,' she said. She was fashionably dressed, and also slightly drunk after lunch with her friends. One or two of them had looked over at the tall, dark and handsome detective chief inspector when Isaac and Larry had entered the restaurant. Isaac had seen the sniggering, the comments passed between the women. He had felt embarrassed. He was on duty and anxious to conclude the current investigations.

'Abigail, was your father involved in crime?'

'Are you accusing him?'

Isaac realised his questioning was probably too direct for a woman unsteady on her feet. He ordered her a black coffee. He needed her sober.

'We've received information that your father was involved in the takeover of Ben Aberman's clubs.'

'Ben Aberman?'

'Are you saying you've not heard of the man?'

'I read the news. His body was found in the back garden of his house.'

'He was the former lover of your father's widow. You must have known this.'

'Not from Helen.'

'We have to consider the possibility that Helen, a woman that no one seems to know fully, had married your father as a means of getting close enough to kill him.'

'By why marry him? Why pretend to love him and to take an interest in his causes?'

'Because if she managed to convince you and your brothers that she loved your father, you would all support her assertion that it was self-defence.'

'But it's absurd. No one could keep up that pretence for so long.'

'She could. She had stripped in a club, yet came away unscathed, she had married your father, and then she fell in love with James Holden.'

'Love?'

'His widow believes she had fallen in love with her husband.'

'Could it have been a pretence with James Holden?'

'Did you know the man?'

'He and my father were friends.'

'If we prove that your father was involved in crime, what would you think of your father?'

'Nothing would change. He did a lot of good with his causes.'

'So did James Holden, and he was killed. There's something else.'

'What is it?'

'We believe your father gave the order for Ben Aberman to be killed,' Isaac said.

'What right do you have to besmirch my father's good name by such accusations?'

'Ben Aberman and your father met on several occasions. Your father was far from the saint you would portray him as.'

'I've not said he was a saint.'

'Did you know Nicholas Slater?'

'Yes, I met him once or twice. Father introduced me to him.'

'He was an acquaintance of Ben Aberman, even went to his parties.'

'My father went to one or two, I know that.'

'Did you know what sort of parties they were?'

'I never asked my father, but I can imagine. Alcohol and a good time.'

'And women supplied by Aberman,' Isaac said.

'Good for my father, if that was the case,' Abigail said.

Larry observed Isaac going easy on the woman. 'Abigail, if what we have been told is correct, it would destroy your father's reputation,' he said.

'It wouldn't concern me. I'm not filled with the need to help others. I'm a selfish person. My father helped a lot of people. My brother is trying to do the same, but he'll not succeed as well as our father.'

'Why?'

'Our father had genuine compassion. He was charismatic, people instinctively liked him. You've met my brother. He can be blunt with people, and he doesn't have the same level of commitment. My brother and I, we're the generation that loses the money.'

'Howard, your younger brother?'

'He was never spoilt by the wealth.'

Isaac could tell that Abigail Adamant was incapable of any great passion. She did not concern herself with right and wrong, only with what gave her pleasure, and whereas she had shown compassion for Helen, she was not interested in whether her father had died as a result of murder or of a woman defending herself. Isaac had to admit that he did not like her very much.

Chapter 25

Two things happened the day following Isaac and Larry's conversation with Abigail Adamant. The first was Richard Goddard coming into Isaac's office to tell him that the audit into the department had been cancelled: it was not unexpected.

'The man beat them again,' Goddard said. 'Even the head of Counter Terrorism Command is back in his old job.'

'It's an admission from Davies that he was wrong.'

'That's not how Davies operates. He'll take the criticism, turn it into an advantage. The commissioner is a man who listens to the rank and file, a man who believes in an open-door policy to his office. The next time you meet him, he'll be friendly, singing your praises.'

'And I'm meant to show him the necessary respect?' Isaac said.

'You'll show him due deference as befits his rank.'

'The plan to remove him has been shelved?'

'It's always there, but he'll stay, at least until his contract is up. I have to give the man his due, he knows how to play the game.'

'The damage he's caused to the Met,' Isaac said.

'It's minor. We're still here, so are the majority of the competent and dedicated.'

The second thing that happened was when Abigail Adamant went home and questioned her brother, Archie.

'I was told our father was involved in Ben Aberman's murder,' Abigail said. She was sitting in the living room of the Adamant house. To one side of her was Howard, his feet hanging over the arm of the sofa. Archie sat square on, his tie loosened, his top shirt button undone.

'So what?' was Howard's reply.

'Did you know about this? Abigail said to Archie.

'Aberman was being difficult. Someone had to deal with him,' Archie replied. He resented being questioned by his sister.

'Are you condoning murder?'

'It's unproven, and since when did you care about our father as long as you had sufficient money to squander?'

'If our father killed Ben Aberman, could Helen have murdered our father?'

Howard turned around from where he had been feigning disinterest and placed his feet on the ground. 'We've been through this before. We supported Helen. If we let the police suspect we have doubts, they'll believe what Abigail has just said about our father.'

'They believe it already,' Abigail said. 'Archie, what is the truth?'

'Our father may have had another side to him. There are some discrepancies in his finances, large sums of money going in, going out.'

'Did Helen know this?'

'I don't know.'

'Did you know about our father when he was alive?' Howard asked.

'Not totally. I knew about the parties at Aberman's house. But that was a long time ago.'

'How?'

'He wanted to talk one day. He admired people such as Aberman, not concerned about their reputations, what people thought of them.'

'Was our father a crook?'

'He was a businessman who lent money.'

'High risk, high interest?'

'To people such as Ben Aberman. Our father enjoyed the subterfuge.'

'You've not answered the question,' Abigail said. 'Did our father kill Ben Aberman?'

'Not personally, but it's possible,' Archie said.

'And since then, Helen's killing of our father?'

'I still believe Helen's account of what happened,' Archie said.

'Archie, did you kill Helen?'

'I've not been responsible for any murders.'

Howard Adamant looked over at his half-brother. He wasn't sure what to believe. Abigail sat down resignedly and looked into space. Her only concern, the impact the truth would have on her lifestyle.

***

Ten o'clock in the morning, and in Homicide the team were focussing on their individual activities. Bridget was dealing with the administration, Wendy and Larry were working on their weekly reports. Isaac was in his office checking his emails.

None of them expected Gwendoline, Daisy's former flatmate, to walk in the door. Wendy saw her first and went over. 'I had to come,' the prostitute said.

'Take a seat and take your time,' Wendy said. 'That's a nasty cut you've got there.'

'It was him,' the woman said. Wendy could see that she had slept rough the night before. Her clothes were in disarray, her hair was tangled, and the handbag she carried was open.

'Him?'

'The man who drugged me when the two were killed in the hotel.'

'What happened?'

'I'm looking at him. There's something familiar, but I can't make out what it is. I've got my money, he's had what he wanted, and I'm ready to go. He's holding my arm. I finally remember who he is. I'm frightened, trying to get free, but he's hanging on. I grabbed a knife from my bag and stabbed him.'

'When was this?'

'Last night. I've been keeping out of sight until now.'

'The cut on your arm?'

'He lashed out at me as I ran out of the room. I caught my arm on something sharp.'

Bridget came in and administered first aid. Wendy gave Gwendoline a hot drink and attempted to calm her.

'Where is he now?'

'I've no idea, and I'm scared to go home. I phoned my flatmate not to go there either, but I doubt if she listened to me.'

'Would he have your address?'

'Some of the contents of my handbag fell out. I can't find some of my cards, one of them has an address on it.'

'The address?'

'15 Brixham Street, Shepherd's Bush, Flat 5,' Gwendoline said.

Wendy made a phone call. 'There's a police car on the way to check it out. You should have come in here earlier.'

'I was frightened. He's killed two people, three if I include Daisy. He could have killed me.'

'Did he take you to that room to kill you?'

'I don't think he recognised me. Before I had red hair, now it's blonde. He wanted me for sex, that's all.'

'Describe the man?'

'I told you before, I don't look. I only do it for the drugs.'

'What do you remember?'

'He smelt nice.'

'Perfume?'

'Aftershave. He was dressed smartly.'

'A suit?'

'Yes, although I don't remember a tie.'

'Anything else?'

'The man, nothing. Maybe you think I'm lying, but I'm not. I never remember them after they've left.

'You'd recognise the smell again?'

'I think so.'

'Very well. Let's get you cleaned up and fed. After that, we can go and see if we can find what the aftershave was.'

Isaac and Larry, realising that Wendy would be the best person to talk to Gwendoline, left her alone. After the woman had eaten breakfast at a café across the road, she and Wendy walked back to the police station. 'I wanted to join the police when I was younger,' the woman said.

'What happened?'

'Drugs. I tried them once, and I was hooked. There's nothing that can be done.'

'With treatment, it may be possible.'

'That's the problem. They give you the methadone, the counselling needed. After that, it's up to the individual to deal with the problem, but the craving, it never goes away.' Wendy, even though she had been nearly two years without a cigarette, still savoured the smell on the street. Wendy knew that heroin was different, and it had destroyed Gwendoline, a woman in her mid-thirties.

Wendy received a phone call. 'Are you certain?' she said.

She then called in Isaac and Larry. 'Gwendoline's flatmate, she's dead,' Wendy said. Gwendoline sat quietly sobbing.

'Wendy, look after Gwendoline,' Isaac said. 'I'll go with Larry to the address.'

'We need to identify the aftershave the man was wearing,' Wendy said.

'Forensics can probably do that if the smell is at the flat,' Larry said.

'Maybe, but it'll help Gwendoline if she's occupied. The man's experienced at killing. He'll not make mistakes with the flatmate. He didn't expect to meet Gwendoline again. He wasn't prepared.'

'She wasn't a bad flatmate, not as bad as Daisy,' Gwendoline said sadly. 'I must be jinxed. Share a flat with me, end up dead.'

***

Neither Isaac nor Larry were impressed with what constituted a flat for two heroin-addicted prostitutes. It was on the second floor of an old council block. The general area was not good either. In the flat, an old kitchen – two of the cupboard doors hanging off their hinges, a cooker that looked as though it had not been used for some time, a refrigerator which hummed loudly. In one corner of the main living area, an old television was switched to one of the shopping channels.

'Where's the body?' Gordon Windsor, the CSE, said as he entered with his team.

'In the other room. We've not been in there yet.'

'And you won't be until you kit up. I don't want you making a mess of the place, destroying the evidence.'

'We know the rules,' Larry said.

Inside the bedroom, a woman was sprawled across the bed. 'She's been shot,' Windsor said.

'We believe it's the same person who killed Helen Langdon and James Holden.'

'If that's the case, there'll not be much evidence.'

'The man's rattled. He hadn't expected to be recognised by the prostitute he'd drugged before.'

Isaac looked around the room: no fairy lights, no massage oil, no sign that the woman brought men back to the flat. On a bedside table stood a photo of a family. Isaac assumed it was of the woman's family in a happier time. A picture of the dead woman and two others, one of them Gwendoline, was taped to the wall.

'Not much to see here,' Windsor said.

'Any observations?'

'She's been shot at close range. There's a sign of a struggle, not much damage to the place. The bullet is probably a 9 mm.'

'The same gun that killed Langdon and Holden?'

'That's up to Forensics, not me.'

On the way out, Isaac and Larry looked into Gwendoline's room. It was the same as the other woman's, devoid of anything other than a bed, a few personal items, a few photos. Isaac picked up some clothes and toiletries, at Wendy's request. Gwendoline was at the police station, and she would not be coming back to the flat. It was a murder scene, and it now represented the best chance to find out the identity of the murderer.

Outside on the street, the usual gathering of onlookers. One of the women standing in the crowd, in her forties, overweight, blotched face, came over. 'I saw him,' she said.

Isaac pulled her to one side. 'What can you tell us?'

'I was waiting at my door for a friend,' she said. Isaac knew she was another prostitute and she had been waiting for a client.

'Your name?'

'Professional or my correct name?'

'Both.' The onlookers, sensing additional gossip, attempted to follow. A uniformed constable kept them behind the temporary barrier.

'Delilah, a hint of forbidden delights,' the woman said. It was clear she had retained a sense of humour.

'Your real name?'

'Mary Alton.'

'Miss Alton, what can you tell us.'

'Call me Delilah. Why don't you treat me to a cup of tea and something to eat? Then we can talk.'

Isaac and Larry hoped it wasn't a con job to get them to buy her a meal.

Inside the restaurant, not far from the murder scene, the three of them sat. A disinterested waiter took the order. Isaac thought the place looked unhygienic. Larry and the woman ordered fish and chips. Isaac settled for coffee only.

'Is she dead?' Delilah said.

'She's been shot.'

'I can't say I knew her. I'd occasionally hear her and her friend coming home, but apart from that, we didn't talk much. I went into their flat once to borrow something or other, I can't remember what.'

Alcohol, Isaac thought but did not comment.

'Gwendoline was okay, the other one could be snooty.'

'Snooty?'

'She thought she was better than us. Supposedly she had grown up in a posh house somewhere. She spoke well, I'll grant her that.'

'You saw the man who shot her,' Larry said.

'I'm waiting for a friend.'

'Client or friend?' Isaac said.

'One and the same. If they've got the money, they're my friend. I've got my door open, just slightly, enough to see who's coming up the stairs. My flat is near theirs. I can see it's not him, so I close my door.'

'Did he see you?'

'No. He would have killed me if I had, wouldn't he?'

'It seems probable.'

'I heard him knock on the door opposite and Annie opening it. That was the name I knew her by, probably not her real name, but most of us, we don't want to remember where we came from.'

'What happened then?' Larry said.

'Annie, she opens the door, and the man enters.'

'You're watching?'

'Not then, but I can hear well enough. The man's looking for Gwendoline, but she's not there. I can tell he's angry and Annie's not saying much.'

'Suspicious?'

'Where I live? The building is full of people like me, like him. If someone's screwing or arguing, I just turn up the music in my flat.'

'Tell us about the man?'

'He's average, nothing special, although he wore a distinctive aftershave.'

'You could smell it?'

'My friend arrived after a few minutes. He thought I'd just had another man in my flat.'

'Did it worry him?'

'He doesn't like it. He's a regular, you see. Sometimes they get jealous, but that's his problem.'

'Did you see the face of the man who entered Annie's flat?'

'Not really. He had on a heavy coat, the collar turned up. He was wearing a hat.'

'It's the same man,' Isaac said to Larry.

'Delilah, you've had a narrow escape,' Larry said.

Chapter 26

Wendy took Gwendoline shopping to try to identify the aftershave the man had been wearing. At the first shop they visited, no success. At the second, the same result. At the third, the smell of the aftershave was unmistakable. Wendy purchased a bottle and then returned to the station, but not before the two women had stopped at a restaurant.

'Not point in skimping on the budget. You're a witness. It's important we look after you,' Wendy said.

'You've been very generous,' Gwendoline said.

Wendy felt sad for the woman, a woman like so many others, just surviving day to day.

Back at the office, Isaac handed Gwendoline a small case with some of her belongings from her flat.

'When can I get the rest?' she asked.

'Wendy will organise it for you. Maybe tomorrow. Do you have somewhere to stay?'

'I've a friend, she'll look after me for a few days.'

'I'll take her there,' Wendy said.

'When you get back, we need to discuss what we have,' Isaac said.

'It's a bit obvious, wearing aftershave,' Larry said.

'The man wasn't expecting to meet Gwendoline. He's flustered, realising his cover's been broken. Whoever he is, he must be one of the men we've been interviewing. Anyone that comes to mind?'

'Archie Adamant, he's a smart dresser, his brother's not.'

'John Holden, when he was alive, may have qualified, but he's dead and buried.'

'I had him down as the possible murderer, but if Gwendoline's correct, it can't be him.'

Wendy returned to the office twenty minutes after dropping off Gwendoline. 'It's a better place than Daisy's was,' she said.

'Housekeeping is not Gwendoline's strong point. The flat she shared with the last murder victim was a mess, even worse than my place,' Isaac said.

'I suppose you don't have stray men over at your place,' Wendy said.

'No strays of any kind.'

'Coming back to the point,' Larry said, 'the only men we've met who are still free are Barry Knox, although I can't remember him smelling of anything, Christine Aberman's current husband, and the two Adamant men. It still doesn't explain who shot Slater and his receptionist, and ruined my best suit.'

'It's been dry cleaned, returned to you,' Isaac said.

'I know, but it's not the same. The blood of two dead people has been on it.'

'You're becoming squeamish.'

'Maybe, but we were there when they were shot. If we'd been in the line of fire, it would have been us that day.'

'Now's not the time to indulge in retrospection. We've got a man out there that we need to find, and fast. Discount Howard Adamant for now, and besides, he's a young man about town, he'll have no trouble finding female companionship.'

'No need of Gwendoline,' Wendy said.

'Focus on the more likely candidates.'

'I've always found Mrs Aberman's second husband to be a little strange.'

'Is it possible?' Isaac said.

'Everyone seems to tie into everyone else. Aberman and Adamant were interconnected. Maybe her second husband is as well.'

'What about Slater?'

'What about him?'

'It was a difficult shot. Could there be more than one murderer?'

'We've got Ugly Pete and Gus for Aberman's death. Nobody for Slater's but neither Ugly Pete nor Gus has any history with guns,' Larry said.

'We've always said the murders of Helen Langdon and James Holden were professional. What do we have on Archie

Adamant? Any history of military training, any experience with weapons?' Isaac said.

The team dispersed. Isaac and Larry left to go and visit Archie Adamant, Wendy to check on Gwendoline, to see if she remembered anything more.

Adamant was not pleased to see the two police officers. He was in his office at the house. He was a sombre man, devoid of any humour. His half-brother took life as it came, made plenty of money and enjoyed himself. Archie looked as if enjoyment was alien to him.

'Is this important?' Archie said. He was sitting down, aiming to look relaxed, not achieving it.

Isaac sniffed the air – nothing. He liked to splash on aftershave, especially if he had a date, but it had been a few weeks since his last one. The woman had seemed pleasant, but on the night of the date she found out that he appreciated a good steak and a glass of wine, whereas she was vegetarian and drank a glass of water. The evening had ended badly, although she had phoned up afterwards to apologise, agreeing that maybe she had been a little sensitive. Isaac knew there would not be a next time.

'Mr Adamant, are you in the habit of visiting prostitutes?' Isaac said.

'How dare you come in here and accuse me of such a thing.'

'We'll need to conduct a search of your house. A warrant is being prepared.'

Larry sat quietly and watched his DCI bait the man. A search warrant for the man's house was not in preparation, and even if it were, it would be up to Homicide to show just reason for it to be issued.

'Yesterday a man paid for the services of a prostitute. That man was also with her in the room opposite to Helen Langdon and James Holden when they were murdered. You, Mr Adamant, fit the description of that man. How are you with weapons? Have you had any training? Will we find any firearms at your house?'

'I'm proficient with firearms. However, I've not visited a prostitute.'

'You're not married,' Larry said.

'What's that got to do with it? Adamant took stock of what he was saying. He did not want the police searching his house with a warrant, concerned that a closer inspection into his business dealings would be detrimental. 'Okay, bring a team to the house. Check what you want and do it now.'

Larry did not need to call for a team. He was more than capable of conducting a detailed search. He checked the bathrooms of the house, the bedrooms, even Howard's. After thirty minutes he returned. 'All clear,' he said.

Isaac was in the other room talking to Howard, Archie's younger brother. 'I'll let Archie know,' Howard said.

Larry noticed that Howard had smartened himself up and he had shaved. 'I've an appointment with a bank,' Howard said. 'I've already told DCI Cook. I've been offered a contract to write an anti-hacking program for them.'

'Your expertise?'

'If you can hack as well as I can, you can also put in place the safeguards. It's big money for me. I may even move out of here, buy my own place.'

'This house is magnificent,' Isaac said.

'It's time to go. Archie can be a pain in the rear end, and Abigail, she turns her nose up when I bring a woman back with me.'

'She seems broadminded.'

'She is, but she disapproves that it's always a different one.'

'What's the problem with Archie?' Isaac asked.

'He had a touch of the prostate, can't get it up.'

'Incapable of maintaining an erection?'

'That's why he's grumpy. The man's in his forties, at his peak, and he's finished. All he's got is his work and a miserable attitude. Me, I'm at my best. Plenty of money, plenty of women.'

Isaac and Larry knew that if Archie could not consummate a sexual relationship, then he was not guilty of murdering Helen Langdon and James Holden. Gwendoline had made it clear that the man she had been with had had sexual intercourse with her.

***

Barry Knox sat in the office at Dixey's. It was two in the afternoon, and the place was quiet, apart from a cleaner out the front sweeping the floor and another polishing the pole in the centre of the stage. Behind the bar, the barman checked everything was ready, placing last-minute orders to the alcohol supplier. Around the back, in the dressing room, none of the women were present; most wouldn't be in the club until after seven in the evening.

Isaac and Larry walked through the club. The new doorman did not need to check their identification; he knew them on sight. They knew him, as well, having already checked him out back at the police station. Doug Maybury had served two years for the violent beating of a man, and for extortion.

'Not again,' Knox said when Isaac and Larry entered his office. 'I'm innocent of any crime. If I didn't know better, I'd say this was victimisation.'

'It's not. Mr Knox, how are you with weapons?'

'What do you mean?'

'Can you fire a gun?'

'I was in the army, corporal. I know how to shoot. Does that make me a murderer? If it does, there are plenty of others with weapons training.'

'We're not interested in any others, only you. Did you visit a prostitute by the name of Gwendoline last night?'

'Why would I? This place is awash with willing females.'

'You told us last time that you'd upgraded the women, and they weren't available, not even to you.'

'Even so, a prostitute. Look at me, a man in the prime of life. Why would I go paying a woman for something I can get for free?'

'Can you?' Isaac said. 'There's not many women who'd like the manager of a strip club, let alone a murderer.'

'Are you accusing me?'

'Slater and his receptionist.'

'What about them?' Knox said. Both of the police officers looked for signs of nervousness in the man.

'Can I use your toilet?' Larry said.

'There's one out in the club.'

'There's one in here.'

'It's not working, doesn't flush properly.'

Larry ignored the man and opened the door to Knox's private bathroom. Inside he found a shower, a sink, and a toilet. He opened the cabinet above the sink. He then returned to where Isaac and Knox were. 'How long have you been using aftershave?' he said.

'Not often. Supposedly the one you saw in there is full of pheromones, drives the women wild.'

'Does it?'

'It's just advertising.'

'The man who used the services of a prostitute last night – the woman was a friend of Daisy, a flatmate of another murdered woman, and she remembers the smell of your aftershave. You were also with her on the night Helen Langdon and James Holden were murdered. Mr Knox, I put it to you that you are the murderer of Helen Langdon, James Holden, Daisy and another prostitute.'

'I've killed no one. I'm innocent,' Knox protested.

'Who paid you? Was it Archie Adamant? We know his father was involved with this club. We know that Aberman was killed on his instruction. Are you willing to go to jail without telling us the truth? Adamant, we can't pin anything on him. We need your testimony.'

Isaac knew that Homicide had enough to arrest Knox, not enough to ensure a conviction. Geraldine would prove to be an unreliable witness, and the smell of an aftershave that was not difficult to purchase would not convict the man.

'Mr Knox, with your testimony, we will arrest Archie Adamant.'

'He's not the father.'

'What does that mean?'

'Gerald Adamant, there was a real bastard, fooled everyone, even me.'

'Was he the person who gave the instruction for Aberman to be killed by Ugly Pete?'

'Gus told me. Adamant was a secretive man. Aberman, he's got the dirt on him, using it as leverage against the money owing. I didn't know, not for a long time, and then Gus, he's in a strange mood, wants to talk.'

'He told you?'

'He told me about that night. He and Ugly Pete had worked Ben Aberman over, Ugly Pete cranking the handle of the generator. Gus, he can be soft sometimes. He goes into the other room, disturbed by the smell of the burning flesh, Aberman arching off the chair. Five minutes later, Ugly Pete comes out and tells him it's all over.'

'What's all over?'

'Aberman, he's signed all the documents. Gus checks on the man. He's tied to the chair, his head flopped forward. Gus walks around to the front, sees the bullet hole.'

'A gun would have made a noise.'

'It had a silencer.'

'He would have heard something.'

'Gus's hearing is not great. He may not have heard.'

'Gus has admitted to burying Aberman. Why are you telling us?' Isaac said.

'I'm protecting myself. Gerald Adamant was the man behind the scenes. He was more dangerous than anyone else. A man devoid of any emotion, other than self-aggrandisement. What people thought of him was all-important.'

'And his son, Archie?'

'I'll not testify against him.'

'In that case, you'll go to jail for the murders of six people.'

'You can't prove it,' Knox said. Isaac and Larry could see that the man was rattled. Isaac knew that if he played Knox off against Adamant, one of them would break.

'Mr Knox, I'm arresting you for the murders of Helen Langdon and James Holden.'

'I've got a club to run. I don't have time for this.'

'Your doorman, he can deal with it. Larry, get the crime scene examiners over here and at Knox's home. You can check as well, see if you can find any weapons. Mr Knox shot Slater and his receptionist, also Daisy and Gwendoline's flatmate. We need the weapon.'

Chapter 27

Barry Knox lived better than Larry had expected. He had a three-bedroom flat on the other side of the River Thames, in Greenwich, not far from the Greenwich Meridian, the line of zero degrees longitude.

Gordon Windsor's crime scene examiners were already on the site. The CSEs focussed on any evidence that would tie in Knox to any of the murder sites. Difficult, considering that very little had been found at any of them, bar the occasional hair, the lint from a piece of fabric. With the CSEs in one room, Larry moved carefully around the flat. There was no sign of a woman being resident, although the place was tidy. Realising that the CSEs would focus on the more obvious, Larry looked for hidden areas, loose tiles, a floorboard that creaked. After thirty minutes he hadn't found anything. He was preparing to leave when above him, just close to the front door, he saw an area of fresh paint. He called over Grant Meston, Windsor's deputy. 'What do you reckon to this?' Larry said.

Meston took a step ladder the team had brought with them. He climbed the three steps and tapped on the area. 'It sounds hollow,' he said.

Larry phoned Isaac. 'Keep Knox on ice. We need fifteen minutes.'

Meston took photos of the area before carefully using a sharp knife to find a crack. 'Here it is,' he said. Gingerly, he continued until he had removed a small square of plasterboard. Inside, a cavity with a package wedged in tight.

More photos and then the package was removed. It was placed on the table in the kitchen and slowly unwrapped. Inside was a gun with a silencer. 'It's the correct calibre, Glock 17, 9 mm,' Meston said.

'Can you confirm it's the murder weapon?'

'Not here. It'll need Forensics.'

Larry phoned Isaac once again. 'We've found a weapon. Forensics will check it out.'

Isaac turned to Knox who was waiting for his lawyer to arrive. 'Detective Inspector Hill has found a gun at your flat.'

'It's for protection.'

'Hidden behind a painted area in your flat? It'll be a couple of hours before Forensics confirms it as a murder weapon, long enough for your lawyer to try and save your arse.'

***

Archie Adamant was panicking. The doorman he had installed at Dixey's after Gus's arrest had phoned him: Barry Knox was in police custody, charged with murder.

Archie knew he did not have his father's natural ways with people and most had found him to be rude and boorish. However, he did have an innate ability to survive. He visited his sister in her part of the substantial home. 'Helen murdered our father. I found out some months ago.'

'How?'

'She had told Holden. He told me.'

'Why?'

'I knew the man. He thought I was the same as my father, full of magnanimity.'

'But why would she tell Holden? She had convinced everyone of her innocence.'

'According to Holden, she was in love. She did not want her present jeopardised by lying to the man.'

'But why did he tell you?'

'He thought he could trust me. He had trusted our father.'

'Holden was a naïve man. Did you kill him?' Abigail asked.

'Do you think I'm capable?'

'Capable enough to find someone to do it for you.'

'She murdered our father,' Archie said.

'Our father was becoming old and irrational. He could have written us out of his will at any time. Does Howard know about Helen?'

'What does he matter? He's only the spawn of that gold-digging woman that our father married.'

'And Slater, what about him? What did he know?'

'He knew too much for too long.'

'Did you kill him? You're a good shot.'

'You know the Adamant motto,' Archie said.

'Unwritten, but our father taught us well: get others to do your dirty work, and for you, an Adamant, to bask in the glory of piety.'

'They've arrested Barry Knox, the manager at Dixey's.'

'Did he kill Helen?'

'Yes.'

'On your authority?'

'I had no option. If Holden knew the truth, so would others. Helen was committed to telling all, and with it would come the checking, and questions about why she had killed our father. I had to do what was necessary.'

'And now?'

'I'm leaving the country. Knox knows too much, and he'll talk. I've arranged a private plane. Do you want to come?'

'I've not done anything wrong.'

Ten minutes later, Archie Adamant attempted to pull out of the driveway, only to find it blocked by two police cars. Quickly, he was bundled into one of the vehicles, his hands cuffed.

'Where are we going?' Adamant said.

'Challis Street Police Station. Detective Chief Inspector Isaac Cook has some questions for you.'

A plane waited at a nearby airport for a passenger who would never come.

***

Archie Adamant did not enjoy the trip to Challis Street Police Station, that was plain to see on his arrival. 'You'll regret this,' he said to Isaac when they met.

'Mr Adamant, we needed to act with urgency. Certain information has come into our possession which identifies you as a person of interest.' Isaac felt no need to say any more. Adamant had a Queen's Counsel coming to the office to represent him. Barry Knox, without the financial resources of the other man, had only a local lawyer.

In the first interview room sat Barry Knox; in the second, Archie Adamant. Outside, in the police station's reception area, were Abigail and Howard Adamant. 'You can't believe our brother is guilty of such crimes,' Abigail said.

'The proof is there. We can prove who killed Helen and James Holden, also the flatmate of one of the prostitutes. They link back to your brother. It's up to him to convince us otherwise.'

Barry Knox waited impatiently. He regretted hiding the gun in his flat, realising that he should have dumped it in the river not far from where he lived. He had always been reluctant to throw anything away, including old magazines and old newspapers, and now it was going to haunt him.

Isaac and Larry entered Interview Room 1. Across from them, Barry Knox and his lawyer. Isaac informed Knox of his rights, the procedure that would be followed during the interview. Knox nodded his head weakly; his lawyer too. Neither of the two police officers believed the lawyer would be able to achieve much.

'Mr Knox, the weapon discovered hidden in your flat has been positively identified as being used to kill Helen Langdon and James Holden. It has also been used to kill another woman.'

'I didn't kill anyone,' Knox said.

'The weapon's in your flat. It's hidden in a cavity in the wall, and the area concealed and painted over.'

'I didn't put it there.'

'Your fingerprints are on the paintbrush that our crime scene examiners found in the laundry. Your continual denial does you no credit. We have sufficient proof for a conviction.'

'Are my client's fingerprints on the gun?' the lawyer said.

'No. The gun is clean,' Isaac said.

'Then you only have circumstantial evidence, not proof.'

'No jury will accept that Mr Knox did not know the gun was in his flat, sealed behind a false façade, his fingerprints on the paintbrush, a pot of paint as well.'

'My client will maintain his innocence.'

'If that is what he wants. We've Archie Adamant in the other room. No doubt he'll be more than happy to blame someone else.'

'Mr Knox, why do you continue to deny this?' Larry said. He could see Knox wavering, wanting to indicate to his lawyer that he was ready to confess, the lawyer pressing on his client's arm to stay still and to let him deal with it.

'My client has no more to say.'

'He's guilty, we can prove it, and if he doesn't talk, then Adamant is going to place all the blame on him,' Isaac said.

'Very well, I killed Helen and Holden. I didn't want to, but Adamant, he was insistent,' Knox said.

'You could have refused.'

'I wanted to.'

'Then why?'

'Adamant knew about my cheating him on the money the club was making. He threatened me with the Aberman solution.'

'You knew about Ben Aberman in the garden?'

'I knew he was dead. I was never sure where he was buried, although I suspected it was the garden. Gus said it was, but with him, I could never be certain.'

'Why weren't you certain?'

'Gus wasn't the brightest, and maybe Adamant had told him to tell me, a warning.'

'This is the older Adamant?'

'Yes, Gerald. He was a tough bastard. Always nice to your face, the sort of man who'd help old ladies across the road. But the man had an evil side. He'd have enjoyed watching Aberman suffer, and then Ugly Pete shooting him in the head.'

'Were you there?'

'Not me. I didn't have anything to do with Aberman's death.'

'Tell us about Archie Adamant.'

'He's worse than the father. Gerald was likeable, but the son's not. The son, he phoned me up, tells me that that Helen had murdered his father in cold blood. He wants revenge.'

'Did he care that much about the father?'

'Archie, I doubt it.'

'How do you know all this?'

'A week after Aberman died, Helen phoned me up. She had left the club by then. We met a few days later.'

'You've known all these years?'

'Not all of it, but over the years other bits of information have fallen into place. Helen, she's confused, not sure what to do. We meet over a few weeks, formulate this plan.'

'The death of Gerald Adamant?'

'Helen, she's a great actor. She knew she'd need to get close to the man, to make him suffer for what he had done.'

'Did she love Aberman?'

'He treated her well.'

'Why did she phone you?'

'You don't get it, do you? Aberman's dead, Helen's still alive and so am I. Neither of us doubts that Gerald Adamant is capable of arranging someone's death. We start spending more time together, end up sharing a bed. After a couple of months, the heat goes out of the romance.'

'Romance?'

'Not the best word,' Knox said. 'We're thrown together by a mutual problem. There's no one else we can confide in, and don't say the police. If we had told you, we'd still be on the street, and Adamant would have dealt with us. The original plan wasn't to kill Gerald Adamant, only to discredit him, expose him for what he was.'

'What changed?'

'Helen saw beneath the veneer. She realised that if he knew he had been engineered into marriage, he would react. She phoned me up the night of his death, told me that she has a task to complete. I told her not to, but she wasn't listening. She hung up the phone. The next day, it's in the newspapers and on the television that Adamant's dead, and Helen's been arrested for murder.'

'Her death benefited you as much as Archie Adamant.'

'Helen phoned me up two days before she died. She tells me she's going to tell all she knows out of love for Holden, and for me to distance myself from London. I panicked, knowing full well that Adamant would start eliminating any potential witnesses, anyone who knew the truth, the same way his father had with Aberman. I met Archie, he told me I had to remove the threat.'

'And you agreed?'

'I had no option.'

'There's a flaw in your testimony,' Isaac said.

'What's that?'

'According to Daisy, the man she arranged for Gwendoline to take to the room in the hotel was a regular customer of hers.'

'I'm keeping a watch on Helen. I see her meet Holden in Bayswater. They look more than friendly. I see them head to the hotel, the concierge inside keeping a close watch of who's going in, who's going out. I know Daisy's into prostitution, and she uses the hotel.'

'You'd been there with her?'

'Once or twice. We go back a long time, and I get a special rate. I phone her up, tell her that I need to meet her in the next ten minutes. She's not available, refers me to the other woman, not as attractive as Helen, not as agreeable as Daisy, but I'm not there for romance.'

'Why didn't you kill Gwendoline?'

'I kill out of necessity, not pleasure. The woman Daisy supplied is unknown to me.'

'What happened?'

'The woman collapses on the bed after I drugged her, and I leave the room. Holden's not locked his door.'

'You enter the room?'

'Old man Holden is going for his life. He doesn't see me. Helen, she's underneath. They're both naked. Helen looks over at me. She realises why I'm there. She attempted to let Holden know what's going on, but there's no time. I shot him first, then her.'

'How did you feel after murdering them?'

'Sickened. I liked Helen, even thought it was love once, and, as for Holden, I had nothing against him. I did what was necessary.'

'It sounds callous,' Larry said.

'I come up against scum every day. I'm one myself. Sometimes you have to do what you know is wrong. That was one of those occasions. After that, I walked out of the hotel and phoned Adamant.'

'What did he say?'

'Not a lot. He wants to stay behind the scenes, not talk to murderers.'

'Barry Knox, you're a self-confessed murderer. Are you willing to sign a confession?'

'I have no option. I'm only sorry that Helen died.'

'Daisy and the other prostitute?'

'I'm sorry about them, but Daisy, she figured it out after a few days, phoned me up. I went over to her place, tried to reason with her. To her, Helen was a saint, and I had killed the woman.'

'Gwendoline's flatmate?'

'I fancied meeting up with Gwendoline again. Macabre, I suppose, but the woman had been unconscious when I killed the other two. I phoned her up, she didn't know it was me. My hair was longer, I even dyed it. We're getting along fine until she remembers. After that, she's out of that room fast.'

'That's when you went to where she lived?'

'She panicked, dropped some papers out of her handbag. I can see the address, so I go out there. I knock on the door, another woman answers. She sees me there, recognises me from another time.'

'You'd used her services?'

'Once or twice. I knew I had to deal with her. I take her into her bedroom, pretend that it's purely professional. She's lying there pretending to be coy as I go through the seduction routine. I reach into the pocket of my jacket, pull out the gun and shoot her. Another one dead. Believe me, it becomes easier after the first couple.'

'And then?'

'I get out of there.'

'Someone shot Slater and his receptionist,' Isaac said.

'It wasn't me. I'd met Slater a few times, and I knew he was involved with Aberman's death, and that he and Gerald Adamant had a special relationship. Apart from that, I know no more. From what I read, it needed a professional shooter to execute the shot, is that correct?'

'Yes.'

'I'm okay at close range, but with long distance, I'm not good. The army tried to train me as a sniper, so I know. You'll need to look elsewhere for their murderer.'

Chapter 28

Archie Adamant was not going to be as easy to crack as Barry Knox had proved to be. The man sat in the interview room; to his side, Geoffrey Westfield, Queen's Counsel. The legal man looked composed and well in control of the situation. Isaac did not like the look of him, knowing full well that he was going to cause trouble regardless of whether the client was innocent or guilty.

'Mr Adamant, we have received a written confession from Barry Knox,' Isaac said after the formalities had been dealt with.

'Let me make it clear,' the QC said. 'My client, Mr Adamant, is a highly respected member of the community. He is not used to being brought to a police station in handcuffs. A formal complaint will be lodged.'

'That is your prerogative,' Isaac said. 'However, there are serious allegations against your client. Allegations that hopefully he will be able to answer to our satisfaction.'

'Very well, proceed.' Isaac recognised an attempt by the Westfield to commandeer the proceedings. He was not going to let it happen.

'Mr Adamant, we can prove that your father, Gerald Adamant, was a criminal.'

'Prove or hearsay?' Westfield interjected.

'Prove. He is no longer here to answer for his crimes, but his son is. Mr Adamant, you were a character witness for your father's third wife, Helen. Is that correct?'

'It is. I, and my brother and sister, never doubted her sincerity, her acting in self-defence. Our father was becoming unreasonable, unpredictable.'

'Why?'

'It's in the records. He was starting to get old, he had a medical condition, and he didn't like it. Helen was there for him to deny the ageing process.'

'Did he marry her for love or for lust?'

'Both. None of us objected.'

'You did at first.'

'We didn't know who she was, although our father was smitten, more so than he had been with any woman for a long time.'

'You must have known her history.'

'Not then, and out of respect for our father, we did not hire private investigators to check.'

'Why? A woman, young and provocative, entered into your house. Aren't you suspicious?'

'We were, but we're not a poor family. If he wanted to squander some of his money on her, it did not concern us, as long as she made him happy.'

'Did she?'

'Yes, but this is well known. She proved to be the ideal wife, loving and caring, devoted to the causes he held dear to his heart.'

'This is all very well,' the QC said, 'but why is my client here, and why the handcuffs? He's not been charged with any crime.'

'We had been forewarned that Mr Adamant was about to leave the country. In fact, there was a plane waiting for him not more than ten miles from his house.'

'Is that an issue?' Adamant said.

'Not in itself, but the flight plan had been lodged at the last moment, and it was an executive jet on hire to you.'

'I often use executive jets.'

'We will be checking the financial records of your businesses and those of the charitable trust. Will we find any anomalies?'

'No.'

'We will also be questioning your brother and sister. Will they corroborate your story?'

'They will, although Howard, he doesn't want to become involved, and Abigail, she's not interested.'

'We've arrested two men in connection with the death of Ben Aberman. One of those men will state that your father gave the order for his murder.'

'I don't believe it. My father was a good man who helped others.'

'He was not there when it happened. He was a man who controlled from a distance. Are you such a man?'

'No. I have taken over my father's interests, business and charitable, that's all.'

'Successfully?'

'Not as successfully as my father, but both are sound.'

'Why not?'

'My father was a unique individual. People instinctively liked and trusted him. I do not have the ready ease he had. It's my personality, and I can't change it. I can only do what I feel is best for the Adamant family.'

'Even if that includes murder?'

'I must object,' Westfield said. 'You are not accusing my client of any crime, only questioning him. Where's the proof that he's done anything criminal?'

'There are enough bodies. Mr Adamant is not the person, nor was his father, to commit any act of violence personally. That is always left to others. We can put forward a strong case showing that Gerald Adamant was behind the death of Ben Aberman. We can also show that Helen Langdon was aware of who killed Aberman and that she executed a plan to marry your father, and to ultimately kill him.'

'That's rubbish. You never saw the two of them together. I did. Helen loved my father. The verdict against her at the trial was erroneous. All three of us knew it, but they dragged up her past history, and she was damned.'

'My client is not here to answer questions regarding his father,' Westfield said.

'We have a statement from Barry Knox, a man who has admitted to killing Helen Langdon, James Holden, and two prostitutes. He has stated that you were the person behind the scenes, giving the orders.'

'For two prostitutes? What for?'

'They're collateral damage. One of them had figured out what was going on, and the flatmate of the other woman had identified Knox as the murderer. We can prove his guilt, and he has given us a full confession. Mr Adamant, yours is not so easy. You've inherited the skill of staying out of sight from your father,' Isaac said. 'Both Detective Inspector Hill and I were in Slater's office when he and his receptionist were killed. Knox did not commit those murders, although you, Mr Adamant, are a good shot. Did you kill Slater, realising that he was getting scared, or he was the only one who could positively identify you?'

'Objection,' Westfield said. 'This is conjecture, not proof.'

'We will obtain the proof. There is enough evidence to overturn Helen Langdon's acquittal. It will show her guilty of the murder of the man who ordered Ben Aberman's death. We can also prove that Slater was at Aberman's house when he signed the documents ceding his clubs to a company associated with your father. Mr Adamant, your defence is based on your father's reputation. Within the next few months, that reputation will be shattered.'

'It's a tragedy what you are doing. My father helped a lot of people around the world.'

'And that excuses him from prosecution?'

'No, but you are wrong, and as Westfield said, it's conjecture, not proof.'

'A father's reputation destroyed, even if you can prove it, does not alter the fact that a person is innocent until proven guilty,' Westfield said.

'The lofty pedestal of the father will be destroyed. It will be more difficult to prove that innocence, and we will have Knox accusing your client.'

'Is that it?' Westfield said.

'For the present,' Isaac said. 'There is one other issue. We will be conducting a thorough search of the Adamant family home and its surroundings.'

'For what?' Adamant said. 'This farce has gone on long enough.'

'Knox did not kill Slater and his receptionist; however, you, Mr Adamant, are a crack shot. We have records of you competing in various competitions in this country.'

'I would request time to confer with my client,' Westfield said.

Isaac adjourned the interview.

'What do you reckon?' Goddard asked outside the interview room.

'Guilt by association, that's all,' Isaac said. The three police officers were taking the opportunity to discuss the case.

'We need his conviction,' Goddard said. 'Any chance of an arrest?'

'We can hold him based on Knox's statement. The proof is up to others.'

The interview resumed, Adamant looking more at ease. His QC leant forward over the table. It was meant to intimidate; it did not work. 'My client wishes to make a statement,' he said.

Adamant cleared his throat. 'I, Archibald Adamant, am not responsible for the accusations levelled against me. My father, Gerald Adamant, a respected member of society, did, at all times, conduct his business affairs in accordance with the laws of this country. He has committed no crime. If he purchased certain clubs, they would have been part of a portfolio, as my father had no interest in places of disrepute. His wife, Helen, was a woman of good character, who myself, Abigail, my sister, and Howard, my younger brother, held in the highest esteem. The charges levelled against her were spurious and took her past lifestyle into account. She loved my father, he loved her. She acted in self-defence and served four years in jail before being acquitted. That acquittal was due to the efforts of James Holden, a believer in the rights of the poor and downtrodden. He arranged her release from jail, the overturning of the original conviction, and her rehabilitation into society.

'The fact that she was in a hotel room with the man when they were both violently murdered does not impact on our fondness for the woman. Why she and James Holden were killed is unknown to me. I was not responsible for issuing a directive to Barry Knox, the manager of the Dixey Club. I knew the man, as I also knew Slater.

'Barry Knox was, and still is, a character of disrepute. I know he had been using the club for prostitution as well as for the sale of drugs. Helen knew this as well, a possible reason for Knox to kill her. I was arrested and brought here in handcuffs. I object to this, and a formal complaint will be lodged. At no time was I planning to leave this country on a permanent basis, and I, as a free citizen, am able to choose my mode of transport as befits my status and my finances. I maintain that I am innocent of any charges levelled against me.'

'Thank you, Mr Adamant,' Isaac said. 'Due to the seriousness of the charges, you will be held while further investigations are conducted.'

Chapter 29

'Not a good interview,' Larry said outside the interview room.

'A disaster,' Isaac said. 'The man's right, our evidence is flimsy, more assumption than fact.'

'You've got thirty-six hours to fix this up, or else Adamant is out of here, and his QC is going to raise the roof,' Goddard said.

Isaac realised he had been premature in bringing Adamant into the station, but there had been no option with the man's impending departure from the country. There was no doubt that he was guilty, but without proof the case against him was going nowhere. Isaac realised that, once again, time was of the essence. He phoned Bridget. 'Fifteen minutes, everyone in the office.'

'Tough day, sir,' Bridget said. She had sensed the frustration in Isaac's voice.

'You're a bit of a hero down at Scotland Yard,' Goddard said after Isaac had ended his call. 'Davies is singing your praises after you wrapped up five murders. Don't stuff it up.'

'Archie Adamant, he's tough. We'll not break him easily,' Isaac said.

'He's got public opinion behind him. Anything other than cast-iron proof is not going to hold up.'

'We'll come up with the proof. The team won't let me down.'

In Homicide, the team sat down. No one would be going home until all avenues had been explored.

'What do we have against Archie Adamant?' Isaac said. 'Apart from Knox and Aberman's ex-wife, do we have anyone else?'

'Gus, the Dixey Club's doorman, and Ugly Pete?'

'Gus had no dealings with the man, and Ugly Pete is a murderer. It will need something decisive and indisputable to ensure a conviction.'

'Abigail Adamant, what do we reckon to her?' Larry said.

'Frivolous, interested in a good time,' Wendy said.

'If Adamant goes down for murder, it's her lifestyle that will be curtailed. She'd not want that,' Isaac said.

'We were there when Slater was shot. He was about to tell us something,' Larry said.

'But why? Whatever he said would have only been to protect himself, place the blame on others. Or maybe he was frightened for his life. Whoever shot him had panicked and seen the danger.'

'Self-protection?'

'Has Slater's office been checked, his clients' files?'

'The man was meticulous,' Bridget said. 'Fraud checked, found nothing untoward. The papers for Aberman's house were there.'

'Wendy, spend time with Aberman's neighbour. Larry and I will stay here with Bridget, see what else we can find,' Isaac said.

***

Wendy found Mrs Hawthorne in a good mood. 'It's her next door.'

'What about her?' Wendy asked.

'Her husband was here last night. They had a terrible argument. I could hear it from my side of the fence.'

Wendy knew that Mrs Hawthorne was just the sort of person a murder investigation needs; the last thing a neighbour wants.

'What was said?'

'I wasn't listening, not particularly.' Wendy knew she was.

'Maybe if we sit down and have a cup of tea,' Wendy suggested.

Knox was languishing in prison, awaiting trial. Adamant was being held at Challis Street, and he was about to walk free, which would only mean trouble. Already the man's QC had been on the phone to DCS Goddard and to Commissioner Davies.

'I only hope you know what you're doing,' Goddard commented to Isaac after he had ended the call from the QC.

Davies's reaction had been more direct. 'Don't let Cook stuff this up.' So much for the honeymoon period, Goddard thought after the commissioner ended the call.

'Mrs Hawthorne, what was the argument about?' Wendy said. Both of the women were sitting comfortably by an imitation wood fire. Wendy was anxious to draw the information out of a woman who was glad of the company.

'She wanted him to stay at the house, he didn't. Something about it being a shrine to a dead man, a man she loved more than him.'

'Is that all?'

'The husband's right. The woman, she fusses around where Mr Aberman's body was found, even erected a little cross.'

Wendy realised the woman didn't only look over the fence, she also had a pair of binoculars. She could sympathise with Aberman's ex-wife.

'What happened with the husband? Did he stay?'

'Not him. He slammed the door hard on his way out and got into his car.'

'The woman?'

'I didn't see her again. She had a visitor later.'

'Do you know who it was?'

'It was Archie.'

'Archie Adamant?' Wendy said. The name had come as a surprise to her. 'I didn't know you knew the Adamants.'

'I don't, not really. Before I retired, I was a teacher at a school not far from here. Very expensive, it was. It was Archie, I'm certain, even though it was twenty, maybe twenty-five years ago. Back then, he was skinny, used to play football for the school team. Now, he's overweight, and no longer attractive.'

'How can you be certain?'

'I always remember my boys. He was a little surly, a bully sometimes, but his academic results were fine, and he was a fine sportsman.'

'We've arrested Archie Adamant for murder,' Wendy said.

'I'm not surprised.'

'Why?'

'I knew his father was successful, although I never met him. The mother would come sometimes, but she died. After that, Archie seemed to spend a lot of time on his own. He used to cheat in the exams.'

'Did you catch him?'

'I saw him do it once, told him I'd report him the next time.'

'Did he stop?'

'Archie? I doubt it, just became more careful. He was always pushing the boundaries.'

'Sneaking young girls into the school? I'm assuming it was boarding.'

'It was, but not Archie. Some of the other boys did. I don't know why as he wasn't a bad-looking boy when he was younger.'

'He's never married,' Wendy said.

'He wasn't gay, or at least, I don't think he was.'

'He wasn't. The man is celibate. What else can you tell me about him?'

'Not much more. I continued for a few years more at the school before retiring. Last night was the first time I'd seen him since.'

Wendy made a phone call to Isaac. 'Archie Adamant's been out to Aberman's house, met with the man's widow.'

'Give me thirty-five minutes, and we'll go and interview her. Is she at home?'

'There's a car in the driveway.'

Wendy turned to Mrs Hawthorne. 'Is she there?'

'She's not been out.'

'She's in the house,' Wendy said to Isaac.

'Make sure she doesn't leave.'

'I'll put my car in her driveway, block her exit.'

'That'll do.'

'The missing piece?' Wendy said.

'I hope so.'

***

Isaac, acutely conscious of the remaining time he could hold Adamant in custody at Challis Street, made the trip to Bray in thirty-two minutes. 'Does she know we're here?' Isaac asked.

'I'm sure she does,' Wendy said.

The two police officers walked down the driveway of Aberman's old house. Wendy knocked on the door.

'Sergeant Gladstone, what do you want?'

'I'm here with DCI Cook. We've a few questions for you.'

'Very well, do come in.'

The three sat in the kitchen. 'It's the warmest place in the house,' the woman said. Wendy thought she was remarkably calm, as if she was making an effort to conceal her true feelings.

'Last night you had a visitor,' Wendy said.

'I had two. My husband, although he did not stay long.'

'Why's that?'

'It's her next door, isn't it?'

'What happened last night should concern you more.'

'My husband has become difficult. He wants to live in London, I want to live here.'

'Is that it?'

'He thinks I'm becoming obsessive about the house, as if it's become a remembrance of Ben.'

'Has it?'

'I can't help remembering the good times we had here, it's only natural, and I certainly don't believe the spirit of the dead man walks the house at night.'

'The room where he died?' Isaac asked.

'My husband planned to make it into a study. If he doesn't want to come here, then I'll find a use for it.'

'Will he come?'

'What option does he have? Both of the houses are in my name. If he wants London, then he can find himself a bedsit.'

'Do you want him to come here?'

'It's up to him. I like it here. He's no Ben, just a man for the cold nights.'

'I've not heard you speak like that before,' Wendy said.

'I'm angry. He's a decent man even if he can be tiresome at times. He'll come, and I'll be glad of his company.'

'Your other visitor interests us more,' Isaac said.

'Archie Adamant.'

'Had you met him before?'

'It was the first time.'

'What did he say?'

'He threatened me. He told me if I said anything it would not be good for me.'

'Should we reconvene at Challis Street Police Station? Do you need legal representation?' Wendy said.

'Why? I've done nothing wrong.'

'On the contrary. We've suspected you for some time. Of all those involved with your husband and his death, you are the only one who has emerged unscathed,' Isaac said. 'Helen Langdon died for what she was going to tell. Slater died for what he knew, and two prostitutes died because they could recognise the murderer, yet you have remained comfortably cocooned.'

'I've nothing to feel guilty about. I was married to a man who became involved with unscrupulous people. It cost him his life.'

'Why did this house remain in your name for all those years, yet it was Helen who looked after the place? Were you party to a conspiracy to conceal the truth? Did you know that your husband was to be killed? And why Archie Adamant?'

'I've told you. He knocked on the door, pushed his way in and threatened me.'

'Threatened you with what? If you're innocent, now is the time to tell us the truth. Archie Adamant is under lock and key. He can do nothing to you at this time.'

'He controls from afar.'

'He controlled through Slater. Barry Knox was the instrument that killed. Both of them can no longer concern you. It is just the police you need to worry about. If you're not forthcoming, we will need to take you to Challis Street and charge you with withholding information. Do you want that?'

'No. I knew my husband had died, not long after his death.'

'Helen phoned you?'

'She told me what had happened and that she had managed to convince Gerald Adamant to leave her with the house to look after.'

'What did you say?'

'What could I say? My husband had fallen foul of people who solved their problems by murder. I didn't want to be another statistic. My life was more precious than that.'

'Your husband?'

'I was sad, but I knew he lived on the edge. His death did not come as a surprise, and we were divorced by then.'

'And you remained in his will as his heir.'

'Ben was a good man, don't let anyone else tell you differently. We were on speaking terms, and there was no bitterness. He wanted his life, I wanted mine. I stayed in Chelsea, and he signed the house over to me. I preferred this house in the country, but he wanted the parties. We agreed, and I always remained in his will.'

'After the divorce, did you see him very much?'

'Rarely, but sometimes we'd meet for a couple of hours.'

'Why did Archie threaten you when everyone else has died? Were you involved with Archie Adamant's father?'

'It was a long time ago. I was divorced, he was on his own.'

'Were you with him when your husband died?'

'Yes. When I heard what had happened, I knew it was Gerald. He never discussed what he did, although I knew. He was a charismatic man, as was Ben. I loved them both, but after what had happened, I left Gerald and found myself a boringly honest man.'

'Do you regret it?'

'I regret nothing. I don't regret Ben or Gerald, and I don't regret marrying a bank manager. Life is what you make of it. Regret for past mistakes and lost opportunities count for nothing.'

'Are you willing to testify against Archie Adamant?'

'What for? What do I know?'

'You know everything,' Isaac said. 'You're playing us for suckers. We've heard about the cross in the garden for your first husband. Is that an act of redemption, to appease your guilt over his death? Did you set up the deal with Adamant to ensure the house would stay with you?'

'No, yes, I don't know.' Wendy knew that Isaac was maintaining the pressure, waiting for the woman to falter.

'Christine Aberman, you've been there all along. Gerald Adamant was smart, staying out of sight, acting as a benefactor of the downtrodden, the weak, the impoverished. And there you are, in league with the man. When did you find out about Helen and Holden?'

'She phoned Knox, Archie told me last night. It was Archie's idea to remove Helen as a threat; he confided in me.'

'Why?'

'His family's name.'

'Slater?'

'That was Archie. You were in his office, and Slater knows what's going on. The police are close to uncovering the truth. Slater's made plenty of money from the Adamants over the years, but he's ready to distance himself, to claim that he was acting on instructions.'

'But he was at the house when Ben Aberman was killed.'

'It was becoming too complicated. Archie was planning to make a run for it. I'm staying here, maintaining a low profile.'

'Why did Archie trust you? Why did Gerald?'

'They both knew a kindred spirit. Archie, he was fond of me, even when I was with his father. He's got this problem, but he could talk to me about it. I was a sympathetic ear, and the Adamants, whatever else they may be, are loyal.'

'You're not loyal to them now?'

'Archie would have turned against me in time. Maybe not this year, but sometime. I'm stopping it now.'

'Will you give us a written statement? Will you testify?'

'Yes. I've killed no one, and the houses are still mine.'

'You won't be seeing them for a long time,' Wendy said.

'A long time, but I will see them one day. That's all that matters. The future, like the past, holds no fears for me.'

Isaac phoned Larry. 'We have the whole story. How did you get on with the gun that killed Slater and his receptionist?'

'We dug up the vegetable patch at Adamant's house. We found a rifle.'

'Forensics?'

'They're checking now. It's the right calibre.'

'How did you know where to look?'

'Instinct. I just thought where I'd hide it.'

'Have you spoken to Adamant?'

'He's admitted to his guilt.'

Isaac phoned Detective Chief Superintendent Goddard who called Commissioner Alwyn Davies. Davies was delighted, singing the praises of the best detective chief inspector in the London Metropolitan Police. Isaac knew he did not mean it.

The End

Murder of a Silent Man

Phillip Strang

Chapter 1

No one gave much credence to the man when he was alive. In fact, most people never knew who he was, although those who had lived in the area for many years recognised the tired-looking and shabbily dressed man as he shuffled along, regular as clockwork on a Thursday at seven in the evening, to the local off-licence. It was always the same: a bottle of whisky, premium brand, and a packet of cigarettes. He paid his money over the counter, took hold of the plastic bag containing his purchases, and then walked back down the road with the same rhythmic shuffle. He said not one word to anyone on the street or in the shop.

Apart from the three-storey mansion where he lived, one of the best residences on one of the best streets in London, with its windows permanently shuttered, no one would have regarded him as anything other than homeless and destitute. Just a harmless eccentric, until the morning when he was found dead in his front garden.

'Never spoken to him, and that's the honest truth,' Jim Porter said. He was a lean man with a pronounced chin, and a strong Cockney accent. 'I've been delivering letters down this street for the last twelve years. Seeing him lying there was the first time I'd ever seen him. Down at the sorting office we called him Ebenezer, no chance of a tip at Christmas, not so much as a thank you. No doubt we shouldn't have, but he's lived in that place for over thirty years, and not one word to my predecessor or me. Weird, if you ask me.'

Detective Chief Inspector Isaac Cook looked at the postman. 'You found the body?' he said. Tall, the son of Jamaican immigrants, and the first in his family to go to university, the first to join the police force, Isaac Cook was an impressive man, as well as a good police officer. Others had told him so, but he was not a man susceptible to flattery, even if he had to admit there was a modicum of truth.

'More by chance. I could see the letterbox was full, the letters no longer going through the slot, and I couldn't take them back with me,' Porter said.

'What do you do when that happens?'

'I can't remember it happening before. Mind you, not many people get letters these days, only bills. I knew about the man inside, so I thought I'd look around, see if I could find a stick or something to push the letters through. Otherwise, he could have been lying there for God knows how long.'

'The lawns are mowed regularly,' Larry Hill, Isaac's detective inspector, said.

'You're right, but it's winter. Once a month would be sufficient. Strange, isn't it?'

'What do you mean?'

'The neglected house, the garden neat and tidy.'

'Is it neglected?'

'I'd say so. I was here once, and I looked through a crack in one of the shutters. There was a single light in the ceiling and some old furniture, decay everywhere. It gave me a cold shiver, almost like one of those horror movies that you see on the television.'

Isaac Cook was not sure about the man. He looked over at the letterbox, noticed that the slot was clear. If the man had found a body, why would he have cleared the letterbox? Isaac decided to say nothing. Once back at Challis Street Police Station, he'd ask Bridget Halloran to check out Jim Porter, the postman, as well as the mansion's owner, Gilbert Lawrence.

***

'Never a word, not Mr Lawrence,' Molly Dempster said. She was a small woman with a slight stoop.

Isaac Cook and Larry Hill were standing in the hallway of her house. The only information they had about the dead man had been a note to Molly, and an invoice in her name with her address as well.

'That's how Mr Lawrence liked it. I'd come in twice a week, iron and press, not that there was much to do. I'd tidy around the few rooms at the back, make him food for the next few days and put it in the fridge.'

'He never spoke?' Isaac asked.

'The last time I heard him speak was over twenty years ago, and then it was only for a couple of minutes.'

'What did he want?'

'A toothache. The man was in agony, and he wanted me to find him a dentist.'

'And you did?'

'I did. But he was generous, at least to me. And you can't understand how good it was to have an employer who never complained, always paid on time.'

'It's still unusual,' Larry Hill said.

'You must have formed an opinion of the man,' Isaac said.

'I've been cleaning for Mr Lawrence for over fifty years. Back when I started, his wife was still here, a lovely woman, although she plastered on the make-up, but always beautifully dressed. Quite the picture she was.'

'She's dead?'

'There were some, gossip mongers, who said he killed her, buried her in the garden, but I don't believe that. I'd seen them together, always loving, never a cross word.'

'Was there an inquiry?'

'One day she disappeared, all her clothes left in the house. Mr Lawrence, he was frantic, and the police dredged the river, organised search parties, put up posters, but nothing.'

'Did they eventually find her?'

'Never. She was a delicate woman, subject to going a little crazy sometimes, but don't we all. Well, not as crazy as her. Two weeks confined to her room, and then she'd be fine. In time, Mr Lawrence came to accept that she had come to some harm due to her craziness, and that was that. And such beautiful children, two of them, although I've not seen them in a long time.'

'We'll check the records,' Isaac said. 'It's before our time.'

'What about the bolted door in the house?' Larry said.

'You've seen how he lives?' Molly Dempster said.

'We've seen it.'

'After Mr Lawrence's wife vanished, he started to become morose. Can't blame him, but before that he had been sociable, and always generous at Christmas. I had a room out the back of the house, above the garage.'

'You were permanent?'

'They needed someone full time.'

'After his wife disappeared?' Isaac said.

'He changed. As though he could never get over it, that close they were. I started to see him less and less, and when I was in one room, he would be in another.'

'Did he go out?'

'Rarely. And then one day…'

'What happened?'

'It was five, maybe six months after Mrs Lawrence had gone. There were men in the house, builders.'

'Doing what?'

'They were installing the bolted door and converting the dining room into a bedroom. There was already a toilet and a small bathroom off to one side of the kitchen. The men were there for five days, and then they left. That was the last time I went past the bolted door.'

'But you still work there.'

'There was a letter on the kitchen sink when I arrived one day. I opened it.'

'What did it say?'

'It was from Mr Lawrence. He thanked me for all that I had done for the family, but he no longer needed a full-time housekeeper, although he needed someone twice a week to clean and tidy up, and to prepare meals for him.'

'Your reaction?'

'Stunned. But what could I say? The man had always been generous to me, and his family were my family. He gave me the address of his solicitor and a time to visit him.'

'You went?'

'Mr Dundas, a stern man, I never liked him. Well, he was polite, asked me to sit down, and made sure I had a cup of tea. Earl Grey, not my favourite.'

It was clear to Isaac and Larry that the woman was glad of the company and wanted to talk. They had a body waiting to be transported to Pathology and a crime scene team at Lawrence's mansion. They wanted to be elsewhere.

'What did Mr Dundas have to say?'

'He was acting under the instructions of Mr Lawrence. I was to be given a house to live in for perpetuity. It was to be furnished to my satisfaction, and I would not be required to pay for anything. Also, I would continue to receive my salary.'

'You accepted?'

'What else could I do? It was all a little strange, but Mr Dundas explained that Mr Lawrence wanted a life of solitude and that he wished to retire from the world. From that day on, I've never paid anything for my house, my salary has been paid weekly, and I've only ever communicated with Mr Lawrence by messages on the kitchen sink.'

'He used to go to the off-licence. You could have seen him there.'

'I never attempted to talk to him, and if I saw him outside the house, I walked the other way.'

'Did anyone visit him?'

'Mr Dundas would come, but it was sporadic. He was in the house three weeks ago.'

***

Back at Gilbert Lawrence's house, the crime scene investigators were still busy. Isaac and Larry arrived back to see the body of the dead man being removed.

'Not much to tell you,' Gordon Windsor, the crime scene examiner, said.

Isaac knew that Windsor would tell him as much as the pathologist, but without the detailed report.

'It's murder, but I suppose that's obvious with a knife protruding from his back.'

'Fatal?' Larry said.

'Not immediately, but the dead man was in his eighties, not in great health. The cold ground would have finished him off.'

'He was reclusive. We've just spoken to the housekeeper.'

'We're checking where he lived. Functional, but not very agreeable. Beautiful building,' Windsor said, looking up from where he was stooped over a broken pot in the garden.

Isaac and Larry had to agree. It was unique for the area in that the mansion was detached and it had a substantial garden.

'There's a couple of cars in the garage, although neither has moved for a long time.'

'What type of cars?'

'Expensive. We've opened the door that was bolted inside the house. Be careful of the dust and the cobwebs when you go in.'

'According to the housekeeper, it's been unused for thirty years,' Isaac said.

'All that money, and mad as a hatter,' Windsor said.

'Was he?'

'What else could he have been. How did he make his money, any idea?'

'We're off to see his solicitor, no doubt he had an accountant. We'll find out, but it appears to be property speculation.'

'We found a filing cabinet inside.'

'We'll need to check it out.'

'We'll leave it where it is for now. Apart from that, the main part of the building hasn't been used, although Lawrence had been in there.'

'Proof?'

'Upstairs, you'd better have a look before you leave.'

Chapter 2

There were not many sights that Isaac and Larry could not deal with, but a dead body propped up in bed, as though it was watching the old television in the corner, was definitely one of the most bizarre.

'My God,' Isaac exclaimed as he entered the room.

Grant Meston, Windsor's number 2, stood to one side. 'Mrs Lawrence, we're assuming,' he said.

'How long?'

'If he bolted the door over thirty years ago, then I'd say she's been here that long.'

'But she's just a skeleton,' Larry said.

'That's what happens to the human body. The hair is still there, so are the teeth, but not a lot of skin. There are relatives, I assume.'

'A son and a daughter. We're contacting them now.'

'How do you tell them that their father has been keeping the dead body of their mother in the house?'

'We've dealt with worse.'

Isaac walked around the bed. There appeared to have been no attempt to clean the body or the bed, not even the room. A lone flower in a vase by the side of the bed was the only sign of any attempt at sanctifying the area, and it had been placed there years before.

'It's a first,' Meston said.

'For all of us. That clarifies whether Gilbert Lawrence was mentally unstable or not.'

'He's been in here,' Meston said. 'Probably not in the room for several months. But outside on the landing, we found his footprints.'

'You'll remove her body?'

'Eventually. The body outside is more important. Mrs Lawrence, what's her history?'

'We're still checking. What we know from the housekeeper is that Mrs Lawrence just upped and vanished one day. Apparently, she had issues. After that, the husband slowly retreated from the world.'

'Makes you wonder, doesn't it?' Meston said.

'Wonder about what?'

'Whether all this money's worth having. Did you see the cars?'

'No. Windsor said they were special.'

'Two vintage Rolls Royces.'

'They're not really important, are they?'

'No. The two bodies are.'

'Then I suggest you concentrate on them,' Isaac said.

'Point taken, DCI.'

'The rest of the house?'

'There has been movement throughout the house, but not much.'

'Gilbert Lawrence?'

'It appears to be only the one person. Any suspects for his death?'

'Not yet.'

***

'My father and mother were very close. Sometimes my brother and I felt left out, not that we were ever badly treated, on the contrary,' Caroline Dickson, née Lawrence, said. Isaac could see that compared to her father's mansion where she lived was smaller, but it was immaculate. The interior walls of the house in Chelsea were lined with paintings, and most of the furniture looked antique.

'It would be better if you took a seat,' Larry said.

A confident and strong-willed woman, Caroline Dickson remained standing. 'I've already been told about my father,' she said.

'Who told you?'

'Molly phoned, the first time in many years.'

'How long since you've seen him?'

'We saw him for a few weeks after our mother disappeared, but then he would walk away from us and lock himself in another room. After that, we haven't seen him since, my brother and I.'

'Not even when he was walking to the off-licence?'

'Once or twice, but it was difficult. I never spoke to him, and I don't think Ralph, my brother, did.'

'Why?'

'Our father was such a dynamic man. You know what he achieved?'

'Property speculation?'

'Speculation is when you played the game, took a chance. With our father, there was no risk-taking. He bought property, fixed it up, and rarely sold it. He was not a man to show off, though.'

'Apart from the mansion and the cars in the garage.'

'He didn't hide his wealth, although he preferred not to talk about it. He had grown up poor, a slum somewhere up north. The mansion was for him and for us. The cars were a childhood passion, not that he ever used them, but they were always polished and ready to go. After so long, no doubt they're not looking so good.'

'We still need you to sit down,' Larry said.

'My father's been murdered. What else is there?'

'Who would want to kill your father?'

'No one that I would know of. Ralph and I will probably inherit, not that it means much to me.'

'Why?'

'Desmond, my husband, is a fine arts dealer, very successful. We have enough money, although I wouldn't mind one of the cars.'

'Why?'

'Desmond's got a thing about vintage cars.'

'Your brother?'

'Ralph's not had it so good. A few failed marriages, a son off the rails, and a couple of businesses that went belly-up.'

'Anything else about him?'

'You'd better ask him. We talk once or twice a year, but Desmond can't stand him. Ralph, unfortunately, is his own worst enemy.'

'Could he have killed your father?'

'He could do with the money, but not Ralph.'

'Sisterly love?'

'The last time we spoke, Ralph was in Spain.'

'He could have flown here.'

'He's in jail.'

'What have you done about it?'

'Nothing. It's not the first time, won't be the last. And each time, he promises to pay us back, but he never does.'

Isaac looked around the room where the three of them were. He could see the affluence, although an art dealer could have the antiques and the paintings on loan. An appearance of wealth did not mean that there was wealth.

It was clear that Caroline Dickson was not going to sit down. Instead, Isaac sat down. 'We've found your mother,' he said.

That was enough to make the woman sit and place her hand across her mouth. 'Where?'

'When was the last time you went inside your father's house?'

'Over thirty years.'

'Your mother is upstairs in the main bedroom. She's been there, we believe, for all that time.'

'We thought she had disappeared, had an accident.'

'Your mother is propped up in her bed.'

'Dead? I suppose that's a silly question.'

'It's not, but yes, she's dead.'

'How?'

'We don't know yet. Pathology will probably give us the answers.'

'Did our father…?'

'Kill your mother? We don't know either. Tell us about the day she disappeared.'

'I want to see her first.'

'It's a crime scene, and your mother has lain in that bed for a very long time.'

'I still have a right to see her.'

'It's highly irregular,' Isaac said.

'Check my records. I'm a qualified doctor. Death holds no fear for me.'

'She's your mother.'

'Will you deny me?'

Isaac called Gordon Windsor at the mansion. 'We've removed her father. If, as you say, she's a doctor, then under the circumstances, we can make an exception,' Windsor said. 'She could have killed her father, you know that.'

'I do.'

At the conclusion of the call, Isaac turned to Caroline Dickson. 'If you're sure?'

'I am.'

***

Nobody said a word on the drive back to Gilbert and Dorothy Lawrence's house. Isaac was in the driver's seat, Larry beside him. In the back of the car, Caroline Dickson with her husband, Desmond. He was holding her hand. Caroline looked impassively forward, her eyes closed. Both of the police officers were unsure about the wisdom of allowing the woman to see the skeletal remains of her mother.

Outside the neglected mansion, Caroline looked up at its foreboding frontage. 'I've not been here for a long time,' she said.

'It's not necessary to do this,' her husband said.

'It is. She's my mother. I always hoped that one day she would walk in the door.'

'You always knew she was dead.'

'Is that true?' Isaac said. He was standing to one side of the woman. In his hands he had coveralls for her to put on, as well as nitrile gloves, overshoes, and a mask.

'What else could I think? She disappears, our father is beside himself, and I'm out there looking for her.'

'Were you still living here then?'

'I was married to Desmond.'

'The house is big enough for you both to have lived here.'

'We weren't, neither was Ralph. I used to come over several times a week, although Ralph never did.'

'Why?'

'My father had little time for him. Ralph had already been married and divorced by then, and he was always after money.'

'Did your father help him?'

'You never knew our father, or you'd not ask that question.'

'What do you mean?'

'We had the best education, and all that was needed to succeed in life. After that, we were on our own. Our father did not believe in children sponging off the parents, no matter how much money they had. He was all into character building, finding your own way in the world.'

'And you?'

'I went to university, studied medicine. I met Desmond while I was studying and we were married. I still practise, three days a week. You can check. You'll find what I've told you to be true.'

'If he believed in his children finding their way, then why will you and your brother inherit?'

'Our mother believed that we should, but our father was circumspect. But he was a great believer in the family, and there's nowhere else he could leave it to. Don't get me wrong. He was a firm but fair father, and I loved him.'

'Your mother?'

'Not as much as my father, but now…'

'We've no proof of death. The room is almost as if it's a shrine to her.'

'Mrs Dickson and one other,' Grant Meston said as he came around the corner.

'I'll go,' Isaac said.

'Very well. Mrs Dickson, you cannot touch the body, is that clear?'

'I've seen dead bodies before.'

'Not like this.'

'Are you sure it's her?'

'Not totally, but the body is in your parents' room. She's dressed in one of her nightdresses.'

Larry stood back, as did Desmond Dickson. 'I could do with a cigarette. This place gives me the creeps,' Dickson said.

'I'll join you. Have you been here before?'

'Once. Gilbert was pleasant. I remember that well enough.'

'His wife?'

'Dorothy, Caroline's mother, was exceedingly gracious. An attractive woman, beautifully dressed. Caroline's not so keen on dressing up to the nines, but her mother was.'

'Ralph Lawrence?'

'Gilbert had no time for him, neither did I. We've not seen him for a few years, and last time, he wasn't looking so good.'

'What do you mean?'

'He'd put on weight, and, as usual, he was only one step ahead of the debt collectors. No money, but it didn't stop him driving a late-model Mercedes, a woman on his arm.'

'What sort of woman?'

'The sort who are impressed by money. Attractive in a tarty way, no doubt a lot of fun.'

Before entering the house, Caroline Dickson was required to sign some forms. After that, a lecture on the procedure to be followed at a crime scene. She nodded her head, said yes and no as appropriate.

The three entered through the back door of the house and moved through the kitchen. 'I'm not so sure now,' Caroline said.

'It's not too late,' Isaac said.

'I want to see her, whatever happens.'

One of the CSEs was standing to one side of the main entrance. An elaborate and vast staircase was on the other side. 'We used to slide down the bannister when we were young.'

'Dangerous?'

'Ralph fell off once and broke his leg. After that, we weren't allowed. Ralph was mischievous. No doubt why we got on so well.'

'Was your father a humorous man?'

'Not father. He thrived on his work ethic. We rarely saw him relax, and he wasn't the sort of parent who'd come and read us a bedtime story.'

'Your mother?'

'She would.'

'Are you sure about this, Mrs Dickson?' Meston said. 'Most relatives have a bad enough time when we conduct a formal identification, but there we've had a chance to make it more congenial.'

'Don't worry, I'll be fine,' Caroline said.

'Is it familiar?'

'Apart from the decay.'

Upstairs, another of the CSEs had strung crime scene tape across the entrance to the door of the main bedroom.

'Anything?' Meston asked the young woman.

'No sign of cause of death.'

Caroline Dickson stood transfixed as she looked into the room. She remembered it when it had been bright and smelt of her mother's perfume. Now it was dark and musty after decades of neglect. 'What about the putrefaction, the pungent smell, the rotting carpet, the sign of insect infestation?' she said.

Isaac looked; the woman was right.

'Your mother was only put there after the process had completed,' Meston said.

'Then where was she?'

'We're checking the cellar now.'

'I want to see.'

'It may help your investigation,' Isaac said to Meston.

'As part of my time at university, I spent a month with a pathologist,' Caroline said. 'There was one murder, an old man who had been shot. I was friendly with the crime scene team. They allowed me to go along.'

'A family member is not the same as an old man you never knew.'

'I know, and I'm sick to my stomach. What went on here? What had my father done? And what about my mother? It's as if my whole belief system has been destroyed.'

'It's not confirmed as murder yet.'

'My father is, though. Why kill him?'

'Because of your mother?'

'But who knew? We never did.'

***

'My father's wine cellar. Also, the boiler for the hot water used to be down here,' Caroline said.

A wooden staircase led down – it creaked. At the bottom, the crime scene team had set up a floodlight, which gave an eerie glow throughout the cavernous area. On either side, a row of wine racks. 'Some of the wines are worth a lot of money,' Caroline said. 'My brother and I used to sneak down here and help ourselves to a bottle occasionally.'

'Your father?'

'He knew, but he never said anything, as long as we didn't take the vintage wines.'

From one end of the basement, 'Over here,' one of the CSIs said.

The three visitors walked over to where the man was standing. 'What is it?' Meston said.

'The soil's been disturbed here. A long time ago, but we believe this is where the body was.'

'That doesn't make sense,' Caroline said. 'We searched the house for days afterwards.'

'Did you?' Isaac said.

'We weren't professionals.'

'It depends what happened. It's possible your mother died elsewhere. Would you suspect your father of killing your mother?'

'No. They were devoted.'

'We'll follow through,' Meston said. 'It's a cold case at the present time. Your father is more immediate.'

'It will be nice to give our mother a proper burial. I can never believe that my father acted other than honourably towards my mother.'

'It's best that way,' Isaac said. If, as appeared to be the case, Gilbert Lawrence had been the only person in the closed-off part of the house since the door was bolted, it did not bode well for the man.

Chapter 3

Emma Lawrence arrived at Challis Street Police Station two days after her brother, Gilbert, had died. It was early morning, and it was raining heavily. 'I demand to see someone,' she said.

'Miss Lawrence, finally,' Isaac said as he met her at reception.

'Why wasn't I informed?'

'We had no idea where you were.'

'I am in the phone book. And besides, you're the police. You should have been able to find me.'

'We had three addresses for you from Caroline Dickson, plus a couple of phone numbers. We checked them all.'

Isaac knew the woman to be seventy-nine, and not close to her brother. She had also remained elusive for some years, not that anyone had gone looking for her. She was colourfully dressed, not like her brother who had adopted drab and dreary as his fashion statement. Lawrence's body was with Pathology, and so far, there was nothing more than the usual. A knife wound in the back, heart failure coupled with blood loss, exposure to the cold weather.

Emma Lawrence, an articulate woman, even if her repetitions about why she hadn't been contacted were annoying, was someone that Homicide had wanted to meet. She was of the same generation as Gilbert and Dorothy Lawrence, and her knowledge of the pair could well be more useful.

Wendy Gladstone, Isaac Cook's sergeant, and in her fifties, could sympathise with the old woman who walked with the aid of a stick, the effects of arthritis. Wendy instinctively liked a woman who still maintained a resilience about her, a woman who did not allow age or infirmity to impede her any more than necessary. It was Wendy who put her close to a heater and gave her a hot mug of tea.

Once Emma Lawrence was settled, Isaac and Wendy questioned her about her brother and his wife.

'I'm sad that he's dead, even though we have not seen each other for many years,' Miss Lawrence said.

'Is there any reason why not?' Isaac asked.

'As children, Gilbert was always intense, always wanting more, not wanting to share.'

'And you?'

'I was easier going, more like my mother. That's why I embraced the hippy movement, an original flower child, even if I was older than most.'

'Free love,' Wendy said.

'Plenty of that back then. Alas, nowadays nothing is free, and as for love, that's a faded memory.'

'You're still active for your age.'

'That's as maybe, but life has a finality. Soon, I'll be reunited with Gilbert and his wife. Then we can get back to what we did best.'

'And what's that?'

'Arguing.'

'Is that why you hadn't seen him for so long?'

'A stupid dispute over our father's inheritance.'

'Did your father have money?'

'Not as much as Gilbert, but we were wealthy. Our father owned an engineering firm, and we lived well. When he died, the money was to be divided between the two of us.'

'And there was a dispute?'

'Isn't there always?'

'Not always, but money often causes conflict.'

'Our father divided his assets between Gilbert and me, fifty-fifty. Our mother had passed away by then. Gilbert reneged on the agreement, only paid me a quarter.'

'Any reason why?'

'I was irresponsible. He was right, of course. I was always falling in love, always falling out. I had racked up an appreciable debt by then, and Gilbert had always bailed me out.'

'Why not your father?'

'We weren't talking when he died. I was close to Gilbert, even if we quarrelled, and he'd complain, but he always helped.'

'I take it that it changed,' Isaac said.

'He changed when he took control of our father's money. Up until then, Gilbert had been buying properties, renovating them and then selling. He was doing well, but once he had the cash injection from our father, he became a different man. Always arguing the cost of everything, checking that nothing was wasted. No throwing out a pot of jam or honey unless it was licked clean.'

'Licked?'

'You know what I mean. The man became a skinflint.'

'Dorothy, your sister-in-law?'

'It was remarkable. Gilbert met her two years after our father died. She was working in an estate agent's office. For whatever reason, my brother fell for her, she for him. They were married within months, and then Ralph and Caroline came along.'

'Did you go to the wedding?'

'I did, not that I could forgive Gilbert.'

'Did you need money from him?'

'Not any more. At that time, I had embraced minimalism, and I was living in a commune. Gilbert didn't approve, and he knew even if he helped, that I'd give it to them.'

'Was he right?'

'Yes. It was silly really, and now I live on my own in a modest flat. Don't get me wrong, I'm not complaining. I have all I need, and I don't need any of Gilbert's money.'

'No reason to wish him dead?'

'What for?'

'Tell us about Dorothy,' Wendy said.

'They worshipped each other and the children. With them, Gilbert was generous and made sure they had everything they wanted. You've seen the house, met Caroline.'

'How do you know we've met her?'

'I read about Gilbert in the newspaper. I phoned her.'

'You've had no contact with your brother for nearly thirty years, yet you knew how to contact Caroline.'

'Why not? And besides, I always met with Dorothy once a year on my birthday. It was our little secret. She was devoted to Gilbert, but she never told him about us.'

'Why was that?'

'I'm not sure. The reasons that separated Gilbert and me were never spoken about. I suppose we just drifted apart. Caroline contacted me a few years ago, and we'd meet occasionally. A lovely woman, similar to Dorothy, although Ralph hasn't turned out too well.'

'How much do you know about your brother's death?'

'I know about Dorothy upstairs in the house. Did Gilbert kill her?'

'Why? Should he have?'

'I'm not talking murder, but Dorothy, she would have these periods where she'd go a little crazy.'

'What can you tell us?'

'Manic-depressive. Not that it happened often, and very few knew outside of the house. Gilbert gave her the best medical treatment that money could buy, and after a few weeks, she'd be fine again. I know she never left the house during those times. That's why there were shutters on every window, to keep her isolated from the influences outside, to keep people from peering.'

'A virtual prisoner?' Wendy said.

'In her own home? I don't think so. If she had been in a hospital, it would have been a straitjacket and isolation.'

'She could be violent?'

'Very. Whenever it happened, Ralph and Caroline would go and stay with friends. They may have known, but probably not the full story.'

'But you did?'

'Dorothy told me everything. The darkness she felt, the despair, the need to lash out or to sit and cry for hours. We became very close.'

'Yet you never spoke to your brother.'

'Never. I don't know if he knew that Dorothy was meeting me, although he may have. Regardless, he never interfered. She could have flung herself down the stairs, broken her neck.'

'Do you know this is what happened?'

'I don't know what killed her. The only certainty is that my brother is not responsible.'

'Let us go back to when Dorothy disappeared,' Wendy said. 'What do you remember?'

'I remember trying to contact Gilbert, but he wouldn't talk to me. I spoke to the housekeeper.'

'Molly Dempster?'

'That was it. She said that Gilbert did not want to have any contact with me.'

'Were you surprised by his reaction?'

'Not really. Gilbert was always a private man, and if Dorothy had disappeared, then he would deal with it himself.'

'She could have been kidnapped, murdered.'

'Molly said she hadn't and my brother was convinced she had had one of her turns and would not be coming back.'

'How could he be so sure?'

'It's too late to ask him now.'

'Are you sad that he's died?'

'I would like to have become friends with him again. To have sat down and reminisced. We had a shared history, a devotion to Dorothy.'

'Are you surprised that he kept her upstairs in the bedroom?'

'He would not have wanted to be parted from her. He was a decent man, even though he had treated me poorly over the years. I had seen him walking out in the street once or twice, but he seemed a broken man. I suppose having his dead wife upstairs in that house for all those years must have driven him crazy.'

'He never spoke one word to anyone, apart from his solicitor.'

'Leonard Dundas. He'll know more than me.'

***

Detective Chief Superintendent Richard Goddard, never far from Homicide when there was a murder, sat in Isaac's office. 'Tough one, the corpse upstairs,' he said. He was a good man, even a friend, but he always seemed to come when Isaac was rushing out of the door.

'We're going back to the house,' Isaac said, more by way of a hint than anything else. Although he had to admit that having Goddard back in charge was preferable to when Superintendent Caddick had been in Goddard's office, and causing trouble with his incessant demand for reports, and his constant incompetent interfering. The man was now consigned out of London, far enough to no longer be a nuisance.

'Macabre.'

'It's out of the ordinary, although Gilbert Lawrence is our priority.'

'It could be related.'

'Only if someone else knew what was upstairs, and if the husband had killed her.'

'Speculation, but it's worth considering. Any suspects?'

Isaac had expected the inevitable question. The chief superintendent was always looking for a quick arrest, but so far there were no clues that led to a killer of Gilbert, no indication that anyone else had been involved with preserving the body of a long-dead woman.

Once free of the superintendent, Isaac and Larry Hill drove over to the Lawrence house. On arrival they walked over to where Gordon Windsor was standing. This time, the man was on the footpath outside the home, coveralls were not required.

'We're convinced that Gilbert Lawrence buried his wife in the cellar for a few years. Once she had decomposed, he cleaned the bones and any loose skin with dermestid beetles,' Windsor said.

'What are they?'

'Skin beetles. Taxidermists, museums, hunters, use them to clean the flesh off a body. They'll only eat dead flesh. It takes time, and he would have had to buy them. We found a tank that he had used.'

'By why clean the bones? The woman's dead. Surely he'd want to see some semblance of her?'

'How would I know? The man's disturbed. He can't bear to be parted from her, but if she was left to decay on her own, can you imagine the insects, the putrefaction, the smell?'

'Okay, we'll accept that the man had lost it, mentally that is, but what does this tell us about how the woman died?'

'It doesn't, not yet. We're taking what remains to Pathology today. Give them a few days, more than the two hours you normally do, and maybe they'll come up with something.'

Isaac knew Windsor was right. As the senior investigating officer, an arrest and a conviction always looked good on his CV. The only problem was that the last three murder cases his department had investigated had extended, not only in time but also in the number of deaths. The current investigation had all the hallmarks of being another one. And what did they have: a body, no more than a skeleton, a body in the garden with a knife in its back, a family at war, although it was more of an uneasy truce. Isaac hoped he was wrong in his summation, but he was sure he was not.

Wendy had liked Emma Lawrence, an elderly woman with a healthy outlook on life, a woman who had embraced the flower generation, free love, and no doubt transcendental meditation and a few drugs not on prescription. Regardless, she still looked sprightly, more so than Wendy, and she knew it.

Caddick, when he had temporarily occupied Goddard's seat, had been desperate to get Wendy out of Homicide by way of a rigorous medical, showing that she could no longer keep up with the workload. Wendy knew it was rubbish, using whatever he could to get rid of her.

She didn't need to be able to run a hundred yards in under twenty seconds, and she didn't need to be able to scale a wall in one bound. But Caddick had been desperate to undermine Isaac's support mechanism of loyal staff: Bridget Halloran, the lead admin person in Homicide, Wendy Gladstone, who had known Isaac longer than anyone, even from when he had been on the beat in uniform, and then there was Detective Inspector Larry Hill. He had handled himself well on an earlier murder investigation, and Chief Superintendent Goddard had brought him across to Challis Street at Isaac's request.

'There would still have been some smell during the process,' Larry said to Windsor outside Lawrence's house.

'Contained, at least within the house,' Windsor said. 'No idea how the housekeeper could have avoided catching a whiff occasionally. Lawrence had done it well, almost professional. Burying the body in the cellar. In time, the body could be removed, and placed in with the beetles. It's all a bit weird for me, but who knows how the man thought. Apparently, he was into real estate,' Windsor said.

'A lot of it, from what we're told. Bridget's doing the research, and we're on our way to meet with the solicitor. No idea about him, but it appears that he was the only one who spoke to Gilbert Lawrence.'

Chapter 4

Leonard Dundas occupied a suite of offices in Pimlico. Isaac had to admit that he was impressed. But then, it was Pimlico, he thought, and definitely upmarket and costly.

'Can I help you?' a young woman asked. She was sitting behind a glass-topped reception desk. It looked expensive. In fact, the whole office did, what with its leather chairs in reception, the open plan office, a man watering the plants around the place.

'Mr Dundas, he's expecting us. DCI Cook, DI Hill, Challis Street Homicide,' Isaac said.

'It's a shame about Mr Lawrence,' the woman said.

'You knew him?'

'As good as. He was our only client.'

'You must have thirty people here.'

'Thirty-four. One's off sick, and another two are out on business. I'll let Mr Dundas know you're here.'

Isaac and Larry made themselves comfortable, but not for long. An elderly man came into reception. He was wearing a suit, his greying hair parted in the middle, a sullen expression.

'Tragic about Gilbert,' he said.

'Mr Dundas?' Isaac said.

'Yes, of course. My apologies. Mr Lawrence's death has thrown us all out of kilter.'

'We're told he was your only client.'

'He was, but that's not surprising. You're aware of his substantial holdings?'

'Not in detail. We're researching them now.'

'Not all of them are in this country. He was a canny man, purchased when the market was low, never sold, or rarely. There's more money in having the properties rented out than buying and selling. The costs only multiply, stamp duty, taxes. I'm sure you know how it is.'

Isaac didn't, as he still had his flat in Willesden, and he had no intention of moving. Larry did, as his wife was determined to buy somewhere larger. The only problem was that she could only envisage the furniture that she would need to buy, the colour of the curtains, the marble-topped counters in the kitchen. She did not consider what Dundas had just mentioned: the hidden costs, the removal company, the increased payment on the mortgage, the solicitor's fees. He knew she would not stop talking about the move, and he knew that without promotion he would struggle with the payments.

'What do you plan to do now?' Isaac asked.

'For me, I'm past my retirement age. I only stayed on with the firm because of Gilbert. My daughter is the junior partner. She looks after the day-to-day operations.'

'What can you tell us about Gilbert Lawrence?'

'Where to start? He was a brilliant man, although after Dorothy died, he changed, so much so that I barely recognised him towards the end.'

'But you met with him. We're assuming he spoke to you.'

'He did, but only in truncated sentences, as he would have a prepared list of actions to follow. I would give him a report, the template we had agreed on many years ago. Our conversations were normally short, no more than a few sentences spoken by either, no mention of the weather, or the family.'

'Are you saying he never asked after his family?'

'Never. Howard Hughes syndrome some would call it, although with Gilbert it wasn't a fear of germs, but the loss of his wife.'

'You're aware of what was in the house?'

'I am now. What can I say? I never went into the main part of the house, never through that door with its bolt.'

'Where did you meet him?'

'In the kitchen. He made sure that the back door was bolted and the blinds were down. He didn't want Molly Dempster to come in.'

'But he kept her on.'

'She had been with the family for a long time. As far as he was concerned, she was the only person he could trust.'

'And you?'

'He didn't trust me. He needed me, and he knew what I did, and how much I should charge. He also entrusted me with buying property for him.'

'Easy to cheat?'

'You can see the office here. He paid for it, the renovations, everything. The man has made me rich. Why would I have cheated him?'

'And now?'

'I have his will and his power of attorney. In the meantime, his empire needs to be tended, and in time sold off, or passed on to those who inherit.'

'Are you able to tell us the contents of his will?' Larry asked.

'Not at this time. It is sealed in a bank vault, duly witnessed. I will read it out to his family and other interested parties in due course. You have to remember that Gilbert, regardless of how he lived, was not a fool. He had amassed over two hundred and thirty properties around the world: shopping centres, office blocks, residential and commercial. We have in this office the deeds to over two billion pounds worth of real estate. He was a tough negotiator, a tough landlord. Such men make enemies, even within their own family.'

'Ralph and Caroline, his children?'

'Ralph was a disappointment, although he would not be capable of murder.'

'Why not?'

'The man would rather scrounge off others. He's a charismatic man, managed to charm a few women out of their savings. But murder, not Ralph.'

'Caroline?'

'She would be capable, but unlikely. She has a good life, and her husband is doing well.'

'Well enough? There are hundreds of millions of pounds at stake here. Irresistible to a lot of people.'

'Not so easy to get hold of. There are overseas trusts, offshore accounts, umbrella companies. Unravelling those, if we have to, will take a long time. We, as a company, will be fully occupied with Gilbert Lawrence for many years.'

'His death doesn't appear to concern you?'

'It does. The man was a friend, even before his wife died, even after he became a recluse.'

'He had what he wanted, his wife with him.'

'Is it related to his death?'

'We don't know. We had hoped you could enlighten us.'

'Not me,' Dundas said. 'I never went in there. The first I knew, the first any of us knew, was when your people found her. She was an attractive woman when she was alive. I suppose she isn't now?'

'Unrecognisable.'

***

'DCI Isaac Cook, what took you so long?' Graham Picket, the pathologist, said. To Isaac, it was a muted welcome, in that the man was usually more vocal when he and Larry walked into Pathology.

'I thought you'd appreciate some more time with Mrs Lawrence.'

'Rubbish. You were busy elsewhere. Otherwise, I would have been chasing you out of here.'

'Maybe. What do you have?'

'Female. No sign of major trauma. From what I can see the woman died of natural causes, although with just a skeleton, it's not possible to be conclusive. No sign of a bullet or a knife or a blunt weapon on the bones.'

'Is that all you can tell us?'

'You've given me nothing to work with. We've confirmed that it's Dorothy Lawrence. Dental records, a DNA swab from the daughter. Apart from that, there's nothing more. The only way you'll know what happened is if the husband wrote it down somewhere.'

The result from Pathology was not unexpected, and the woman's death was not the primary consideration, Gilbert Lawrence was. The two police officers returned to Homicide. It was time for a meeting with the team.

'What about the son?' Isaac asked. It was the first time he had sat down in his office for some time. Wendy Gladstone was in the office, as were Larry Hill and Bridget Halloran.

'Ralph Lawrence has a history of failed businesses, broken marriages, and a troubled son along the way,' Bridget said. Office-bound, and glad of it, she was the person who could find her way around a search engine. Isaac had asked her to put together a profile of Gilbert Lawrence, a dossier on him and his family. 'Ralph Lawrence is in Spain, speculative real estate sales to English tourists. I contacted the local police there, and the man's been released from jail on the understanding that he leaves the country immediately.'

'To where?'

'London. I assumed you would want to talk to him.'

'Is he being picked up?'

'He is. I've organised someone from the station.'

That's what Isaac liked about his team, always thinking ahead, taking the initiative. And yes, Ralph was a person of interest, although if, as it seemed, he was in Spain, he could not be the murderer.

'What else?' Larry said. He was standing, his usual pose. Both Wendy and Bridget were sitting down.

'You and DCI Cook have met with Leonard Dundas. Is he providing you with a list of Lawrence's assets?'

'He is, but we would rather hear it from you. Dundas will be considering what to tell us, and what not to.'

'Very well,' Bridget said. 'This is what we have. Gilbert Lawrence, eighty-two years of age. He purchased his first property when he was nineteen, a small studio flat in Clapham. Nothing special and it was rented out. By the time of his twenty-fifth birthday, he had sixty-three properties throughout London. Some were shops, others were offices, although the majority were residential. From what I can gather, he was cutting a swathe through London, and I've found newspaper articles showing the young property magnate. Their words, not mine. He had met and married his wife when he was twenty-two, purchased the house where he died when he was twenty-nine. Before that, it had been converted into flats. He had it renovated, and Dorothy decorated it. It featured in a couple of magazines at the time. I've included copies of what it looked like back then, although I suppose it looks vastly different now.'

Larry looked at the magazine article. 'It does,' he said.

'Any history on Dorothy Lawrence?' Isaac asked.

'If you're referring to her bouts of madness, there's very little. She was born in the north of the country, went to school there. I've managed to obtain a birth certificate. After her marriage to Gilbert, two children, Caroline and Ralph. You've met one, the other is due in the next few hours. I'm checking with the private hospitals around the country that deal with people who have her condition.'

'Why private?'

'Gilbert Lawrence was a private man. He would not have wanted any more people than necessary to know if his wife was ill.'

'She could always have been signed in under a false name.'

'How many properties did Dundas tell you about?' Bridget said.

'Over two hundred.'

'I've found close to one hundred and fifty through companies that are registered in his name or companies that he controls in the UK. The other properties may be overseas or hidden from view. Also, in the thirty years that he remained reclusive, he has expanded his empire considerably. He may have retreated from the world, but he continued to make money.'

'Which means that whatever the reason he decided to hide in that house with his dead wife, he was still mentally astute.'

'It makes you wonder what makes people tick,' Larry said.

'Or how they can form enemies who want to kill them.'

'That makes no sense. Gilbert Lawrence spoke to no one, offended no one, and he didn't get involved with his son and daughter, and yet he's killed. The man was old and frail. He couldn't have lasted much longer anyway.'

'Long enough if you're to inherit.'

'Ralph?'

'Or Caroline. And what about Ralph's son?' Isaac said. 'Where is he?'

'The last we have on him is an arrest for drug possession six months ago. After that, nothing.'

'Wendy,' Isaac said.

'Leave him to me.'

'What about Gilbert and Dorothy's daughter?'

'Caroline married Desmond Dickson thirty-three years ago.'

'Were Gilbert and Dorothy at the wedding?'

'It's in the files I've given to all of you. Yes, they were. It's also the last record I can find of Dorothy.'

Larry studied the newspaper article. 'The two Rolls Royces in the garage,' he said. 'They were used at the wedding.'

'Caroline and Desmond Dickson have two children,' Isaac said. 'What do we know about them?'

'Both are employed, steady jobs. The daughter is married with a child under one. The son is single. Neither has been in trouble with the law.'

'And Desmond Dickson?'

'A fine arts dealer, well respected. We've nothing against him.'

'Statistically, it's a family member or someone Gilbert knew,' Isaac said.

'Ralph or his son. They're the most likely,' Wendy said.

'The most obvious, although Ralph wasn't in the country, and the grandson is a junkie.'

Chapter 5

Wendy Gladstone, from when she had been a constable in the north of England finding child runaways to tracking down persons of interest in a murder investigation in London, had an enviable reputation. Her skill, she knew, honed over the years, was to adopt the mindset of those she was looking for. A rich person is not about to hide in a derelict property, a drug addict is not likely to check into a five-star hotel.

Ralph's son Michael, Wendy knew, was dossing down somewhere with his addicted friends, sharing needles, and whatever food they could scrounge or steal. And he was not likely to be close to his grandfather's house, the area too upmarket for derelict properties, or squatters.

Of more immediate importance was that Ralph Lawrence had arrived in London on a flight from Barcelona, and he had failed to meet up with the constable sent from Challis Street to pick him up at Heathrow. He, Wendy thought, would be easier to find.

From what they knew, Ralph Lawrence was a man who appreciated the finer things in life, regardless of whether he could afford them, or whether they belonged to someone else. He would either be at a friend's house if he had not outstayed his welcome on previous occasions, or he would have checked in under a false name at a quality hotel, enjoying the minibar and the restaurant, using an invalid credit card if needed. He was a slippery character, everyone in the department knew, although his criminal record had amounted to no more than passing false cheques in his teens. Since then, some investigations into the fraudulent use of credit cards overseas, unpaid hotel bills, and a litany of other misdemeanours, although none had been substantiated.

The upside was that Ralph had no record, except for a miserable credit rating. The downside was that he could not be escorted off the plane at Heathrow. He had left Spain as an undesirable, but in England, he was English, and he was free.

Bridget was assigned the task of checking with the other police stations in London, contacting the homeless agencies and other charities, in the hope of locating Michael Lawrence. As with Ralph, he was a person of interest only. No one in Homicide felt that he was responsible for the death of Gilbert Lawrence. Whoever had killed the old man had been careful to leave no incriminating evidence. Apart from a smudged fingerprint on the knife, the only other evidence at the scene was a crushed plant in the garden where the murderer had placed his boot, and a trace of blood on the gate handle as he exited the property. The blood had been found to be that of Gilbert Lawrence. Another trace of blood had been discovered ten yards south down the street. The traffic camera mounted on the corner of the road had failed to identify the individual, as the area was busy at the approximate time of the man's death, and besides, what were they looking for? Was it a man or a woman, tall, short, fat, thin? Did they have on a coat or not, and what about their age? The reality was that Isaac and his team had very little.

And the woman upstairs had apparently died of natural causes, although that did not obviate her being poisoned, a skeleton unable to reveal that possibility.

'It's the inheritance,' Isaac said. In the office, Larry Hill and Chief Superintendent Goddard, his uniform proudly worn.

'It's for the presentation of a gallantry medal to the constable who was shot when he was protecting a woman from an irate husband,' the chief superintendent said.

Anything to promote himself, Isaac thought. Goddard was looking to take over Counter Terrorism Command when the time was right, although that wasn't likely to happen as long as Alwyn Davies was the commissioner of the London Metropolitan Police, and the man wasn't in a hurry to vacate his post.

Davies, the man who was going to reform the Met, bring it into the twenty-first century, but instead had proven himself to be an adroit political animal, had done little in the way of reformation, more in demoralising. At least that was the opinion of Isaac and Goddard, although there were others who had prospered.

'No chance of an early arrest?' Goddard said.

'Not yet. We've not got a motive for the murder. Sure, the man had money, but not in the house, and no one's gained anything yet. Once the man's last will and testament is read, we'll have a better idea.'

'And when's that?'

'Tomorrow. The family will be gathering at Leonard Dundas's office at ten in the morning. I'll be in Dundas's office, although I'll probably not be at the reading. However, I will be given a copy afterwards.'

'Not all the family will be there,' Goddard said.

'Ralph probably won't be. The father may not have liked him, but he's probably included in the will somewhere.'

'No guarantees. It would help if you were in when the will is read.'

'Outside will be fine. I'll see the people as they come out from Dundas's office.'

***

Ralph Lawrence prowled up and down in his hotel room in Kensington. It had cost plenty, more than he could afford, but what did it matter. He would either pay for it with one of the cards he possessed or he wouldn't. He knew that his return to England, not that he had any option, was a necessary risk, and there were some people not far away who wanted money in cash, and he could not pay. And he knew how they dealt with those who crossed them.

'One month from now you will be in here, or we will find you,' they had said. And now he was back in their part of the world, and he still remembered the man with his shattered kneecaps groaning in agony, their idea of a warning.

'Just so you don't forget, take a close look at him,' one of the three had said. Criminal nobility, that was what Ralph Lawrence knew their lead man to be.

If only I hadn't tried to cheat those men in Spain. How was I to know that the British tourists, a sweet and gullible husband and wife team, were part of a sting to trap me? Ralph Lawrence thought in a moment of introspection.

And now he was in England, and the repayment to the man and his thugs could not be avoided. He knew being here was a risk, but his father's death had been providence from heaven. A chance for the miserable old skinflint of a father to pay for all the suffering he had caused him, and as for the others, his son, his sister and her husband, what did they matter. Once the gangsters had been paid off, he was going straight, straight from Heathrow and back out to where it was warm, to purchase himself a good house, a good car, and find himself a willing woman. Ralph Lawrence was not a vain man; he knew that he had the gift of the gab, and this time, he would not need to pretend with the woman. This time he would be rich.

***

Molly Dempster, for the first time in her adult life, found herself without a routine. She did not like it, having been used to her twice-weekly visits to the Lawrence mansion. She did not know why she had been invited to the office of Leonard Dundas on the following day. She knew it had to be important, but she had never asked for anything from her employers and had never once been tempted to take anything from the house: not a bar of soap, nor washing up liquid, nor even some money occasionally. All that she purchased for the home she accounted for in her neat and meticulous handwriting. She felt great sorrow for the man who had died, even sadness for a woman who had died decades before. She could only imagine the anguish that her husband must have gone through. If she had known, she would have made an effort to soothe the man.

Caroline, she knew, was a compassionate woman. She'd ask her tomorrow at Dundas's for three months to move out of the house that Gilbert Lawrence had let her live in. She had saved some money and could afford to pay the rent for a while. After that, she could live with her sister, though she didn't want to. Molly knew that as much as she loved her sister, the woman could drive her mad with her untidiness, her need to smoke in the house. Gilbert's death had signalled to Molly the closing of her life, and all she could do was resign herself to the inevitable. She sat down again on the kitchen chair and shed a tear, not only for Gilbert and Dorothy but for herself.

Chapter 6

An auspicious occasion, the reading of the last will and testament of Gilbert Aloysius Lawrence: recluse, property magnate.

Isaac knew that the accolade of philanthropist would not be used in any obituary, not even at the man's funeral, as he had never given much to anyone outside of his family, and only to charity when it came with a sizeable reduction in tax.

Bridget, in the office, had checked back for any press cuttings in the last thirty years and had found very little. The name of Lawrence had appeared in the financial sections of the newspapers from time to time, but apart from that, there was not much of interest.

Ralph Lawrence had more column inches devoted to him, due to his behaviour in his teens, starting with drunken and loutish and culminating in appearing in court on a charge of passing fake cheques.

As Bridget had said to Isaac, the man's a habitual conman, no perceivable morals, good or bad, a rotten egg as her father would have said. All that could be found about Caroline Dickson, née Lawrence, were the details of her wedding, as well as a photo.

Isaac sat in the reception area of Leonard Dundas's office; he was early. The young woman at reception had given him a coffee and a magazine to read, although those coming in through the door were of more interest. Jill Dundas, Leonard's daughter, came over and introduced herself. Isaac found her to be polite, but not friendly, purely professional. He judged her to be in her forties. She was wearing a dark blue jacket with matching trousers, a white blouse. If her look was anything to go by, she was a worthy person to take over from her father, Leonard, who had come into the office looking tired, more so than the first time Isaac had met him.

'It's a nightmare,' Leonard Dundas said. 'When Gilbert was alive, he kept his finger on the pulse. But now, his death has left a lot of people anxious.'

'What sort of people?'

'Tenants, lending institutions, overseas banks.'

'Why? Surely everything is secured.'

'Secured, yes, but people are people, they panic. And besides, what's to worry about? Gilbert was solvent, and no lease agreements have been impacted.'

'Was Lawrence still buying?'

'He never stopped.'

'New instructions?'

'It depends who inherits.'

'Ralph gave us the slip at Heathrow. We're trying to find him and his son,' Isaac said.

Caroline Dickson entered the office, nodded at Isaac. Her husband accompanied her, as did Emma, Gilbert's sister. Molly Dempster came in looking a little unsure of the surroundings. The receptionist gave her a cup of tea, and showed her where to go, and ensured she was seated comfortably. Isaac could see through the open door that Caroline gave the housekeeper a brief hug.

The door to where Dundas was to read the will closed soon after. Isaac strained to listen but could hear nothing. A man walked into the solicitor's office. He was puffing, and he looked as though he had had a rough night. Isaac knew that he was face-to-face with Ralph Lawrence.

'Where's the meeting?' Ralph said to the receptionist.

'Your name?'

'Ralph Lawrence. Sorry for being late, traffic.'

'I'm Detective Chief Inspector Cook,' Isaac said, standing up to introduce himself. 'We missed you at Heathrow.'

'You didn't miss me. I missed you. Subtle difference.'

'There are some questions we have for you.'

'After we've dealt with finding out who my father has given his money to. He was a difficult man, we never got on, although I suppose you know that. And my mother upstairs in the house. I thought he was smarter than that. Did he kill her?'

'Not that we can prove. Is there any reason he would have?'

'None that I can think of. I liked him when we were young, but then he became remote, thought that throwing money at our education, paying for overseas trips, was the solution.'

'Challis Street Police Station after the reading, okay?'

'As long as he hasn't given it all to the Battersea Dogs Home, that'll be fine.'

Ralph Lawrence rushed away, entering through the door into the room where the rest of the family, as well as Molly Dempster, sat. Isaac craned his neck to see the reaction of the others but could see little. The one man who had remained elusive, the one man that his family had not wanted to see, and for whom Wendy had been searching, had walked into the solicitor's office.

Isaac took his phone out of his pocket. 'Wendy, Ralph is at Dundas's. Get down here, take a good look at him, and make sure he doesn't give us the slip again.'

***

Leonard Dundas rose to speak. The others in the room held their breath, looked nervously around them, all except Molly who sipped her tea. She would have admitted to being baffled as to why she was there, and what was being said. She had an aunt who had left her a teapot once when she had died, but the handle had fallen off long ago, and all she received from her parents, who had been as poor as church mice, was a demand from the council to pay the electricity or it would be cut off.

And there in that room was Ralph, looking much older than the last time she had seen him, vaguely smelling of aftershave and alcohol.

Such an attractive young man, she remembered, always trying to sneak a girl into the house, never getting past his father, but he had charmed Molly as well as the girls, and if the coast was clear, she had turned the occasional blind eye – not that she approved. She was strict Presbyterian, and they didn't do such things, not before marriage. Not that it stopped a few in the congregation, she knew that.

Caroline sat on the other side of the room. She was clutching her husband's hand, hard.

I, Gilbert Aloysius Lawrence, presently of 47 Atherton Street, Kensington, London, England, hereby revoke all former testamentary dispositions made by me and declare this to be my last will.

Those present listened as the preliminary declarations were made, and the nomination of Leonard Dundas as the man's executor. In the event of his being unable to complete his duties, then Jill Dundas was to take the role of executor. Caroline Dickson and Ralph Lawrence waited for the distribution of the estate. The fact that their father's solicitor had been nominated as the executor concerned Caroline, not so much Ralph, as long as he received his fair share.

To Molly Dempster, a person who has shown great loyalty to the family, I extend my thanks.

The housekeeper looked up when her name was mentioned. Ralph was instantly suspicious that Molly and her father had been involved, but he took a further look, and realised that both of them had been too old, and Molly had always been the eternal spinster, but…

The house that she currently occupies will be signed over to her. The deeds will be made available in her name, and she is to continue to receive her salary until her death. Also, all costs relating to council rates, electricity, gas, and maintenance will be paid out of my estate. A fund will be established to cover this. As well, a one-off payment of one million pounds will be deposited in a savings account for her use.

One house down, over two hundred more properties, Caroline and Ralph thought. Neither of them had any problem with Molly receiving the house and the money. Molly sat stunned, not sure what to make of what had been said. Ralph leaned over and whispered in her ear. 'He's given you the house,' he said.

'Does that mean I don't have to go and live with my sister?'

'You're rich. You don't have to go anywhere. Our father has looked after you well.'

'Oh, good. I am pleased,' Molly said. Leonard Dundas could see that the woman was confused. He would have a word with her before she left.

Dundas continued.

> *To my son Ralph, a disappointment, in that he has frittered away an excellent education, a stable upbringing, and chosen not to embrace frugality and sound business practices, I bequeath nothing.*

'What the …?' Ralph jumped to his feet. 'He can't do this, not to me. I have debts to pay, people with demands.'

'Sit down, Ralph,' Caroline said. 'Hear what Mr Dundas has to say.'

'I can't leave here with nothing, I can't.'

'Mr Lawrence, Ralph, if I could have your forbearance, there is more,' Dundas said. Jill Dundas sat quietly taking in the interactions of the people. It would be her who would have to deal with them afterwards.

> *However, he is to be offered redemption. If he can hold down suitable employment for one year, with no cheating, no harebrained get-rich schemes, and no seduction of gullible women, then subject to the recommendation of a group of eminent persons that I have assembled, a sum of five million pounds is to be given to him. That money will be transferred to him over a five-year period in monthly instalments.*

'Who came up with that?' Ralph said.

'Your father,' Dundas said. 'I believe the term is that you've been snookered.'

'I'll challenge the will.'

'At the end of this reading, it will be necessary for those present to sign that they will not contest the will. If they do not, then all monies to them will be forfeited.'

'And given to who?'

'The money will be held in trust for another generation. Mr Lawrence was an astute man. He had thought this through very carefully, and with my advice.'

'He was mad, mentally incapable. There's no court in the country would believe that he was a sane man, thirty years in that house with our mother, a corpse. What kind of man does that, and did he kill her? We don't know that yet.'

'Be quiet,' Caroline said. Ralph sat down, a scowl on his face. Desmond Dickson looked at the man, remembered him from when they had last met, eleven years ago at least. He hadn't liked the man then, he liked him even less now.

Michael Lawrence, my grandson, through Ralph, has become a person of weak character. A fund sufficient for his rehabilitation has been set up, and he will voluntarily check into a private facility that will treat his addiction. He is an intelligent young man, poorly guided by a father of low repute. If, after one year, Ralph's son, with Ralph's active encouragement, is still clean and contributing to society, then Ralph will receive an additional payment of one million pounds. Michael will also receive one million pounds at that time. If, as I expect, he has not re-entered society, then Ralph will not receive either the five million pounds or the additional one million pounds. I will further add that I do not believe that any of the money bequeathed to Ralph and his son will ever be paid. I cannot, in death, profess to like my son and my grandson any more than I did when I was alive.

Ralph sat quietly. He knew people who would deal with the high-and-mighty Leonard Dundas.

To Caroline, my daughter, a person that I have missed over the years, but could not bear to see, on account of her mother, I bequeath five million pounds. An additional one million pounds are bequeathed to each of her and Desmond Dickson's children. Both of them have taken their place in society, and I can only express my admiration for them. Unfortunately, I have never met either, except when they were very young, but I have received regular reports, as I have on all those present here today.

'What does that mean?' Emma Lawrence asked. So far, she had sat quietly.

'Yearly reports were prepared by a private investigator, a discreet man. Mr Lawrence led the life of a recluse, but he was well aware of what went on. His mind was still alert, his business acumen was sound.'

'He was as mad as a hatter, locked up in that house,' Ralph said. He had been quietly seething, knowing full well that a will was invalid if signed by an incapacitated person. And he knew madness when it was there staring everyone in the face.

'Gilbert Lawrence's will has been updated every year. He was a sane man, and tests were conducted to prove that he was.'

'The man never left the house. How could he have been sane?'

'Proof will be supplied if required.'

'Whoever did these so-called sanity checks, did they know that my father had his wife upstairs, a skeleton that he had prepared in the cellar of the house?'

'That knowledge was not available,' Dundas said.

'Then we are wasting our time here. I've better things to do than sit here and listen to the last words of a madman,' Ralph said.

'Under the terms of the last will and testament of Gilbert Lawrence, you will forfeit any claim on his estate if you do not sign your agreement here today.'

'Let me remind you, Dundas. My father was mad, and his will is worthless. I will find someone competent to deal with its legality. I am entitled to half of what he's worth, not a measly five million pounds, and then only if I hold down a job. What do you, what did he expect me to do? Get a job in a shop, work in an office? I'm an entrepreneur, not someone's lackey.' With that, Ralph Lawrence stormed out of the room.

'Mr Lawrence,' Wendy said, as the man tried to exit the building.

'Yes, what do you want?'

'Sergeant Wendy Gladstone. We have a few questions for you.'

'Not now. I'm busy.'

Wendy could see the anger in the man's face. His eyes were bulging, his cheeks were flushed, his hands were shaking. 'Unfortunately, I must insist.'

'Not now. Can't you see that I have other things to do.'

'It's either voluntarily or in handcuffs.'

Lawrence looked at the two uniforms standing by. 'Very well, but I will lodge a formal complaint.'

'That's your prerogative. I'll give you the contact details once we get to Challis Street. Mind your head as you get in the back seat of the police car.'

After a short break, while everyone calmed down after the disruption by Ralph Lawrence, Leonard Dundas continued.

To my sister Emma, I bequeath one million pounds. I cannot say that I approved of some of her decisions in life, but they were hers, and I respect her for that. The money is hers to use, wisely or otherwise, although with age comes wisdom.

Leonard Dundas and his daughter will maintain my property portfolio. To Leonard, one million pounds. To Jill Dundas, one million pounds. Caroline and Desmond Dickson will take responsibility for my property portfolio, in consultation with Leonard Dundas and his daughter, although Caroline will be the only one given voting rights. They will not be able to liquidate more than five per cent of the assets in any two-year period. The children of Caroline will be asked to join the committee in time, and with voting rights. What has been set up will remain with the Lawrence family.

'What about the mansion in Atherton Street?' Caroline asked.

'It will become part of the Lawrence property portfolio. What is inside belongs to you.'

'The cars?'

'They are yours,' Leonard Dundas said.

Chapter 7

Ralph Lawrence slouched in a chair at Challis Street Police Station.

The information received from Spain had shown that with an excellent website and his charm Ralph Lawrence had managed to induce British holidaymakers enamoured of the sun and the local culture to place down payments on a speculative property development venture. It was a scam. The Spanish knew it, as did Homicide at Challis Street, but that was a technicality in as much that he had not broken any laws in England.

Isaac looked at the man, well aware that he had been dealt a body blow at the reading of the will. Leonard Dundas had updated the DCI about the contents of the will, and the reactions of the people present. He explained that even in death, Gilbert Lawrence had no intention to give his fortune to non-deserving causes. And according to the father, the son was not deserving.

'Mr Lawrence,' Isaac said. 'We're investigating the death of your father, Gilbert Lawrence.' Wendy Gladstone sat next to Isaac. Ralph Lawrence sat on the other side of the table. He did not have legal representation.

'That bastard screwed me.'

'I have been updated by Leonard Dundas,' Isaac said. 'The conditions placed on you are harsh. It is understandable that you are angry, although it does not obviate the fact that the man was murdered. That is what concerns us, not your enmity towards him.'

'I didn't dislike the man, only the way he lived, even when we were young.'

'According to your sister, he fulfilled his responsibilities, and neither of you suffered.'

'She's right, but she was always the favourite. He would confide in her, even ask her advice sometimes.'

'Did he take it?'

'Who knows? Probably not. With me, nothing.'

'Your childhood, unsatisfactory as it may have been to you, does not have any bearing on the death of your father, or does it?'

'What does that mean? I was in Spain, you know that, so do the Spanish police.'

'Along with some unfortunate tourists who put down payments on property they'll never own. How much did you make there?'

'We broke no laws. And besides, what do people go on holiday for if it's not to waste money?'

'Mr Lawrence, your reputation precedes you. Whether you conned them does not affect our enquiry. Your father was murdered, and we need to find who was responsible.'

'Why am I here? It can't be me, and I hadn't seen the man for decades.'

'But you know people who are capable of murder. Did you expect to receive half of your father's property portfolio?'

'I did.'

'Had that been promised to you? Had you seen a will to that effect?'

'No, but what else was he going to do with all his money? He couldn't take it with him, although he would have if it were possible.'

'You've been told what was in the will. Your father has placed his trust in Leonard Dundas.'

'My father trusted no one. If Dundas has the assets, he's there now figuring out how to realise on them. I know what the promise of easy money does to people. The holidaymakers in Spain, believing that they are getting a special deal from another Brit. Do you think they considered the poor soul who was losing money? Do you think they worried if someone else and their family were to be reduced to begging on the street?'

'I doubt if they did,' Isaac said.

'That's what makes it so easy. Greed, the most powerful human emotion, and my father has given Leonard Dundas the keys to the vault. That man and his daughter will cream the money, not that anyone will ever know.'

'Smart?'

'Smarter than me. They'll never be caught.'

'According to Mr Dundas, your father was of sound mind, and had been checked each year for his mental stability,' Wendy said.

'How? You tell me. My father never left the house, apart from once a week to walk down to the off-licence. He has our mother upstairs, a skeleton, and everyone says he's sane and the great financial mind.'

'Are you suggesting we check on his mental condition?'

'It's highly suspicious to me. Okay, in that room at Dundas's, I blew it, but I'm right, and everyone knows it, even my sister.'

'She's happy with your father's bequest,' Isaac said.

'And why not? She's got voting rights, and no doubt access to any decisions that Dundas and his daughter make. With all that property, maybe it doesn't need to be sold. I've been cheated by others who want the fortune for themselves. Believe me, there's skulduggery involved, and Leonard Dundas is a large part of it. Caroline maybe, although I wouldn't trust that husband of hers.'

'Desmond Dickson. You have your suspicions?'

'Not as such, but the man knows the value of money. He'll make sure he and Caroline have plenty.'

'Molly Dempster?'

'Let her have what my father bequeathed her. She deserves it.'

'We have difficulty believing that she did not know what was going on in the house,' Isaac said.

'When I was younger, I used to suspect her and my father.'

'An affair?'

'We used to see more of Molly than our mother sometimes. It was just a childish fantasy, that's all.'

'Your father and Molly were friendly?'

'Forget I said it. To me, Molly is the one good person. I'll not hear a word against her.'

'In the meeting at Dundas's, you stood up and stated that people have demands on you. What did that mean?'

Wendy noticed Ralph Lawrence shift uncomfortably in his seat.

'I needed the money, that's all.'

'What will you do now?'

'Find someone to contest the will.'

'That will cost money. If Dundas and his daughter are as smart as you say they are, they'll have covered their tracks well. According to Dundas, a lot of the money is tied up in overseas banks, trusts, offshore-registered companies. Not so easy to get hold of.'

'That's why I need a good solicitor. They're out there.'

'I suggest you do not break the law, Mr Lawrence. The English police are not as forgiving as the Spanish.'

'They weren't forgiving either. Strings were pulled.'

'What does that mean?'

'What I said. Do you think they would release me just because my father died?'

'Why are you telling us this?'

'Insurance.'

'Against whom?'

'Just remember that whatever happens, I didn't kill my father and that Leonard Dundas is not to be trusted.'

'These people? The sort that kill to get what they want?'

'Yes.'

'Did they kill your father?'

'I don't know, and that's the honest truth.'

'We need to stay in touch. As much for your protection as for our investigation.'

'Your son, where is he?' Wendy said.

'I've no idea. I've not seen him for a few years.'

'Is he in trouble?'

'Not to my knowledge. I found alcohol when I was younger, he found heroin.'

'Does that upset you?'

'He's an adult. My father was a self-made man. I wanted to be, but my son, he's a hopeless case.'

'His mother?'

'No idea where she is now. A few wives, a few other women since then.'

***

The interview with Ralph Lawrence had brought a new element into his father's death. Chief Superintendent Goddard had joined the scheduled meeting in Homicide.

It now looked as if the investigation was going to be prolonged, and this time with the addition of possible organised crime interference.

'Ralph Lawrence is in trouble,' Isaac said.

'You could see that he was putting on a brave face, but he was frightened,' Wendy said. 'He's going to disappear again.'

'You've got a watch on him?'

'I have, but if he's in deep with the loan sharks, they'll not wait long.'

'What are you suggesting?' Goddard said.

'Either Ralph has borrowed money beyond his ability to repay, and the father's death came as a godsend, or else he's borrowed against his perceived inheritance,' Wendy said.

'If organised crime had killed Gilbert, that would explain the lack of clues,' Isaac said.

'Are we suggesting that the man's death was prearranged, murder to order?' Larry said.

'It's possible. Ralph may have known that entering an arrangement with the loan sharks came with some conditions: pay the money back with interest, we'll deal with your father.'

'Would he have entered into such an agreement?'

'Is Ralph the type of person to read the small print or to care about his father?'

'Unlikely,' Wendy said.

'According to Leonard Dundas, the man has survived by charming gullible and rich women.'

'And once he had his money and tired of them?'

'Cast off, flotsam to the sea. Tell us, Bridget and Wendy, you're both mature women. Wendy, you've met the man, Bridget, you've seen him. Pretend you're rich and lonely, and Ralph Lawrence comes up to you and lays on the charm.'

'Twenty years too old for me, and the man's going to seed,' Wendy said.

'He didn't appeal, not from what I could see,' Bridget said.

'That's it,' Isaac said. 'The man's survived due to his charisma, his good manners, his expensive education and his posh voice. He's never needed to borrow heavily before, but now he's getting old, and Spain was the make or break. He also knew he only needed a few more years before his father died of natural causes.'

'Men like Gilbert Lawrence don't die that easy,' Goddard said. 'They refuse to accept the possibility. He could have lasted another five, ten, maybe fifteen years.'

'Okay, we'll concede the possibility, but Ralph's aware that one day he'll be fine. And he's a chancer. He's had a litany of failed ventures. It could be that he wanted to settle down, get a house in the country, a garden, grow vegetables.'

'Conjecture, short on facts,' Goddard said.

'That's the problem,' Isaac said. 'We don't have facts. We have a dead man knifed in his garden, no clues of any significance. We have a great deal of money, and according to the man's solicitor, a great deal of property.'

'But not going to the man's children.'

'Not in itself. Caroline, the daughter, received a five million pound one-off payment.'

'Enough?'

'Not if you expected a great deal more. Greed, yet again. Caroline Dickson and her family are stable people. No reason to suspect them at this present time.'

'Money corrupts, you know it,' Goddard said. 'I suggest you don't leave anyone out of your investigation.'

'We won't.'

'An early arrest?'

'Not looking good,' Isaac said.

'I was hopeful. You've got my confidence but be careful. If the son is involved with dangerous people, who knows where it will end up.'

With Goddard leaving, Isaac turned to Wendy. 'Ralph Lawrence's son, any updates?'

'I've got one,' Bridget said. 'I did some searching on the internet.'

'And?'

'He's moved on from being a layabout squatting somewhere or other. He's now an anarchist, committed to the overthrow of capitalism, and the redistribution of wealth to the needy.'

'With him being one of the needy. Where do we find him?'

'Idiots Incorporated,' Bridget said.

'Apart from that, do they have a title?'

'Anarchist Revolutionaries of England. Their address belies the fancy title. You'll find them in a lockup garage down in Putney. Wendy's got the address.'

'Violent?' Isaac said.

'Their website states that they are committed to the overthrow of the current government. By any means, according to them.'

'It's either rent-a-crowd who do little except philosophise or people who believe that murder is acceptable.'

'And Ralph Lawrence's son had a grandfather who represented the worst excess of what they abhor.'

***

There was one thing that concerned Isaac, the sanity of Gilbert Lawrence.

Isaac phoned Jill Dundas, made an appointment to meet with her later that day. Meanwhile, Larry Hill and Wendy Gladstone were getting acquainted with London's very own anarchists. Not that Wendy, a committed socialist, had any problems with people who wanted a better deal for themselves, but violence and extremism did not sit well with her. Larry had formed his opinion the moment they drew up alongside the ramshackle lockup garage, pre-war by the look of it, with its two wooden doors literally falling off their hinges. Outside on the street, four men stood. One was tall, and academic in appearance. 'All he needs is a soapbox and a spot down at Speaker's Corner in Hyde Park,' Larry said.

Wendy switched off the car engine and looked to where Larry had been pointing. She could see what he was talking about. The academic, judging by his corduroy jacket and his faded jeans, had the other three assembled around him. He was making a speech.

'The workers need us, and they need us now. For too long they have been downtrodden and made to feel the boots of the capitalist overlords on their backsides. That will change when we take control. When we ensure the distribution of the wealth amongst the people. I live for that day, and so must you.'

'Sorry to disturb you,' Wendy said, although she wasn't concerned if they were upset. A check on the Anarchist Revolutionaries of England website had identified the academic as Professor Giles Helmsley, faculty member of the London School of Economics until he staged a demonstration inside the main building complaining about the disparity in salaries between the teaching faculty and those working in administration. Once evicted from the LSE – Bridget had done the research – he had drifted from organisation to organisation, demonstration to demonstration, until he had founded the ARE.

'A smart man, once,' Larry said.

'Disturbed,' Wendy said.

Helmsley had taken no notice of her the first time. 'Mr Helmsley, a moment of your time,' Wendy shouted again.

Helmsley, temporarily interrupted, looked Wendy straight in the eye. 'The filth, I suppose,' he said to his audience of three.

'If, by that, you mean a police officer charged with protecting you and every other ratbag from themselves and others, then I am. Sergeant Wendy Gladstone. A few minutes of your time, if you please.'

'We do not recognise your right to be here. We have dispensed with the need for the capitalist lackeys.'

'No doubt you haven't dispensed with their fortnightly handouts of money for the unemployed, the vacuous, and the just plain stupid. And a public footpath is open to all people, even the police.'

'Is that an insult? If it is, I will be forced to take action.'

'What? Sue me? Threaten me with violence?'

'I will defend my rights as a citizen of this country. Neither you nor anyone else has a right to criticise me or take action against me.'

'Freedom of the masses, is that it?'

'If you understood our manifesto, you would agree.'

Helmsley, realising that he had met his match, turned away from the three converts and came over to where Wendy and Larry stood.

'What do you want? I've not broken any law,' Helmsley said.

'We're not saying you have,' Wendy said. 'We need to find Michael Lawrence.'

'Never heard of him.'

'He's on your website. Five feet eight inches, dark hair, spikey. He's got a tattoo on his arm of an eagle.'

'I've no idea who you're talking about.'

'That's fine,' Larry said as he took out his phone. '16 Grantly Street, Putney. A lockup garage, currently occupied by the Anarchist Revolutionaries of England. Check it for class A and B drugs, weapons, subversive literature, incitement to riot. You know the drill.'

'You can't do that,' Helmsley said.

'Do you want me to cancel it? It's up to you.'

'Okay, I know him. One of our most fervent.'

'Where is he?'

'I don't know.'

Larry reached for his phone again.

'Very well. 246 Hazelmere Road. It's a five-minute walk from here. He shares with some of the other comrades.'

'You've been there?'

'Not me. I've got a place not far from here.'

'No doubt you share it with your fellow revolutionaries.'

'I do my bit.'

'And what bit is that? The bit where you incite them to violence? The bit where you take a share of their benefits? Mr Helmsley, you've never been arrested, other than for causing a minor affray. Fifty pound fine, is that the limit of your anarchy?'

'You don't understand what we are trying to achieve. Some of us need to remain at a distance, to provide leadership and guidance.'

'And have a good time,' Wendy said. 'Is Michael Lawrence having a good time?'

'He's into heroin, a hopeless drug addict.'

'Do you know of his family?'

'I do.'

'Did you kill his grandfather? You must have hated what he represents.'

'One of the elites. I am glad that he is dead, but no, I did not kill him, nor did any of our members.'

'And what's going to happen when you succeed?' Larry said. 'Tumbrels taking the capitalists to the guillotine? The women sitting there knitting, the men cheering?'

'It won't be like that. The people will welcome us, even those who oppose us now.'

'Mr Helmsley, you're full of hot air. If we don't find Michael Lawrence, we'll be back, and this time, not only to your headquarters but also the house you own. You're no different from

Lenin driving around in a Rolls Royce: just a hypocrite. We'll meet again, Mr Helmsley, and soon.'

Chapter 8

Ralph Lawrence, free of Challis Street Police Station, realised there were imponderables for which he had no solution. He made two phone calls. The first was to a psychiatrist whom he had known from his school days, an eminent man in his field now. The second was to a man who would either assist him or would see that he never walked again. Ralph plotted his course very carefully.

If, as he suspected, his father with only a corpse to keep him company, had been irrational and eccentric, then the man's sanity could be disputed. But even if the will was invalidated, how much of his father's wealth would come to him, and how much would remain hidden? After all, Leonard Dundas and his daughter had had a long time to distort the truth and to hide the whereabouts of swathes of property and legal documents.

The first call revealed that a case could be made to dispute Gilbert Lawrence's sanity, although it would be costly and prolonged. If Dundas had been controlling his father for many years, then his father had been merely a shell, rubber-stamping Dundas's instructions. He knew that he needed the truth, he needed allies.

'Caroline, we need to talk,' Ralph said as he stood at the door of his sister's house. He had in his pockets the sum of one thousand five hundred and fifty-two pounds. Not much to show for a lifetime of playing the game, he knew, but he had hoped for a fortune.

'Come in, if you must,' Caroline said.

Once inside the elegantly decorated terrace house of Caroline and Desmond Dickson, Ralph quickly found a radiator and sat down close to it, removing his suit jacket. He had to admit that his sister had done well for herself, but then, she was the more sensible of the two. She had always looked for stability in her life, whereas he had searched for adventure.

'Life's taken a turn for the worse for you,' Caroline said. They had been close when they were young, and seeing him down and out, a body blow straight in the chest after the reading of their father's last will and testament, she could only feel compassion.

Before Desmond had come along, the most important man in her life had been her brother, even if he had not been the best influence or the most honest.

'Our father was not sane, you know that,' Ralph said as he slowly warmed in the heat.

'I know it, but what can we do?'

'Leonard Dundas controlled our father for years.'

'I've spoken to Desmond about it. We will accept the money offered, and I'll take up the offer that Dundas made at our father's request.'

'That's a smoke screen. You're to be given voting rights. Voting on what? The truth? Will you be given full visibility?'

'It will give us five million pounds, our children one million pounds each, and more importantly, it will give us time.'

'Time for what?'

'Time to find out the truth.'

'I've received nothing, not unless I agree to conditions that cannot be met.'

'We can only sympathise with your predicament.'

'Sympathy will not help,' Ralph said. He moved away from the radiator and sat in an armchair near to his sister. 'I need money, and I need it now. Holding down a steady job is not going to work, and as for Michael, he's barking mad.'

'What do you know about him? Where is he? What is he doing?'

'The last I heard he was into heroin. He was looking for money from me.'

'Did you give him some?'

'I sent him ten thousand pounds. What else could I do?'

'He is your son. His mother?'

'No idea.'

'Did you come here for money, or just to complain about how your life has turned out?'

'I'm desperate. What we were working on in Spain hasn't worked out. The police down there are tough. They've seized our assets.'

'Assets?'

'Okay, just a rented office, a couple of cars, and our laptops.'

'The money you had managed to part from the gullible?'

'That as well. It was a sound business proposal. They would have had secured tenure.'

'Ralph, save the advertising for others. You've lost your money, probably borrowed plenty. And now you're looking for a handout, and support to take on our father, is that it?'

'That's what I said before.'

'We will take no further action at this time until we have more knowledge of the intricacies of what our father and Dundas have been doing for the last three decades. We have time on our side, you do not. What do you intend to do?'

'I'll fight.'

'With what?'

'Whatever I've got.'

'You're playing with fire, not for the first time, but fire nonetheless. You're going to get burnt, not by Desmond and me, but by others. Did you kill our father? You'd be capable.'

'Not me. I was incarcerated in Spain, you know that.'

'What about Michael? He was in England.'

'Not him. He's barely capable of looking after himself.'

Ralph knew his sister would not help him, and he did not intend to plead. His situation was precarious, and he had been in tight jams before. He would get himself out of this one.

***

The young anarchist Michael Lawrence was found at the address given by Giles Helmsley. In keeping with the beliefs of the organisation, or because they were just bone-lazy, the house that three of the anarchists occupied was only fit for keeping animals.

'Mr Lawrence, we've a few questions,' Wendy said. She stood back more than ten paces on account of the mess. The man who wanted to right the wrongs of the capitalist state was lying on a mattress on the floor. It looked neither clean nor hygienic. To one side, there was a syringe and a bottle of beer.

'If you're the filth?'

'Sergeant Wendy Gladstone and Detective Inspector Larry Hill,' Wendy said as the two officers showed their warrant cards.

'I've nothing to say.'

'That's fine. We can continue our discussion down at the police station.'

'You can't come in here and tell us what to do,' one of the others said.

Larry moved over close to the man who was dressed in a tee-shirt with the words 'Down with the Capitalist State' emblazoned across the front of it. 'Now, look here, my anarchist friend,' Larry said, enunciating his words, 'if you don't want to be arrested and charged for having heroin in here, a firearm on the shelf behind you, then I suggest you shut up and leave us to deal with your friend.'

'There are no guns here,' the would-be tough man said. Wendy could see that Larry was ready to give him a swift kick in the stomach and a slap across the face.

The other anarchist remained curled up, fast asleep. On the arm of a chair next to where he slept, an empty bottle of whisky.

'Not much revolution today from that one,' Larry said, looking over at the man.

Wendy returned to Michael Lawrence. 'What is it? Here or down at the police station?'

'I've done nothing wrong.' Wendy could see the similarities between him and his father. She imagined that the young man could even be handsome underneath the tattoos and all the rings, some in his ears, one in his nose, another in his left eyebrow. If he was an indication of what the end of capitalism was to bring, then she was glad it was not going to happen anytime soon. One of her two sons had come home with a tattoo once. She remembered hitting the roof, not that he had taken too much notice as he had been drunk, but the next day, he felt her tongue. After that, she had to put up with the occasional tattoo, liking some, not liking others.

Then she and Bridget on holiday in Italy had dared each other, and both had had a small butterfly tattooed on their left ankle. It had been down to too much of the local vino, and Wendy's sons had given her hell when she got back to England.

'Okay, here, if you must,' Michael said, attempting to sit up and to lean against the wall.

'We've spoken to your father,' Larry said.

'Him? What for?'

'What do you know of your grandfather, Gilbert?'

'Not much. I've never met the man.'

'What else do you know?'

'According to my father, my grandfather is rich.'

'He's one of those that you're against.'

'It won't be long before you and your masters will be gone. Plenty for everyone.'

'Someone will need to work. Will it be you?' Larry said.

'Not me. Giles says the revolution will need soldiers.'

'I thought it was to occur when the people of England embraced the cause. There'd be no need for you then. Mr Lawrence, you're just a layabout, spouting nonsense as long as you are able to doss here. Helmsley told us where you were. He's done a con trick on you and the others, but that's not why we're here.'

'My grandfather. What about him?'

'Do you know where he lives.'

'No. Should I?'

'Your grandfather was killed.'

'Should I be sorry? Shed a tear? Is that what you want?'

'Mr Lawrence, did you kill him?' Wendy said.

'Are you joking?'

'Did you know anything about him?'

'Giles wanted me to find out more. He asked lots of questions.'

'What did you tell him?'

'I knew where he lived, that's all. I never went to the house or spoke to anyone.'

'Your father's sister?'

'I left home at fourteen. I've been on the street ever since. I may have met her when I was a child.'

'What would you do for some of your grandfather's money?'

'Anything.'

'Including detoxing from drugs, finding a job?'

'Anything.'

'Mr Lawrence, your grandfather has offered you one million pounds if you are willing to enter into a private drug rehabilitation clinic to sort yourself out. After that a job. Will you do it?'

'Yes, for a million pounds.'

'Very well. Make a phone call to this number,' Wendy said as she handed Michael Lawrence the number written on a piece of paper.

Outside on the street, the figure of Giles Helmsley. 'Not willing to go in, is that it?' Larry said.

'I'm here to ensure that the comrades are not subjected to police brutality.'

'What would you do if they were? Wise up, Helmsley. You're a charlatan preying on vulnerable people who neither understand nor care about what you're talking about, as long as they have their drugs and a place to sleep.'

'Did you feed that errant nonsense to the comrades?'

'Don't worry. The comrades are beyond caring about what we have to say,' Larry said.

Wendy and Larry walked to their vehicle.

'You were pushing it,' Wendy said.

'Michael Lawrence could have killed his grandfather, but it would have needed Helmsley to make him.'

'A blow for the cause?'

'Helmsley's cause. He could have hatched a plan to kill the old man, assuming that the grandson would get some money. And then he'd convince Michael to hand it over.'

'It's a possibility, but far-fetched.'

'It's no worse than any other scenario.'

'No better, though.'

***

Two weeks after the death of Gilbert Lawrence, five letters were sent. Two days later, four of them were signed for. The first recipient, Molly Dempster, opened hers and almost collapsed to the ground. The second, Caroline Dickson, phoned her husband. The third was delivered to Emma Lawrence. She was disturbed to receive it, not altogether surprised. The fourth was received by Leonard Dundas. He was shocked by the thoroughness of what he read. The fifth, to Ralph Lawrence, was not delivered due to the man not being at the hotel where he was staying.

The first that Homicide heard of the letters was when Molly Dempster appeared at Challis Street Police Station. It was Wendy who escorted the nervous and shaking woman up to Homicide.

Isaac and Larry, who had been out following up on the few leads they had, returned to the station as fast as they could.

Once back, the team sat with Gilbert Lawrence's former housekeeper.

'When did you receive it?' Larry said.

'This morning. It's from Mr Lawrence, from his grave.'

The team studied the envelope. It was from another solicitor in London. It was dated two days previously. On the outside the details of the person it was addressed to, and in the far-right corner in capital letters, 'TO BE OPENED AFTER MY DEATH'. Inside, three sheets of paper. The letter was dated 28th April 2017. Only one year old.

'I couldn't read it,' Molly said. 'It's as if he's writing to me from beyond.'

'Bridget, phone up the solicitor that sent this after this meeting,' Isaac said. 'Either they come in here, or we'll go out there.'

No doubt you are all wondering what to make of me, and whether I was sane or not. My death, whether it was in my sleep or after an illness, or whether my end was violent, I cannot know, as I cannot predict the future. Those who have received this letter will know by now what they have been bequeathed. Some will be pleased, others will be neutral, and some will be angry. The question about my beloved wife, Dorothy, is also a question that must be answered.

But first, my reasons for the division of my assets. I was a careful man in life, generous to those I loved, difficult and belligerent to those I did not. While I have tried to be scrupulous in my business dealings, I have at times been forced to deal with unsavoury characters. These are not people of my choosing, and I have always kept them away from my family. Some of them have been villains, no doubt some of them would be capable of murder. That explains the reference to my death and the possibility that it could be violent. I have never sought the company of dishonest people or criminals, but with some of my more significant acquisitions, it was sometimes inevitable. I should say that this letter has been updated annually since I first put pen to paper over twenty-five years ago. Nobody, not even Leonard Dundas, knows of this letter and its contents. It has changed to some extent as the years have moved forward, as has my will.

If you are reading this now, then I am dead. Molly is no doubt confused, but the remainder of her life will be as agreeable as I can make it. Caroline, my daughter, is also provided for. Ralph, my son, has become a disappointment. I had hoped to give him and Caroline the control of my empire, but, alas, it was not to be. I know that I could have given it to Caroline instead, but I wanted the family to control it. Desmond Dickson is a good man, I've no doubt of that, but he is not of my blood. I could not give all that I have strived for to others. Caroline's children will be eventually brought in, when and if they show the necessary acumen. I have engaged another firm to monitor their progress. By necessity, I am forced to rely on others, but I have put checks and counter-checks in place to ensure compliance and accountability of those charged with the responsibility. An additional letter will have been sent to Leonard Dundas and his daughter with full details of the auditing process, as well as the auditing of Dundas and his company.

Leonard Dundas has served me well over the years, and whereas I could trust him when I was alive, I cannot give him my unqualified trust when I am dead. His daughter, Jill, will take over the reins soon, and those checks will apply to her too. Caroline will have the most significant role in the years to come, and that is why there is to be a strict liquidation of assets policy in place.

No doubt my directives will dissipate in time, yet I hope in death, as I did in life, my legacy will continue.

My beloved wife, Dorothy. I grant that some may see my isolation from the world and my reclusive behaviour as symptoms of madness. They are not. Dorothy had suffered all her adult life with a debilitating mental condition. It had become worse in the last six months before she vanished from the world. She was a proud woman who did not want people to know. If she had died, there would have been an autopsy. Such is the burden of men as successful as I have been. There was also a substantial life insurance policy in her name. Suspicion would naturally have arisen. On the day my wife died of natural causes, I closed all the shutters in the house and placed my wife in the cellar. The possibility of her vanishing from the house and dying as a result of misadventure was plausible and ultimately accepted.

It is strange to reflect that the preparation of my wife to allow her to be placed in her bed was a calming experience. She was there with me, and I wanted nothing more. Some people will see it as macabre, others as a sure sign of madness, but believe me, it was neither. It was a sign of love.

I had never been a sociable man and the attention that I received as I became all the more successful did not sit easily with me. Being reclusive in the house with Dorothy suited me admirably. Molly continued to look after me and was never involved in any way with Dorothy's disappearance.

In time, as I aged, I have become more careless in my appearance and my health. I contacted three companies of psychoanalysts. Their names are with Caroline and Dundas. I did not meet them, although I would speak to them once a year, and go through their questionnaires, their attempts to understand the state of a person's mind. They will attest to my sanity. Of the three companies, one is in the UK, one is in the USA, and the final one is in Australia. If an attempt is made to dispute my sanity, a well-honed team of lawyers is in place to deal with it, and a fund in place to pay for their services. Yet again, a process of checks and counter-checks between the companies has been set up. Collusion by anybody or any group will not be possible.

I cannot allow my legacy and the love of my wife to be destroyed by unfettered greed. That is all. Gilbert Lawrence.

Chapter 9

Ralph Lawrence rarely regretted any decisions that he had made in his life. He was a man with an unrelenting belief that life was what you made it, and luck had nothing to do with it.

As he sat on the chair in the back room of a disused warehouse in the east end of London, he was beginning to regret his philosophy. He had returned to England primarily because the Spanish authorities wanted him out of their country, but secondly because his father had died.

Not that he had felt any sadness. On the contrary, the man's death, tinged with intrigue about how he died, gave him the best hope for the future. Yet now he was in trouble, and he knew it was not going to be so easy. The man sitting opposite him in the seedy back room that smelt of damp and decay was not likely to be swayed by smooth words.

'Lawrence, I staked you money for your venture in the sun. Where is it?' Gary Frost said.

'I need time. There's been a problem,' Ralph said. On either side of him were two men who looked as though they were used to beating people for a living.

'Gilbert Lawrence, a relative of yours?' Frost said. He was a small man, quietly spoken. He was dressed in a navy-blue suit, a red tie, and a white shirt. He looked like a banker, and that was what he was: the banker of last resort.

Ralph had done the sums. The cost to set up the scam in Spain was more than four hundred thousand pounds. No use skimping on a cheap website, and then there were the advertisements, and transferring the money overseas, and the bribes, a lot of money in themselves. His Spanish partner, another charmer, still languished in a cell in Spain. He had also borrowed money, and it had been going well. They had managed to sucker over one and a half million out of the tourists, another two million to be followed up on. And the money was not there. Lawrence was not sure why, although he suspected the bribes they had been paying hadn't been enough. No doubt his Spanish partner would be making a deal to get himself out of jail.

One of the men standing over Ralph grabbed hold of his shoulder, almost lifted him out of the chair. 'You never answered the boss's question.'

'He was my father.'

'Then why are we here having this unpleasantness,' Frost said. 'Let go of Mr Lawrence. He is our honoured guest. And what is four hundred thousand? How much was your father worth?'

'Somewhere close to seven hundred million pounds, probably more.'

'And your share?'

'It'll take time to realise on his money, but it should be three hundred million pounds.'

'Why didn't you tell us before? I was prepared to let my boys go to work on you. You know what that would have meant?'

Ralph flexed his legs, imagining the pain of a low-velocity bullet penetrating his kneecaps. 'It may take time to get the money.'

'What does it matter. We can wait. Six weeks, is that long enough for you?'

'It is,' Ralph said, hoping that it was long enough to get out of the country.

'Give our guest a whisky,' Frost said.

One of the heavies poured the drink and gave it to Ralph. The man now receiving the VIP treatment was shaking so much he was barely able to hold it.

'I'm a reasonable man. It's only business, you know that.'

Lawrence knew it wasn't. It was sheer desperation on his part that had led him into the clutches of the loan shark. He was shaking now because he had just been saved from a savage beating, and his kneecaps possibly being shattered. He knew that once he was free of Frost and his men, he would be shaking until he had distanced himself from them. But what to do for money: he had none.

***

Caroline Dickson realised that her father had made a strategic error. A possible indication that the man had been slipping in his later years. It would have been understandable, given his advancing years and his morbid account as to what he had done to her mother, and how he had kept her in her room. She could imagine him up there with her, discussing business, updating her on the economy and what was outside, and how she was better off where she was.

Ralph may be a fool, and his outburst when the will had been read had not endeared him to anyone, but Caroline knew that the brother she had not seen for eight years had been right. Their father had been mad, but the medical and psychoanalytical reports showed clearly that the checks had been conducted correctly, and her father's responses had been above average. *How could that be?* Caroline thought. *Do I want to rock the boat?*

She knew she had voting rights, and as a direct descendant of the dead man she had precedence over Dundas, but the man and his daughter had control. She had had to look up where the Marshall Islands were, as there were five million two hundred and fifty-nine thousand dollars in an investment fund there. The Cayman Islands she knew, as well as Cyprus and Mauritius. She needed the accounts in her name, and that had not occurred yet. She could see the hands of the Dundases pulling strings. They had access to all the bank accounts, the title deeds of all the properties, and yet they were all in the name of Gilbert Lawrence and the companies that he had set up. Caroline knew that it would be a battle royal.

Desmond, her husband, was an honest man, and he would help, but he was used to dealing with trustworthy people, not with Leonard and Jill Dundas. But Ralph knew crooks, and he knew how to deal with them. She needed him as her special adviser.

***

Isaac Cook and his team in Homicide studied Gilbert Lawrence's letter from beyond the grave. The distribution of the wealth was not the primary concern, although it was important. What concerned them more was what the dead man had revealed about the death of his wife, Dorothy. Wendy Gladstone and Bridget Halloran abhorred the cavalier manner with which he had described his wife in the cellar. Larry Hill was more intrigued by the process. All, including Isaac, could not believe it was the behaviour of a rational man, a man capable of satisfying three respectable psychoanalysts on three continents that he was sane.

The experts' results were of no concern if they were legitimate, but what if the tests had been falsified? If they had been, as seemed possible, then it would invalidate Lawrence's will, which in turn would throw the motives behind the man's death into confusion.

'How do we prove this?' Bridget said.

'Research these companies, see what they have to say.'

'I've done some research, not of the companies, but what constitutes insanity.'

'And?' Isaac said, knowing full well that Bridget would have been thorough.

'If the will is to be contested…'

'Assume it is,' Isaac said. 'Ralph Lawrence has been left out of any immediate money, and Caroline Lawrence is only to receive a minor amount.'

'Five million pounds, minor?' Larry said. He was struggling with finding fifty thousand for his wife's house-hunting plans. To him, Caroline Lawrence had received a fortune.

'The dead man had a property portfolio in the billions. And it's still with Leonard Dundas. If that man has concealed some of his client's money and property holdings, there's no way that anyone could find out the full extent of what the man owned.'

'He's either the greatest crook or naively honest,' Wendy said.

'Have you met any honest men lately?' Larry said.

'My husband was, but he could only lay claim to a small pension and a bungalow. Apart from him, there aren't too many, especially if they're worth hundreds of millions.'

'We can debate this ad infinitum,' Isaac said, 'but what is important is whether Gilbert Lawrence was sane.'

'As I was saying,' Bridget said.

'Apologies, we digressed.'

'This is what I've found out. The person must be of "sound mind, memory, and understanding" when making a will. That person must understand the nature of the act and its effects, the extent of the property of which he/she is disposing and must be able to comprehend and appreciate the claims to which he/she ought to give effect.'

'Is that it?' Larry said. He had had an aunt who had died and had given her money to the church instead of her family. He remembered his mother, his aunt's sister, saying over the dining room table that the woman was mad, but the money remained with the church.

'There's one more clause. It's in legalese. "And must not be affected by any disorder of the mind that shall poison his affections, pervert his sense of right, or prevent the exercise of his natural faculties and that no insane delusion shall influence his will in disposing of this property and bring about a disposal of it which, if the mind had been sound, would not be made."'

'The précised version,' Larry said.

'If he had been declared sane and he had the necessary proofs at the signing of his will, then it's valid. Remember, most people don't get their sanity verified while they're alive. It's up to the beneficiaries, or those who believe they should receive something from the person's estate, to contest it afterwards.'

'Are the three certificates valid?'

'They are.'

'Did they have all the facts?'

'How could they? Nobody knew about Dorothy Lawrence upstairs in the house.'

'The will is contestable?'

'Without a doubt. And if Gilbert Lawrence was so smart, he wouldn't have left loopholes in the will.'

'There was a clause at the end for those present to sign their agreement,' Isaac said.

'That may have been legally binding, but Ralph Lawrence didn't sign.'

***

Ralph Lawrence made contact with his sister one day after his encounter with Gary Frost, a man who had an unenviable reputation as to how he called in his debts. Ralph had not wanted to use the man, regretted it now, but he had been down on his luck, and he needed out from the predicament he had found himself in.

The first day he had made contact with Frost was the first time for a very long time that he felt trepidation about what he was doing.

Ralph Lawrence knew himself to be a supreme optimist, fully aware that not many ventures had turned out bad. Some, his sister and their father included, would have said that a failed business venture was indeed that, a failure. To Ralph, his definition was that if you lost money, it was. But he had not lost money; others had. On every venture he had been creaming off the top and squirrelling the money where no one else could get hold of it, including his ex-wives, bloodsuckers all of them. But he had chosen them for their youth and beauty, or for their money. The last woman had been smarter than most and had seen through him early on. She had found some of his bank accounts, the cryptic passwords, and had helped herself to over two hundred thousand pounds before sending him a letter from an unknown destination: 'The weather's fine, so is the hotel and the man I picked up in the bar last night. And don't expect me to wish you were here.'

'Where have you been? I've been trying to contact you,' Caroline said.

The siblings met at a restaurant. Caroline knew she would be paying.

'I was occupied,' Ralph said.

'You didn't pay for the hotel. I phoned them.'

'Did you pay?'

'Hell, I did. What sort of trouble are you in?'

'Money trouble, the usual.'

'Where are you staying?' Caroline could see that her brother was looking the worse for wear and that he had a tired, faraway look about him.

'A cheap hotel. It's not much good.'

'Why? You could always check into somewhere better.'

'The deal in Spain has gone all wrong. It's left me in a predicament.'

'You're hiding out. Why?'

'Some people want their money. The sort of people who don't take no for an answer.'

'I need your help,' Caroline said. 'Dundas has got us over a barrel.'

'Didn't you figure that out when he was reading the will?'

'I wanted the five million first.'

'You signed the clause at the bottom, no contesting the will?'

'It's not enforceable. The tests of our father's sanity are invalid. We can dispute that.'

'Caroline, supposing I agree to go in with you, what's in it for me?'

'Two hundred thousand pounds today, and forty per cent of whatever we find.'

'Assuming the will is invalidated, and we become the sole beneficiaries?'

'We'll never find it all. Dundas will have covered his tracks well. That's why we need you,' Caroline said.

She called the waiter over. 'Another bottle of wine, please,' she said. This was a time to celebrate.

'We? You and Desmond?'

'Regardless of what you and he may think of each other, he realises that he's not up to what's required.'

'And I am?'

'You know the tricks, what Dundas could have done. Where the titles to the properties are, the bank accounts.'

'It will cost.'

'I've offered you two hundred thousand pounds.'

'We'll need a top-notch computer hacker, someone to go through Dundas's office, check the files, take copies.'

'Illegal?'

'Do you think he'll respond to a legal demand?'

'We need to know before we force him. How much for the additional help?'

'Probably another three hundred thousand pounds.'

Caroline was suspicious. He was her brother, and she knew him better than anyone else. Give the man an inch, he would take a mile, and then disappear, brother or no brother. 'You want me to give you more money?' she said.

'Not this time. Our father owes us a lot more than a pittance. I'll play it by the book, but I need your assurance that you'll help out if I can't fend off the money lenders.'

'Violent?'

'I was desperate. I had no option. But now, with you and me, we'll deal with Dundas. Our father was crazy, you know that?'

'I know it. Our mother up there in that room. Have you seen the body?' Caroline said.

'I'm not sure if I want to.'

'I have. It's ghoulish. Whether it was her death or not that turned him, there's no way to know. And are we sure he was making the decisions all these years, with Dundas implementing them?'

'How can we be? How can anyone be?'

'We'll never know. The will, we are assuming, is genuine.'

'Maybe it is, maybe it isn't, but whatever you do, don't dispute it for now. You, Caroline, need to be with Dundas. He must never know of our meeting here today.'

'Agreed. I'll transfer the money to your account when I have the details. Play this fair, and we'll deal with that bastard Dundas and his scheming daughter.'

Chapter 10

Homicide still wrestled with where Molly Dempster fitted into the investigation. There was no reason to believe that she was involved in her employer's death or that of his wife, but she had spent more time in the house than any person other than Gilbert.

Isaac and Larry found her at her house. There were signs of her new-found wealth: the two men at the front of the house painting the windows and the door, another man tending to the garden.

'I had to do something,' Molly said. 'Mr Lawrence gave me the money to look after myself.'

She seemed to be unaffected by the wealth of her lifelong employer and spoke of him and his children in a loving, almost childlike manner, as though they were her family. Not unusual, he supposed, as checks into the woman had revealed a life of modest means: no man in her life, no pets, nothing.

Inside the house, also being subjected to modest renovations, Molly Dempster sat in the small living room. Isaac and Larry sat nearby. A tray of tea and biscuits on a table in front of all three.

'Miss Dempster, for all those years you were in that house with Mrs Lawrence upstairs,' Isaac said. He had helped himself to a cup of tea and a biscuit. Larry, conscious of the need to keep his weight down, only had a cup of tea.

'I know. Somehow, I find it romantic, but then I was always the first to cry if there was a love story on the television, you know the type, where one of them dies young, the other left on their own.'

'Do you understand why Mr Lawrence would have wanted his wife there?'

'Oh, yes. They never wanted to be apart, neither of them. If he was late coming home, or she was, the other one would be fretting.'

'But what concerns us is that you were there twice a week, and Mrs Lawrence was buried in the cellar. After that, Mr Lawrence had to prepare his wife's body, and that is not the easiest of the processes. There must have been some odours, and not pleasant either.'

'Maybe there were, but I wouldn't have taken any notice.'

'Why's that?'

'Hyposmia, virtually no ability to smell. I've had it since I was young. It's no use talking to me about the smell of a flower. Once, I nearly gassed myself. The oven hadn't lit, and I was trying to find out why. I almost passed out until Mrs Lawrence came and pulled me free.'

'Your friendship with Mr Lawrence?' Larry said.

'Ralph was trying to make something out of it, but he was young and adolescent. His hormones and his imagination were getting the better of him. And besides, I had no need of a man or a woman. Never have, never wanted to. I just want my routine, the chance to sit down at the end of the day and turn on the television.'

'How could the man have kept away from you? You must have seen him occasionally.'

'Maybe I did, but he wanted to be alone. Once he left the door unbolted, so I snuck in for a quick look.'

'How long after he had gone into seclusion?'

'One, two years. I don't remember exactly, but it was a long time ago.'

'And what did you see?'

'Nothing. It was dark with the shutters closed and very dusty. I might not be able to smell very well, but my hearing was fine. I could hear a sound from upstairs, so I returned to my part of the house. After that, I never tried to look again.'

'Did he know you'd been in there?'

'It was never mentioned, although, as I said, he always wrote his instructions down for me. The door was never open again while I was in the house.'

Both Isaac and Larry could not fault the woman, although no physical contact, no conversation, made no sense.

'Let's go back to when he needed a dentist. What did he sound like, look like?'

'He was quiet, as though he hadn't spoken in a long time, which I suppose he hadn't. I made the appointment, and he left when I wasn't in the house. All I know is that three hours later, he was back in the house. After that, I never spoke to him again.'

'The dentist?'

'Brian Garrett. I've got his phone number. I suppose he must have seen more of Mr Lawrence than me.'

***

Gary Frost, unscrupulous and on the periphery of crime, knew what he had with Ralph Lawrence. A man who had come to him five months earlier needing money. It wasn't the first time he'd seen men such as Lawrence, men who lived on the edge, scoundrels more than criminals.

Frost understood that Ralph Lawrence was weak, not like his father, Gilbert. He did not tell the son that he already knew of the father. Frost had done further research, not difficult considering the amount of interest in the man's murder. It made for great headlines – England's own Howard Hughes, dead with a knife in the back. The reclusive billionaire with his wife dead in her bed, the battle for his fortune.

The estimates of the dead man's wealth varied from one billion up to somewhere close to infinity. No one, certainly not Ralph and his sister, knew precisely how much. The only person who seemed to have any idea was the father's former solicitor and his only confidante.

Frost was reclining on a chair, taking in the sun through the window in his penthouse flat. The flat was big enough to double as his accommodation and his place of work. It was on two levels, the lower one for his office and his support staff. With Frost, an agreement to lend money came with a handshake and an email setting out the terms and conditions: the money to be transferred to any nominated location, either a deposit into a bank account or cash. The payment schedule, principal plus interest of ten per cent per week, payable on demand. Default penalties, not included in the email but given in person or by phone, were simple. Non-payments or delays in adhering to the agreement would be settled by extreme violence.

'It's sure-fire, can't lose,' Ralph had said when told of the conditions of the loan.

Frost remembered his words only too well. If it was sure-fire, it could only mean that it was not strictly legal, and it would either make a fortune or it wouldn't. But then men such as Lawrence were all too ready to play into the hands of men such as him. And now he had the son of Gilbert Lawrence. What could be achieved? He needed his man in the prime seat, but there were problems. Even without the media, Frost could see delays, also the possibility of Ralph being sidelined and receiving none of the fortune, or so little as to render him irrelevant. Frost could not allow that to happen. If Lawrence was entitled to half of his father's wealth, then that was what he would get.

Ted Samson, small, barely five feet four inches, his name not indicative of the man, stood before his boss. He was dressed casually, yet expensively. The ideal man for going here and there without raising suspicion.

'I've got a job for you,' Frost said.

'Whatever you want,' Samson said.

'Ralph Lawrence. He's not seen you, has he?'

'Nobody sees me unless I want them to.'

'Good. I want you to keep a watch on him, never let him out of your sight.'

'Twenty-four hours, seven days a week?'

'Exactly. Your brother can take over when you need a break.'

'And what do you want, boss?'

'Don't let him out of your sight, report back all that he does. And if he attempts to do a runner, well, you know.'

'Call you, and then grab him.'

'Exactly, but don't let him know that you're keeping watch.'

'You can trust me, boss.'

***

Chief Superintendent Goddard was under pressure, which meant that Isaac Cook and the entire Homicide team were as well.

'It's like this,' Goddard said as he sat in Isaac's office. 'Gilbert Lawrence is receiving a lot of press interest, understandable given the man's lifestyle, and his wife upstairs.'

'Not to mention the fact that he owned a lot of property,' Isaac said.

'The man's will, has it been resolved?'

'Not to everyone's satisfaction. The only problem is that the main beneficiary appears to be Lawrence's solicitor.'

'Complicated, but why? Normally the children would inherit the majority.'

'That's the problem. Lawrence wasn't normal, was he?'

'Who gained from the man's death?'

'The solicitor. Lawrence's daughter inherited five million pounds, and her two children one million each. Ralph Lawrence, his son, nothing, although there were conditions under which he could inherit.'

'Cut out of the will?'

'Without question, and Ralph's son is an anarchist, as well as a drug addict.'

'Dead within a month, if the drug addict got hold of some of the money. Anarchists would have no issue with Gilbert Lawrence being murdered.' Goddard said.

'They're only pretend anarchists. A brick thrown at a bank, a demonstration somewhere else. Just assorted ratbags, although their leader, Professor Giles Helmsley, is a unusual character.'

'What do you mean?'

'Academic, well-spoken, and up until six years ago, a member of the faculty of the London School of Economics.'

'Any reason to suspect him of the murder of Gilbert Lawrence?'

'No proof. That's the problem, the man is killed, nobody sees anything, nobody hears anything. The housekeeper is not a suspect either.'

'Why not?'

'No motive. She's been working for the family for decades, even before Lawrence went crazy. And she received a million pounds in the will.'

'If she knew about the wife upstairs, she could have felt the need to do something.'

'No one had been up there, not for a very long time, apart from the dead man. The CSIs have been over the place with a fine-tooth comb. We had a concern about what Molly Dempster may have known, but we've not come up with anything. The off-licence where he used to go once a week is not in the best area. Someone could have followed him home, seen the opportunity to accost the man, steal some money.'

'Did the people in the street, the off-licence, know who he was?' Goddard asked.

'Some would have.'

'And nothing from the CSIs?'

'There was a clear sign where the housekeeper had walked, as well as the postman, but nothing more.'

'Then it's not someone off the street, is it?'

'Gilbert Lawrence sent a letter to everyone important outlining certain facts, including why his wife was upstairs. No document has been received with accounts, real estate holdings, passwords. Everything is with Dundas.'

'And Lawrence is certified as sane?' Goddard said.

'We're checking, but we're expecting Ralph Lawrence to dispute the will. He may be a con artist, but he's got a point. An evaluation of sanity can only be based on the facts presented. And not one of these experts knew about how he had taken his wife, buried her in the ground underneath the cellar floor for some months, and then exhumed her, removed what he could of the excess skin and internals, and then had her remaining body eaten by dermestid beetles until she was virtually only bone.'

'But she could have been murdered?'

'It's possible. Unprovable, though.'

Isaac realised he'd given his senior very little. As soon as he'd left he called in his team.

'What do we have?' Isaac said.

'Ralph Lawrence met with his sister,' Wendy said.

'How do we know?'

'I've been keeping a watch on him after I found him at another hotel. Since meeting with her – they met at a restaurant – he's moved out of the hotel and back into something decent.'

'What about Dundas and his daughter? Any movement there?'

'They've done nothing wrong that we can see,' Larry said.

'Yet they have gained the most from this.'

'On the face of it.'

'Larry, we need to go and interview the postman who found Gilbert Lawrence,' Isaac said.

Chapter 11

'I still had to deliver the mail,' was not the comment that Isaac and Larry were looking for.

Jim Porter, the postman, had been found at his home five miles from where he had discovered the body of Gilbert Lawrence. Judging by the condition of the flat he lived in, he was a slovenly man. He had not been pleased to see two police officers at his door, although it was a block of flats which the local police would have been only too familiar with. It was grim, low rent, and definitely not the sort of place that Isaac liked. His small flat in Willesden was not much larger than the postman's, but it did have a pleasant outlook, whereas the view from where the three men stood was of an old industrial site.

'They're putting up some fancy high-rise for the wealthy, not for us,' Porter said as he looked out of the window.

'Gilbert Lawrence was wealthy,' Isaac said. 'You must have been tempted.'

'Who wouldn't be? I'd heard stories about the man: reclusive, never spoke, the smell of rotting fish.'

'Rotting fish?'

'That's what they said at the off-licence.'

'Who else have you spoken to about him?' Larry said. He looked around the flat, realised his wife wouldn't have crossed the threshold. He had to admit his wife looked after him, the children, and the house well, and with her, there were no dirty cups in the sink, no magazines thrown haphazardly across any vacant space.

'Nobody, not really, but sometimes people liked to talk, and old man Lawrence was as good a subject as any other.'

'Molly Dempster?'

'She liked to talk, but if I asked about him inside, she'd clam up. I was never sure what to make of her.'

'What do you mean?'

'You've been in the house; didn't you feel it?'

'Feel what?'

'As though it was evil, which I suppose it was.'

'You had been in?'

'Only as far as the kitchen. Sometimes she'd ask me in for a cup of tea. I always got the impression that she was glad of the company.'

'Did you ever see Lawrence?'

'Not me. Once I heard a noise from inside, as though something had fallen over and smashed on the floor, and once or twice the sound of footsteps. I'm not squeamish, far from it, but I never wanted to stay there for long. Do you reckon Molly's all there?'

'What do you mean?'

'I don't know. It's just the feeling that something wasn't right. Now we know it wasn't, but Molly, she must have known something.'

'According to her, she hadn't. She served the family all her adult life, that was all.'

'I read in the newspaper that Lawrence had given her a house and money.'

'He had. For loyal service to him and his family.'

'But he never saw his children.'

'Not since he locked himself away. Had you ever seen them there?'

'I saw the daughter once or twice, but she only ever spoke to Molly from the footpath outside the front gate. The son, Ralph, he never came around, but Molly said he was a lovely child, not so good when he grew up.'

'You never saw him?'

'Not me. Molly may have, but she didn't say much, although I could tell she was fond of the man inside the house. Supposedly at night, he'd come out into the kitchen, eat his meal and then retreat back to his place.'

'For a postman, you seem to know a lot about Gilbert Lawrence and his family history.'

'Just snippets over a few years. I saw him once shuffling down to the off-licence. I walked past him, said hello, but nothing.'

'Why did you talk to him?'

'Just curious. He didn't reply, didn't even look my way. What would have happened if someone got in his way? Would he have reacted?'

'Porter, at some time we'll find out the full story of Gilbert Lawrence, who killed him and why. We'll also find out if you've been lying or failing to tell us the full story. If you didn't kill him, then it would be better to be honest now. Later on, you could be charged with obstructing justice. Do you understand this?' Isaac said.

'I understand, but I'm just the postman, a bit too nosy sometimes for my own good. You'd be surprised what I've seen over the years, but Lawrence, I don't know what to say. I didn't kill him, and no doubt you've checked, but there's no criminal record against me.'

'We've checked. You're clean, but you must have seen something of the man, seen something that would help us with our enquiry.'

'Once or twice, when I was delivering letters along Lawrence's street, I'd see a man standing by the post box, looking in the direction of his house.'

'Checking the house?'

'I don't know. It only happened a few times in the weeks before his death, and it wasn't always the same man. I know what I saw, but why they were there, and what they were after, I can't tell you.'

'Would you recognise these men if you saw them again?'

'Probably, but if one of them is a murderer, I'm not too keen.'

'We'll give you protection if it's needed.'

'And when's that? When you find me dead? Whoever they were, they weren't there to make sure the old man was well and in good spirits.'

'It's more than that,' Larry said. 'The man did leave the house on an occasional basis. If they had wanted to do him harm, they could have then.'

'Anything else?' Isaac asked.

'His letterbox used to fill up occasionally, and I always pushed the letters through. I couldn't go back to the post office and say that I couldn't deliver them when there was a letterbox in the door of the house, could I?'

'You could have given them to Molly Dempster.'

'I could have if she would have accepted them, but she wouldn't.'

'Any idea why?'

'She never said. Anyway, there was this one time. It was about a year ago, and don't ask me the date, as I can't remember back that far. The letterbox was full, and I've got a letter to push through. It's thick and in a padded bag. So I give the letters a shove, and they fall out of the back of it and onto the floor inside. I kneel down to hold up the flap on the letterbox to push the letter through. Now, most letterboxes have a weak spring on them, but Lawrence's is heavy duty, and it's hard to hold open.'

'What happened?'

'I've got the flap open, and I have the letter halfway through when it was snatched from me.'

'Gilbert Lawrence?'

'It had to be.'

'Did you see him?'

'I did. He was kneeling down on his side. Our eyes made contact. Nothing was said, he grabbed the letter, the flap closed, and I grabbed my bag and beat a hasty retreat. Not before I took a second look, though.'

'Why?'

'Maybe it's too many horror movies, maybe not, but I was scared.'

'But nothing happened.'

'I know it didn't but looking back at those eyes scared me.'

'Did you see anything else?'

'He swore, but to himself, not to me. I had seen inside the house, and I saw him standing ten feet, maybe fifteen, back from the letterbox.'

'Why didn't you just put the letter through and leave?'

'Curiosity. I couldn't help myself. I kept looking, and then he disappeared. After that, I never looked again.'

'The men across the road, what about them?'

'There's not much more I can say. I'm paid to deliver the mail, not to speculate on who's watching him.'

'Molly Dempster, do you think she knows more than she's saying?'

'I would have thought so.'

***

Ralph realised that with his sister he had to play it by the book. With her, he would act honourably, but he still had the issue with Gary Frost and that little man who appeared at regular intervals. If he was to assist his sister, he needed Frost off his back. He needed to meet with the man.

Ralph had spent most of his adult life in the shadows between legal and illegal, and it wasn't the first time that someone had been after him. He'd seen the man watching him outside the restaurant where he had met Caroline, and then at the bank, and the last time in the foyer of the hotel where he was now staying.

'I'm not about to take a runner,' Ralph said as he sat down next to Ted Samson on the seat in the hotel foyer.

'I beg your pardon,' Samson said.

'Tell Frost I want to meet with him in public. I don't fancy my chances with his heavies.'

'When, where?'

'Here, two this afternoon. I could do with his help.'

With that, the little man walked out of the front door of the hotel and melded into the crowd outside. Ralph walked up to the bar and ordered a whisky. He knew he was taking a risk, but he and Caroline needed help. They needed to understand what Dundas was up to, and they needed to follow up on the trail of deception he had created.

Caroline had attended one of the meetings with Dundas; her voting rights were not needed. All Dundas and his daughter had spoken of were taxation liabilities for the current year, rental increases, and maintenance issues. It had been a smokescreen to confuse her, Caroline knew that, with superfluous nonsense, and yet the full extent of her father's assets still eluded her.

She had signed at the end of the will reading, agreed to take no further action to contest it. It had to be Ralph who would contest the will, and he had little credibility. It was a narrow line that they walked, Caroline and him. It was all or nothing. The thought of her mother propped up in her bed still gave her occasional sleepless nights.

***

Leonard Dundas knew the truth, having spent more time with the reclusive man than anyone else, and now Ralph was threatening to cause trouble.

'Father, we cannot let this collapse. All that you have built up, gone in an instant,' Jill Dundas said.

'How can it? You know the subterfuge that we have created, the false trails, the hidden bank accounts.'

'Admittedly it will be difficult, and we are open to criminal investigation.'

'We are open to legal challenges, that is all. It will take them more than my lifetime, probably more than yours, to get to the truth, and then it will only be what we allow them to see.'

'Caroline Dickson?'

'We'll ensure she has the sweeteners that we have agreed on. She'll not want for money.'

'Ralph?'

'An idiot, dangerous though. The man's savvier than his sister. He could cause us trouble.'

'Are you suggesting…?'

'Not yet. We have enough to deal with at this time,' Leonard said. He knew that he had schooled his daughter well. Gilbert Lawrence may well have made a fortune, but that did not mean that it belonged to his offspring. It was a dog-eat-dog world, and he, Leonard, had been tutored by the best, by Gilbert Lawrence. When he had been at his peak he had been unassailable, and many had fallen foul of him, forced to sell their properties below their true value.

Sometimes it had been Gilbert who had created the situation, sometimes it was the economy, but the man had profited at the expense of others, not caring as to their fate. Why should he, Leonard Dundas, a man who had put up with that dishevelled man of few words for the last thirty years, care if the man's children were deprived of their inheritance? Caroline, he knew he could deal with. Ralph, he was not so sure. He would wait and see, but not for too long.

Chapter 12

Gary Frost did not appreciate being summoned to a meeting by someone he considered of little worth. 'Lawrence, what is it?' he said disparagingly once the two men were seated in chairs close to the hotel bar.

'I believe the situation has changed, don't you?' Ralph said. 'It is no longer me that needs you, it is you that needs me.' Caroline would not approve of what he was doing, but then she was naïve in so many ways. Too many years of affluence had weakened her ability to see what they were up against.

'I don't see how,' Frost said.

'The money I owe you is unimportant,' Ralph said with bravado. It was a habitual error on his part that had got him into trouble on a few occasions. He should have remembered Spain and what had happened there. But there he had been giving the spiel about how investing in Spain was low-risk, an easy way to secure a financial nest egg at a discount price, not knowing that the couple attentively listening to his advice were English civil servants, and not only that, from the inland revenue. Bob and Deidre Marshall, a couple in their forties, had considered buying a small house in Spain, not far from Barcelona. Deidre had the money from a favourite aunt who had just died, and they had researched the subject thoroughly. They understood the legal aspects of a foreign purchase, the taxation implications, and above all, the real cost, not what the man with the smooth tongue was telling them.

It was they who had reported Ralph and his partner to the English authorities, who then passed on the information to their Spanish counterparts. The end result was that Ralph and his partner had been arrested and flung into a damp cell where the mosquitoes kept them awake at night, as well as the cockroaches that scurried over them once the light went off.

'It's still my money that I want from you, plus the interest,' Frost said. He did not appreciate or trust people who were overly confident. They were the most likely to let him down. 'I've given you time on account of who your father was.'

'And what you could hope to gain from it,' Ralph said.

'I know Dundas has got you and your sister tied up. The man's smart, smarter than the two of you.'

'That's why I've summoned you here.'

'*Summoned.* I suggest you be very careful in how you talk to me. Your position is still tenuous.'

'Okay, I'll concede that you've come to see me at my request,' Ralph said. 'The problem is that Dundas had somehow managed to obtain certification that my father was sane.'

'Your mother upstairs propped up in the bed, is that it?'

'Not the act of a rational man, and then he signed over control of his fortune to Leonard Dundas.'

'How much do you know of your father's holdings?'

'Not enough.'

'And your sister?'

'She will not play her hand at this time. I intend to contest the will, but Dundas has all the information, not me or my sister. We need to know more.'

'What do you want me to do?'

'Five per cent of whatever you find over and above what we have already. Remember that not all can be liquidated quickly.'

'Do you intend to liquidate?'

'I want money, not property. If I have enough, then I'll be overseas and enjoying life.'

'Hustling?'

'Not for me. I'll be an upright citizen, may even settle down.'

Frost knew the money that he was owed was inconsequential compared to what was on offer. 'What do you want from me?' he said.

'Call off your dwarf, and then help me to chase what's out there.'

'It's a deal.'

'And cancel the money I owe you.'

'It's a lot of money.'

'I'm offering you a fortune.'

'Or nothing?'

'As you said. It's a risk on your part, on mine.'

'Where's the risk to you?' Frost said.

'I don't trust you, Frost. You're a man who succeeds through thuggery and intimidation. You could still have me kneecapped or killed.'

'There's no risk from me. You're too valuable now. Keeping you alive is my only concern.'

Ralph ordered a bottle of champagne to celebrate. For the time being, he and Gary Frost were united. But behind the smiles and the polite conversation both men knew that the other was treacherous, and neither would relax until their business arrangement had come to a conclusion.

***

Caroline Lawrence attended the next meeting at Dundas's office. It was clear that it was to be a repeat of the previous one: the minutes read, an update from Jill Dundas on profit and loss, tax liability, the year ahead. Caroline could see that she needed Ralph in the meetings.

Caroline listened as Jill Dundas droned on about provisions for the next year's projected downturn in rentals, and the possible selling of five per cent of the real estate, a shopping centre not far from London, where the vacancy rate was higher than the national average and only likely to get worse.

'How much?' Caroline asked. It was the first item in the otherwise dull meeting that interested her.

'Forty million pounds, if we act now. If, as we suspect, the major tenant, a supermarket, pulls out, the value could go down five million.'

'Won't any purchaser know that?'

'Not yet. The supermarket chain will not reveal what their long-term plans are.'

'But you know?'

'We pay to know.'

'Someone on the inside?'

'Someone who will keep it under wraps for the time being,' Jill said.

'How much will that cost?'

'A lot less than the five million drop in value if we don't act now.'

'And the proceeds?'

'After costs, twenty per cent to you.'

'And the eighty per cent?' Caroline asked. She had to admit that close to five million pounds excited her.

'That will be invested, probably into another property, and then there are our costs.'

'How much to you?'

'It will be documented. After costs of sale, then approximately ten per cent to our account.'

'The bribe?'

'That will not be recorded.'

'Illegal?'

'Debatable, but Caroline, do you care? We are offering you a lot a money.'

'But when and how often?'

'The sale will take some time, maybe four to five months. After that, we will make a payment to you.'

'And after this, what then?'

'Your father's instructions were clear, no more than five per cent divesting of assets in any two-year period,' Jill said.

'But how can that be valid? He's dead, and I am his daughter. Surely that decision belongs with me.'

'Not according to your father's instructions,' Leonard said. 'He named me as the executor of his will and his legacy, and I, as his friend, will uphold what he has requested.'

'Even if it's not legally binding?'

'Any attempt to interfere will result in your immediate exclusion from this meeting and any subsequent ones.'

'Are you taking over from my father,' Caroline said.

'The empire that he created will continue, and you, Gilbert's daughter, will be provided for, but let us be clear here and now: it will be me and my daughter and this company that make the decisions.'

'Is this legal?' Caroline said meekly.

'It is. I've spent half my life with your father. I know what he wanted, what I believe is correct. There is no further discussion. You, Caroline, in accordance with your father's wishes, are welcome at these meetings. You will receive substantial sums of money for your compliance, but any attempt to take over from me and my daughter will result in your non-attendance, and no information as to what we are doing,' Dundas said.

'Which means you will make the decisions. It is for me to rubber stamp them.'

'Stamp or otherwise, it makes little difference to us.'

'You certainly screwed my father, and you say he was sane.'

'He was, ask the experts. Let me know what your decision is. Either you are with us, or you are not, but I have had a long time to ensure that the Dundas family is in control. You may regard this as a hostile takeover if you like, but remember, the law is on my side, not yours.'

Caroline looked over at Jill Dundas, could see the smug look on her face. Now, Caroline knew the truth. For all those years, as her father had slowly declined, her mother propped up in her bed upstairs, Leonard Dundas had been subtly engineering his control of the empire her father had set up. She could not speak, other than to weakly nod her head.

Chapter 13

Michael Lawrence, now under the tutelage of Giles Helmsley, the eccentric leader of the Anarchist Revolutionaries of England, was, for once, not drunk or drugged. He was coherent and feeling as sick as a dog.

He was in Helmsley's flat, not the dosshouse which was more in keeping with the disreputable state of the grandson of the property mogul: his lank hair, the tattoos, the smell of alcohol, and the years of living rough.

'Michael, it's our chance to strike a blow for the cause,' Helmsley said. If the young man had been awake and aware, he would have noticed the insincerity in the tone of his leader's voice, the man almost choking as he spoke what he did not believe.

'Go away, I'm ill. I need a fix,' Michael said as he retched, his stomach incapable of emitting any more.

'You need to stand up and be counted. It is time for us to strike at the system.'

Michael Lawrence moved away from the chair where he had been sitting and leant over the kitchen sink. His head throbbed, his body shook, and he was shivering, even though the flat was warm. Helmsley knew he needed Michael functional, although he was not sure how he could use him, or how long it would take. He did not relish the man occupying the bed in the second bedroom, but for the cause, his cause, he would suffer.

'I need a fix,' the young man said yet again. Helmsley knew he had a poor specimen of manhood, but he had no option but to use him.

Within his group of degenerates, one or two were committed to the cause, the others were only interested in banging whatever drum it was that gave them what they wanted, which in the case of Michael Lawrence was a ready supply of heroin and alcohol, coupled with the occasional woman. And now Helmsley could see the way to move his cause forward, while at the same time embellishing his bank account.

Luckily for him, he knew, he had within their midst the grandson of a wealthy and dead man, a grandson who must surely be entitled to some money. Not that the complaining youth cared, but Helmsley was a man of strong personal convictions, a man who had dedicated his life to the less fortunate and found most of them lacking in the moral fibre and tenacity that he possessed.

'I need you to stand up and claim your inheritance,' Helmsley said. He thrust Lawrence under a hot shower and liberally applied the soap to him. It was not the first time that the leader of the Anarchist Revolutionaries of England had been excited by the sight of a naked man, but now was not the time and the place.

Once Michael was out of the shower and dry, Helmsley removed his earrings and studs. Not much could be done with the tattoos, only a long-sleeved shirt to cover them the best he could. Once he looked more normal, Helmsley took him to a hairdresser to get his hair cut into a more conventional style.

Two days later, a man entered the office of Leonard Dundas and his daughter. It was Jill, the daughter, who invited him into her office after he had said who he was.

'I believe that my grandfather has died,' Michael Lawrence said.

'You were mentioned in his will, but how did you know?' Jill said. She looked at the man in front of her. If this was the Michael Lawrence that they had been told about, then either the information had been wrong, or the man had changed.

'I believe there are conditions placed on me.' He was dressed in a red-striped shirt, a pair of blue trousers, and a navy jacket. He did not like the look, but Helmsley had explained it all to him carefully.

'Play your part, help the cause,' Helmsley's repetitive chant over the last few days. He, Michael Lawrence, knew what was required of him, and if it was dressing in clothes that he did not like, pretending to be one of those he despised, then that was what he would do.

'How do you know about the conditions?'

'I was told. It doesn't matter, does it?' It did to Jill Dundas, but she chose not to comment.

'Are you still on drugs?'

'I'm clean, although I need help.'

'One of the conditions is that you will check into a drug rehabilitation centre. Is that acceptable?'

'Yes.'

'Today?'

'I'll need money for expenses.'

'At the centre, you will need nothing, but I will authorise payment of five thousand pounds to your bank account.'

'Thank you.'

'It is not for drugs.'

'I will adhere to the conditions,' Michael said, his stomach cramping.

Michael Lawrence had prior to meeting with Jill Dundas, and with Helmsley's prompting, contacted his aunt, Caroline, who had told him what was required. She had then phoned Ralph to update him. 'It's playing into our hands,' Caroline had said, although she was not sure if it was or how.

Ralph was suspicious of his son's resurrection, not having had any contact with him for several years, and the last time they had met, he had deemed his son a hopeless case. But according to his sister, who had met him, her nephew looked presentable, although pale and definitely undernourished.

Jill Dundas booked the young man into the Waverley Hills Centre, a stately home on the outskirts of London, in an area complete with rolling hills and fresh air. Michael, driven down by Caroline, looked at the place as they drove through the main gates and up the sweeping driveway. He did not look forward to it, having attempted to get off the drugs a few years earlier. But that had been a detox centre alongside a charitable institution in one of the rougher parts of London. That hadn't worked; he wasn't sure if this would, but he had Caroline in one ear, Helmsley in the other, both offering encouragement, although neither had met and were unlikely to.

'Good to see you, Mr Lawrence,' Ian Grantly, the medical director at the drug rehabilitation centre, said. The sign outside made no mention of its function, or that it catered to the rich and famous. Caroline saw one of her favourite singers as she walked through the building with Michael and Grantly. At another time and place, she would have felt inclined to stop and talk to him, but as Grantly had said, 'We're all equal here.'

'Leave me, Caroline,' Michael said. 'I'll play the game.'

'It's up to you,' Caroline said. She had to admit that after so many years of not seeing her nephew, she had been surprised by his better than expected appearance. He was also polite, and he had inherited the charm that his father had in abundance.

'Once an addict, always an addict,' Grantly said as he escorted Caroline off the premises. 'Visiting hours, Monday and Wednesday, 2 p.m.'

'Can you get him off the drugs?'

'We can control him in here, but outside, that's when the problems start. He looks as though he's had it rough.'

'There's not been a lot of guidance from his father, and as for his mother…'

'Long gone?'

'The mother, no idea where she is. His father is here, although he's been absent for more years than I can remember.'

'That's the problem. Michael needs a support mechanism.'

'I'll try, but I'm not going to be a nursemaid.'

'I'm informed that all costs will be borne by his grandfather's estate.'

'They will, although you'll be submitting them to a Leonard Dundas. He's as careful with money as my father was. I'd suggest that you don't commit to any treatment out of the ordinary unless you've run it past Dundas.'

'I read about your father,' Grantly said.

'No doubt you formed your own opinion.'

'Your mother, that's what I assume you're referring to. Hardly the actions of a rational man, but I suppose you don't need me to tell you that.'

'I don't. Ralph, my brother, Michael's father, is also not always easy to understand.'

'It doesn't make it easier when there's eccentricity in the family.'

'But you'll try. I need Michael on my side,' Caroline said.

'And his father?'

'If you have a centre for stupidity, he could do with a few weeks there.'

'Bad decisions?'

'In the past. I just hope he's wiser now.'

'Do you think he is?'

'No.'

***

For once, Ralph was welcomed into Caroline and Desmond Dickson's house, but not because the two men liked each other. On the contrary, Ralph regarded Desmond as a pompous snob; Desmond considered his brother-in-law worthless.

'The situation's changed,' Caroline said. She was holding a glass of red wine and leaning back on the dining room chair. She had to admit that she was slightly tipsy.

'Not to me, it hasn't,' Ralph said. He had drunk as much as his sister, but he was a regular drinker, Caroline was not. 'Dundas is still in control.'

'But your son is attempting to reform.'

'He's a weak man, a major disappointment.'

'The pot calling the kettle black,' Desmond said in a moment of derision. For the last few hours he had been civil to Ralph, but now, when all three were winding down after a meal prepared by Caroline and three bottles of the best wine from the house's cellar, the reluctance to speak their minds had dissipated.

'Desmond, you may be married to my sister, but it doesn't stop you being a pain in the rear end.'

'Please,' Caroline interceded, not very successfully as the effects of the alcohol were impairing her usually coherent speech. 'We need to work together. The enemy is Leonard and Jill Dundas, not each other.'

'Caroline is right,' Desmond conceded. 'I spoke in error. Ralph, please accept my apologies.'

'There is no more to say. My son will assist or he won't. It doesn't stop the issue with Dundas and his scheming daughter, and what they have control of. Caroline, you've attended their meetings. Are you able to update us with any more than what you have already told us?'

'Not really. We can assume there are more properties than we know of, more bank accounts, but unless Dundas tells us, we're blind.'

The three of them moved to another room. Caroline prepared coffee, black for everyone, and she made it strong.

'I have a contact. I don't trust him,' Ralph said.

'A criminal?' Desmond said. He didn't like where the conversation was heading. He did not need to walk on the dark side. He had a successful business, upstanding members of society as his customers. He had met the occasional villain, realised to what lengths they would go to maintain their importance or to achieve their aim.

'We need to hack Dundas's computers, check out the files in his office.'

'We need someone on the inside, not a crook,' Caroline said.

'Anyone in mind?' Ralph said. He was about to suggest bringing in Gary Frost, but he knew the man could not be trusted.

'Someone in Dundas's office must be willing to help if we pay enough.'

'That's the easiest way to get yourself evicted from the meetings.'

'Your contact?' Caroline said. She wanted the money from the sale of the shopping centre, but that was months away, even more time for the Dundases to put additional blockers in place.

'What do we know?' Desmond said.

'We know of three bank accounts in the UK, two overseas.'

'Passwords?'

'Not to any of them.'

'And how much in total?'

'Seven million pounds approximately.'

'So where is the rest? There must be more cash,' Ralph said. He couldn't see how they could progress further by talking about it. There was a time to bring in help, and that time was now.

The three studied the figures that had been presented to Caroline by Leonard Dundas. According to what they had in front of them, there were twenty-five million pounds deposited in various bank accounts, the locations not specified, as well as a total of one hundred and eighty-three properties, the majority in the

UK, others around the world. Nobody believed that what they were being shown was the true situation, purely what had been prepared for them to see, and an independent audit of Gilbert Lawrence's assets would not reveal much more, cleverly concealed as they would be.

'I don't trust my person,' Ralph said.

'Then we need someone in Dundas's office,' Desmond said. For once he found his brother-in-law making sense. 'Your son, Michael?' he said.

'I've not seen him yet. Caroline, what did you reckon?'

'It may be time for you to reacquaint yourself with him. His return may be suspicious.'

'What do you mean?'

'He was, according to what I've gleaned from the police, involved with anarchists.'

'Do we have them in this country?'

'Apparently we do. They call themselves the Anarchist Revolutionaries of England. It's run by Giles Helmsley, a disgraced academic.'

'Him?' Ralph said.

'Do you know him?'

'We were at school together. Back then he wasn't an anarchist, just odd.'

'What do you mean?'

'He always saw himself as superior. Academically brilliant, always on about the ruling classes.'

'But you went to an elitist school, even members of the aristocracy in your year.'

'But Helmsley was different. He was working class, won himself a scholarship. Supposedly an attempt by the school to make itself out to be egalitarian.'

'Was it?'

'Not at all, but I suppose there were brownie points to be gained for those in charge. Anyway, Helmsley was there and he was keen, keener than any of us. He always sat up the front of the class, looking for an opportunity to show us how smart he was.'

'Was he?'

'He was. We were at the back of the class, only interested in playing up, getting a few drinks in, making plans to meet up with the local girls.'

'Helmsley?'

'Not him. We always thought he was gay, not that there was any proof, but it was unnatural. Teenage males are hot for anything in a skirt, but Helmsley, he'd be there, his face in a book.'

'You've not changed,' Desmond said.

'Thankfully, I haven't,' Ralph said. 'Anyway, Michael. What's he up to?'

'Are you suspicious?'

'Of Michael? Like father, like son. If he's willing to sort himself out, it can only be with someone at his back. I was always weak if temptation was there, but Michael, he was worse. If there was alcohol, he'd down the lot, and then he was into drugs, running with the crowd. Quite frankly, I assumed he'd OD at some stage.'

'It didn't concern you?' Caroline said.

'It did, but he's an adult, and even if I was more responsible, I couldn't take him on. I have enough trouble looking after myself.'

'And his mother?'

'The last I heard, she was swanning around the Caribbean. A beautiful woman in her day, probably still is, but she was never the maternal type.'

'Not much of an upbringing for your son,' Caroline said.

'No worse than ours. The first thing that our parents did was to ship us off to boarding school, come home at long weekends, holidays, and even then, we were soon sent off on an activity somewhere.'

'That was our mother and father, devoted to each other.'

'Not normal, though.'

'We survived.'

'Who knows if what they did was right or wrong. And besides, it's Michael that we're talking about. The man is sorting himself out, a weak and feeble person susceptible to drugs. The condition of our father's will was that he had to stay clean for a year, get himself a job. I can't see him doing that.'

'What if he's cleaned up? What are the chances of getting him into Dundas's office? Could we trust him? Would Dundas let him in, give him a job?'

'If I agree to Dundas's conditions, he might,' Caroline said.

'What conditions?'

'If I agree to rubber stamp everything that charlatan and his daughter do, then maybe they'll agree.'

'Try it on,' Desmond said, 'and Ralph, go and see your son, make your peace.'

'And Helmsley?' Ralph said.

'Let's see what he does. If he becomes a nuisance, we'll need to neutralise him.'

Chapter 14

'No, we never met Mr Lawrence,' Kingsley Wilde, the senior psychoanalyst, said. He was broad-shouldered, with grey hair and a beard trimmed short.

Isaac and Larry were in the offices of Wyvern Psychiatrists, one of the organisations that had declared Gilbert Lawrence sane and able to sign his will.

'If you never met the man, how can you declare him to be of sound mind?' Isaac asked.

'It was an unusual request,' Wilde said, as he sat upright, looking at the two police officers with a keen eye.

'We're not here for evaluation,' Larry said. He found the man unnerving.

'Apologies. I'm not conducting an analysis of you. No doubt you're both subjected to vigorous checks of your physical and mental status by the police doctor.'

'We are,' Isaac said. 'We're concerned that for the last twelve years you have given Gilbert Lawrence a clean bill of health, when the man lived an unusual life and, as we now know, his dead wife was upstairs in the house.'

'How a person lives does not decree whether he or she is mentally impaired. We had realised that he was eccentric, but our tests are not there to deal with what we would believe to be unusual. Our requirement was to ascertain whether the man was capable of signing his last will and testament, that is all.'

'Are you saying that living in that house as a recluse does not indicate a person with severe mental issues?' Isaac said, not sure if Wilde was on the defensive and trying to justify his position or whether he genuinely believed what he was saying.

'We conducted standard tests in writing and via phone.'

'No video?' Larry said.

'At the request of his solicitor, it was only audio.'

'And how did the man sound?'

'He sounded like a man of advanced years. He was coherent if a little slow in his responses. Apart from that, he was found to be in control of his faculties. And let me make this clear. If the man's last will and testament is to be contested, it is up to those contesting it to prove that he did not have the required mental capacity or did not properly understand and approve the content of the will.'

'Will you stand up in court and defend your position?' Isaac said.

'Detective Chief Inspector Cook, we are a reputable organisation. There is no need for us to defend what we have stated. The standard tests were conducted, the results were appropriate. As far as we are concerned, the man was sane.'

'Even with his wife upstairs in her bed for thirty years.'

'Even then, although we did not know of that. A murderer, a rapist, those who commit outrageous and disturbing abuses against other people or commit terrorist acts could all be sane. It may be that others will say they are not, but the tests are specific in so far as Mr Lawrence was concerned. His wife in her bed will no doubt sway the general public, but in law it will have little bearing. If others wish to dispute the will the man signed, then they can, but the law is not on their side in this matter. I realise that is not what people would expect, but the onus of proving mental incapacity is on those disputing.'

Wilde, no doubt, had a list of clients impressed by the letters after his name. To be associated with a disputed will, with him having to argue in a court of law that a man who he had declared sane had in fact been living with the skeletal remains of his wife, was not going to be well regarded in the media.

Isaac could only imagine the headlines in the press: 'Billionaire sane even though his dead wife was propped up in their bed,' says a prominent psychoanalyst. Other media outlets might not be so kind, running quizzes on how to determine your sanity: 'Do you have your dead wife upstairs? If you do, then you're sane'; 'If she's in the kitchen making you tea, then suspect borderline mad'. Facebook could well have a field day, with the amateur pundits providing comedy.

'Mr Wilde,' Larry said, 'are you seriously expecting us or anybody else to believe that your tests, as detailed as they may have been and even if they were in line with agreed procedures, were not impacted by his dead wife being upstairs? And before you answer, remember that not only did he put her in the bed, he had previously buried her for some months and stripped her carcass, cutting chunks off her body, before putting her in with flesh-eating beetles. Can we be expected to believe that the man was sane, can any court of law, can you?'

'I hold by what I said,' Wilde said. He sat down, a dejected look on his face. 'I know what you're saying. There are some who still regard what we do as charlatanism, an opportunity for the criminally insane to get off serving a sentence in a normal prison, to be confined to a mental institution with three meals a day and daytime television, even after they've murdered or committed other ghastly crimes.'

'We intend to contact two other psychoanalysts,' Isaac said. 'One in America, the other in Australia. Will they answer the same as you?'

'They will.'

'Any gain to yourself?' Larry said.

'We were paid for our services, that is all.'

'A lot of money?'

'Yes, but that's to be expected. Any legal challenges to the man's inheritance were expected to be rigorous. Anything other than total diligence on our part would have left us open.'

'And Leonard Dundas?' Isaac said.

'I have no idea what Dundas's arrangements were. All I know is that Gilbert Lawrence understood what he was signing and that he had the mental faculties to do so. Regardless of how your investigations turn out, we acted correctly.'

'And if he murdered his wife?'

'Did he?'

'We have no proof, but if he did?'

'The tests were conducted according to accepted criteria.'

***

A father and son meeting after so many years should under normal circumstances be a cause for celebration, Ralph Lawrence realised, although he could not see it that way. He had never been paternal, no more than the mother of the boy had been maternal. It had always been agreed between Ralph and the then Mrs Lawrence that no child should result from their union. However, when Ralph had been flush with money, and the alcohol had flowed, as well as ganja, in Negril, Jamaica, the one-time hippy resort that had become the playground of the rich and famous, Yolanda had become pregnant. Neither she nor Ralph had been excited at the time, each blaming the other, but nine months later the boy had been born on a rainy day in London.

A cause of celebration it should have been, but Ralph had taken one look and decided fatherhood wasn't for him. His wife had taken a look as well and felt maternal love for what she had produced. For the sake of the child, active and healthy with a fine pair of lungs as he went through teething, the reluctant parents had tried their best, even ensuring that their son was well looked after. By the time of his fifth birthday, the young Michael was sent off to school. With him out of the way for most of the day, Ralph reverted to type and started to stay out longer, Yolanda also finding herself another lover.

Ralph had known that his wife was easy, the reason he had been attracted to her in the first place. He had never wanted the perennial wallflower, the stay-at-home wife, the meal on the table at dinnertime sort of woman. He had wanted someone wild and free, the same as him.

Both Ralph and Yolanda looked across the table one night, as the young Michael sat in his chair eating his meal.

'We're not cut out for this,' Ralph said. It was the first time in several months that he had said something that his wife could agree with, the arguments, the separate beds, having become the norm.

'He's still our son,' Yolanda said.

'What do you suggest?'

'When he reaches seven we can send him to a boarding school. In his holidays, he can come and stay with either of us.'

And that was that, so much so that in the years from his seventh birthday up until he was eighteen, father and son had not seen each other more than a handful of times. And even then it had always been for short periods, and neither felt comfortable in each other's presence. Not that Yolanda, the mother, had been any better: always off here and there with one wealthy lover or another. Very soon the periods away from boarding school became a succession of brief contacts for the young Lawrence with his parents, intersected with activities such as hiking in Scotland or learning to surf in Hawaii, or whatever else the wealthy did with their children until they grew up.

The drugs came about after a weekend with the son of a banker at his house in the north of England. Two friends who had boarded together for the last five years, each looking out for the other. Michael Lawrence, extrovert and charming, his friend Billy, shy and introvert. It was the former who secured the two women, both eighteen and attractive, working class. With an empty house, the two friends seduced the women, not difficult given the amount of alcohol in the house, and it was them who introduced Michael and Billy to heroin.

Neither had been able to resist the descent into hell. Billy had died at the age of twenty-three, alone and destitute, after his father, desperate to protect his reputation, had thrown him and Michael out of the house after coming home early and finding the two of them cavorting with the women in the indoor swimming pool.

And now Ralph Lawrence found himself in the same room as his son. Each looked at the other, and then out of the window at the rehabilitation centre. Outside the weather was frosty and overcast, reflective of the mood in the room.

'It has been a long time,' Ralph said.

'Time moves on,' Michael said. He stood calmly, sedated or whatever the centre did to a person; Ralph didn't know, didn't want to either. He had spent a lifetime drinking, never once succumbing to anything more harmful than cocaine, the occasional joint of marijuana, and as for injecting into a vein, that wasn't for him. He had seen it, who hadn't in the circles he had moved in, but a fear of needles and an aversion to the sight of blood had served him well.

'You're looking well,' Ralph said.

Both men struggled to come to terms with the current situation, and neither was enamoured of the other. Even when Michael had been growing up, and on the rare occasions that they had met, it had been difficult. A few hours away from the school at the weekend, a meal at a restaurant, a brief chat about school and what the other was up to, and then back to the school, both of them breathing a sigh of relief.

And now the two of them together, one older and supposedly wiser, the other in his thirties. It was the only time in nearly twenty years that both had been sober or detoxed. An uneasy stillness filled the room. Eventually, Michael took the initiative and approached his father, his right hand held out. Both men shook before Ralph put his arms around his son and embraced him. 'Sorry,' he said. 'We've both stuffed up, but now's our chance to put it right.'

The two men left the room and walked down the corridor outside. Both of them felt a little embarrassed about their momentary show of emotion. Ralph had to admit to feeling good for the embrace, Michael was not so sure. To him, this was the man who had deserted him, had thrown his mother away. Whatever Yolanda Lawrence may have been, Michael, through the years at boarding school, had maintained a vision of his mother as someone of loveliness, someone who would come and rescue him. But she had never come, and Michael could only blame the man at his side.

'It wasn't wise, you coming here,' Michael said as the two men sat down next to a coffee machine in the centre's dining room. Ralph took two coffees and gave one to his son.

'I wasn't sure if I should, but Caroline said it was important. How is the treatment?'

'The need remains.'

'Unpleasant?'

'It has been, but there is a greater cause.'

'My father's fortune,' Ralph said.

'I cannot wait a year.'

'The drugs will return?'

'I don't know. I'm not used to feeling normal. Is this what it's like?'

'If you mean boring and uneventful, then yes,' Ralph said. 'Normality is that. I miss my previous life, but then I'm older.'

'My mother?'

'We'll find her. The last I heard she was in the Caribbean, but that's a few years ago.'

'Why are you here, father? To gloat?'

Ralph shifted uncomfortably on his seat. The man he was talking to was a stranger, although the resemblance between the two men was noticeable. 'You went to Caroline and then to Dundas, why?'

'There were two police officers.'

'DCI Cook?'

'He was one of them. They told me about the one million pounds if I straightened myself out.'

'The money would not have convinced you to change.'

'It didn't, but Giles Helmsley encouraged me.'

'I know him, did you know?'

'He never mentioned it.'

'No doubt he wouldn't. I was told that he was an anarchist.'

'He is. He understands what needs to happen, and the cause needs money.'

'Giles Helmsley needs money. Is he still the same malignant worm?'

'He is a great man.'

Ralph realised that even without drugs, his son had fallen under the influence of Helmsley, a man who had few redeeming features.

'Then we must disagree as to what you want, but it is still possible for us to work together for our mutual benefit, would you agree?' Ralph said. As much as his son was alien to him, he had to admit that he liked the man, even if his attachment to Helmsley was of great concern.

'For our benefit, then yes. But you, father, must do your part. If I am to work with you and my aunt, then you must agree to mend your ways.'

'I'll not get a job in an office, but let's see. I can still sell, maybe there are opportunities for me in this country.'

'And no hustling, breaking the law. We must be beyond reproach.'

'We will be. It is strange, Michael. I almost feel excited at the prospect.'

'I do not. It will be hard for me, but with you and Giles, I will persevere. I also want to see my mother one more time.'

'Why only one?' Ralph said.

'Neither of us was put on this earth to live to a ripe old age, and neither of us has a woman who is devoted to us, we to them.'

Ralph said nothing, only thought to himself that Yolanda, wherever she was and whoever she was with, would look good dead and in bed. His son had reopened wounds that had been closed for too long.

Chapter 15

The atmosphere in Homicide was tense. It had been six weeks, and not one person had been put forward as the possible murderer of Gilbert Lawrence. The question of Dorothy Lawrence was still unresolved, and her remains had not been released for burial.

'Update,' Isaac Cook said. His mood had worsened in the last week, understandable given the current situation. In the past, the DCI's temperament had remained constant even when the pressure was on, but now he could see unresolved questions begging for an answer.

Larry Hill was standing, his usual pose, Bridget grasped a file of papers in her hand, and Wendy Gladstone nursed her left leg, not wanting to show that her arthritis was giving her trouble, not fully conscious that rubbing the sore area only made her pain more noticeable to the others.

'Ralph Lawrence is visible,' Wendy said.

'Doing what?' Larry asked.

'He's moved out of the hotel and into a small flat in Bayswater.'

'Not his style, is it?'

'Not at all, but the man's inheritance is conditional on him and his son sorting themselves out.'

'That was for one year,' Isaac said. 'Neither of them is going to last that long. The son's a hopeless junkie.'

'He's still in rehabilitation and doing well by all accounts,' Bridget said.

'How do you know?'

'I phoned them up.'

'They may have just given you the standard response,' Larry said.

'They may have, but you can check, can't you?'

'We can.'

Wendy was unsure what to do. In the past, she would have been involved looking for someone who was missing, but now all the main players were visible. Leonard Dundas and his daughter were most days at their office, Caroline Dickson and her husband, Desmond, were to be found at Desmond's place of business or at home, and Ralph Lawrence was either at his flat or out at the son's rehabilitation centre. And Molly Dempster could be found at her small house most days of the week.

'Bridget, the papers you're holding?' Isaac said.

'I've checked with the psychoanalysts in Australia and America. They've applied similar tests to Kingsley Wilde, and I've checked on the internet to see if there have been similar cases to this that would set a precedent.'

'Have there been any?'

'Not with a dead wife upstairs. Disputed wills can take years to resolve and a great deal of money. There was one case in the United States where so much money was spent to secure the inheritance that the legal costs were more than the money the complainant ultimately received.'

'Has a case been registered yet by any of Lawrence's family?' Isaac said.

'Not yet. They have twelve years to dispute the will, indefinite if fraud is proven.'

'Ralph Lawrence has to stay out of trouble for a year, the same as the son. Neither of them is capable. Is Giles Helmsley still around?'

'He's visited Michael on a couple of occasions. On the third, he was ejected after making a scene about his right to see his friend whenever he wanted without visiting hours.'

'Quoting the anarchist bible?'

'According to the person I spoke to,' Bridget said, 'he made a fool of himself, spoke about the upcoming revolution when he and his people would take over, and he would remember those who had removed him from the building.'

'If he took Wilde's tests, what do you reckon?' Isaac said.

'He'd pass.'

***

Leonard Dundas, almost as old as Gilbert Lawrence, knew that his days as a solicitor were numbered, even his days on earth. Not a spiritual man, he could only reflect on what he had achieved. The son of a minor civil servant, a man who punched the time clock at work every morning, a newspaper under his arm. And then at the end of the day, he punched out and took the bus to his council house in a nondescript suburb, with a non-descript wife, only to sit by the radio of an evening smoking his pipe.

Dundas remembered it only too well: the sheer drudgery, the infinite boredom of a father who every year took his two-week holiday and booked into the same boarding house in the same seaside resort. And there would be the man with his wife and children, strolling up and down the promenade, sitting on the beach in rented deck chairs, and then, for a treat, fish and chips.

The one positive, Leonard Dundas realised as he sat at his desk, that his father had been a disciplined man, a trait inherited by the son. His father was a creature of circumstance, the son was as well, but he had had the benefit of an education and the chance to see some of the world. His mind was not closed to the opportunities, and a chance encounter with a young man about town by the name of Gilbert Lawrence had been opportune for both of them. To Dundas, Gilbert was a friend, as was his wife, but the children, Caroline and Ralph, were of little consequence.

He judged Caroline to be competent, although financially not astute. Ralph had been the bane of Gilbert's life, and neither father nor son had much in common apart from a mutual disdain for each other, not like his daughter, Jill. To Leonard, his daughter was a person of great worth, even to Gilbert who had expressed his admiration for her. And now, Leonard knew, as he sat calmly in an attempt to slow the shaking of his hand, to ease the aching in his back and the throbbing in his chest, he had complete confidence that Jill would maintain Gilbert's legacy, and his as well.

'What is it, Father?' Jill said as she came into his office. She had seen the glazed look in the man's eyes, and him sitting motionless, almost like a statue. She also knew that he had pushed himself too hard in the last month securing Gilbert Lawrence's fortune, making sure that the loose ends were tied up, and that his daughter had signing rights to all the accounts around the world, and that her name had been given on any proxies needed.

'I've done what I can,' Dundas said. And with that, his head fell forward. Ten minutes later, Leonard Dundas was in the back of an ambulance and on the way to the hospital, a mere formality, as he had been declared dead by the medic who had arrived with the ambulance.

The first that Homicide heard was a phone call from Caroline Dickson. 'Leonard Dundas has suffered a heart attack. He's dead,' she said. It had been just five minutes after he had left for the hospital that she had arrived at his office for another of the scheduled meetings.

Bridget contacted the hospital to confirm it and then informed Pathology that they had another body to check.

***

With Leonard Dundas dead, the scheduled meeting at his office was cancelled indefinitely. Not that either the man's death or deferring the meeting concerned Caroline. To her, he had been the devil incarnate, the man who had engineered himself into her father's confidence and then stolen everything he could lay his hands on. She knew how Dundas and his daughter lived, very well in fact. A house in town, better than hers, and a place in the country.

With the senior Dundas out of the way, Caroline met with Ralph and Desmond to discuss the way forward. Desmond had to admit that his brother-in-law had changed. No more the flamboyance, the endless patter of the 'what I can do for you' and 'to our mutual benefit' jargon that he was usually only too keen to roll out.

'It's Michael,' Ralph said. 'He's getting out in a few days.'

'A problem?' Desmond said.

'You know it is. He needs somewhere to stay, and I don't think that he and I should share, do you?'

'Not here, if that's what you are suggesting.'

'We need Michael the way he is now. I went and saw him a couple of days ago. He's straightened himself out, and he's sure got my gift of the gab. He was charming one of the young nurses. I wouldn't be surprised if the two of them haven't got a thing going on when the lights are low.'

'I thought there were rules about fraternising with the patients,' Caroline said.

'It's not a hospital. More like a hotel with rules, that's all. Good luck to him if he is. She was a cracker to look at.'

'Has he said that he wants to stay with you?'

'It's either me or he'll be back with Helmsley. He was back out there again, and this time they let him in.'

'Why?'

'He played their game, apologised for his previous outburst. Even gave them some cock and bull story about him suffering from an addiction.'

'And they believed it?'

'No reason not to. The man's an oddball, and he can talk. No doubt they weren't checking too hard either. There was another celebrity checking in, one of those holier-than-thou types. Outside there were some reporters and cameras. The centre was under pressure, and Helmsley took the opportunity.'

'Any damage?'

'To the centre?'

'To your son?'

'Michael started on about the cause again. I don't know why, as he was a smart enough lad when he was young, and then there's the nurse. If he could stay on the straight and narrow, she would do him a world of good, but there you are.'

'Like father, like son,' Caroline said. 'You had it made with Ralph's mother, but you blew it.'

'There was more to it than that. You only saw one side. She used to play around, did you know?'

'So did a lot of people back then, especially the crowd you hung around with.'

'Maybe, but she left us high and dry. Michael wants to see her.'

'What have you done about it?'

'I found her. I don't know why, but I thought she may have calmed down, not that I want to see her, but I had spoken to Michael's doctor out at Waverley Hills Centre. He agreed, even spoke to her on the phone. She's arriving in the country in two days' time.'

'Where's she staying? Not with you, I hope.'

'She's booked herself into a hotel. Apparently, she's got money, although not much else. She sounded upbeat, but it was a pretence.'

'Is she pleased to be seeing her son?'

'With Yolanda, it's hard to tell. Maybe she regrets what happened.'

'And maybe she realises that you're on the cusp of a financial windfall,' Caroline said.

'Am I?'

'Dundas is dead, his daughter's in charge. We can deal with her.'

'How? She's been schooled by her father, and she's no pushover.'

'We'll find out. The next meeting, you're coming as my adviser.'

'And Michael?'

'One week at the same hotel as his mother. We have the funds to do that. After that, we'll meet with him, as well as Yolanda if necessary. Leonard Dundas's death couldn't have come at a better time.'

'We still need to know where the money and the assets are,' Ralph said.

'We can afford to give it a couple of weeks. Jill Dundas may prove to be more flexible.'

Chapter 16

Graham Picket raised his eyes from the desk and let out a deep sigh. There, standing in front of him, DCI Isaac Cook and DI Larry Hill.

'Wouldn't it have just been easier for me to send you an email with my report attached?' Picket, a humourless man of few words, said.

'Probably, but you're a busy man. Rather than waiting for the full report, we were just interested in your professional opinion,' Isaac said. Neither Picket nor Isaac had much in common. Isaac was personable, the sort of person that people opened up to; with Picket, most people turned away, and the man knew it, but he had come from a dour family, and he wasn't going to change, the reason he was a lifelong bachelor.

'Seeing that you're here. If Dorothy Lawrence had been murdered, there's no way that I can ascertain the truth. Analysis of the bones reveals nothing, other than she had broken her left arm as a child and a leg in her thirties. Approximations though, and no doubt you can check the records. But you'll not bring a case against her husband even if you wanted to. Unless you have any reason to delay, it would be possible to release what remains of her for burial.'

'Cremation?' Larry said.

'I would suggest burial,' Picket said. 'That way if you need to exhume her remains, they'll still be there. Gives me the creeps thinking about her in that house.'

'Hold off for now with Dorothy Lawrence. What about Leonard Dundas?'

'Apart from the normal ailments of a man in his late seventies, Leonard Dundas was in good health. He suffered a heart attack, nothing more. I'll send you a report, more technical, but his death is not suspicious.'

'His body can be released?' Isaac said.

'I'll sign a death certificate and release the body to his family if that is what you want.'

***

It was clear that Leonard Dundas's death was going to have repercussions. As had been suspected by Homicide and the

Lawrence family, the man had been calling the shots for a long time.

Isaac and Larry visited Dundas's house, found the man's daughter dressed in black. 'Sorry about your loss,' Isaac said.

'He was a great man, always cared for his family,' Jill Dundas said. It was the first time for the two police officers in the house, and it was, as expected, impressive.

The woman was on her own in the house, save for a cat asleep in one corner of the room.

'You live here on your own?' Isaac said.

'With my father. I'm not married, but you know that already.'

'Your career took precedence?'

'I was married once, but it didn't work out. He wanted children, I didn't. Nothing sinister, and we keep in contact, the occasional weekend away together.'

'It's unusual.'

'Not to us, it isn't. He's still single, so am I. We should never have married, stayed as lovers.'

'And his wanting children?'

'He had them with another woman, but it was me he wanted, not her. She was purely the vessel.'

'It sounds cold-hearted.'

'I suppose you harbour illusions of romantic love, happy families, the children with their friends, birthday parties. None of that drives me, apart from the romantic love, and I have that from Carl.'

'Do you have someone coming over to be with you?' Isaac said. He had met the woman on a couple of occasions, but this time she seemed hard, as if she was pretending to be strong and resilient when she wasn't. He wasn't sure what to make of her, but then he had never been sure of her father.

'My father knew his time was up. He had completed what needed to be done, and we had spoken about his death. It is not a time for overt displays of sadness or joy, just time to reflect on his passing, and what he and Gilbert Lawrence had achieved.'

'Gilbert and your father?'

'Yes. What else did you think? Gilbert was another great man, but as with Alexander the Great and Hephaestion, or as with

Lennon and McCartney if you want a more contemporary reference, he needed someone with whom he had an infinity to implement his ideas, to deal with the legalities, the financial controls.'

'And now you have the most complete knowledge of what Gilbert and your father set up.'

'I do, and if the Lawrence family thinks I'm an easy touch, then they are very wrong. I was schooled by two great men. They taught me well and believe me when I say that I was a great student.'

'Which means you'll be walking into the lion's den the next time you meet with them.'

'With them, I'm the lion.'

'Why are you telling us this?' Larry said.

'I'm telling you because you will be talking to Caroline and Ralph Lawrence, and no doubt Michael. If the young anarchist thinks he's going to get special treatment because he's cleaned himself up and because he's a charmer, he can think again.'

'You seem to know a lot about Michael,' Isaac said.

'It pays to know who you're dealing with, their foibles, their strengths, although with Michael, he'll soon turn back to the easy road, even with Giles Helmsley in his ear.'

'You know about Helmsley?'

'I know everything. Even Caroline and Ralph meeting, planning on how to take control, but it's not going to happen.'

'It's a big challenge for you. Aren't you frightened that whoever killed Gilbert Lawrence could target you.'

'Why? I have the key to the vault, no one else. Gilbert never did, but his death brings the murderer closer to me, I realise that.'

'Are you convinced that Gilbert was murdered for his money?'

'What else? And none of the Lawrence family knew of the man's will.'

'You did, so did your father.'

'Why would we kill him? We had access to every facet of the man's empire.'

'The man was getting older, possibly senile, dementia setting in. At some stage there was a risk that he wouldn't be able to pass the sanity checks, and even if he did, they don't hold much weight in law,' Isaac said.

'They've kept the family at bay, and even though Gilbert had met with no one for many years, except for my father, he was well aware that the rats were ready to pick over the bones.'

'Did you ever speak to him?'

'Yes. My father always said it was only him, but sometimes we would receive instructions, and I would speak to him, but only on the phone, never in person.'

'And what did he sound like?'

'Lucid, although a little slow, but his mind was sharp. Sometimes he'd even share a joke with me. He may have been eccentric, but he and I got on well. He once said that he wished I had been his daughter.'

'Derogatory about Caroline and Ralph?'

'Don't get the impression that we had long conversations. They were always formal, business-related, but sometimes… It was almost as if he regretted the life he led, and he would make a personal comment.'

'Such as his respect for you?'

'Yes. And one day you'll be in my office, or down at your police station, trying to get me to admit to the murder.'

'Why would we do that?'

'I'm innocent, and you would be clutching at straws. No one had any immediate gain on Gilbert's death, and there was no clear direction as to who would benefit. The only two people who knew the contents of the will were my father and me. My father wouldn't have killed him, but I could have.'

'Is this pre-emptive? Assuming that by giving us the scenario we would have come up with, it will somehow exclude you from our investigation.'

'In part. I did not kill Gilbert, I'm just letting you know. If you take me in for questioning, you will need to be sure of your facts. And now, if you don't mind, I would prefer to be on my own.'

'She would be capable of murder,' Larry said once he and Isaac had left.

'I liked her,' Isaac replied. 'The woman may be hard, but there's a vulnerability about her. She misses her father greatly, and regardless of what she says, she is a woman who has forgone a lot for her ambition. In her quiet moments she must be very sad.'

'She could still be a murderer.'

'It's possible that she is. She is, as she said, the person with the strongest motive.'

Chapter 17

Gary Frost, a man who had lent money to Ralph Lawrence when he was high-risk, did not relish taking a back seat. But that was what had happened. So much so that the man had chosen not to answer his phone calls. Ted Samson, the short man who had been tailing Lawrence, had been replaced. Now there were two, sometimes three and they were varying their schedules. Now his tails were a housewife in her forties, a retired army officer, and a schoolboy in his teens, all appreciative of the extra cash in hand.

Frost phoned his men downstairs. 'Bring Lawrence in but be careful. No witnesses, nothing suspicious, and no roughing up.'

Yolanda, the former Mrs Ralph Lawrence, sat in her hotel room; she was bored. She had been in London for two days: the first, jet-lagged, the second talking to her former husband and preparing to meet a son she had not seen for a long time. As she walked down Oxford Street, her eager eyes on every shop window, her gold-plated credit card firmly in her handbag, Gucci, of course, she had to admit to feeling slightly better, although the climate was not to her liking.

Easily solved, she thought, as she deviated from her route and entered one of the shops. Forty minutes later, a uniformed doorman opened the door as she left. She walked further on, no more feeling the cold, a fur-lined coat wrapped around her. She cared little for the man she had left behind in Antigua, but his credit card had not let her down. She knew she was callous, but if Ralph were about to secure the golden egg, to become almost as rich as Midas if he had his way, then she could see a change in her affections.

Ralph had a talent for spotting people keeping tabs on his movements, his wife did not. From across the road, at two different vantage points, two people kept watch.

It had been Frost who had seen the complication. The word was that Yolanda was no pushover. Ralph had made his money through his charm and his ability to set up plausible if ultimately worthless investment strategies. Yolanda had the looks and the ability, even in her early fifties, to seduce men, the richer, the better. The man in Antigua, pushing seventy, was barely able to keep her satisfied, but it was not what drove her. The fortune he had made in shipping or transport or something – she was never sure what, never cared either – came with a credit card, the best jewellery, and an expensive car wherever she was. In London, the car wasn't critical, although the jewellery was first-rate, and the credit card glinted each time she showed it. A jewellery shop beckoned, and she went inside. Outside were two people, neither aware of the other. Both took their phones out and made their calls.

***

While Yolanda enjoyed herself, or as much as she could, knowing that the meeting with her son was scheduled for the following day, Ralph could not say the same for himself.

As he left his flat in Bayswater a man that he knew came up to him. 'Mr Frost wants to see you,' he said. He was big, at least a head and shoulders taller than Ralph.

'I said I would be in contact. Things are progressing,' Ralph said, knowing full well that his dismissal of Frost's request would have little effect.

'Mr Frost, he doesn't like to be kept waiting.' The tone was polite but menacing.

'Tomorrow.'

The firm hand on the collar, the bundling into the back seat of a BMW 7 Series was not violent, although sitting wedged between two burly men who looked like they were wrestlers at the weekend was not welcome.

'I'll have something to say about this to your boss,' Ralph said, more sheepishly than when he had been standing out on the street.

'Do what you want. We're following orders. Mr Frost, he doesn't like to be kept waiting.'

No more was said until the car pulled up outside Frost's place. This time Ralph got out of the car on his own, no hands on him, and walked to the lift. He pressed the button for the penthouse.

'Ralph, good to see you,' Frost said as the door opened on Ralph's arrival. 'It's been some time since we sat down for a chat.'

'I thought we had an arrangement.'

'And so we do.' The man was effusive and overly friendly. Ralph knew that this was when he was at his most dangerous.

The two men sat on comfortable chairs in the living room. A view of the River Thames, the skyscrapers of Canary Wharf on the other side of the river. Each man held a glass of red wine. Ralph Lawrence feigned relaxed; he was not. He knew the man to be vicious and able to impart pain through his heavies at any time.

Frost sat nearby, attempting to assess the man opposite. Was he a major player? Was he trustworthy? Would he ever get any of his father's money, or should he just break one of his legs now and squeeze him for whatever was owing? Or should he pressure the son, even the new-found ex-wife?

'What do you want?' Ralph said as he put his drink to one side.

'What I always want: money. And your friendship.'

'Frost, you're not the sort of man who wants or needs friends. You enjoy threatening people, gaining an advantage, and having them thrown into the back of a car and brought to you here.'

'There was no throwing, just gentle coercion. You've kept away, Ralph, not even answering my phone calls. I was worried, thought you may be ill, coming down with a cold.'

'Cut it out, Frost, and get to the point.' Ralph knew that acting firmly with the man was risky, but he had little to lose, and besides, he had leverage, money leverage. With his sister and him working together, even his brother-in-law, there was a possibility that they might bring it off. Now they only had Jill Dundas to deal with, given that her father had done them all a favour and keeled over with a heart attack.

'You're pushing your luck here, Ralph.' That was one thing about Frost's intimidating tactics, he always maintained the same calm manner of speaking. No bad language, no raising of his voice, no leaning over the hapless fool who had got into his clutches. It was more frightening than a thug looking you in the face from one foot away and shouting at you, Ralph knew that. He wanted to leave, but he couldn't.

'I still intend to pay you back. The situation's changed.'

'I know that. Dundas has died, and your wife is back in town.'

'Ex-wife. We haven't had anything to do with each other for many years.'

'She's a gold-digger from what I've been told.'

'Just you leave her alone. Our arrangement is between you and me, not Yolanda, not Michael, and definitely not my sister. Is that clear?'

'You still owe me money.'

'If I pay you now?'

'The original four hundred thousand plus interest.'

'How much?' Frost's offer seemed the preferred option to Ralph, but he wasn't sure how to get the money. Gilbert Lawrence's fortune would take years to sort out, although with the money he had been given by Caroline, plus a share of the shopping centre sale, another three to four hundred thousand, then it may be possible.

'Pay me today, and it's just over one million two hundred thousand.'

'How? That's outrageous!' Ralph said, getting up from his chair and pacing around the room. 'I can give you two hundred thousand now, more when the sale of one of the properties goes through.'

'How much and how long?'

'Four to five months, and then I can only give you another four hundred thousand.'

'What a shame,' Frost said. 'Such a pleasant meeting and you go and ruin it by giving me bad news.'

'What do you mean? You're ahead on the deal.'

'You're forgetting the interest. It's ten per cent per week.'

'I never agreed to that. That means I can never pay you.'

'Pay me now what I want, or in four months when we have another conversation, it will be at least five million, probably closer to six.'

Ralph had been feeling good that morning when he had woken. The first meeting since Dundas's death had been scheduled for the following day, and he was going along as Caroline's adviser, not that Jill Dundas would approve. She'd complain, both he and his sister knew that, but not as effectively as her father. And now, as he sat with Frost, Ralph knew that he was back where he had been before. In Spain, he had had the money, or he did until his partner upon release from prison had absconded with the lot. It was either pay Frost what he wanted now, and only Caroline could help, or he could not afford to wait for his father's fortune. He'd have to make a run for it, hope that Frost and his men could not find him, and then somehow ensure he could maintain his stake on his father's fortune. And then there was the added complication of Michael and his association with the anarchist fool Helmsley. And what about Yolanda? She still looked lovely, though mercenary, and when he had picked her up at the airport, he had recognised that she was still fond of him, and he of her. It had only been money that parted them, but now he had the chance for that money. He had known when she had come out from customs that he wanted her back in his life.

But Frost was in the way, and if Caroline wouldn't help with the money, then Yolanda wasn't possible.

Ralph knew he was compromised. He had to act quickly and decisively. He was afraid. 'One week,' he said. 'The money in full.'

Chapter 18

Michael Lawrence met up with his mother on a Tuesday in a restaurant not far from the Waverley Hills Centre. Neither was comfortable in the presence of the other.

'Mother, a long time,' Michael said.

A pregnant pause before Yolanda responded. 'You're looking well,' she said. She looked inside herself for the emotions that she knew a mother should have for her child.

'Twelve years since I've seen you.'

'A long time.'

Ralph Lawrence, who had driven Yolanda to the meeting of mother and son, watched from outside. It was not intended that he join them, as he had made his peace with his son, difficult as it had been. It was now time for the mother, but he knew it would not be easy. Yolanda had left her son in the care of others, mainly the various boarding schools he had attended, and apart from the occasional difficult weeks during holidays when it had been impossible to avoid, they had barely sat down together. But now they were two adults, the son older than the mother had been when she had abrogated her responsibilities.

Yolanda moved forward and wrapped her arms around her son. A brief embrace, followed by a longer and more sincere one, though neither felt the warmth that should exist. Ralph watched from outside as they sat down at their table. He then returned to his car to wait and ponder his next move.

'Why did you come?' Michael said.

'Your father told me that you wanted to see me,' Yolanda replied, realising that the child she had emotionally rejected as a babe in her arms had grown into a good-looking man. She liked what she saw, unable to make the connection between mother and son. It had been a rainy day the last time they had met in a café in Hyde Park, not far from Buckingham Palace. Michael had been at his worst, his speech slurred, a new tattoo showing the redness of being freshly inked. On his arms she had noticed the needle marks, the sign of the tie-off that had been wrapped around his upper arm to make the vein more pronounced. Then she had been ashamed of him, and apart from having a cup of tea and a sandwich neither had said much to the other. Their parting had been no more than a brief embrace, as one shuffled off looking for somewhere to sleep, the other to find a taxi to take her to Heathrow and the first-class cabin on the flight to the Caribbean. She remembered that she had shed a tear in the taxi cab.

And now, here was a person to be proud of, a son to show to her friends. 'It is hard to answer. I had not heard from your father for many years. He phoned, I came,' Yolanda said, her voice choking with unexpected emotion.

'Not for my grandfather's fortune?'

'I don't need it, and that's the truth,' Yolanda said, but it meant staying with a man in Antigua who did not move her the way that he should. Ralph still did, although he was older and definitely fatter, and the innate charm he'd had when he was younger had diminished. She knew that she would choose him over her current man. Ralph had been a dreamer who was always living on the edge, one day rich, another poor, but if he could secure some of his father's fortune, then maybe…

'I sorted myself out for it,' Michael said.

'You were in a bad way the last time I saw you.'

'Once an addict, always an addict.'

'And this Giles Helmsley that your father mentioned?'

'I'm not sure now although he made sense before.'

The two, if they would admit it, would have said that they were enjoying talking to each other. Ralph Lawrence took another quick look through the window of the restaurant, anxious to ensure he wasn't seen by Michael. He returned to his car and made a phone call.

'People like Helmsley prey on the weak and vulnerable,' Yolanda said. 'Are you vulnerable?'

'If I hadn't been neglected, then maybe it would have been different.'

'Don't lay your guilt on me.'

'I'm not. Off the drugs, I realise that life is not certain. Sometimes, certain events are for the better, sometimes they aren't.

If we had lived a conventional life, you and my father, as well as me, it still would have given no guarantees.'

'It wouldn't, and you've fared well, although you've made some bad decisions, so has your father.'

'Have you, mother?'

'Your father still moves me, but he was not a steady provider. He could have made something of himself, but in the end, he only managed to stay one step ahead of the law, and to bed as many women as he could.'

'Mother, you've bedded enough men from what I've heard.'

'I'm not innocent, none of us is, but I'm here in England. What are we going to do? Can you forgive? Can I love you as I should?'

'We can try,' Michael said.

Neither drank alcohol, ordering instead orange juice. Yolanda knew that she had been drinking more than she should in recent months, an attempt to compensate for the boredom of living in a hot country, and friends who judged you by the money in your bank, not your worth as a person.

'Then we need to help your father,' Yolanda said.

'If I have money, I'll weaken. You must know that?'

The two finally ordered a meal and made idle conversation. Yolanda talked about her travels, not mentioning all of the men, even the ones who had treated her badly, one who had even hit her. Michael talked about his time on the street, his attempts to sort himself out, the places he had slept, the people he had met. Even the woman he had wanted to be with, but she had overdosed on heroin one night, and he had watched her die.

It was late when they left the restaurant, Yolanda walking with her son to the centre, leaving him at the door and kissing him on the cheek, Michael responding by putting his arms around his mother and holding her close.

Outside on the road, Ralph waited. Once she was in the car, they spoke, but not for very long. Yolanda, emotionally drained, soon succumbed to sleep as Ralph drove. At the hotel, Ralph escorted her to her room. He did not return to his car that night.

***

Molly Dempster walked into Challis Street Police Station. She was well dressed and had applied make-up. Isaac and Larry did not recognise her at first, although Wendy did.

'Miss Dempster, what brings you here?' Wendy said.

'I've got a confession to make,' Molly replied, her voice quivering.

Wendy feared for the worst and called over Isaac. 'It's not that,' Molly said. 'Is there somewhere we can sit?'

An interview room was found along the corridor. It was not intimidating, and it was just the three of them. Isaac felt obliged to follow the correct procedure and to advise the woman that her conversation was being recorded. She acknowledged the fact.

'You spoke of a confession,' Wendy said.

'I'm embarrassed to tell you. It complicates your enquiries.'

Apart from the standard activities, the investigation into the death of Gilbert Lawrence had stalled, and it was causing problems, not only within Homicide and for Detective Chief Superintendent Goddard but with Commissioner Alwyn Davies, the head of the London Met. Neither Isaac nor Goddard had any time for Davies, with both regarding him as the worst head of that august organisation in living memory, but he couldn't be ignored.

'Take it nice and slow,' Wendy said. In another situation, she would have gone and sat with the woman, but in the interview room, she sat alongside her DCI.

The two police officers waited while the woman composed herself.

'Ralph is my son,' Molly said. Wendy almost fell off her seat, Isaac's mouth opened with a gasp.

'This comes as a great surprise,' Isaac said.

'It's something I've lived with for many years. Nobody knew except for Gilbert and Dorothy, and now they're both dead, the secret could have gone to my grave.'

'You'd better take your time,' Wendy said. She felt a flush of emotions come over her: horror, disgust, love, confusion. She didn't know which one was prevalent, although she had always regarded the housekeeper as one of life's gentle souls, a person who never sought attention or fame or wealth but completed her daily tasks and went home to watch the television or to read a book. And in one sentence, the woman had changed totally, no longer the innocent, but a woman with a history.

'I had been with Gilbert and Dorothy for a year, and Caroline was there, a lovely little girl, similar in so many ways to her father, but she had her mother's looks. I never wanted much out of life, just somewhere to live. My father had been a good man, hard-working, but with a reckless streak. That explains Ralph's impulsive behaviour. My mother was the same as me, a stay-at-home mother who always ensured we were clothed, and there was a meal on the table when my father came in. It was a good life, but when I was seventeen, they both died suddenly. My father from too many years down the coal mine, my mother from grief. I was distraught and had nowhere to go. I thought to go into service, work in a grand house somewhere, a domestic. I found an agency, and they put me in contact with Dorothy. We hit it off straight away, and I moved in above the garage. I was happy. I knew my place and they treated me well. Gilbert was always exceedingly polite to me, not abusing his position, no pushing up against me in the house, pinching my bottom. Always the perfect gentleman. I grew to love them both very much.

'One day, Dorothy was in the kitchen. She was sad. I went over to her, and she told me what the problem was. It seemed that Gilbert was desperate for a son, but Dorothy couldn't give him one. She had had a difficult birth with Caroline, and she was incapable of bearing another child.'

Wendy sat transfixed by the story, Isaac couldn't say a word, only to listen to Molly recount an incredible tale.

'I had never considered motherhood, not for myself. All I wanted was a quiet and simple life, but I could see the anguish in Dorothy. I offered myself.'

'Her reaction?'

'Shock, what else? To me, it seemed the ideal solution. They were my family, and I was always a practical person. I could see a way out of any dilemma.'

'She agreed?'

'Not then, but over a few months she'd occasionally raise the subject, and I would always reply in the positive. It was a great deal of trust we placed in each other, in Gilbert. Not once did the bond break between the three of us. Eventually, we all sat down and discussed the matter. It was me who convinced them that I was the best, the only opportunity for them to have a son. No guarantees you realise, as it could have been a daughter.'

'Any legal agreement between you and them?'

'I would never have accepted it. They were family. This was my gift to them.'

'You became pregnant how?' Isaac said.

'Men, they always see the difficulties,' Molly said to Wendy. 'It was a long time ago, no visits to a fertility clinic. I slept with Gilbert on three separate occasions, Dorothy and me calculating the optimum times.'

'Dorothy?'

'She wasn't there when I slept with Gilbert. She always went out those times. Anyway, the third time I'm pregnant. six months later, I left the house and checked into a place up north, Dorothy coming with me. Caroline was at a boarding school for two months, and then she spent the next holiday with Gilbert and then a cousin in Cornwall. After the birth, Dorothy and I returned with Ralph, his mother holding him close to her body.'

'Dorothy was now the mother?' Wendy said.

'Oh, yes. I was delighted in that I had given birth to Gilbert's son. You must have realised that I always loved him. Dorothy was pleased, and her husband now had a son.'

'After that day?'

'I was there as my son grew up, although he never knew, and I never spoke to Gilbert and Dorothy about the matter. Nothing changed after our return, and I loved them both all the more.'

'Did you…?'

'Never. Apart from becoming pregnant, Gilbert and I never slept together again.'

'Yet Ralph became trouble, a disappointment to his father.'

'It was my side of the family, don't you see. My father could be reckless, but I still loved Ralph regardless. He was a lovely boy, a charming man, and he has never found out the truth.'

'Why have you told us this?' Isaac said.

'I had to. My friends are dead, and I am slowing down. One day it will be my turn to pass on. I need, at least once, to hold my son and for him to recognise me for who I am. It's the foolish request of an old woman, and it might cause complications, but I had to tell you first.'

'Why?' Wendy said, a lump in her throat, a tear forming in her eyes.

'Someone murdered Gilbert. Your investigations need the facts, and my relationship with Gilbert and Dorothy may have some bearing on your investigation.'

'Do you think anyone else knows the truth?'

'It was a long time ago, and none of us ever spoke of the matter. It was always our secret. You must understand why I have come here today.'

'We do,' Isaac said, feeling the same emotions that Wendy did.

Chapter 19

Michael checked out of the rehabilitation centre, and after a few days at Yolanda's hotel, moved in with Ralph. It was not an ideal situation. For one thing, both men still felt uneasy in the other's presence, and also Michael proved to be untidy, open toothpaste tube in the bathroom, dirty clothes thrust into the washing machine looking for someone else to wash and dry them.

Ralph prided himself on his appearance, his clothes arranged on hangers in his wardrobe, his washing done by a lady who came in once a week. And she was now complaining, wanting more money, not to mention having to clean the sheets after Michael had brought a young woman over for the night. Although Ralph, who had been with Yolanda, a not infrequent occurrence, had to admit on his return to the flat that apart from the signs of debauchery, there were no signs of drugs and alcohol.

Yolanda still stayed in her hotel, her gold-plated credit card working fine, although regular phone calls to Antigua were a requisite, and even a long weekend back there to ensure maintenance was carried out on the benefactor. The day she left, Ralph had driven her to the airport. He had felt a pang of sorrow that she was going to give herself to someone other than him in exchange for money. Not that he hadn't been guilty in the past of such indiscretions, but with Yolanda he felt comfortable, as if somehow it was meant to be, and the years apart had been a mistake best forgotten. But then, he remembered as he bade her farewell, the two of them had been a lot younger, and the fire had burnt stronger then.

Ralph, conscious that he was in his fifties and not in peak physical condition, took to exercising, a few laps in a swimming pool each day as well as walking three times around a park across the road from the flat that he and Michael occupied. Yolanda kept fit walking around London with her credit card. Michael, sober and responsive, looked for work, one of the conditions in his grandfather's will, not that the thought inspired him. He was, he knew, an inherently lazy person, although he could see a future in sales, given that his natural charm and his looks made him likeable, but he had no track record.

'I'm in a spot of bother,' Ralph said as he sat down with Caroline at a pub not far from her house. At any other time, Ralph would have appreciated the open fire, the bonhomie of the place, the horseshoes nailed to the timber beams of the sixteenth-century former coach house. But he could see the look on his sister's face, the look that clearly said no.

'It's money, this loan shark that you got yourself involved with, isn't it,' Caroline said. She was keeping to mineral water, Ralph had a glass of red wine in his hand. Neither was smiling.

'If I don't pay him, it's a broken leg, maybe worse.'

'How much?'

'It's over one million pounds.'

'Give him what I gave you and pay the remainder when you can.'

'It's not that easy. There's the compound interest.'

'You're not going to be much use to Desmond and me, are you? If you can't keep out of trouble, how are you going to keep Michael off drugs, and is he working? I've got some sway with Jill Dundas, but you're going to destroy this, you know that?'

'I'll pay you back once the shopping centre sale goes through,' Ralph said.

'It's still not enough, is it? And loan sharks don't lend money at five per cent per annum, do they?'

'That's the problem. The deal in Spain was going well. We had the money, but my business associate took the lot.'

'I saw promise in you, I really did. Now you are back with Yolanda, and Michael is making an attempt, but yet again you're a loser.'

Ralph could see that the bond between him and his sister was not there. She had needed him, still did, but she was going to throw him to the wolves. The evening ended badly, and neither felt the need to wish the other a good night.

***

Back at the flat, Michael was occupied filling out another job application, the third in as many days. To one side of him on the sofa was Giles Helmsley. Ralph, alarmed at seeing the man on his return but remembering when they had been younger, initially felt the need to be polite, but soon realised that the eccentric former professor was not there for his son's benefit; he was there for himself.

'What are you doing here? This is my place, not yours,' Ralph said. He sensed his temperature rising, the short temper that he had possessed since he was a young boy coming to the fore. It had not been a good day. His sister had rejected him, his son too now from what he could see, and Yolanda was in Antigua sleeping with another man. And then his phone rang.

Absentmindedly, without first checking, he brought the phone to his ear. 'Ralph, I was expecting you to come and see me,' Frost said. In sheer terror, Ralph pressed the off button on his phone and lurched forward at Helmsley, grabbing him by the collar, causing a cup of coffee on the small table in the centre of the room to tip over.

'Lawrence, what do you think you're doing?' Helmsley said. He knew that if Ralph hit him, it would hurt, but it was good, better than he had hoped, the chance to begin bringing back Michael to him.

'Giles is helping me to get a job. We are not talking anarchy or politics at all. He is here as a friend,' Michael said, hoping to calm the situation.

Ralph, beside himself with anger and frustration and not sure what to do, took a seat to one side of the room. He looked across at the now-smiling face of Helmsley, wanting to punch him in the face, but realising that he was not the problem, it was his sister. She had more than enough money to pay off Frost.

'My apologies,' Ralph said. 'Helmsley, I don't trust you, you know that. I don't even like you, never have, but you have a right to my son's friendship.' He didn't know why he had said what he had. He did not believe it for one minute.

'Michael needs our help, and you need mine,' Helmsley said, going into charm mode.

Ralph left the flat and went downstairs and out onto the street. It was a bright night, and he looked up at the sky.

A car pulled up alongside him, the same BMW 7 Series that he had been in once before. Ralph reacted with alarm and attempted to move away and back to the safety of his flat. As he approached the main door to the building, an arm blocked his way. 'Mr Frost wants to see you,' its owner said.

Ralph looked around and then up at where the voice had come from. It was one of Frost's heavies. 'I have an arrangement with Mr Frost. My time's not up.'

'Mr Frost, he wants to have a little chat, remind you of the seriousness of the situation. That's what he told me, anyway.'

'Tomorrow.'

'Today. He said you needed reminding.'

Ralph could only remember the first blow that hit him in his stomach outside his block of flats. After that, a blur as he was manhandled into the back of the BMW, his head pressed firmly down into the footwell.

'Ralph, you hung up on me,' Frost said when Ralph regained consciousness.

Ralph realised that he could not move. He struggled, felt ropes binding his arms that were stretched skywards. He could see the beam above him. He felt the wetness in the crotch of his trousers.

'What is this? What have I done?'

'You've forgotten our agreement, haven't you? I've been told that you and your ex-wife are getting cosy.'

'You've been spying on me,' Ralph said. He was feeling distinctly uncomfortable, his feet barely touching the ground, his right leg cramping up, the rope biting into his wrists.

'Protecting my investment, that's all.'

Ralph wanted to tell the man he was a liar, but he knew that his situation was precarious. He was strung up as if he were a side of beef in a butcher's shop, or maybe freshly slaughtered and in an abattoir. He was confused, not sure what to do, not sure if he would leave the warehouse alive, or if he did, if he would be able to walk again.

'You've soiled yourself,' Frost said. 'We're only here for a little chat, nothing more.'

'But I'm hanging here. Let me down, please.'

'If you insist, but my men will stay nearby. If our conversation is not to my satisfaction, you know what will happen.'

'I do.' With that the rope that had been holding the frightened man was loosened, and Ralph collapsed onto the ground. Picking himself up, he sat down on a wooden chair that was to one side of him, the wetness in his trousers causing him discomfort and acute embarrassment.

'Now when will I see my money?'

'Next week, as I told you.'

'Your time is running out. And remember, the interest accumulates. Your wife is an attractive woman, so I've been told. It'd be a shame if she had an accident, wouldn't it?'

'Leave her alone. Your issue is with me.'

'That's where you're wrong, Ralph. Before, it was with you, but now you have a sister, a son, a lover. Any of them will do if you fail to pay me back. Today would be better, tomorrow at the latest. If you want another week, that's fine, just add another eighty thousand pounds to your pay-out.'

'I can't.'

'Can't or won't?'

'I can't get that sort of money. My sister won't help.'

'Then maybe we should talk to her first. I'm sure she will want to see you safe. Or what about her husband? He's got himself a good business, lots of rich clients. How many children does she have? Two, isn't it?'

'You bastard. You would do anything to anybody for your benefit.'

'You would cheat poor gullible tourists out of their retirement funds. We are very much alike, you and me, Ralph. Neither of us has too many morals. The only difference is that I use violence as a tool.'

'And what if I don't pay?'

'You know what will happen. I'm giving you another week, interest-free.'

'Why?'

'Because I like you, or maybe you'll need that week to recover, let the others see what will happen. Maybe your wife can convince the old man in Antigua to help. Your sister, what will she do? Help you out?'

'Give me a week, and you'll have your money,' Ralph said, his body shaking from cold and fear. A rat scurried by. Over to one side, lying on the floor, his jacket and shirt.

'Boys, you know what to do,' Frost said.

The first that anybody else knew was when Homicide received a phone call from the hospital.

'It's Ralph Lawrence,' Bridget Halloran said as she walked into Isaac's office. 'He's in casualty. He's been severely beaten.'

Chapter 20

Jill Dundas smiled when she heard about Ralph Lawrence and his accident, falling off a roof and onto a concrete floor. At least that was what Ralph had said it was, his own silly damn fault for not looking where he was going.

The team at Homicide were under no illusion, even if the man in the hospital bed said otherwise. He had received a severe beating. Sure, as the doctor had said, he had a dislocated shoulder, but there was no way that the bruising on his body had been caused by anything other than a man's fists.

'It's the truth,' Ralph said, his son on one side of his bed, his sister on the other, a nurse hovering nearby checking his temperature, ensuring that he was comfortable.

'Why lie to us, Mr Lawrence?' Isaac said, even though he understood why. It wasn't the first time that a man had lain in a hospital bed, too frightened to tell the truth.

'Why protect those who did this to you? You could have been killed.'

'I wasn't, that's all. I've no more to say. Can't you accept that?'

'Leave my father alone,' Michael said. 'Can't you see he's in agony?'

'You're playing this wrong,' Larry said. He had seen the flowers arranged around the room, noticed one bunch from Jill Dundas, another from Yolanda, now on a plane back from the Caribbean, her credit card revalidated. Another bunch from a mysterious sender, just a blank card, the only words 'Get well soon' printed in bold letters on one side in red. That one needed checking out.

'Whoever did this, they'll be back,' Isaac said. 'These people are professionals. Your only protection is with us.'

Ralph stirred in his bed, attempted to sit up, grimaced in pain, and lay down again. 'It was an accident. My fault for being on that roof. It wasn't that high, maybe fifteen feet, and I thought I'd be fine.'

Caroline Dickson came close to her brother and whispered in his ear.

'What did you just say, Mrs Dickson?' Isaac said, having noticed the sister leaning in near the brother, but not able to hear what was said.

'I just gave him my love. He's my brother, I care.'

'Mrs Dickson, let me remind you. If you and your brother, even Michael here, are concealing the truth, for whatever reason, it could have serious repercussions.'

'We've broken no law,' Michael said.

'The law you can deal with. Whoever did this is not held back by rules or regulations or the law. They believe they're invincible, and they'll be back. Maybe not today or next week, not even for a few months, but mark my words – these are dangerous men who could have killed Mr Lawrence but chose not to for a reason. And we all know why, don't we?'

'Do we?' Caroline said.

'They want something. This is a warning, and none of you here is capable of standing up to whoever it is. If they can't get it through Ralph, they'll get it another way.'

***

The inevitable presence of Chief Superintendent Richard Goddard in Isaac's office, not that anyone could blame him, certainly not in Homicide. The savage beating of Gilbert Lawrence's son was a development, the first for some time.

'Are you sure he was meant to live?' Goddard asked. He was sitting across from Isaac. In one corner, a potted plant that Bridget and Wendy had given Isaac some time ago after another of his failed romances. On the wall, a picture of Isaac when he had graduated from university, his face beaming, proudly holding his certificate.

'We don't know who it was,' Isaac said. 'But we're sure he didn't fall off that roof. Why would someone risk bringing attention to themselves? It's not as if Ralph Lawrence received any money from his father. He's currently renting a two-bedroom flat, nothing special, and his son's there as well.'

'His sister did, and what about his ex-wife? Plenty of money there.'

'We're investigating all scenarios. Nothing's certain, but we believe Ralph's owing money to someone, and he's having trouble paying.'

'Evidence?'

'None, just a hunch. We've seen it before. There's no point killing the borrower. A few days in the hospital, a few broken bones, and the borrower's more compliant, may even commit a crime to pay it back.'

'Loan shark?'

'Gangsters, loan sharks, even one of the man's dubious friends. It wouldn't be the first time Ralph Lawrence has found himself in hot water. He may have meted out similar treatment to others when he had been flush with money.'

'Whatever, whoever, don't take long on this one. Questions are being asked.'

'They always are,' Isaac said. As much as Isaac respected his senior, it was as if the man was playing the same old record. There was always a budgetary issue, the key performance indicators were down, he needed the current murder solving, or there was pressure from above.

Although the pressure, as both of the men knew, was through the office of Commissioner Alwyn Davies, the head of the London Metropolitan Police, a man who did not rule by consensus and professional leadership but by adroit political manoeuvring and intimidation. Goddard and Isaac were very much in the man's line of sight, having crossed swords with Davies on more than one occasion, and the commissioner wasn't a man to forget. To both of the men, how Davies survived was of concern, but as Goddard had said before, get on and do your job, I'll deal with the commissioner.

With the superintendent out of the office, Isaac called in the team. It was still early in the morning, the best time Isaac always thought to formulate the actions for the day.

Wendy Gladstone was first in, closely followed by Bridget Halloran, the office supremo, and then Larry Hill, Isaac's detective inspector.

'Find out who gave Ralph Lawrence a good beating, is that it?' Larry said.

'Critical, but his sister knows something. We need to talk to her first.'

'Before we plan the day's activities, let's recap on yesterday. Bridget, what do you have?'

'More details from Spain as to what Lawrence was up to. The man's associate was released from prison two weeks after Ralph Lawrence returned to England. He cleared out any bank accounts and disappeared, left a string of debts behind him.'

'Debts someone wants to be paid?'

'The company had leased a couple of vehicles through a local company, and the premises they operated from were owned by a local businessman. Apart from that, and the tradesmen who fixed up the office, there doesn't appear to be anyone with any criminal connections.'

'It depends on whether Lawrence's colleague borrowed from loan sharks,' Isaac said.

'There's no way to find out, and besides, that's a Spanish problem. If Lawrence is beaten up here, and there were signs that his wrists had been bound and he was missing one shoe when found, then he almost certainly borrowed in England. Any idea how much?'

'Not yet. It's not a loan that would have been registered.'

'Any luck with bank accounts?'

'We know that the scam in Spain had almost two million pounds in a local bank. The Spanish police have supplied us some information, not all.'

'Why?'

'They're investigating a crime in their country. We're not the most important, although they've been helpful up to a point.'

'What do you mean?'

'A murder in England is not their priority. The current government is attempting to cut down on corporate crime, scamming of tourists. The normal thing that gets the country a bad reputation, keeps the tourists away, as well as the genuine investors. The police, no doubt, are feeling the heat. The only person I've been in contact with is a junior officer, good English, and she's tried her best.'

'Should we ask Chief Superintendent Goddard to speak to his counterpart in Spain?' Wendy said.

'It won't help,' Bridget said. 'You soon hit bureaucracy, and the wheels will grind slowly.'

'Bridget's right,' Isaac said. 'Any indication as to how much Ralph might have borrowed?'

'There was a cash injection into one bank account of four hundred thousand pounds. It may not be money that Lawrence borrowed, but it seems possible. The money had been transmitted by an offshore bank, and the bank's not telling whose account, but I've been on to Fraud, and they reckon it's probably an English account holder.'

'Okay, enough said. We need to find whoever gave our man Ralph a few days in the hospital. Bridget, keep checking, Wendy, you can come with me to see Caroline Dickson.'

'I'll get down on the street. Start checking out who's lending big,' Larry said.

'We're dealing with someone who's not averse to violence, and a police officer may not scare him. Easy enough to take him out, never to be found again,' Isaac said.

'I'll find out a few names first, and then we'll discuss it. After that, we can figure out what to do.'

***

Caroline Dickson agreed to an interview at her house.

'Mrs Dickson, I need to caution you,' Isaac said. 'There is vital information that you are withholding from us, we know that now.'

'I've been totally honest with you, so has my husband,' Caroline said.

'Your brother is in trouble, and you know it. He told you something in the hospital.'

'He's borrowed money he can't pay back.'

'Are you going to help?'

'I don't know. It's a lot of money, and these people can't be trusted.'

'If they can do that to him,' Isaac said, 'they are capable of more, even murder.'

'Ralph's frightened, and he told me not to tell you. It complicates matters.'

'Not for us, it doesn't. Your father's murder, could it be related?'

So far nobody in the Lawrence family knew of Molly Dempster's remarkable confession. The revelation that Ralph was her son may well have provoked an interesting reaction from Caroline, but now was not the time and place. Ralph was in the hospital not because of who his mother was, but because of his father. Isaac could see Gilbert's death as related, but it was a long shot.

'My father's death, why?' Caroline said. 'He was old, not in good health, and he would not have lived forever.'

'Five, ten years, long enough for someone to have become nervous, become desperate. Now we know your brother didn't kill him, proof from the Spanish police on that one, and we've ruled out Molly Dempster.'

'Molly's a saint, always has been. She brought us up as if we were her own children,' Caroline said, showing more affection for the woman than she did for her brother.

Wendy looked over at Isaac, saw an imperceptible shake of his head. Both the police officers knew that the woman had said something closer to the truth than she would ever know. It was clear that at some stage Ralph would have to be told. He was illegitimate, the bastard son of a wealthy man and the family housekeeper. Further scandal for a family that had had its fair share. And how would Caroline take the news? Would she distance herself from her half-brother? Neither shared an unbreakable bond; maybe when they were younger, but they had spent many years apart, and Caroline led a decent life with a man she loved, whereas Ralph had become disreputable, a disgrace to his father and to her. Caroline's children were upstanding members of society, Ralph's son was struggling to find his way, full of the weaknesses that had blighted his biological father.

'Molly had lived above the garage, and then spent the remainder of her time looking after your father, only once venturing into the main house. Doesn't that sound strange to you?' Isaac said.

'That was Molly. She was just a good person. You'll never find either Ralph or myself say a bad word against her. And as for killing our father, not possible. Even if she suspected what was upstairs, it would not have changed her. She was devoted to my parents, even loved them.'

'Explain love,' Wendy said.

'A deep friendship. Once, my mother, I was in my teens by then, told me that if something happened to her, I was to ensure that Molly was looked after.'

'What did you take that to mean?'

'I was in my teens, the silly teens, too much alcohol, too many late nights, and no doubt too many unsuitable men. She was trying to tell me something, but I wasn't listening that closely, trying to get out of the house. Molly came in, and that was the end of the conversation.'

'You're older now. What do you think she meant?'

'The love that Molly felt for my mother was sisterly. For my father it was romantic. We always knew, Ralph and me. Sometimes we'd tease her, not that she said or did anything, only smile. Our mother wanted Molly to be with our father if she was not there.'

'Did your mother sense an early death?'

'Sometimes she would have these episodes where she would need to be confined to the house. No doubt she would have been suicidal, into self-harming.'

'Any proof?'

'Not really. We were away a lot of the time, although Molly would have seen it. My mother was clear that she didn't want our father to be on his own, and if it wasn't her, it was to be Molly. To Ralph and me, she was a second mother, but she never interfered in the family. She'd just be there, always in the background, always trustworthy.'

'In the end, Molly wasn't with your father, was she?'

'After our mother disappeared, although we didn't know that she was dead and upstairs, our father became reclusive. He became what you know of him. The loss of our mother must have affected him greatly.'

'And Molly?'

'She was distraught, but she continued regardless. Always stoic, always a meal on the table. I never saw her cry.'

'Some people don't,' Isaac said. 'Sometimes they just bottle it up, keep busy, although when they're on their own, they let go. Molly could have been one of those people.'

'Probably, but she was the rock when our father went to pieces with grief.'

'And you?'

'I was at the house every day after our mother disappeared, out on searches for her. We dredged the canal, the ditches, looked in manholes, checked the train station, local buses, taxis, but nothing. The police were involved. You must have records.'

'We do, but what about Ralph?'

'He wasn't there. By then, he had gone overseas, and it was two years before he made contact again. He was in Thailand, or maybe it was Cambodia. It appears he had met someone and he was planning to stay. When I told him about his mother, he came back, not that there was any point. Our mother was gone, we even held a memorial service for her at the local church, and our father was already in seclusion. He only started going to the off-licence in the last ten years. Before that, Molly would deal with everything. A list of requisites in the kitchen of a morning and she would buy what was needed, prepare his meals, change his bed, the one that had been placed in the room off the kitchen.'

'Why did she do that for all those years?'

'That was Molly.'

'Coming back to Ralph,' Isaac said. 'What are we going to do to help him?'

'He needs to tell you the truth. The money can be dealt with, but do the people who put him in the hospital take what's given and leave well alone?'

'They probably will, but it's a different circumstance here. Your father was incredibly wealthy. A temptation to most people, not only the criminal.'

'We've had enough begging letters and emails. My family of long-lost relatives is over two hundred now. You wouldn't believe that I have family on all continents.'

'We've seen it before; lottery winners are the more susceptible. Some have even squandered their wealth on the more deserving cases,' Wendy said.

'Were they?'

'Who knows. It's not criminal to beg, not criminal to give. It wasn't a police matter, only if it was a scam.'

'We've got a big bin, that's where they all go,' Caroline said.

'It doesn't stop them knocking on your door, jumping out in front of your car, feigning an injury.'

'It's happened. Desmond's considering hiring a guard for outside the house, but for how long? Has Molly been pestered?'

'We don't think so, but we'll check. There are some questions for her.'

'Don't trouble her too much. She's just an innocent. All this is beyond her,' Caroline said.

Chapter 21

Larry worked his contacts, attempted to find out who was lending big, who was likely to use violence if anyone defaulted.

Harry Eckersley, a low-life that Larry had heard of before, operated out of a shop in Hammersmith, no more than a couple of miles from Challis Street. The shop was rundown, full of second-hand phones, laptops, and computers, assorted bric-a-brac and more than enough family mementoes, deposited there for sale or return to the owner if they came up with the ready cash. It was not the sort of place that Larry liked, and he knew that some of the merchandise wasn't legally acquired. He didn't expect a friendly welcome.

'Detective Inspector Larry Hill, Homicide, Challis Street. Are you the owner?' Larry said as he showed his warrant card, his photo and name displayed.

'No one's died in here, copper,' Eckersley replied. 'No need to kill anyone for what they leave here in exchange for some of my hard-earned.'

Insults from the general public weren't unexpected. Larry had heard it before, even in the pub he visited on a Friday night for a quiet drink of beer. The rough element that sometimes got in there knew that the police were powerless to respond to verbal threats, and after a few drinks, some had attempted to bait Larry and other police officers more than they should, usually being egged on by their drunken mates.

Larry had experienced one a couple of weeks previously. It was close to closing time, and the man who had been hurling names had come out of the pub feeling pleased with himself. He didn't see the man standing to one side out on the street, not until it was too late. He fell to the ground after one blow in the face from a clenched fist. 'Next time, it'll be your groin,' Larry said.

'That's police brutality. I could report you.'

'No witnesses,' Larry said. He knew he had been wrong to hit him, but sometimes enough was enough. The next time Larry encountered the man, he had walked over, patted him on the back and bought him a pint of beer.

'Sorry about the other week. Too much beer, not enough brains,' he said.

'Forget it. You're not the first, you won't be the last.'

'I pity the poor guy who you hit in the balls. You packed a punch.'

'Just make sure it's not you, or any of your smart friends.'

'It won't be. You've got our respect.'

Larry looked Eckersley square in the eye. 'I'm here about murder, not whether half the stuff in here is stolen. Unless you want this place turned over by the uniforms looking for stolen merchandise, I suggest you stop your insults and give me some answers.'

The miserly little man reflected on what to do. 'Okay, Inspector, what do you want?'

'It may be better if you close your door, or we can talk out the back.'

'Here's fine. It's a mess back there.' Which to Larry meant that the evidence of stolen goods hadn't been dealt with yet.

With the door at the front closed the two men sat down on a couple of chairs produced from behind the counter. 'We'd better make ourselves comfortable,' Eckersley said.

'We're looking for big lenders. I'm told that you're one.'

'I lend if the risk is acceptable. But I have a limit.'

'What is it?'

'One hundred thousand, but I'm reluctant. If they don't pay me back, I'm out of pocket, not much I can do about it either.'

'You can threaten them, give them a taste of what will happen if they don't pay you back with interest.'

'Even if I did, that doesn't mean I'll get it back, does it? And besides, that's not how I operate.' Larry knew when he had been told a lie. Eckersley was just the sort of man to send in his men if someone was giving trouble, late on his repayments, had given some dumb tale about next week and paying in full.

'Don't feed me nonsense,' Larry said. 'I'm not here for you. I'm here for someone who lent four hundred thousand, someone who's not averse to giving someone a serious beating, someone who would probably kill if the debt couldn't be recovered.'

'No profit in that, only a lot of hassle.'

'Let's assume this person can afford to carry the debt if there's no other option.'

'There are one or two, but if they find out that I've spoken to you…'

'They won't. And don't give any of that "I'm just an honest man trying to make an honest quid" nonsense. It's an insult to my intelligence.'

'You're a tough bastard, Detective Inspector Hill,' Eckersley said.

'I'm a good friend if you help me. Help me, I help you. Deal?'

'It's a deal.'

'Good. Who do you have?'

'There's one not far from here. Goes by the name of Dennis Bartholomew. Some call him Dennis the Menace, after the cartoon character in the boy's magazines back in the fifties, or maybe it was the sixties, not sure which now. Find an original, and they can be worth money.'

'Why the nickname?'

'He's not into the rough stuff. With him, you sign a contract, sign over your car, jewellery, whatever you've got of value. He'll charge high interest, not as high as some, and with him, it's a regular beating every few days until you settle. Anyway, that's when he becomes a menace.'

'It's violence, it's criminal, but our man is much more violent. Break bones, put you in the hospital violent.'

'There's one I've heard of. Low profile, rarely seen out on the street. I've heard him referred to as the lender of last resort.'

'Nowhere else, that's where you go?'

'Tough bastard. I heard of one mug who borrowed heavily from him. He took the money he had made and skipped the country, failed to pay back the loan,' Eckersley said.

'What happened?'

'Rumours, may not be true, maybe that this lender put it about to make sure anyone else who borrowed from him paid up.'

'Assume they're true. We believe this individual to be dangerous. He's already put someone in the hospital.'

'It could be him. Anyway, the story is that this fool, he came from around here, has got this great idea for an illegal gambling club, high-rollers, no limits. These clubs appear from time to time, make their money and close. The bribes are too high, the security's a nightmare, and then there are the extortion merchants. Illegal gambling doesn't always attract the best clientele. The club opens, the guy is pulling in serious money, dealing with those trying to rip him off, breaking a few arms if anyone's caught cheating. Very soon, he's got himself two million in cash sitting in a safe in his office, another one and a half shipped out of the country. The lender staked him a quarter of a million, and he wants it back along with the ten per cent per week interest.'

'Ten per cent per week?'

'That's what I said. And he's not slow to show you what will happen if you borrow, normally some hapless fool on the floor or strung up who hasn't kept up the payments.'

'How do you know this?'

'Someone who came in here, nasty divorce, cleaned him out. He wants to get back into business, the banks are not biting, telling him to go take a running jump. You know what they're like?'

Larry did, having renegotiated his mortgage to accommodate his wife's plan to buy another house. The manager had sat there, telling him what a privilege it was to be able to help one of our fine police officers, before slapping the offer down on the table. Larry had looked at the proposal, looked at his wife, looked at the bank manager. He knew that he could just about make the payments, although his wife's reaction to the disappointment if he had not signed, meted out for the next few weeks, he couldn't. Larry even managed to thank the sanctimonious parasite who had just suckered him into more debt.

'I know,' Larry said.

'This man I'm telling you about. He'd been over to see this person we're talking about. He's on the other side of the Thames. The conditions were laid out. A volunteer, not that he had any choice, was on display to show what happens if you don't pay. They shot out the man's kneecap, then dumped him fifty miles away.'

'He could have told them who had shot him.'

'Not him. It's either keep quiet, or it's the other kneecap or the concrete boots. Anyway, this guy with the gambling club. He's skipped the country, not paid his staff or the lease on the premises he'd been using, not that they can do much about it. But our lender, he's got connections, and he finds out where the man's gone. Supposedly, he's swanning around Dubai, a couple of Russian tarts in the back seat of the Mercedes with him. They come up to an intersection, outside of the city, in the desert, so I've been told. A couple of motorcycles pull up alongside, passengers on the pillion seats. They level a couple of Kalashnikovs into the car, killing the man, the two whores, and the driver. After that, the man's hotel room is broken into, the safe is opened, and out pops the best part of seven hundred thousand in fresh notes, some in Euros, some in American dollars.'

'Tough justice.'

'Not to this man whose name you want. You sure you want to get mixed up with him? He'll not have any issues with a nosy policeman.'

'Your friend, the one with the divorce?'

'The deal with the lender is, if you don't take the loan, then no issues, just never tell anyone what you've witnessed. At least the man's fair. Anyway, the man with the divorce comes back here. I lent him fifty thousand, not what he wanted. He's got a small shop down the far end of Portobello Road. He's making a living, and his kneecaps are safe, even found himself another woman. And he paid me back.'

'The name of the lender?'

'Gary Frost. He's got a penthouse down in Greenwich. Ask around, you'll find him. Don't blame me if you get yourself shot.'

'I won't.'

'And for the record, the merchandise in here is not stolen, not by me. It all belongs to those who are desperate. I give them money for it. It's then on sale, and either someone else buys it, or they repurchase it.'

'I'll trust you,' Larry said, not that he believed Eckersley, but the man had helped.

Chapter 22

Homicide had the name of someone with a dubious history, although with no criminal record. Of the two men who were always close to Gary Frost, one had served time for grievous bodily harm, the other was known to the local police in Greenwich as a man with a foul temper and likely to drink more than he should on a Saturday night, and then to take to brawling. The last time, according to a police sergeant that Larry had spoken to, it had taken three police officers to subdue the man. The next day, sober and in the cells at the station, he had been contrite and exceedingly agreeable. The sergeant reckoned he was the more dangerous of the two.

Gary Frost remained an enigma. He kept a low profile and was rarely seen out in public, and if he was, it was invariably in the back seat of a top of the range Mercedes.

Everyone in Homicide was focussed on the man who gave out money and violence in equal measure. The man with the busted kneecap that Eckersley had mentioned had been found. He had been doing it tough since his release from the hospital, and he limped badly, a crutch under one arm, but he was alive. Attempts to find out if others had not fared so well were proving unsuccessful. The gambling club owner who had made it out to Dubai, found himself a couple of Russian women, as well as a surfeit of bullets as he and the women had been gunned down, appeared to be just one of the colourful tales on the street, although Isaac and Larry weren't so sure it was just a story. It may not have been Dubai but somewhere less desirable, and the Russian women, attractive and readily available in the city in the desert built on money and oil and not much else, could instead have been a couple of local slappers of no great beauty and not that young either.

The limping man with the destroyed kneecap wasn't talking, nor was Ralph Lawrence, who kept to his story that he was inspecting a property he was interested in purchasing and he had slipped. Isaac and Larry had pressured the man, could see that he was nervous, wanted to speak, but wouldn't.

Outside of the building where Frost's penthouse was located, Larry stood, unsure of what to do next. It wasn't the best of days, and the wind was biting. He wasn't sure what he was trying to achieve, knowing full well that knocking on the door would not get him far, may even get him into trouble: police intimidation, upstanding citizen, no criminal convictions. That was the problem, Larry knew. The most accomplished criminals, those with the mental acumen, always ensured that someone else did the dirty work, leaving them clean.

'I need you back at the station,' Isaac said on the phone to Larry. 'Leave Frost for the moment, we've got something to deal with.'

Larry made the trip back over the Thames to Challis Street, parked his car, noticing that the weather was better there than it had been over in Greenwich where it was more exposed.

In the office, all the key people were there. 'What is it?' Larry said as he sat down.

'Ralph Lawrence is out of the hospital and back at his flat. If Frost was responsible for having the man beaten, then he's not going to give up because of us. And Helmsley's in Michael's ear. We're expecting fireworks. In fact, we should consider creating them. We need Ralph to talk, then we can pressure Frost. He's a definite suspect, not sure how and why, but he's the sort of man that kills.'

'Molly Dempster knew more than anyone,' Wendy said. 'Does Ralph know about her?'

'Not yet. It may be time for him to find out his background. We can judge his reaction, see if it makes any difference.'

'How do you want to do this?'

'Caroline Dickson's house, make sure all the key people are there. Make it for tonight, six in the evening. Bridget, make a few phone calls, make sure Caroline and her husband are there, also Ralph and the reluctant Molly.'

'She'll not like it,' Wendy said.

'You can go and see her, tell her it's necessary if we're to solve who killed Gilbert. And besides, she said that she wanted to hug her son once and for him to recognise her as his mother. Tonight might be the night, although the reactions may be hostile.'

'What's the point of upsetting an old woman?' Bridget said.

'I can understand your sentiments, but this is a murder enquiry. We have Ralph who won't tell us who put him in the hospital, Molly who knows more than she's telling us, and Caroline who's playing a strategic game with Jill Dundas. Everyone's hiding something. We don't know what yet, but we need to move the investigation forward.'

'I'll look after Molly,' Wendy said. 'I don't like this. She's a nice woman who just wants a quiet life.'

'No doubt you're right, but she could have killed Gilbert for retribution. Even though she loved him, at least when he was younger, he had kept Dorothy, a person Molly loved as a sister, dead and in her bed for all those years. And can you imagine the kind of horrors that the man must have perpetrated on his dead wife, burying her in the cellar, stripping her flesh, feeding her to those beetles? If it were a movie, we'd all be out of our seats or out of the cinema. Larry, you and me, we've got a door to knock on.'

'Gary Frost?'

'Who else? We'll need a police car outside just in case our visit is not welcome. Is the man at home?'

'He is. I've got the local station updating me as to his movements. If we let on that we know he's lent money to Ralph, it could get nasty.'

'That's what I'm hoping for. And the kneecapped man, where is he?'

'Not far, but he'll not talk,' Larry said.

'If he doesn't, we'll let him know that we're talking to Frost, may let it slip that we've told his lender that he's been very helpful.'

'Not strictly by the book.'

'I know it, but we're only implying. We need the man to tell us the truth. Frost could be Gilbert's killer. The man's smart. He could have realised that he'd lent money to the wayward son of a real estate mogul. He may not have known it when the money was lent, but he finds out and takes a calculated risk that the death of one would lead to another gaining the wealth. We need to frighten everyone, raise the emotions, look for the reactions. Bridget, any more from Spain?'

'Nothing. The police are too busy with their own problems down there to worry about us.'

'There goes the trip to Spain to meet up with our Spanish colleagues, the chance to get a suntan,' Isaac said.

'No problems for you, sir,' Wendy said.

'I could still do with some warm weather.'

'We all could, but it's not likely to happen soon, is it?'

***

Isaac had to admit to being impressed with where Frost lived. He and Larry had called in at the local police station, met with Inspector Emily Matson.

'Frost is loan sharking,' Isaac said.

'We're aware of the man's reputation, but we've had no reason to bring him in, and besides, there's been no complaints, nothing criminal,' Matson said. Isaac judged her to be mid-thirties, maybe closer to forty, attractive in an efficient way, with her hair pulled back tight, minimal make-up, blue eyes. She was dressed in a blue suit, not regulation, but civilian. 'I'm giving evidence at 11 a.m. Fraud caught a man using false credit cards, not uncommon around here. I was the arresting officer, so I can't come with you to Frost's.'

'That's fine. We can deal with him on our own.'

'Just watch out for his men. One of them spends time here occasionally. He goes by the name of Ainsley Caxton. Tough individual. He put one of our guys in the hospital for a night after three of ours tried to take him down outside a pub one night. Apparently, a couple of drunks inside had started making fun of his name, putting on funny walks, telling him it was a little girl's name. Mind you, they weren't smiling the next day. One of them ended up concussed after Caxton rammed his head into the pub wall. The other copped a boot right where it hurts, brought tears to his eyes. From what I heard, he sings soprano now. The other tough that Frost keeps nearby is Hector O'Grady. He's not been in trouble with us, but he's a big man, bigger than Caxton.'

'We'll be careful. We were just letting you know that we're following up on a homicide in our part of the world.'

'Frost responsible?'

'Nothing's proven, not yet.'

Isaac and Larry left the police station and drove the short distance to where Frost lived. Outside, a police car, two patrol officers inside. 'We'll call if we need you,' Isaac said. He had brought them two coffees, which was appreciated.

'We'll be here. Be careful with Caxton. He put me in the hospital once,' one of the uniforms said.

'Inspector Matson told us. And the guy singing soprano?'

'He always had a squeaky voice, but it's a good story.'

Isaac rang the bell at the security door to the block of flats. A gruff voice answered. 'What do you want?'

'DCI Cook, DI Hill, Challis Street Police Station, Homicide.'

'You've got a warrant?'

'We can get one, haul your sorry arse down to the police station. Tell Mr Frost we want a few words with him, or we'll come back later with a piece of paper, make it official.'

'Very well. I'll press the button. Enter the lift and enter 756 into the keypad.'

Outside Frost's penthouse, the two men stood, Caxton and O'Grady. One was squat and menacing, the other taller, fitter, and altogether a better-looking man, although that was subjective, and neither would have been regarded as handsome. Caxton had a scar above his left eye, O'Grady had broken his nose on more than one occasion, and the bridge was skewed to one side.

'Mr Frost doesn't like uninvited guests,' Caxton said.

'Then maybe he shouldn't go roughing up people, lending them money they can't afford to pay back,' Isaac said. Larry thought Isaac was playing a dangerous game, baiting the heavies even before they had met Frost. It wasn't the first time Isaac had gone on the offensive, and most times it worked, produced the appropriate reaction, but they were on the seventh floor of the building. It was a long way down, and the security door at the front of the building would be strong enough to hold any help at bay for long enough.

'Mr Frost isn't going to like you coming in here accusing him.'

'Tell him we're here. We don't have all day.'

'Go easy,' Larry said. 'We're in Frost's territory here.'

'We need a reaction. A black eye won't do you any harm, and if they do hurt us, we'll have the measure of them, know that Frost is our man.'

Inside, sitting on a brown leather chair, was the man himself. The penthouse was too warm for Larry, just right for

Isaac. 'What can I do for you?' Frost said as he got up from the chair. Even though he was at home, he was dressed in a suit, white shirt, and a tie.

'We understand that you lend money?'

'Nothing wrong in that. I'm even registered, an office in the city. More of a broker really, put those who want the money in touch with the lending institutions, take the commission.'

'You don't work from there?'

'What for? Employ people, that's the secret. Ideal for me, ideal for them.'

'Okay, that's the legitimate side of the business,' Isaac said. 'What about the other side, the high-risk clients, those who can't get money from the banks?'

'I can't do much for them. If they've got themselves in trouble, destroyed their credit rating, that's their problem, not mine.'

'Why the two men outside? If you're legit, you've no need of protection.'

'Not all those that get loans can pay them back. The bank forecloses, divorces occur, and then the man is on his own, looking to blame someone. He can't take on the bank, but he can take on my company and me. Caxton and O'Grady can deal with anyone who comes near me, plus drive the car, run errands.'

'Mangle kneecaps part of their job description?' Isaac added.

'Chief Inspector, you've been reading too many gangster books, watching too many films. That's not how it works in real life.'

'It does. We've seen it before, and you're involved. What about the man you had kneecapped, walking with a permanent limp?'

Frost appeared agitated, started walking around the room. Larry could see Isaac getting under his skin.

'I've let you in here in good faith. I thought I was helping with your enquiries, not aware that you intended to insult me, accuse me of being a criminal.'

'Mr Frost, we know all about you, not that we can prove it, not yet. No one's speaking. It appears that they're more frightened of you than they are of the police. Why is that?'

'I've done nothing wrong. If people want to borrow money, that's up to them. If they can't pay it back, I can be sympathetic, but I'm not a charity.'

'Ralph Lawrence, you lent him money?'

'I'll not say I've never heard of the man, as I read the newspapers, surf the net, the same as everyone else. He's the son of Gilbert Lawrence, the madman with all the money and his dead wife upstairs in her bed.'

'And you've never met him?'

'What for?'

'The man's borrowed money, a lot of it. We know he came to the lender of last hope, he came to you.'

'I suggest you leave. I would call the police, but you're here already. I'll be making a complaint.'

'Do what you want, Mr Frost. We'll be watching you, and the next time you put someone in the hospital, we'll be there. And remember, neither Ralph Lawrence nor the kneecapped man has spoken to us. They keep telling us it was an accident, although how you can shoot yourself in the knee is a mystery to us.'

Isaac and Larry got up to leave. Larry turned around and looked at Frost, already on his phone making a call. 'Where was it? We were told it was Dubai where you had Steve Samuels killed.'

'Samuels?' Frost said.

'The gambling club owner who borrowed a lot of money from you, skipped the country, a couple of Russian whores in the car. You had him killed.'

'Inspector, I'm not a man without influence, my name counts for something, at least it does in this city.'

'Any action against Lawrence and the other man and we'll be back. And if we see Caxton and O'Grady anywhere near them or us, we'll take them in for questioning. No doubt we'll find something to charge them with,' Isaac said.

'A fertile imagination, Inspector Cook. I hope the Met treats you well when you're back in uniform.'

Chapter 23

Jill Dundas, now without the guiding hand of her father, realised the responsibility and burden on her shoulders. Not only was there Gilbert Lawrence's substantial real estate holdings to concern herself with, but there was also Caroline, Gilbert's daughter, close by, attempting to find out more, and now Ralph. As far as she was concerned, he was a man of little worth, a man who had justifiably been derided by his own father. What worried her was that there were people out there who used violence as a weapon, and she was the most likely target. Even a modicum of information from her, a password, an account number, could be worth millions. And some people knew how to hack computers, even though her father had been fastidious about ensuring that no one other than the two of them knew the full extent of Gilbert's wealth, and the office computers, the internet connection, had the best protection that money could buy.

Jill knew of the account squirrelled away in the Cayman Islands, one of the places in the world that didn't enquire too closely into where the funds came from. That was her father's special account, unknown to anyone in the office, and even she didn't know the passwords, but she knew where to find them. There was also a house there, set back from the beach, no more than two miles from the centre of Georgetown, the capital. Idyllic when the tourists weren't there, annoying when they were. All in all she believed that with her father's tutorage she was well placed to deal with all financial matters, but violence frightened her. Even as a child, a fight in the school playground would upset her for days, but that was other people, and if whoever had confronted Ralph hauled her off to some dingy room and threatened her, even hit her, she knew she would weaken.

And now Caroline was adamant that Ralph would come along to the meetings at the office as her special adviser. It was a weakening of her position, Jill knew. Ralph may be many things, most of them negative, but he wasn't naïve about how to conceal money in foreign bank accounts, how to set up companies and trusts to hide assets. Jill was aware that he would be asking pertinent questions, questions that she couldn't divert with legalese and financial jargon. The man was a threat, and if she knew who it was that had beaten him, she would have asked them why they hadn't finished the job.

Jill Dundas made a phone call. 'Caroline, we need to meet.' She hadn't wanted to make it, she knew she had to.

The two women did not meet at the office of Dundas and daughter, nor did they meet at Caroline's house. The conversation was important, and they met at the Savoy hotel in the centre of London, in Westminster, on the Strand.

'Caroline, we have a problem,' Jill said. There had been a brief embrace when first meeting, more a courtesy than a show of affection. Caroline was under no illusion, and she had not brought Ralph with her, at Jill's request, 'to each other's mutual benefit' had been the words that the solicitor had used. Ralph was still convalescing, drinking too much, and complaining at not being fully mobile, and Michael bringing his girlfriend over every other night, their bed banging on the shared bedroom wall, was making him crankier by the day. Caroline knew that with his current temperament he wasn't much use to her anyway.

Ralph's temper, justified at the reading of their father's last will and testament, was not needed now. Now, it was time for reasoned argument, a breaking down of the barriers that Leonard Dundas, and now his daughter, had put up.

'It's just you now. What are you going to do?' Caroline said. She was not in a mood to be conciliatory.

'Ralph is in trouble, isn't he?'

'That's Ralph, but what's it to you? You're not the bleeding-heart type, and I doubt if you care what happens to him, to us. To you, Ralph and I are like something the cat dragged into the house.'

'Honest words, Caroline,' Jill said. 'Neither of you deserve any of your father's money. The man was a genius, my father's friend. What are you and Ralph, the spawn of a great man? Your only skill was to be born his child. I worked hard for what I've got, so did my father, so did yours.'

At least the woman is honest, Caroline thought. 'You've opened up, but why and now?'

'Ralph's just a pawn, a charming nonsensical pawn. It's me that's the target. I'm the one with all the information, and I'm willing to admit that I'm afraid, more so than ever before.'

They were sitting in the Thames Foyer. Jill ordered afternoon tea, a favoured pastime of the hotel's guests and tourists to the city of London. She helped herself to a cake, Caroline chose a homemade scone with clotted cream and jam.

'What are you suggesting? That we make some kind of a deal?'

'We need to protect ourselves, and at this time, you'd quite happily see me go to the devil,' Jill said.

'You and your father have stolen our legacy. I don't know how, maybe I never will, but your father had managed to control my father and to take his money.'

'Your father was eccentric, maybe even slightly crazy with your mother upstairs, but he still knew what he was doing. Your father had amassed a fortune, and he put in safeguards to ensure it was not squandered. And yes, my father helped himself to plenty, but he wasn't going to throw it away, and nor am I. Work with me, Caroline, to protect ourselves, and I'll make it worth your while.'

'Pretty words, purely because you're frightened, but what do they mean? The police are out looking for who put Ralph in the hospital. What happens when they catch them? Will you renege on what we decide here today? And what about Ralph? He may be all that you say, but he's still my own flesh and blood. I can't cast him off just because of something you say.'

'They could come for you as well, you know that,' Jill said.

'I know. What do you suggest?'

'Ralph's owing money?'

'He is, and I know how much.'

'We pay his debt, make a deal with him, and then get him out of the country.'

'And leave me high and dry? How can I deal with you? Jill, you may sit there with your mouth full of cake, a cup of tea in your hand, looking pretty, but you're still a devious woman. You're no better than those who dealt with Ralph. I'd be putty in your hands.'

'Not if I pay you out, as well.'

'How much?'

'Fifty million pounds.'

'How much is my father worth, and the truth?'

'Six hundred and twenty-five million, but you can't realise on it all, only a fraction.'

'Why?'

'It's tied up in real estate, bonds, investments. It would take years to liquidate.'

'Fifty million, when?'

'As soon as Ralph is dealt with.'

'You're still exposed.'

'I need protection, but I need to know, are you interested? It's a generous offer, and I'll make sure that I keep you informed, ensure another two million a year for the next ten.'

'We can deal,' Caroline said. She had no interest in attending meetings, pretending to understand finance when she didn't, and Ralph was always going to be unreliable; it was in his DNA.

***

Yolanda was back in town and attempting to nurse Ralph back to health. With Michael and his girlfriend, an attractive tattooed young woman, monopolising the flat, Ralph had moved in with Yolanda for a few days, not that either was committed to the other. Even on the drive over in a taxi, the two of them had argued. Yolanda was concerned that the man she was transferring her affections to wasn't worth the effort, and he'd never have the money to look after her as well as her man in Antigua, who was keen and exceedingly generous, did. Ralph didn't want a nursemaid, and Yolanda was high-maintenance, and if he scored big time with his father's money, then he'd get himself into shape and play the field. A man with a fortune could have as many young and willing partners as he wanted; no need to be with a woman who complained and was starting to show her age, even if she was the mother of his son. Not that he could profess to any strong emotion for him, and now a bottle of alcohol had snuck its way into the flat. Michael, he knew, was on the downward spiral, aided and abetted by the girlfriend, vacuous and well-meaning, who was not helping at all. As the doctor at the rehabilitation centre had warned, a lot don't make it.

Yolanda had raised objections when Ralph had insisted that the 6 p.m. get-together at his sister's house was necessary and she wasn't invited. The police were to be there, and there was to be an update on his father's murderer. If his father was proven to be insane, then the man's will could be challenged, and if Leonard Dundas had been involved in the murder, it would be another plus for his and Caroline's case.

Chapter 24

At Caroline's, the front door was open. Inside, the assembled cast. On one chair, Molly Dempster sat. Wendy had brought her along and was seated nearby. Isaac could see that Wendy was the mother duck and she wasn't going to let anyone upset her duckling. Isaac preferred raw emotions to be the order of the night, and his sergeant close to one of those assembled could be a problem.

Caroline sat with her husband, Desmond. On the table in the centre of the room, a bottle of red wine, sandwiches, sausage rolls. Larry was hungry. He had had a busy day with Inspector Matson out at Greenwich, going through the case against Gary Frost, checking CCTV to see if Ralph had been in the area, also the man with only one functional kneecap, but it was like looking for a needle in a haystack. Too many people in the area, too many cars, and no clear idea of dates and times. Emily Matson had been interested when told about the gambling club owner, and she was making enquiries overseas. Larry had been more interested in recent cases pertaining to Ralph Lawrence, possibly Gilbert, but drawing blanks.

Ralph sat on another chair. Isaac could see that his condition had improved. Apart from slight bruising on his face, and the fact that he was squirming to get comfortable, he looked almost back to normal.

'Thanks for coming tonight,' Isaac said.

'It wasn't far for us,' Desmond said.

'It was either here or at Challis Street,' Isaac reminded him.

Isaac felt trepidation about what he was doing, realising that the emotions of those in the room would be challenged, but it was a murder enquiry, and those closest to the dead man had skeletons, and skeletons cause conflict, subterfuge, concealment. Someone in the room may know something hitherto unrevealed. He needed the raised and raw emotions, he needed people to open up.

'This is what we have,' Isaac said. 'Ralph is involved with a villain by the name of Gary Frost. Neither will admit to it, but it was Frost who put Ralph in hospital. He would have used two thugs named Ainsley Caxton and Hector O'Grady. We've been to see Frost, and we and the local police where Frost lives are following up on a few cases of violence meted out to those who get on the man's wrong side. We've found no connection between Frost and Gilbert Lawrence's death, and we don't think we will. Lawrence was killed with a degree of finesse. Frost's thugs are slash and burn, and none too subtle. Ralph has got off lightly, just a savage beating, although the marks on his wrist indicated that he was bound, and we don't believe his story that he fell off a roof.' Ralph sat quietly and said nothing, not even making eye contact with Isaac.

***

Molly Dempster sat in her chair; she was not looking up, not drinking from the cup of tea placed in front of her. Wendy could only imagine what was going through her mind, the reality of what she was about to tell the people in the room. Isaac and Wendy knew, had checked DNA with Forensics. What Molly had said was true, she was Ralph's mother, and now her son was sitting on one side of the room, she on the other. The young boy that she had raised with Dorothy, spent more time with than the woman who had disappeared all those years ago – tonight the grown man would find out the truth.

'Caroline is in contact with Jill Dundas, a woman she doesn't trust, neither do we totally,' Isaac said. 'Now, we're not accusing her of murder, but the bequeathment by Gilbert is not usual. Whatever Jill Dundas and her father came up with, they've certainly done best out of the man's death. It may be what Gilbert wanted, it may not, but neither Caroline nor Ralph has the full picture. We've had people checking, and it's not that easy to know exactly what Gilbert Lawrence's wealth is, only that it is appreciable. We've also called on our overseas colleagues to do some checking. Caroline's received five million, her two children a million each. Not bad for most people, but Caroline and Ralph were expecting hundreds of millions. Am I correct?' Ralph and Caroline nodded in the affirmative.

'I'd have stayed in Spain if I'd known that I was going to be cheated,' Ralph said, the first words of any consequence he had uttered since entering his sister's house.

'Not likely,' Isaac said. 'You were deported, lucky that we were in contact with the authorities down there.'

'I would have come to an arrangement. A few pesetas here and there, problems disappear quickly.'

'It's euros now,' Isaac said. Wendy was keeping quiet, so was Larry. Their DCI was on a roll, he wouldn't appreciate their chipping in with a few comments, not that they had any. Wendy felt sorry for Molly, knowing that Ralph, her son, was a man of little worth, but then the old woman had admitted that Ralph's behaviour was only like her father and her grandfather, decent men but dreamers, always taking a chance when the odds were against them.

'Euros, pesetas, I'd still be back there.'

'You would still have had Frost to deal with.'

'I could have paid him off.'

'You've heard about Samuels and Dubai, the two Russian women?'

'Who hasn't? It's folklore out on the street. And besides, it was Belgium, a couple of streetwalkers, and it wasn't a Mercedes, it was an old Peugeot. Doesn't sound so romantic, though, that's why Frost embellished the truth, made him sound more important, more dangerous.'

'Are you admitting to your involvement with Frost?'

'Okay, I borrowed some money, but it was a roof that I fell off. With my father's money, I was hoping to buy somewhere in England, settle down with Yolanda, even find a place for Michael.'

Isaac had an admission that Ralph had borrowed money from Frost, the first time the man had spoken the truth. 'We'll bring Frost in at some stage. We'll not linger on your denials for now. Caroline, you met with Jill Dundas in the West End, correct?'

'There's no harm in that,' Caroline, on the defensive, said.

'Unusual, considering that you've been disparaging of her in the past.'

'You've not heard me say anything, have you?'

'We keep our ears to the ground. Jill Dundas controls all of your fortunes. She's one woman, what if anything happens to her?'

'We're lost. We need her alive, even if we don't trust her. Nobody in her office knows where everything is.'

'You've tried bribing some of them?'

'No. One of them came to us, offered to help for a cost.'

'And what did you do?'

'Nothing at this time, and besides, what would a junior know? Leonard Dundas was a smart man, the same as our father. He'd not leave loose pieces of paper around. Even if this junior could help, it would be limited. Jill Dundas is the key. That's why I was at the Savoy, afternoon tea, very expensive, but she was paying.'

'What was said?'

'She's frightened, interested in making a deal.'

'Frightened?'

'You'd better talk to her.'

'We're here talking to you. What's she frightened of?'

'What do you think? Ralph's half-killed, and he only owes a million and a bit. Jill's controlling hundreds of millions, and she can lay her hands on twenty, maybe thirty without any difficulty, and she's not a brave woman. She admitted to me that she's scared, and I don't blame her. If Ralph weren't such a fool, we'd all feel a lot safer, even Desmond and I.'

'You're right to be scared,' Isaac said.

'Can't you arrest them?' Desmond said.

'No proof. No one's talking, not even Ralph, not even the man they kneecapped. Caroline, you've fared well enough with your father's death. Could you have killed your father?'

'Not me. I still loved him, even though we hadn't spoken for many years, and I didn't need the money.'

'But what if you had known about your mother?'

'I don't think I would have done anything, other to have taken down that door that was always bolted with a sledgehammer, and to make my father tell me the truth. Did he kill her? It could have been one of her episodes. She could have slipped, fallen down the stairs. He could have been frightened of what would be said, confidence could have fallen in his empire, his line of credit could have dried up. Even if it was an accident, mud sticks, you must know that.'

Isaac knew, but he wasn't about to elaborate on his involvement with a Swedish au pair when he was younger who turned out to be a serial killer, or how, when DCI Caddick had temporarily occupied Isaac's seat in Homicide, the man had laid all the department's ills on the previous incumbent. It took the best part of a year after the man had left for Isaac to overcome the negativity and the aspersions made by Caddick. Even now there were still some who believed that Caddick was a competent police officer, and Isaac was just smoke and mirrors, a good-looking charmer with a mild Jamaican lilt in his voice.

'Let's recap,' Isaac said. 'Ralph was beaten half to death by Caxton and O'Grady on Frost's orders, a warning to pay up, deal us in on your father's fortune, or else. Caroline's talking to Jill Dundas, finds her more willing, probably willing to deal Ralph out. And that's because she's scared that those who beat Ralph may come for her, string her up, apply lighted cigarettes to her, and God knows what else until she opens the safe, hands over the account numbers, gives the passwords. Frost would only need a laptop and an internet connection, and he could bleed her for millions, maybe even arrange an accident in the River Thames afterwards, swimming lessons with weights. Caroline, Desmond, he could even go for you. If I were you two, and Jill Dundas, I'd be working on Ralph, get him to talk. He's scared enough, and if we go near Frost, bring him into the station and charge him, we can't make it stick, and he'll grab Ralph wherever he is. Quite frankly, I don't have much hope for him. He's a weak specimen of manhood, and I can't blame his father for being critical.'

'You can't talk to me like that,' Ralph said.

'Why not? You've not got long to live. How are you with swimming? Or maybe they'll string you up, take your manhood with a sharp knife. Not a pretty sight, and we've seen it before. What will Yolanda say, how about Michael? I'm not sure your sister will care much.'

Wendy could see that Isaac was pushing, probably harder than he should. The line between police questioning and harassment was clouded in grey, and Isaac was feeding the man, wanting him to agree, rather than let him volunteer it.

'Stop,' Molly said. The first word that she had said all evening. 'I need to tell the truth.'

Caroline looked over at Molly, expecting her to say that she had killed her father, not wanting to believe it was possible. After all, this was Molly, the one constant in her and her brother's lives, the one person they could always turn to, never to receive an admonishment, only a willing ear and sound advice. It had been Molly she had gone to when her first boyfriend had dumped her, on her birthday even, and the first person she had told when she had met Desmond, and how they had made love on their first date, and now the woman was on her feet and wanting to confess. Caroline couldn't believe it, didn't want to.

'Are you sure, Miss Dempster? I could do it for you,' Isaac said.

'It's my responsibility. It's been a secret for too long, but with Gilbert's death and Ralph's condition, I must speak now. It is not something I want to take to the grave. I want to go with a clear conscience and to be judged with respect, not derision. Caroline,' Molly said, looking over at the woman, 'I have loved you as if you were my daughter, you must know that.'

'I do, and we have always loved you,' Caroline replied, not sure what was coming next.

'When you were young, your father and mother were desperate for a son. Of course, you were too young to realise this. Your mother had had a difficult birth with you. She couldn't have any more children.'

'But she had Ralph.'

'She did not. Her name is on his birth certificate, as is his father's, but Dorothy, your mother, did not carry him for nine months and give birth to him in a private hospital in the north of England. Your mother was there, she was the first to see him.'

'What are you saying?' Ralph said. He was no longer looking down, attempting to sit comfortably and not exacerbate the pain he still felt in his chest. 'Caroline is not my sister, I'm not a Lawrence?'

'Ralph, dear Ralph, you can't remember suckling at my breast, can you? You are a Lawrence, Gilbert was your father.'

'That's proven,' Isaac said.

Molly shifted on her feet, her knees buckling as she spoke. Wendy stood up and put an arm around her, only to have it pushed away. 'Sorry, I must do this now, and on my own.'

'Who is the mother?' Caroline said. She was not sure what to think. Ralph, troublesome as a child, disreputable as an adult, had always been there. They had a bond, a bond that couldn't be broken, and now Molly was on her feet and telling them that she and Ralph were not related.

Molly calmed herself, took hold of the arm of the chair where she had been sitting. 'I loved your parents, both equally. Dorothy was like a sister to me, and Gilbert was the kindest, most gentle man that anyone could imagine. They were so much in love, and I was happy for them. They were my life, as you and Ralph were. I would do anything for them, even bear the son that they so desperately wanted. It was my gift, my honour.'

'It can't be,' Ralph said. He looked over at Caroline, could see the horror on her face, the bewilderment, as if it were a movie, not real life.

'I loved Gilbert as much as I loved Dorothy. Dorothy told me if she wasn't around, that I was to be with Gilbert, but we never had an affair, although Ralph thought we might have had when he was younger. But then he was young and pubescent. His mind was not in his head but somewhere else. Ralph, do you remember me looking the other way when you brought a young girl home with you, telling you to be careful?'

'But how? If you're my mother, can it be proven?'

'It has been,' Isaac said. 'We've taken a blood sample from you, saliva from Miss Dempster, and we already had Gilbert Lawrence's DNA. There is no doubt that you are the son of Gilbert Lawrence and Molly Dempster.'

'Don't you see? I did it out of love.'

'But how?' Caroline said.

'It was a natural conception. I only slept with your father to become pregnant. Apart from that, we never slept together before or after. If Dorothy hadn't been there, then maybe, but my act of love, our lovemaking, was for the purest intent. Surely you must understand. You and Ralph are brother and sister, and Gilbert is the father of both of you. It was Dorothy who was Ralph's mother.'

Caroline went over and placed her arms around Molly, tears streaming down her face. 'Thank you,' she said.

Ralph did not move. 'It makes sense now, doesn't it? I always sensed something, I never knew what.' He then raised himself from his chair and went and hugged his mother. Wendy was in tears, Isaac wasn't sure what to feel, Larry was mute, and Desmond Dickson sat in his chair, shaking his head.

'I'm sorry,' Isaac said when everyone had calmed down. 'To solve the murder of Gilbert Lawrence, we need openness. The secret you've just heard had to be told, either now or later. Emotions are frayed, and no doubt you will need to discuss what has been said here tonight. It still doesn't bring us any closer to solving the crime, though.'

'I'm not sure what to think,' Ralph said. 'On the one hand, I'm pleased to know the truth, on the other I'm confused. Molly, or should it be Mother, has always been special to all of us, but what she has said brings in another dimension.'

'Your mother's a target if this gets out,' Caroline said.

'Very well, I will give DCI Cook a full and open statement as to who and what Gary Frost is. The police, in turn, must ensure the safety of my mother and Caroline and her family, also Michael and Yolanda.'

'We will,' Isaac said, although he knew they were dealing with a man who gave little credence to the police and the law.

Chapter 25

Bridget Halloran, an inveterate computer junkie, was pleased with herself. She loved nothing better than surfing the internet, both in her spare time, although there wasn't much of that at present, and at work in Homicide, diving deep into police databases, or scouring for information about places and people and procedures. Now she had hit the jackpot.

'It's your show,' Isaac said in his office. It was late afternoon. Larry had been hoping for an early night; there was a school play, his eldest had two lines to say, and his wife was adamant that he had to be there to show support for the family.

'I've passed on the information to Larry's contact out at Greenwich,' Bridget said. It was not usual for her to be so excited.

'Belgium?' Larry said, the primary area of interest for Inspector Emily Matson at the police station in Greenwich, as well as his. If Frost could be linked to an actual crime, something that could be proved with a chance of a conviction, then so much the better.

Ralph Lawrence had given a full account of Gary Frost, his two henchmen, and how he had been trussed up like a Christmas turkey while Caxton and O'Grady had worked him over. Also, how the money was sent to his account overseas, the interest payments, what would happen if payment was not received on time or if he tried to cheat. He had recounted how Frost had bragged that the police were irritants, no more annoying than a mosquito of a summer's night, and how he had contacts in the right places.

Emily Matson had taken exception to Frost's assertions, seeing that her station was the closest to where the man lived, and any official police enquiry would focus on Greenwich Police Station, and then fan out from there. Two years previously, an inspector by the name of Fredericks had been charged after he had been exposed for taking backhanders from a local drug dealer. He had been Inspector Matson's boss at the time; she had been a sergeant on the rapid promotion ladder: young, female, university degree. She was seen as indicative of the future of a modern, educated, and professional police service, and association by default had impacted on her.

She had suspected him at the time, although she had failed to report it: no proof. Larry understood where she was coming from when she told him the story. It was one thing to inform on a dishonest police officer, it was another to prove it, and for several months she would have been ostracised by some of the others in the station. A word in the ear of the offender, a talk with his colleagues was seen as better, but even that had its risks. Another policeman in the station had taken that course of action. A trio of thugs on his way home, and two weeks in the hospital for him, and then he had left the service, taken a job as a security guard; better pay, though.

The promotion to Inspector for Matson had come about one month previously, a reward for good work, and a new superintendent in the station who recognised good people and ensured they received the recognition they deserved. And now an email in her inbox from one of DI Hill's colleagues outlining in detail what she had been trying to find. Little did she know that Bridget was not a two finger typist with limited computer skills, but a whizz who could type a hundred words a minute, and could access the overseas databases of a myriad of police stations, strictly legal, look for the keywords, and then run any document through an online translation service.

At Challis Street, Bridget told the team what she had already sent to Emily Matson, copied to Larry, who hadn't had a chance to read it yet. 'Nineteen months ago, a Peugeot car was sprayed with bullets in Belgium,' Bridget said.

'Confirmed?' Isaac said.

'I've a copy of the police report at the time, as well as an English translation. The occupants of the vehicle included the driver, Alain Courtois, 38, a Frenchman living in Brussels, the capital. He ran a private taxi service, cheap and reliable according to his website. Also, in the backseat, three passengers: two females, one male. The females were subsequently identified as Freya Brepoels, 29, prostitute, and Sonia Colen, 26, prostitute. Both of the women were Belgian nationals.'

'The man?' Wendy said.

'English, false passport. I've run his photo against that of the dead man. It's Samuels.'

'I thought he had taken off with a fortune,' Larry said.

'Maybe he had,' Isaac said, 'but if he thought Frost could find him, then a low profile would have been more appropriate, or maybe he liked Peugeots and local tarts.'

'How do we tie him into Frost?'

'We can't,' Bridget said. 'They were shot near a small village outside of Brussels, a wooded area. No witnesses and the vehicle had been pushed off the road into a ditch. Someone in the vehicle that rammed them had got out and sprayed Samuels' vehicle with one hundred bullets from a semi-automatic rifle. Apart from that, nothing.'

'No link back to Frost?'

'The Belgian police never made the connection between the dead man and Samuels. If there's a connection, it's up to us to make it.'

'No joy from the kneecapped man?' Wendy said.

'No. He's still frightened, so is Ralph Lawrence, but he's still carrying on. Not sure if we can protect him and the others,' Isaac said. He could see a lot of possibilities, no proof, and the primary case, the murder of Gilbert Lawrence, was going nowhere.

'If Samuels was killed in an assassination, that means someone paid, and plenty. And why? Frost would have wanted his money back, and a dead man isn't going to give him any.'

'Maybe he did have the money or some of it. We know that Frost is devious. Samuels was making plenty at his club, but was everyone losing? And Samuels would have had to ship the money out of the country. He's hardly likely to have been carrying it on him.'

'Bank records?'

'I'm looking,' Bridget said. 'So far no luck. But he could have opened an account anywhere in a false name. All he'd need after that is the account number, the password, and a debit card.'

'Not much of a life for someone who supposedly stole millions,' Larry said.

'He was meant to be in Dubai: Mercedes, Russian women out of the Cyclone Club, not in Belgium, a Peugeot, and a couple of locals.'

'Made up to suit tough man Frost's image?'

'It's possible,' Isaac said. 'Larry, phone up Inspector Matson. Tell her that tomorrow she's on a trip to Belgium with you. Bridget, you make the bookings, and I'll phone Matson's boss to okay it. Check out the area where Samuels was staying, the murder scene. There must be witnesses somewhere. No reflection on the Belgian police, but they may have just put it down to an English gangster getting his comeuppance, a drug deal gone wrong. They've got their hands full over there with all the migrants trying to get across the channel.'

***

Yolanda was dismayed at Ralph's pathetic attempts to gain some of his father's fortune, only to get himself put in hospital, and her son was no better, succumbing to his old habits. The last time she had seen Michael, a few days previously, he had been drunk, and it had been clear that he had been smoking something other than cigarettes.

A pragmatist, Yolanda knew that father and son were weak individuals, more suited to each other than to her. In Antigua, there was a house and a good life with people such as herself: expats away from the cold and the bleakness, lapping up the sun, playing golf or bridge, or lying next to a swimming pool drinking cocktails. Ralph knocked on her hotel door, looking for a bolthole away from Michael and his girlfriend who had moved in on a permanent basis at the flat in Bayswater. That was when he found out that she had checked out, the hotel taking her to the airport.

Ralph knew the situation was tenuous. He was no longer Dorothy's son but Molly's, not that it concerned him as much as it should. And so it was that at three in the afternoon the only son of Molly Dempster and Gilbert Lawrence presented himself at his mother's door.

'Mother, I've come to stay for a few days, if that's alright.'

Molly looked at the man, not the best specimen with his two-day stubble, his breath smelling of beer, his clothes creased. She knew that if it had been anyone else she would have said no, but it was her son: the babe in arms, the young boy who had come to her for sympathy after falling out of a tree, the pubescent youth who had struggled with growing up. She had looked after him through those years, and even though he was in his fifties, he still needed caring for.

'Come in,' she said, overjoyed to be able to spend time with him, good or bad. It had come full circle from the child to the father and back to the child. For her, regardless of what others may say, Ralph was her son, and she was proud of him. 'I'll make up the spare room for you.' Molly knew that she was happy.

Michael meanwhile languished in his bed, his woman by his side. On one of the bedside tables, a syringe. He was back in heaven or purgatory, he did not care which. His girlfriend, a woman whom he loved when he was drugged, unsure about when he wasn't, was in euphoria.

A knock on the door. Michael stirred from the bed and opened it. 'What have you done to yourself?' Helmsley said. Dressed in a checked jacket, a pair of blue jeans, a large scarf around his neck, he looked every part the eccentric professor that he was, not that the young Lawrence could see him, his eyes blurred. He only wanted to go back to his bed and make love to his girlfriend, knowing she would not refuse him. After all, hadn't it been him who had used the money from Jill Dundas to feed her habit, and if she refused, then there were others. He was flush with money, sufficient for his life. A flat belonging to another, a woman, a drug dealer who sold only the best and at a reasonable price. The only blight on his life was the man standing at the door, disapproving, the same as his mother. He had spent a lifetime on his own, neglected by his parents, and he did not care for either or where they were.

'The cause needs you clean,' Helmsley said as he pushed through the door and into the flat. The girlfriend came out of the bedroom, took one look around. 'Who's he?' she said. She was stark naked, as was Michael. Helmsley looked at them both: the seductive young woman with the tattoos and the needle marks and Michael, young, masculine, with bulging muscles. He knew which he preferred, but now was not the time to put the young woman back in her room and to attempt the seduction of a young man who probably would not resist, probably would not remember. Instead, Helmsley put on the kettle. 'Strong coffee and plenty of it,' he said. 'And get rid of that woman.'

Chapter 26

At St Pancras Station, Larry carried a small bag, Emily Matson arrived pulling a suitcase.

'It's only overnight,' he said.

'Better to be prepared, just in case,' Emily said. It was seven thirty in the morning, the Eurostar direct to Brussels was due out in one hour, and then a trip of just under two hours. Larry reflected that he had got up, showered, driven to the airport, parked his car, and waited for the train, in total nearly three hours, almost long enough to travel under the channel and to return to

London. And if he and Emily had travelled out to the airport, it would have taken even longer.

'A coffee?' Emily said. Larry could see that she had purchased new clothes for the occasion, crisp and still showing the mark on the blouse where it had hung on a hanger. She wore a red skirt, high boots, and around her shoulders was draped a shawl. 'I've got a coat in the case if the weather turns.'

'Not snowshoes, I hope,' Larry joked. He had to admit she was agreeable, competent, and most of all, enthusiastic.

'Married?' Larry asked as the two sat down at a table in the coffee shop, keeping their eyes peeled for an update on their train. It was Larry's first time on Eurostar, Emily's second.

'Not yet. I've got a live-in boyfriend. We've been together for a few years, but he's a bit slow on the uptake. I've given him enough hints to get down on his knee.'

'Necessary these days?'

'The wedding ring, down on the knee? Not really, but it's romantic. I'd like him to do it, just the once.'

'And then marriage?'

'If he's for me, we'll stick together. No need for a piece of paper.'

At 8.31 a.m. the train pulled out of the station; two hours later it pulled in to Brussels Midi Station. Inspecteur Jules Hougardy, a distinguished looking man in his fifties, met Larry and Emily as they left the station.

'Pleased to meet you,' he said. 'I was involved with the original investigation.' His English was excellent, which was as well as Larry's French was rudimentary, and Emily's good enough to order a meal, find a hotel, ask for directions, but certainly not up to the standard required for a murder investigation.

'I've prepared a full day,' Hougardy said, 'but first, lunch. It'll give you both a chance to update me, me to update you. We've been working on the case ever since you contacted us.'

Emily hoped for something traditional for lunch, not the fish and chips that the Inspecteur chose.

'We'll drive out to the murder scene. We've been around the local village with the photos you sent over, with some success.'

'The Peugeot?'

'It's an old case. We can have a look at it, but you'll not gain much from it. You're both booked into a hotel in the centre of town, adjoining rooms.' Emily didn't like the look in the Belgian's eyes. She had heard that the French were incurable romantics, always looking for a dalliance. She didn't know that it applied to the Belgians as well. And besides, the man may dream, but the reality was a solid day of policing and an early night, alone and without interruption.

The trip out to the murder scene took twenty-five minutes. They passed through a small village before coming to an isolated area. To one side there was a ditch, large enough for the front end of a car.

'A four-wheel drive rammed the Peugeot near here,' Hougardy said as he slowed down.

'Did you find the vehicle?'

'Never. Although if it had bars at the front, it might not have sustained a lot of damage, and if it had been used off the road, as many are of course, then it would not have been distinguishable, not around here anyway.'

'Make, model?' Larry asked.

'We believe it to be a Toyota, but that's supposition. We found a trace of paint on the Peugeot. Forensics ran it through a spectrometer, conducted solvent tests, came up with a Toyota green. Unless someone had resprayed the vehicle, we believe it to be a Toyota Land Cruiser, 1985 to 1992. There are a few around here and the borders are open.'

'The photos?'

'We've one witness to someone buying food in a supermarket not far from here. The man was English, no French, and not very pleasant. He became agitated that the person behind the counter didn't understand what he was saying.'

'Sounds like the English they get down in Spain,' Emily said, having been embarrassed by her fellow English on holiday there, getting drunk, making fools of themselves. In her teens she had been there with a few friends, but they hadn't enjoyed themselves, what with the local lotharios fancying their chances, and the English louts assuming that every English woman was there for their benefit.

'Not the person we've got here. Big, muscled, not the sort of man to sit on a beach.'

'We've got two people of interest. Any chance of meeting this person who was abused?'

'Next stop.'

In the town square of Herzele, an attractive village not far from the murder scene, the three police officers entered the shop. Jules Hougardy spoke French most days of the week, but the shop owner, a woman in her sixties, small and neat, shook the hands of the two English police officers, especially Emily's, and spoke in a language that neither Larry nor Emily could understand.

'It's Flemish,' Hougardy said. 'Most people speak both. In Brussels you'll find the majority of conversations are in French, but outside of the big city, some prefer French, others Dutch, and some converse in Flemish. It pays to be trilingual if you want to be a police officer in Belgium.'

'And you are?' Emily said, noticing that Hougardy had no trouble talking to the woman.

'I was brought up in a Flemish-speaking family, but regardless, at the station, we can speak in all the languages of our country. Not like the British, am I correct?' Hougardy smiled.

'Only English, and not even the Queen's,' Larry said, responding to the gibe.

Emily held two photos for the woman to look at. She studied them for a few minutes, putting on her glasses, before pointing at one of them, pulling a face to indicate non-verbally what she thought of him. She even gripped the tip of her nose and pulled at it. The definition of a stinker translated across countries and languages.

'You know this man?' Hougardy said.

'We do. Please thank the lady for us,' Larry said. 'Would she be willing to testify that he came into her shop?'

'She would. I've already asked her. We have another witness. Our people found him this morning. He nearly had an accident with the Toyota.'

'Let's go and see him,' Emily said, as she shook the hand of the old lady, who in typical Belgian fashion grabbed hold of her and kissed her on both cheeks.

'She likes you,' Hougardy said. 'She thinks you're attractive and that you should find yourself a good Belgian man to settle down with, her son, for instance.'

'Thank her for the offer, but I'm taken.'

Outside the small shop, where Emily was still feeling a little embarrassed by the woman's exuberance, a man stood. He was a robust individual, ruddy complexion, extended belly. Larry liked the look of him. He was farming stock, his clothing indicative of that, as well as the tractor that stood not far away.

'This is Monsieur Mathy. He is quite happy to converse in French.'

Emily tried out her French. Surprisingly, it wasn't as bad as she had imagined, and Mathy grabbed both of Emily's hands in his and shook them vigorously.

'You're a hit here,' Larry said. 'Maybe you should come back and marry the son.'

'Maybe I will if there's any more cheek.'

Emily showed Mathy the photo. He responded in French, Emily understanding what he said.

'It's confirmed. What else do we have today?' Larry said to Hougardy.

'A meal tonight with my team, a copy of our case files, in French originally, but we've translated most of them for you. And tomorrow I'll drop you off at the station.'

Larry took the opportunity to phone Isaac on the way back into Brussels. No action would be taken until he and Emily were back in London. Two witnesses of the one person was not sufficient proof in itself. They still needed to find additional evidence, and they didn't want the man to disappear.

Jules Hougardy drove past the police holding area where the Peugeot was stored on the way back. As he had said, the Peugeot did not reveal much in itself. It was severely dented at the front, the bodywork was peppered with holes where the bullets had pierced the metal, the windows were all broken apart from one side window, and inside there were still bloodstains.

'The women?' Emily said.

'Locals, off the street. Both were addicts, neither was attractive. Sorry about the lack of detail, but there's not much more to say about them. They had been picked up an hour earlier, heading out for the night to a house in the country. Samuels, now we know his name, made the booking in the name of Smith, Airbnb. It was just their bad luck, the same as the driver.'

***

Giles Helmsley had control of the grandson of Gilbert Lawrence, a useless lump of a drug-addicted attempt at manhood, whose only delight was to screw the bitch who had just left, no doubt intending to come back as soon as he had gone. Helmsley wasn't sure what to do. He wanted to stomp out of the flat, find another willing recruit and to bleed him and his family for what he could, but no one else had the wealth of the Lawrence family. He plied Michael with coffee, put him into a warm bath, only to see him almost collapse, his head slowly sinking below the surface of the water. It was a hopeless situation, he knew that.

All that money at the rehabilitation centre, and one woman, one syringe, and the man was as bad as he had ever been. He needed him clean, he needed help. He made a phone call. Forty minutes later, the two men that had dossed with Michael were at the door. Fully dressed – Helmsley had had to dress him – the grandson of the wealthy man was soon downstairs and in the back of Helmsley's vehicle, a late-model Jaguar. *No use in driving around in an old bomb*, Helmsley thought as he pulled away from the kerb, hoping that Michael Lawrence wouldn't throw up or urinate in the back seat, hoping the other two wouldn't either.

'I want my girl back,' Michael mumbled, the others in the car attempting to get him to shut up. Back at the dosshouse, the man was roughly thrown back on the mattress where he had come from. Helmsley administered the heroin into his vein, not sure what he was doing, only knowing that he needed Michael quiet for now while he planned his next move. He knew that heroin was the last thing that Michael needed, but he needed him to stay and to sleep. Tomorrow, the man would detox the hard way: cold turkey.

At the back of the dosshouse was an old washroom, a solid lock on the door. When he entered the austere room, Michael Lawrence would have gone from the five-star luxury of the Waverley House Rehabilitation Centre for the rich and feeble to a flat in Bayswater, then back to his old doss house mattress, and

373

then to a washroom with concrete walls and a concrete floor. Five days in there, maybe six, and then he would be let out, cleaned up, and sent off to get more money, to the same place he had obtained money before.

And to hell with the revolution, Helmsley thought, not that he didn't believe in it, but what was the point. Those he collected to his side were only the disenfranchised, the lunatic fringe, the people that he despised.

If only the London School of Economics hadn't been so rigid, he could still be there, formulating the manifesto to take the next step forward in his quest for justice for the people of England: equality and prosperity in equal measure. Not once did he consider that he, Giles Helmsley, could be mad; that was the arrogance of the man.

Chapter 27

Emily Matson did the rounds at Challis Street, Larry doing the introductions. She liked the freshness of the police station, the camaraderie that existed. She had confided to Larry on the Eurostar coming back to London that the environment at Greenwich Police Station was toxic, the after-effects of her previous inspector who had been found guilty of taking bribes.

And now everyone in the station was careful to be on their best behaviour, excessively documenting everything, looking for flaws in others. Even she had been reported for not informing the

Admin Department that she would be out of the country for a few days, although the station superintendent had been notified in a phone call from Isaac. Regardless, there'd be some on her return to the station who would make disparaging remarks about her getting ahead of herself, becoming involved in Homicide when she should be focussed on theft and the cat burglar who had been making his way around the area.

'There's one DCI who was hostile that I became involved with Challis Street. He thought that his seniority should have ensured that I handed the investigation into Frost over to him.'

'And?' Larry said.

'He complained to our superintendent when the Belgium trip came up, said it was his right to go, not a junior.'

'Which meant?'

'Not a woman. He's a chauvinistic misogynist. The super told him to button his lip, and to get back to work. The superintendent's a good man.'

'This DCI, what did he hope to gain in Belgium? And besides, we would have scuttled him.'

'Nothing to do with the case. For him, it would have been Belgian chocolates, Belgian beer, a sampling of the local talent.'

'Fancies himself?'

'He's the only one that does. The superintendent's been trying to get him out, but the man sticks like glue. He gave evidence against the other DCI, gained a few more brownie points, a friend of the commissioner.'

'Alwyn Davies?'

'You've met him?'

'We've had our problems. He had DCI Cook and Chief Superintendent Goddard out of their seats for a while. The man's odious, but he plays it smart.'

Isaac's office was too small with Emily in the department. Down the hall, a conference room was secured.

'Emily, Larry, an update,' Isaac said.

'There's no doubt that Hector O'Grady was seen in the village of Herzele. We've two independent corroborations, one the owner of a small shop, the other a farmer who states that O'Grady's vehicle nearly caused an accident.'

'O'Grady driving?'

'Nobody recognised a photo of Ainsley Caxton,' Larry said, 'although the murder of Samuels would have required some time. It's logical to assume that one person did the shooting, another the driving.'

'Is there any way to find out if Caxton and O'Grady were in Belgium at the time?' Wendy said. She was anxious to be out of the office and following the two heavies would have suited her fine.

'It was nineteen months ago,' Emily said.

'Still, there must be CCTV here and in Belgium. Two men travelling in a green Toyota Land Cruiser must have been seen.'

'Without a doubt, but that's a lot of work, going through all the videos, and would they still be available?' Bridget said. She had previously been the CCTV viewing officer, a skill she had been trained for. She would find proof if anybody could, she knew that.

'Two people identifying O'Grady won't hold up in court. It's supposition, not proof. Emily, Larry, good work, but we need to follow it up,' Isaac said. 'What's the current status of the two thugs?'

'They're still in Greenwich. O'Grady's been out and about, Caxton was seen three days ago, but nothing since then. We believe he's in the area, though,' Emily said.

'You're maintaining surveillance?'

'Low-key. We don't want to let on that we're closing in.'

'We need something we can pressure them with. And then we can go after Frost, make the man sweat. His arrest may lead us to whoever killed Gilbert Lawrence. Wendy, work with Emily and her people. Find out the movements of Caxton and O'Grady, see if they're predictable, see if they're committing any crimes. Emily and her people are obviously doing a good job, so liaise, no need for you to be pounding the pavement any more than necessary.'

Wendy could see her DCI aiming to protect her, to keep her increasing immobility concealed for as long as possible. She had to thank him for his consideration, regretted that it was necessary. Regular exercise, massaging, and medication were helping, but the decline was continuing. And besides, Greenwich suited her fine for a few days. She had wanted to get up to the Greenwich Observatory for some time, a chance to see the Prime Meridian, zero degrees longitude, and the Cutty Sark, an old clipper ship, its restoration complete after a devastating fire. She had been there with her husband in their courting days. It would be good to go back, nostalgia for her, a remembrance of what a good man he had been, even if he had been difficult sometimes. She had to admit that she still missed him.

'I've been checking names with Eurostar, the ferries, the airlines,' Bridget said. 'So far, no Caxton or O'Grady, although the checks are not that rigorous. Easy enough to forge documents, and no one is keeping a record of the photos on them,' Bridget said.

The team was excited. For once, some decisive action. Emily was pleased to be in an office where negativity did not abound. She thought she could enjoy being in Challis Street on a more permanent basis, but her boyfriend was over the other side of the River Thames, and she did not see him that often as it was. Homicide involved much longer hours than she had worked before. It was the conflict between being a professional police officer and a person in a relationship. She knew she was not willing to make the ultimate decision of one at the expense of the other. She had seen too many relationships fall apart, she was not about to allow hers to become one of those as well.

'The vehicle seen in Belgium, left- or right-hand drive?' Isaac said.

'No one's sure,' Larry said. 'The lady in the shop did not see the vehicle, the farmer swerved to avoid it. It's important to know, but there's no way we can tell.'

'Bridget, any luck?'

'Nothing registered to Frost and his associates. I've been checking with records, stolen vehicles. There are two possibilities for UK registered vehicles. A Toyota Land Cruiser, 1990, stolen to the south of London, found abandoned in Brighton. Another vehicle, 1991, reported missing in Earls Court. The dates tally, and of the two, only one has been recovered.'

'Is anyone checking?'

'Forensics have the vehicle. Inconclusive at this time. The vehicle had been returned to the owner, and he subsequently tidied it up and sold it on.'

'Dented, condition indicative of an accident?'

'The owner was a keen member of an off-roaders club. The vehicle was not in good condition when it was stolen, no better or worse when it was returned. According to him, it was a good workhorse, had given him lots of fun, and he had been sorry to see it go.'

'Why did he sell it?'

'Child on the way. No doubt his wife had something to do with the decision.' Larry understood. Before he had married, and before his wife had become pregnant with their first, he had been driving around in a two-seater, an MGB. A lot of fun, but not very practical. He had been sad when he sold it, even sadder when he drove out of the dealer's with a four-door Ford Mondeo. He had mourned the change, a sign of passing from youth to adulthood and married responsibility.

Isaac phoned Forensics, received an update on the Land Cruiser. After two minutes, he put his phone down and spoke to the team. 'It's probably the vehicle in Belgium. Damage at the front is consistent with hitting another car, and they found paint from what looks to be the Peugeot. They've been in contact with Belgium, received a detailed analysis of the Peugeot's paint. Bridget, you've a registration number, run it through the system, see what you can find.'

'Will do, also I'll access the databases in Belgium, talk to Inspecteur Hougardy.'

'Get yourself on Eurostar and sit with their CCTV viewing officer. If we have a vehicle, we have a driver and a passenger. No problems over there, and they've probably kept records. It's the most lit up area on the planet, lights on all the motorways, so no trouble with visibility.'

'I can access our records from over there. I suggest that I continue here for the next two hours, and then take the train. We need to know if Caxton and O'Grady are in the vehicle in the UK, but we need to place them near to the scene of the crime.'

'Sorry, Wendy,' Isaac said. 'You'll need to stay in London, no souvenirs for you, no late-night drinking with Bridget.'

'That's understood,' Wendy said.

Bridget leant over, touched her on the arm. 'Don't worry, I'll bring you back a big box of chocolates, as well as a bottle of beer.'

'I'd rather the farmer that took a fancy to Emily,' Wendy said, Larry having recounted the story earlier.

'If he fits in my bag, I may just do that,' Bridget said.

***

Giles Helmsley may have been credited with a high intellect, a PhD from Oxford University, but he was not the man to administer drugs, especially the narcotic kind. It was five in the morning when one of the two men who had helped Helmsley with Lawrence knocked on the door of his flat.

'It's Michael,' the man said. His visit was not appreciated in the building where the radical academic lived, a door opening on the floor below, a curious person looking out, telling whoever it was to keep the noise down.

'Mind your own business,' Coyote said, with a few expletives. It was not the addict's name but the moniker taken from a cartoon that he answered to. He thought it made him sound cool; it did not. It only made him appear to be more stupid than he actually was. A typical anarchist follower, Helmsley would have admitted if pressed.

'What's up with him? Has he left?'

'He's not moving. I've tried shaking him, even threw water on him, but nothing.'

Helmsley pulled Coyote inside the flat. 'Shut up and sit quietly while I get dressed.'

Coyote wrestled with the concept of quiet, and he moved around the flat, looking at this and that, staring out of the window. He was shaking and sweaty, and in need of a fix, and the professor had taken his drugs and given them to Michael the night before.

Helmsley came out from his bedroom, put on a coat that was hanging from a hook on the back of the door to the flat. He then grabbed the addict, not willing to call him by his silly name, and dragged him out. On the landing outside, Coyote said, 'It's Michael, he's dead.'

'For Christ's sake, be quiet,' Helmsley said, increasingly annoyed that the man knew his address.

As they walked down the stairs, Coyote was still complaining, grabbing hold of the bannisters, brushing up against a couple of the doors. One of the disturbed residents opened his door and made a comment; Coyote tried to get free and to smash him one. 'That's all they understand,' he said.

Giles Helmsley had kept his anarchist beliefs separate from where he lived. He had a cause to follow, a cause that required sacrifices, but not his. To his neighbours, he was a quiet, studious man, and now that was unravelling as Coyote continued to cause trouble. Outside, on the street, he gave the addict a smack across the face with an open palm – it had some effect. In the Jaguar, cold at first, but soon warmer with the heater, the two men drove to the dosshouse.

Inside on the floor, lay Michael Lawrence. 'He's not dead,' Helmsley said. 'He's still breathing.'

'He's OD'd,' Coyote said. The other occupant of the room, another addict who preferred being called 'Stud' to Gerald, continued to sleep, his snoring raucous. Helmsley opened a window, the cold air taking some of the smell in the room. He phoned Emergency Services.

Chapter 28

When Bridget arrived at the railway station in Brussels, Jules Hougardy was waiting outside for her. She was as impressed with the man as Emily and Larry had been. It was late afternoon by the time she arrived, and although she had spent the morning checking through the databases, attempting to access CCTV footage of the cross-channel tunnel and the ferries, it hadn't been entirely successful. Forensic analysis of the Land Cruiser had not come up with anything more. The vehicle, returned to the owner after its now known sojourn on the continent, had been patched up, driven along rough tracks, had its underside bashed, its bodywork scratched, before being subjected to an amateurish three-month restoration by the owner. It had then been sold on to another off-road enthusiast. Any evidence of Belgium, Caxton, and O'Grady was long gone, apart from a sample of the Peugeot's paint. The only piece of good news was the confirmation that the vehicle had crossed into mainland Europe three days before Samuels died, and had returned two days after. No doubt the delay in the return had been to check that the vehicle wasn't wanted by the police: the usual practice being to park it somewhere prominent, somewhere legal, somewhere the police would have been checking. If it was still there after a couple of days, then it was safe to drive.

'I've booked you into the same hotel as Inspectors Matson and Hill,' Hougardy said, 'but first, we must have dinner. I've arranged a local place, somewhere the tourists avoid. All they want is fish and chips, but for you, the works.' Bridget remembered Emily's comments about the Belgian police officer's love of fish and chips, but that was not what she ate. For her, it was Carbonnade Flamande, a beef casserole cooked in wine. For dessert, waffles and ice cream. The meal was delicious, the company excellent, and she made sure to phone Wendy on her return to her hotel.

'Perfect gentleman,' Bridget said.

'The evening wasn't a total success then,' Wendy said.

'It was. Tomorrow I'm meeting with his team and spending time with the CCTV viewing officer. Not all of it's available. Hopefully, it'll be enough. They've got cameras everywhere.'

'Nowhere has more than London but focus on the farmer's village.'

'I'll go and see the farmer for you, see if he's your type.'

'He will be. Hurry back soon. The office is not the same without you, and I've got another report to file. I could do with your help.'

The next day, Bridget tucked into a good breakfast. The hotel offered either continental or English. She chose the English, realising that she was falling into the trap of the reluctant tourist, wanting to see the exotic as long as it was accompanied by a cup of tea and bacon and eggs.

At the central police station in Brussels on Rue du Marché au Charbon, Bridget met her counterpart, a moustached man who smelt vaguely of mothballs. She imagined Hercule Poirot, but this man was not short or rotund, and his moustache was neatly trimmed, not curled up at the ends. He was also talkative and did not use his little grey cells to the same extent as Agatha Christie's most famous creation.

'Bridget Halloran, I am pleased to meet you,' Hendrik Brun said, his Belgian accent strong, his English understandable. He also took her hand and kissed it. Bridget blushed. She could never imagine her DCI or her DI kissing her, hand or cheek.

'We've got a lot of work to do,' Bridget said. The office was better than Challis Street, more modern, more open. To her, it lacked the charm that Challis Street offered, the homely touches she had brought to it. She took out her laptop, logged on using the police station's Wi-Fi, the password supplied by Brun.

'We've obtained records from the cameras out at Herzele,' Brun said. 'One of the cameras was faulty. Also, the videos from another have been deleted. We do have two others. With your permission, we'll concentrate on them. For our purposes, I suggest we divide the videos, you taking the time after the murders, and I'll take before.'

Bridget could see that the man was no-nonsense, straight down to work, and as competent on a computer as she was. They first checked the videos at the ferry port where the vehicle had entered the country. The date and the time were now known. It was not difficult to spot the Toyota coming off the ferry and driving up the ramp and onto the dock. The road markings took the cars from driving on the left to the right, and numerous signs reminded the drivers that this was Belgium, and all vehicles were left-hand drive, and great care was to be exercised.

'The windows are darkened,' Brun said. 'We can't see the driver or the passenger.' Bridget could see that he was right. The vehicle that had been recently checked in England had clear windows. Someone had applied a film, probably purchased at an automotive store. Whoever had done it had complicated their work. None of the CCTVs in Brussels were of any use, as the department responsible prided itself on erasing all footage after six months.

Herzele was a different situation. The records were kept in Ghent, a city not far from Brussels, and the deletion of video files was not so rigorous. Bridget sat on one side of Brun's desk, he sat on the other. In front of them, a large monitor each. Brun slowly scanned back from the closest time to the shooting, Bridget scanned forward. The video from one of the two cameras was clear, the other was blurred and out of focus.

It took two hours before Brun saw the vehicle in the village. He and Bridget then focussed forward from that time. It was another twenty minutes before he had traced it as far as he could, which was still two kilometres from the murder scene. With times established, he used enhanced imaging technology to look for additional detail. 'The tinting is only on the windscreen and the front windows, the rear tailgate has none,' he said.

Bridget wondered why they had not picked up the Toyota at the time of the murders. But then, as Brun explained, English tourists driving around were not that uncommon, and the registration number wasn't easy to read. In fact, it was almost impossible, the first and last letters covered in mud or rust or both, the numbers scratched and unreadable. It was either done on purpose or the result of bashing over muddy tracks or logs with the off-roaders.

After nine hours solid looking at the monitor screens, neither of the two officers was able to focus any more. Bridget phoned Wendy who brought in Isaac on speaker. The time in Brussels had been successful in that the vehicle had been identified. It would need another day, when she and Hendrik Brun would focus in detail on the time that one of the men had entered the shop in Herzele. The almost accident with the farmer had been outside of the village, in an area where there were no cameras. Nothing would be gained by trying to look for further verification from the farmer or any other drivers on the road. It had been a overcast day when the murder occurred and the road had been mainly deserted, the reason that the farmer had pulled his tractor out into the centre of the road without due care and attention.

***

In Belgium, the prosecution case was firming against Ainsley Caxton and Hector O'Grady. In London, there were other developments, in particular, the hospitalisation of Michael Lawrence.

The first Homicide heard of him being there was when the hospital administration had phoned, his name being on a database of concerned persons, a possible drug overdose. The second was when Molly Dempster called to tell Isaac that Ralph was on his way to see his son.

In intensive care at St Mary's Hospital, where Alexander Fleming had discovered penicillin, and not far from Paddington Station, two doctors stood by Michael's bed, three nurses hovered close by. The man was Gilbert Lawrence's grandson, and as Jill Dundas had said, money was not an issue. She wasn't sure why she had said it when she had arrived at the hospital ten minutes after Ralph, five minutes after Isaac and Wendy. Larry had taken over following up on Caxton and O'Grady, attempting to find more evidence against Gary Frost, anything that could stick.

An intravenous drip was to one side of the bed, the patient lying flat on his back. Only Ralph had been allowed in initially, Isaac after he had shown his warrant card and insisted that it was vital to see the patient.

Michael's face was covered by a mask supplying oxygen, an ECG machine standing by. 'It's not good,' one of the doctors said. 'The man had three times the normal amount from what we can see.'

It was known that Giles Helmsley had made the phone call for the ambulance, but he was not at the hospital. Isaac made a phone call to Larry. 'Pick up Helmsley, make sure he's at Challis Street within the hour.'

On the bed, Michael moved, not conscious of his actions. Ralph was present, although Isaac had left and was talking to Jill Dundas and Molly Dempster.

'Waste of time getting him detoxed,' Jill Dundas said. Isaac could see the hardness in her face. She had professed sadness at Gilbert's death, at the death of her father, but had it been feigned? Isaac couldn't be sure.

'Too long without treatment. We could have helped him earlier, but now? There's possible brain damage as well,' one of the doctors said as he came out and spoke to Isaac. 'Not much of a life, not much of a death either, although he'll not know much about it.'

Michael Lawrence died at 11.08 a.m. on a Thursday morning. Ralph was heartbroken, so was Molly. Jill Dundas stood nearby in the reception area, mouthing the words the others wanted to hear. She did not shed a tear, neither did Ralph, although Wendy and Molly did.

Larry phoned; Helmsley was at the police station. After another twenty minutes at the hospital, Isaac left, leaving Wendy with Molly. She would look after the woman who had aged in that short time at the hospital. She had gained a son, a grandson, and now one of them was dead, and the other was not the healthiest, and his future looked bleak.

At the station, Helmsley sat quietly. He was holding a cup of tea: Earl Grey, at his request. He looked into vacant space, saying nothing, seeing nothing.

'I found him at the dosshouse,' Larry said, 'lying down on that filthy mattress that Lawrence used. He looks as if he can't take it all in. Bizarre when you think about it. A brilliant man they said down at LSE, and yet he's out there leading the good fight, believing that people are waiting for the revolution.'

'Genius level intelligence comes with its own problems,' Isaac said. 'Better to be like us, smart enough to know what's good for us, smart enough to leave the rest well alone.'

Larry led Helmsley into the interview room. He had committed no crime as far as was known, and legal representation was offered but declined.

'Mr Helmsley, you phoned Emergency Services,' Isaac said.

'One of Michael's friends woke me up, told me that he was in trouble. I went over there, found him on the floor. That's when I made the call.'

'The other man could have,' Larry said.

'Coyote, that's the name he likes to use, was the same as Michael, an addict.'

'But Michael was with Ralph. What happened?'

'Michael was weak. I was at his place. He had a woman with him, doped up as well. The two were on heroin, and Michael needed help.'

'The woman?'

'I've no idea. I kicked her out. Michael could have served the cause, but what does he do? He finds himself a drugged-out female. The two of them, naked in that bed, a syringe to one side. I took Michael, thrust him into the shower, plied him with coffee and brought him back to where the woman couldn't find him, neither could his father.'

'Even if we accept what you've told us, it doesn't explain why he had OD'd, does it?'

'One of the others must have injected him,' Helmsley said. Larry noticed the twitch in his face when he spoke.

'You're lying, aren't you, Mr Helmsley? A drug addict is not going to waste perfectly good heroin on someone else. You injected him for your own purposes.'

'I was going to put him in a room at the back of the house, make him go cold turkey. A fancy rehabilitation centre in the country with its five-star accommodation and runs around the lawns couldn't fix him, no doubt charged thousands as well. But that's the capitalist system: screw the poor, bleed the rich.'

'Mr Helmsley, we don't need a political party broadcast. Did you inject Michael Lawrence on that mattress?'

'I did it for him. My intentions were honourable.'

'Your intentions have killed him, and they were not honourable, they were for your own distorted purpose. You're a hypocrite, you wanted his family's money. You will be charged with involuntary manslaughter. Further charges may be laid against you. I suggest you find yourself a good lawyer.'

Chapter 29

Bridget had to admit she enjoyed being in Brussels. Hendrik Brun was proving himself to be a man after her own heart, a computer aficionado. He had admitted the previous night that he enjoyed surfing the net, learning from the computer, and his typing was even faster than hers.

Bridget was confident the following morning that the day would wrap up her time in the Belgian capital, so much so that she checked out of the hotel, booked herself on Eurostar for six o'clock that evening, and arranged for Wendy to pick her up on her arrival at St Pancras Station.

In the office at the police station in Brussels, there was no need for Bridget to set up her laptop, having done it the previous day. The two of them, she and Brun, went straight into reviewing the CCTV from outside the shop in Herzele, the one monitor between the two of them. Scrolling back, the vehicle could be seen entering the town square, and then parking.

'See there,' Brun said. 'You can see Caxton getting out of the passenger's side.' Bridget looked closer, could see another person in the driver's seat, a large man, even larger than Caxton. Bridget was sure who it was, but it wasn't conclusive.

The pair moved to another monitor with higher definition. Zooming in helped but blurred the man. An overlay of O'Grady was imposed on the monitor, an attempt to align features: the nose, the mouth, the chin. The identity was required first, the proof later. Both admitted defeat. Scrolling forward from where the vehicle had parked, it stopped just before driving out of range of the camera. Two men got out of the car. This time their features were unmistakable; it was Ainsley Caxton and Hector O'Grady. O'Grady could be seen picking up the phone: a time, as well as a location.

'Traceable,' Brun said. He sent an email, Bridget could not understand what was written as it was in Dutch. 'A colleague. He'll give us the number phoned.'

'You don't have O'Grady's number.'

'We must assume he dialled an English number. My colleague is very thorough. He will not let us down.'

Inside the Land Cruiser, with a brief side view in through the passenger's door, they could see a weapon, its barrel visible.

'There's proof,' Brun said.

'Proof that they committed the crime. Wherever the weapon is now, it's long gone. They could have brought it over from England, tied it to the chassis underneath, or they could have purchased it locally.'

'Only on the black market. The laws are strict here: residency, proof of address, police check.'

'The same as in England,' Bridget said, not sure of her facts.

'They would have brought it from England. Coming into Belgium, the checks are not that strict. Unfortunately, the trade in illegals, contraband, drugs, is one way, not two. The checks will be more vigorous going back to England. They would have dumped it; the river is the most likely. No chance of finding it now.'

'The deaths of Samuels and the others are murder,' Bridget said. 'It will be difficult for the Belgian authorities to prove a case.'

'Almost impossible. Circumstantially, yes, but the defence lawyers are smart. It'll never be proved. I'm afraid it's up to you in England to bring these two men to justice.'

***

Ralph Lawrence, no longer evicted from his flat, moved back. His mother was holding up, tearful at first, then stoic. For a reason he could not explain, he was sad. It wasn't as if Michael had amounted to much, but he was his son. He reflected on a cheerful baby, a playful young boy. Even Yolanda had eventually found some affection for him.

He had once caught her singing a lullaby as her son gurgled in his cot, only to pull away and make some excuse about trying to get him to sleep. She had a busy day the next day: socialising, a meeting at the magazine where she submitted the occasional article. He knew that she cared, but the woman was driven to better herself, and wasted emotions were not needed.

Two years later, she was away more than she was at home. He had followed her once, found out that the articles and the magazine were no longer needed. She had found herself a fancy man, a banker in the city. Ralph remembered the confrontation that night, where she defended her position, the child crying in the other room. After that, they never slept together, until she had finally left when Michael was six, old enough to be boarded out for five days a week at school, and then at seven years of age for the full week, long weekends and holidays excepted.

Yolanda had gone, he had an empty house, and he needed money. It was a friend from school who had told him about the rich pickings in the South of France and the Costa Brava. An Englishman, well-educated and speaking with a plum in the mouth, could get anything, be anything, he had told Ralph.

Two weeks later he had been in St Tropez, only visiting, checking if his friend was right, when a woman approached him. 'You must be a lord,' she said. Ralph knew that he had dressed well, something he always prided himself on. Instinctively he had replied. 'Lord Lawrence, the second son of the Earl of …' somewhere he couldn't remember now.

'My husband and I, we love the Royal Family.'

'Oh, yes. I get to spend time with them, went to school with one of them.'

Ralph unintentionally had struck the mother lode. His friend who had said it was easy pickings stood back in amazement as Ralph was whisked off to dinner, and then invited to stay at the mansion the woman and her husband had rented for the season. Over two weeks, he continued to spin them tale after tale: how the castle was in need of repairs; if only they could come over sometime, but it wasn't suitable for them; how he could introduce them into society, maybe even be able to get them to meet a prince.

It had been so easy, only interrupted because Michael was coming home for two weeks. As he left the mansion, the wife thrust a cheque for fifty thousand pounds into his hand. He had done nothing, hurt nobody, not even committed a crime. All he had done was entertain them, give them a thrill. The money to them was nothing, to him it was a godsend.

Michael, on his father's return, had found him to be generous and attentive, but he was still only young. It was the last time that they had spent any time together until the flat in Bayswater, and now he was dead, the victim of drugs, the victim of callous and shallow parents, the victim of Helmsley. The man had annoyed him at school, and now he had taken his only child from him.

Ralph Lawrence took a handkerchief from his trouser pocket and blew his nose, as well as dabbing his eyes. He then picked up his phone and dialled Antigua.

***

Bridget had debriefed Homicide on her return to Challis Street, also giving Wendy the largest box of Belgian chocolates that she could buy.

The team watched the edited video replays from Herzele, crystal clear images of Caxton and O'Grady, the rifle inside the vehicle. 'It's them,' Isaac said. 'The only problem is that it's not proof, just more evidence if we manage to secure enough evidence against them for a trial.'

'The weapon?' Bridget said.

'Without it, Forensics can't do bullet analysis. Regardless, we do have a case against the men. We can pull them in, make them sweat. We've got Ralph Lawrence's evidence as well. Anyone else?'

'Not yet,' Larry said. 'Give me twelve hours while I go and talk to the man who put me onto Frost. He knows more, I'm sure of it.'

'He's not going to allow himself to be compromised,' Wendy said.

'Who knows how these people think. If Frost is out of the way, then there are more suckers for them to bleed. My man's no saint, even if he pretends he is. I'll push, see what I can get. Maybe best if you phone up Emily Matson, tell her to keep a close watch on Frost and his henchmen, and to be prepared to pull Caxton and O'Grady in at short notice. Not Frost, though. We need him to sweat some more. Without them around, who knows? Easy to be tough when you're protected, not so good when you're on your own.'

Emily Matson intensified the surveillance on Caxton and O'Grady. The DI whose nose was out of joint was once again complaining to the station's superintendent about being sidelined while his junior was getting all the glory. He had been quick on the phone after leaving the super's office, Emily overhearing the gist of what was being said, certain he was speaking to Alwyn Davies.

Larry told Emily to stay focussed and to ignore the office politics. She had the full support of Challis Street Homicide and Chief Superintendent Goddard. He only hoped her superintendent was up to the task. If he wasn't then Isaac and Goddard would make a personal representation at Greenwich, endeavour to bolster the superintendent, a man with just over one year to go for his full pension and retirement, and who did not crave the ignominy of a reduction in his rank and his pension.

Caxton was out and about, buying McDonald's one day, a pizza the next. O'Grady was not so visible, although he had been seen in a local gym pushing weights. Both men were feared in the area, both as likely to grab someone by the collar than wish them a good day.

If they were to be brought in, Emily knew, it would have to be one at a time. Indications were that they would not come voluntarily. Neither had committed any offence in England, not in recent years, although Caxton had picked up more parking fines than most, but that wasn't an arrestable offence as he had paid them all on time. O'Grady had nothing against him.

The hotel in Brussels where Caxton and O'Grady stayed had been found, the bill paid, no trouble from either man, although they had drunk too much in the bar. Isaac knew the case was weak, and he could bring them in, but a smart lawyer would have them out within a couple of hours. Ralph Lawrence would testify, but only if Frost had murdered his father and was locked up, otherwise he wasn't going to confront the lender of no hope and his henchman purely on the say-so of the police that they would protect him. They had not managed to protect Michael, and he had seen the police protection already offered to him and his family: minimal at best, useless if the truth were known. No doubt subject to budgetary constraints or some other jargon that everyone seemed to use.

'The kneecapped man, what about him?' Isaac said to Larry. They were out of the office, walking around Gilbert Lawrence's mansion, trying to go over what they had so far. Arresting Frost looked possible, especially if they could get Caxton or O'Grady to break. But Frost had no apparent connection to Gilbert's death, no prior knowledge that Ralph and Gilbert had been related.

Inside the previously bolted off main section of the building, the two police officers could see that the CSIs had been careful, no fingerprints, no footprints, but they had walked through with their equipment, and the floor, previously covered in dust, had been disturbed. Larry and Isaac had ensured to put on gloves and overshoes and to let Gordon Windsor know that they were in the house, a matter of courtesy rather than a procedural requirement. They climbed the sweeping staircase, the steps creaking as they moved. It was not a pleasant place to be, still smelling of decay and death, although the death was more imagined than real.

At the top of the stairs, a cold breeze. Larry froze, not sure what to do. He had read his children a bedtime story the previous night, a fairy tale about a princess in a draughty castle. It was recommended for ages five to seven, although it had a touch of the melodrama about it, not that it concerned them at the time, or even him. But now he and his senior were in that castle, even though it was smaller, and the princess, a dead body, had been in the second room along the landing. Isaac opened the door, saw that the bed remained, although the body was long gone. He phoned Picket in Pathology. 'Any reason why you can't release Dorothy Lawrence for burial?'

'I'll write the death certificate.'

Isaac phoned Caroline Dickson to tell her; she was relieved.

Outside the mansion, decaying after such a long time of neglect, the two officers stood to one side of where Molly Dempster had found Gilbert lying on the ground. The area was still marked off, but the grass had since grown.

'It could still be Ralph, even though he was with the Spanish police,' Isaac said.

'He could have arranged someone else. Not Caxton and O'Grady, bulls in a china shop, those two.'

Chapter 30

Jill Dundas made contingency plans. There had just been too much interest in Gilbert's death, too much sentimentalising about Michael's death, too much morbid interest in Dorothy. Her father had been a brilliant man, a man to be revered, but he was not mentioned, while a drug addict and a skeleton were given preference.

The popular press continued to write on the subject. Michael's death, and the subsequent arrest of a known agitator for involuntary manslaughter, raised speculation in the scurrilous newspapers and on social media about the possibility of demonic practices in the case of Dorothy, the sacrificial death of Gilbert, the just reward from God for Michael's death.

Jill knew that none of it was true, but it was not possible to give a truthful account of all that had transpired. Gilbert had indeed been senile but showing moments of lucidity. His business mind had remained detached from his social behaviour: the death of his wife Dorothy unhinging him for many years. It was only her father who had been able to get near to the man, and he had known, he must have, of the horror that was on the second floor of the mansion. But not once did her father reveal what had been committed, not until the last few months when she came to know that her father's time was up, the doctor picking up an ongoing degradation in his health, a fluctuation in his heart.

'Jill, you must know the truth,' he had said. It was late at night, and he had been sitting in his favourite chair, a glass of port in his hand. As she sat there, he recounted the saga of Gilbert Lawrence, Dorothy's death, the irrational and unsound mind of his friend as if he was having a brainstorm, the pressure too much for the most lucid of men. It had been her father's decision to ensure Gilbert Lawrence's legacy. It had required the signature of the great man, gladly given as he suffered, unsure whether he was alive or dead. After that, her father had told her, Gilbert vacillated between sanity and utter madness, not willing to leave the prison he had created. The trips to the off-licence, even though they had commenced years previously, were the man's attempts to reconnect.

Her father had convinced her that it was better to let sleeping dogs lie, and not to resurrect the past, to never let on what had happened in that house to that man, that woman. Dorothy had been an ill woman for a long time, her father said. A woman who had hurled herself off the top step of the staircase, dying at the bottom, not from a broken neck, but from despair complicated by grief over her son, anger with her daughter for marrying Desmond and moving away, from internal bleeding.

'Don't you understand,' Leonard said that night to Jill, 'Gilbert blamed them all. Dorothy for dying, Ralph for what he had become, Caroline for upsetting her mother. It was only me that he would see, not Molly. She raised other emotions in him, not that I always understood why, but he cared for her. He never mentioned an affair, but…'

And now Jill knew about Ralph, and Molly being his mother. Legally it did not impact on Gilbert's last will and testament, although it may give her leverage, a means to delay what would become certain in time: that Gilbert had been mad, but he was becoming saner, and even at his advanced age he had decided to ease out of seclusion and to take control of his empire, to make his peace with his family.

***

The man didn't phone often, but Frost knew he was worth the monthly retainer that he paid, a package left under a bench at the entrance to Greenwich Observatory on the first Thursday of every month at eight thirty-three in the evening, the man arriving at the spot two minutes later. The news was disturbing. Caxton and O'Grady were liable to be picked up at any time. Frost trusted Caxton, not so much O'Grady. The evidence was flimsy, and the police technique would be to arrest the men, pressure them heavily and hope that one would crack. He knew one of them would; he could not take a chance.

Frost knew that it was all due to Ralph Lawrence, a malignant sore of no worth. Lawrence had brought the police to his doorstep, and they were putting two and two together, coming up with three, but soon it would be four. And then it would be him at the police station, the connections made with Lawrence, with Belgium. A private man, Frost knew that if he wanted to stay where he was, free and not in prison, he would need to break the links joining him to the crimes that had been committed.

Inside his penthouse, he summoned one of his men. 'How do you like fishing?' he said.

'We go out occasionally, rent a boat not far from here.'

'Good. Take your partner out today. Make sure he doesn't come back.'

'Can I ask why?'

'It is better that you don't know. And make sure that he rents the boat and picks you up somewhere else, somewhere you will not be seen.'

'Are there more?'

'The first must be today. The others, if there are to be any, we will discuss after you return.'

Frost, a man who did not procrastinate, felt calmer, confident that he was making the right decision. Two previous decisions were proving troublesome, he knew that. First, the murder of Samuels, motivated more by the man's intransigence about paying the interest, although he had repaid the principal, done as a warning, and then lending money to the weak and insignificant son of Gilbert Lawrence.

Another phone call from his informer. 'Tomorrow afternoon.' Two words only, but it was enough for Frost. The police were getting closer, and he could not hold them at bay indefinitely. Whatever he did, he needed to ensure his survival, Caxton's if he could, but if he couldn't, then he would have tried. Frost logged onto his laptop, checked his bank accounts. He started transferring money out of the country: somewhere warmer, somewhere that not too many questions were asked, somewhere he did not want to go, but freedom was better than the alternatives.

By the time he had finished two hours had passed. He had seen the boat go by on the Thames. It was not a large boat but sufficient for two. In the small cabin, dressed in wet weather gear, was Hector O'Grady. Further down the river, close to where Caxton had parked his car, O'Grady would pull in before the two men headed out into deeper water, a fishing spot that both knew. Fishing was a passion of O'Grady's, and Caxton had been out with him on a few occasions, invariably bagging more fish.

'Unusual for the boss to let us off for a few hours,' O'Grady said.

Caxton looked over at the man he regarded as a friend. The water was choppy, the beer was cold, and both men had to admit to enjoying themselves. A container ship went past, its wake rocking the small boat. O'Grady's rod started to move, a fish testing the bait, and then the rod bent further, the fish hooked.

'I've got one,' O'Grady said. He started reeling in the line, the fish fighting him, Caxton to one side leaning over the stern of the boat, a net in his hand ready to scoop up what had been caught.

'Keep the net there,' O'Grady shouted.

Caxton took two steps back and drew a small gun from his pocket. 'Sorry,' he said. 'The boss wants you out.' He pulled the trigger and shot twice, one in the back and another in the man's neck, his aim deflected by the rocking of the boat.

Lying prostrate on the boat's decking, his fishing rod discarded, O'Grady gasped, 'Why?'

'It's nothing personal,' Caxton said. He retook aim and shot O'Grady through the brain. He then pulled up the anchor, secured it firmly to the body of his former partner and then threw him over the side. With the man sinking to the bottom of the river, Caxton started the engine on the boat and headed for shore. Once he was within ten yards of it, he turned the boat around and pointed its bow out into deeper water. He then took his gun and shot two holes in the wooden hull, before enlarging them with a safety axe that had been secured to a bulkhead. He set the throttle to maximum, the engine revving, the boat gaining momentum. He then jumped over the side of the boat and swam to shore, although he almost didn't make it as the cold water sapped his strength. Ashore, he made for his car, felt on top of the front offside tyre, and retrieved a key. He started the engine and turned on the heater. On the back seat, dry clothes and a towel.

Chapter 31

The number that O'Grady had phoned from the village of Herzele in Belgium had been traced back to Gary Frost. Even more evidence for the case against him. The content of the conversation that had lasted for less than one minute was not known.

A sorry-looking man was brought into Greenwich Police Station at two in the afternoon. He had not resisted when Emily Matson took him into custody on suspicion of murder, as well as the grievous bodily harm of Ralph Lawrence. The kneecapped man was still not willing to talk. The evidence in both cases was dependent on Caxton admitting that he was guilty, and Larry had been with her when the arrest was made. There was no sign of Hector O'Grady, and the low-key surveillance of the two men had missed his disappearance.

Technically the murder of Steve Samuels was the responsibility of the Belgian police force, and Inspecteur Hougardy was on his way to England, although he wouldn't be present in Greenwich for the first interview with the man who had been detained. The proof was flimsy, purely a chain of events leading to an inevitable conclusion, and although Caxton and O'Grady had been identified by two people in Herzele, another in the hotel in Brussels where they had checked in under false names, there were no fingerprints, no forensic evidence. Emily would be conducting the interview, her first of a murderer. Larry would also be in the interview room, and Isaac would be outside, chafing at the bit, knowing that he would go in harder than the other two, although he hoped that Larry had learnt enough by now to get Caxton flustered and to make the man contradict himself.

Alongside Caxton sat the offensive figure of Edward Sharman, which surprised Isaac, not sure how the man, a singularly ill-mannered and belligerent person, had managed to find his way across the river. Sharman was competent, Isaac knew that, good at getting the guilty off on a technicality. Isaac knew that DIs Matson and Hill had drawn the short straw. They were going to be hard pushed to break through, and Sharman would be doing the majority of the talking for his client.

Outside in the reception area of the police station, Gary Frost was conspicuous by his absence.

A full team of uniforms had been mobilised, even bringing in more manpower from Challis Street, to look for Hector O'Grady. The last that had been known of him was that he had gone out fishing, not unusual in itself, the man at the boat shed said. 'Hector, he's keen, even when the weather's not good. No doubt he takes some liquid refreshments to keep him warm. Always brings the boat back in good condition, even cleans it for me. And yes, he took it out yesterday, not a good day, but the fish should have been biting, not that I'd eat them myself, too small mainly, but Hector, he would have. Tough guy from what I've been told, but when the boat never came back, that's when I started worrying.'

The evidence about the boat was still coming through; another fisherman had seen it sink into the water. The detective inspector who resented Emily Matson usurping him, especially with the trip to Brussels, had been assigned to look for O'Grady. It had been a direct order from his superintendent, a directive he accepted graciously, although he had been seething behind his clenched teeth. 'Don't you worry, Superintendent. Always pleased to help a fellow officer.'

On the river, the local coastguard, the Thames River Police, and a couple of men who worked at the boat shed where the boat had come from trawled up and down in the vicinity of the area identified as O'Grady's most likely destination. Each boat used GPS to keep to their path as they crisscrossed an area of five square miles. The tide was on the turn as they moved up and down, ideal for finding something, but another two hours and a stiff breeze from the east would come up, and if anything was floating, then the chances were that it would be lost.

In the station, Emily Matson followed the correct procedure, informed Ainsley Caxton of his rights, asked everyone to state their name, and in the case of the two police officers their rank. An immediate rebuff came from Sharman, stating on the record that his client was not guilty of any crime. Isaac had briefed Emily beforehand to take the blustering, the rhetoric, in her stride and to keep focussed. She heeded the advice, but she still felt unnerved by a man in a three-piece Savile Row suit, a man who had practised law for as long as she had been alive, a man who knew all the tricks, and a man who was very expensive, more expensive than Caxton could afford, but Frost could.

Isaac knew that Frost was not protecting Caxton for Caxton's benefit. He could see that the heat needed to be raised on Frost, and soon. The surveillance of the man was tighter now, and it was known that he was in Greenwich. Isaac and Wendy left the police station and drove the short distance to the man's penthouse, the man himself answering the intercom on the door this time.

'Detective Chief Inspector Isaac Cook, Detective Sergeant Wendy Gladstone, Challis Street, Homicide. We have a few questions for you.'

'I'm not talking to the police without my lawyer being present.'

'An innocent man would let us in, but maybe you're not. Sharman's going to be busy for some time with Caxton, no doubt he'll weasel him out of there, but how about you, Mr Frost?'

The latch on the door released. 'Come up, I've nothing to hide.'

Isaac turned to Wendy. 'He's feeling vulnerable. O'Grady's not here, and Caxton's under pressure. We can break this case yet.'

'Gilbert Lawrence?'

'The pieces are falling into place. Deal with this, then we raise the heat on the others. Ralph's still not in the clear, neither is his sister. And as for Jill Dundas, a nasty piece of work behind that façade, she will still need further questioning. Once we start solving one case, everyone's nerves will become ragged.'

'Of course, I'm supporting Caxton. He's been with me for years,' Frost said. He was standing at the window of the penthouse, staring out at the river. The weather was looking increasingly wild.

'Hector O'Grady, what can you tell us about him?'

'He's been with me for three years. A good man, and his not being here is out of character.'

'How did you manage when they were in Belgium?' Isaac said.

'And when was that, Inspector?' Frost said. He moved to the other side of the room, sat down on a sofa, beckoned the two police officers to make themselves comfortable. Wendy thought him to be an attractive man, not that it didn't make him guilty.

'When they killed Samuels. We've got the dates, the time that O'Grady phoned you. An error using your number. Arrogance on your part, I suppose, believing that you could thumb your nose at the Belgian police.'

'I receive a lot of phone calls. No doubt some of them are from overseas. It doesn't, however, prove that Caxton and O'Grady were in Belgium. I knew Samuels, I'll not deny that. From what I was told, he had skipped the country, owing me and others money.'

'You didn't pursue him?'

'I tried to find him, but with no success.'

'And if you had?'

'The man knew the conditions of the loan.'

'Violence?'

'Not me. That's not how I operate.'

'It is, so don't give me your nonsense. You use violence as one of the conditions of default. Kneecapping, trussing a man up and beating him senseless, following another overseas and murdering him, and then letting it be known it's what happens to defaulters. What do you think we are, fools? And how do you keep one step ahead of us? Do you have corrupt cops feeding you information? Where are they? Who are they? Mr Frost, you will be next at the police station, and I intend to make sure you can't wriggle out of this one. The case will be so watertight that even Sharman won't be able to help you.'

Frost sat back on his chair, a grin on his face. 'DCI Cook, you have got it all wrong. I am an innocent man. Successful, I'll grant you, and tough with those I deal with, but I am an honest and peaceful man, the sort of person who feels sorry for an animal in distress. I even donate to several charities in the area. Ask around, you'll find that people don't always like me, but there is respect.'

***

Ainsley Caxton, a man who had learnt the art of saying little in a police interview, knew nothing about boats, especially the type that showed up on echo sounders. One of the boats from the boatyard, equipped with one to show fish shoals, the depth of the water, picked up the unusual shape.

The initial detection was relayed by the river police to Greenwich Police Station and then on to DCI Isaac Cook, the highest-ranking officer attached to the investigation, even though he was operating outside of his area.

It would be two hours before the police divers could be on station at the location. The boat, almost certainly the one of interest, was resting on the river bottom at a depth of twenty feet. The visibility was virtually zero, although one of the two police boats carried a submersible camera. Lowering it over the side, and taking into account the slow-moving tide, the boat moved up and down over the area. On the third run, with the camera at a depth of fifteen feet, an image could be seen on the monitor in the cabin. It was not clear, but it was recent, and it could only be O'Grady's boat.

The interview with Caxton was halted for six hours, long enough to allow a full investigation of the sunken boat in the River Thames. Caxton had been brought in for murder, so the twenty-four-hour deadline before charging or release did not apply. He could be held for thirty-six hours, subject to the inevitable paperwork being dealt with, long enough for the boat to be brought up from the river bottom and for Gordon Windsor and his team of crime scene investigators to check it out, and to bring in Forensics if needed.

At the penthouse, Gary Frost was being kept up to date on developments. At St Pancras Station, Inspecteur Jules Hougardy was climbing into the back seat of a taxi, and at Greenwich Police Station, Ainsley Caxton sat in a cell calmly eating a pizza, confident that his boss would get him out.

The Lawrence family, especially Ralph, were also being updated, a ploy by Isaac to relax their stance, to make them believe that Frost was more than likely the murderer of Gilbert, or the man behind the murder, and that he had engineered it to allow him to close in on Ralph. Not that Isaac believed it, but he wanted the guilty to feel as though they had got away with the crime. Caxton and O'Grady were known villains, men who had made a career of violence, but they had not killed Gilbert. Frost was not a murderer, just a smart man who used those capable of such crimes to his advantage.

Larry sat with Emily at Greenwich Police Station, anxiously waiting for updates. The inspector who had taken umbrage at her usurping him hovered in the background, coming in close sometimes, attempting to draw Larry away. It did not work. Larry had spent time with Inspector Emily Matson, knew that her lack of experience was offset by her dedication to the job and that she was honest. From what Larry had heard of the other inspector, he did not trust him. The superintendent had come down, introduced himself to Larry, told him that he and Chief Superintendent Goddard were friends from a long time back.

Out on the water, the two river police boats waited. A barge was on its way from upstream, as was a floating crane with straps suitable for lifting the sunken boat. It wasn't a big boat, no more than twenty-two feet, but it was important that no evidence was destroyed unnecessarily. Typically, a sunken boat would be brought up if it was a hazard to navigation, or if there were extenuating reasons: insurance, valuables on board, a dead body. The first of the divers had been inside the cabin, found no corpse. The second diver had scoured around the immediate vicinity. Both divers were tethered to the surface by lines, another diver on standby up above just in case one of those down below got into trouble, but he was not needed.

Seven hours and twenty-five minutes after the boat had first been located it broke the surface of the River Thames. Even after such a short time, it was covered in mud and a few crabs, some crayfish, as well. It was eased onto the barge and secured. The nearest land where it could be tied up was close to the boatshed it had first set out from.

Isaac was at the dock as the barge tied off. Frost watched from his penthouse, disturbed by what he could see. The instruction to Caxton had been explicit enough, but then the man wasn't the smartest. He should have known the river that close into Greenwich was not that deep. A more intelligent man would have taken the boat further downstream and into deeper water, but Frost realised that nothing could be done now.

On the boat, now starting to dry out, Gordon Windsor was standing. He had donned his coveralls, his overshoes, his gloves, and he wore a mask, not so much to prevent contamination but to minimise the smell of the river and the drying mud.

Inside the small cabin, Windsor picked up a jacket, inside it the name of Ainsley Caxton. He held it up for Isaac and his team to see.

'It wasn't there when the boat went out,' said Joe Garibaldi, second-generation English with Italian grandparents. 'I always check when the boats go out that they're clean and no one's left anything in them. Sometimes they leave a phone when they come back, or a wallet. You'd be amazed at how careless some people are.'

Isaac wasn't.

'Isaac, kit yourself up. Inspector Matson, Larry, you as well,' Windsor shouted.

The three moved closer to the boat after following instructions. 'No need to come onboard,' Windsor said. 'Just look underneath.' The three could see the holes. 'What does it mean?' Isaac said.

'The boat has been scuttled. There are signs of a bullet being fired through the hull, not that it would have been a big enough hole to have sunk it that quickly. Someone's gone at it with something bigger, an axe probably. No sign of the gun or the axe, though.'

'Anything else missing?' Emily asked.

'The anchor. If your man has killed someone out on the river, he's probably been thrown over the side with the anchor tied to him.'

'Any chance of finding the body?' Larry asked.

'Don't raise your hopes too high. A few weeks and a body will be down to bones and a few bits of flesh: natural putrefaction, plus the fish and the crabs. After that, the bones could go out with the tide, the current can get strong out there. We're checking for fingerprints, but don't hold out for us finding anything conclusive.'

Bridget phoned, Larry answered. 'That's great. I'll be there within the hour.'

Larry turned to the others. 'Keith Waters, the kneecapped man, he's heard about Caxton being taken into custody, also that O'Grady's missing, presumed dead. He's willing to give a statement.'

'That means we can bring in Frost, and make it stick,' Isaac said.

'For grievous bodily harm, not for murder.'

'Okay, leave Frost to stew for the time being. Larry, you and Wendy take the man's statement. Emily, it's your show,' Isaac said. It was her jurisdiction, and he recognised the need to bow to her authority and input.

'A few more hours won't do any harm. I'll make sure that Caxton knows what's going on. Let him sweat a bit longer.'

Chapter 32

Yolanda had been sad when Ralph Lawrence phoned to tell her about the death of her son. He had wanted to see her again, to make her come back to him, but he knew she would not. 'He's gone, Ralph,' she said. In the background, Ralph could hear the sound of people laughing. In the Caribbean, she had a life and money and friends. All he could offer was a two-bedroom flat in Bayswater, and possibly years of legal wrangling while he, and hopefully his sister, took on Jill Dundas.

'I understand,' Ralph had said. 'Will you come back for his funeral?'

'Not now. I will mourn in my own way. One day I will return and visit his grave, place a few flowers, shed a tear. I loved you, Ralph, you know that, but we will never meet again.' And then she was gone, back to her life in the sun. It suited Ralph to think that she would sit down in her quiet moments and reflect on her son, on him, the love that all three had once had, but he knew she probably wouldn't. She had been a selfish woman back then, she still was, but he would miss her.

***

Keith Waters gave his statement, Larry and Wendy witnessing it. Out at Greenwich, Inspecteur Jules Hougardy looked out at the River Thames from Zizzi's restaurant on Greenwich Promenade. On the other side of the table, Isaac and Emily. It was Italian, and all three were eating pasta.

'We have an old-fashioned fish and chip shop in the town,' Emily said. 'We'll take you there before you go back, as long as you don't mind it soggy with vinegar.'

'A pint of warm beer afterwards,' Hougardy replied. 'But, for now, what do we have?'

'If we can prove that Caxton murdered O'Grady, then he's subject to English law. Whatever happens, he can be sentenced for grievous bodily harm.'

'The case against him in Belgium is still circumstantial. We know he's guilty, but our defence lawyers are as good as yours. Are you searching the river for O'Grady's body?'

'We are, but it's like looking for a needle in a haystack. Unless it catches on something, the chances of recovery are slim. Larry and Wendy will be back within the hour. Then Emily and Larry can go to work on Caxton again.'

***

Caxton was led into the interview room at Greenwich. He had now been formally charged with the murder of Hector O'Grady, a fingerprint having been retrieved from the sunken boat, as well as the lesser charge of grievous bodily harm inflicted on the persons of Keith Waters and Ralph Lawrence. The recovered boat continued to dry at the wharf, no more than two hundred yards from the police station.

Emily was taking the lead role, Larry backing her up. In another room sat Jules Hougardy, Isaac and Wendy.

'My client wishes to make a statement,' Edward Sharman said. Procedurally, they were remiss in not advising him of one late development, but Emily, as well as the rest of the team, wanted the final blow to come as a surprise.

'I, Ainsley Gregory Caxton, of 15, India Street, Greenwich, wish to state that I was not involved in the disappearance of Hector O'Grady, a colleague as well as a friend. The boat he had rented and which has subsequently been found indicates the worst. I had been out with him before, and I can only hope that he is recovered alive and well. The statements by Ralph Lawrence and Keith Waters are lies. They are both weak men who had failed to keep their finances under control. They are using fraudulent untruths as leverage against my employer, a man who lent them money in good faith.'

'Is that it?' Larry said after Caxton had finished.

'The evidence is circumstantial,' Sharman said. 'I am insisting that my client is released immediately.'

'It's not so easy, Mr Sharman,' Emily said. She remembered Isaac's advice: 'Start gently, slowly raise the tempo, keep your final arguments for last. Fluster, confuse, get them to make mistakes, not you.' She knew that at the first interview she had not followed the advice given and that Sharman had bettered her. She was not willing to let it happen a second time.

'Why?'

'Mr Caxton and Hector O'Grady were in Belgium when Steve Samuels was murdered along with a taxi driver and two prostitutes. We have impounded the Toyota Land Cruiser they took to Belgium; CCTV footage and facial recognition technology have confirmed it to be them. They were travelling on false documents. We also have two witnesses who saw them there. If Mr Caxton is released from this station, an extradition order is in place for him to be rearrested, pending extradition to Brussels. Whatever happens here today, your client is in for a lengthy prison term. Bail will be refused here and in Belgium. Mr Caxton's track record is not good; no judge will allow him freedom while he waits to be tried.'

'I've done nothing wrong,' Caxton said. He looked over at Sharman who took no notice.

'A bullet has been recovered from the boat,' Emily said.

'Is that proof?' Sharman said.

'The bullet is with Forensics.'

'And what do you intend to do with it? It's a bullet, not a gun. There are no fingerprints on a bullet.'

'But there is on the boat, and we do have Mr Caxton's jacket.'

'I lent it to him. It was a cold day, and his jacket wasn't as warm as mine,' Caxton said.

'Even if it was, and you're telling the truth, it still doesn't explain the fingerprint.'

'I'd been out on the boat before. Maybe it's old.'

'We've checked with the owner of the boat. You had never been on that boat. There are three boats for hire. One was out of the water for maintenance. The other one was already rented out. We have full records and the testimony of the owner. You had been on that boat once, and that was when Hector O'Grady was shot and thrown over the side. Mr Caxton, you are guilty of murder. Now is the time to own up,' Emily said.

'It was an accident, I swear it. Hector was in a funny mood, someone had taken his girlfriend. We went out with a few beers, a can of worms and a couple of fishing lines. He was my friend. I wanted to help him.'

Sharman looked at his client, shook his head. The first rule of defence, never admit to anything, no matter how inconsequential.

'Why kill him?'

'It was an accident. He's out there, he's argumentative, and the beer is getting to him. He was never a big drinker, and now he's into his fifth. I tried to stop him, attempted to take the gun off him. He's going wild, shooting into the water just because the fish aren't biting. I grab the gun, it goes off.'

'He's dead?'

'Dead, yes, he was. I'm panicking. You would never believe it was an accident. What was I to do? I couldn't come in here, throw myself on your mercy.'

'O'Grady's body?'

'He fell off the side when the gun went off. I tried to grab hold, but I'm not good with boats. Hector knew all about them, I didn't. I always wore a life jacket out there. Hector said they were only for young girls and weaklings. He could sometimes be insulting, not that I took much notice most times, but out there he was dangerous. I'm telling you the truth.'

'And the axe through the bottom of the boat, the bullets as well?'

'I was panicking. I've told you this. What more do you want me to say?'

'How did you get to shore? You've told us you wore a life jacket, but we found both of them on board the boat.'

'I swam.'

'You scuttled the boat first. And why didn't you get on at the boatshed, the same place as O'Grady? Was this part of the plan?'

'My client needs time to consider,' Sharman said. Emily continued with her questioning.

'Mr Caxton, you've lied about being in Brussels, you've lied about Ralph Lawrence, about Keith Waters. Why should we believe you now?'

'Because it's the truth. I didn't mean to kill him.'

'Mr Caxton, you will be held pending a trial. You will also be charged with the murder of Steve Samuels in Brussels. Also, the charges of grievous bodily harm will stand. Whatever happens, you, Mr Caxton, will be spending many years in prison.'

***

'Five years for grievous bodily harm,' Isaac said. 'That's the maximum for what Caxton did to Lawrence and Waters, concurrent sentences. The judge may decide on consecutive, but it's unlikely.'

The team, including Jules Hougardy, were sitting in the Prince of Greenwich pub. Everyone had a pint of beer, including the Belgian police inspector. Caxton was locked up, Frost was still sweating it out in his penthouse, and a search of the River Thames downstream from where O'Grady had disappeared, presumed dead, had found nothing. The sunken boat had provided no more clues, and the case against Caxton for the murder of O'Grady was based on the man's confession, although he was holding to his story that it was an accident.

'No chance of a conviction in Belgium, either,' Hougardy said. He had to admit to enjoying himself away from his office in Brussels. Even Bridget had made the trip across the Thames, one of the few occasions that her routine varied from Challis Street to home and back. Both she and Wendy were making a night of it: a few too many drinks, a couple of sore heads in the morning.

'We'll bring in Frost in the morning, lay it on heavy. He'll have the indomitable Edward Sharman with him,' Emily said, jubilant about how she had handled herself during the interview with Caxton. Outside the pub a river mist was closing in, a clear sign that the search for O'Grady would be called off.

Gordon Windsor and his team had concluded their work on the boat and were now back on their side of the river. The bullet recovered was with Forensics, although it would only reveal the calibre, not the make of the gun and who had fired the shot. Even so, breaking Caxton had been a good result. The car taken to Brussels had yielded nothing more of interest, only that off-roaders were a breed unto themselves in that they could take perfectly good machinery and subject it to so much abuse.

In the pub, Hougardy talked, his accent endearing him to the police officers and the other patrons in the pub. He was a hit, and he appreciated the warm welcome afforded him.

It was eleven in the evening, and the team were on their last drinks. Downstream from Greenwich, an elderly couple were walking their dog along the shore. They spotted a dead dolphin, not seen often in the lower reaches of the Thames, but with the cleaner water of the last few years, not unknown. The man, more agile than his wife, who was relegated to using a walking stick, followed his dog down to the rotting carcass. It was covered in seaweed and slime, and it was neither pleasant to look at nor to smell. Albert Gravelly, a retired bus driver, forty-two years with the same company and never an accident, took the stick that the dog always carried in its mouth. Looking at the carcass again, the moonlight reflecting off it, Gravelly prodded it with the stick. It was not what a man with a weak constitution needed. He shouted to his wife who was sitting on a bench ten yards away. 'You had better phone the police,' he said.

Albert Gravelly, a man who had seen many things over the years, especially on the late-night shift, had never seen what his dog had wanted to sniff. He took the stick and threw it for the dog as he walked back to his wife.

Chapter 33

'You'd never make a sailor out of Caxton,' Hougardy said. The full team from the pub were present at the site where O'Grady had washed up, all except Bridget who had left, not to go home, but to update her records in Challis Street. A former lover had accused her of being a workaholic, but she knew she wasn't. She was just a person who enjoyed her job, and if the others in Homicide were out and dealing with an unexpected development, she would have felt guilty just going home.

The crime scene investigators were on the scene, floodlights had been installed, and a generator was up on the path above. The Gravellys, both in their eighties, had been taken back to their small cottage, the dog barking in the back seat of the police car. Larry and Wendy were taking their statements. They had found the body or, more correctly, the dog had, and apart from that, there wasn't much more they could say.

Gordon Windsor and his team attempted to place a crime scene tent around the body, although a wind was blowing, and it was very exposed. In the end, a decision was made to move the body to a more sheltered position. A thorough check was completed in the immediate vicinity first.

Five uniforms had come over from Challis Street, another four from Greenwich Police Station. They were moving up and down from the crime scene looking for further evidence, although that was deemed unlikely, as the body recovered was fully clothed.

'Not much of a sailor?' Emily reminded Hougardy of his earlier comment.

'If he had wanted the body to remain undiscovered, he'd have made sure to weigh him down, tie him off to prevent him floating to the surface. There's still a piece of rope attached to the body, a sloppy knot.'

'Are you into sailing?'

'When I was younger. The man had tied a granny knot, not a reef. Not that either is ideal if he wanted the body to stay submerged. Are we assuming the man had been tied to the anchor?'

'We are.'

'Under the water, there are currents that ebb and flow, some colder than others. And knots are subjected to that movement, and they and the rope are buffeted. Some will loosen, some will stay in place, even tighten, and others will eventually unravel. That is what has happened here.'

'He's right,' Windsor said. 'The condition of the body indicates that it has been submerged, and not just floating on the surface. Also, the man had been shot three times, one of them in the head, area of the brain. There are signs that crabs have been on the body, but not many, as the body has not started serious decomposition yet.'

'Murder?' Emily said.

'Three bullets, one in the head, it seems likely,' Windsor said. 'We're not staying here any longer. The body will be taken back to Pathology. Isaac, you can go and annoy them later on this morning.'

***

Gary Frost, updated by his source, could only see the noose tightening. If it hadn't been for Ralph Lawrence, none of this would have happened. He felt intense anger towards the man, a need to strike out. Used to making decisions, he wasn't sure what to do. He was dithering, he needed out of the penthouse, out of Greenwich.

Downstairs, in the garage beneath the building, a car. He took the keys, left his penthouse and found the Mercedes. He did not drive often, but this time he would. As he came out from the garage, a police car opposite saw him and reported it to Greenwich Police Station, to the inspector charged with keeping a watch on Frost.

'Let him go,' had been the instruction. 'We'll keep a watch from here.'

The two police officers who had kept watch overnight complied with the instruction. After all, the man was their senior.

One of those in the vehicle, a smart young man, ambitious as well, phoned Emily.

'What did he say?' Emily reacted with alarm. It was still early, and she had just fallen asleep. She had set the alarm for two hours, not fifteen minutes, but the information was startling.

'Inspector Camberwell told us to let Frost go. It made no sense to us, but we followed instructions.'

'Any idea where Frost is now?'

'None. He took off, heading west.'

Emily phoned Isaac to update him, then her superintendent. He was straight out of bed and on the phone. 'Camberwell, fifteen minutes, my office.'

Bridget, also woken up, was at the office at Challis Street within twenty-five minutes, and logging into the CCTV cameras in Greenwich. The registration number of the Mercedes that Frost was driving was known, and the police cars in London were equipped with automatic number plate recognition.

Meanwhile, Frost had parked across from Ralph's flat in Bayswater. He was in a side street, concealed from view.

An arrest warrant had been issued, with instructions for Frost to be detained and taken to Greenwich Police Station, suspected of being an accomplice to murder. He was not considered dangerous, but officers were advised to approach him with caution.

At Greenwich, Jules Hougardy was back in the police station. He had stayed the night in a hotel no more than five minutes' walk away. Isaac and Larry were finding their own way back across the Thames. Wendy was with Bridget, helping if she could, lending moral support if she couldn't. Both women were feeling the effects of a heavy night, although now was not the time to complain.

Edward Sharman arrived at Greenwich Police Station at ten minutes after nine in the morning. He was not in a good mood. Emily was pleased, so were the other members of the team. He had been updated as to the situation, a full report of the current status at his disposal. Ainsley Caxton, on being advised that Gary Frost had left his penthouse and was nowhere to be found, realised that he was vulnerable. He had admitted to the charge of assault, minor to him, as he had committed far worse crimes in the past. Sharman had chastised him for his outburst in the interview room. 'You bloody fool,' he had said. 'All you had to do was to keep your mouth shut, and I would have got you out, but where are you now? Five years, if those fools testify.'

'You can fix it,' Caxton had said in reply.

But now, the situation had changed. Gary Frost was no longer around, a warrant was out for his arrest. He would be defending himself, not one of his employees, and where was the man, what was he doing? Was he running, or was he planning something more serious?

Sharman and Caxton sat together to discuss the situation. Sharman reflected on his fee for services rendered, realised that he was committed to continuing for the time being, but unless Frost transferred money to his account, then he and Caxton could find someone else.

'O'Grady's been found,' Sharman said. As usual, he was wearing the three-piece suit, his hair immaculately parted down the middle. 'Three bullets, one in the brain.'

'It was an accident. He was out of control.'

'They'll not go for it. How do you want to plead?'

'What will happen if I admit to it?'

'Sixteen years minimum.'

'And the grievous bodily harm?'

'Five each, although we should be able to get all sentences served concurrently.'

'You can't get me off?'

'Not on this one, and now Frost has done a runner. They'll take what you've admitted to, the statements from Lawrence and Waters, the proof of you and O'Grady being in Brussels, no more than one mile from where Samuels and three others were killed. I can cause confusion in the jury, raise an element of doubt, but you'll be convicted of the murder of O'Grady, and if you're not, the Belgian police will have you extradited. No chance of their proving their case, but Frost has made fools of the police. They'll not forget.'

In the interview room, Emily and Larry sat. On the other side of the table, Ainsley Caxton and Edward Sharman.

Outside, listening in, Isaac, Jules, and Wendy. In another part of the building, Inspector Camberwell was clearing out his desk, with another inspector checking that what he took wasn't police related, only personal. He had been suspended on full pay while a disciplinary hearing was convened, a chance for him to explain why he had called off the surveillance of Gary Frost. His badge was with the superintendent, as was his phone. He knew that if they checked the numbers dialled, they would find the calls to Frost. He knew that he should have used another phone to call the man, but in the last few days, with the frenetic pace, the information that needed passing on, he had not had a chance to add credit to the phone that he kept hidden underneath the dashboard in his car. There was nothing that the police force disliked more than a bent policeman, and if he were in prison, there would be some that would remember who had put them there. Commissioner Alwyn Davies had brought him into London, put him out at Greenwich, and he was not answering his phone.

Camberwell snuck out of the office and headed to the nearest pub. He needed a stiff drink, and he needed it now.

Chapter 34

Ralph Lawrence turned in his bed. It had been a late night, what with Yolanda on the phone, yet again not wanting to return to London. In the end, he had drunk a full bottle of whisky before collapsing. He blearily opened his eyes, realised that it was daylight outside and that someone was knocking on the front door to his flat.

Without checking, he turned the latch on the door and opened it. On the other side, Gary Frost. 'You bastard,' he said as he pushed his way in. 'You're going to testify against me.'

Ralph struggled with the situation. He was larger than Frost, the man was alone, but why was he here, what did he want? He slapped some water on his face from a tap in the kitchen, before looking at Frost again. The man was standing firm: his face red, his hands raised in anger.

'Frost, what do you want? We had an arrangement, but you wouldn't wait.'

'You've given the police a statement saying that I had you beaten.'

'What else would you want me to say? That you're a good fellow, a good mate? Get real. You're in trouble, and you're lashing out. When I came to you, what did I get? Sympathy, a shoulder to cry on? Not from you. I got Caxton and O'Grady beating me up, showing what would happen if I didn't give you what you wanted, and now O'Grady's dead.'

'How do you know?'

'It's on the news. And Caxton's singing like a bird.'

'He won't.'

'Without you to hold his hand, he'll be putty to the police.'

'I need to get out of the country,' Frost said.

'Why look at me? My father left me high and dry. Look how I live. Nowhere as fancy as you, although you can't go back, is that it?'

'I'm desperate,' Frost pleaded.

'Not such the big man now, are you? It's easy to be tough when you're on top, but down below, where I've been, you're frightened. Now, if you haven't got anything to add to our conversation, I suggest you leave while I call the police.'

Ralph picked up his phone, speed-dialled Detective Chief Inspector Isaac Cook. 'I've got a Mr Frost in my flat if you're interested.'

Frost rushed out of the door. 'You bastard, I'll get you for this.'

Ralph knew he would not.

***

Edward Sharman knew that the situation was hopeless as he sat in the interview room. On one side of the table, the two police officers were sitting up straight, full of pride because they had brought an investigation to a successful conclusion. On his side, Ainsley Caxton had shrunk in his seat. Before O'Grady's body had been found, and before he had discovered that Gary Frost had run out on him, Caxton had been full of himself, almost cheeky with the police constable who had brought him his breakfast, but now, it was over.

The confession had surprised even Isaac. Caxton had not spoken since entering the interview room and would not until he had left, except to give his name and to read his statement.

'I, Ainsley Gregory Caxton, do admit to the killing of Hector O'Grady. I was acting on the instructions of Gary Frost. He has been responsible for other murders, none of which were committed by me. I am guilty of the maltreatment of Ralph Lawrence and Keith Waters. O'Grady was proving to be unreliable. Frost demanded that I dispose of the man. I followed orders as a soldier would if given a command by an officer.'

Larry could see Sharman's clever wording. An attempt to convince a jury that his client Caxton, a man who did have a good army service record, was a man who did what he was told, a humble man who deserved leniency. It was a clever ploy, but Larry, like Emily, knew full well that with the litany of crimes against Caxton it would not lessen the sentence. He was going down for sixteen years at the very least.

'Frost's business empire was under threat. He needed to reduce his liabilities. O'Grady was a man likely to talk. He was physically strong, mentally and morally bankrupt,' Caxton continued. 'I joined the boat two miles from the boatyard. We had pulled in there before, and both of us were familiar with the place. Sometimes we'd make a small fire, cook the fish and then have a few drinks. I shot him, not because I wanted to, but because I had to. In Belgium, it had been O'Grady who killed Samuels. I was merely the bystander, but Frost intended, if there was no hope, to lay the blame on me. If I did not agree to kill O'Grady, he would implicate me in Samuels' death. It was known that he had received a phone call from Belgium, and the evidence was mounting against him. I had regarded Frost as a friend, but when he told me to kill O'Grady, I knew he was not. That is the end of my statement.'

Caxton was formally charged with the murder of Hector O'Grady and taken back to his cell. 'Where's Frost?' Sharman said.

'We're still waiting for him,' Emily said.

'Give me a call when he gets here. I'll be representing him.' Sharman stood up and walked out, not shaking the officers' hands, not saying goodbye.

***

Frost did not return to his car. He cut a sorry figure as he walked, keeping to the side streets as much as possible. He met Ted Samson, the small man who had kept a watch on Ralph Lawrence on his ignominious return to England.

Samson was pleased to see Frost in the coffee shop, knowing that their meeting would come with four fifty-pound notes being slipped across the table.

'Mr Frost, what do you want?' Samson asked. He had ordered a café latte, the man opposite to pay. 'I told you what I saw at Gilbert Lawrence's house.'

'You were looking for Ralph Lawrence, but he was in Spain.'

'That's right. You never paid me.'

'How much?'

'Another five hundred. In cash and now.'

Any other time, Samson would have been hanging upside down from a beam for his impertinence, but now the man who saw all, said nothing unless paid, was in control. Frost reached into his wallet and withdrew ten fifty-pound notes. He passed them across the table, the little man hurriedly putting them into a pocket.

'You're a little bastard,' Frost said.

'Little, I'll agree with, but not a bastard. You're in trouble, and the police are looking for you. The word is that Caxton's pleaded guilty, put the blame on you. The police have your photo on a list of the most wanted. You'll be lucky to stay free for more than a few hours.'

'How much?'

'Another ten of what you just gave me. A disguise, is that it?'

'I need to get out of the country. Can you arrange it?'

'A good passport costs money. I can't help you there.'

'Okay, a disguise. What do you have that you haven't told me?'

'I kept a watch on Gilbert Lawrence's house. I saw people going in, people going out.'

'Which people?'

'The housekeeper, the postman, the old recluse.'

'Anyone else?'

'Another five hundred.'

Frost was running short of cash, but he managed to give the man what he wanted.

On a piece of paper, Samson wrote down the name of one more person. 'That's who'll get you a passport.' He also handed over a timed and dated photo from his iPhone.

'I could have bled this person for a fortune,' Frost said.

'You still can. I've no need of a fortune,' Samson said. 'Just a quiet life, enough for my needs, a couple of pints of an evening.' And with that, he left. Fifteen minutes later he returned and placed a bag on the table. 'That'll cost you two hundred,' before he disappeared once again, this time not to return. For the first time that day, Gary Frost smiled.

***

Jill Dundas sat in her office, the door was closed. At the reception, a man stood. 'Tell Jill I'm here about an unpaid debt. Tell her it's personal.'

The lady on reception made the phone call. Jill Dundas came out of her office. 'Yes, what do you want?' she asked as she looked across at a man with a mop of black hair.

'Look at this,' Gary Frost said, as he opened his wallet to reveal a time-stamped photo.'

'Come into my office, please.' The woman maintained her cool.

Inside the office, Frost removed his wig. It had itched, and it had made him look stupid. It had, however, allowed him to walk past two police cars. 'My name's Gary Frost. I'm about to be charged with murder, and you, Miss Dundas, are going to get me out of the country.'

'Why, how?'

'You saw the photo. It is you, isn't it?'

'But what does it mean?'

'Let me tell you a little story,' Frost said. 'I had lent a lot of money to Ralph Lawrence. I did not know of his family connection. And why should I? But then Ralph's a naughty boy, and he's not answering his phone.'

'Get to the point.'

'I don't know what to do. I need time to consider, and I get one of my men to watch out for him, but he keeps the information to himself, bleeds me for more money.'

'Is there a point to this?'

'My man finds the father's house, realises it probably the one place that Ralph will come to. He sees the housekeeper, the postman, old man Lawrence. He's a devious man that I employ. He's like a ferret, here and there, scurrying around, taking me for money, taking it from whoever else. Maybe he took some from you, but it's not important now. Anyway, my life's taken a turn for the worse, and I met with the ferret. He tells me that he knows something, something that I've not paid for. He may be right, or maybe he's been paid off. He gave me a photo, the one I just showed you. I've taken a copy, emailed it to the police, a twenty-four-hour delay before it's sent. I could cancel it, but that's up to you.'

'I'll deny it all, the best lawyers.'

'If he's as good as mine, you'll be arrested for murder.'

'What do you want?'

'Not money. I want to get out of this country, a false passport.'

'That can be arranged, but it takes time.'

'How long?'

'Eight hours.'

'Where?'

'To the north of London.'

'You've done this before,' Frost said. He had to admit he admired the woman: cool as a cucumber, a heart of pure ice.

'I've not admitted to anything.'

'Nor should you. Get me out of the country, a false identity, and your secret is safe with me.'

'Can I trust you?' Jill said.

'What do you think?'

'I think that you will honour the agreement. You will have your passport.'

Frost could see no reaction in the woman: no sweating, no nervous twitches, no sign of panic.

Outside, in the reception area, the noise of people entering. Frost stood up. 'You've called the police.'

'I haven't. They must have followed you. Our agreement stands. Get yourself out on bail, and I'll get you out of the country.'

'It's a deal.'

***

Gary Frost sat in the interview room at Greenwich Police Station. On his right-hand side, Edward Sharman. Across from them, Emily Matson and Larry Hill.

'We received a tip-off,' Emily said. 'What were you doing at the offices of Jill Dundas?'

'My client has no comment,' Sharman said. 'He has given you a statement stating his innocence. He is a wealthy man who is being accused by others in an attempt to discredit him.'

'Mr Frost will be charged with conspiracy to murder. We have sufficient proof to secure a conviction for that charge. Mr Sharman, you have seen the evidence against your client, as well as the testimony of three other persons. It would be advisable to prepare his defence.'

'I know what I need to do,' Sharman said.

Outside of the interview room, Sharman shook the hand of Emily. 'Not so good for my client, but you did a good job.' With that he left the police station.

'Who tipped us off about Frost being with Jill Dundas?' Isaac asked.

'We don't know,' Larry said. 'A squeaky voice said something about Frost having cheated him out of a hundred pounds. Unlisted number, so no point in tracing it.'

Emily arrived at Inspector Camberwell's home at eight in the evening. The man was still asleep after a twenty-four-hour bender at home and in the pub. A security camera had picked up Caxton placing the package under the bench near the Greenwich Observatory, Camberwell picking it up a few minutes later, even checking that the full amount had been paid. It had been another piece of information that Caxton had put forward in an attempt to deny his guilt and to portray himself as a weak man. It was not going to work, but it did allow Camberwell to be arrested: the most heinous of crimes, a police officer guilty of taking bribes. He would be detained in the cell next to Frost.

Nineteen hours after Frost had been remanded, almost twenty-four from when he had sat in Jill Dundas's office, an email arrived in Isaac's inbox. He opened it and forwarded it to the team. Bridget printed out a high-definition jpeg and pinned it to the evidence board in Homicide.

Jill Dundas was arrested later that day. She protested that the photo was a fake, an attempt at extortion, and that was why Frost had been in her office. She was charged with murder; the date matched the time of death, the blood stains visible on the hem of the dress as she had left Gilbert Lawrence's mansion. At her house, the dress was retrieved. The woman may have been financially smart, but she did not understand forensics. There had been an attempt at cleaning the dress, but the marks remained inside the fold of the hem. Forensics were confident that they would be able to extract enough to match Gilbert Lawrence's DNA.

'I had to. All that work of my father's, and Gilbert wanted to come out of seclusion, to make contact with his family. For them to forgive him, for him to forgive them. I couldn't allow it. I had to kill him.'

Ralph Lawrence and Caroline Dickson were stunned at the revelation. The full extent of their father's assets, or whatever could be recovered, would be theirs.

Yolanda phoned from Antigua on hearing the news. She intended to be on the next plane to London. Ralph told her not to bother.

The End

Murder has no Guilt

Phillip Strang

Chapter 1

Giuseppe Briganti had come over from Italy fifteen years previously with a smattering of English and not much else. Life had been tough back home for Giuseppe, or Peppe as everyone called him, the third son of a farmer. Not that he had reason to complain, as his father was a good man, and he loved his mother dearly. It was just that Peppe was not cut out for farming. So much so that at the age of twenty he left for Milan.

He learnt his trade well, so well that within five years he was at the top of his profession, and constantly in demand in the hairdressing salon that was owned by a man who treated Peppe as if he was his own son.

Yet it was the salon's owner who had by his actions been responsible for Peppe's hasty departure for England; the reason Peppe was in his salon in London cutting the hair of Alphonso Abano, another immigrant to England, although Abano came from Sicily, mafioso country.

Back in Milan, Peppe had been in love, but she had preferred the salon owner, clearly apparent when Peppe had walked in on the two, in flagrante delicto, in the back room of the salon.

Peppe knew that he should have hit her first, and then the old man second, but he did neither. Without saying a word, he moved back out through the salon, only stopping long enough to pick up his scissors and a couple of combs. Peppe was never a man for material possessions, and it took him just one hour to pack his suitcase, pay the outstanding rent, and catch the first train heading north. One day later, a train pulled into London, and Peppe stepped off. He had sufficient money not to worry for a few days, and he checked into a hotel.

On the fourth day, he answered an advert for a hairdresser at the salon where he now worked, and in time purchased the business from the man who had first employed him.

Life now consisted of enjoying his nights alone, his days in the salon catering to celebrities, the upwardly-mobile bankers and financiers, and, thankfully, only one gangster.

In Italy, Peppe had catered to both sexes, but in Kensington, on Kensington High Street, not far from the palace, it was strictly men only, although women came in with their men.

In one chair sat Guy Hendry, talk show host, a man about town, and a man who graced the front page of the celebrity-obsessed magazines on account of his film star looks, his perpetual suntan, and the women he took out. Peppe thought he was a Dorian Gray character, in as much as the man was ten years older than when he had first walked in the door of the salon, yet his women had become progressively younger, and the one he had now in tow, Gillian Dickenson, was five years younger than the previous one.

Peppe would have said she was vivacious, with a permanent smile, a bust that looked artificial, and a skirt that barely covered her underwear, and yet she looked as if she had just left school.

On another chair, having his hair cut, the vain and obnoxious Paul Waverton. The whizz kid they called him in the press for his ability to read the financial markets and to make the right call. His Bentley was parked outside, close enough to be admired by Waverton and the people on the street, illegally enough to get a ticket for parking where it shouldn't be. Not that it worried Waverton as he flaunted his money, even giving a fifty-pound tip to whoever worked on his hair. And work was the word, for Waverton, in spite of all his financial acumen, was an unattractive man with hair like steel wool, almost like a Brillo pad, and as hard to keep in shape.

Peppe focussed back on Abano. 'Not so busy today,' the little man said. Peppe would have happily refused his custom, but Abano was not a man to fall out with, the sort of man who had friends in low places who wouldn't have any issues about giving someone a savage beating.

'It will be later,' Peppe said as he combed Abano's hair back over the top of his scalp, the expensive treatments for premature balding not working, and certainly not willing to tell the gangster.

Abano liked to talk big and to show off, not that Peppe wanted to hear the stories, only to take the man's money and to shuffle him out of the salon. Time at Peppe's salon was by appointment only, and in another forty minutes an important customer was due, a friend of royalty. He was more the salon's type of customer, as were Hendry and Waverton.

It didn't happen often, but sometimes people without appointments came in, and as it was a Tuesday, typically the slowest day of the week, there was a spare chair and a spare hairdresser. But the person who came in was not a well-heeled man, nor a celebrity, not even a gangster. It was a celebrity seeker, a woman in her thirties, carrying more weight than she should, and definitely drunk.

'Mr Hendry, Guy,' she gushed as she made her way over to the man. Gillian Dickenson stood up to impede the woman's progress, but she was pushed to one side. One of the other hairdressers attempted to grab the woman's arm, but she wrenched herself free.

'I need your autograph and a photo,' she said to Hendry.

'Not now, later,' Hendry said in a friendly manner, in an attempt to maintain his on-screen persona.

'Now, it's got to be now. My friends will never believe that I met Guy Hendry.'

'Please, now is not convenient. Send an email to my publicity company, and I'll make sure you receive a promotional package and an invite to a recording of one of my programmes.'

'You're like all the rest of them,' the woman sneered. 'All smiles and teeth on the television, but total bastards in real life.'

'Please, will you leave,' Peppe said.

'Who are you to tell me to do anything?'

'I'm the owner, and this is private property.'

'I'll go once Guy Hendry gives me an autograph and a photo.'

'Very well,' Hendry said, raising himself from where he had been sitting, running his fingers through his hair.

'Hey, you can take the photo,' the celebrity-obsessed woman said to Hendry's girlfriend.

Nobody looked at the door to the salon, only at the commotion to the rear of the room. Peppe was nervously pacing around the room, Abano was on his phone calling for a couple of his men to wait outside the salon and to deal with the woman if she didn't leave.

Hendry, seriously annoyed and not in a good mood, smiled through gritted teeth, not even complaining when the woman put her arms around him and thrust her breasts forward.

'The real stuff, you don't know what you're missing,' she said.

'That's enough. Out of my establishment,' Peppe said.

A man who had come in unannounced stood just inside the door of the salon. He looked around him and at the people assembled. From inside the long coat that he wore, he withdrew a semi-automatic rifle. He released the safety and sprayed the salon, making sure that no one avoided the bullets. He then walked around to each of those lying or slouching or still groaning. He withdrew a pistol from his pocket and shot each person at close range in the head.

In all, a total of twenty-eight seconds from first shot to when he left the salon. Outside, he casually walked away down Kensington High Street. Once clear of the area, he deposited the rifle and the pistol in a rubbish bin.

Back at the salon, the screaming of the people on the street could still be heard, as could the sirens of the police cars and the ambulances. The man knew that they were too late and all they would find would be dead bodies. A most satisfying day, he thought.

Chapter 2

Kensington High Street, with the rush hour traffic building and multiple homicides, was not something that the local police were prepared for, although practice for terrorist attacks had helped. With no option, the busy thoroughfare had been closed, causing anger with those already stuck in traffic, and frustration with the other motorists as they were diverted around the area.

Outside the hairdressing salon, Detective Chief Inspector Isaac Cook, the English-born son of Jamaican immigrants who had come over in the sixties, stood. He cut a striking figure: tall, athletic and erect. Alongside him, Detective Inspector Larry Hill, Cook's second in command, and a man who struggled with his weight, self-induced as he was partial to overeating and drinking too many pints of beer, much to the consternation of his loyal wife.

'Not good,' Hill said, a typical understatement from the man, as he peered into the salon.

Isaac Cook looked as well. The crime scene investigators were already on site checking the bodies, conducting their examination of the scene. On the street, barriers were being erected to isolate the scene from the view of the curious onlookers who were aggressively taking photos on their smartphones, and talking amongst themselves and to others.

The two police inspectors donned coveralls and gloves, as well as overshoes, before entering, stepping to one side to clear the body of a young woman lying on her side, her heavily-bloodied face still visible.

'Gillian Dickenson,' Isaac Cook said.

'She's always on the television. Supposedly she was going around with Guy Hendry.'

'She was. He's over the other side.'

Larry Hill, a man who had seen death more than once, looked around and at the young and very dead woman. 'You never get used to it, not totally, do you?' he said.

Isaac Cook realised that he had, and that he felt inured to the scene. It had caused him concern on more than one occasion, and it had even ended one of his relationships when he had come home ambivalent about a murder scene. That time it had been a husband and wife who had been shot by a disturbed son. The girlfriend at the time, blonde and in love with the DCI, had seen the murders on the television. She was close to tears at the story of how the dead couple had adopted the son as a child, knowing of his mental difficulties, and then the person they had heaped love and care on had murdered them.

'It's so tragic,' she had said. Isaac's reaction had been to turn off the television. Two days later, she moved out.

Larry Hill's ever-loyal wife continued to pressure him to achieve more, to allow them to upgrade their house again for the third time in ten years. He knew that he had neither the motivation for study nor the inclination for promotion with its added responsibilities. He was a man who enjoyed being out on the street, meeting with the villains, solving the crimes, not sitting in an office.

And whereas he had the greatest respect for the man who had brought him into Homicide at Challis Street Police Station, he had no wish to take Isaac Cook's position as the lead officer in the department once he had moved on.

'It looks like a terrorist attack,' Gordon Windsor, the crime scene examiner, said. He was a small man with thinning hair who Isaac Cook respected enormously.

'But it's not,' Isaac replied. The three of them were standing to one side of the salon.

'As you say. What we have are eight bodies, each with a bullet to the head.'

'It looks as if they were shot more than once.'

'We'll send the bodies to Pathology, so you'll have a more exact idea of what happened.'

'Your initial observations will suffice for now.'

'Okay. We believe that one person came in to the salon and used a semi-automatic rifle. We've no idea what make, although we've retrieved a bullet from the wall. It will help to narrow it down, but that's about all. After that the man...'

'Man?' Larry said.

'An assumption, and besides, we've got shoe prints. Typically, it's men who commit these sorts of crimes, that's all.'

'Assume it's a man,' Isaac said. 'What else do we have?'

'The killer then shot each person in the head, a precise shot.'

'Not all could have been the target, and this was not the act of a hot-headed idiot.'

'Hot-headed idiots don't eradicate the witnesses with such precision, and normally they have a death wish, end up shooting themselves. This was professional,' Windsor said.

'Not typical of London.'

'It is now. You've recognised some of the dead?'

'Gillian Dickenson and Guy Hendry.'

'There's one more you know.'

'Who's that?'

'He's not so easy to identify, not from here.'

'His name?'

'Alphonso Abano.'

'Minor villain, drug dealer?'

'That's the one.'

'He'd not be a target, not for a killing this elaborate,' Larry Hill said.

'Larry's right,' Isaac said. 'He's the sort to end up knifed in a back alley. These murders were orchestrated, which means whoever did it was paid well, and may not even be a local, not even English.'

'That's for you to figure out. We're not sure who the others are, except for Giuseppe Briganti. His photo's up on the wall.'

'We'll ID them later.'

With the traffic so heavy Isaac and Larry left their car and walked two hundred yards to where they could be picked up by Sergeant Wendy Gladstone, a woman in her fifties, with enforced retirement closing in on her due to her arthritis and her general low level of fitness.

'It's chaos out there,' she said.

'It'll be chaos for the next five to six hours. They're attempting to clear one lane on the road which should help, but the traffic will be backed up for miles,' Isaac said.

'The ghoulish hanging around?'

'As usual, not that they'll see much.'

'You'll need to make a statement. There's a camera crew at the police station already.'

'And at the crime scene, not that I intended to talk to them there,' Isaac said. 'And besides, the details are sketchy. What do you know about Guy Hendry?'

'He's one of my favourites. Is he…?'

'Dead. As well as Gillian Dickenson. Some of the others we've not identified yet, apart from that slimy weasel, Alphonso Abano.'

'Guy Hendry and Gillian Dickenson were an item. The latest in his long line of conquests,' Wendy said.

'She doesn't look so attractive now.'

'Professional?'

'That's what we reckon, but why? Whoever did this must know the pressure will be on us to solve it as soon as possible, no stone unturned.'

'No shortage of resources, either.'

Wendy Gladstone eased her car through the London traffic, difficult at the best of times, horrendous as she had to divert to make her way through, even flashing her badge a couple of times to ensure the police officer on traffic duty let them through.

***

Challis Street Police Station, an edifice that had been built sixty years previously, had been modernised over the years. The Homicide department on the second floor was not the best area in the station: that was reserved for Detective Chief Superintendent Richard Goddard up on the top floor. However, Homicide was clean and modern and suited those that worked there.

Bridget Halloran, a long-time friend of Wendy Gladstone, looked after the administrative side of the department. She and Wendy had pooled their resources and moved in together a couple of years earlier, when Bridget, a woman in her late forties, had kicked her layabout lover out of her house, and Wendy's husband had died.

In Isaac's office, apart from the plant in the corner, a gift from Wendy and Bridget when one of his previous romances had ended, the furnishings consisted of a filing cabinet, a desk replete with laptop and monitor, a chair for the incumbent, and three more for the department's core team.

'We need to identify those at the scene,' Isaac said. He was leaning back on his chair, glad of the chance to rest. The night before the team had worked late wrapping up a murder investigation, the death of an old man. In that case, it had been the daughter desperate for the man's money who had been arrested, but now all she was going to get was a lengthy stay in prison. And besides, unbeknown to the woman, her father had changed his will six months previously, writing the daughter out.

'Who do we have a positive ID on?' Bridget asked.

'Guy Hendry and Gillian Dickenson. Also, Giuseppe Briganti, the owner of the salon.'

'Hairdresser to the Stars.'

'Is he?'

'Even to the Royals, so they say.'

'They?'

'The magazines that obsess about such matters.'

'Pure nonsense, just entertainment. But Briganti is well known and expensive.'

'Alphonso Abano was there as well. Two of the others appear to be employees of Briganti's, so they shouldn't be too difficult to identify. That leaves two others, a man in his thirties dressed in a suit. There was a car outside, appeared to be his. Follow up on the registration.'

'I have,' Bridget said. 'Paul Waverton, banker.'

'Who's taken responsibility for informing the next of kin?'

'It's your job, although they won't suppress Guy Hendry's identity for very long.'

'You've got the addresses?'

'I have.'

'Very well. Let's go. There was also another woman there. She didn't look to be an employee, and she was dressed cheaply. Not a customer, and not related to anyone else in the salon. Also, she was clutching a magazine, the type that you two like.'

'A fan of Hendry's?'

'It's probable. Let's deal with the next of kin first. Who's nearest?'

'Gillian Dickenson's mother lives five minutes from here.'

'Okay, we'll start with her. Wendy, it may be best if you come with me. Larry, return to the crime scene, follow through on the unknowns. And see if there's any more evidence that we can work with.'

'If it's professional, then it's unlikely.'

'Then find out who the target was. The others would have been dispatched to prevent witnesses.'

'It's very sad,' Bridget said.

'It's those who are left behind that suffer the most. And besides, we're here to do a job, not to get emotional,' Isaac said. 'One more thing, I knew Gillian Dickenson. Nothing in itself, but she was at a party I went to about six months ago.'

Chapter 3

'It's Gillian, isn't it?' Maureen Dickenson, an attractive woman in her late forties, said as she opened the front door to her house. She was dressed similarly to the way her daughter had been when she was killed. Wendy thought that on another woman it would have made the person look cheap, but not with her.

'Can we come in?' Isaac said.

Inside the house the woman sat on the edge of her seat.

'I'm sorry, but your daughter has been killed.'

There was no initial reaction for what seemed like an eternity.

'How?' Maureen Dickson eventually said.

'There's been a shooting. Your daughter was an unfortunate consequence,' Isaac said.

'Was she with Guy?'

'She was. He has died as well.'

'I knew no good would come of her associating with him.'

'You knew him?'

'I was younger than Gillian when I went out with him, but I saw through him soon enough, the same as she would have. But now, she'll not get a chance. Can I see her?'

'Later today, maybe tomorrow,' Wendy said. 'We'll need an identification. It's either you or her father.'

'Her father's dead, five years ago.'

'Can I ask how?' Isaac said.

'There's not much to say. He died in a car accident one night. It was late, not one block from here when a drunk ran a red light and slammed into Gerry's car. He was a good man, strong on discipline, and we brought up our daughter well. But you know the young, always looking for that extra bit of excitement, and Guy was that.'

'Is there anyone who can be with you?' Isaac said.

'My sister. Her number's in my phone.'

Wendy took the woman's phone and called the sister.

'Five minutes,' Wendy said after she had ended the call.

Isaac returned to talking with the dead woman's mother. 'Sorry about this, but I must ask some questions.'

'If you must.'

'We don't know who was targeted. We're assuming it wasn't your daughter, but what can you tell us about Guy Hendry?'

'I told you. I knew him when we were both young, and then, he's there with Gillian. I told her to be careful. The man's a charming rogue, or should I say he was. I was with him for a few months in my teens before he became the big celebrity. I fell for him in a big way, but I could see no future in it. Gillian would have enjoyed the lifestyle for a while, and then she would have left him and looked for someone more suitable.'

'She was part of that lifestyle. I've seen her on the television, the occasional game show,' Wendy said.

'Gillian always had a good moral compass, the legacy of her father and me, but she was ambitious, and you've seen her. The sort of woman who turned men's heads, as I did in my day.'

'You still would.'

'I try to look after myself, but now it doesn't seem so important, does it?'

'It does,' Isaac said.

'You're a charmer too. I can see that.'

In the nearly thirty minutes they'd been in the front room of the terrace house, Maureen Dickenson had not once shed a tear or expressed remorse at her daughter's death. Isaac thought it unusual but knew that different people react in different ways. He assumed that, behind the façade, the woman had experienced sadness and disappointment and heartache in her life, and one more blow, as severe as it was, was not going to cause her to break down and show her true feelings. He imagined that once they were gone, she would relent and let the emotions flood over her.

After twenty minutes, more than the five initially promised, a knock at the door.

'I'm Gillian's aunt, Maureen's sister. How is she?' a woman who looked older than her sister said.

'She's holding up.'

'Was Gillian with him?'

'She was.'

Inside the house, the two sisters embraced; Stephanie, in tears.

'You mentioned Guy Hendry when I opened the door,' Wendy said when the two women eventually sat down.

'I didn't like him, not like Maureen and Gillian,' Stephanie said.

'It goes back a long time,' Maureen said. 'He wanted Steph before me, but my sister you'll come to realise is more sensible than me. She rejected him at the first instance, and that's when he came on to me. No doubt Gillian was the same to him, a plaything on the rebound from another.'

'That's not something that a mother would be pleased to think of their daughter,' Wendy said.

'Gillian had her head screwed on, and if a middle-aged lecher wanted to fritter his money, and if she wanted to think it was love eternal, then no harm has been done. And besides, she wasn't the sort to come home pregnant.'

'Were you?'

'I suppose I was foolish back then, but don't try and read anything into it. Guy had been my lover, and now he's Gillian's.'

'Men such as Hendry make enemies: jealous husbands, disgruntled boyfriends, discarded women.'

'Hendry was a total bastard,' Stephanie said. 'Not that there weren't some who didn't hate him, but killing him and Gillian in cold blood, that makes no sense.'

Wendy looked over at Maureen and could see that the enormity of what had occurred was starting to sink in. 'Do you have a doctor we could call?' she said.

'I'm a qualified doctor,' Stephanie said. 'I'll stay here and make sure my sister is fine. It may be a good time for you both to leave.'

'If there are further questions, we'll come back. I'm sorry that we had to be the bearer of sad news,' Isaac said.

'You're only doing your job. Just make sure you get the bastard who did this.'

'We will.'

Outside the house, the two police officers stood for a while.

'How do you think it went?' Wendy asked.

'Better than most. The one part of the job I hate, telling parents that their child is not coming back home again.'

'She took it well.'

'I know,' Isaac said as the two of them walked to their car. Gillian Dickenson was the first, she wasn't the last visit for that day. Guy Hendry's family had to be told next, and then there were the others who had died in that salon that day; Larry Hill could deal with some of those.

As for the others, additional police officers would be charged with the responsibility of informing the nearest and dearest. The time to inform had to be that day, as it would not take long for the identities of those in the salon to become known, and Guy Hendry would be on the evening news – a television personality, a man about town, a lothario, was always good copy.

As Isaac and Wendy drove away from the area, Isaac glanced up at the Dickenson house. Wendy phoned for a uniform to be assigned to the house to keep away the media and the onlookers.

***

Kensington High Street, and four hours had passed since the shooting. The traffic was lighter on Isaac and Wendy's return to the crime scene. Gordon Windsor was standing nearby, a coffee in his hand.

'They've all been identified,' Windsor said. Isaac thought the man looked drained, more than usual. They had worked together on many cases before and had seen sights that no sane person should see: headless corpses, bodies decayed after years in shallow graves, throats cut.

'Worse than most?' Isaac said.

'The women are the hardest to take.'

'I had met Gillian Dickenson once before,' Isaac said, realising that he had not mentioned it to the woman's mother.

'We've all seen her on the television. Very attractive once, I suppose, but now it seems ghoulish to make comments about how pretty she had been. She'll not look so good after Pathology's checked her out.'

'They'll all be subject to a full autopsy. Any clues as to who was the primary target?'

'None. Alphonso Abano was a criminal, but hardly justifying an assassination.'

'That's what it was,' Isaac said. He was now holding a coffee courtesy of a uniform who had fetched it from a café across the road that was doing sterling business with the additional customers. One lane of the road had reopened to traffic and the barriers were being pulled further back to allow the regular transit of vehicles in both directions. The front window and door of the salon were being covered to block prying eyes.

'Any ideas?' Windsor asked.

'Not yet. The other woman?'

'Sal Maynard according to her driving licence. She's not from around here. There's an address.'

'What can you tell us about her?'

'There's a photo on her phone with her arms around Hendry. Not the sort of woman that Hendry would go for.'

'What do you mean?' Wendy said, taking umbrage at Windsor's comment.

'No offence, purely an observation. Sal Maynard came from Stockwell, a ten-storey tenement, low-rental.'

Wendy realised that Gordon Windsor was only profiling, a necessary part of a police investigation, but her socialist leanings were offended when a dead woman was degraded in comparison to another who, by her mother's admission, was sleeping with the man that she herself had slept with in the past. Again, Wendy could see that the wealthy and the famous were excused for their failings, but for the poor and unknown and unattractive, a different set of rules applied.

'She could have been a decoy, paid to distract the others while the killer entered the premises, measured up the situation,' Isaac said.

'But she was killed as well,' Wendy said.

'Collateral damage. Who knows what she had been told, and what her history is. It could be relevant. We'll check her out next.'

Chapter 4

Neither of the two police officers was impressed when they parked outside Sal Maynard's address, the urge to comment muted on account of the woman's violent death. Due to their delay in arriving at the ninth-floor flat in the drab concrete and poorly maintained building, the local police station had taken the responsibility of informing the next of kin.

A uniform was stationed outside the entrance to the flat. He sharpened up, stood to attention upon seeing the senior officers. 'Not much to say,' he said when quizzed by Isaac. 'They've been informed, that's all I can tell you.'

'They've? You know them?'

'Down at the station, the Maynards are well known. Fencing stolen goods, stealing cars and a quick respray, the occasional incident down at the pub when the eldest gets drunk and starts throwing his weight around.'

'Sal Maynard?' Wendy said. She was not impressed with the uniform's attitude. A family was grieving, yet he showed no compassion, only disdain for those inside.

'She didn't get into trouble, not too much anyway. A few too many drinks sometimes, and she was argumentative. A conviction for shoplifting when she was younger, but nothing recently. I can't say I liked her very much, a foul mouth, but that's about it. Sorry for talking bad about the woman, but I thought you'd like the truth. Inside, you'll no doubt receive the saccharine version.'

'No doubt we will,' Isaac said. 'The neighbours?'

'A few want to get in and offer their condolences. A few just want to be nosy. You know how it is.'

'Unfortunately, we do. High crime rate in this building?'

'Not as high as you would expect. There are a lot of recent arrivals in the building, the women covered up, the men trying to do their best. I can't say I understand them, but on the whole they cause little trouble. There are others here who'd steal anything, and sometimes the drunks will bait the immigrants. One day there'll be trouble, hopefully not today.'

'Not sure I appreciate his take on the Maynards and the locals,' Wendy said as she and Isaac waited for the door to the flat to open.

'Don't judge him too harshly. They've got a difficult job with the disparate society down here,' Isaac said.

The door opened, a heavily-tattooed and burly man stood on the other side.

'DCI Cook, DS Gladstone, Challis Street Homicide,' Isaac said.

'Come in,' the man said, exhaling cigarette smoke over the two officers.

Isaac and Wendy walked down the narrow hallway, brushing against the coats hanging on hooks to their right. A dog barked from behind a closed door. There was a distinct smell in the air of perspiration, stale smoke and alcohol. Isaac felt like taking his handkerchief and holding it over his nose.

'A saint, I'm telling you she was,' a female voice shouted from the room at the end of the hallway.

Isaac and Wendy passed through the doorway to find a group of people sitting around. On the table in the centre of the room, a half-empty bottle of whisky.

'DCI Cook…'

'Don't bother with your names. You're not welcome here, nor is he outside,' the woman who had shouted, said.

'You are?'

'Beverley Maynard, her mother. Have you found the bastard who killed my daughter?'

'We're still conducting enquiries.'

'Then why are you here? We didn't kill her.'

'We're assuming that your daughter wasn't the primary target,' Wendy said. 'We need to ascertain her movements, to check if she or you may have seen anything. What can you tell us about your daughter?'

'She was a good girl, not like the others.'

'The others?'

'My two eldest. Alex, you've met. He's always in trouble for this and that. The other layabout sitting sheepishly, that's Harry, a nasty piece of work, and to think I carried him for nine months.'

'Mum, you shouldn't say that, not to them. They're the police, even if they're not wearing a uniform,' Alex said. He was leaning against the wall, a cigarette hanging from his mouth, a glass of whisky in his hand.

'I'll say what I like. I'm the mother, and I'm sad, even if you're not. You two made Sal's life hell, even when she was younger, and now look at what's happened. Snatched away from me, the only one who cared, and who's going to look after me now?'

'Mrs Maynard, if we could come back to your daughter,' Isaac said. He could empathise with the uniform outside. This was clearly a fractious family who not only gave the police trouble but would not have been liked in the area. He was sure that if they enquired they would find few that would speak kindly of the family in flat 923.

'What do you want?'

'Your daughter's movements. She was in Kensington. Did she go there often?'

'Sal liked to look in the shop windows. She was obsessed with those who had money and fame. I don't know why as she wasn't much to look at. When I was her age, I was a looker, mark my words.'

'You're a liar,' Harry Maynard said. 'Our old man, before you nagged him to death, said you were selling yourself not far from here. That's where he met you, said you were cheap, and not too fancy even back then. At least Sal didn't do that, not that she did much else.'

'Sal helped out at the supermarket for two or three days a week. Casual, so they didn't have to pay her much,' Alex said. He was on his third whisky since Isaac and Wendy had arrived in the flat.

'We're certain that she was at the murder scene because Guy Hendry was there.'

'He'd not fancy her. Apart from working sometimes, she'd sit in front of that television and read those magazines. She was keen on Hendry, not that I could see much in him. And as for that Gillian Dickenson, skinny as a rake.'

'She died, as well,' Wendy said.

'It's been on the news. No mention of Sal, only that an unidentified female had also died. They mentioned Hendry and the tart he was with, but nothing about my Sal.'

'The names are not revealed until the next of kin are informed. You must know that,' Isaac said.

'Of course I do. But it's not right. My Sal was a good girl, and they report it as if she was a nobody, whereas the suntan and the teeth, and his fancy woman, get their pictures splashed across the television. And what about Sal, nothing, not even a mention of what she meant to me.'

'Mum, stop talking nonsense. You didn't care for her, any more than you do for us,' Alex said, his words slurring.

Isaac and Wendy were glad when they left the flat. On the face of it, there was no more to be gained at the Maynards', but Isaac knew that with the most inconsequential, the most unlikely piece of information, they could be back there. Sal Maynard may have been of little consequence, at least at the murder scene, but she could have seen something, heard something at another time, which could have required her death. Nothing and nobody could be regarded as trivial.

***

Larry Hill left the crime scene at Briganti's salon and headed into the area's criminal underbelly. He knew that Alphonso Abano's death would ensure that the criminal community was on edge and they would be closing ranks.

The first stop, the Wellington Arms in Bayswater. Inside, one of his informers, a man of moderate height and intellect, yet taciturn, and very careful in what he said.

'Seamus, a pint?' Larry said to the man, who was sitting to one side of the main bar.

'I thought you'd be in,' Seamus said.

'What's the mood on the street?'

'Just talk, nothing more. Abano's not a great loss, and no one believes they were after him.'

'Any names?'

'Not for the killing. Abano was not a major player, even if he fancied that he was,' Seamus said, his Irish accent still noticeable even though he had lived in London, on and off, for over twenty-five years. He was dressed casually: a pair of faded jeans, a white tee-shirt, his receding hair parted to one side, the grey starting to show in the shoulder-length hair.

Seamus Gaffney was not a criminal, although he skirted on the edge of legality. Apart from running errands for an illegal gambling syndicate, and the occasional favour for some of the criminals in the area, he was clean. He'd spent three months in prison as a youth in Ireland for passing false cheques; he had even managed to purchase a car with one of them, only to have it break down after fifty miles, and when he had returned to take umbrage with the man who had sold him the dud, he was up and gone.

Gaffney had put it down to one dud in exchange for another.

'I'd agree,' Larry said. 'Who could have been the target at Briganti's?'

'Nobody knows, and that's the truth. Maybe they're careful not to speak in case they end up dead, but on this one, Inspector Hill, you'll need to look further afield. It could be someone brought in from overseas for the one job, and then shipped out.'

'We've considered that possibility. Whoever it was, they dumped the rifle and pistol in a bin as they left.'

'No fingerprints?'

'Nothing. We've got Interpol onto it, but no details.'

'The villains don't like someone coming in here and causing trouble. It makes it more difficult for everyone.'

'A downturn in crime for a few days, some small benefit,' Larry said.

'Briganti was a decent man, kept to himself, and Hendry doesn't seem likely.'

'Did you know either?'

'Briganti in passing. He'd sometimes have a glass of wine of a Saturday in here. Hendry I know from a long time back, before he became the big star.'

'How?'

'Not much in itself, but he used to do some modelling. Back then, he was a good-looking man, no money, but he always seemed to be able to find himself a woman. Some reckoned that some of them were paying him for his time.'

'Prostitution?'

'Escorting, more like. If he was, good on him.'

'Not something either of us would have been paid for,' Larry joked.

'Not a chance,' Seamus agreed, his empty glass pushed across the table.

'Make that three,' a voice from behind.

Larry looked up to see the menacing figure of Nicolae Cojocaru, a man that the detective inspector kept his distance from. Cojocaru, wanted in his home country of Romania for extortion and murder, but claiming immunity from deportation due to his notoriety back there not affording him a fair trial, walked tall in London. Even the police gave the man a wide berth, knowing full well that he kept a team of henchmen on hand.

It was only the third time that Larry had spoken to the man. The first was when Cojocaru had told him to back off on prosecuting another man, not that it had done any good, and Larry had not complied. But the man, according to the word on the street, had some dirt on the Romanian crime boss, and if he was incarcerated, then he might talk. Not that it was relevant now, but his first day in prison the man had had an unfortunate accident and was now dead and buried. The second time had been in the pub they were in now. Cojocaru had seen Larry sitting in his regular seat, and had made a disparaging comment about the police in general, and Larry in particular. On that occasion, Larry had stayed seated, and the man had moved on, evicted someone else from their spot close to the bar.

Cojocaru was a charmless man who ruled by intimidation and overt violence. Larry did not feel comfortable with him sitting alongside him, two of the gangster's henchmen standing to their rear.

'It wasn't my people,' Cojocaru said, leaning in Larry's direction.

'Not your style?' Larry said sneeringly.

'Now look here, Mr Policeman, I've sat here in an act of conciliation. Whoever was responsible, they frighten us.'

'You're a known criminal and not someone with a good reputation. Too many people have died around you. Why should we be discussing this matter?'

'I keep my ears to the ground. I know that you're someone who can be trusted. You want to solve this crime. I want those responsible out of here.'

'There are some who would want you out as well.'

'No doubt they would. I'm an honest businessman, although I'm a tough bastard. Those who get on my wrong side end up regretting it. You don't want to be one, do you?'

'Are you threatening a police officer?'

'I don't threaten. I say it as it is.'

'Very well, Mr Cojocaru, what do you know about the shooting?'

'My contacts tell me it was someone who was brought in from overseas and then flown out.'

'But why? It makes no sense to be so visible.'

'It sends a warning that whoever it is can act with impunity.'

'Are you frightened?' Larry asked.

'Only a foolish man has no fear. Whoever it was could come back and finish the job.'

'Why? And who was the target? Alphonso Abano doesn't seem worth it.'

'He wasn't.'

'The others are clean.'

'Nobody's clean, you know that. Everyone's got skeletons, some criminal, some not, that they'd rather not be known.'

'What do you want from me? I'm not going to look away while you maim and kill and ship your drugs into this country,' Larry said.

'Let's just say that I'm an honest businessman who sees the neighbourhood going downhill.'

'You can say it, I can't. But I don't want any escalation in crime. Tell me what you know, and we'll agree to act civil to one another.'

Larry wasn't sure, and ideally, he would have called his DCI for advice, but time was of the essence. He knew that men such as

Cojocaru did not offer help often, and if the killer was an import, the Romanian, a swarthy man in his fifties, could assist.

'Another time, you and I will not be having this conversation. Get in my way and you know what happens.'

'A display of the rough justice from where you come from.'

'Not much of a legal system either. It's men such as me who maintain control, and fear's a great motivator, a deterrent as well. Anyway, what we have is a Mafia-style killing. I've put the feelers out, and it's not someone from Romania.'

'You would have known in advance if it was?'

'I would have stopped it if I had.'

'Late at night, local tip?'

'Inspector, don't keep baiting me, or I'll let you deal with this.'

'Very well. Who was the target?'

'I've heard about Hendry and his woman, Briganti as well. He came over from Italy, check him out, although I suppose you are.'

'Complete dossiers are being prepared on all those who died. The question is, as you say, why kill them all? There's nothing to be gained.'

'There is. An overseas syndicate wanting to establish their mark in this country. The easiest way to frighten any who would get in their way is to show their dominance, their willingness to use violence.'

'A threat to you?'

'An honest businessman, as we've agreed.'

'I forgot.'

'Hypothetically, assuming I was what you think I am, that sort of person would be seriously worried.'

'A bastard thing to do, killing innocent people.'

'Nobody's innocent. You'd learn that in my country. You're either the one in control or you're the flotsam, and of no consequence.'

Larry realised that the gangster had no concept of right or wrong, only in ensuring that he remained the most vicious crook in the area, the man that everyone else was afraid of, a man who could have used the hairdressing salon as an example.

'Keep in touch, Hill. We need each other,' the parting words from Cojocaru as the men separated, a brief handshake. 'Remember, take care with me. I'm a good friend to those who understand me.'

And a savage and malignant bastard to those that don't, Larry thought.

Chapter 5

Guy Hendry had an ex-wife and two children, that much was known. Failing any others, they were the next of kin, although according to the tabloids, the relationship between Guy and the former Mrs Hendry was acrimonious.

'I've no issues with Guy,' Liz Hendry said after she had opened the door to her house in a leafy suburb near Richmond Park. 'The man can't help himself, but he's looked after us well.'

The two police officers found themselves sitting in two chairs in the main room of the house. It was well decorated, the sort of place that featured in magazines.

'Guy paid for all this, not that he couldn't afford it.'

'You seem very composed given the circumstances,' Wendy said.

'I reported from a few war zones earlier on in my career, saw things no person should ever see. Guy's death, as well as Gillian's, has come as a shock to my children and me.'

'Your children, where are they?'

'They've left home now. Two daughters, the oldest is twenty-two and married, the youngest is nineteen, and living with her boyfriend. They've been over to see me, and my sister's in the other room, so is Guy's.'

'You knew Gillian Dickenson?' Wendy asked, her initial concerns about the woman in part allayed by her pleasant manner.

'I knew of his conquests. I was one when I was younger. I liked Gillian, and some may have said she was with Guy for his money, but he was still great fun. I would have had him back in a flash, but that's not how he was wired. One of the reasons that he's been so successful. He knew of his appeal to women, and he knew how to turn on the charm.'

'Sergeant Gladstone's right,' Isaac said. 'You don't come across as the grieving widow.'

'I am. Ask me what you want, and then if you could, please leave me in peace. At least for a few days. I will take responsibility for the funeral arrangements, along with his sister.'

'We should interview her while we're here.'

'She's not bearing up as well as me.'

'The truth is that we don't know who the intended target was,' Isaac said. 'The shooting was well-executed. Apart from a local criminal, no one of interest was in the salon.'

'Loved by all, was Guy. Loved by too many, the occasional discarded boyfriend might have said. Sometimes, the women would come on to him, and one or two might have been married or in a relationship. The one fault, minor I suppose, is that sometimes he couldn't say no.

'Any incidents that you know of?'

'One or two. Guy would phone me up occasionally to let me know, and when the children were younger, we'd all go away on our annual holidays together. Some may have seen it as strange, but we didn't, the reason our daughters are so well-balanced.'

'He should have stayed with you,' Isaac said. He had to admit that he liked Liz Hendry, a person with a refreshing honesty about her.

'He tried, but then the fame and fortune came along. When we first met, he was struggling. The occasional photo shoot for a men's clothing line, an in-store magazine, and we had no money to spare. But then he got the first game show to host, and for a while he was impossible to live with. We used to live in a one-bedroom bedsit, and then we had a four-bedroom house.'

'We've only heard good reports about his affability, although there was an autograph hunter in the salon. The photos of her with Guy don't show him as being overly friendly with the woman.'

'You'll not hear a bad word from me about him, nor will our daughters say anything against him. Our youngest has taken it badly, and she'll come back later to be with me. The eldest is more stoic, more like me in many ways.'

'Jealous husbands and discarded boyfriends don't hire professional killers,' Isaac said.

'Guy wasn't the target, nor was Gillian. I liked her and she thought it was love, no doubt Guy did, but after about six to nine months, there's another temptation. Don't get me wrong, he was a good man, as good as you could hope for. Now, if you don't mind, I've spent enough time putting on a brave face.'

'That's understood,' Isaac said. 'If we could meet with Mr Hendry's sister.'

Liz Hendry shook Isaac's hand and then Wendy's. She then left the room, a handkerchief in her hand.

After a few minutes, Guy Hendry's sister came into the room. It was clear that she was older than her brother by more than a few years.

'Step-brother,' Pamela Vincent said. 'We were close as children. I was more like a mother to him than our father's third wife was. She was a bitch, the wicked step-mother, and our father was a charmer, the same as Guy, but he didn't have the inherent decency that my brother had. More my influence than his parents.'

'Your mother, Guy's mother?'

'They both took off, and we rarely saw either of them. We came from money, yet Guy didn't want any of it. That's why he was down in London with Liz and struggling to make ends meet. If it had stayed that way, then he'd still be alive.'

'We can't control our destinies,' Isaac said, knowing full well that if he could, he would be happily married to Jess, but she was long gone and now had two children with another man. He suddenly felt sad, reminiscing about the one woman that he had really wanted.

'I stayed with the money, inherited enough to live well, but Guy never touched any of it. He made his fortune through sweat and hard work.'

'Any enemies?'

'Our father was a ruthless businessman. He would have made enemies, but not Guy.'

'Where is he now?'

'Dead and buried. A lifetime of smoking cigars, drinking whisky and burning the midnight oil. A driven man, he had a coronary at the age of seventy-one. Guy never went to the funeral, there was that much hatred between the two.'

'Your brother was capable of anger and hate?'

'Not towards any of us. It was our father he hated, almost as much as he hated his mother for deserting him.'

'Is she still alive?'

'She is. She's old now and lives in the country. I'll give you her address. I'll let you form your opinion when you meet her.'

'Your opinion?'

'I've never formed a judgement against her, no more than I have against my own mother. She's dead, by the way. Guy's mother was a frail woman, even when she lived with our father. And with our father, you were either with him, or you were out, and totally.'

'Are you saying she may have had no choice but to leave Guy with his father?'

'I could understand the rationale at the time, but I was nine years older when she left that night. Guy was only eight, so he didn't see these things in the same light. Whatever the reason, I don't believe he has met his mother more than a few times in the years since. I wish my brother were still alive, but he isn't, and we'll have to deal with it. I just hope that you're able to solve this horrendous crime as soon as possible and to bring whoever did it to justice.'

'That's our intention,' Isaac said.

***

The unexpected visit of Nicolae Cojocaru to where Larry and Seamus Gaffney had been sitting in the pub had not been a pleasant encounter, and Larry, usually not a man to express his prejudices, could not act with indifference towards the man. Cojocaru, with his adroit manipulation, his money, and his henchmen had cut a swathe through the area. In the past, the villains had been English, then Irish, then from the Caribbean, Jamaicans mainly, and the last group had been vicious enough. But compared to the Romanian gangsters, they were as children.

'Tough bastard,' Seamus said.

'He frightens me,' Larry said. 'He could have done it.'

'Too close to home, he's not responsible.'

Larry knew that while Cojocaru was capable of ordering violence, he was not a man who carried a gun or committed the acts personally. He was a godfather figure in his community, and there were those from the old country who looked to him for assistance; people not in a position morally or financially to condemn the man's criminal activities.

That night, late as usual, Larry found his wife waiting for him when he arrived home, her typical stern look not apparent.

'Busy night,' she said with almost a touch of affection. Larry knew that she wished he'd leave the police and get a job that wasn't so dangerous and didn't come with the temptation of boozy nights. He knew she had been right on a previous case when the Homicide team were getting close to solving some murders, and he had ended up in hospital, severely beaten. If it hadn't been that the hoodlums who had gone at him with baseball bats were ineffectual, he would have been dead. As it was, he had escaped with no more than severe bruising, a couple of broken ribs and a dislocated shoulder blade.

'You've seen where I've been on the television,' Larry said.

'Guy Hendry. Why would anyone kill him?'

'They killed his girlfriend and six others, a bloodbath.'

'And you're mixing with those who did it?'

'Not this time. We don't think it's local-based, and Hendry was not the target. Never can be sure on that, though.'

'He always seemed a charming man, but then on the television, these celebrities let us see what they want of them.'

'DCI Cook and Wendy have met with his family, also Gillian Dickenson's. According to them, Guy Hendry was a decent man. Gillian Dickenson came from a good home, as well. They had to tell the mother that her daughter was dead.'

'Not you this time?'

'Not this time, thankfully. Just hope there are no more villains out there with semi-automatic rifles.'

'And you in the middle of it. You know I worry.'

'I wouldn't love you if you didn't. Someone's got to deal with this.'

'But why you?'

'Let's not go there again. You know I'm not leaving.'

'I know. Your dinner's in the oven if you're hungry.'

'I'm starving. Any chance of sleeping upstairs tonight?'

'Just make sure you brush your teeth and use some mouth freshener. I can't be angry tonight, although I should be. Any suspects?'

'I met Cojocaru.'

'He gets as much publicity as Guy Hendry,' Larry's wife said as she walked out of the door to the kitchen.

'Not good, though. He's a man who frightens me.'

'He frightens a lot of people. Don't go getting yourself killed.'

'I don't intend to,' Larry said.

'But Cojocaru. He's a killer.'

'I'll make sure to call him sir every time I meet him.'

'Not you. You're more than likely to have a beer with him.'

'Reluctantly,' Larry said, knowing that Cojocaru was a man who would know what was happening before anyone else, even the police.

Chapter 6

Giuseppe Briganti's mother, an elderly woman, her back bent from years of working outside tending to the cattle and the vegetables that they grew for sale, sat in the corner of the farmhouse. In another corner, a television was on. For the woman, it was her only connection to the son she had seen three weeks previously when he had been on one of his frequent visits. She remembered the joy that he had given her when he had told her how successful his business had become. He had told her about where he lived and how he preferred to be on his own. She regretted that he had not married and given her grandchildren, but she knew the anguish that had driven him to London.

'I'll not last for much longer,' she said, desperately sad at the loss, aware of her own mortality; the stroke last summer, and now the inability to walk more than a few paces. She was sixty-eight, but life had been tough, and Giuseppe had offered to take her to London and look after her and to make sure that she received the best medical care. Once, eleven years ago, she had visited him, the one time she had left her Italy, and she only remembered the cold and the rain, and the fact that she did not understand what everyone was saying. Not that they were unfriendly, on the contrary, but she was a village woman, as was her mother, and her mother before that.

Her husband had died five years previously, and Giuseppe had visited to organise the funeral and to say a few words praising his father and mother for giving him life, and for caring for him. He had said that he wanted to stay, but his mother knew that it was just words for her, and he had never been a farmer. He had been destined for more, and she had seen him achieve that.

Around her in the farmhouse, her brothers and sisters, the ones still alive, as well as half the village. It had been a good life, the woman had to admit. She raised herself from her chair to make sure that everyone had something to eat and drink. A sudden pain in her chest and she slumped back in the chair. Ten minutes later the village doctor pronounced her dead.

***

Early morning in the office, DCI Cook's mandatory practice: the six o'clock meeting during a murder investigation. The others in the team had no trouble agreeing, only with complying. Bridget Halloran had worked late the previous night dealing with the paperwork, and setting up the reporting structure that a bureaucratised police force demanded. Not that she complained, as she enjoyed her work immensely and had great respect for her DCI. It had been two in the morning when she had left the office, and a twenty-minute drive, less than three hours sleep, and then back to the office.

Isaac could see that Bridget was suffering, as were the others, as was he. He had only slept for one hour. He'd lain in his bed for longer, but the events had been churning over in his mind. Wendy Gladstone, the ever-loyal sergeant, yawned. Larry Hill was another person who had had a late night, but his had been tinged with alcohol and Nicolae Cojocaru.

'Thanks for making it,' Isaac said. 'I needn't tell you the seriousness of what we have here.'

'We understand, sir,' Wendy said. 'Why can't the villains let us have a good night's sleep?' she said by way of lightening the sombre tone of the room.

'We'll ask them sometime, but in the meantime, what do we have? Larry, you first.'

'The word is that it's someone from overseas aiming to muscle in.'

'Cojocaru?'

'I met with him yesterday, not that I intended to. Most times the man keeps out of the way, but he wanted to talk.'

'Update us on what he said.'

'His arrival in the area has changed the pecking order amongst the criminals.'

'What about the West Indian gangs? You were friendly with them before.'

'They're still there, but they're maintaining a lower profile. Cojocaru is the most savage we've come up against, and according to the man, someone else is out there that frightens him.'

'Keep in contact with him, find out what else he knows, and keep us updated as to where you are. That man kills, whether you're a police officer or a gang member.'

'I know that. With the West Indians, I felt safe enough, but with Cojocaru, I don't.'

'Wendy, what do you have?' Isaac said. He'd noticed that the woman's arthritis had been troubling her less in the last few weeks, a sign that the weather was improving, and early-morning frosts had not been seen for some time.

'I'm working through the others in the salon. You've met with the more significant people, so I've concentrated on the other two hairdressers, Baz, short for Barry, Hepworth and Frank Boswell. Hepworth was Australian, and I've got the local police in Sydney dealing with informing his family and interviewing them. If there's any need, I'll set up a video link from here, but the man seems clean. His father was English, and Barry Hepworth had an English passport, no immigration issues. The man paid his taxes, and Briganti's books seem to be in order. Frank Boswell seems to be clean as well. He's English, born in Liverpool. From what we know so far, he came from a middle-class family, the father is an accountant, his mother teaches at a local school. Nothing on him other than drunken driving a few years ago, and he'd been apprehended once for buying cocaine off the street. He was probably still snorting it, and Forensics and Pathology will confirm if that's the case. I'll go up to Liverpool if we find any negatives against him. Sal Maynard is of more interest. Her family has had more than its fair share of run-ins with the law. One of her uncles had been in Maidstone prison for five years for theft, cars mainly.'

'Delve into the others with Bridget,' Isaac said. 'Anything untoward and we'll follow up.'

'Cojocaru could be leading us down the garden path.'

'What do you mean?' Isaac said.

'A diversionary tactic.'

'He's savage enough to have been responsible.'

'The man's not stupid. Antonescu and Becali, his two offsiders, are not too smart, and I reckon that Antonescu would have no compunction in shooting innocent people, nor would Becali, but this time I reckon that Cojocaru's levelling with us.'

***

'I don't care who the bastard is, I want him dead,' Cojocaru said as he stomped around the living room in his penthouse flat. Standing not far away, afraid to sit, were his two henchmen.

Crin Antonescu, the first of the two, a squat pug-faced man, a wrestler in his youth, enjoyed violence, although only if he was not on the receiving end. He still remembered the time when he had been, the result of not throwing a championship match on which a gambling syndicate had staked a fortune. Not only had they lost millions, but Antonescu had lost the full strength in his left arm after four men had gone to work on him for not following orders.

'You live to tell others who may think that they are smarter than us,' one of the four men had said, and now Antonescu sat in the room in Kensington listening to the man who had controlled that syndicate.

Antonescu hated Cojocaru, although the thought of betraying him brought the pug-faced man out in a cold sweat.

Cojocaru knew that fear brought with it respect and devotion, the same way a maltreated dog will continue to follow its master, even after it had been starved and beaten.

The second of the two men in Cojocaru's presence, a tall, slender man with wavy hair and a dark complexion, went by the name of Ion Becali. He did not fear Cojocaru, only loved the man for what he had done for his family when he had been desperate and struggling to make ends meet in Romania.

'He's not a local,' Becali said, referring to the shooting at Briganti's.

'Ion, I'm not a fool,' Cojocaru said.

'Abano wasn't much of a target,' Antonescu said.

'He may have fancied himself as an important man in the area, but he was just small time. What was he involved with?'

'We used him a few times to sell drugs for us. We paid him well enough, and he kept his mouth shut.'

'You two are my eyes on the street, but you're coming up with nothing.'

'Nobody knows, or else they're clamming up.'

'I don't care what you do, who you hurt, but I need to know. If it's someone from the old country we'd know by now. If it's someone from elsewhere with fewer scruples than us, then it's war. Are we ready?'

'If it's locals, then yes. We've got them under control, but if it's unknowns from overseas, no chance,' Antonescu said.

'What are you suggesting? That we bring in more people to help?'

'How many of the locals did we kill when we came to this country?'

'You tell me.'

'Over twenty, but most of them were Jamaicans, the rest Irish, some from Scotland, and a few English, but they weren't used to our kind of violence. Or at least the English weren't, lily-livered the lot of them.'

'The police, any issues?'

'A few uniforms can be paid to look the other way, or if they don't take money, they'll respond to threats.'

'What sort of country is this, where the police are honest, the villains are harmless?' Becali said.

'The sort of country that has made us rich and feared. The sort of country where we can hold our heads up high.'

Becali thought back to Romania and how he had scratched out an existence, stealing what he could, fencing what he couldn't. And now he was living in an upmarket flat in Bayswater, a couple of women on tap, a cabinet full of drink, and the best hashish that money could buy. It had been a good eight years in a country that respected his right to be there, even paying him government money in the first few months while he established himself, while he and Antonescu with Cojocaru's planning had methodically eliminated all opposition. If the authorities had known what atrocities they had committed, especially against those from the Caribbean, the police would have been more diligent.

Concern over gang warfare had been raised in parliament at the time, and in the media on occasions, but not much had come of it, just blustering and grandstanding by a few. Cojocaru knew, as he had back home in Romania, that society needs discipline, not vague rules and regulations. The area that he controlled was calmer than before; there was a lower level of street crime, and areas that had been no-goes late at night were now safe to walk in by the law-abiding majority.

The master gangster looked out of the window of his penthouse flat and surveyed his domain. He knew that the move to England had been right, as back in the old country there was a new government that had been elected on a platform of law and order.

They weren't achieving much of either, but they had become a nuisance.

In England, the presumption of innocence before guilt had served him well, and apart from a few attempts by the authorities to muscle him and his men out of the country in the early days, he had managed to stay. And those that had shown the possibility of securing his deportation were either in his pay now, or keeping out of the way, or dead. Of the three options, Cojocaru knew which he preferred.

'The Russians would be capable of hitting Briganti's,' Cojocaru said, a shiver running down his spine.

'But why? We take the heroin they ship out of Afghanistan, pay them plenty for it,' Antonescu said.

Chapter 7

Detective Chief Superintendent Richard Goddard was not a happy man, Isaac knew that. The two had worked together since one had been an inspector and the other a constable on the beat. The relationship, akin to friendship, had served the two men well, although as Isaac, now a detective chief inspector, was well aware, it did not obviate the need for his Homicide team to provide a result.

'Isaac, I've got my seniors breathing down my neck, the same as I am down yours. What's going on, and what are you doing to prevent a repeat?' Goddard asked in the sanctity of his office.

'We're struggling on this one,' Isaac admitted, knowing full well that his senior appreciated an honest answer, even if it was not the one he wanted to hear. 'Apart from a minor villain in the salon, we can't find any reason to kill the others in Briganti's. We're still conducting enquiries, interviewing the next of kin, checking on the street for what's being said, who's suspected.'

'And?' Goddard said from the comfort of his leather-backed chair. His DCI had to do with a wooden chair, and not very comfortable at that.

'It appears to be a warning to the crooks in the area. Larry Hill's been in conversation with Nicolae Cojocaru, and the man believes that's what it is.'

'We take the word of a gangster?'

'Not normally, but it's more his style,' Isaac said. 'Not that we can pin it on him.'

'Men like Cojocaru don't get their hands dirty, you know that,' Goddard said. Isaac could sense a tenseness in the man. He'd thought he'd be heading up Counter-Terrorism Command by now, but was still stuck in Challis Street Police Station, courtesy of a police commissioner by the name of Alwyn Davies, an acerbic political animal who neither Isaac nor his chief superintendent liked, having had more than a few run-ins with him.

Davies should have been out on his ear after a string of terrorist acts in London. And then there was his bringing in of his own people into senior positions, temporarily removing both Isaac and DCS Goddard on one occasion and bringing in an incompetent to take their places.

But now stability reigned at Challis Street, even if there was an unease about the place. Isaac, in his younger years, had featured in a promotional for the television-viewing public as the face of the modern and cosmopolitan London Metropolitan Police: urbane, black, degree-educated. There were some who saw him as a future commander, even commissioner, but now he'd been languishing for too long in Homicide. Not that it concerned him unduly, not in the last year anyway, as his team were efficient, and he had just managed to upgrade his flat in Willesden for one in Hammersmith.

Detective Chief Superintendent Goddard was a political animal, but not with the savagery of Alwyn Davies, the senior officer in the London Metropolitan Police.

Goddard had gone out of his way to protect his protégé, Isaac, on a couple of occasions, both woman-related. The first time, a more youthful and less-experienced Isaac had slept with a woman who had later turned out to be a murderer. The second time was in the north of the country, when he had been snapped in an embrace with a woman. It had happened at a party in the hotel where he was staying during the hunt for a woman who had killed several men. A group of three women, all inebriated, had grabbed him to take a photo of them all before one of them had taken a picture of just the two of them, smiling, arms around each other. Isaac had thought no more of it until later that night when the woman – the murderer – had loaded the photo onto social media. For a while, he had become a laughingstock, although in the end he had regained some creditability by arresting her, but not before she had stabbed him with a knife.

'How do men like Cojocaru manage to evade the law?' Isaac said. He knew that it was a rhetorical question.

'Have you met the man?' Goddard said, choosing not to answer his DCI's question.

'Larry Hill has, I haven't.'

'Any advantage if you do?'

'If the man is frightened, then there's no harm done.'

'If someone's muscling in on his action, either they are planning to strike a deal with the man or to eliminate him.'

'They could have done that instead of killing innocent people.'

'Innocent?'

'Alphonso Abano is no great loss, but the others didn't deserve to die purely because there's a war going on out there.'

'Cojocaru was bad enough in dealing with the local villains before, but now this has taken a turn for the worse.'

'It has been quieter for a few months, up until Briganti's, that is.'

'A temporary lapse. Meet with Cojocaru, see if he'll help us. We can deal with him another time.'

Isaac knew that it was a compromise, in that dealing with one villain at the expense of withholding access to another, more violent, more unpredictable, more unknown, was necessary. He left DCS Goddard's office with the intention of getting Larry Hill to set up a meeting.

***

An air of palpable tension pervaded the air as Larry, fishing for information, entered into his and most of the villains' favourite pub, the Wellington Arms.

In one corner, propping up the bar, Crin Antonescu. He cast a steely glance over at the police inspector, a brief nod of his head in acknowledgement. Larry responded in the same manner, not pleased to see him there, not disappointed either. Ion Becali, the other of the two men closest to Cojocaru, was sitting down at a table, a woman in her twenties close by, her arm around his shoulder. Larry knew her by sight and by name: Betty Acton, black, beautiful, although starting to show the effects of selling herself and the drug abuse she had subjected her body to. It wasn't often that she came into the pub, nor was it usual for Cojocaru's two men.

Larry strolled over to Becali, passing by Seamus Gaffney and giving him his pint. He wanted to speak, but Larry had a more pressing question for another.

'Where's your boss?' Larry said to Becali, who had pretended not to notice the police officer approaching him.

'Our night off,' Becali replied. Not a good enough answer for Larry. Betty grabbed hold of Becali's face and pulled it forward to hers before kissing him firmly on the mouth, a clear sign to Larry to leave them alone. Usually, he would have. Becali was a violent lover, known to be so because another Betty lookalike had ended up in the hospital badly beaten and bruised. She had wanted to bring a case against the man, supposedly a dispute over the final payment for her services. In the end, the woman had left the hospital and moved out of the area. Larry had made some low-level enquiries, but nothing had come of them. Either she had found herself face down in a ditch somewhere, or she was feeding the fish and the crabs at the bottom of the river, or she had changed her name and was standing on a street corner somewhere selling herself for whatever she could. Regardless, no one, not even a next of kin or a friend, had come forward after the woman vanished.

'It's the first time I've seen you and Antonescu in the pub together without your boss.'

'Nicolae Cojocaru's not a man for drinking.'

'He's game for anything else.'

'What does that mean?'

'The last time I saw you, it was in here with Cojocaru. He was worried then, so were you, and here you are with your fancy woman. No doubt you've got a night of pleasure planned. I hope we don't have to visit the hospital later tonight or tomorrow to find her in intensive care.'

'Ion treats me well,' Betty said, the needle marks visible on her skin.

'We need to meet with your boss,' Larry said. 'If he's in the country, that is. If he's not, where is he?'

'He's here. Others are looking out for him. And he's entertaining tonight, the same as I am. Antonescu's keeping himself comfortable with a few beers.'

'He's not a lover?'

'He is, but he likes a drink now and then. For myself, a couple of pints and a good woman.'

'Betty's the good woman? I thought you had a couple of classy whores in your stable.'

'How dare you insult me,' Betty said indignantly.

'Take no notice,' Becali said. 'Detective Inspector Hill's just leaving.'

'It's my night off, Hill,' the man said, turning his gaze to Larry. 'And If I fancy a bit of rough, then that's my right. It's a democratic country where a man can make his own decisions.'

Larry sat down and looked over at the young prostitute. 'Betty, you heard the man, you're the rough. Just make sure that you don't end up as the beaten or even the dead.'

'Cojocaru will see you tomorrow morning,' Becali said. Larry could see the redness in the man's face, the tightening of his grip on his glass, the look of an angry man.

'I'll be there with Detective Chief Inspector Cook. There's a gang war brewing, and we want to stop it before it gets out of hand.'

'So do we. Now if you'll excuse us, go away and talk to your informer friend. And tell him to be careful. We don't like people sticking their noses into our business.'

'I'll tell him, but I'll be keeping an eye out for what you're doing. We're not sure that you weren't involved in what happened at Briganti's.'

'Okay, Mr Policeman, you don't like us, and we don't like you. Mutual dislike and distrust, is that it?'

'It is, but I've got the law behind me, you haven't.'

'Idle threats. Mr Cojocaru doesn't take favourably to people who threaten him.'

'We know his solution, and you and Antonescu carry it out.'

Larry stood and walked away, observing the look between Becali and Antonescu. Betty sat to one side of Becali; she was not holding him as tight as before. Larry hoped that the woman would not regret selling herself to a vicious man for the night.

***

Seamus Gaffney, a man who appreciated a few pints of beer of a night after a hard day of not doing much, was waiting for Larry to come over to where he was sitting. That day he had organised the location for an illegal dogfight where bloodthirsty men would bet on the outcome of two half-starved dogs fighting each other, the victor being accorded the accolades, the other, either maimed or dead. Gaffney didn't appreciate the spectacle himself, but he had bills to pay, the same as everyone else.

There was a wife, a homely woman who preferred to stay back in Ireland, although he went over there every six weeks to see her. Not that he was idle back there, as there were six children and another on the way. He liked it there, and the cottage where his family lived was paid for. The only problem was that the community was honest and law-abiding, the sort of place where everyone went to church on a Sunday, and where he didn't fit in. In his childhood, he'd been hyperactive, and in his teens, he had been into graffiti and vandalism, painting the church door with his impression of art: bright orange and blue. And then as an adult, it was false cheques and a few months in prison. He had become a leper in Ireland, yet Sheila, the next-door neighbour's daughter, had always been there, even during his childhood and his adolescence, and then his time in prison. They had married on a Saturday, a small affair at the church where he had adorned the church door. Even Father O'Rourke, the village priest, had made a joke of it at the time of the wedding, although the day after the defacing of the Lord's house, he had turned up at the Gaffneys' home with a cane in his hand, and he had tanned the young Gaffney with it, putting him in bed for a week.

Seamus's mother had wanted O'Rourke to be prosecuted, but Seamus had pleaded with her not to do it as he would be ostracised from his friends, and Father O'Rourke was right in what he had done to him.

In time, life in the small community moved on, and Seamus never defaced the church again, even stopping every time he passed the place to enter and offer a prayer to be forgiven, and to apologise to the Almighty for what he had done.

England was the only place for Seamus Gaffney after he left prison, and although he had tried his hand at labouring, and then serving in a shop, he was a restless man. He was, however, reliable, and those in Notting Hill and the adjoining suburbs recognised that. He always had his ear to the ground, and he knew how to set up activities on the edge of illegality. Gambling on fighting dogs, bare-knuckle fighting, although there wasn't much of that in the last few years, and arranging a cheap car for someone: stolen, resprayed, the engine markings removed on more than a few occasions. He had spoken out of turn once and had inadvertently given a clue to the police; the outcome of that an arrest, and a man had spent two years in jail. On his release, he had grabbed Seamus by the collar, marched him up to the pub.

'You owe me a skinful of beer,' the released prisoner said.

'Why's that?'

'They never found out about the other crime. The money's safe from that one, and later tonight you're going to drive me to the airport. I've got plenty, and after two years that I spent inside courtesy of Her Majesty, I'm well ahead.'

Seamus had been relieved when the man had boarded the flight to Thailand, and a life of bargirls, cheap alcohol and drugs. The word came through six months later that for all his luck the man had been on the receiving end of a beating in a bar in Phuket and had died of his wounds.

'Seamus,' Larry said, having visited the bar in the Wellington Arms to order another pint of beer for the man, one for himself. 'What can you tell me?'

'You've been talking to Becali.'

'Why not? The man knows more than you do, or does he? He's a vicious bastard, so's Antonescu, but we need to find out who shot up Briganti's. Have you found out any more?'

Seamus took a drink, downing almost half the contents of the glass in one gulp. 'The rumour mill is working overtime. Everyone's got a theory. Most think it's the Romanians aiming to tighten their grip.'

'Their grip is already tight. Are there any dissenters?'

'Some of the gangs are in discussion.'

'To form an alliance against the threat?'

'If it's not the Romanians, then they need to be ready. There's talk of bringing in more weapons. It could get nasty.'

'That's why we need to meet with Cojocaru, the other criminal syndicates, the gangs.'

'*We*! Count me out. I'll talk to you here for a few pints and some of your money, but don't ask me to meet with any of them.'

'Seamus, you're letting your mind get away with you. It's the police who'll be talking with them. You can help with letting me know who's talking to who, or I can find out from them direct.'

'They'll not talk openly to you, not yet. Another incident and they may do.'

'Another incident planned?'

'That's the problem, just rumours. There are some that say the hit on Briganti's was aimed at the man himself, others say it was the hot-shot banker, others reckon it was Guy Hendry or the woman he was with, even the Maynard woman. Myself, I think they're all wrong.'

'What do you reckon?'

'I read that they shoot up places overseas.'

'It's not part of our culture.'

'You may be right,' Gaffney said. 'I've heard there is a shipment of weapons coming in.'

'A rumour?'

'It could be, but if it's correct, they'll be available to the highest bidder. You'd better be prepared.'

'We will be,' Larry said as he downed his last pint. He had kept it to four; he would not be sleeping on the sofa that night.

Chapter 8

Pathology had completed the autopsies of those who had died at Briganti's. Isaac read through the reports in his office. He had been joined by Bridget and Wendy; Larry was out on the street attempting to meet with the various gang members and villains, those that would talk to him.

'According to the reports,' Isaac said, 'Abano had been drinking, nothing excessive, and Briganti was clean, as were the other two hairdressers that died, although one of them, Baz Haywood, was found to have traces of cocaine.'

'Guy Hendry and Gillian Dickenson?' Wendy said.

'Nothing to report apart from Gillian Dickenson being two months pregnant. Paul Waverton, the banker, was heavily into cocaine. And as for Sal Maynard, her autopsy reveals that she was verging on obese, no sign of any other ailments. What do we have on her?'

'The family has some criminal history, hardly enough to warrant execution,' Wendy said. 'I'm following up in detail with Bridget on all those in Briganti's. We're not excluding that one of them was targeted and that Cojocaru is not responsible.'

'Correct,' Isaac said, knowing that he had trained his team well. 'We can't assume anything. Larry's out there trying to find out more details, and we're meeting with Cojocaru.'

'Be careful,' Bridget said.

'I've already run it past Detective Chief Superintendent Goddard. He's given the go-ahead, and we'll have armed backup not far away.'

'So will Cojocaru,' Wendy said.

'The fact that the man's worried indicates that it's a foreign syndicate attempting to take over.'

'But why Briganti's?'

'Depends on the reason. An arrogance on whoever's part that the English police are ineffective, a warning to the Romanians and the other criminals in the area.'

'Are we ineffective?'

'We go by the book. It's still more effective than the alternatives, and we're not dealing with terrorism here.'

'It's worse than that,' Bridget said.

'Terrorism is usually committed by low-intellect, religiously dogmatic and radicalised peoples. Organised crime overseas is not run by fools, but by people who are smart and know what they're doing,' Isaac said.

'As I said, it's worse.'

'The upsurge in weapons in the area?' Wendy said.

'There are enough already, but there could be more. We'll see what Larry's got to say, and what Cojocaru tells us.'

***

Four men sat in a room heavy with the smell of ganja, the Caribbean name for marijuana. Their collective criminal empires overlapped and included the area covered by Challis Street Police Station: from Paddington in the east, through Bayswater and Notting Hill and Holland Park to the West, up north as far as

Ladbroke Grove and then south taking in Shepherd's Bush and Kensington.

The house where the men sat was not affluent Kensington or Holland Park, not even Bayswater, but Ladbroke Grove and a council property. The men, leaders of their various gangs, did not often meet, and then only on the street and mostly late at night when a dispute had to be settled that invariably resulted in violence.

Larry, who had smelt ganja many times before, had to admit to a feeling of light-headedness as he waited in an adjoining room. Across from him, two Rastafarians.

'They're not sure what to do with you, copper,' one of them said. Larry could see the glazed look in the man's eyes, the colourful and expensive clothes he wore. He could also see the knife in its sheath pushed down the front of his trousers. Larry knew him as Delroy Williams, a man who had spent time in jail for selling crack cocaine. He wasn't the only one in the house who had served time, but of the four leaders, only one had. He had been caught in an affray three years earlier, stating that a man had come at him with a knife and he had defended himself.

'Talk to me, that's what they'll do. They're scared,' Larry said. He had liked Rasta Joe, a former gang leader and part-time informer, when he had been alive, as big a villain as any of the four in the other room, but he had been charismatic too. Delroy Williams was not, and he had a surly manner about him and a hatred of the police.

'We're scared of no one,' Williams said, although Larry had the measure of the man. Williams was a coward, feeling brave on account of the four men in the other room, and the fact that he was spaced out on ganja. Larry chose not to indulge in any more conversation with him.

The other man in the room, a short, unattractive individual, was unknown to Larry. 'Your name?' he said.

'Liston Hayes.'

'After the boxer?' Larry said, assuming that he had been named after Sonny Liston, a former world heavyweight boxing champion.

'Never heard of him,' the man said.

'How long have you been here?'

'A couple of hours.'

'This country, I meant.'

'I was born here, up in Manchester.'

Larry looked intensely at the man, recognised the speech patterns, knew that the man had not been in England for more than six months to a year.

Liston Hayes was only small, but he had a look about him that Larry didn't like. As if he was a man who was more than he seemed, a possible murderer brought into the country in anticipation of the gang warfare which could explode at any time.

The door beyond opened, a man stood at the entrance beckoning Larry to enter. The smell from the room was stronger than where he had been sitting.

'Don't worry, Larry. We'll open the windows, put a fan on high for you. We don't want one of London's finest corrupted by us,' the man said sarcastically.

'Long time, no see,' Larry said. 'I thought you were doing five to ten in Pentonville.'

'I served three, out for good behaviour. I'm a model citizen now.'

'Not you, Marcus Hearne, you'll always be a villain.' Larry remembered the man from before his imprisonment: good-looking, polite and friendly, a dealer in drugs, a loyal friend to those he liked, ruthless to those he did not. In the end, he had served time for the drug dealing, not for the murders that had occurred on his orders. Personally, Larry liked the man; professionally, he did not. But he knew one thing: if Hearne was one of the four, then he would be safe. Outside on the street, two blocks away, an unmarked patrol car. Larry made a phone call. 'I'm fine. Don't stay where you are, leave,' he said.

Information was coming through from sources on the continent about Briganti's. Larry would use it if it helped with the discussion, keep it to himself if it would not. The information was dynamite, and the West Indians were touchy at the best of times; he didn't want them rushing to mobilise their people. He also did not want them arming themselves more than they already were.

***

'What did you find out?' Cojocaru, an even-tempered man most times, said. He was sitting in a leather chair in his penthouse. It was early in the afternoon, and the view out over the area was excellent, not that he could enjoy it, not that day.

'No one knows anything,' Becali said. He was standing up, as was Antonescu. To sit in the presence of their boss without his express permission would be a marked show of disrespect, almost a challenge to his leadership.

'It's the Russians,' Cojocaru said.

'None of our contacts have confirmed that,' Becali said.

'Your contacts are just the minnows, mine are the sharks.'

'What are you going to do?'

'I need to meet with them.'

'But why? If they don't like what you say, you don't return.'

'We need a neutral location where I'm safe.'

'In London?'

'Here's as good as anywhere.'

'But what do they want? We take whatever they send to us.'

'There's a bumper crop in Afghanistan of opium poppies. It'll drive down the price, and the Russians don't want to ship more to maintain their margin, they want to increase their profits.'

'But how?' Becali said.

'They'll go through England and Europe taking out whoever opposes them, drop the price of the drug, ensure more addicts, and then bring up the price. The strategy is good, the only problem is that they want to cut us out.'

'They've always hated us,' Antonescu said.

'They hate Romanians as much as we hate Russians. What's new? We can still do business with them.'

'How did you find out their plans?'

'Yuri Aliyev.'

'He's our primary contact with the Russian mafia?'

'Bratva if you want to use their Russian name. And yes, Aliyev has served us well, ensured that the shipments arrive on time and the quality is good.'

'Do you trust him?'

'Aliyev is one of them. He can't be trusted, but business is business. I need to convince those in their senior hierarchy that we are the best option.'

'Are we?'

'We have to be.'

'This meeting with the police, are we prepared?' Becali said. 'What will you tell them?'

'I will judge at the time how much they need to know and how much we confuse them. We weren't responsible for Briganti's, and I don't want them trying to pin that on us.'

'You don't intend to tell them it was the Russians who shot up the hairdresser's?'

'I may hint, I may not.'

'Are you sure it's the Russians?'

'Aliyev is the messenger. He could have lied. He may not even know the truth. A loyal lieutenant, no more, the same as you two. Now, what do we have to confuse the police and to give us time to negotiate with the Russians?'

Chapter 9

Isaac paced around Homicide; his team were letting him down, which meant that his leadership was not up to par, and he had seniors to answer to. Not only was DCS Goddard looking for results, so was Commissioner Alwyn Davies, and he was not a man to take no for an answer, let alone an 'I don't know'.

And that was precisely what the man had received from Goddard, although couched in police jargon, and now Goddard was in Isaac's office, and he wasn't looking happy.

Unable to avoid the confrontation, Isaac entered his office, a perfunctory shaking of hands before sitting down.

'Isaac, you're stuffing around on this one. A man can't just walk into a hairdresser's, shoot the place up, and then walk out of the door and down the street. Hell, he could have been sat across the road, a cappuccino in front of him, a cream bun in his mouth, having a laugh at you, at us.'

'We interviewed everyone in the vicinity. He wasn't there.'

'If this is someone from outside the country, then it's organised crime. Have you contacted Serious and Organised Crime Command?'

'I have. They're looking at that angle. Although, if it's the Russians, what happened is not their normal modus operandi in this country.'

'That's what's worrying everyone, even Davies. In the confines of this room, the man's a fool, but then we're both agreed on that. We answer to him, he answers to the politicians, the prime minister, the general public. If there's to be an upsurge in violent crime, he intends to stamp it out ASAP, with your help and mine, or without.'

'Has he threatened?'

'Not in as many words, but we know what happened last time. We've been out on our ears before, and it wasn't a pleasant experience. Returning me to Challis Street must have stuck in his throat when he issued the directive, and the man doesn't forget. And if you hadn't arrested the damn woman, being stabbed for your troubles, receiving a commendation for meritorious service, then you'd be out on the beat, back in uniform.'

'We brought the woman in,' Isaac said by way of defence. He realised that it was a lame response, but it was the only one he had. Goddard was right, Isaac knew that, but what could he say. Serious and Organised Crime Command was running with the information provided so far, including a detailed analysis of Nicolae Cojocaru and his organisation. Not that they had to do much as the man was well known to them.

And as for the others in Briganti's that fateful day, Guy Hendry's body had been released and buried, a moving ceremony according to the evening news on the television channel which had covered it, as well as a one-hour documentary on the life and times of the man.

Isaac had watched it at home with Jenny, his latest girlfriend, a willowy part-time model from a small town to the south of London, as white as he was black. One friend had commented that the two of them together was like a rerun of the Black and White Minstrel Show, popular in the sixties on television. Isaac had taken it in jest, Jenny had not, and the friend was now off the Christmas card list, and not welcome at the flat that Isaac and Jenny shared.

The documentary on Hendry, the subject of a meeting in the office the following day, had emphasised the man's achievements, the charities he supported, loved by his colleagues. It had not dwelt on his female conquests, only to say that he was beloved by many, male and female. Gillian Dickenson had been one, and she had been buried in the family plot in her hometown, a smaller gathering than for Hendry, but Isaac had attended, noted that the man's first wife, the mother of his children, had been there and she had shed a tear for the dead woman.

The body of Baz Hepworth, one of Peppe Briganti's employees, had been sent back to Australia, and that of Fred Boswell, the other stylist, had also been released. Briganti's body still remained in the mortuary, as did the bodies of Paul Waverton, Alphonso Abano, and Sal Maynard.

Richard Goddard, normally agreeable, could be irritating on occasions, and now was being just that. Isaac could sympathise with the man, as he had to deal with seniors who were not always pleasant, and most of them were driven by ambition and internal politics. Goddard was a master of both disciplines, but his ambition was being thwarted, as was Isaac's, and neither wanted Alwyn Davies's stooge, the incompetent boot-licker Superintendent Caddick, back in Homicide.

'This Russian angle? Is it likely to hold up?' Goddard asked.

'Eighty–twenty,' Isaac said.

'Your estimate or that of Serious and Organised Crime?'

'Both. I'm meeting with one of them later in the week. No point before as they're in contact with their counterparts overseas.'

'In Russia?'

'They prefer to deal through Interpol: more efficient, less bureaucratised, more unlikely to have a mafia man on the inside.'

'A problem in Russia?'

'There's big money at stake.'

'It's not much to go with. I'll hold Davies at bay for as long as I can, but any more deaths or shootings, and you know what happens.'

'I know. Not something any of us want, and non-productive. If it's Caddick who comes through the door, then all bets are off. He'll only stuff it up.'

'If it happens, then make yourself scarce and keep working on it. Policing would be a lot simpler if everyone was competent.'

'A lot simpler if we didn't have criminals either, but that's life. Whatever happens, the team in Homicide won't let you down.'

'I know that, Isaac. While you and Serious and Organised Crime are working on the eighty, make sure your team continues with the twenty. It may still be homegrown.'

'We're still following through on four of the bodies. Everyone's got skeletons, and the four have histories of wrongdoing. Three of them are minor, and Abano was a criminal, but of little note. We should wrap up our investigations into them in the next couple of days and then we'll release their bodies.'

***

It was late in the day when the phone call came through. Bridget answered the phone, took the message, and called the others into Isaac's office. Larry had been dealing with paperwork, entering his day's activities into his laptop; Wendy was doing the same, although her typing was woeful, and her spelling was suspect. She was pleased that Bridget would fix it up for her afterwards, a ten-minute job for her, an infinity for her.

Isaac looked at the clock on the wall. It was nine-thirty in the evening, another hour for him in the office. He'd been running through the investigation so far, messaging his contact at Serious and Organised Crime.

'It's serious,' Bridget said as she took the seat in the far corner of the office. Wendy sat down alongside her, Larry remained standing and leaning against the door.

'What is it?' Isaac said.

'A phone call from the Irish police.'

'Why would they phone us?'

'Seamus Gaffney.'

'He visits every few weeks,' Larry said. 'A family man who commutes to Ireland on a regular basis. Devoted to his wife, and I asked the Garda, the Irish police, to keep tabs on him.'

'They found his rental car five kilometres from the airport, Gaffney inside.'

'Dead?' Larry said.

'Two bullets to the head.'

'Cojocaru?' Wendy said.

Larry looked ashen-faced. 'First Rasta Joe and now Gaffney,' he said.

'Occupational hazard,' Isaac said. 'He probably found out something he shouldn't have. Any contact with him, Larry?'

'Not since the last time I met with him. If he had found out something, he was either keeping it to himself, or he was aiming to see who'd pay the most.'

'Assume the latter. Larry, get yourself over to Ireland. There should be a flight tonight.'

'It'll be tight. Bridget, update me on the way. Contact, phone numbers, and book a hotel close to where I'm heading.'

'Get to Dublin, rent a car. I'll place an order on the rental company, should save you some time.'

Larry left the office; Isaac phoned DCS Goddard to update him. 'Forewarned, forearmed,' Goddard replied. 'His death is not likely to be major news, or is it?'

'It's unlikely, but whoever killed him and for whatever reason is worried.'

'So are we. Cojocaru?'

'Too obvious,' Isaac said. 'And the man knows we've been keeping a watch on him. Bridget will check out the flights to Ireland, see if Antonescu or Becali have been there, although the man has others who could have killed Gaffney.'

'Stay with it. I'll consider how to keep the commissioner off our backs. The man's death in Ireland is another complication we could do without.'

'It means that someone's frightened. The question is what did he find out.'

Isaac turned to the other two in his office. 'We've got some work to do. Five minutes, get a coffee, and let's see what we've got.'

It was going to be a long night, and the meeting with Cojocaru was scheduled for the next day at a pub outside London. It had been intended for Larry to go with him, but Isaac knew that wasn't possible, and he wasn't going to cancel the meeting.

Upon her return, with a cup for him as well, he spoke to Wendy. 'How do you feel about meeting a vicious thug tomorrow?'

'He won't be the first I've met.'

'He makes the West Indians look like Sunday School teachers.'

One in the morning, the three left the office. An itemised list of questions to ask the master gangster and a file opened for Gaffney, although the man had been killed in another country so strictly speaking it was their case. Isaac had worked with the Irish police before; he knew there would be full cooperation between the two police forces.

***

Larry arrived in Dublin late, the last flight. He picked up his car at the rental company, a woman handing him the keys. 'The local police have been on the phone, so has a Bridget Halloran. There's a purchase order, and your driver's licence has been forwarded. No more to do, just sign on the dotted line,' she said.

'Thanks,' Larry said. It had been a long day, an even longer night. He found the car quickly enough, a local police car waiting alongside.

'Detective Inspector Hill?' the patrol officer, a ruddy-faced man carrying more than a few extra pounds, said.

'Yes, that's correct.'

'Fine. We've been asked to show you the way, save you trying to find it.'

With the patrol car leading, a late model Ford with a broad yellow stripe bordered by a thick blue line on both sides of the vehicle, it took fifteen minutes to make it out to where Gaffney had died. A Nissan, the same as Larry had rented, although his was green, Gaffney's blue.

'Nasty business,' Detective Inspector Buckley said as he shook Larry's hand vigorously, a bear-like grip.

'Not the first you've seen,' Larry replied. He liked the look of the man. It was well after midnight and the DI, although obviously well-primed at the local pub and expecting a night off, was alert and interested, and above all, an asset.

'The same as you, I suppose. Not that I expected to see Seamus like this. Harmless he was, although an idiot as a child, not much better as an adolescent. But as I said, harmless. Not the sort of man to offend anyone. You knew him?'

'As an informer, but you're right. I liked him in some ways, but he was into villainy, one step ahead of the law, and free on the street as long as he gave us the occasional titbit as to what was going on in the area.'

'What was going on?' Buckley said. 'I heard about the shooting. Your neck of the woods?'

'It was, and Gaffney was sniffing around. I assume he found out more than he should.'

'It looks professional. We found where the shooter had been, and he must have known Gaffney was on the way.'

'Which means advance information.'

'Someone back in London had tipped off whoever it was that did this. The man was regular as clockwork visiting. Every six weeks he'd be here, usually a Friday and then back to London on Monday.'

'You knew him well?'

'I came from the same village. I was even the best man at his wedding. I liked Seamus, and his wife, Sheila, is a lovely woman. Happy as can be, those two were, although an unusual arrangement. But then, I see my wife every night, and happy is not a word I'd use. How about you?'

'We're close. Mostly argue over money and my drinking, but apart from that, we get on well.'

'Goes to show, doesn't it? I have one Guinness, and I'm in the doghouse, although you didn't come all this way to hear me griping, did you?'

'Later over a Guinness we can talk, but for now, what do we have? Any evidence?'

'I've got the men in the dust coats on the scene seeing what they can find.'

'You mean the crime scene examiners?' Larry appreciated the man's relaxed manner, although he wanted answers. He needed to phone back to his DCI, knowing that the man would be waiting for his call.

'Yes, them. A good bunch, and if there's anything to be found, they'll find it. What we've got so far is a shot from a distance as the man slowed at the intersection, and once he'd veered off the road and into the ditch, the second bullet to the head.'

'The same as what happened at Briganti's.'

'What do you mean?'

'The person who killed those in Briganti's hairdressing salon shot the people at random with a semi-automatic, and then went around them individually and shot them in the head.'

'The same person?'

'It's a possibility.'

'The most obvious is usually the most reliable. Any idea as to height, weight, dark or light hair?'

'Dark hair, we've got a sample. Although in a hairdresser's, it's not so easy to be sure. Forensics are not willing to commit to it. If you've got anything here, they'll be interested. It's important to know whether we're dealing with the same shooter or someone else.'

'It sounds as though you've got a tough case over there,' Buckley said. 'Here, put on some protective gear, and we'll go over nearer to the car and where the first shot was taken.'

Larry phoned Isaac to update him, raised the possibility that the Briganti shooter was not on mainland Europe, but could still be in England, and as of six hours previously, in Ireland. Isaac phoned Bridget who issued an update to the points of entry into Ireland, the ferries and airlines, although the details were vague. The chance of apprehending a professional assassin by such an obvious tactic seemed remote. It was three in the morning. Isaac turned in his bed for another thirty minutes before deciding that sleep was going to elude him for that night. He got out of the bed, careful not to disturb Jenny who looked at him with one eye, said nothing, and went back to sleep. Isaac knew she'd not complain at his leaving the flat at such an hour.

Isaac arrived at Challis Street just before 4 a.m. to be greeted by Bridget. 'Work to do,' she said. He phoned Larry.

'Inspector Buckley, Ryan, is with me. He's done a great job. We're working with the crime scene team. We've got a hair sample, a shoe print, and a possible piece of clothing from where the shooter took the first shot. It could be the same man as at Briganti's, but we'll need Forensics to work overtime on this one,' Larry said.

'If there is the possibility of a gang war, then that's what they'll do. The murder belongs to the Irish police. Any issues?'

'Not here. We'll work together on this one. The inspector's a family friend of the Gaffneys. We're off to see the man's widow.'

'Do that, and then take a couple of hours to clean up and rest. Unless there's any reason to call earlier, we'll talk again at 10 a.m. We're meeting Cojocaru at 11.30 a.m. I'm taking Wendy.'

'I'll stay another day, follow through on the same shooter possibility. I'll aim to take the flight back to London late at night.'

'Time for a Guinness?' Isaac said.

'Buckley's fond of a drink. I'm sure we'll manage a couple.'

Chapter 10

It was early in the morning in Homicide and activity was at a high level, Larry having phoned from Ireland, although he had been instructed to get some rest and not contact them before ten that morning. Detective Chief Superintendent Goddard was in the office as well. The death of Gaffney in Ireland, the possible forensic evidence connecting the shootings at Briganti's and in Ireland, were at the forefront of the DCS's mind.

Commissioner Davies was watching closely to see how Goddard and his team were performing and whether he should bring in additional help. It wasn't his decision to make, but as Goddard said to Isaac, 'Don't wait for the man to follow procedures, and don't expect any civility from him. His skin's more important than those that died, and if there's to be warfare on the streets, he wants himself clean, he wants scapegoats.'

Isaac, a detective chief inspector, did not need the old and by now tiresome reiteration that the sword of Damocles hung over his head. Davies was a difficult man, but sometimes Isaac wondered if DCS Goddard wasn't using the man's name for effect, in an attempt to impose his authority and to sharpen up Homicide by using the name of another. Whatever the truth, Isaac was pleased when Goddard left the department and retreated back upstairs to his office.

It was still not eight, and Isaac and Wendy were on heightened alert, an adrenaline rush due to the impending meeting with the Romanian.

'We leave here at 10 a.m.' Isaac said. 'That'll give us plenty of time to get to the meeting point.'

'Where?' Wendy asked.

'Cloak and dagger on this one. Cojocaru's not given us the final destination. He's frightened that we'll get our people in there before and bug the place.'

'Would we?'

'I'll not jeopardise the meeting for the sake of incriminating evidence against the man. What's possibly brewing out there is more important than putting that man behind bars, or getting him deported back to Romania.'

'It's a golden opportunity. If the man's frightened of others, his guard is likely to be down. He could say something, not to us, but to others, that could give the courts enough to deal with him.'

'Serious and Organised Crime Command is interested in what's discussed, and they'll want a full report.'

'Are we wired? Or are our smartphones on record?'

'Not this time. We'll meet the man in the pub, but Antonescu and Becali will not be far away. They'll check us out first.'

'I thought it was just him.'

'It is. Larry met him in a pub full of patrons, but we have to go through this subterfuge.'

'Why?'

'It wouldn't pay for him to be seen talking to me, and we don't know who else is watching. The man's neurotic, we can't blame him for that. If others are coming in to threaten his empire, he'll be weighing up the pros and cons, making sure to tell us what we need to know, not the full truth. Larry says he's smart, so watch out for him manipulating the conversation. And above all, be agreeable with the man. We're there to solve nine deaths now, not to express an opinion about the malevolence of the man.'

'I'll not say anything,' Wendy said. She was not willing to admit that she was nervous. The man they were meeting had a bad reputation, and those in the area where he operated gave him a wide berth, some even crossing the street as he approached, others doffing their caps, standing to one side for him. She had not seen the man in the flesh, only checked him out through the police records. Nicolae Cojocaru, forty-six, formerly from Bucharest, Romania, although born about ten miles to the north. A list of convictions as a youth, and then, in his early twenties, the leadership of a group selling drugs. From there, a rapid rise in the criminal echelons until, at the age of thirty-two, he was one of the four major criminal leaders in the country. Suspected of widespread bribing of politicians, the police, and the judiciary, a dozen unsolved murder cases attributed to his name, but unproven. His move to England had occurred nine years previously on the election of a new government in Romania; the man who headed it was known to be honest, and he had campaigned on a platform of law and order.

Of the four most significant crime figures in Bucharest, two had been jailed, one had been killed in a police shootout, and the other, Cojocaru, was in England, and not intending to go back. Apart from two judges and three senior police officers, nobody else had been arrested in the purge against corruption in the country. The honest prime minister had lasted twenty-three months before a bomb under his car had ended his period in power. After that, the habits of the past returned, yet Cojocaru, according to an Interpol report, was unlikely to go back to his home country. A new criminal elite had arisen in the intervening years, and Cojocaru would have had to start afresh, to forge new contacts, to acquire politicians, judges and police officers to protect him.

Wendy put down the report and focussed on the current day. Larry phoned again, spoke to Isaac. The conversation was brief, and Isaac made no comment when he came out of his office and left Challis Street with Wendy. On the drive south, she asked him what Larry had said.

'He's just curious, disappointed that he'll not be there when we meet with Cojocaru.'

Wendy questioned no more, not sure that there wasn't more to the conversation. The final destination had been messaged to Isaac who had entered it into his GPS.

'I don't trust Cojocaru, and he could end up feeding us nonsense,' Isaac said. 'Larry's not so sure now that Gaffney and Briganti's are related. There are some differences.'

'Is that what he was talking to you about?'

'Sorry. I was distracted before. Alwyn Davies is sticking his nose in, and then we've got Serious and Organised Crime Command to update.'

'Superintendent Caddick?'

'Davies will use any excuse to get his man back, and in truth, we could do with some help, not Caddick obviously.'

'Serious and Organised Crime Command will be able to offer backup, more their case if Briganti's is proven to be the result of organised crime.'

'Cojocaru probably knows by now, although we can't be sure he'll tell us the truth.'

Wendy looked out of the car window: at the people driving to work or to the shops, the school children in their uniforms, heavily-laden backpacks containing their books. Every other child she could see had a smartphone and was busy texting. In her day, there had been no smartphones, no internet, no ability to send a message to someone around the world, or ten yards down the road. She missed those times: calmer, safer, more agreeable. A time when a child rode a bike to school with no helmet, no fear of abduction, and where the mother would be at home on the child's return after school, as her mother had been. But now, for most of those at the schools they passed, there would be an empty house, a meal in the refrigerator for reheating in the microwave, a computer in the child's bedroom for skyping, or Facebook, or for watching pornography. And now, she and her DCI were off to meet a thug, a man who prospered from the misery of others, a man who should not be in the country.

Sometimes, on the days when her arthritis troubled her, she felt that her time for policing had passed. Those were the times when she missed her husband the most, difficult though he had been in his final years with dementia setting in and an increasingly narrow view of people other than Anglo-Saxon and white. She knew what he would have thought of a Romanian gangster. It was a good job he was not in the car with them as they pulled into the pub car park.

'The Black Rabbit,' Wendy said as she looked up at the sign outside the building. 'Hardly seems appropriate, does it?'

'It depends who's the rabbit, him or us.'

Across from their car, Antonescu and Becali.

'They'll want to check us for weapons, recording devices.'

'We've no protection,' Wendy said. 'I don't like the look of the shorter one.'

'Crin Antonescu, a former wrestler, violent, and apparently he enjoys it.'

'I've read their files. The other one, Becali, looks more agreeable.'

'Socially, maybe, but he's a murderer. We don't think they were in Ireland with Gaffney.'

'Any reason why not?'

'They were in London four hours before the man's death, and two hours after. We've got witnesses who'll attest to that.'

'Reliable?'

'One was an off-duty policeman, the other, the publican of the Wellington Arms.'

'We're clean,' Isaac shouted across to the two men.

'Where's Hill?' Becali said.

'In Ireland. I've brought Detective Sergeant Gladstone instead.'

'What's in Ireland?' Antonescu said. He was standing on the other side of the car to Becali, alongside Wendy. She looked up at him; he, down at her. Neither smiled. Wendy could see that his eyes were too close together and his muscles bulged under a jacket two sizes too small for him. He reminded her of a Smurf, a cartoon that was still popular, but without the blue skin, and definitely without the smile.

The two police officers got out of their car. Becali patted down Isaac. 'Police business. I've left the phone in the car.'

'And how about you?' Antonescu said to Wendy.

'Clean.'

The man shrugged his shoulders and moved away.

'He's inside. Don't trick us or he'll not be pleased,' Becali said as the four walked towards the pub's low door.

'Don't worry. No one's coming if that's what you're worried about, and no one's listening in,' Isaac said. 'Let's hope Mr Cojocaru is going to tell us something. It was a long drive for just a drink.'

'What he tells you is not our business. We only follow orders,' Antonescu said.

Inside, the pub was typical of so many: horseshoes on the walls, old newspaper articles and photos of the area stretching back a hundred years and even longer. One picture of the pub, horses and carts outside, the men with their stiff collars and hats, the women dressed in their Sunday best.

'I've bought three pints,' Cojocaru said as he shook Isaac's hand.

Not wishing to be impolite, although not wanting to return the gesture, Isaac smiled and offered the typical, 'Pleased to meet you.'

'I though Inspector Hill would have been here.'

'He's in Ireland. Seamus Gaffney was shot.'

'I heard about it, tragic. I believe he was a friend of Hill's.'

'Not so much a friend, but Gaffney had his ear to the ground.'

'Too close. No doubt he upset someone, spoke out of turn.'

'This is Sergeant Gladstone,' Isaac said.

'Pleased to meet you,' Cojocaru said as he shook Wendy's hand. She thought the man pleasant, dressed as he was in a navy suit with an open-necked white shirt. He smelt of aftershave, the same one as her husband had favoured. 'You'll not want a pint, I assume. Let me get you something else.'

'Beer is fine,' Wendy said.

'No one's going to disturb us,' Cojocaru said. 'I've paid the publican to keep anyone else out, at least for the next hour.'

'Why here?' Isaac asked.

'Neutral territory. I prefer wandering eyes not to see us or to speculate.'

'Here is hardly secret.'

'I agree, but it's better than nothing. And besides, what I know is not that secret anyway. I just wanted us to meet and talk, a mutual problem.'

'Mr Cojocaru, if you don't mind me saying,' Wendy said, 'we don't have anything in common.'

'Under normal circumstances, I might agree. But I thought that if I scratch your back, you'll scratch mine. An English saying, I believe.'

'It is,' Isaac said, 'but Sergeant Gladstone's right.'

'Let me finish. I've had feelers out overseas, back in Romania and elsewhere. There's a group in Russia who are eyeing England and other countries for a major expansion.'

'Drugs?'

'Yes. They want to expand, cut out the middlemen, drive up the price. They're ruthless, and nothing or nobody will dissuade them.'

'This is England,' Wendy said. 'We will.'

'Unfortunately, the typical English resilience won't help you. Of course, you can stop whoever, but you know how English law works, how people think in general. A slow intrusion here and there, the occasional act of violence, the increased level of drug activity on the streets and people adjust. How many people are talking about Briganti's now? Not as many as on the day and nobody stops outside the salon. They just walk by, their faces glued to the screens of their phones, or earpieces listening to music.'

'I'll agree with you there,' Isaac said. 'But why should we work with you on this one? You're hardly a saint.'

'An honest businessman, if you want our meeting to continue.'

'Honest men don't concern themselves with criminal activities,' Isaac said, aware that he was testing the man, pushing more than he should, less than he would have liked to. He wanted the man in jail or out of the country, but for the present he was a man to be friendly with.

'I'll ignore your comment, a lady present. DCI Cook, there's a problem bigger than either of us, bigger than the London Metropolitan Police, and that's the Bratva. You know who they are?'

'The Russian mafia, the brotherhood.'

'They're well-organised, structured along the lines of a large business: a CEO, board meetings, lieutenants, rank and file hoodlums. And they're vicious.'

'Proof, names?'

'Briganti's was the starter. A test to see how the police would respond, your weak spots, your strengths, not that there are many of those.'

'Insults won't get you far,' Isaac said. He lifted his glass of beer and took a drink. He was aware that he needed to hold his own with Cojocaru, aware that the man was educated, able to converse in good English.

'Not insults, facts. What have you done so far? Checked out those in Briganti's, found out nothing, other than Abano was a criminal, two of the others used cocaine, and Hendry had good taste in women. While I, a man with contacts around the world, know more about the truth than you do.'

'Seamus Gaffney, relevant?'

'Not here. The man was useful to some, but he was an informer. His killer will be found in due course. You are aware of the gangs, the Rastas, as well as some others who are arming up, ready for a battle royal?'

'We were told they were not arming against the Russians, and what about this shipment? Do you know when it's coming in and how?'

'Believe me, Cook, I don't want this to escalate any more than you do.'

Wendy was not sure what to make of the man. On the one hand, he was pleasant, he spoke well, and he seemed obliging and generous in what he was telling them. Yet she had read his record: the violence, the torturing, the killing of others at his command.

'What do you want, Mr Cojocaru?' Wendy said. 'An amnesty, that we'll leave you alone for the duration?'

'Not me. I've done nothing wrong.'

'We'll not go further with that discussion,' Isaac said. 'But the Russians are disturbing. How do we find out more, and where are they? Who shot up Briganti's?'

'The name of the man is not important. It is the person behind the man, not the man behind the weapon. You know that as well as I do. I will give you a name, and we will talk again in two days.'

'The Russians are not going to be satisfied with our part of London,' Isaac said as he emptied his glass. The conversation was coming to an end.

'They're using us as the litmus paper, the toe in the water to check if the water's warm or cold.'

'Why us?' Wendy said.

'You'll need to ask them,' Cojocaru said.

Isaac knew, but he chose not to mention it. It was because Cojocaru was the funnel through which the Russians had been working. They were testing him, ascertaining whether he was up to the task or not.

'The name that you are going to give us?'

'Stanislav Ivanov. Check him out.'

Cojocaru shook hands with Wendy and Isaac and walked out of the door. Outside, he got into the back seat of his black BMW, Becali in the driver's seat, Antonescu alongside.

'What do you reckon?' Isaac said after the man had left.

'Charming, yet vicious. I wouldn't want to be on the wrong side of him,' Wendy said.

'He could still have given the order for Gaffney's murder. We need to know if that's the case. When Larry's back, the two of you check on Gaffney's movements, see if he saw or heard anything and if he was trying to set up a deal.'

'It'll not be easy.'

'That's why I've got the best team in Homicide,' Isaac said.

Chapter 11

Sheila Gaffney said little, her eyes red from crying. Ryan Buckley sat beside her, his arm around her shoulder.

'I know he was a rogue, but I loved him, he loved me, and he always had time for the children,' the woman said eventually. She had a happy look about her, Larry decided. Apart from the fact that she was pregnant, she was a short, roundish woman with red hair, rosy cheeks and a freckled face.

The house where the three of them sat was small, with no more than three bedrooms judging by the size of it, but it had a loved look.

'Your children?' Larry asked.

'They're not far away. The eldest, she's the most sensible, the closest to her father, is next door with her best friend. She'll be back here soon enough. The others are in the garden or with the neighbours. Seamus loved it here, and he was looking to come back on a permanent basis. Not that I had any idea how he'd fit in. He upset a few when he was younger, and they've forgiven him. But my Seamus wasn't the sort to stay at home.'

'Is that what he was planning to do?'

'He said it was. Something about how our future was going to be better. Not that I wanted anything to change. He's away for a few weeks, then back here for a few days. It was like a honeymoon every time, and now he's not going to walk in the front door again, is he?'

'Sorry, Sheila, but no,' Buckley said. Larry could see the man's genuine affection for the woman.

'Do you know who? I know that people could get angry with him, but killing someone, that's different, isn't it?'

'It is,' Larry said. 'Any enemies that you know of?'

'Not Seamus. Was he involved with crime in London?'

'On the edge. He was crafty, managed to avoid too much trouble. We let him go a few times with a warning, a swift kick up the rear end.'

'Literally?'

'Metaphorically. I used to meet with him occasionally, talk about this and that.'

'He gave you information for money?'

'He did.'

'I told him that it would get him killed, but he kept telling me not to worry, and it was only general knowledge that he was passing on.'

'Sometimes it wasn't. Easy to upset people doing that,' Larry said.

'That's what got him killed, talking when he shouldn't. Mind you, he never wasted his money, and he looked after us well.'

'We believe it was something more serious than that. Have you seen anyone suspicious around the house lately?'

'I should get you a cup of tea. Forgetting my manners. Seamus wouldn't like me doing that.'

'It's not important,' Buckley said.

'I must,' the woman said as she got up from her seat and left the room.

'You'd better go with her,' Larry said. 'Delayed shock.'

Five minutes later the two returned, Buckley carrying a tray with three mugs and a bowl of sugar, a jug of milk.

'Mrs Gaffney,' Larry continued after all three had settled again, 'we believe this was not a local with a grudge. If anyone's been around the house that looked out of place, we need to know.'

'Well, there was this one man looking for directions, a foreign accent and I didn't understand what he was saying at first.'

'Could you describe him?'

'Apart from the accent, he was about average height. I noticed that he limped with his left leg.'

'How was he dressed?'

'Smart. He wore a suit which was unusual for around here, apart from a Sunday.'

'Sunday?'

'Church. We're all firm believers around here, even if Seamus wasn't too keen. When he was back here, he came with me, never failed. Not so sure if he did in London. Probably not, I suppose. And he did like a drink, and he was close to the children.'

Larry could see the woman drifting. The initial tears had dried up. They were soon to be replaced by inconsolable anguish. After that, there'd be no more questions for some time.

'Mrs Gaffney, would you recognise this man again?'

'I would.'

Larry took out his phone and scanned through the photos of people of interest that he had on it.

'No, it's not any of them, although he looks similar,' Sheila Gaffney said, pointing at a picture of Crin Antonescu.

Outside, their collars turned up against a cold wind, Buckley lit up a cigarette, gave one to Larry.

'Was it him?' Buckley said, referring to the picture of Antonescu.

'We can prove that he was in London, and he doesn't limp. The person that Sheila Gaffney met may just have been a tourist.'

'We'll keep checking, but this time of the year the place is full of them.'

***

Isaac dropped Wendy off at Challis Street. She had work to do after their conversation with Nicolae Cojocaru. He continued on to New Scotland Yard, parking his car on the street outside, a police-parking designated spot. He walked through the security at the entrance, showed his warrant card and received a badge to display inside the building, before proceeding through the first door to the main building and taking the lift to the fourth floor.

'Isaac Cook, long time,' Detective Chief Inspector Oscar Braxton said.

'It's not often I get an invite to such a hallowed place,' Isaac replied in jest to a man he'd known for some years.

The two men, one black, the other white, sat down at a desk and spoke about old times, out on the beat, training, and what life had brought them both. Braxton, married with three children; Isaac, still single and hoping for the patter of little feet one day. Isaac could see that the man, a similar age to him, looked older by at least five years, but then, Braxton was a smoker and a drinker, and Isaac was neither, apart from the occasional social drink or when he was meeting with villains, as he had that day.

'Nicolae Cojocaru, slippery bugger,' Braxton said. 'We've been watching him, but he plays the game well. Apart from the deaths that occurred in his name, none proven, he maintains a low profile. We suspect him of being a major player in importing illicit drugs into this country, but he uses middlemen. Men who don't know who the others are, except over a phone, and the points of entry into the country change. And if they're storing the goods for any length of time, a factory unit on a weekly or monthly hire. With no actual contact linking back to Cojocaru, we can't prove anything.'

'How about his bank accounts?'

'We managed to gain access to one in the UK, but the money was legit. If he's being paid, it's offshore. The money moving around can't be spent that quickly, anyway.'

'Any reason?'

'What can you buy with it? A castle in Scotland, a Greek Island, a fleet of Rolls Royces?'

'Cojocaru lives well,' Isaac said.

'He's got enough businesses and property in London to justify his lifestyle. The man even pays taxes.'

Isaac realised that Braxton was expressing a personal view on the distribution of wealth. He thought it a naïve outlook for a man working in Serious and Organised Crime. Men such as Cojocaru, Isaac knew only too well, were not satisfied with sufficient; they wanted all they could get, a way of keeping score.

'He can't be the only player in this country,' Isaac said.

'He's not, but he concerns us more than the others. And he's been dealing with the Russians, but you must know that,' Braxton said.

'We do, but we're Homicide, not Serious and Organised Crime. If someone's murdered we're there, but drug smuggling and whatever else goes on in our patch is of interest, but not our primary focus. Briganti's is murder. Otherwise, it's up to you, and you're telling me you can't pin the man down.'

'Not entirely true,' Braxton said, irritated by the impertinence of someone from Challis Street, not the prestigious surroundings of New Scotland Yard.

'Sorry if I'm blunt, but I've just spent time with the man in question, and he gave us the runaround, gave us a name.'

'Everyone thinks we've got it easy,' Braxton said. 'They know who the criminals are, so they expect us to go out there and arrest them. But it doesn't work like that, you know that. Cojocaru can afford the best legal advice, and the prosecution, good men and women, are paid by you and me out of our taxes. This is not Romania or Russia or the Middle East where these ratbags come from. We can't just go and pick them up, put on a show trial, slam them in prison or make them disappear. We're accountable, and they know it. No doubt they have a good laugh at our ineffectiveness, but that's the way it is.'

'We have the same problem,' Isaac said. 'What about Stanislav Ivanov? Cojocaru gave me his name.'

'What do you know about the Russian mafia?' Braxton asked. An air of cordiality existed between the two men.

'Not a lot, other than they're organised and dangerous.'

'That's it. They are exceptionally well-organised, and they regard crime as a business, not as anything dishonest, and now, in Russia with so much corruption, they're thriving. Ivanov heads the Tverskoyskaya Bratva, one of the most influential of the crime gangs.'

'What does the name mean?'

'Tverskoy is a district in Moscow. Skaya translates as belonging to. The Tverskoyskaya Bratva was formed in Tverskoy. Most of the mafia gangs take the name of the place where they were formed or where they're based. Bratva, I assume you know what that means.'

'The Brotherhood, although not much brotherly love from what I've heard.'

'None at all, and if you're a member and in trouble, you're hauled before their executive. If found guilty punishment is swift. No chance of an appeal with them, no right of reply.'

'Tough justice,' Isaac said.

'Don't feel sorry for whoever's on the receiving end. They're bad news, and so far, we've kept them out, but now, if it's Stanislav Ivanov, we've got trouble.'

'Tell me about him?'

'He's well known in this country. Fifty-two, educated in Moscow at the Lomonosov University. A master's degree in economics, a bachelor's in English. The man speaks flawless English. No convictions against him and he has a dacha outside of Moscow, heavily fortified.'

'Protection?'

'Men such as Ivanov get neurotic about their own importance. He's only in charge as long as there are no pretenders to the throne in the wings.'

'Where does Cojocaru fit into all this?'

'We're not sure. He wouldn't be a pretender, and he's only a small cog in the wheel. But he's a weak point, and the Russians are making a move.'

'Any proof?'

'We have our sources in this country and overseas. Not that the locals know any more than we do, but overseas there is a power struggle between the various mafia gangs in Russia.'

'I'm interested in solving the murders. The possible incursion of the Russians only concerns me if it has some bearing, if it will precipitate more murders.'

'It will, you can be sure of that.'

'So what do we do?'

'Prayer might help. What we really need is for Cojocaru to open up. He does not intend to allow anyone to come in and usurp him. He'll be in contact with the Russians, but be warned, don't get too close, or you'll end up regretting it.'

'From Cojocaru?'

'He'll play it strategically. Have you seen any Russians?'

'We don't know who we're looking for.'

'Okay, I'll give you a rundown on who is who, as well as photos. We'll be monitoring the airports in case anyone comes in. But Ivanov is not a criminal in his own country, no one would risk saying anything to the contrary, and it's not likely to change. He's got those who could change his status in his pocket, and he visits England on a regular basis. He's got a house, more like a mansion, close to the River Thames in Richmond, a place in Bayswater. His wife comes for the shopping, he comes for Ascot and the football, but most of the time she's at one place, he's at the other indulging in what crime bosses do.'

'What's that?'

'High-quality women. Sometimes he brings them with him, sometimes he sources locally.'

'No crimes against him in England?'

'None, and if Cojocaru is right and Ivanov is planning something here, it's a frightening development.'

'Cojocaru only mentioned the name.'

'He must be scared if he's talking to you.'

'He's still dangerous.'

'He'll double-cross you or anyone else if it helps him,' Braxton said. 'Keep in contact, and be careful.'

'I will,' Isaac said. He needed to get back to Challis Street. Larry was back from Ireland, and he had to be debriefed, and the additional information disseminated amongst the team.

Chapter 12

Wendy continued with her investigations into the others that had been in the salon that day, placing emphasis on the four whose bodies still remained in the mortuary. She discounted Waverton, the banker, soon enough. The man had no criminal record, no known associates, and although he was financially sharp, there had never been any suggestion of anything untoward. With him out of the way, her focus turned to Sal Maynard, once again travelling out to where she had lived.

Time had moved on for the Maynards, not a close family, in that though it was only a few weeks since the daughter had been shot, there was a raucous party in full swing at the depressing flat in Stockwell. Wendy parked her car, careful not to leave anything inside that suggested it was a police issue, and walked up to the tenement, pushing past a group of youths attempting to look menacing, but looking stupid instead. Wendy took the lift to the ninth floor where it stopped with a shudder.

At the flat, Sal's heavily-tattooed older brother opened the door to Wendy's knock. 'Bad time?' Wendy said.

'It depends, doesn't it?'

'On what?' Wendy took two steps back as she didn't want to get too close to the man, who was clearly drunk.

'Are you here to party or to cause trouble?'

'I'm here conducting further investigations into the death of your sister.'

'Not partying, a shame. I like older women, more experienced.'

Wendy retreated from the door and back to the relative safety of her car parked on the street below. A teenage boy riding a bicycle, his shirt hanging out and a cigarette in his mouth, approached her.

'Are you here about Sal?' he said.

'Yes. What do you know about her?'

'Knowing too much around here only causes you problems.'

'It'll cost, is that what you're saying?' Wendy said.

'A man has got to make a living somehow, and you look as though you've got plenty.'

'Man? You should be in school.'

'What's the point? All they want to do is to teach us about other places, and how to spell and write and to add up. What use is that to me?'

'It'll get you a job.'

'Not me. I make enough.'

Wendy's two sons were a credit to her, both married with children and holding down good jobs, but the individual in front of her, no more than sixteen, was unlikely to make thirty, she thought, if he continued the way he was. His future, she decided, was either drugs or prison or both. Regardless, she needed to know what he was referring to.

'How much?'

'A good feed first, McDonald's will do. And five hundred pounds.'

'For what? To tell me that Sal Maynard didn't do much and the Maynards are criminals. Is that it? Or are you going to tell me that they robbed the local newsagents? I'm investigating Sal's murder, not chasing petty criminals.'

'It's more than that.'

'Very well. Fifty pounds and another ten for McDonald's. You can go on your own afterwards.'

'It's a deal. There's a park not far from here, down the end of the road, the second turn on the right. I'll meet you there.'

'If this is a trick…'

'It's not. It's good, you can trust me, and Sal, she wasn't such a bad sort. A bit stupid, but she would always talk to me, sometimes buy me a drink.'

'You're underage.'

'The publican doesn't worry too much, and besides, I go around the back. Sal deals with him, you know what I mean?'

'I'm not sure that I do. What's your name?'

'Ralph, although everyone calls me Ralphie.'

'Okay, Ralphie, you need to earn your money. The park or down at the local police station.'

'No deal. They know me down there.'

'And what will they tell me when I check with them?'

'They'll tell you I'm a liar and can't be trusted. But what do they know, stuck in that station of theirs? It's tough, and the police don't like it up here, and they don't like the Maynards, and they don't like me.'

Wendy could understand why. 'What's your surname?'

'I don't want to give it,' the youth said.

'Don't be stupid. You've told me your name is Ralph, and that you prefer to be called Ralphie. You ride a bike, you know Sal and the local pub, and you've got two earrings and I can see a tattoo in the shape of a cross on your arm, or I assume that's what it's meant to be. Did it yourself, did you? I'm sure the police could tell me your full name, where you live, the crimes you've committed, even the days you failed to go to school. Fifty pounds and a Big Mac is dependent on you playing ball with me.'

'Okay, Ralph Ernest Begley. Satisfied?'

'For the moment. Five minutes, at the park.'

Wendy phoned Bridget, updated her as to her movements, before driving the short distance to the park. Ralphie was waiting on her arrival, his bike propped up against a bench where he sat.

'You'll be seen,' Wendy said.

'That's alright. The others know I'm here, and I'm taking them all to Maccas afterwards.'

The highlight for the local hoodlums, McDonald's, Wendy thought but did not comment to the young man, knowing full well that he probably came from a dysfunctional home, his parents in and out of work, drinkers, and the father possibly with a criminal record. Ralphie's problem was that his outlook on life was an inherited trait.

'What do you have?'

'The money first.'

'If you think you can be smart with me, then you've got another think coming,' Wendy said as she opened her handbag, withdrew a small purse and handed over the money.

Ralphie looked at the money, the most he had seen in a long time, before stuffing it into the left pocket of his jeans. 'I saw Sal on the television. They said she worked in a shop,' he said.

'She sometimes did.'

'That's not all.'

'What do you mean?'

'Sal and me, we were friends. Nothing like what you're thinking, but we used to talk.'

'Why you?'

'I don't know. Maybe she saw that my life was similar to hers. She had ambition, did Sal. Not that she expected anything to change.'

'Why?'

'You saw Sal?'

'I saw her dead body.'

'Sal wasn't attractive. Heavy-boned she used to say, and she could hold her drink. She tried to better herself, but her family are trash. You know that.'

'I do.'

'Anyway, Sal told me about this man. It seems he fancied her, don't know why. That's her words, not mine.'

'Is this man important?'

'If Harry Maynard finds out that I told you, he'll find me and give me a good belting.'

'Why?'

'Harry is possessive. He regarded Sal as his property, not that he ever touched her. But Harry, he's bad news. Alex, the younger brother, doesn't do much, and the mother is a tyrant. I don't like her either. Strange really, that from that flat came Sal. If she had been pretty and slim, she could have made something of herself. Always had her head in a magazine about celebrities and movies stars.'

'An unhappy woman?'

'She was, but with this man, he used to pay her money, she was fine.'

'Prostitution?'

'Sal didn't think it was, but I saw him once.'

'Describe him?'

'Tall, foreign looking. Sal said he was from Europe somewhere.'

'Romania?'

'Where's that?'

'If you went to school, you'd know it was a country.'

'I've heard of Romans,' Ralphie said.

Wendy did not intend to give a geography lesson to someone who wasn't interested, and besides, she hadn't known a lot about the country before Briganti's and Cojocaru. And now, something about the Maynard woman. A woman who five minutes previously had been a bit player in the murders.

'Did Sal sometimes sell herself?'

'Harry, if he ever finds out it was me, he'll go crazy.'

'I'll not tell him it was you, but it's important. You want us to find out who killed her, don't you?'

'I suppose I do.'

'What does that mean?'

'I'm frightened. If they killed her, they could kill me.'

'Why?'

'I don't know. But I watch those programmes on the television.'

'That's fiction, this is reality. Sal wasn't the target, we're sure of that. But this man, he's important. Once again, was she selling herself?'

'Her mother did when she was younger, I know that. But yes, Sal was. Not often, not that she minded much. She would have done anything to get out of here. And those actresses in Hollywood, they're doing it all the time.'

'Ralphie, you need to get your head out of your backside and look around. What they write in the magazines and put on the television isn't fact, it's pulp for the gullible.'

'Sal believed it all, but then that was the way she was. Simple in some ways, smart in others.'

'Smart?'

'This man was promising to find her a place where they could meet, upmarket, with a concierge and all. She was excited, and she thought that he loved her.'

'Did he?'

'Not him. I saw him with her, the look on his face as he drove away.'

'Did you tell her?'

'Once I tried to, but she wasn't listening. And besides, I know who he is. I saw him on the television, standing not far from where she died. He was in the crowd.'

'You'd recognise him again?'

'I would.'

Wendy scrolled through the photos on her smartphone. 'That's him, that's the man that Sal used to go around with,' Ralphie said.

After Ralphie had gone, she made a phone call. 'DCI Cook's office, thirty-five minutes.'

Bridget hung up her end of the phone line and arranged for everyone to be in the office. Wendy had not told her what it was about, but she had known the woman for many years. Whatever it was, it was important.

***

Larry had attempted to leave Ireland, even getting as far as the airport in Dublin and checking in, returning the rental car on the way. The same lady who had taken his keys was surprised to see him standing back at the counter twenty minutes later.

'I'll need to extend. If you can use the same purchase order, it would be appreciated,' Larry said. He needed to be home, one of the children was not well, and his wife was fretting, but events in Ireland had taken precedence.

'I rented him the car,' she said.

'Who?'

'Seamus Gaffney. He's a regular, every six weeks, and he never misses one of the children's birthdays or a school open day.'

'How do you know all this? Larry asked.

'As I said, he was a regular. Sometimes you get to talking with the customers, and after so many years, we got to know each other well.'

'Strictly business?'

'Oh yes. Seamus was a family man, devoted to his wife. Not that I ever met her, but a good woman from what he said.'

Larry was anxious to be on the road as time was of the essence, but the clerk behind the counter had possible information. He could spare her a few minutes, and then he'd be off, returning to conduct a formal interview with her at a later time.

'He picked up the car from me the day he died. He was in a good mood, but then he always was when he came back to Ireland. I can understand that. I spent two years in England, not that I liked it that much. Apologies if I insult your country.'

'No apology needed. What can you tell me? What is there that would be of interest? Something has come up, I've got to go,' Larry said. His wife was on the phone, and she wanted to know why he would not be home that night.

'It was strange, not that I thought much about it at the time.'

'What was?' Larry said, eyeing the clock, running the car keys through his hand.

'I could swear he was being followed.'

'Any idea who? Can you describe the person?'

'That's it. I can't, not really. You tend to get an eye for people in this job, those who are going to feed you a stolen credit card, forged driving licence, those who should pay extra for additional insurance. Too many of them, I'm afraid. They rent a cheap runabout and then think it's a supercar or a four-wheel drive. And then they're back here with the vehicle claiming it was in that condition when they rented it, not that they get anywhere as they had a chance to complain at pickup, and we have photos before they leave. The insurance saves us a few arguments, that's all.'

'If you're so perceptive, how come you didn't figure this person?'

'Average height, average look, average clothes. It's as if he was experienced at blending in.'

'Professional, you might say.'

'Anyway, Seamus is off, and this person is agitating for his vehicle quickly. But if he's not booked ahead, or he's not on the database, it takes time.'

'Did he get the car?'

'He had to take one of the more expensive vehicles. Literally ran out of here, took off with his foot to the floor. The car's back here now, and there was no damage, so I assume he was a competent driver.'

'What luggage was he carrying?'

'Nothing special. A small suitcase, the type you can take on the plane with you.'

'His name?'

'It's on file.'

'English?'

'It's hard to tell these days, but yes, I'd say he was. Good-looking, if he wasn't so shifty.'

'Was he? How would you know?'

'It was him, wasn't it?'

'What do you mean?'

'He must have killed Seamus, such a nice man.'

'A nice man who saw and said too much,' Larry said, not elaborating on what he meant. 'I'll need you at the police station. I'll phone for a vehicle to pick you up. Is that okay?'

'Not really, but if it's important.'

'It is.'

Larry made a phone call, a patrol car arrived within five minutes. Larry left the office and jumped into the rental car. Twenty-five minutes later, he arrived at his destination. The crime scene was crowded with police officers, an ambulance, the crime scene examiners, the obligatory onlookers, the media. He flashed his warrant card at a police constable and was waved through. He parked back from the crime scene at a distance of twenty yards.

'I need to get up there,' he said to another constable who wasn't letting him through. 'It's important.'

'Not unless you're kitted up, it isn't,' the constable replied. Larry knew he was right, but it was urgent. Over to one side he saw one of the officers who had met him at the airport the day before.

'Can you get onto the crime scene team, get me some overshoes, gloves?' Larry said.

The officer walked over and gave him what he needed. 'We always keep some in the vehicle. It's tense here.'

'That's understandable,' Larry said as he ducked under the crime scene barrier. To the left of the road, a couple of floodlights. To the right, Ryan Buckley's car.

'In his driveway as he was coming home. You could be the last person to have spoken to him,' Fergus Turnley, the crime scene examiner, said after Larry had introduced himself and explained that he had only left the man a couple of hours previously.

Larry looked in the vehicle. Ryan Buckley was leaning back, his face covered in blood. His mouth was open, his eyelids still slightly open. Not far away, at the front door of the semi-detached house, a woman in her dressing gown could be seen. She was being held firmly by someone Larry assumed to be a neighbour or a friend. Larry remembered that Buckley had said that it wasn't a happy home, but the woman, thought to be the wife, looked sad, or maybe it was shock, or perhaps she had killed him.

Larry put the last option to one side; he knew that speculation served no purpose. The only known certainty was that Inspector Ryan Buckley, a man he had shared a Guinness with, was dead in his car, the result of a shot to the head at close range. The similarities to the murder of Seamus Gaffney were all too obvious.

Larry phoned Isaac to update him. They both kept the conversation short.

'If Seamus Gaffney and Buckley have been killed by the same person, that means the murderer knows you by sight,' Isaac said.

'I know, and I don't mind admitting it, I'm not feeling very comfortable at this time.'

'Work with the local police, keep us updated.'

'We might have a witness to the murderer, the lady at the car rental company. We'll go through the usual: photos of known criminals, the passengers coming into the airport, driving licence, address.'

'Get back here as soon as you can. The situation is becoming more difficult,' Isaac said.

'I'll need two days,' Larry said.

'No more. See if you can find out who it was, and why.'

Chapter 13

Ralph Ernest Begley, a distinguished name for such a worthless individual, Wendy thought, but it wasn't her call to make character evaluations. Her responsibility had been to follow up on Sal Maynard and to confirm if she had been tied into what had happened at Briganti's, even if that proof came from an individual who would quickly be discredited as a witness in a court of law. Wendy knew how a smart defence lawyer would work, the soft build-up, pretending to be the man's friend, lulling him into a sense of security. And then, the shift in tactics, the ability to convince the witness that it could have been another day, another time. And had the witness been drinking, or maybe taken drugs?

Wendy knew that Ralphie wouldn't stand a chance, and even if they questioned the man he had identified, it wouldn't hold up, certainly not enough for a prosecution, not even enough to hold the man for twenty-four hours.

Isaac, not so pessimistic as Wendy, saw it differently. It was the first definite link between the crime at Briganti's and one of the victims, and now the triangle had been completed, and one of Cojocaru's associates was involved.

Ion Becali at home, occupied as he liked to be on a day away from his boss with a bottle of whisky and a woman, didn't appreciate the knock at the door, the two police officers standing there, requesting his attendance at Challis Street.

'Give me two hours, and I'll be there,' Becali had replied.

Two hours later, Ion Becali walked through the door of Challis Street Police Station. He was dressed in a suit, a white shirt with a tie. Isaac looked at him, knowing full well that the man's sartorial elegance wasn't going to save him from stiff questioning.

As Larry was still in Ireland, Wendy was seconded to sit along with her DCI in the interview room. The time was 2.30 p.m. Becali's breath still smelt of alcohol, although he was sober, and his face wore a scowl. Alongside him, Jerry Zablozki, a lawyer known to Challis Street. The man was a Jew, third-generation English of

Polish descent. Outside of the interview room, Isaac liked the man: affable, open to discussing the law, his family; but inside, representing his client, the man wouldn't let anything pass. Isaac knew he would need to be careful.

Anything prejudicial or an inappropriate accusation would be noted by Zablozki, and if Becali came to be charged and standing up in front of a judge and twelve good people, the jurors, on a charge of murder, then Isaac's or even Wendy's statements would be used in the man's defence.

Isaac completed the formalities, informed Becali of his rights, the procedure to be followed. The man nodded his head, said yes as appropriate, gave his full name and address.

'My client regards his attendance here today as an affront to his integrity. He is an honourable and upstanding member of his community,' Zablozki said.

Isaac wanted to say the vicious and violent Romanian gangster community, but he did not. He merely said, 'Mr Becali is helping us with our enquiries. No charges have been laid against him, and we appreciate him coming here of his free will.'

'And if I hadn't?' Becali said.

'There are still questions to be answered.'

Zablozki turned to his client. 'Let it go. If you hadn't come, they would have obtained a court order, and you would have been regarded as a hostile witness.'

'I'm here,' Becali said. 'Let's get on with it.'

'Very well,' Isaac said. He had leant forward on his chair to assert his authority and to emphasise what he was to say. 'We have proof that you, Mr Becali, were meeting with Sal Maynard on a social basis.'

'What makes you think that? And yes, I know who she is.'

'It is necessary for you to state who she is, and what she has to do with my client,' Zablozki said.

Isaac knew the man was deliberately being obtuse.

'Sal Maynard was a young woman who was brutally murdered with seven others at Briganti's hairdressing salon. Mr Becali was meeting with her. The question is why didn't he tell us this before.'

Becali shifted uneasily on his seat. 'I meet with a lot of women.'

'Maintaining your image?' Wendy said.

'What image is that, Sergeant Gladstone?' Zablozki said.

Isaac gave Wendy a poke under the table, a 'keep quiet, don't bait the man' nudge.

'A man about town,' Wendy murmured.

'My client's personal activities are of no concern to the police or to anyone else. If he wishes to entertain a woman that's his prerogative. I'm sure you and your DCI would agree.'

'We would,' Isaac said. 'But the fact remains that we have irrefutable proof that Mr Becali and Sal Maynard were involved. We believe that the arrangement was commercial, at least on Mr Becali's behalf, although the information that we've received indicates that Sal Maynard was enamoured of Mr Becali, and even saw it as love.'

'Even if this was true, and we strenuously deny this, what has the woman's death got to do with my client?'

'Mr Becali was in the crowd outside Briganti's on the day of the shooting.'

'I don't deny that. I had heard about it, so I went down to look. Not that I stayed long.'

'Why not?' Isaac asked.

'I've seen shootings before.'

'In England?'

'Not here, but back home they happened from time to time.'

'And when you realised that it was a woman that you had been seeing?'

'If it was someone I knew, then she wasn't using that name.'

'Can you supply us with a list of names?'

'Not all of them, and sometimes they don't give a name. I don't spend time with them for their conversation. I saw a picture of the woman afterwards, not my type.'

'Plain, frumpish?'

'That's it. I like to spend a bit more. If you know what I mean.'

Wendy didn't appreciate the man's dismissive attitude towards a woman who had not met his ideal of perfection. She remembered back to her teens when she had been the plain Jane and she had hung around with the prettiest girl in the village, the beauty and her friend. Sure, it had made her feel better, and there was always the drunken throwaway who'd give her some of his time, even make love to her in the back seat of a car, or behind a hedge. But Wendy knew her history had been different, in so much as her parents had been good people who had loved her, and she had been good at school. And then she had joined the police force, met her husband and married, had children. But Sal Maynard had had none of that. She had been doomed from the start, and she had followed her mother down the path to despair, and she had died because of it.

'Our witness will state that you dropped her off at the block of flats where she lives,' Wendy said.

'I don't make a habit of dropping them anywhere, not the rentals.'

'Neither my client's behaviour nor his morality are of any concern to the police,' Zablozki said, conscious of Becali's derogatory view of women.

'We are not here as arbiters of his beliefs,' Isaac said. 'We are trying to establish that he had a relationship with Sal Maynard. That does not mean that he was involved in her death, although it is suspicious.'

'Assuming I knew this woman, why would I want her dead? I've nothing to hide, and believe me, she wouldn't have learnt much from me, or maybe the art of lovemaking,' Becali said.

Isaac could tell that the man was becoming obnoxious on purpose, a belief that he had the interview in his control. Isaac knew that was when people started to make mistakes and to relax their guard.

'Mr Becali, are you categorically denying any knowledge of Sal Maynard?' Wendy said.

'I deny nothing. If I had been with her, I can't remember, and as for dropping her off, where did she live?'

'Stockwell.'

'Not me. It's a dump up there, not my sort of place.'

'Your continuing denial does you no credit,' Isaac said. 'We will continue to check, and there are CCTV cameras across London. It may take some time, but if you were with Sal Maynard, here or in Stockwell, we will find proof. Your visit to this police station will not be so cordial the next time.'

'Is that it?' Becali said. 'I've got one on the boil. I'd like to get back to her if I may?'

'Plain and frumpish?' Wendy said. She couldn't resist another go at the man.

'Beautiful and expensive,' Becali replied.

Isaac wrapped up the interview. Becali left, a car waiting outside for him. Wendy retreated in disgust back to Homicide and her desk. Zablozki came up to Isaac as both men stood outside the police station. Isaac had needed the fresh air after an odious encounter with a man who was known to kill people, although Sal Maynard seemed unlikely. He had been disgusted by Becali's dismissive condemnation of and disinterest in the woman, even if she had been part of life's flotsam. Whatever she had been, she deserved better in death.

'DCI, you're wasting your time with Becali,' Zablozki said. A short man, he barely came up to Isaac's shoulders. On his head, a kippah, or what most people referred to as a skull cap.

'I hope they're paying you well. It's not over yet.'

'Maybe I shouldn't mention it, but the rumours on the street are talking about the Russians. Any truth in it?'

'It's part of our investigation. I assume you're not too fond of them.'

'They were ruthless in my homeland. The reason my grandfather came to England. He was penniless then, worked hard, a lot of prejudice back then, still is in certain areas.'

'You've done well.'

'I'm English through and through. I took advantage of all this country has to offer. If the Russian criminal class is coming, I'd not like to see it.'

'Nor would we. What do you know of the Bratva?'

'The Russian mafia. Not a lot, only that they're ruthless.'

'Cojocaru's frightened.'

'DCI, we're heading into areas we shouldn't discuss. I'll bid you goodbye.'

As Zablozki walked away, Isaac shouted to him. 'Your client?'

The man turned around and smiled.

Isaac knew that his position was easier than Zablozki's. He had no illusions about guilt, all he had to do was to prevent further deaths, and find the culprits of those that had already occurred.

Chapter 14

Nicolae Cojocaru knew the man sitting opposite him, not personally but by reputation – Stanislav Ivanov.

Cojocaru had wanted the meeting to occur in England, Ivanov had not. A villa in the South of France was not of the Romanian's choosing, but he had had no option. The command had been given, and he had obeyed. To have not met with the head of the Tverskoyskaya Bratva would have been an affront, and as had often been with others, a death sentence.

Cojocaru studied Ivanov, careful not to be too obvious, aiming to gain an understanding of a man who had a fearful reputation. Cojocaru was nervous in his presence, the intended effect of someone who had the earthy look of a man of the soil, but clothing of the finest cut.

Surrounding the villa, there were expansive gardens. At the perimeter of the property, a high wall protected it from the view of those outside. Every fifty yards along the wall there was a man dressed in a suit, a Kalashnikov held firmly across his chest. The villa was a fortress and he, Nicolae Cojocaru, was inside it.

So much for a neutral location to hold discussions, Cojocaru thought. He was cornered, as was Antonescu. The squat man sat resolutely outside the room where the two crime bosses met.

'You have handled our business successfully for the last six years, but now there's a need to change,' Ivanov said. The message was clear. Do what I say, and you will survive. If you don't, you will die.

'Why the need to change?'

'Nothing is static.'

'Why here? Why not in London as I suggested?'

'I decide what happens. You will do what I command, or you will not see London again. Do I make myself clear?'

'You do,' Cojocaru said, seething at the way the man was dismissing him as if he were no more than a cockroach to tread under foot. He wanted Antonescu to come in from the other room and to shoot the man in the chest, but he knew that was not possible. In London, a possibility, but not in France, knowing full well that Crin Antonescu was unarmed and in the company of two of Ivanov's men.

'There are some who say that we should just take over, but I do not agree.'

'Tell me what you want. We have handled the distribution for you up till now.'

'You're a businessman. It's a scale of economics. We, the Tverskoyskaya, can lower the costs, increase the price, maximise the margin. You, Nicolae Cojocaru, cannot.'

'We have suppressed the competition.'

'Only in your area, and what are they, a bunch of spaced-out junkies from the Caribbean, no more than a handful of brain cells between them.'

'We agree, then.'

'Not on what is important. You've killed a few, frightened the others, no more than sheep, but what about the police? Are they in your pocket?'

'Some are, but England is not the same. They still have their rules and regulations, and most are incorruptible.'

'Then get rid of them. If you don't, we will. And what about that dwarf outside?'

'Crin Antonescu. He was a wrestler, I'd trust him with my life.'

'That is all well and good, but does he kill for you?'

'He has and often.'

'We showed you what we are capable of. Would he have been capable of that?'

'Was it necessary?'

'A man with morals. You'll not go far. I don't think we can use you,' Ivanov said as he raised himself from his seat. 'It seems another example is needed.'

Ivanov called to the other room. A bloodied Antonescu was dragged in, unable to stand without assistance.

'Will you work with us or will you die here, Cojocaru?' Ivanov said, pointing at Antonescu.

Realising that he was cornered, Cojocaru meekly replied, 'We will work together.'

Ivanov pulled a gun from inside his jacket and handed it to the Romanian. 'A sign of your loyalty. This way, I will know that you mean what you say.'

'Not Crin. He's been loyal to me, almost a friend.'

'There are no friendships in the Tverskoyskaya Bratva, only blind loyalty. Are you loyal?'

'I am,' Cojocaru said. He raised the gun and walked over to Antonescu. 'Sorry, my friend, I must do this.'

The former wrestler, then gangster, and now a victim, said nothing. Cojocaru pointed the gun at the man's heart and pulled the trigger.

***

Larry met again with the lady from the car rental company. It was surprising how upset she was.

'I saw him, the man who killed Seamus and now Inspector Buckley. I could have prevented it if I had reported the man.'

'Reported what? Larry said. Alongside him was Inspector Annie O'Carroll.

'You were not to know,' Annie O'Carroll, a career police officer, fifteen years in the Garda, and highly experienced, said. After Buckley's death there was an agreement with Buckley's and

O'Carroll's superintendent and DCS Goddard for the two police forces to work together, a joint sharing of the case, given that the two murders had occurred in Ireland, yet the initial investigation remained in England.

The consensus was that the two men had been killed by the same man, although that was still awaiting final confirmation from Forensics and the crime scene examiners.

Seamus had been shot twice, the first with a rifle from a distance, a skilled shot. Ryan Buckley's shot had not required a great deal of skill, just the knowledge of where the man would be and when, the nerve to approach his vehicle in a lighted area and to pull the trigger. Buckley's street had been residential, and no CCTV cameras were nearby, although a person out late at night walking his dog had seen a car driving away at speed at the time of the murder. The description hadn't been good, only that the vehicle was medium sized, white or yellow, and the driver wore a cap.

The Garda, like the London Metropolitan Police, regarded the death of one of their own as a crime of the highest seriousness, even more so than the death of Gaffney. Larry could understand the sentiment, having seen one of his partners die at the hands of a crime syndicate, a hit and run as he had crossed the road outside the police station.

'It doesn't pay to dwell on what might have been,' Larry said to the distraught woman. 'I could have had another drink, and who knows, Ryan Buckley might still be alive. What is important is that we apprehend whoever did it. Now, let's go back over what you told me. You said that the man was in a hurry to follow Seamus.'

'I did.'

'Are you sure it was Seamus? It could have been that the man was late for an appointment.'

'No, it was Seamus, I'm sure of it.'

'Why?'

'He wrote down the registration number when I gave the car keys to Seamus.'

'Assuming you're right on this, let's go back over what he looked like. And what about the vehicle he borrowed.'

'He returned it soon after Seamus died. He only had it for five hours, paid the full day rate.'

'We've checked the licence he showed you. It was stolen two months ago. Did you check the photo on it with the man?'

'I think I did, but I may have just taken a note of the name, the date of issue, the date of expiry. That's what the insurance people want.'

'The picture on the licence and the man could have been different?'

'I would have taken a cursory glance, but every day there are a lot of people renting, returning, extending. His insistence for me to hurry up didn't help.'

Larry could see that the seemingly unflappable woman who stood behind the counter was actually a nervy woman. He wasn't sure how much credence could be given to her testimony; however, the stolen driving licence was of concern.

'Not conclusive,' Inspector O'Carroll said. A red-haired woman in her forties, Larry had to admit to being impressed by the way she handled herself. Ryan Buckley, a hearty, friendly man had not impressed him. Sure, he had been competent at Seamus's murder scene, even handled himself well with the man's widow, but he had not had the attention to detail, the enthusiasm Larry expected.

'He wasn't the easiest,' Mrs Buckley had said when Larry met her. 'Sometimes we didn't talk for a few weeks, not that I can blame him totally. We're both fiery, and Ryan would drink too much, and then there was the occasional smell about him.'

'What kind of smell?'

'Another woman.'

'Any idea who?'

'I never asked, never wanted to know.'

'An unusual reaction,' Larry had said.

'I can deal with ignorance. The truth would have eaten at me. Not that it mattered, not after the first few times, and he kept to his room, I kept to mine.'

'You weren't sleeping together?'

'Not for four years. I suppose he had to do something about it, but I would have preferred us to be closer.'

'Then why weren't you?'

'It just became a habit, him and me, and now someone's killed him.'

'Anyone you can think of?'

'It'd be better if you ask down at the police station. There are plenty in prison because of him.'

After Sheila Gaffney, Larry couldn't help but make the comparison. Sheila was soft and comforting, even in her distraught state; Buckley's wife was not the same. A similar age to the other woman, she had maintained her figure, and it was clear that her appearance mattered to her more than it did to the other woman. He could warm to Sheila, but not to Dervla Buckley, a woman who had a husband that strayed. Larry resolved not to think badly of Ryan Buckley and to assist Inspector Annie O'Carroll to the best of his abilities. But London was where he needed to be, and even if the murderer was still in Ireland, the Irish police were as competent as those at Challis Street.

It was after midnight when Larry arrived back at his home in London, his wife waiting for him, a hot cup of tea and a meal. Not that he needed either, he was just glad to be home. For now, he would forget all that had occurred and savour his wife, and in the morning, it would be him that drove the children to school. He realised that if his wife was sometimes demanding and difficult, she was still the woman for him. He gave her a kiss, had a shower, and went to bed, asleep within five minutes.

***

Cojocaru arrived back in England no more than two hours after Larry. For the gangster, there was no welcome home by a loving wife, a meal on the table. All that he could look forward to was his penthouse flat with its view of the River Thames. Suddenly it did not seem so important. He made a phone call.

'The police are fishing,' Becali said on answering.

'They've got nothing. My place, twenty minutes,' Cojocaru said.

Becali wanted to say he was busy, but the tone in Cojocaru's voice told him that the female company he had was less important than a direct request from the man who had saved him from a dismal life in Romania.

'Antonescu is dead,' Cojocaru said as Becali walked through the door at the penthouse.

'How?' Becali said as he instinctively headed to the drinks cabinet to pour himself a whisky, another for his boss.

'They killed him in front of me, an example of what will happen to us if we don't comply.'

Becali knew that he should feel sad for the dead man, a colleague and someone who could always be trusted when there was violence to commit or murder to carry out. It was a time to say a few kind words about him and to reflect on the good times, the benevolent and generous acts he had committed, his goodness, but Becali could not. He could only remember the negatives, the Jamaican Rasta they had held down while they forced the man to give the names of those who could threaten Cojocaru, their strengths, their weaknesses, who they loved, where they lived. The man had said plenty before Antonescu had taken a brick and smashed it against the man's head. Apart from that, nothing came to mind. No times of sheer jocularity with the man, when both had been at ease with the world, and now he was dead.

'But why? We could have helped them.'

'We can and we will. The situation is difficult, and now you, Ion Becali, must raise yourself up and work with me. We are no longer the masters of our destiny, and what happened to Antonescu could happen to us.'

'We are doomed, you know that.'

'Our only hope lies in preventing the Russians from taking control, but I don't know how.'

'You spoke to the police. They could help.'

'They cannot stop this. Set up a meeting with the West Indians, let them know that the situation has become more serious.'

'Briganti's, did Ivanov admit to it?'

'Yes. It was a warning to us and to others.'

'I was hauled into Challis Street,' Becali said.

'Why?'

'One of my women died.'

'Zablozki?'

'He was there. They couldn't hold me, although they were trying to make a case out of it because I was seen outside her place, and then in the street outside Briganti's.'

'What is so important about her?'

'She was in Briganti's when it was attacked.'

'Hendry's woman?'

'The other one.'

'Why? You can afford better.'

'Sometimes, I fancy them that way. Reminds me of the old country when my choice was limited.'

'Why eat peasant food when you can afford the best?'

'It may be better in the old country for me now,' Becali said. A wave of nostalgia flowed over him, even a tinge of remorse that Antonescu was dead. He could not help but feel that Nicolae Cojocaru was not telling him the full story; the man never had in the past, only issuing commands. But now he was talking to him almost as an equal. Regardless, he would set up a meeting with the West Indians, knowing full well that they would be suspicious.

Chapter 15

Larry sat in a café on Portobello Road. It was early in the day and whereas he had often been there for breakfast, now it was for a meeting with Marcus Hearne, one of the four at the house where they had met with Larry, put forward their concerns, even their willingness to open up on what they knew, what was happening. They had been worried then, and now Hearne admitted that they worried more.

'It's like this,' Hearne said. 'We met with you that day, told you what was going down, and how Cojocaru had taken over.'

'Not enough to bring the man in for murder,' Larry said.

'You'd need witnesses, a body.'

'And neither of them is likely.'

'That's why we brought you to the house.'

'Almost poisoned me, though.'

'Medicinal,' Hearne said, a wry smile on his face, the only sign of ease in the man. Larry couldn't warm to him in the same way he had to Rasta Joe, the beer-drinking Rastafarian. Larry, out on the street and ferreting around, heard plenty, always without proof. He knew for instance that Marcus Hearne was a murderer and that he had killed a man eight years previously in a vicious gang fight on a vacant block of land not far from Regent's Canal. It had been a settling of grievances between two rival gangs as to who controlled which part of the area. Larry would have said the police, if asked, but the gangs considered themselves masters of the area, although that had been before Cojocaru.

'I didn't feel any better for it,' Larry said. He ordered a coffee for himself, as well as breakfast. The importance of the meeting with the gang leader had exempted him from Homicide's early-morning meeting.

'We're willing to work with you on this,' Hearne said.

'You told me that before, but I don't remember anyone coming forward with anything worthwhile.'

'There wasn't much to tell you. After Briganti's, it went quiet.'

'There's always something happening, and you know it.'

'I'm not an informer.'

Larry felt no need to comment. Hearne had served time in prison before; he would be back there again, and if he, Detective Inspector Hill, had to be the person to arrest him then so much the better.

'Cojocaru, is that why we're here?'

'You know it is. What happened to Antonescu?'

'We don't know,' Larry admitted, not mentioning that it was known that the missing man had left England with Cojocaru and not returned. The French police were helping, at the request of the Met, and Braxton at Serious and Organised Crime was interfacing with Homicide.

'He's dead.'

'How do you know?'

'We don't need proof.'

'Do you know why?'

'Don't go wasting your time on him. He's not worth it.'

'It's still murder.'

'According to you, and what about Cojocaru wanting to meet with us?'

'When?'

'One day's time, a location of his choosing.'

'And what do you want me to do? Come to the meeting?'

'Of course not. But if we don't return, we want you to know about it, who'll be there and where.'

'You suspect a trap?'

'We do. Cojocaru never consulted with us before. All he did when he took over was to start killing anyone who got in his way. The man has his back to the wall now, and he wants our help.'

'If you let us know where and when we'll keep a look out for you. But you've got to level with me, no playing me for a sucker.'

'Not this time. If Cojocaru is going to issue ultimatums, it's going to get nasty.'

'And you and the others will be at the meeting unarmed and without backup.'

'We have no option.'

'I need something from you.'

'Name it.'

'Ion Becali and Sal Maynard, one of the women who died at Briganti's. We know he was messing around with her, although he denies it.'

'What do you suspect?'

'It's possible that Becali was involved. Possibly used her as a decoy. The woman was susceptible to the man's charm, saw it as love. He could have spun her a story about robbing the place. We don't have proof of anything, and it may be nothing, but we need to know if there was any more to it.'

'Becali hedging his bets, playing both sides?'

'Find out what you can and let me know. I'll protect you the best I can, but once the threat's been removed, I'll be after you for the crimes you've committed.'

'I'm not admitting to any.'

***

Two in the morning, Inspector Oscar Braxton phoned. Isaac took the phone call. 'Not too late for you, is it?' Braxton said.

'That's fine. I've not heard from you for a while,' Isaac said as he got out of bed, not wanting to disturb his girlfriend, and went into the other room. Instinctively he put the kettle on to make himself a cup of tea, knowing full well that a phone call at such an hour meant only one thing – developments.

'I'll do it,' Jenny said as she came into the room. Isaac had had problems with other romances, when the hours he worked, the midnight phone calls, had been something they said they could deal with, but none had, not until Jenny. She understood and he was grateful.

Isaac looked out of the window of the flat, saw a few lights in the other flats in the building, a couple arm-in-arm on the street, a drunk slowly making his way home. It was remarkable, he thought, that one of the world's major cities could be so quiet.

'Are you still there?' Braxton said.

'Yes. Just waking up.'

'Easy life at Challis Street, nine to five.'

'I wish.'

'Don't worry. I won't tell anyone you've got a cushy number.'

Isaac remembered the light-hearted repartee of the man from when they had first met years before. He took Braxton's comments in the spirit they were given.

'We followed up on Cojocaru in France. Disturbing news.'

'Give me the details.'

'Stanislav Ivanov.'

'I gave you the name,' Isaac reminded him. 'Cojocaru gave it to us, told me that he'd contact me in a couple of days, but never did.'

'Cojocaru and Antonescu were picked up at the airport in Marseilles and transported to a villa along the coast.'

'How do you know this?'

'Our counterparts in France keep a watch out for anyone of concern.'

'Cojocaru?'

'Not him. Ivanov has a villa down there. Surveillance picked up one of his cars at the airport and took a photo of the two men getting into it. It didn't ring a bell at the time, not a big one anyway. After we contacted them, passed on the details, they checked further. The car entered through the gates of the villa twenty-five minutes after leaving the airport.'

'Ivanov inside the villa?'

'He was, and some of his men. The French know he's got weapons in there, not that they can do much about it.'

'Why?'

'Model resident. He doesn't break any laws down there, uses it as his primary residence. Too hot, not the climate, in Russia, and he's always under threat of assassination. Makes sense if you're Bratva to keep out of the country.'

'Listening devices?'

'Not in the villa, and the area's been swept by Ivanov's men. Anywhere that could have been used to eavesdrop has been removed, including a couple of houses where the residents were obliged to sell.'

'Or else?'

'That's it. Anyway, Cojocaru leaves the villa after fifteen hours. He's on his own, and the same car drops him off at the airport. That's all we know.'

'Antonescu?'

'He's not been seen since.'

'Larry Hill's been told that he's dead.'

'A reliable source?'

'Not one hundred per cent, and there's no way whoever told Larry would have been in that villa.'

'Unless Antonescu appears we'll assume that he is,' Braxton said. 'The ball's in your court. Find out what's going on. And one other thing, a shipment of weapons was intercepted in France.'

'Forwarding address?'

'Cojocaru, not that it was on the manifest documents, but we know of a few aliases and how they get the drugs in.'

'Which means there's another shipment that you've missed.'

'The quantities indicate something major. You'd better get extra people on the street.'

'We're working on it.'

'Okay. I'll let you get back to sleep,' Braxton said.

'Not much chance of that now.'

***

Inspector Annie O'Carroll continued with the investigation into the deaths of Seamus Gaffney and Inspector Ryan Buckley. Forensics had given a ninety per cent probability that the two men had not been murdered by the same person. No gun had been found at either location, even after dredging the local waterways and scouring through the usual places where they could have been dumped.

Feeling the effects of being a woman in a male enclave, the eyes of others on her performance, she phoned Larry in London.

'Any chance of you coming back here?' she said. 'Ryan Buckley's death is professional, and we've no leads. Seamus Gaffney's is probably local.'

'What about the car that followed Gaffney from the airport?'

'Kathleen Pearse from the rental company has proven to be an unreliable witness. We found the driver here. He had dropped the car back at the airport but didn't catch a flight. He's in custody for a burglary he committed four years ago. We had him on our radar, that's why the false driving licence, the bogus address.'

'The reason for him hurrying off?'

'His mother was on her deathbed. He got there five minutes too late. Still, once we caught up with him, we had to arrest him. No doubt he'll be allowed to attend the funeral.'

'Which means Seamus Gaffney is still unsolved, and no leads.'

'I'm not getting a lot of help from my colleagues with Gaffney, plenty with Ryan. And we can't assume that the man had an English accent, doesn't hold weight now.'

'Not really. If he were Romanian, it would help.'

'Not that I'd know Romanian from Bulgarian or Greek,' Annie O'Carroll said.

'No one would. If we could link it to Cojocaru and his men, it would be a bonus. Although one of them is not around now.'

'What happened?'

'Went on a trip to the south of France, never came back. Serious and Organised Crime is putting him down as missing in action, presumed dead.'

'Murdered?'

'Poetic justice if he is. There's an attempt to bring in a large shipment of weapons from the continent, and the gangs are nervous, even meeting with Cojocaru. And then we've got Stanislav Ivanov not far behind.'

Larry had to admit to enjoying his conversation with the Irish police officer, but unless the situation changed, he'd have to stay in London.

Wendy had spent more time with Ralphie; his family, not as dysfunctional as Sal's, although still uncaring, had not impressed Wendy when she had met them. His father lounged in a well-worn chair, the television showing the horse races, his phone at his side to place the bets. Apart from that, the man did little other than complain about how they had laid him off at work, a menial cleaning job, on account of his bad back, and he was going for worker's compensation for the permanent injury that he had suffered. Not that Wendy had seen much of the injury when the man jumped out of his seat when his horse had won.

'See, I told you that I could pick them,' he said to his wife, Ralphie's mother.

'About time,' the only words to emanate from the woman. Even when Wendy had questioned her about Sal Maynard, her replies had been monosyllabic, just yes and no. Ralphie's father had been more forthcoming in saying that Sal's mother was just a tart and the daughter was no better, just a useless lump of lard. Wendy could only sympathise with Ralphie, and she vowed to help him if she could.

Outside the house, Ralphie had been apologetic, although his vocabulary was interspersed every few words with a four-letter expletive.

'Did Becali kill Sal?' Ralphie asked.

'We've no proof.'

'You don't need proof to know whether he did or not.'

'We don't think so. And whatever you do, keep well away, the man's violent. I don't want you getting involved.'

'It'd be more interesting than around here.'

'It probably would be, but Ralphie, mark my words. Becali is not a person to be trifled with and never approach him. You must promise me that,' Wendy said, speaking to him as she would have her own sons when they had been younger.

'I won't. Promise.'

Wendy left Ralphie, having gained no more information. She had only come back to the area after Becali's importance in the investigation had risen. With Antonescu out of the picture, the murder of Buckley could have been at Becali's hand. A window of opportunity had been discovered for the second murder in Ireland, long enough for the Romanian to have made the trip over, probably using a false name and identification. And no need to use a rental car, as local transport, especially the train from the airport to a station, no more than a five-minute walk from Buckley's house, ran at regular intervals.

Becali was front and centre, and at Challis Street, the team met again. This time in the presence of DCS Goddard. The man was not happy, not that anyone else was, and an air of inadequacy had settled over those present. A team honed through numerous murder investigations, sometimes challenging, sometimes procedural, but now the clues were too few and far between.

Larry was the first to speak, that is after Goddard had given his usual speech about working 'the hours required, I expect everyone to do their bit, the eyes of the commissioner are on us'. They had all heard it before, and it hadn't been necessary, but Isaac could see that the man was wearying of the battle to keep Commissioner Alwyn Davies out of Homicide, as well as his man, Superintendent Caddick.

'Inspector O'Carroll believes the hit on Ryan Buckley was professional. If it was, then Becali's a possibility, and what about him and Sal Maynard?'

'I feel sorry for the woman,' Wendy said. 'She had a dreadful home life, and then scum like Becali treat her like a piece of meat.'

'We're not here to discuss the injustices of the world,' Isaac reminded her. 'Only who's guilty and who's not. And what about Seamus Gaffney? Larry, you knew him, what do you reckon, the sort of man to make enemies?'

'Apart from informing, I'd say not. A likeable man, but he knew what was going on, and was willing to part with some of it for a price. But I reckon he kept quiet on some things, too dangerous otherwise.'

'Would he have known about Briganti's?'

'Who knows? We're assuming Cojocaru didn't. Otherwise, he wouldn't have met Ivanov in France.'

'According to Oscar Braxton, you don't debate whether to meet the man or not. A command is what you receive, and failure to attend is at your peril.'

'Becali didn't go to France,' Wendy said.

'No chance. He was here with us, and we were keeping a watch on him. And if he was in Ireland, then he was busy. Maybe he wasn't summoned to France.'

'Which means he could be working for the man.'

The name of Stanislav Ivanov had filtered through to Westminster, and politicians on both sides of the House were out trying to gain brownie points by accusing the other of inaction over terrorism in the past, and now organised crime.

The team in Homicide knew which of the two was the worst. Terrorism was ideological, organised crime was commercial, and money speaks, and Ivanov had an unlimited amount. Yet the man, with no criminal record, freely entered England on a regular basis, travelling in his personal jet, a retinue of staff with him, a Rolls Royce on arrival, a house in Bayswater. To those who would see him in the best restaurants and the best clubs, at the football or the races, he was an example of the new Russia. To those who had examined his history and that of Russian organised crime, he was the most malevolent and foul sore to blight that country.

'Larry, the venue for the meeting with Cojocaru and Marcus Hearne and his colleagues?' Goddard asked.

'Colleagues? A generous term.'

'Compared to what we've got now, they're almost gentlemen.'

'Hearne hasn't got the venue yet. He's on the way, diverting here and there. He reckons it's a farce, but then he's not a patient man.'

'What would Ivanov say if he knew about it?'

'The Russians hate the Romanians, and they'll not take commands from Cojocaru.'

'Bridget, follow up with Larry. Once he's got the venue, attempt to set up the best surveillance we can,' Isaac said.

'Isn't that a job for Serious and Organised Crime?'

'We're working together on this.'

'I'm meeting with Davies,' Goddard said. 'The man wants answers.'

'We've not given him much.'

'I'll keep him off our backs for now. Rome wasn't built in a day, and the team's handling the case well. Mind you, I'd rather meet with Cojocaru. At least the man wants to negotiate. With Commissioner Davies, it's a one-way decision-making process.'

'The best of luck,' Isaac said.

'Don't worry about me. The worst he can do is throw me out on my ear. You're messing with people who kill.'

'We'll be careful,' Wendy said.

Chapter 16

Marcus Hearne never made the expected phone call about where the meeting was to be held. Larry was at the crime scene within forty minutes of receiving the notification.

'It's a messy killing,' Gordon Windsor said. He was standing to one side of the ditch, looking down at two of his team in the water. The body was face down, although its wallet had floated to the surface, a driving licence providing identification. 'What do you know about him?'

'Marcus Hearne, gang leader, someone I used to meet with from time to time,' Larry said.

'You pick your friends well.'

'We needed Hearne,' Larry said.

'That's why he's dead.'

'It makes no sense.'

'Is this to do with Briganti's?'

'Yes.'

Larry could see no more to be gained at the murder scene. He drove back to Challis Street. He was not in a good mood.

The first person he saw on his arrival at the police station, the obnoxious and unwelcome Superintendent Caddick. 'Bad day,' the man said.

'Not the best. What are you doing here?'

'What are you doing here, sir,' Caddick replied. Larry could see that the man hadn't changed: overly impressed with his own importance, incompetent without equal. The man was a walking disaster, and he was in Challis Street.

'Are you coming back, *sir*?' Larry said, adding emphasis on the 'sir'. It was close to impertinence, but he didn't care, and if Caddick wanted to write a report about his attitude, then that was fine. Larry walked away and left Caddick standing where he was.

In Homicide, the welcome face of Isaac in his office.

'Caddick's downstairs,' Larry said.

'He's been in here. I gave him his marching orders. If the man wants to make something of it, that's up to him. Marcus Hearne?'

'Dead, one bullet.'

'No idea where Cojocaru is?'

'The general area, but it doesn't help us.'

'Stanislav Ivanov landed in his private jet ninety minutes ago,' Isaac said.

'To attend the meeting?'

'We don't think so. He's at his house in Bayswater. We've got people staking it out.'

'Is he on his own?'

'A couple of women, they looked expensive. And then there are some bodyguards.'

'Armed?'

'Not on arrival.'

'It's all coming to us,' Larry said. 'And Caddick?'

'He's just sticking his nose in. The man's come to gloat. He'll wait until we've got the case almost solved. Then he'll be back to take my seat or DCS Goddard's.'

'We'd better solve it sooner than later,' Larry said.

'Marcus Hearne, what did you expect him to tell you?'

'If Cojocaru had offered him a sweetener, he might have told me nothing.'

***

The revelation, coming later in the day, was a shock. So much so that Larry had taken the first flight to Ireland. Upon landing, Annie O'Carroll had been there to welcome him. To see her there, a half-smile on her face, lifted the dark mood that he had carried all day.

'You've cracked it?' Larry said.

'One of them. I've booked you into the same hotel as before.'

'Not sure if I can stay. The situation in London is fluid. Ivanov's in the country, and Cojocaru's missing, as are three of the West Indian gang bosses. There's a palpable tension on the streets. No one wants to be caught in the action if anything happens.'

'Is that likely?'

'People panic, especially when they are being fed rumours from opposing sides. But if Ivanov has had Cojocaru and the others killed, then who knows?'

The two police officers drove in silence; Larry took the opportunity to close his eyes for a few minutes.

Inside the house they had driven to Sheila Gaffney sat silently in one corner of the room. 'I'm sorry about this,' she said.

'Why didn't you tell us before?' Larry said.

'I was upset over Seamus's death. I did love him, but he was away for so long each time. I had hoped he would have come back to live with us, and when he said that he would, I told Ryan that it was over.'

'How long had you been having an affair with him?'

'Five years, on and off. Ryan couldn't accept what it was, just a casual fling. He saw it as love, and no doubt with Dervla being difficult, I seemed the ideal choice for him. He became angry when I told him.'

'When was this?'

'The same day as Seamus arrived, early in the morning. Long enough for, well, you know.'

'We know now.'

'Mrs Gaffney, you're pregnant,' Annie O'Carroll said.

'It's Seamus's, I know that. I wouldn't have done that to him.'

'The full story, in your own time,' Larry said.

Sheila Gaffney got up from where she had been sitting and walked around the room before sitting back in the same chair. She seemed to have visibly shrunk.

'It was after the third child. Before that, they came at regular intervals, and I was always busy looking after them. And then a spell where I failed to get pregnant. Seamus was still commuting, supporting us as he always did. I became lonely, maybe because I wasn't expecting, and from loneliness comes melancholy and then reflection, and finally the need to do something. It was on one of Ryan's visits. He was always dropping in to see how we were. Seamus, the rogue that he was, and Ryan, a police officer. It's hard to believe the friendship between the two men, but it never wavered.

'Ryan is here, and I knew that he always liked me, always commenting if only his wife could be more like me, and then it happened. I wanted to say no, but I couldn't. And afterwards, I thought I should feel guilty, but I didn't. I felt loved, and by two men. After that, he'd come over occasionally, but he started to become serious. He even spoke of my divorcing Seamus, he divorcing Dervla, and for us to get married. I had wanted to end it for some time, always too afraid to do it, and then Seamus is on the phone saying that he's coming back for good.'

'Ryan Buckley's reaction?' Larry said.

'He stormed out of here, ever so angry. He said he was going to have me one way or the other.'

'Which you interpreted as meaning that he intended to murder your husband?'

'No. Ryan could be hot-headed but I could never have imagined that he would harm Seamus.'

'We've proof?' Larry asked Annie.

'We had never considered Ryan as the murderer. A fellow police officer, a loyal friend of the family.'

'And?'

'When Sheila told me, we re-examined the evidence, checked on Ryan's movements. His car was fitted with GPS monitoring. We backtracked where it had been driven and found a layby where he had pulled in. Our people went there and found the weapons. It's conclusive. Ryan murdered Seamus,' Annie said. She had her arm around Sheila Gaffney.

Larry realised there were no words that he could offer that would alter the anguish and the shame that Gaffney's widow felt. He left the house and returned to Annie's car. Five minutes later she came out of the house.

'It came as a shock, but we have our murderer,' Annie said.

'What about Buckley's killer?'

'That still remains unsolved.'

'I should get back to London. If you could drop me back at the airport, I'd be grateful,' Larry said. He had spent just under three hours in Ireland before he boarded the plane for the return journey; his despondent mood had returned.

***

'It sticks in your throat,' Oscar Braxton said. Isaac and Larry were at New Scotland Yard in Braxton's office. On the television, a football match, and in the owner's box, Stanislav Ivanov. 'That's the trouble, people just don't care. Look at them fawning over him, making him out to be something special instead of the grubby gangster that he is.'

Isaac could sympathise, knowing full well that there were more villains outside of the prisons than in, and with enough money anyone was innocent. He realised that it was a pessimistic view of the law, and any attempt at meeting with Ivanov, possibly bringing him into Challis Street, would be met with a barrage of Queen's Counsels, all of them at the pinnacle of their legal prowess.

The philanthropic businessman was how the football team saw him, the general public if they knew of him, but never as the head of a violent criminal gang, only separated from the hoodlums causing trouble of a Saturday evening after a few too many drinks by his wealth.

'We can't touch him, I suppose?' Isaac asked.

'He doesn't break any laws in this country, and back in Russia, he's protected. Friends in high places protecting his back, him protecting theirs. And now, the man is making a move in this country.'

Larry, glad to be back home with his wife and their children, having arrived the previous night, said little, although the events in Ireland had unsettled him. Sheila Gaffney, the dutiful wife, a person who caused no harm to anyone, now tainted as a scarlet woman in the press; the reputation of Ryan Buckley in shreds.

'Look at that,' Braxton said. On the television, Ivanov making a speech about how he was honoured to be the owner of such a prestigious club, and how he was looking forward to making England his home.

'He wants the place for himself,' Isaac said.

'He intends to run his criminal empire from here. And there's nothing we can do about it.'

'Any more on Crin Antonescu?'

'He never left Ivanov's villa. And now you have another death, Marcus Hearne. He'll not be missed, I assume.'

'Not by us,' Larry said. 'His family maybe.'

'Not really relevant, is it? What about the other so-called leaders of their communities? Any chance of finding out what was said at the meeting with Cojocaru? He must be quivering in his boots with Ivanov coming here on a permanent basis.'

'They're not talking at present. Since Hearne died, I've not heard from them.'

'Cojocaru has left the country,' Braxton said.

'Where to?'

'Romania. He knows he's the meat in the sandwich. It would help if we knew the story of what happened to Antonescu.'

'We may never find out,' Isaac said. 'Was there a reason for us coming up here?'

'We've had a lead on who may have killed Ryan Buckley.'

'Who and how?' Larry said.

'We checked with our counterparts in Russia, the ones we can trust.'

'Some you can't?'

'Corruption's endemic there. You're either part of the system, or you're dead. But there are one or two who keep a low profile, take the backhanders, keep us informed. We checked on a couple of names we received from them, men who Ivanov uses outside of Russia.'

'Do you have photos on file, any other details?'

'We've checked on the movements of the two men. One of them is arrogant enough.'

'Has he been in England?'

'He's French, and he's been in Ireland, as well. We've checked with the police over there, and we've had our CCTV people looking for him. He came in through Belfast and then took a train to Dublin. From there, he disappeared for a couple of days, probably stole a car or hired one using false ID. From Dublin, he crossed to Wales on the ferry and disappeared. The French police have a lead on him. I'm going to France on Eurostar tonight. I assume you'll both come with me.'

'I will,' Isaac said. He had promised to take Jenny out that night to a restaurant, a celebration of six months together, but he knew she'd understand.

'I'll pass,' Larry said. 'I need to be back in Ireland. If he's been there, we'll need proof that he spoke to Sheila Gaffney.'

'Agreed, that's a plan,' Isaac said. He had a phone call to make at the conclusion of the meeting; he had to phone Richard

Goddard. The wolves were closing in on the man again, and a fresh lead, a link between a murder and an organised crime leader, would give Goddard and the Homicide department a breather of a few days before further questions as to why the shooting at Briganti's was still without a murderer.

***

The three remaining gang leaders considered their position carefully. As had been agreed with Cojocaru, they were lying low for a few days, a house on the south coast, a supply of good food, good drink, and five women, recent arrivals in the country who did not speak English, other than a smattering. Of the five, two had been known to Becali in the old country. They were there to ensure the men did not leave the house until the all-clear had been given. The other three were there for entertainment.

'It's either Stanislav Ivanov or me,' Cojocaru had said. 'You're smart men, you'd not want the Russian mafia, and they'd not want you.'

At the end of four hours, during which Cojocaru had stated his case and told the three about the barbaric acts committed by Ivanov, and that the man had admitted to the attack at Briganti's, there was an agreement to give the Romanian three days. After that time, they'd decide as to whether the Romanians and the other gangs would combine against a common enemy.

The second day. 'We're in trouble here,' Devon Harris, a tall man from Barbados, said. Back in the West Indies, he had been hustling the tourists out of their hard-earned money, but with an English grandfather who had been white, and a brother who had permanent residency in England, he had managed to deal with the bureaucracy and to legally enter the country. His contribution to the country that had taken him in: two murders, another maimed for life. And what had it given to him? The opportunity to use his streetwise cunning to build up his gang until he was supplying Notting Hill up through Bayswater and Paddington with drugs. He would have said that he had done well for himself, but now he wasn't so sure.

'Cojocaru has given us his word that we are safe,' Jeremy Miller, the second of the gang leaders, said. Second generation, born in London, he was a softly-spoken man, his Jamaican accent the result of growing up in Trench Town, a wild and lawless suburb of Kingston, the Jamaican capital. The left side of his face had a scar from just below the eye down to his upper lip, the result of a knife fight when he was fifteen. He shouldn't have been in his parents' place of birth, but his father had died after he had cheated on another gang leader in London, and Miller's mother had quickly taken the three-year-old back to Jamaica. Not that the place was much safer, but the threat against her son was reduced by distance. At the age of eighteen, Miller had returned to London and had used his quiet yet authoritative manner to work his way up through his gang, using his innate intelligence and his ruthless ability to remove anyone in his way by whatever means seemed appropriate.

'Cojocaru's word meant little when he came to England. Do you believe him now?' Harris said.

'He can never be trusted, but what can we do?'

'If we are to throw in our lot with Cojocaru, what guarantees do we have that he will honour what has been agreed?'

'What has been agreed? And what of Marcus Hearne? And these women can't be trusted, junkies the lot of them, apart from those two over there.'

The third gang leader, Claude Bateman, older than the others, sat without saying a word. He looked over at one of the three women who had just walked in the door. 'While you two debate, I intend to keep myself occupied. He grabbed the woman – blonde, no more than nineteen or twenty – and led her away. The two other women in the room, supposedly not available, looked at Devon Harris and Jeremy Miller.

'I'd take the one on the left,' Harris said.

'They understand what we're saying, or she does. Did you see her reaction when you mentioned her? We used to control everything, and now we're here, no more than children waiting for the parent to decide what to do with us.'

'We may not leave here alive, have you considered that?'

'I have. What do you suggest?'

'For now, nothing. Bateman had the right idea. If we leave here, then we have the Russians to deal with. If we stay here, then it's Cojocaru. I trust neither, but we must wait and hope that the cards are in our favour.'

'You are an optimist when there is no reason for optimism. We're sitting ducks in here, targets out there.'

'Then I'm taking the one who pretends she doesn't understand English. You can choose amongst the others.'

The woman who had previously resisted any advances by the three men stood up and took hold of Harris's hand. The other gang leader sat in his chair, pensively weighing up the options.

Chapter 17

Emotions were running high at New Scotland Yard in Commissioner Alwyn Davies's office. The man could see from the reports that the investigation into the murders at Briganti's was far from resolved. Goddard had nothing to say, not in defence of his position, and for once the blustering, belligerent and political animal Davies was right.

'We've got a lead on who killed Inspector Buckley in Ireland,' Goddard said.

'What's Ireland got to do with this? It's London I'm concerned about, and especially your part of it. I put you back there against my better judgement, and this is how you repay me. You could have got rid of Cook. The man's a walking liability with his laid-back approach to policing.'

'I don't believe that's a fair assessment of the situation and of DCI Cook.'

'Fair! When did fair come into it? We've got hoodlums running around the streets, arming themselves from what I hear, and you talk about fair. Get real, man. You're a chief superintendent, not a welfare counsellor. You need to ride your men, be there every minute, following up on every aspect of the case. But what do you do? Leave it to them, and now this. This Cojocaru, how long's he been in the country?'

'Nine to ten years.'

'And he's a major distributor of illicit drugs?'

'He is.'

'Why? You've had long enough to get him under control.'

'Attempts are being made to get him deported.'

'You can't deal with men like him through the courts. More QCs than you and I have had hot dinners. You need to bait him, let him show his true colours, force him to commit a crime. Time's against you on this one, and Caddick's waiting for the say-so from me. Give me one good reason why I shouldn't dump your Cook and put Caddick in. He'll not mess around.'

'Sir, with all due respect,' Goddard said, 'Superintendent Caddick is the last person we need at Challis Street at this time.'

'Don't give me "with all due respect". You don't like Caddick, nor does Cook, but that's not the point. We need to show action on this matter, and you're telling me it's under control and we have a suspect. Frankly, it does very little to quell my nerves. A gang war is the last thing we want at this time.'

'That's what we're trying to prevent. Isaac Cook is in France with Serious and Organised Crime. Inspector Hill is in Ireland checking on the Frenchman, gathering evidence.'

'I read the report of Stanislav Ivanov. A nasty piece of work if Serious and Organised Crime is correct.'

'They invariably are. We can't touch the man, not legally, and he's well-protected.'

'Why do we let such scum into the country?'

'You'd better ask the government. Obscenely rich and you're welcomed in. Poor and desperate and the doors are bolted.'

'Yes, we know all that, but what are you going to do? And don't give me your usual platitudes. The situation is not under control. Are we going to have a repeat of what happened at the hairdressing salon?'

'It's unlikely.'

'And how do you know this? The reports indicate that Ivanov is probably involved, yet you can't make the connection. So how can you say it's unlikely?'

Davies paced around the room, did not speak for what seemed to be an eternity to Goddard, but was less than twenty seconds.

'One week,' Davies said.

'And then what, sir?' Goddard asked.

'To come up with some results. And if there are any mass murders in the interim, don't bother reporting, just send me your resignation, an email will be fine.'

Davies had broken every rule in the book by his dismissive and derogatory dressing down of a chief superintendent. Goddard knew he would be wasting his time taking the matter forward.

***

With Larry in Ireland and Isaac in France, Wendy Gladstone was in the office with Bridget Halloran. One variable remained outstanding: the presence in Briganti's of Sal Maynard.

'If she was there as a distraction,' Wendy said, 'she wasn't looking to get herself killed.'

'Her life wasn't that good. Was she stable, mentally?'

'According to Ralph Begley, she was.'

'You reckon that if the woman was in there, it was because of Ion Becali?'

'Yes. Which would mean that he was involved.'

'Becali's playing it both ways?' Bridget said.

'Men have died for less, but why? Becali's a disgusting man, but he's not stupid. If you cross Cojocaru, you end up dead. If you cross Ivanov, you end up dead. Not good odds whichever way you look at it.'

'If you're faced with two imponderables, you choose the path of least resistance, the winning side.'

'Who's the winner?'

'Us, hopefully. But if I had to stake money, I'd say Ivanov.'

With no more to discuss, Wendy went back to her desk. The office felt cold without the other two police officers. She sat and looked at the blank screen of her laptop, realising that a feeling of negativity had come over her, negativity she could not shake. Inaction and apathy, two conditions that she had always avoided, had surfaced with a bang. She stood up with a start, pushing her chair back with such force that it upended.

'What's the problem?' Bridget said, not used to seeing her friend in such a state.

'Impending doom. As though there's something in the air so tangible that you could cut it with a knife, yet we can't see it.'

'You were talking about Ion Becali before. Is that it?'

'I'm not sure. The injustice of it gets to me sometimes. Becali is out there larger than life, Cojocaru is enjoying the sweet life, and Stanislav Ivanov acts as though he owns the country. And there's Sal Maynard who did nothing wrong in her life, except wanting to better herself; and there she is, forgotten and not even missed by her own family.'

'She wasn't the only one in Briganti's,' Bridget said.

'I know that, but the others had been loved, even Alphonse Abano. But with Sal, nobody.'

'There's Ralphie.'

'It's not sufficient.'

'Welcome to the human condition. If she wasn't loved, there's not much you can do about it.'

'There is. I can give her justice.'

'How?'

'By making sure whoever talked her into going into that salon and draping herself around Hendry is brought in and charged with being an accessory to murder.'

***

Cojocaru sat in his suite at the Radisson Blu Hotel in Bucharest. Located on Calea Victoriei, it was not far from Revolution Square, the scene of a disastrous speech by another Nicolae, Nicolae Ceausescu, the former president, who had been deposed and shot after a show trial, the guilty verdict predetermined. The irony was not lost on Cojocaru. He reflected on what he had achieved on his return to the land of his birth. It had been good to visit his parents' grave, to see the house where he had grown up, even where he had shot his first man, but Bucharest had changed. No longer as easy as it had been, it was now full of shops and cars, and the government, if not totally incorruptible, was not as pliable as before.

He had contacted one of the crime syndicates, a group that he had dealt with before. Back then, the leader had been a man his age, but he was dead, and in his place, his son, a smart thirty-two-year-old. Cojocaru realised that he was a man whose time was past, a man who did not belong. He had made a few phone calls, only to receive impersonal replies, or on two occasions the clicking in his ear as the phone was hung up on him. The visit had been a disaster, and he knew that the surly confidence he had had in London had gone.

Cojocaru turned on the television, found nothing of interest, walked out of his room, and went and sat by the swimming pool. The evening climate was balmy, and he was dressed in shorts and a polo shirt. He felt some serenity as he leant back on a reclining chair.

'Stanislav Ivanov will not be pleased,' a man who came up to him said.

'Your boss has no need to worry. I am here visiting my parents' grave, that's all.'

'Do not lie. The best thing you can do is to return to London and to pray that Stanislav Ivanov has a forgiving nature.'

'Does he?'

The man looked Cojocaru directly in the eyes. 'Not that I've ever seen it.' He then walked away.

Panic seized the gangster, the realisation that he was no longer the hunter but the hunted, and that Romania was no longer his home, nor was London. The only hope lay with the West Indians, but he knew that was futile. They did not have the tenacity to deal with the situation. But did he? The situation was too difficult to comprehend, but nothing could be resolved from Romania, and now Ivanov had men following him, men who at a command could kill him. He went to his room, packed his suitcase, and took a taxi to the airport.

In London, Becali received a phone call from his boss at eight in the evening. 'Pick me up at the airport, 11 p.m. flight.'

'Any success?' Becali asked. His situation had become difficult as well. His link to Sal Maynard would be confirmed in time, and regardless of what he had said, he had enjoyed his time with her. It wasn't love, but it wasn't hate or indifference. With him, she had been genuine. With the women who cost a great deal more, the show of enjoying his company was fake, but that simple and uncomplicated woman who had lived in a depressing ten-storey tenement building had confessed her love for him, her willingness to trust her life to him, her blind obedience if that was what he wanted.

'None. Ivanov has people here, and the old contacts are gone. London is where we are, where we must do what is necessary.'

'Is there no alternative?'

'None. You, Ion Becali, are the one who must do this. There is no one else who I can trust.'

'We will succeed, you and I.'

Cojocaru did not answer as he did not know what to say. Becali had always been a loyal servant to him, but now the man was about to become more. Whatever the outcome, Cojocaru knew that the relationship between the two men would be inexorably altered.

***

Larry was tired of being away from home. One of the children had a cough, another had a 'parents meet the teachers' function in three days. He wanted to be home for both of them.

'Buckley's wife?' Annie said.

'Any suspicions there?'

'Not with her. It's not as if Buckley had much to show for his years in the police force.'

'Neither do I. It's the life we choose, isn't it?'

'It is. Although with my husband and myself working, we're not so badly off, and Ireland is a lot cheaper than London.'

'Is Dervla Buckley at home?'

'She will be. I've phoned to tell her we're coming.'

Larry could tell that Annie O'Carroll still had a lingering sorrow for Buckley.

Larry had no such sentiment; a crooked police officer had abrogated his right to sympathy and concern.

Dervla Buckley was not in a dressing gown on their second visit. This time, she was dressed in an ankle-length dress, her hair coiffured, her makeup immaculate. She was welcoming to the two police officers.

On a table in the sitting room, a spread of sandwiches, freshly-brewed coffee, and a pot of tea. 'I thought we'd make ourselves comfortable,' Mrs Buckley said.

'Thank you,' Annie said, 'but we've got a few questions. There are disturbing aspects to your husband's death.'

'I don't miss him if that's what you expect me to say. I know about Sheila Gaffney.'

'How?'

'She came over here to offer her condolences.'

'What did you do?'

'I was angry at first. Seamus had died, and although she had been sleeping with Ryan, it just doesn't seem that important to bear any malice against her.'

'Have you known her for long?' Larry asked.

'A long time, almost as long as I knew Ryan. A good woman, good mother, and before what she admitted to, a loyal wife. It goes to show, doesn't it? People assumed I'd be the one to stray, not that I did, and humble and sweet Sheila is there, flat on her back, my husband on top of her.'

'There's another issue,' Larry said. 'We've identified the man who probably shot your husband. We believe that Seamus had told Ryan something of value. And that was why Ryan killed Seamus, hoping to grab the money for himself.'

'I never considered him to be dishonest. He loved being a police officer. I can't believe that of him.'

'Inspector O'Carroll would prefer to believe the same, but the facts are indisputable. Your husband died as a result of an order from a foreign crime syndicate. We need to know why it's important. Is there anything he said to you that seems obscure?'

'Nothing. We were barely talking, only what was necessary.'

'I hope you're telling the truth. Two people have died in Ireland, I don't want you to be the third,' Larry said.

'I don't know anything, believe me. Ryan's life insurance is still valid, although I don't expect his police pension is. I have been left financially secure, at least I can thank Ryan for that.'

On the drive to the airport, Annie spoke. 'Did you believe her?'

'The money that Ryan's life insurance will pay is not going to last indefinitely, no matter what she said. However, I do believe her. Just hope that others are of that opinion,' Larry said.

Chapter 18

Claude Bateman, the most ruthless of the gang leaders who had enjoyed Nicolae Cojocaru's hospitality, was the first to leave the house where he and the two others had been wined, dined, bedded, and given the runaround.

He had been spotted in the Wellington Arms. Larry heard of the man's reappearance through a contact who phoned him from time to time, a fifty pound note, a few drinks given in return as payment.

Bateman was in a corner of the pub when Larry walked in. This time he had brought Wendy, a woman who was also partial to a drink, but the visit was business not social, although Larry ordered a pint of beer for each of them.

'Over here, Inspector,' Bateman shouted.

Larry and Wendy sat down at the man's table. Around him, four men, members of his gang: Tony Hammond, a young man, skinny as a rake. Good with a knife if the word on the street was accurate, six months in prison at twenty for theft. Victor Powell, short, in his thirties, an open-necked shirt with a large medallion proudly showing. Larry hadn't seen him before and assumed he had been brought in if there was to be violence. The third gang member, Marlon Morris, a surly-looking individual who didn't like the police under any circumstances, and he had elbowed Wendy when she sat down. She had made a mental note to check him out with Bridget. To her, he looked more than a rank and file hoodlum. The fourth man, good-looking, well-spoken, and polite had shaken the hands of the two police officers, as had Bateman. His name was Colin Ross. Wendy thought he was charming, Larry did not.

'Where are the other two?' Larry asked Bateman. A woman came over and put her arms around the man's shoulder; he pushed her away.

'One of your admirers?' Wendy said.

Bateman, not responding to the question, looked over at Larry. 'The bastards killed Marcus Hearne.'

'There have been others in the past. Why are you concerned and why are we talking in this pub?'

'Where else? Either I declare my position or I sit on the fence.'

'And you intend to work with the police on this?'

'I intend to survive.'

'Your men here, what do they reckon?'

'They'll do what I say.'

'Until you're deposed.'

'Others have tried.'

'And died. Isn't that how you decide who's in charge?'

'Inspector, let's focus on our common position. You don't want an escalation in violence in the area, nor more drugs coming into the country, correct?'

'We want no violence and no drugs.'

'You're living in cloud cuckoo land,' Bateman said. 'This is the real world, crime happens, people take drugs, people get drunk, even you in the past when Rasta Joe was alive.'

'My habits are not of concern. What do you want from me? What are you going to give in return?'

541

Bateman turned away from Larry and Wendy and focussed on the other four at the table. 'Leave us alone. I've got two police officers to protect me now,' he said.

The four gang members moved away, taking up a position close to the bar. Of the four, Morris kept his eyes firmly on Bateman, Larry and Wendy.

'I don't like the look of him,' Wendy said.

'Marlon? He's harmless, just likes to look big and strong,' Bateman replied. His tone was mocking. Wendy didn't believe the man.

'What do you have for us?' Larry asked. His glass was empty. He looked over at the barman and held up the empty glass, a nod from the barman in return. Bateman followed suit as did Wendy. Soon there were three more pints of beer on the table.

'Devon Harris and Jeremy Miller will be here soon enough.'

'Why not now?'

'Cojocaru has been trying to make a deal. He's frightened of the Russians, so are we.'

'They killed Crin Antonescu, almost certainly were responsible for Briganti's and one other murder in Ireland.'

'We can't trust the Romanians, no more than the Russians. What do you suggest we do?'

'Seamus Gaffney knew something. He told someone else what it was, and he's dead. Whatever it was, it was lethal. I need to know what the man knew,' Larry said.

'You want a lot. We know less than you, and that we're unsure what to do. If Gaffney had found out something, why didn't he tell you?'

'It had more value if he sold it on, or offered his silence if they paid enough.'

'Gaffney was always a fool, playing the margins, listening where he shouldn't. He was going to die one day on account of his big nose.'

'Maybe that's true. What else do you have? Hearne's dead, yet you stayed with Cojocaru.'

'He told us about Antonescu, not that we cared for the man. Marcus was talking to the police, and secrecy was vital.'

'You accepted that? He did no more than what you're doing now.'

'We didn't accept it, but we needed to know what Cojocaru had to say. Men die, men live, and Hearne led a violent life.'

'The same as you.'

'The same as me. One day, one of those at the bar will challenge me. You know this.'

'Cojocaru's been in Romania, although he's back now. Have you seen him?'

'Not since that day when Hearne died. Cojocaru told us about Ivanov and what he's capable of. Is it true what he said?'

'That Ivanov is a mafia boss, more violent than anyone else you've ever encountered, and that one of his men shot up Briganti's?'

'That's about it.'

'He didn't lie.'

'That's what we thought, not that we trust Cojocaru. But the man had a message, we had to listen to it.'

'Why were the three of you out of touch with your people?'

'We weren't, not totally. Hammond knew where I was, but he was keeping quiet. We agreed to give Cojocaru three days, but then he never came back. We enjoyed his hospitality, and Harris and Miller are still there.'

'It must be good hospitality,' Wendy said.

'It was,' Bateman said. 'The best.'

Wendy needed to know no more.

Larry looked over at the four gang members. He could see that two of them were drinking heavily, Victor Powell and Marlon Morris were not.

'You need to stop Ivanov,' Bateman said.

'With what? The man's got no criminal record, not even a parking ticket, whereas you do.'

'I'm not the problem, Ivanov is. We've learnt to live with Cojocaru, even do business with him, but this Ivanov may cut us out altogether.'

'He may just remove you, chop you into little pieces and feed you to the fish.'

'We'll fight.'

'On a street corner, knives and fists? Not a chance. The Russians will be armed with guns, and they'll know how to use them. If this is not stopped, it's you who'll lose. What was Cojocaru's plan?'

'I don't think he knew what to do. He just needed to know that we'd be with him and not the Russians.'

'Will you?'

'We represent our community, not his or Ivanov's.'

'If you had to choose?'

'Better the devil you know than the devil you don't.'

Wendy could see that Bateman, the same as Marcus Hearne, was looking for de facto support from the police for the criminals. She knew that would not happen, and that Bateman was not a man to be trusted.

Marlon Morris came over, a scowl on his face, a disparaging look at Larry and Wendy. He carried a half-full glass of beer. He drank it before speaking. 'Devon Harris is back,' he said to Bateman.

'Where?'

'Not here,' Morris replied. Larry knew that what he was saying was that he was wherever the police weren't.

Larry stood up, offered his hand to Bateman, which he shook. 'Keep in touch and don't get yourself killed. You're playing with the big boys now, and they won't have any scruples about killing you and your men.'

'According to Cojocaru, they kill the police as well.'

'None of us is safe, you'd better remember that. If you want to meet Harris without us being present, then so be it. But don't blame us if you end up on the pathologist's table, cut open from top to bottom.'

'I'll be in touch,' Bateman said as he leant over and shook Wendy's hand.

Larry wasn't sure if he would see the man again. The West Indians were playing a dangerous game, a game they were not prepared for.

***

At 10.02 a.m. Stanislav Ivanov walked down the four steps outside his Bayswater residence. On the street, three men stood close to a Rolls Royce. On the other side of the road, another man looked up and down, checking. All four men were bodyguards, as were the two on either side of the leader of the Tverskoyskaya Bratva.

Ivanov was in a good mood: the latest financial statements were all in the black, and the planned expansions throughout Europe and England were progressing well. The two men at either side of him were anxious to hurry him away from the house and into the car, but Ivanov wanted to look around, to look at the garden, even to say hello to a woman pushing a child down the street in a pushchair, to wave to a man walking his dog. Those protecting the man knew that it was out of character for their charge, and that in France he stayed concealed most of the time, and in Russia he travelled in a convoy of ten to twelve vehicles.

The bodyguards were disturbed with the change in the man, the result of his decision to stay in England on a permanent basis, his belief that England was safe.

On the pavement Ivanov stopped once again to talk to a group of schoolchildren, not that they knew who the man was, other than he was wealthy and influential. He asked them about their lessons, and what smartphones they used, and were they on Facebook. The guards attempted to hurry him along, careful not to touch his person.

From a window on the upper floor of a block of flats one street away, another man watched the scene. He opened the window, confident that with distance came protection. He took aim with the rifle set on a tripod, its telescopic sight tested many times for accuracy. He loaded one bullet into the rifle and pulled the trigger. He then left the room, the rifle still in position. He had no need of the weapon again, no need to gloat over his handiwork, only to feel a wave of relief surge over him.

The bullet's target lay motionless on the footpath, the schoolchildren screaming in horror, the bodyguards unable to comprehend the scene, conscious of their fate if the man died, and even if he didn't, they were guilty of negligence.

An ambulance arrived five minutes later, a medic stabilising Ivanov before putting him in the back of the vehicle and transporting him to the nearest hospital, the Rolls Royce following as well as two other cars.

The first that Homicide heard of the shooting was a phone call from Isaac. 'I'm with Oscar Braxton. Get over to St Mary's Hospital in Paddington. Ivanov's been shot.'

Both Wendy and Larry were familiar with the place, as it was on Praed Street, just up from Paddington Station.

'We're heading back on Eurostar. We'll come to the hospital on arrival. Expect a media circus there.'

'Buckley and Briganti's murderer?'

'That's still ongoing. Stanislav Ivanov is the key, and if he dies, there'll be no Russian incursion into England. But if he survives, you can imagine the consequences.'

'Revenge?'

'And lots of it. The man is not the "forgive and turn the other cheek" kind of person. Whoever shot him must have known this.'

'Who? Any suspicions?'

'Not yet. Find out where the shot was taken from. No stone unturned on this one. I'll phone DCS Goddard. He's bound to have Commissioner Davies onto him soon enough.'

'Caddick?'

'God help us if he appears,' Isaac said. 'Got to go, taxi to the station. See you in a few hours.'

***

Not far away, Devon Harris met with Claude Bateman; Jeremy Miller was on his way. Everyone, including Cojocaru, the West Indians, the police, knew that whatever happened, a day of reckoning was coming when the opposing forces would be lined up against each other, either to come to an agreement or to fight.

At St Mary's, the police were attempting to keep the media at bay, setting up an area across the road, and bringing in metal barriers. At the entrance to the hospital, two uniforms stood, backed up by a patrol car.

Larry waved his warrant card at the uniforms. They let him and Wendy through after a call from DCS Goddard to tell them that the man in the operating theatre was part of a homicide investigation. The uniforms, nervous due to the importance of the man inside, had only been doing their duty, Isaac knew that. A high-profile patient, and forged identification papers, easy enough to come by, could have been used by the media, or by the assassin if the man showed up to check on his work.

'I need an update,' Larry said to the lady at the desk outside the operating theatre.

'I can't do that,' she said. 'I'll get a doctor to see you.'

Across the room, an elegantly dressed woman.

'Mrs Ivanov, I'm Sergeant Wendy Gladstone, Challis Street Homicide. Could I take a few minutes of your time?'

'Why? What has my Stanislav done? We intended to come and live in England but after this? Such a good man.'

Wendy could have said because he was a thug who controlled the most powerful criminal gang in Russia, the Tverskoyskaya Bratva, a man who killed and tortured people without a care, a man who had a couple of high-class women at his place in Bayswater, while, she, the wife, lived in Richmond in a mansion. Wendy could see a hardness in the woman's face and realised that she would not have cared about the negatives, only the positives – the man was rich and generous, and he left her alone.

'Have you received any updates on his condition?'

'They told me to prepare for the worst,' Elena Ivanov said. At her side sat another woman of a similar age, although not as well-dressed. She held the other's arm in a sign of friendship.

'We will need to question him.'

'Not Stanislav. He does not answer to anyone.'

'This is not Russia. Here in this country, the police have the right to question. With citizenship comes responsibility. It is important that we find out who shot your husband and to bring that person to justice.'

'He will talk to you if he can,' Ivanov's wife said. Wendy was sure it was only an answer to make her go away.

Wendy knew that whoever had pulled the trigger would receive punishment. The answer to who would administer it remained unknown. With the British legal system, the man would be afforded the benefit of a fair trial. With Ivanov's cohorts, the man would be condemned and killed with little formality.

Wendy left the woman and returned to Larry. 'She'll not tell us much,' she said.

'Ivanov's wife. She would regard us as no more than insects to squash underfoot.'

'Not if she wants to stay in this country. Ivanov wants to be here, so does she, but why? He doesn't need to be in London to run his organisation.'

'Ivanov doesn't feel as secure as he did before. He wants out, he wants England and a peaceful life.'

'Peaceful to men such as Ivanov is subjective,' Wendy said.

Chapter 19

Nicolae Cojocaru sat back in his chair; he was a contented man. On one side of him, a bottle of whisky; on the other, mounted on the wall, a flat-screen television tuned to a news channel. The breaking news, the shooting of Stanislav Ivanov, the latest report from the hospital stating that the man's chances were not good. A brief synopsis followed of the man's career. How, at the age of ten, he had been abandoned in the height of winter, surviving by sleeping in heated basements when he could find them, underneath stacks of cardboard when he couldn't. How he had been taken in by an orphanage and had educated himself, taking every opportunity to better himself, eventually leaving university with two degrees. After that the television report became sketchy. There was mention of the ending of communism with Gorbachev, the rise of the oligarchs, Ivanov being one of the most prominent. Cojocaru knew that most of the story of the man's past was not true, having been put out there by a loyal employee. Cojocaru wondered how long before the veneer started to crack and the truth was revealed.

Becali sat in another chair. 'A great day,' he said. He lifted his glass of whisky in the air, a salute that the worst was over.

'It will be when they take him out of there in his coffin.'

'There is no question of his death.'

'That is what you said before.'

'They'll not give up on him that easily, but it was a good shot, I'll vouch for it.'

'On this, Ion, I trust you. What of the three West Indians?'

'They have left the house.'

'Good. Give them a bellyful of food and drink, a few women, and it's as easy as leading a camel to water.'

'With Ivanov gone, they'll go back to what they were before. Will you honour your agreement with them?'

'What agreement?'

'To deal with them in a more consultative manner in the future; to fight the Russian threat together.'

'Ion, still so naïve. No wonder you were starving in Bucharest. I never made any agreement, only suggestions. Are we ready for what happens?'

'The weapons are here, and Ivanov's people are ready to start shipping the extra quantities of drugs. Are you sure about this?'

'I am sure. What Ivanov planned, we will implement.'

'The Russians have agreed?'

'Whoever killed Ivanov has done them a service. They are very grateful.'

'They must never know.'

'Not from me, they won't. What now for you, Ion?'

'Today, I intend to celebrate. Tomorrow, day one of what has been agreed. It has all worked out better than could have been expected.'

'As long as Ivanov stays dead.'

'His bodyguards?'

'Some have disappeared, the others have been told to not indulge in reprisals. And besides, they don't know who was responsible.'

'Does it matter to them?'

'No, but without Ivanov and the Tverskoyskaya Bratva giving them clear instructions, they'll hold back.'

'Let's hope the man's dead, for all our sakes,' Becali said.

'I can feel it in my bones,' Cojocaru said. 'He's dead, and for once, I will join you in your celebration.'

***

As fast as Eurostar was, it wasn't fast enough for Isaac. As the train was pulling into St Pancras Station, he was off and running; Oscar Braxton, not such a fit man, struggled to keep up with him. In the taxi, Isaac caught his breath; Braxton tried to look at ease, but his face was red, and he was gasping for breath.

At St Mary's Hospital, the two men soon found Larry and Wendy. Updates on Ivanov's condition were slow in coming. Braxton, his tie still undone after loosening it in the taxi, contacted his department. Serious and Organised Crime, New Scotland Yard, had more clout than Homicide, Challis Street. He spoke to his commander who phoned the hospital's director of communications.

'There'll be a power struggle in Russia, survival of the fittest,' Braxton said to Isaac.

'Deaths?'

'It's probable, but it'll be internal and in Russia. It's not our concern. What's happening here is, though.'

Ten minutes later, a surgeon came out from the operating theatre.

'I'm Brian Forsythe, you'll need an update on the patient,' the surgeon, a man in his fifties, greying at the temples and as tall as Isaac, said.

'You're aware of who the man is?' Isaac replied.

'Not that it matters, but yes.'

'He's still alive?' Larry asked. A blunt question, he knew, but he had spent enough times in hospital to know that the surgeon would feel the need to give a description of the effect of the bullet entering a man's skull, the prognosis, how long he may or may not live, the difficulties in stemming the internal bleeding, and so on.

'It's important,' Isaac said.

'The patient is still alive. There was internal bleeding in the brain, fracturing of the skull. His survival is still dependent on a number of factors. We've put him into a medically-induced coma.'

'How long for?' Isaac asked.

'It depends on how he progresses. Anywhere from a few hours up to two weeks.'

'Ivanov wore body armour under his jacket, that's why the shot was to the head.'

'I only know the man from the media reports,' Forsythe said. Isaac could see that he was anxious to get away.

'What you've read is only part of the story,' Oscar Braxton said. 'I'm from Serious and Organised Crime Command, DCI Cook is from Homicide. The man is not what he seems.'

'He's still a patient. But what I can tell you is that even if he regains consciousness, he may not remember anything that has happened. And there is a possibility that he may be in a vegetative state for a long time.'

'Are you able to quantify the possibility?'

'Not at this time. We will issue a bulletin that our patient is receiving the best medical care and his chance of survival is good.'

'Stanislav Ivanov, whether he lives or not, will be the signal for a power play in Russia, a call to arms for organised crime in this country.'

'That I cannot help you with. Now, if you will excuse me, it was a difficult operation, and I have others to see,' Forsythe said.

***

Apart from one, Ivanov's bodyguards had vanished, not unexpected as questions would be asked as to who they were and what they knew of the assassination attempt, as well as why they had been carrying weapons. The one remaining was at Challis Street, voluntarily.

Wendy returned to the police station to work with Bridget. Isaac, Larry and Braxton went to the crime scene.

'What can you tell us?' Isaac said to Gordon Windsor.

'Here, not a lot.'

'Why?'

'Where the shot came from is more important.'

Windsor stood from where he had been kneeling. 'Up there is a possibility,' he said, pointing to a towering nondescript block of sixties' architecture, one of several in the area that had been built for the working class, and rented out, although some of the flats had been purchased under the government's Right to Buy policy that was introduced in 1980. Isaac knew this, as he had contemplated the purchase of such a flat before buying in Willesden.

'Have we people up there?' Isaac asked.

'We do, although it's a slow job. Not everyone is keen to see the police marching through, and some of the flats are empty or bolted shut. It's got to be on the top floors, twentieth and above.'

'I need to meet with Claude Bateman,' Larry said.

Isaac and Braxton drove the short distance to the block of flats. Outside, on the street, the obligatory crowd of onlookers, some hostile about the excessive police presence.

'Never here when we need you, are you?' one of the crowd shouted.

'If you're rich, it's a different law for them,' another screamed.

'Take no notice,' Isaac said to Braxton. 'It's not the first time in this building for us, not the last.'

'A lot of crime?'

'No more than other parts of London. The building's occupied by disparate people, some good, some bad. It's just that they're hemmed in, unable to get out.'

'There are plenty of other places.'

'If you've got money. The gang members, not Cojocaru's, like these places. Easy to hide.'

'Why would someone shoot from here?'

'Why not? It's some distance, but Ivanov was hit in the head.'

'We need to know if it's the same person who killed Buckley and carried out the attack on Briganti's.'

'Sal Maynard is still involved somewhere in all of this.'

'We keep coming back to Becali, but it wasn't him.'

'Not at Briganti's, but who knows. No one had a clear view of the man. That's the problem, the man on the street is not trained to observe.'

'We'd better follow through on what they find here,' Braxton said.

The two men entered through the front door of the building, a uniform checking their warrant cards before letting them through.

'He's keen.'

'New in the station.'

On the twentieth floor, two officers from Challis Street were working their way methodically through, flat to flat. 'We're getting a warrant to open up the flats if no one's at home.'

'How long?'

'Bridget Halloran is working on it for us.'

'Not long,' Isaac said. 'No luck yet?'

'Not yet. We've got others on the floors above. Gordon Windsor reckoned the bullet was fired from up high.'

'I'll take his word,' Isaac said as another flat door opened, a woman hiding in one room, covered head to foot in black.

'You can't come in here,' a man with a full beard said. He was dressed in the traditional clothing of Pakistan.

'We believe someone has used one of the flats to shoot at someone down on the ground.'

'I'm just home from work, and my wife won't let anyone in when she's on her own.'

Isaac, sensitive to the situation, phoned for a female police officer to come up to the flat.

After five minutes, Constable Jill Albertson reported for duty. 'Pleased to help. The crowds down below are restless. Some want to get home, and we're not letting them.'

'We'll need to set up a mobile canteen, toilets.'

'There's a church hall nearby, and the locals are helping out. But it's not the same, is it?'

'No.'

'Constable Albertson will check your flat, is that acceptable?' Isaac said to the man, now identified as Fahad Shaikh, a recent arrival in the country with his wife and three children.

'We are a law-abiding family. And yes, the constable can come in. Thank you for your understanding.'

Jill Albertson entered the flat, checking each and every room, placing emphasis on the windows looking out and over to Ivanov's house. She returned, thanking the Pakistani for his assistance and wishing him well.

'The flat on the corner,' she said to the police officers.

'You saw something?'

'It juts out from the other flats. It must have an extra bedroom. There's a small window that I could see in. I didn't want to mention it to Mr Shaikh.'

'What did you see?'

'A rifle.'

Isaac phoned Gordon Windsor to update him. Two crime scene investigators arrived soon after, their boss with them.'

'Are you sure of this?' Windsor said.

'I'm sure,' Constable Albertson said.

'We have to hold back until Armed Response arrives. We don't know who's inside.'

'Nobody, you know that,' Windsor said.

'I don't want to have to write a report on how you or one of your team were shot,' Isaac said.

'Fair enough. We'll get ourselves organised. It would be best if they didn't have to smash the door in.'

'Armed Response won't care too much for what you want. If there's to be shooting, they'll not be too fussy.'

'Understood. Regrettable, though. We should clear the people out on this floor.'

'Constable Albertson, up to the task?'

'Yes, sir. Leave it to me.'

'And keep it quiet. Those closest to the flat, set up some sort of a barrier as you bring them out, in case there's some shooting.'

As anxious as Isaac was to enter the flat, it was another thirty-five minutes before the all-clear was given. Armed Response was in place, Sergeant Northam in charge.

A knock on the door, no answer, Northam keeping to one side, protected by body armour. Isaac and the others waited at ground level. The arrival of the police officers with their weapons had increased the number of onlookers, some even leaving the church hall and their food to watch and to offer comments, some congratulatory, some critical, and some racial about the occupants in the block of flats.

'One more time and we go in,' Northam said. He hit the door hard with a metal bar. 'Police, we're armed. Come out at once with your hands up in the air.'

A break of sixty seconds for a reply. None was forthcoming.

'Okay, break it down,' Northam issued the command to one of his men.

The battering ram, known as the enforcer, made short work of the door, one attempt all that was needed before the door opened. Inside, a clear view through to the front window.

Down below, Windsor winced at the amount of evidence that the men would disturb. A formerly pristine crime scene devalued by the tactics of a group of men whose function was to secure the flat, not to concern themselves with where they walked and what they disturbed.

On the twentieth floor, Northam gave another command. 'Stand back.'

He then called out once again. 'Police, we're coming in, and we're heavily armed. Resistance is not advised, and we will shoot to kill.'

No answer.

'It's empty,' one of the other armed officers said.

'Okay, maximum care, and keep your weapons ready to shoot.'

At the rear of the flat, the rifle was found on its tripod. No person was discovered. The flat was declared safe.

Chapter 20

A hastily-convened press conference at Challis Street Police Station, and Richard Goddard's one failing would become apparent. Numerous courses and plenty of practice had convinced him of one thing – he was a lousy public speaker, his monotone voice tiring on the ear, his need to pause, when no words emanated other than 'Arrgh' and 'you know'.

At the back of the room, three cameras were mounted on tripods; at the front, iPhones on record. Goddard rose to speak.

'Ladies and gentlemen, thank you for coming. The recent upsurge in violent crime is of concern to all of us. That is why we are meeting here today. Let me thank Detective Chief Inspector Cook from Homicide for being here, as well as Detective Chief Inspector Oscar Braxton from Serious and Organised Crime Command. They will both make a short speech, after which there will be time for questions. I would ask that you allow them to make their speeches first.'

'What about Stanislav Ivanov?' a man in the second row of the assembled media contingent asked.

'And you are?' Goddard said.

'Colin Bartlett, Fox News.'

Isaac cringed. Everyone knew who Bartlett was. The man was the bane of the police force, forever criticising it for its inability to control terrorism. He had been scathing two nights previously on the television about the progress on the Briganti shooting, and now the chief superintendent was trying to control the man by belittling him. It wasn't going to work, Isaac knew that, and the press conference was a shambles before it had started.

In Russia, a group of men sat around a table in a boardroom, watching a live feed streaming into a laptop and then onto a screen on the wall. At a penthouse in London, two men watched smugly, confident that whatever happened their future was secure. At the Wellington Arms in Bayswater, the television was tuned to the press conference, although it was only the rank and file hoodlums who watched. The three gang leaders that Cojocaru had attempted to bring onto his side were ensconced in the house where Larry had met them previously, but then there had been four; Marcus Hearne now dead and in the mortuary.

'We'll answer your questions after DCI Cook and DCI Braxton have spoken.'

Bartlett sat quietly. Isaac knew it would not be for long.

'Detective Chief Inspector, would you speak?' Goddard said, directing his request at Isaac.

Isaac, confident in what he wanted to say, approached the lectern. 'Ladies and gentlemen. The first matter of interest is the attack at the hairdressing salon of Giuseppe Briganti. We have eliminated all those inside of any involvement, and all the bodies have been released to their families.'

'Why did you hold on to the body of Sal Maynard?' Bartlett shouted.

Isaac could see that the man had no intention of being quiet.

'Some discrepancies needed to be resolved.'

'She was involved with a major crime figure, sleeping with him.'

It was clear that Bartlett had inside knowledge – knowledge that was confidential.

'I am unable to comment on specific details of the case,' Isaac said. 'We have proof that the crime at Briganti's was committed by a foreign national. We have identified one person, and we are working with overseas police forces to bring this man to justice. We also believe that he was in Ireland and that he killed another man there.'

'From what was reported, Inspector Buckley killed Seamus Gaffney, a known informer, a man in regular communication with Detective Inspector Larry Hill.'

A general air of unease was apparent in the room. Richard Goddard took hold of the microphone. 'I would suggest that any questions are held for later,' he said.

Isaac knew that the man was wasting his time. Barely ten minutes into what was slated as a twenty-five-minute presentation, and nothing of importance had been said.

'Let me come back to where we are,' Isaac said after reclaiming the microphone. 'An overseas crime syndicate has been attempting to enter this country and to take over a large part of the illegal drug trade. They intended to base themselves primarily in the local area and to fan out from there. This has caused tension in the wider community, and unfortunately some deaths.'

'Why Briganti's?' A voice from the back of the room.

'The evidence we have received is that it was a show of strength, a warning to deter others who may resist.'

'Has it?'

'At this time, we believe it has.'

'There's a power vacuum, isn't there?' Bartlett said.

'There are elements in the community, as there are in other areas of the city and throughout the country, who believe they are above the law.'

'Elaborate on that statement.'

'At this time, I cannot. We are attempting to defuse the situation and to prevent further violence. Outlining our plan at this time would be counter-productive.'

'Let Braxton speak,' Goddard whispered in Isaac's ear.

Isaac stood to one side; Braxton came to the microphone.

'Detective Chief Inspector Braxton, Serious and Organised Crime Command,' he said. 'We have been working together with DCS Goddard and his team. An attack on a hairdressing salon by an organised crime syndicate, where innocent people were killed, was a senseless and cowardly attack and must be condemned.'

'Wonderful words, but worthless,' a woman in the front row said. Isaac recognised her, Lisa Saunders. The woman was on the television every night, debating law and order with a panel of so-called experts. She had a soothing and mellow voice, the type that sucked you in before she spat you out.

Braxton ignored the woman and continued. 'Organised crime, as in any major city, is unfortunately present here. The efforts of the police and the community have kept it at controllable levels up till now. I have been in France with DCI Cook, consulting with the French police. An arrest is expected soon.'

'Then why did you come back to England after Stanislav Ivanov was shot?' Bartlett asked. 'Is it because he is a major crime figure? Is he, in fact, the head of a Russian mafia crime syndicate that calls itself the Tverskoyskaya Bratva? A group of people who will stop at nothing to ensure their aims.'

'There are no criminal cases against Mr Ivanov.'

'Not in this country, not in Russia, but you know all about him. Everyone is careful in what they say, the result of his influence and wealth, but behind closed doors, what's the truth, what do you say about him?'

'Mr Ivanov has been shot. His life hangs in the balance. Speculation will serve no useful purpose.'

Isaac could see Braxton being pushed into a corner. He had thought that the man's attendance had been ill-advised, but Goddard had been adamant, and now the conference was being railroaded by the media.

'We are here to discuss the murders and attempted murders, not to speculate,' Isaac said.

'We're here for the truth. Marcus Hearne, a local gang leader, has been murdered, another drinking friend of Inspector Hill.'

'Inspector Hill is above suspicion.'

Lisa Saunders decided it was her turn to speak. An attractive woman, Isaac had to admit, but with a viper's tongue and a wasp's sting. 'In recent years, there has been a disturbing rise in the number of criminal gangs from eastern Europe entering England. Is that correct?'

'That has been reported by us,' Braxton said.

Isaac could see the subtle drawing in by Lisa Saunders, making her target relax his guard.

'There were some deaths some years back when one major crime figure entered this country, true or false?'

'There has been an escalation at times of criminal activity. Criminal gangs operate throughout the city, that's true. But it would be wrong to lay the blame on one group of people based on their ethnicity or their religion.'

'Why? Because it's not politically correct?'

'Apportioning blame to one group or another serves no purpose.'

'Are you telling me that you sit in your office in Serious and Organised Crime Command, and don't mention where someone comes from, their background? Are you telling those assembled here, and those watching on the television, streaming it over the internet, that you don't make decisions based on these factors?'

'We are conscious of the differences, and yes, we do discuss such matters, converse with our counterparts overseas.'

'Then, Detective Chief Inspector Braxton, why the subterfuge? Do you think we're all fools?'

Touché, Isaac thought, *Braxton's been taken hook, line, and sinker.*

'It is our responsibility to not exacerbate the situation by making claims without proof.'

'Nonsense. We have one such criminal, a Romanian by the name of Nicolae Cojocaru, running a crime syndicate. Isn't that true?'

'There are no crimes recorded against Mr Cojocaru.'

'Yet you have a case file on him, and there have been several attempts to deport him, a man who has been labelled a criminal back in Romania.'

'Speculation,' Braxton said.

'Did Cojocaru arrange for Ivanov to be shot?'

'Mr Ivanov is a successful businessman, the owner of the football club that I support.'

Isaac winced at Braxton's attempt at levity. The woman asking the questions wasn't going to be distracted by such a tactic.

Richard Goddard took hold of the microphone. 'Ladies and gentlemen, this press conference was scheduled for twenty-five minutes. We've run over time, and as you can appreciate we are busy.'

A flurry of hands from the other reporters in the room; a retreat by the three police officers.

'Disaster,' Isaac said. 'Was Commissioner Davies watching?'

'He would be,' Goddard said.

'Then you either drop your phone out of the window or you and he will be having a conversation soon. Oscar, you shouldn't have been there. You've connected Ivanov with organised crime, made it obvious that the man is of interest.'

'I'd disagree. Cojocaru was mentioned as well. Both of them will be very nervous now.'

'One will be. We should meet with him,' Isaac said.

560

****

'A Steyr SSG 69 PIV, Austrian, bolt-action, .308 cartridge,' Gordon Windsor said. 'It's been fired.'

'You've looked down the scope?' Braxton asked. He and Isaac were back at the flat where the shot had been taken to kill Ivanov.

'Kahles ZF84 10x magnification scope. More than accurate for the distance. It was focussed on where Ivanov had been standing.'

'A bulky item to bring up here. Someone may have seen whoever brought it in.'

'Too bulky to take out afterwards if you're aiming to get away, and if Ivanov's men had figured out where the shot had come from. There's not much to see in the flat. It's empty, and apart from the toilet being used, nothing to tell you.'

'The person who fired the shot?'

'He would have used his right shoulder against the butt.'

'Conclusive?'

'Yes.'

'How long do you reckon the person was here?'

'We're assuming anywhere from thirty minutes to three hours. It's cold at night, and there was no heater, no electricity either.'

'If it was thirty minutes, the shooter must have known of Ivanov's movements.'

'That's for you to find out,' Windsor said. 'If it were only thirty minutes, then the rifle would have had to be set up in advance, possibly another target to zero in the scope.'

'Needle in a haystack looking for another shot. Any help on that?'

'None. Some noise when fired, but it did have a silencer.'

'Around here, not too many people would have been asking questions even if they heard a shot.'

Wendy took responsibility for the door-to-door interviews in the building. The rifle had been removed and was with Forensics for further testing, not necessary according to Gordon Windsor, but required nevertheless as it was vital evidence.

As expected, no one had heard anything, except for the wife of Fahad Shaikh, but as she had explained to Constable Jill Albertson and Wendy, she had not seen anyone. In the two women's presence, she had removed the cover from her face. The two were astonished by her beauty. She looked no more than nineteen or twenty; it was found out on checking that she was twenty-two, her husband older than her at thirty-eight.

Bridget had checked out the shooter's flat and found out that it had been sold two years previously, and up until three months before the shooting it had been rented to a family of four. Apart from that, a dead end.

'Someone must have known that the place was empty,' Isaac said at his early-morning meeting in the office. 'And whoever it was may well be the breakthrough we need.'

'It was sold to a company, they've purchased a few in the building and throughout the area,' Bridget said.

'The principals of the company?' Larry asked.

'I'm checking, but it seems that efforts have been made to conceal their identities.'

'Suspicious?'

'It could be part of a complex tax-reduction strategy, not necessarily illegal, or it could be an overseas company hiding dirty money.'

'Criminal?'

'It doesn't mean they're the murderers.'

'We need the names of whoever they are,' Isaac said. 'Dirty money could mean drug money, and we've a few names there.'

'I'll keep checking,' Bridget said. 'It may take some time.'

'Time is what we don't have. And no one's going to come forward with a description of this man.'

'The same person as in Ireland?'

'Whoever it was, he was capable of it, but it wasn't a difficult shot, not if the person was trained and the scope was lined up. According to Windsor, two shots had been fired before taking the shot at Ivanov,' Larry said. 'Even if we found the target for zeroing, it'll not tell us much. CCTV cameras?'

'We're checking, but if the man were organised, he'd only have to change his clothes. Some of the women in the building are covered, some of the men wear traditional dress.'

'An abaya?'
'It's always possible, although it seems bizarre.'
'I'll check,' Bridget said.

Chapter 21

Wendy Gladstone had thought that her time in Stockwell was at an end. She had conducted interviews with Sal Maynard's family, not that they had revealed much, in as much as the family were neither articulate nor still interested in a dead family member more than a few weeks after her death. It had saddened the police sergeant on the times she had visited the house, the drunken and foul-mouthed mother, the tattooed and violent elder brother of the dead woman, the drugged younger brother vacantly staring into space.

And now, a phone call from Ralphie.

Wendy and the young man met at McDonald's, which according to Ralph Ernest Begley was the best food that money could buy. Not that Ralphie was paying. Wendy ordered a Big Mac and extra fries for each of them, as well as a milkshake.

'What's this all about, Ralphie? I'm not out here on a wild goose chase, am I?'

Ralphie spoke between mouthfuls. Someone else was paying, and he was going back for seconds. 'It was something Sal said once. I didn't remember it before, and I suppose I wasn't listening.'

'Did you do that often?'

'What?'

'Not remember or listen.'

'Both. Sal could talk, and sometimes I just switched off. Not that she realised. I liked her, but you know that already. But she could talk rubbish sometimes, especially about celebrities and their perfect lives.'

'They have their problems the same as everyone else.'

'They don't have to live around here.'

Wendy realised that Ralphie wanted better, but as he sat eating it was clear that his time to change was limited. He was generationally unemployed and uneducated, his parents leading by example. The only hope for him was to leave the area, find himself a good family, re-engage with his education. She had already passed his details on to the local church and welfare services, but she knew they were inundated with worthier persons. And besides, she had three grandchildren, the eldest approaching school age, and she wanted to spend time with them, not to be a nursemaid to someone else's child, knowing full well that at the end of the day he would return to the negative influence of his family and friends. And even if Ralphie married, it would be the repeating cycle in that he would become the uncaring parent, possibly someone who would take a belt to the child.

'Do you want another Big Mac?' Wendy asked.

'My friends reckon I'm foolish talking to you.'

'Do you?'

'Not if you feed me and give me some money.'

Wendy left the table and went and ordered another Big Mac, bringing it back after a few minutes. 'Now, what have you got to tell me?'

'And the money?'

'Tell me what you know first.'

'Sal, it was the week she died. She was in a good mood, talking about this man and how he was going to take her away from here, put her on a pedestal.'

'Do you know what a pedestal is?'

'Not really, but Sal thought it was special.'

'It is, but who was this man, and why?'

'That's it. The one I saw was tall and slim, but that's not how she described him to me.'

'What do you mean?'

'She said he was the same height as her. And she didn't say he was slim.'

'But she was sleeping with Becali, the man you saw.'

'I'm certain of that, but I told you before that Sal made extra money.'

'You told me that Sal was keen on Becali?'

'I did, but I also told you about the face he pulled when he let her off that one time.'

'Can you be certain that it was Becali she was keen on?'

'Maybe I didn't hear right, and sometimes I'd tell her to slow down, but if she'd seen a celebrity, she'd not stop going on and on. I belong around here, so did she. It's okay to dream, but that's all it is.'

Wendy knew that she could have told him that life was what you made of it, but she did not, she had more pressing issues to deal with. If Sal Maynard did have another man, then who was he and where was he?

Yet again, the young woman had been thrust front and centre into the investigation. Not that she was guilty of any crime, but whatever she was, she was dead because of it.

Ralphie, his meal eaten, cycled away, fifty pounds in his back pocket. She had no intention of contacting him again unless it was vital. She sat at McDonald's for another ten minutes going through what he had said, wondering about the truth of it, and how to find Sal Maynard's mysterious admirer. She realised that it was not going to be easy.

***

Nicolae Cojocaru did not regard the presence of the two police officers as anything more than an inconvenience. In the past, back in Romania, if an officer of the law had not succumbed to gentle persuasion, either financial or with a gift, a car, a woman, then that officer had been sidelined or removed from circulation permanently. In the old country, when he had been a man of note, the bribes had been extortionate, and there was always a senior officer who would deal with a recalcitrant lower rank. In some ways, the gangster missed the old days where everyone and everything had a price or a solution. His recent trip to Romania had shown him that he was no longer a significant player and that a young class of villains had taken over. Even if he had wanted to go back, he couldn't, not without committing himself to violence and a large capital outlay to secure allegiances, to re-establish himself.

And now, back in England, two men who were incorruptible, two men he could not remove.

'Stanislav Ivanov is still in a medically-induced coma,' Isaac said.

'What has that to do with me?'

'You visited him in the south of France,' Oscar Braxton said.

'Did I?'

'Are we going to go around in circles on this?' Isaac said. The three men were meeting in a restaurant in Notting Hill, at Cojocaru's suggestion.

'I'm not sure what you mean,' Cojocaru said. He leant back in his chair, stifling a yawn.

'Are we keeping you up?'

'Busy night.'

'Celebrating that Ivanov is in the hospital?'

'How many times do I have to tell you that the man does not interest me?'

'We know the truth, even if you continue to deny it. We know that you were picked up in a car belonging to Ivanov at Marseilles Airport and that you entered the man's villa. Antonescu never left there. We believe he is dead.'

'You're living in a fantasy world,' Cojocaru said. He looked away and beckoned the waiter.

'A whisky for me,' he said. 'How about you two, or are you on duty?'

'I'll take a beer,' Braxton said.

'Likewise,' Isaac said. He didn't want to drink, and certainly not with the man opposite, but they needed to find out what he knew or what he was willing to tell.

'Crin Antonescu travelled with you to France, we can prove that,' Braxton said.

'And if he did, then so what? Travelling out of the country is not a crime. Maybe he's taking a holiday,' Cojocaru said, a tenseness in his voice.

'We're suspicious that you would meet with the head of the Tverskoyskaya Bratva after you had given us his name.'

'You cannot ignore people purely because you dislike them.'

'Let us be honest, Nicolae Cojocaru. You are the head of a crime syndicate in England,' Isaac said. 'We can't prove it, not sufficiently to arrest you and to send you back to the hovel you came from, but there is a more pressing matter, the shooting at Briganti's.'

'I thought you were going to say Ivanov.'

'He is another grubby individual who hides behind a veneer of respectability.'

'No doubt you don't say that to his face.'

'There are no investigations into his activities in this country, although we believe he was behind the shooting at Briganti's, also the death of a police officer in Ireland.'

'Then you'd better talk to him.'

'We will when he regains consciousness. And when he does, we'll tell him that you ordered his assassination. How do you think he'll respond?'

'I did not organise it.'

'Then who did?'

'I don't know.'

The two police officers could see that Cojocaru was not going to respond. Not that they had expected him to, but if he was unnerved and frightened then maybe he would act irrationally.

'We can't prove it yet, but it has to be you,' Isaac said. He looked over at Cojocaru, hoping to see the tell-tale signs of a man who was lying: the eyes looking away, the twitching hand, the beads of sweat on his forehead.

'We are trying to find out who owned the flat where the shot was fired from,' Braxton said. 'We will make the connection to you, and then it will not matter whether Ivanov lives or not. We don't even have to bother arresting you. All we need to do is to let Ivanov's Bratva know that it was you. Or maybe they've figured that out already. We're told there are a few after Ivanov's position.

Whoever takes his position won't be coming over to England to thank you. He'll be looking to carry on Ivanov's work, and maybe he'll use you for a while, or maybe he'll just have you killed. One way or the other, you, Nicolae Cojocaru, are a dead man.'

'Time will tell,' Cojocaru said.

'And this drug shipment that's in the country. Do you intend to distribute it?' Isaac asked. He took a drink of his beer, realising that in the company of evil it did not taste the same. He put it to one side, not intending to drink any more.

'I am an honest businessman.'

'You are a malignant parasite on society. If Ivanov doesn't get you, we will. In fact, your best chance is to level with us, turn Queen's evidence.'

'Detective Chief Inspector Cook, Detective Chief Inspector Braxton, I'll bid you both farewell. I do not find your company agreeable,' Cojocaru said as he stood up from his seat. He then walked out of the front door of the restaurant and got into the back seat of a black BMW, Ion Becali in the driver's seat.

'We made him feel uncomfortable,' Braxton said.

'We did, but what next? He could still strike a deal with the Russians. Cojocaru has residency in this country, they may not.'

'We still don't know what's going on, do we?'

'If Ivanov regains consciousness, he'll be looking to reassert himself. We should follow through on that angle,' Isaac said. 'But this investigation has deviated from what it was. Challis Street was looking for whoever shot up Briganti's, but now we're working with you on organised crime. The focus has been lost.'

'The focus hasn't, but how do you find out what happened? If, as we believe, Ivanov was responsible for Briganti's, and that Cojocaru was behind shooting Ivanov, then the person who took the shot in that flat is important. Get one, you get them all.'

'No one's come forward, and the gun on the twentieth floor wasn't registered, and there were no prints.'

'I'll get back to Serious and Organised Crime, find out what information is coming in from overseas,' Braxton said.

'I've got to get back to Challis Street. Sergeant Gladstone has an update, one of her people. Keep in touch,' Isaac said.

The two men shook hands, one heading down the road to his car, the other heading up.

Chapter 22

One of Stanislav Ivanov's bodyguards remained at Challis Street, not because he provided protection to the Russian businessman but because in a drain close to the assassination scene a gun had been found, the obvious deduction being that one of them had dumped it there.

Isaac looked across at the man in the interview room. 'Your name?' he said.

'Gennady Peskov,' the heavyset man replied. His English was acceptable although guttural. A translator was offered, but declined, as was legal aid. In the man's passport, a visa entitling him to carry out business in England, although no mention of his protection activities.

'How long have you been here?'

'Eight weeks.'

Larry sat to one side of Isaac. 'Why did you stay at the crime scene?' he asked.

'It was my job.'

'You provide personal protection for Stanislav Ivanov, is that correct?'

'I do.'

'And you carry a gun?'

'In Russia I would, but not in England.'

'Yet we found a gun near where Mr Ivanov was gunned down. Was it yours?'

'Not mine, but some of the others may have carried them.'

'Even if it is illegal?'

'Even if it was. Not that Ivanov would have approved. He's an honest man, but men such as him are always under threat.'

'What sort of man? A criminal, the head of the Tverskoyskaya Bratva?'

'One of the wealthiest men in Russia. People such as him make enemies.'

'You've been schooled well,' Isaac said. 'We've checked you out. In Russia, you spent time in prison for violence, almost killed a man once.'

'When I was younger, and the law is not always honest as it is here in England.'

The two police officers realised that Peskov, a gun for hire even if he denied the fact, was not a stupid man and that he had the innate street sense to say the right words and to not exacerbate the situation.

'Stanislav Ivanov is in the hospital.'

'I will stay by his side. The other bodyguards were not concerned about him, I am.'

'Why?'

'We grew up in the same village. To me, it is more than my job. To me, it is an honour.'

'Your visa is in dispute. You are not here to be employed, only to conduct business meetings.'

'I do attend the meetings, and I am not paid in this country. I don't think that you will deport me.'

Isaac knew they wouldn't. Even if Peskov had been carrying a weapon, he was a witness to a crime.

'Let us come back to the crime scene,' Isaac said. 'You are there with Ivanov, yet he gets shot. Why?'

'He enjoys the freedom in England. He wants to act as if he's English. Sometimes he gives us concern by his actions.'

'At the crime scene?'

'He wanted to talk to the people in the street, to look at his garden. We were hurrying him from the house to the car. He was not allowing us to do our job.'

'Are you saying it was his fault?'

'Not entirely. And it's not ours, not mine, that he was shot.'

'And what will Ivanov's reaction be, assuming he regains consciousness?'

'He will be angry and he will blame others.'

'Who?'

'Those who did not stay at his side, those who were responsible.'

'Do you know who it was that shot him?'

'No. Once I am free of here, I will be at Stanislav Ivanov's side.'

'There are no charges against you, Gennady Peskov. Where will we find those that ran from the crime scene?'

'I've no idea. If they could, they would have left the country by now.'

'Back to Russia?'

'Yes.'

'Thank you, Mr Peskov. You're free to go,' Isaac said.

Gennady Peskov walked out of Challis Street and hailed a taxi. 'St Mary's Hospital,' he said.

***

Nicolae Cojocaru's initial optimism was starting to wane. His nemesis, Stanislav Ivanov, had now been in intensive care at the hospital for nine days, and each bulletin from the hospital always said the same – the patient's condition is still critical, although there are signs of recovery.

Cojocaru could see the implications if the man made a full recovery, the consequences even if he did not. So far, the Tverskoyskaya Bratva's approaches to him had been low-key, no mention of how and why and who had shot their leader, only concern about how to maintain business, how to increase the distribution of the drugs out of Afghanistan.

The Romanian was under no illusion, and his denial if they asked about his involvement in the man's shooting would mean little to them.

Ivanov alive was a threat, dead he was also a threat, but in the half-world that the man occupied, he was an enigma; he made everyone nervous.

Cojocaru turned to Ion Becali. Both were in Cojocaru's penthouse.

'While Ivanov is in the hospital, we are safe,' Cojocaru said.

'We have taken control of the latest shipment, and we are setting up more distribution outlets for the Russians.'

'At the reduced price?'

'That is what Ivanov planned, and we have complied.'

'What about the gangs in the area? Any trouble?'

'We've taken them on to help with the distribution, although there are some complaints about the lower payments.'

'We're still maintaining their percentage at the old rate. They've no reason to complain.'

'Even so, it's more work for them, more chances of being caught.'

'They know the alternative,' Cojocaru said as he looked away from Becali. The man had gone from loyal employee to friend, even a junior partner, but now with Ivanov hanging on, Cojocaru could only see a man who had failed him; a man who had said his marksmanship was without equal. And yet he had been unable to kill Ivanov.

Cojocaru picked up his coat and headed out of the penthouse. 'You're driving,' he said to Becali.

'Where to?'

'St Mary's Hospital. I want the truth.'

'Is there any concern that what they are reporting is not correct?'

'It is always a risk. If he's dead, we will last longer, maybe even long enough to plot our return to the old country.'

'But we are not wanted back there.'

'I must maximise the profits in the short term. Back in Romania, I will buy myself a house in the country and grow vegetables.'

'Nicolae Cojocaru, you are not a man of the soil.'

'Becali, it is better to plant the vegetables than to be the fertiliser that makes them grow.'

'I don't want to go back to my old life,' Becali said as he grabbed the car keys. 'I want to stay here. I will deal with the problem on my own.'

In the basement of the building was Cojocaru's Mercedes. Becali eased it out of its parking spot and left the building, heading east in the direction of the hospital.

***

Serious and Organised Crime Command was watching the unfolding events with concern. The Russian mafia had, so far, had minimal impact in England, although they had made inroads into the former Soviet satellite states, but now their influence was starting to increase in London. A mansion in Kensington had been bought by Alexei Koch, a colleague of Ivanov's.

Reports indicated that whereas Ivanov was a man with some charisma and education, Koch could not be tagged with the same attributes.

According to Oscar Braxton, the man who had bought into one of the best streets in London was known for his savagery, a man who had personally murdered and tortured back in Russia, a man who had ascended up through the hierarchy of the Tverskoyskaya Bratva, a man who frightened many.

In Isaac's office at Challis Street, the team assembled, as well as Braxton.

'Ivanov's condition has improved,' Isaac said.

'Any signs of retribution for his shooting?' Braxton asked.

'Not yet. He's in for a long period of convalescence, whatever happens.'

'And in the meantime, we wait,' Larry said.

'Any better ideas?' Isaac said.

'Bateman's worried. The Russians are becoming too visible.'

'We're keeping a watch on them,' Braxton said.

'And doing what?'

'As long as they don't break the law, and they've no crimes against them back in Russia, it's difficult to refuse them a visa.'

'And with enough money, no one's looking too hard.'

'Can't we pre-empt the situation?' Isaac said.

'What do you mean?'

'Ivanov's the key. No one is going to act decisively while the man's life hangs in the balance. What if we issue a bogus report on his condition, and then watch what happens.'

'Are you suggesting that you're willing to allow an upturn in violence while the Bratva fight it out amongst themselves in Russia, and Cojocaru and Becali attempt to quell the local villains?'

'Can we control it?'

'It would require senior management to buy into it. If it goes wrong, it's on our heads.'

'And the lives of a few villains, and possibly a few innocent bystanders.'

'You've been on the streets, what about the cut-price heroin out there? Neatly packaged and brought in from Afghanistan, a stamp of quality marked on the outside.' Larry said. 'Do we have an option?'

Isaac made a phone call; Detective Chief Superintendent Goddard appeared within three minutes.

'Davies suggested something similar. You'll never get permission,' Goddard said.

'What are the options?' Isaac said. 'The streets are being flooded with low-cost heroin, and the police are only making a dent in it. We'll not win on this one, and everyone knows it. We could handle the West Indian gangsters, barely contain the Romanians, but the Russians have the muscle and the money to ride over us.'

'DCI Braxton, put it to your boss, and then I'll want a joint report from both our departments as to what is proposed, the risks, the rewards, the collateral damage.'

'And then?' Isaac asked.

'I'll take it to Commissioner Davies, get his input.'

'What are the chances?'

'It depends on your report. Davies doesn't want the street flowing with Russian gangsters and cheap heroin. What will happen after they've flooded the market, increased the number of drug addicts?'

'The price goes up, and so does the crime rate.'

'Get me the report, and we'll see. In the meantime, what are you doing?'

'Continuing with the investigations into the murders of Marcus Hearne and Ryan Buckley and the deaths at Briganti's.'

'Buckley's death is a matter for the Irish Garda,' Goddard said.

'His murderer could still be in England.'

'Very well. Just keep busy and arrest someone. I don't like what you're suggesting. Too many variables, too many opportunities for a mistake.'

Chapter 23

Wendy Gladstone had confronted death many times, and the sight of a body hanging from a beam, or with a bullet in it, did not bring her to tears. But the body lying on the ground did. A cord was tied around its neck, the bike that the man had been riding was off to one side, propped up against a tree. It was a bike that she knew; it was the bike of Ralph Ernest Begley, or Ralphie as he preferred to be called.

In the times she had spent with the young man, she had seen a decent soul wanting to make a difference, unable to break the cycle that condemned him. And now he was dead, and Gordon Windsor was with the body.

'You knew him?' Windsor said.

'Ralph Ernest Begley,' Wendy said.

'Who found the body?'

'I received a phone call from him ninety minutes ago. I came out here to meet him.'

'Here?'

'We used to meet nearby, and then I'd pay for a feed at McDonald's for him. It was how he liked it.'

'And when you got here, he was dead?'

'He said it was important.'

'You're not sure if it was?'

'With Ralphie, you could never be certain. He may have just wanted a feed and some money.'

'He was killed for a reason,' Windsor said as he stood up. 'The others in my team can complete the investigation.'

'Strangulation?'

'A neat job, no signs of resistance from Begley.'

'Which means that whoever killed him, knew him, or they were in conversation.'

'A local?'

'Not from around here,' Wendy said. 'The area is full of minor villains and layabouts, but not murderers. What else can you tell me about the death?'

'Whoever did it was strong.'

'Anything more?'

'Not at this time. The investigators will go over the area. You'll have an updated report later in the day. Next of kin?'

'The local police have informed them. I'll talk to them after here, but I don't expect much from them.'

'Someone that's killed before, I'd say.'

Wendy left Windsor and headed for the Begleys'. *No time like the present*, she thought.

The front door was opened on the second knock by a young woman. 'What do you want?' she said.

Wendy looked at the woman; assessed her to be in her teens. She was wearing a tee-shirt two sizes too small, a pair of faded jeans and her feet were bare. On both arms, tattoos were visible, and she had a ring in her right nostril. Apart from the affectation of disreputability, Wendy could see an attractive young woman already destroyed by the environment and the system, the same that had condemned Ralphie.

'Sergeant Wendy Gladstone, Challis Street Police Station,' Wendy said.

'A bit late, isn't it? He's dead.' It was the reply of someone who didn't care or was incapable, stupefied by the effects of one or another recreational drug.

'I came to offer my condolences.'

'Suit yourself. They're in the other room.' The young woman left and went back to the front room of the house, music blaring loudly. Inside the room, Wendy briefly saw an older man. Wendy held her handkerchief to her face, not to stifle the tears, but to lessen the smell of sweat mixed with marijuana and tobacco. In the back room of the house, a group of people sat or stood. Leaning with his back against the kitchen bench, the elder and violent brother of Sal Maynard.

'You still here?' the man said on seeing Wendy.

Wendy felt the urge to rebuke him and to tell him what she thought of him and his family, as well as what she thought of the Begleys, but did not. Ralphie and Sal Maynard had become friends out of a need to better themselves. Sal had become obsessed with celebrity to find her way out of her malaise. Ralphie had seen McDonald's and its hamburgers as his salvation. Neither had stood a chance, and here in this kitchen, was all that Wendy despised. She wanted to turn around and leave, but there were questions to be asked; answers, if there were any, to be drawn from people who did not trust the police.

'Mrs Begley,' Wendy said. She could see Sal Maynard's mother with her arm around a small woman, the tears rolling down her cheeks.' I'm sorry for your loss.'

'What are you doing here, tormenting this poor woman?' Mrs Maynard said.

'I liked Ralphie. He was a decent young man.'

'He said you were alright,' Ralphie's mother said.

'With some help, he may have achieved something.'

'We'll never know now, will we?'

Ralphie's father leant against the far wall. In his right hand, he held a bottle of beer.

Wendy could see some worth in the mother, none in the father. The other drug-consumed brother of Sal Maynard was not present. The blaring music from the front room continued to impede the conversation.

'Could that music be turned down?' Wendy said.

'No one dare interfere when she's entertaining,' Mrs Begley said.

'Why?'

'She does what she wants.'

'How old is your daughter?'

'Fifteen.'

'And you, Mr Begley, allow your daughter to prostitute herself in your house?'

'She's not mine.'

'We were separated for some years. Ralphie was ours, Rosy is mine,' Ralphie's mother said.

'I came here to offer my condolences and to ask you a few questions.'

'I'm not sure we can help.'

'Very well. Could the Maynards leave us for half an hour?'

Sal Maynard's brother opened the fridge door, took a can of beer and left soon enough. After a few more hugs and kind words from Mrs Maynard, she left as well.

Three remained in the back room, Wendy and the parents of Ralphie Begley. Fred Begley took another beer for himself, gave one to his wife. No sign of affection between the two was shown. In the other room, the music continued to blare, together with the sound of the daughter and the man she was with. To Wendy, the noises were not of an innocent fifteen-year-old female who should have been at school.

'Excuse me,' Wendy said. She left one room and walked down the narrow hallway and opened the door of the other; she did not knock. 'Get your clothes on, and get him out of here. Your brother has just died, and you're screwing around.'

'It's my house,' Rosy said.

'What business is it of yours?' the man said.

'Your name?'

'I've done nothing wrong.'

'A female of fifteen, under the age of consent, and truant from school. There's a police car outside, a couple of officers. They'll have a few questions for you on the way out.'

'She told me she was seventeen.'

'Ignorance is no excuse.'

'I'm not a tart, and Billy, he looks after me.'

'And Billy is over thirty, and if he's giving you clothes and money, taking you to fancy hotels and restaurants, that's prostitution. You, young lady, need discipline, but I suppose there's not much in this house.'

'You're not my mother.'

'If I were, you'd feel the weight of my hand on your backside. Now get Billy out of here, and I'll be pressing charges against him. You, Miss Begley, will come into the other room with your parents now.'

Wendy opened the front door of the house and beckoned one of the officers over. 'Check out Billy here. Book him for having sexual relations with a minor, and then take him down to Challis Street, get him checked out. I want the book thrown at him.'

'We know Billy Jepson,' the officer said. 'Smarmy individual, sells drugs around the back of the pub of a Saturday to minors. We'll make something stick.'

'This is police brutality,' Jepson said.

'It's justice,' Wendy said.

Wendy returned to the back room, Rosy with her.

Mrs Begley sat quietly sobbing, her husband stood, his back resting against a wall. Rosy crouched on the floor. Not one of the three spoke to the other.

'Rosy, let me start with you,' Wendy said.

'Why me?'

'Because I've not spoken to you yet. You were too busy with Billy Jepson before, but now I need to ask you a few questions.'

'If you must.'

Wendy saw another lost soul, but she couldn't feel the warmth for the young woman that she had for her brother. 'What was your relationship like with Ralphie?'

'We'd talk, that's all.'

'Is that it?'

'He was alright, but we didn't have anything in common.'

'I don't think anyone has in this house, do you? Rosy, you don't seem to be upset that your brother has died.'

'Why, should I be?'

It was clear to Wendy that the young woman was hostile, although she wasn't sure if it was a result of her abrupt removal from her lover, or whether it was the woman's natural state. Regardless, she needed to talk.

'Rosy, let me be plain here. If you've been selling yourself to Billy and others, I'll have you remanded and placed in care. Do I make myself understood?'

'You can't talk to Rosy like that,' the mother said.

'I can and I must. You seem to be upset over Ralphie's death, although your husband and Rosy don't.'

'Has your father ever laid a finger on you?' Wendy asked Rosy.

'I've never touched her,' the father said.

'I'll be reporting Rosy and her behaviour once I'm back at Challis Street. You, Mr Begley, if it is found that you have touched your daughter, then charges will be laid. Now, Rosy, has your father ever made any inappropriate actions against you?'

Rosy sat mute, her eyes looking down.

'No need to answer,' Wendy said. She knew the truth; others would deal with the father in due course.

'Ralphie was worried, I know that,' Rosy said.

'What do you mean?'

'He liked Sal, not me, but she was fat and plain.'

'Ralphie told me that he identified with Sal. Both of them wanted something better out of life, so do you. But giving yourself to Billy Jepson and others is not the way to achieve it. Sal Maynard thought that associating with celebrities would be her way out, Ralphie had no idea of how to get out and had resigned himself to his fate. But you, Rosy Begley, believe that giving yourself to older men is the way. You're still a child, even if you have the body of a woman.'

'It's better than what they do,' Rosy said, lifting her head, glancing over at her mother and father.

'It's not the solution. I'll ensure that you receive counselling if that's what you want.'

'Ralphie said you were a good person.'

'Not that good. I was wild at your age, but I had good parents.'

'Mum's fine, even if she's unable to control us.'

'Rosy, what did Ralphie tell you?'

'It was earlier today. He told me he was going to phone you, but he was frightened.'

'Of what?'

'He knew who the second man was.'

'That Sal Maynard mentioned?'

'Yes. He'd seen him somewhere, and the man frightened him. Ralphie was thinking of disappearing, and he wasn't sure of what to do.'

'Did you advise him?'

'I told him to vanish, and now he's dead.'

'Did he give you a name?'

'I can't remember what he said.'

'Why?'

'I wasn't listening.'

'Or maybe you were spaced out on drugs.'

'I might remember later.'

'And if you do, what will you do? Phone me or try to make some money for yourself?'

'I'll phone you.'

'Ralphie was probably killed because of this name. If you try to make a deal, he will kill you. Do you understand?'

'Yes.'

'Unfortunately, Rosy Begley, you don't. One of the men that Sal Maynard was involved with was a Romanian gangster, not a Stockwell villain, not a Billy Jepson. These men kill without conscience. If they or he suspect you know, then your life will be forfeit, as will your parents' lives. Does everyone in this room understand?'

Wendy looked at the other two, both nodding in acknowledgement. She knew they did not.

Chapter 24

In St Mary's Hospital Stanislav Ivanov opened his eyes for the first time since he had been shot. The time had come to see whether the football club owner, entrepreneur, and Bratva Godfather was to be a vegetable for his remaining days, or whether he was to make a full recovery.

Detective Chief Inspectors Isaac Cook and Oscar Braxton stood back from the bed.

Ivanov slowly moved his head, looked at his wife and smiled. She came closer and kissed him on his forehead. A nurse checked the patient's pulse, a doctor felt proud that the medical care that had been provided appeared to have been successful.

'What happened?' Ivanov said to his wife.

'There was an assassination attempt,' she replied.

'Who?'

'The police don't know.'

'They are unimportant. Where is Gennady Peskov?'

'He is here, but you must rest.'

'I need Peskov.'

'Your wife is correct,' the doctor said. 'We need to ascertain your intellectual acuity, conduct further tests. You are still under mild sedation, and will be drowsy for the next few days.'

Ivanov moved his head towards his wife and spoke, his voice still slurred. 'Peskov knows what to do,' he said. His wife nodded but did not speak.

Isaac Cook and Oscar Braxton heard the words but did not understand; a police sergeant, the child of Russian immigrants, stood next to them.

Outside Ivanov's room, the police sergeant reported all that she had heard spoken in Russian.

'Peskov's the key,' Isaac said.

'The key to what?' Braxton replied.

'We're none the wiser, but Ivanov seemed coherent.'

Gennady Peskov came out from Ivanov's room, as did Ivanov's wife. Isaac walked down the corridor with the woman, Braxton stayed with Peskov.

'Mrs Ivanov, you must be pleased that your husband will recover,' Isaac said.

The woman did not miss a step and kept walking. 'Yes,' she said.

'There will be violence. We cannot allow it to happen in England.'

'I am the wife of Stanislav Ivanov. What he does or does not do is not my concern.'

'It is your concern. So far, he has not committed a criminal offence in England. If that changes, it could jeopardise your welcome in this country.'

'Inspector Cook, I am powerless in such matters, the same as you.'

The automatic doors at the exit to the building opened and Mrs Ivanov stepped into the back seat of a black Mercedes, the chauffeur opening the door for her. The vehicle sped away, leaving Isaac standing by the side of the road. He returned to where Gennady Peskov was standing with Oscar Braxton.

'Peskov tells me that there is nothing of concern,' Braxton said as Isaac arrived.

'Mr Ivanov has placed his trust in you. You must know what he wanted you to do,' Isaac said.

'It is for me to let others know that Stanislav Ivanov lives and that it is business as usual.'

'Business – commercial or criminal?'

'With Ivanov, commercial. I need to bring in my own security,' Peskov said.

'There has always been a police officer outside Mr Ivanov's room,' Braxton said.

'But Mr Ivanov is awake.'

'Do you expect another assassination attempt?'

'Your police officers will be no match for someone determined.'

'Are you suggesting that the Tverskoyskaya Bratva will attempt to kill him, or will it be closer to home?'

'I am not suggesting anything. Stanislav Ivanov needs more security, that's all I'm saying.'

'We are wasting our time with Mr Peskov,' Isaac said to Braxton, ensuring that the Russian heard the disdain in his voice.

'If anything happens to anybody in this country, then you, Gennady Peskov, will be our primary suspect. Is that clear?'

'That is clear,' Peskov said as he walked away.

'There's going to be trouble. What about Cojocaru? If he was behind the assassination attempt, then he must be worried,' Braxton said.

***

Larry met with Claude Bateman who had taken the role of lead police communicator for the West Indian gangs in the area. Bateman was affable, more so than on the previous occasion.

The Wellington Arms in Bayswater, the venue for their meeting, was full, mostly with locals enjoying a quiet drink, a few tourists winding their way through the area, a few West Indians, some gang members, some not, sitting quietly or propping up the bar. Larry sat towards the back of the pub; on his left, Bateman, and on his right, one of Bateman's men.

'What will happen?' Bateman asked. He had a cigar in his mouth, he offered one to Larry. The two men took a puff on their cigars before expelling the smoke; neither spoke for a minute.

'What will you do? Are you clean?' Larry said.

'Becali took the shot at Ivanov.'

'Did he take the shot, the truth?'

'He had been in that building before.'

'Why didn't you tell us before?'

'Tell you what? If you knew that he had been seen there, what would you have done? Nothing, other than to confront Becali and Cojocaru. You wouldn't have arrested them. And then what?'

'You'd be exposed.'

'Discretion is the better part of valour. If you arrest Becali for attempted murder, cast-iron evidence, then the person who saw him in that building will testify. Until then, nobody will say anything.'

'You're telling me now.'

'The situation has changed. Ivanov will live, others will die.'

'Becali entered the building, took the shot from the flat and left. Did your person see this?'

'Not the flat, but the man entering and leaving the building, yes.'

'It's still circumstantial.'

'That's why you've not been told. You can't prove it, nor can we, but Ivanov does not need proof.'

'You've not told the Russians?'

'If we told one of his men, could they be trusted? Would they believe us? They hate us more than they hate Cojocaru.'

'Have you had any more contact with the man?'

'He's keeping a low profile, and with Ivanov recovering he must be worried.'

'And worried people do stupid things.'

'We will not become involved. The Russians are smarter than Cojocaru, more violent, and better resourced. We'd not stand a chance.'

'Neither would the police. What can you do to help us?'

'What do you want?'

'Keep us informed at all times, no matter how insignificant. Any strange faces on the street?'

'Russians?'

'Or Romanians.'

'How do you tell the difference?'

'I'm not sure, apart from the language. Have you seen Ion Becali?'

'He was in here a couple of days ago, drank a couple of beers and left.'

'Did he speak to you?'

'He wasn't in a talkative mood. He met up with a woman, left with her.'

'Is she important?'

'She's known in the area, but no, she'd know nothing.'

Larry felt that his time was wasted with Claude Bateman and that the West Indians were bit players in the unfolding drama. A phone call from Isaac, an excuse to leave the pub.

Outside, Larry got into his car, acknowledged one of Bateman's men who had been keeping a watch on it for him. Graffiti, a nuisance in the area, had been on the rise, and a police car was a prime target for a quick spray, the words artistically applied, yet derogatory. No one would dare touch Bateman's car, but a police vehicle was fair game, and for those who indulged in such behaviour, a badge of honour.

At St Mary's Hospital, Ivanov was sitting up and enjoying a good meal. No hospital food for him, it had been brought in from a Michelin-starred restaurant.

'This would not have happened in Russia,' he said.

Larry had arrived at the same time as Isaac, and both had entered the man's room together. To one side of Ivanov's bed, Gennady Peskov. There was no sign of Ivanov's wife.

'We've tightened security,' Isaac said by way of an apology, which he knew was an inadequate response. 'We'll ensure that it doesn't happen again.'

'No doubt, but it doesn't help.'

In Ivanov's previous room at the hospital, one floor up, Gordon Windsor and his crime scene investigators were commencing their investigation, the bullet hole in the window clearly visible.

'We believe it was the same person that shot you before,' Isaac said. Larry said nothing, disturbed that with the security they had provided for the Russian gangster, no one had thought to check the possibility of another shot being taken from outside the building, the same as when the man had stood on the street outside his house.

'I thought the English police were the best, but it appears they are not. I may have to re-evaluate my time in your country. It may be that Russia is a safer place for me.'

Isaac knew this was rhetoric on Ivanov's part and that this incident would be breaking news in the media: a prominent and respected Russian businessman, the intended victim of a brazen assassination attempt, the second since the man had returned to England, the first since the football team he owned had won the FA Cup.

'Our investigation has been thwarted by a wall of silence. Mr Ivanov, who took these shots?'

'I am a powerful man, and in Russia, powerful men have powerful enemies.'

'Are you saying that the attempts are orchestrated from Russia?'

'I have said no such thing. Do not try to trick me with your English language. I am suitably fluent not to fall for such tricks. In Russia, business is sometimes conducted with a gun, but here in England, I thought it was not.'

'It is not an Englishman who shot you, and you know this. It was either a Romanian or a Russian. We are aware of your connections in Russia, of the Tverskoyskaya Bratva.'

'I am a legitimate businessman who abides by the law and the ethics of the country that I operate in.'

'Are you saying that the Bratva is legitimate?'

'It is you that mention the Bratva, not I. And may I remind you that I am an influential man, and any aspersions that I am in some way guilty of any crime are slanderous, and I will ensure that your superiors are informed of what you are saying.'

Isaac knew that once the words 'influential', and 'I have friends in high places' were mentioned, then the person saying the words was rattled, and they were guilty.

'If you'll excuse me, I will go and check on your previous room,' Isaac said. 'What will you do about this second assassination attempt?'

'I will rely on the British police to apprehend who is responsible and to bring them to justice.'

Both Isaac and Larry knew that the man would not.

Upstairs, in the room previously occupied by Ivanov, Gordon Windsor was busy, as were three of his colleagues. Outside, along the corridor, some of the other patients in the adjoining rooms were being moved. It was a crime scene, and it was neither as quiet as it should be nor as hygienic. A middle-aged woman from the hospital administration made herself known to Isaac, expressed her concern at what had happened, and asked how long it would be before the police were finished and that it was a hospital for the ill, and not there for a police training exercise.

Isaac soothed the woman, ensured her that all efforts would be made to keep the disruption to a minimum, but a man had almost been shot in the hospital, and that had to take precedence. After ten minutes of his best diplomacy, the woman left.

Isaac and Larry kitted up in coveralls, gloves, overshoes, and entered Ivanov's previous room.

'Not a good record,' Windsor said. He was looking out of the window at a building across the road.

'The police or the assassin?'

'Both. You'll be hauled over the coals on this one. The man was in our protective custody this time.'

Isaac did not respond. He knew that Windsor was correct. Stanislav Ivanov had been provided police protection. It was not so much an oversight, more a realisation that it was the first time that a bullet had been fired into a hospital, and this time, the point of the bullet's departure could be clearly seen, an open window no more than fifty yards distance.

'We've got people over there?' Larry asked. 'It was only luck that Ivanov moved to one side in his bed at the right time.'

'The shooter's been sloppy this time. We found some prints.'

'Larry, get over there,' Isaac said. 'Find out what you can and make an arrest. If you don't, we're in for a rough time.'

***

Two days after the second attempt on Ivanov's life, the man checked himself out of St Mary's Hospital and returned to his home in Bayswater. However, this time Gennady Peskov ensured that the security provided was the best possible, no more low-grade thugs from Russia, other than a core group of four personally chosen by Peskov. A private English security company were to patrol outside the house; they were not armed, not even with pepper spray or tasers, a result of stringent English laws restricting the carrying and use of weapons, and although Peskov thought it foolish, Ivanov could not agree. With the money being paid, and the incorruptibility of the men employed, he knew that he was safer with men who regarded security as a profession, not just a chance to carry a gun and act important.

Peskov and his chosen four, fellow villagers back in Russia, had an arsenal of weapons in the house, although when they left the building they ensured that only two of them would discreetly carry guns. In the event of a gun being used, that person would be whisked out of England before the authorities could question him.

Ivanov sat in his favourite chair, his wife nearby.

'I want to stay in England,' the wife said. She was holding her husband's hand, but not with the attendant affection that would be assumed, but then, Ivanov knew that didn't exist. They had married young and had had three children. One of them, the only daughter, was a doctor in Moscow, and she used her mother's maiden name, and never mentioned that she was the child of Stanislav Ivanov. The two sons, one was killed in a shootout in St Petersburg, the other, a lieutenant in the Tverskoyskaya Bratva. Of the three children, Stanislav and his wife were fond of their daughter, not the remaining son. Each year the three of them would meet at a dacha near to a Black Sea resort. For ten days, they would be a family and no mention would be made of where the wealth had come from.

'I intend to stay as well,' Ivanov said. 'You can stay at the country house, I will stay here. And let us not pretend with each other.'

'I was worried.'

'So was I, but we maintain the pretence. You are the face of respectability, but I have no need of you,' Ivanov said.

'And I have no need of you,' the wife said. 'I will return to my home with your permission.'

'It is granted. I have work to do.'

'Be careful, the police are not fools. They will be watching.'

'It must be done. I have upgraded your security, just in case.'

'Thank you, my husband. I will check on you from time to time, and if you need me at your side, then call.'

As soon as Ivanov's wife had left, Gennady Peskov entered the room.

'Is all ready?' Ivanov said.

'It is ready. When?'

'Five days. I want everyone to be lulled into a sense of complacency. I want everyone to believe that my return does not upset the equilibrium. Cojocaru?'

'He is outside.'

Ivanov raised himself from his chair, Peskov assisting. 'Let him in,' Ivanov said.

Nicolae Cojocaru entered the room, the sweat beads on his forehead clearly visible. It was what Ivanov had hoped to see. The last time they had met, the Russian had forced the Romanian to shoot Crin Antonescu, one of Cojocaru's henchmen, one of the very few that the man could trust. And now the Romanian was back in the lair of the Russian godfather, a lair where he, Nicolae Cojocaru, was a mere pawn.

'I am pleased to see that you are well,' Cojocaru said.

'I thank you for your kindness. As you can see, I am fully recovered,' Ivanov said, struggling to maintain an upright posture. 'Please sit down. We have matters to discuss.'

Cojocaru sat down, bolt upright; Ivanov slumped back onto his chair, hopeful that it looked as though it was planned, and not as the need to take the weight off his feet as soon as possible.

'The distribution goes well, up nine per cent on last week,' Cojocaru said, his voice quavering.

'That is not why you are here.'

'I don't understand.'

Peskov stood to one side of Cojocaru, his right hand inside his jacket pocket.

'I want you to kill Ion Becali and to bring his head to me,' Ivanov said calmly.

'Why?'

'I need a sign of loyalty that I can trust you. You killed Antonescu, but you did not learn that my benevolence is limited, my wrath infinite. You have attempted to kill me on two separate occasions, and you have failed on both. I should be dead, yet I live. You, Nicolae Cojocaru, live because I have need of you. Either you comply with my request, or you will not leave here today.'

'The police are watching this house, you must know that.'

'Let me rephrase what I've just said. You will leave this house as a free man innocent of all crimes, or you will leave as a condemned man, the date of execution not yet determined. Which is it to be?'

'I wish to live, but for how long?'

'I will make you a promise. Do what I want without hesitation, and I will leave you alone. You are not the first to attempt to kill me, and some have died, some have lived. I do not blame you, I only pity your stupidity. Now, admit that you wanted me dead.'

'I did, but purely for my own survival.'

'Then we are honest with each other. Cojocaru, I do not like you or any of your Romanian friends, and you don't like me and what I represent. Openness is the way forward, and I want Becali dead as a token of our agreement here today.'

'And afterwards, when my usefulness has been exhausted, then what?'

'You will be free to do what you want.'

A confused man left the house, a man who knew that he was condemned whichever way he turned, but then he had known that since Ivanov and his Bratva started to make inroads into England. Peskov smiled as Cojocaru walked down the steps to the road. At that moment, Cojocaru wished that Becali was still in the flat that he could see up above him; he wished that the man was there to take a shot at him, and not to miss.

Chapter 25

Wendy attended the funeral of Ralph Ernest Begley, and watched as the young man's mother mounted the steps to the lectern at the front of the church and spoke of her son.

In the front row of the church, Begley's father and Rosy, the fifteen-year-old child who has flirted with danger and promiscuity. The two did not sit close to each other. On the left-hand side of Fred Begley, a police officer sat. To compound Ralphie's death, investigations into Fred and his step-daughter revealed that the man had been guilty of crimes against her, and he was now on remand awaiting trial. Rosy was dressed in black, the nose ring removed, the tattoos covered. Wendy looked over at her; she smiled back. At the conclusion of Ralphie's mother's eulogy, Rosy got up and helped her back to her seat. The young woman then mounted the steps to the lectern and spoke from the heart. The mother had been tearful but her eulogy devoid of any content other than a mother's love for a son and how he had always been a good child, rarely crying, and how his future had looked promising, and that she would miss him. Rosy, her face no longer caked in makeup, spoke of her brother, and how they would talk, sometimes into the night, and to her, he was the most important person in her life. She did not mention the father, nor did she look at him. To Wendy, it was as if she was talking to her, and it brought a warm glow to her; as if the death of Ralphie had not been in vain, and that the young woman had a chance of redemption, the chance her brother had never had.

Outside the church the young woman came over and put her arms around Wendy. 'Thank you for coming. Ralphie would have appreciated it,' she said.

'He wanted to be someone better. You seem better equipped to succeed.'

'I am. I was always top of my class at school, and I've refocussed myself on my studies. Please stay in touch. My father will not be around, not that he ever was, not when it was important, and my mother, well, you know what she is.'

'Call me if you need me,' Wendy said as she walked away and to her car. She had a smile on her face; for once, amongst all the misery and despair, a ray of sunshine, the possibility that she may have made a difference.

As she reached the car, Rosy came running up. 'I remembered the name of the other man. Anton something.'

'Antonescu?'

'That's it. Crisp?'

'Crin?'

'That's what Ralphie said. Do you know him?'

'I know him, but he's dead.'

'Are you sure?'

'As sure as I can be.'

'I hope it helps.'

'It does,' Wendy said as she gave Rosy a hug. 'Look after yourself.'

'I will.'

***

Commissioner Alwyn Davies was angry, and it was Detective Chief Superintendent Richard Goddard who was on the receiving end of the man's invective.

'How do you think this is going to reflect on the London Metropolitan Police?' Davies said. 'Twice they've tried to kill him, and the second time he's in intensive care at St Mary's Hospital, a guard on the door. What did you think, that they'd give up after the first attempt?'

'We provided the best security we could,' Goddard said. 'It was touch and go if the man would live after the first attempt.'

'But he did, and now he's back at his house. Do we have security there?'

'He's employed a private security company, very expensive, professional. They provide security to diplomats in the city, influential visitors.'

'Questions are being asked about Ivanov,' Davies said. His tone was almost conciliatory; before it had been combative. Goddard didn't like the change. He knew Davies to be a political animal, more concerned with his own survival than that of others.

'Enough money and questions go away.'

'What does that mean?' Davies's voice once again combative.

'Not bribery or corruption, but Ivanov entered this country with his pockets full of money and no criminal convictions overseas. He came on a Tier 1(Investor) Visa, two million pounds to invest. After two years, he injected another fifty million, although the minimum requirement was ten. He followed the correct procedures and we can't deport him.'

'If he's a legitimate investor in this country, then why are people trying to kill him?'

'It's in the report.'

'Goddard, don't get smart. Tell me why.'

'Stanislav Ivanov is the head of a criminal organisation that calls itself the Tverskoyskaya Bratva. Mafia, if you like. He'll claim that he isn't the head, and even if he is, there are no convictions against him, and he's done nothing wrong in this country.'

'What about the Romanians?'

'Serious players in the importation of illicit drugs and distribution. The Russians are attempting to muscle in, either use them or kill them.'

'And in your patch?'

'That's where Nicolae Cojocaru, the most significant of the Romanians, is based, but his operations spread out from there.'

'Yes, I've heard this all before, but what are you doing about it? What are you doing about Ivanov? These rogues sneak into our country, flashing their money and we do nothing.'

'We're here to police the wrongdoers, not to say who comes in or not,' Goddard said. 'We need to wrap up the shooting at Briganti's first. Serious and Organised Crime Command have Ivanov in their sights, but unless the man makes an illegal move, they're powerless.'

'He won't.'

'DCI Cook is maintaining the pressure on Nicolae Cojocaru. He's behind the attempted assassinations, not Briganti's though.'

'Can you be sure of that?'

'There's one inconsistency which doesn't make sense.'

'Which is?'

'Sal Maynard, a celebrity-obsessed woman, was in Briganti's, died there. It appears that she was spending time with Cojocaru's two lieutenants.'

'Then that's a clear tie-in, or am I missing something?'

'Cojocaru had no reason for Briganti's, Ivanov did. It's Ivanov for Briganti's, yet Sal Maynard is tied to Cojocaru. Not that she probably knew, not too bright according to reports, and now her friend from where she lived is dead as well. The trail continues to lead back to Cojocaru, yet we know it's not him.'

'Goddard, I've little confidence in your DCI Cook, you know that. I'd prefer my man Caddick in charge, but I've kept him out for the time being, hoping that you'd deal with the investigation.'

'Superintendent Caddick would not be advisable at this time,' Goddard said. He knew that a direct statement that the man was Davies's lackey and incompetent would have met with an immediate rebuke.

'Very well, have it your way. Goddard, for once you make sense. Now go and stir up your team, and leave me to deal with running the Met. You're not the only one who worries me.'

Richard Goddard sensed that for once the man did not mean what he had just said. It was as if there was a begrudging admission from Commissioner Davies that Chief Detective Superintendent Richard Goddard was a good police officer doing a decent job under difficult circumstances.

Goddard could not think the same of his commissioner, a man he still loathed.

***

'I've told you because I don't want to kill you,' Cojocaru said. The two men were in Cojocaru's penthouse; neither was interested in the view.

'If Ivanov knows that you are telling me, he'll have you killed,' Becali said. 'We will not succeed a third time. Have you admitted to our previous attempts?'

'I had no option. If I kill you, then I will survive a little longer.'

'Then do it,' Becali said.

'Why?'

'I don't mean me. Kill someone, make it out to be me, body destroyed beyond recognition.'

'You would do this?'

'For you, Nicolae Cojocaru, I would.'

'But who?'

'Does it matter?'

'Ivanov will want proof of your death.'

'Then Ivanov must die. What about the other Russians?'

'Ivanov's Bratva will do nothing, business is more important to them. As for the other Bratvas, they will not act. The only risk is Gennady Peskov. He is loyal to Ivanov, the same as you are to me. He will forfeit his life if necessary to avenge Ivanov's death.'

'Then he must die as well.'

'But how?'

'You must stay here. This time I need to get close to the man.'

'You will die.'

'If I survive, get me out of the country,' Becali said. 'And I want the truth of what happened to Antonescu.'

'It seems that we will both be growing vegetables back in the old country,' Cojocaru said.

'The truth.'

'I was given an ultimatum in France. Either I shot Crin, or they would shoot both of us there and then.'

'And you shot him in cold blood?'

'They had severely beaten him. I apologised before I pulled the trigger. He forgave me before he died.'

'You had no option, but now, we do.'

***

At Challis Street Police Station, a quandary on how to move forward. Larry met with Claude Bateman, the second time in as many days, a café close to Notting Hill.

'The calm before the storm,' Bateman said. 'It's a wait and see, and none of us wants to be involved. Ivanov's recovery frightens us. We do not believe that Cojocaru will live long, now that it is proven that Becali shot at the Russian twice.'

'Proven?'

'Yes, we know that he did. I did not tell you the full story last time, too dangerous. Becali was seen going into that flat. I have a witness who will come forward when needed.'

'Who? There is only one we know of, a covered woman in one of the flats on the same floor.'

'It was not her.'

'Then her husband.'

'He will not talk without certain assurances.'

'Such as?'

'Protection and the right to stay in this country.'

'You cannot give him that,' Larry said.

'But you can. If he gives you what you want, it is the lever to deal with Cojocaru, the opportunity to free ourselves from his influence.'

'Would you welcome this?'

'What option do we have?'

'You're admitting to criminal activity. I could have you arrested. Our conversation here today could be used as evidence.'

'You will not arrest me or others,' Bateman said. He took out a cigar from his pocket, put it back again.

'Why not?'

'The chance to rid yourself of Cojocaru is more important than arresting me. And besides, if what we plan works out, we can re-establish ourselves. And maybe Ivanov will go, and I will take the Romanian's place.'

Bateman was not a fool, Larry knew that, but the man was indiscreet and naïve. He had seen how Cojocaru had dealt with those he did not trust or want. The West Indians were violent and handy with a knife and a gun, but they still retained the Caribbean sentimentality, and death, even if they were responsible, was met with sorrow by them and the community.

'You are taking a risk, you must know that,' Larry said.

'There will be winners and losers, but to stand on the sidelines will achieve little. You can have Fahad Shaikh once you have satisfied his concerns.'

'We can pull him in anytime. Why does he trust you?'

'Who else can he trust? He has exceeded his visa, and he has been working two jobs, cash in hand. He came to me, not out of fondness, but out of desperation. He knew what would happen if he had come to you directly.'

'We would have secured his visa for as long as necessary.'

'For as long as it took to convict Becali. Shaikh needs more, and now, you have a man you can arrest. How much is this worth to you?'

'Why have you protected him for so long?'

'Leverage. He wants a commitment from you, in writing. I want your word that you will remove the malaise of Cojocaru and Ivanov.'

'Guarantees I cannot give. Cojocaru is possible, Ivanov is uncertain. The jobs that Shaikh has been doing. For you?'

'It is better that I do not answer, wouldn't you agree?'

'I would. Where can I find Fahad Shaikh?'

'He is at his flat. No agreement and he will not talk. He has placed his trust in me, not you.'

Larry knew that Bateman was right. Fahad Shaikh would give the team their first arrest and with the man's testimony their first conviction.

****

'Can't be done,' Richard Goddard said. He was sitting in his office on the third floor at Challis Street. On the other side of his desk, Isaac Cook and Larry Hill.

'But the man's a material witness. We need his evidence.'

'Where is he now?'

'Sergeant Gladstone is with him. I've organised two officers from Armed Response to ensure his safety.'

'Okay, put him and his family in a safe house. I'll see what can be done. Becali's trial will stretch out for some time. I'll make a few phone calls on behalf of the man, pull in a few favours. No promises, but it's the best we can do for now.'

Isaac left his chief superintendent's office and travelled out to Shaikh's flat.

'Everyone's curious as to why we're here,' one of the armed officers said.

'We're moving the family,' Isaac said. 'A safe house.'

'Now?'

'Yes. I need to go in.'

Isaac knocked on the door, Wendy answered it. 'I need to talk to Mr Shaikh.'

'He's frightened. They had a rough time back in Pakistan, and neither he nor his wife wants to go back.'

'We can get him a year in the UK, and DCS Goddard's trying for more. Becali's conviction will go in his favour.'

After five minutes, while Fahad Shaikh's wife moved to one of the bedrooms, Isaac entered the previously forbidden flat. He explained the situation, offered no guarantees, only emphasised the British sense of fair play and decency. Shaikh listened intently, finally agreeing with what he had been told. Two hours later, Wendy left with the family and five suitcases, the extent of their worldly goods in England. It wasn't much, Wendy had to admit, but it was probably more than where they had come from. Shaikh's wife grabbed her arm as they left the flat for a small house in the country. Fahad carried one of the children, his wife, another, and Wendy held the hand of a pretty girl of four.

Downstairs, a four-wheel drive waited for them. Wendy followed in her car for the fifty-minute drive. Whatever the future held for the Shaikhs, it was better than the depressing little flat they had left, Wendy thought.

***

An all-points warning had been put out for the arrest of Ion Becali, possibly armed and dangerous. Oscar Braxton was in Isaac's office, as was Richard Goddard, who left soon after to phone Commissioner Alwyn Davies about the breakthrough.

At the same time, a desperate man, unaware of his fate, sat in a café two streets from Ivanov's home. He knew what needed to be done, but not how to do it. He had walked up Ivanov's street fifteen minutes earlier, suitably disguised, and had seen the security, professional and alert, not like the Russians who stood to attention when needed, slouched when no one was looking.

Becali left the café. He was not thinking straight, and his plan, which had seemed plausible at Cojocaru's, now seemed foolish. There he had been willing to sacrifice his life for the man who had saved him from a life of subsistence and had brought him to England, but now he did not want to die, only to live. The future lay with Ivanov. He walked the two streets to Ivanov's house and shouted to the bodyguards on the road.

'I want to see Ivanov,' Becali shouted. 'I'm laying my weapon down.'

'Slow and easy. Which side of the body is the gun, right or left?' one of the men shouted back.

'Left.'

The four men standing outside the house moved behind a Range Rover on the street.

'Remove the weapon using your left hand and put it on the ground.'

Becali complied. He knew that the men ahead of him were English and unarmed, but from one of the windows to the left of them, two pairs of eyes watched. They would be armed, he knew.

'Now lie down spread-eagled, arms and legs stretched out. One of us will come over and check that you're not carrying any other weapons.'

Becali complied with the request; another man came over. He placed one of his boots firmly on the Romanian's back, pinning him to the ground.

'Don't move, not till one of the others has checked you out.'

A second man came over and frisked Becali thoroughly, pulling his wrists together behind his back and securing them with a cable tie.

'You can stand now,' the man said.

'I need to meet with Stanislav Ivanov,' Becali said. The cable tie was unexpected, and he knew it had to be removed.

'The police have issued an all-points for your arrest.'

'I need to see Ivanov first, it's important.'

'We're here to protect the man, not to let scum like you through. A police car will be here soon enough. You can either comply, or I'll flatten you. Your choice.'

'I'll comply.'

Becali realised that his chance to strike a deal with Ivanov was gone, but he was still alive. It wasn't the outcome that he had wanted, but it could have been worse.

Chapter 26

Nicolae Cojocaru realised forty-eight minutes after Ion Becali had left that he had made the wrong decision. A man stood in front of him, a man he had not expected to see.

'Becali has been seen close to Stanislav Ivanov's house. What did you expect? Did you imagine that he would be successful on his third attempt?'

'I killed you in France,' Cojocaru said.

'Ivanov was right. You are a fool, easily duped.'

'We were friends.'

'We never were. To you, I was a man who committed violence when it was needed, nothing more. You were willing to kill me to save your life.'

'I had no option. Neither of us would have left Ivanov's villa if I hadn't.'

'You were told to kill Becali. Stanislav Ivanov is a forgiving man to those who are loyal to him, indifferent to those who aren't.'

'I could not kill Becali. He has always been loyal to me.'

'Ivanov was willing to abide by his agreement, the same as he has with me, but now, your fate is sealed.'

'Can we make a deal? It is not too late to save us, you included. Anyone who knows what Ivanov is in England, the crimes he has committed, will die.'

'I have seen nothing, nor will I. The man has my allegiance, you do not.'

'But I shot you.'

'A subterfuge to test you. You did not check the gun, it contained a blank, and I was wearing a bulletproof vest. Ivanov wanted to know if you were capable of violence and whether you would shoot me in the chest.'

'It makes no sense.'

'Not to us, but we are not smart men, not as smart as Ivanov. I had to decide, the same as you. I chose Ivanov, you chose to die,' Crin Antonescu said.

Cojocaru, not sure what to say or do, sat down on a chair. Antonescu sat too, always ensuring that the gun he held was pointed at his former boss.

Neither man moved, except to maintain their gaze at the other. Cojocaru could see the impassiveness in the other's eyes, but he was not surprised. Crin Antonescu had always been emotionless when violence was involved, whereas Ion Becali had followed orders, and now he was in police custody.

'It would be better if you shot me now,' Cojocaru said.

Antonescu shot Cojocaru once in the head, the man's lifeless body slumping forward. After the man had died, Antonescu reflected on what he had just done, feeling a pang of regret.

He knew that Cojocaru, for all his faults, had supported him, and what he had done in France was only what he would have done if the positions had been reversed. He left the penthouse with a heavy heart and drove back to his hotel. He had re-entered England under a false name, his dark hair dyed blond and cropped short. Life was as uncertain for him as it had been for Cojocaru and for Becali. He knew that he needed to leave the country as soon as possible.

***

Ion Becali sat in the interview room at Challis Street Police Station. In front of him, a cup of tea, to one side, his lawyer, a naturalised British citizen from Romania. Across from the two Romanians, Isaac Cook and Larry Hill.

Isaac followed the procedures required, informed Becali of his rights and that what he said could be used in evidence. He had said it many times in the past, and he knew it verbatim, but it was imperative that Becali, a man with a good level of fluency in English, understood it as well, the Romanian lawyer ensuring that he did.

'Mr Becali, you have been arrested outside Stanislav Ivanov's house. You were armed. Why?'

'My client has nothing to say,' Klaus Ponta, the lawyer, said. The man's English was flawless. He was in his mid-forties, starting to put on weight, his hair beginning to thin. Isaac felt that Becali had chosen his lawyer well.

'Carrying a loaded gun is a crime in this country,' Isaac said. 'There is a minimum five-year prison term for the offence. Mr Becali needs to be made aware of this.'

'I am,' Becali said.

'What was your intent on approaching Mr Ivanov's house?'

'I wanted to talk to him, to reason on behalf of Nicolae Cojocaru.'

'With a gun?'

'I knew that Ivanov would have guns in the house. It was for personal protection.'

'Are you telling us that Ivanov is a criminal?'

'I am not.'

'Then why would Cojocaru want to make a deal with Ivanov? Ivanov is a man without a criminal record, but we all know in this room that Cojocaru is responsible for distributing large quantities of illegal drugs throughout the area and the country.'

'No charges have been laid against Mr Cojocaru,' Ponta said. 'Supposition is not the basis for an interview, neither is putting words into the mouth of my client, who may or may not fully understand the legal implications.'

'Mr Becali, we can prove that you were in the flat where the first assassination attempt was made. We believe that you intended to try a third time, although that would have almost certainly resulted in your death.'

'I am not guilty of murder.'

'As an assassin, you have proved your incompetence. As a prisoner, you may be more effective. The choice is yours. If we release you with no charges, then Ivanov may choose to remove you, or maybe Cojocaru will. And what about Sal Maynard and the shooting at Briganti's? Was it you?'

'I've told you before, I may have been with the Maynard woman, nothing more.'

'We now believe that she was also involved with Crin Antonescu. Did you know this?'

'It's possible.'

'Ryan Buckley, an inspector with the Irish police, was murdered. We know it wasn't you, although it is possible that you know the reason why.'

'Why should I?'

'Buckley was a friend of Seamus Gaffney, a man who kept his nose to the ground. We believe he knew something which he told Buckley. Buckley, we know, killed Gaffney and then attempted to strike a deal with someone, either Cojocaru or Ivanov.'

'It appears that you have nothing against my client, other than carrying a weapon,' Ponta said.

'You can try if you want to dismiss that charge, but the charge of attempted murder still applies.'

'How?' Becali said.

'We have a witness,' Larry said. 'A witness that will testify that you were in the flat where the shot on the first attempt was made. Also, on the second attempt, CCTV footage of a person fleeing the area, as well as a shoe print. We have enough to make a conviction stick. Mr Becali, I would suggest that you start to tell the truth.'

'Why? You intend to convict me of crimes I didn't commit.'

'We have sent a vehicle to pick up Nicolae Cojocaru. He will be offered the chance to make a statement. If he knows you are to be convicted of attempted murder, what do you think he will say?'

***

Isaac had to agree that the evidence against Becali was not tight. The man was guilty, but it was mainly based on incomplete evidence. Even the gun recovered from outside Ivanov's did not have fingerprints, Becali having worn leather gloves on account of the cold morning. And Fahad Shaikh, a recent arrival in the country with his young wife, probably a first cousin as was the tradition, and his involvement on the periphery of crime, would be regarded as a marginal witness. Careful manipulation of the jury by a skilled defence lawyer would ensure prejudice against the Pakistani, and his testimony would be debased as a result.

Even so, it was a win of sorts, and the first arrest in an investigation that had gone on for too long.

Isaac sat on his chair in his office, his hands clenched behind his neck, leaning backwards, the weariness of the long hours starting to tell. He would have remained there for longer except that Brigitte came rushing in.

'Cojocaru,' she said. 'He's dead.'

Isaac left Challis Street soon after, Wendy with him. Larry, who was out of the office, cancelled his meeting with Bateman and headed out to Cojocaru's penthouse.

On the street, the crime scene tape, the barriers being erected. A uniformed police officer let the three of them through,

Gordon Windsor did not. 'Get kitted up if you want to go in,' he said.

'Have you seen the man?' Isaac asked.

'One shot to the head. One to two hours ago.'

'Who phoned the police?' Larry asked.

'The man's housekeeper. She's available,' Windsor said.

'Wendy, talk to her and get a preliminary report. I'll go up with Larry,' Isaac said.

Three men, kitted up with coveralls, gloves, and overshoes, entered the penthouse, stepping to one side of a crime scene investigator who was on the floor checking for evidence. At the other end of the hallway, the main living area, a man slumped on a chair.

'Not a pretty sight,' Windsor said.

'Any signs of a weapon?' Larry said.

'Not here. It's a clean kill, and whoever did it was smart enough to black out the CCTV cameras in reception.'

'Fingerprints?'

'Not yet. Don't hold your breath on this one.'

'Becali?' Isaac said.

'If it's one to two hours since the man died, Becali didn't shoot him,' Larry said.

'This may loosen his tongue,' Isaac said.

Chapter 27

Two days passed; two days when the initial flush of success after the arrest of Ion Becali had ground back into a routine.

The team at Challis Street met each morning early, and the days stretched into the nights, no one going home until late; nobody complaining either.

The body of Nicolae Cojocaru had been examined by Pathology, the man's penthouse had been checked by Gordon Windsor and his team, and Forensics had conducted tests on the bullet removed from the body. Nothing new had been found, and frustration at the lack of progress was felt by all.

Commissioner Alwyn Davies had been on the phone to Chief Superintendent Richard Goddard who had been in Homicide attempting to rally the team – it was not needed.

Stanislav Ivanov stayed in his house, apart from a brief excursion out to his football club for a function, his wife accompanying him. The man had made a speech about how pleased he was that they had won the most prestigious footballing competition in the country, the FA Cup, and sorry that he had not been there to cheer them on, but he had been otherwise occupied.

Ivanov made light of the assassination attempt, and Isaac, who had made sure to be in the back of the room at the function, could only imagine what the man really thought.

Annie O'Carroll had been on the phone from Ireland to let Larry know that leads had dried up there, and whoever it was that had shot Ryan Buckley, he wasn't Irish, but that was known already.

Another man sat in his hotel room; a man not used to inactivity and apathy; a man who needed to get out from the four walls and room service.

At four in the afternoon of the third day after Cojocaru had been shot, Crin Antonescu stepped out through the front door of his hotel and walked down the street. He needed a drink first and then a meal. The pub he chose, five miles from where Cojocaru had lived, five miles from the West Indian gangs and Challis Street, seemed safe enough for him.

He ordered a beer and a pub lunch. He then sat down in the corner of the bar. It was not ideal, but it was better than nothing, he realised. He looked up at the television mounted high on one wall and saw the face of Ivanov beaming back; it was a face he had trusted, but now the man was not answering his calls.

Without finishing either his beer or his lunch, he walked down the street, absent-mindedly, not knowing where he was going. He reflected on what had been, the early years in Romania, the setting up in England, on Ion Becali, on the woman who had fallen for him, and even though he had not loved her, there was a warmth in her, a genuine wish to be with a short, stocky ex-wrestler from Romania. But she was dead in that hairdressing salon with the others. He had sent her to her death, and he was sorry, an emotion he did not feel comfortable with. He phoned Stanislav Ivanov one more time – no answer. Gennady Peskov answered on the second ring when he phoned again.

'You were told to wait,' Peskov said. He had hated Antonescu from the first time he had met him in France. A man who is willing to change sides was not a man to be trusted, and now the man was phoning him.

'I have completed my task. It is for you to protect me, to get me out of the country.'

'Then wait.'

'For how long?'

'For as long as is needed. Ivanov does not forget those who are loyal, and you have done what is required. Your hotel has been paid for, and extra money has been given to you. You have no reason to complain.'

Peskov cut the call; Antonescu kept walking.

It was after nine in the evening when Crin Antonescu walked into the police station at Challis Street. The appearance of the man caused consternation in Homicide and alarm with Ivanov when he heard.

'I will tell you what I know,' Antonescu said in the interview room. He did not have a lawyer with him.

'We have always assumed you to be dead,' Isaac said.

'I am guilty of entering this country under a false name and with a false passport. I wish to return to Romania.' The man spoke slowly and with great thought.

'What other crimes are you guilty of?'

'I have committed no other crimes in this country.'

'Ion Becali has been charged with attempted murder. Nicolae Cojocaru is dead.'

'That I know.'

'How?'

'It is on the news.'

'Why have you come here?'

Isaac realised that his questions were inane, but he wasn't sure what else to ask. Across the table from him and Larry was a savage killer, the man who had probably killed Cojocaru, almost certainly had murdered Ralph Begley, yet there was nothing to tie the man to the crimes. It was as if Antonescu was playing with them, but Isaac knew he was not. Antonescu was not an intellectual, not a strategist, but a man who thought a passport violation would get him transported out of the country.

'There's no reason for me to be here now.'

'You came in illegally. Couldn't you leave the same way?'

'There are others who will not let me leave alive.'

'Why? Because you have murdered for them? And what's the truth with Sal Maynard?'

'She was a decent person and I mistreated her.'

'By making her go into Briganti's?'

The man's behaviour concerned Isaac and Larry. Antonescu had spent his life as a violent criminal, and now he was being circumspect and remorseful. It was an act, and it was convincing, and if the man's history had not been well known, others might have been duped.

Isaac knew that whenever a villain was contrite, it meant something else. The man had said that others would not let him leave alive, but why?

'Before we can help you, we need to know why they want you dead, and why did you return to this country illegally?'

'I needed to make peace with Nicolae Cojocaru.'

'A phone call would have sufficed. What happened at Ivanov's place in France? You went in but never came out.'

'I am out now, and I am willing to tell you what you need to know.'

'The truth?'

'All of it.'

'Then let's start with what happened in France.'

'Cojocaru shot me.'

'Why?'

'Because Stanislav Ivanov wanted proof of his loyalty.'

'An unusual way to test a person.'

'Not with the Bratva. I cannot blame Cojocaru.'

'Would you have done the same?'

'With a gun to my head if I didn't?'

'That's not an answer. I'll repeat the question. Would you have shot Cojocaru if the positions had been reversed?'

'Yes, and so would you.'

Isaac ignored the man's attempt at justification. 'Have you killed a man before?'

'In self-defence.'

'In England?'

'Never. Nicolae Cojocaru was always careful to ensure that we trod lightly with breaking the law.'

'Was the man importing drugs into this country?'

'Yes.'

'Then you are guilty of more than a passport violation.'

'My job was to protect him, not to become involved in his business.'

'Yet you stayed in France and now the man is dead. What do you say about this?'

'I failed in my duty.'

'And France?'

'What could I do? I either sided with Ivanov or I was dead. Cojocaru would have taken the shot, and I would not have been wearing a bulletproof vest.'

'Your story makes no sense,' Larry said.

'Then release me, and I will chance my luck on the street.'

'Ivanov has not committed murder in this country. Why is your life in danger?'

'If you guarantee that I will be protected and you will deport me to Romania, then I will tell you all.'

'Including how you killed Marcus Hearne?'

'I didn't kill him and you can't prove that I did.'

Isaac could see that they were hitting the proverbial brick wall. A conviction for Ion Becali was based on the testimony of an illegal migrant, not on forensic evidence. A smart lawyer would have argued that Ion Becali wanting to see Ivanov was not unreasonable and there was no proof that his intent had been murderous. Men such as Ivanov, men as rich as Midas, received requests all the time from people down on their luck.

'Then who killed Hearne?' Larry asked. 'We can't help you if you don't cooperate.'

'I was wrong to come in here. I want to leave this country; not admit to a murder I did not commit.'

'Tell us about the meeting. What happened?'

'I don't know. I was not there.'

'Let me come back to Becali. Did he kill Marcus Hearne?'

'If I say he did, you will keep me in this country.'

'As a witness.'

'What life is that for me? I will be on the street and Ivanov will have me killed.'

After one hour of questioning, a break in the proceedings. Antonescu asked for a pizza, which was duly delivered to the police station. Isaac and Larry went back to Homicide, and Larry phoned Annie O'Carroll in Ireland.

'What do you have?' Larry said after he had updated her.

'Unreliable witnesses, a possible man on Buckley's street twenty minutes before he was shot.'

'Possible?'

'Someone was taking selfies with an iPhone. There's a man in the background. The time's right, but we can't recognise him.'

'Short, stocky?'

'We've been through this before,' the Irish police officer said.

'Humour me.'

'Very well. The man that we have is short, but we've been through the faces you sent before. Came up with nothing.'

'Okay, try this. Blond, hair cut short, not as stocky as before.'

'It's probable, but it's an image from an iPhone, not in focus either.'

'We've got Brigitte checking through the flights to Ireland and the ferries crossing the Irish Sea. Any chance for you to check with the car rental companies in Dublin?'

'We checked before, went nowhere.'

'That was before. We've got one man for attempted murder, another at Challis Street who's claiming to be innocent. He was thought to be dead, but here he is, and he's altered his appearance. A thug, as bad as they get, and not too bright. If he were in Ireland, he could have made a mistake. Check the clubs, pubs, anywhere a degenerate could get to, and the man's accent is strong, so he would probably stand out.'

'Briganti's?'

'It's possible he's involved. We don't know how long he's been on Ivanov's team, but they've dumped him now. Probably trying to distance Ivanov from Cojocaru's death, but why they left Antonescu on the street, we're not sure. It seems to be an error on their part, and Ivanov doesn't make many errors, but if it wraps up the murder investigations, then we'll pursue it at all costs. Annie, bring in whoever you can and let's get this man.'

'Send me an updated photo.'

'Five minutes and you'll have it. We can't hold the man for long. He's here voluntarily.'

Isaac phoned Gordon Windsor. 'Any updates on Cojocaru?'

'The man's with Pathology, but they'll not be able to tell you much more. We've not found any clear evidence at the murder scene, other than a blond hair.'

'Is it with Forensics?'

'It is. Significant?'

'Test it against Crin Antonescu. You should have a sample of his DNA.'

'Should we? I don't think so, not unless he's on our database.'

'Very well. Send one of your people down to Homicide, and we'll get you a sample.'

***

Crin Antonescu, who in an act of desperation had willingly walked into Challis Street Police Station, now found himself charged with the murder of Nicolae Cojocaru. Not that the proof was certain, Isaac knew that, but they needed Antonescu's DNA to move forward. With an arrest, the man would be forced to comply.

The sample was with Forensics within the hour, a swab from inside the man's mouth, a strand of hair. Antonescu had complained, but legally he had no option.

Back in his cell, the Romanian sat quietly, taking his meals when they came, and asking for coffee every twenty minutes. Isaac and Larry looked at the man on the camera in the cell, unable to make any sense of a villain who came into a police station uninvited. It was behaviour they had not experienced before; the assumption was that he was more frightened of Ivanov than of the police. That was understandable, but why had he returned to England, why not go somewhere else? Ivanov frightened Isaac and Larry. The man was distinguished, and some would say charismatic, and the general view of the populace was that he was a man who had made good in the new Russia.

Oscar Braxton was over from Serious and Organised Crime Command. He was sensing a victory of sorts, but not total. 'We'll never get Ivanov,' he said.

'Any worth in talking to him again?' Isaac said. The three, including Larry, were sitting in Isaac's office.

'He'll not admit to anything, and Becali outside his house is circumstantial. Damning to Becali and to us, but Ivanov will have the best legal minds with him. He'll come out clean, and if he was behind Briganti's and Cojocaru's death, where is the connection?'

'Leave him for now, focus on wrapping up the murders. Any word from Inspector O'Carroll?' Isaac said, directing his glance over to Larry.

'Not yet. She's trying, but there's no forensics to back it up. We may get Antonescu for Cojocaru, but not for Buckley, even if he's guilty.'

A phone call from Gordon Windsor, a look of relief on Isaac's face. 'Bring Antonescu back up. We've made the connection to Cojocaru. He's already been charged, but this time it's up to him to see if he's willing to admit to the crime and whether he's willing to implicate others.'

Chapter 28

Annie O'Carroll phoned from Ireland. The indications were that Antonescu had been in Ireland, although the photo, enhanced as best as it could be, was not good enough to be proof positive. It appeared that the murder of Buckley would remain without a convicted murderer, although there was no doubt about who was responsible.

Antonescu sat in the interview room once more. Klaus Ponta, who had represented Becali, sat to his side, the charged man having relented about the need for a lawyer.

'Mr Antonescu, you've been charged with the murder of Nicolae Cojocaru. Is there anything you want to say in your defence?' Isaac said.

'Your evidence is circumstantial,' Ponta said. 'My client has not admitted to the crime.'

Isaac respected Ponta; the man was just doing his job.

'It's not, and with added focus, we'll find more evidence. We're also certain that Antonescu shot Inspector Ryan Buckley in Ireland. Your client, if he is not able to offer an alternative explanation of why he was at Cojocaru's penthouse, and why he was in Ireland, will stand trial.'

'I didn't do it,' Antonescu said. He slammed the table with his fist, almost causing a glass of water that Larry had brought into the room to topple off and onto the floor.

'There are unresolved questions,' Isaac said. 'The first is what did Inspector Buckley find out from Seamus Gaffney that condemned him? And who did he tell it to? The fact that he wasn't killed by Mr Antonescu indicates that Gaffney either hadn't revealed what he knew or that Buckley killed him first. Antonescu, what do you have to say?'

'Ion Becali killed Buckley. Seamus Gaffney had dirt on Cojocaru, not Ivanov. I wasn't involved,' Antonescu said.

'But you know the story?'

'I'm not saying anything. All I know is that Gaffney was trying to blackmail Cojocaru and that Becali killed Buckley.'

'It wasn't Becali. We can trace his movements at the time of Buckley's death; yours, we can't.'

'My client has no more to say,' Ponta said.

'Let's move on,' Isaac said. He was feeling increasingly comfortable with the situation. Oscar Braxton was listening in from another room, as was Richard Goddard.

'To where?'

'Marcus Hearne.'

'The black man,' Antonescu said sneeringly.

'Do you have an issue with people of colour?'

'Not me. I knew him, didn't like him, although I suppose you did.'

Isaac could tell that the Romanian was racist, not that it impacted the investigation, unless it was a motive.

'Cojocaru attempted to bring the West Indian gangs in, the reason that four of their leaders accepted his hospitality. Claude Bateman, Devon Harris and Jeremy Miller made it to the meeting, Hearne didn't. Why?'

'I'll not answer that question.'

'Because you can't, or you don't want to?'

'My client has been charged with one murder. We will address the falsehood of that, not other purported crimes,' Ponta said.

'Dead in a ditch is not purported,' Larry said.

'To you it's important, but not to my client who is innocent. He is concerned with a false accusation against him. He came to this police station, not to be charged with murder, but for assistance. He is fearful for his life, and now you have jeopardised it further.'

'Why?'

'Nicolae Cojocaru has powerful friends in Romania. They will not take his death lightly.'

'The man had no friends in Romania. He was a social pariah, convicted of crimes in absentia, derided by the villains there. Let's not pretend otherwise. The man's dead and no one is going to miss him.'

'Then someone did you a favour,' Antonescu said.

'They did, but it's still murder, and you did it.'

'Gentlemen, this is going nowhere,' Ponta said. 'Mr Antonescu wants to help, but with a murder charge against him, he is reluctant to say more. If an accommodation could be made, then it may be possible that he can further assist.'

'We can't grant him immunity from prosecution, not for murder,' Isaac said.

'Then he has no more to say.'

***

'What can Antonescu do against us?' Gennady Peskov asked. He was in Ivanov's house, a glass of whisky in his hand, the same as Ivanov.

Ivanov touched the plaster on his head, felt a slight pain as he applied pressure. Apart from that he felt fine, although he realised that his mental acumen was still not up to speed. He had erred with Antonescu, underestimated the stupidity of the man.

'Antonescu can do nothing against me,' Ivanov said. 'You allowed him to be arrested. What do you intend to do?'

'But you commanded me to tell him to kill Cojocaru.'

'And then you were meant to kill Antonescu and to ensure his body was never found. Why didn't you?'

'It was planned. He may have sensed that others were coming for him.'

'He sensed nothing. He is just a mindless thug. The same as you, Gennady Peskov, have proven to be.'

'I gave instructions for him to be killed after he left Cojocaru's.'

'You are not the mastermind, I am. I entrusted you with more responsibility after you stayed by my side in the hospital, but it appears that my weakness in crediting you with brains was a mistake.'

'I will discipline those that have failed us.'

'Failed you. Can your command be tied back to you, to me? Can these men be trusted again?'

'Not in this country.'

'Then they must leave immediately. Where are they now?'

'They are nearby.'

'A plane is waiting for them, make sure they are on it. I want them out of England within two hours, is that clear?'

'And what of me?'

'You will stay. You will protect me at all costs, even your own life. But you are a fool. I will need to keep a watch on you from now on.'

'I will not let you down,' Peskov said.

'If you do, I will not be so generous the next time,' Ivanov said. He knew that he was not generous, only astute. Gennady Peskov, for all his faults, was the one man who would stand between him and a bullet.

In another part of London, a group of police officers discussed the situation.

'Marcus Hearne?'

'Becali or Antonescu, probably both,' Isaac said.

'Ivanov is still free,' Larry said.

'And will remain so,' Oscar Braxton said. 'He's taken on a couple of Queen's Counsels to protect him legally, and a PR company to deflect the negative publicity that's stuck to him. Expect to see more of Ivanov at charitable functions in the next month or so, overly-generous donations as well. We can't beat him, not while money speaks.'

'Briganti's?' Wendy said.

'It still needs to be solved. Marcus Hearne knew something, or Cojocaru couldn't trust him, not after he was speaking to me,' Larry said.

'He's not the first person who's given you information that has died,' Isaac said.

'Not the first, not the last,' Larry agreed, 'but Wendy's right. What about Briganti's?'

Isaac made one more phone call, Gordon Windsor answered.

'Antonescu was at Cojocaru's penthouse; we can prove that from a strand of hair on a chair that he sat in,' Windsor said. 'It's recent, the chair had been cleaned in the last couple of weeks. We've also checked Antonescu against Briganti's. No shortage of hair there, a hairdressing salon, but we found proof that he had been in there as well. Not blond and dyed, dark and natural. How the man pulled it off and managed to walk out of there unseen, we don't know. But he's your man. He killed those people at Briganti's.'

Isaac relayed Windsor's findings to the team. 'He must have been working for Ivanov for a long time,' he said.

'Poor Sal,' Wendy said. 'She thought it was love and then the man killed her.'

'The others didn't deserve to die either. What about Ralphie, who killed him?' Isaac said.

'Antonescu. Sal used to speak to Ralphie. He phoned the man, probably trying to get money out of him and was killed for it.'

Isaac picked up his phone and made one more call. The phone at the other end was answered.

'Detective Chief Superintendent Goddard,' the voice said.

'Antonescu killed the people at Briganti's, Cojocaru as well. The other murders are either him or Becali; both are in custody. You can phone Commissioner Alwyn Davies.'

'And Ivanov?'

'Expect to see him on the television and gracing the social pages of the newspapers. He's on a charm offensive now, and there's nothing we can do about it.'

'The biggest villain walks free, is that it?'

'It is,' Isaac said.

The end of a long-running murder investigation should have been a time for satisfaction at a job well-done. No one in Homicide felt in the mood for a pat on the back or a celebratory drink at the pub.

The End.

Phillip Strang

Printed in Great Britain
by Amazon

63689771R00369